Also by Rowena Cory Daniells

The Outcast Chronicles
Besieged
Exile
Sanctuary

The Chronicles of King Rolen's Kin
The King's Bastard
The Uncrowned King
The Usurper
The King's Man (*ebook*)

ROWENA CORY DANIELLS

BESIEGED

BOOK ONE OF THE OUTCAST CHRONICLES

SOLARIS

First published 2012 by Solaris
an imprint of Rebellion Publishing Ltd,
Riverside House, Osney Mead,
Oxford, OX2 0ES, UK

www.solarisbooks.com

ISBN: 978 1 78108 011 5

10 9 8 7 6 5 4 3 2 1

A CIP catalogue record for this book is available from the
British Library.

Designed & typeset by Rebellion Publishing

Printed in the US

The seeds of every conflict are planted in the past, and so it was in the last days of the Late Golden Age of my people. When the war started, no one knew all the facts, and not one person was properly prepared, least of all me.

Taken from Imoshen's Private Journal

Chalcedonia and the Five Kingdoms

PART ONE

Chapter One

Year 290
(290 years since the Wyrds signed the accord
with King Charald the Peace-Maker)

'THEY ALWAYS SCREAM.'

Oskane flinched at the baron's tone. This was his cousin's daughter, not some bitch whelping puppies. Luckily, no one was watching him. They had eyes only for the young woman labouring on the royal bed.

He'd been in this very room for the king's birth twenty-seven years ago, which was the last time he'd seen a woman in her extremis. A high priest did not attend women in childbirth, unless it was to witness a royal birth.

He was glad. Birthing was a cruel process.

'It is a woman's lot in life to suffer,' the baron continued. His colleague, and rival, Baron Nitzel, called himself a scholar. But Oskane knew him to be a consummate manipulator and master strategist.

Which was what had been needed when the King, Charald's father, died on the battlefield, leaving him the throne and a kingdom in chaos. Between them, he and Nitzel were the reason the fifteen-year-old boy-king had been able to curb the barons and unite Chalcedonia, while holding back the kingdom's greedy neighbours. For twelve years, King Charald had done nothing but fight to survive.

Now he wanted an heir.

And this woman writhing on the royal bed was the means to that end. A single sheet covered the swell of a belly that looked too big for her small frame. At fifteen, she was the same age Charald had been when he was thrust onto the throne. Until now, Oskane had thought her role less demanding.

Sorna was the daughter of a powerful baron whose claim to the throne was almost as good as Charald's, and her marriage to the king had guaranteed her family's loyalty. In return, Oskane's family gained the king's ear and a crown for the baron's grandson. All Sorna had to do was birth a healthy boy, to ensure King Charald's claim on the future.

'I said I'd plant a child in her belly within the year. Didn't I?' King Charald stated, pleased with himself. 'A son is just what I need.'

'True, sire. An heir is what the kingdom needs,' Nitzel agreed smoothly, and it must have cost him, because the girl was related to Oskane, not him.

'With any luck he'll be a fine strapping lad. I'll call him Cedon, after my father,' King Charald announced. He was a handsome man, despite the scar on his chin, which pulled one corner of his mouth down. He had very fair colouring, with ice-blue eyes and a receding hairline. A big man, he was as tall as one of the T'En race, not that anyone would say this to his face.

King Charald was a True-man and proud of it, just as he was proud of his strength.

Oskane had seen it over and over. What King Charald wanted, King Charald got. He did not rest until he achieved it, going days with almost no sleep. The eager boy-king had turned into a single-minded bully, and Oskane had come to regret the role he'd played in securing Charald's throne. But this child...

He had such hopes for this child.

'Is there nothing you can do to speed up the birth?' Charald demanded of the saw-bones. 'She's been at it all night.'

'It's a natural process,' Etri said. Perhaps five years younger than the king, the man was very ambitious, but not without skill.

Skill, that is, in sawing off men's legs after they festered from battlefield wounds. What did he know of birthing? That was women's business. Oskane only knew as much as he did because he'd consulted a midwife, when he heard the king wanted his son born into a man's world. Charald had hung the symbol for his patron god over the bed. The Warrior, the belligerent one-eyed god, seemed out of place in a birthing chamber. If women had a choice, they chose the Mother to watch over them.

In the space between contractions, Sorna caught her breath. Sky-blue eyes glistening with pain and fear searched the faces of the men surrounding her: her father, her two brothers, the king, his advisor, the saw-bones and the high priest.

Fewer witnesses than the day Charald was born. Oskane had been the high priest's personal assistant, back then. An ambitious priest of twenty summers, he had believed it was a woman's place to suffer. Now... now he no longer knew what he believed. With the loss of his faith, there was nothing but a hollow ache where once he'd held conviction. All he had left was his duty, and he clung to that like a drowning man. He was here to bear witness to the birth of a prince.

If it *was* a boy.

If it was a girl, Charald would farm the babe off to a wet-nurse and get Sorna with child again as soon as possible. She would then have to go through this all over again – the bruises on her flesh from Charald's love-making, the brave smiles. Since the morning after the wedding, when Sorna had called for the high priest, she'd prayed every day, but not one word of complaint had passed her lips.

Now Oskane wanted to reach out to ease the panic in her eyes.

Another contraction took her, and she gave a keening groan that rose in pitch to a scream.

'Can't you do something for her?' the older of her two brothers asked, having to raise his voice. His younger brother looked on, eyes darting from face to face, out of his depth.

'It is a woman's lot to bear children,' Baron Nitzel said. 'I've gone through three wives. The first two died in childbirth. The third is with child now. You miss them, but you get used to it.'

Oskane fought the urge to throttle him.

'What about pains-ease?' the younger brother asked as her screams subsided.

'Pains-ease?' Charald echoed. 'Don't like it. Never touch the stuff. Makes you weak.'

'Not everyone has your fortitude, sire,' the saw-bones said, with a smile. Then he turned to the younger brother. 'Too little pains-ease has no effect. Too much makes females insensible and risks the baby's life. The woman has to be conscious to do the work of birthing.'

'Besides, females don't feel as we do,' Nitzel added. 'They are simpler creatures, closer to animals. The gods did not give them finely-attuned minds and souls like ours so they could endure childbirth.'

The brothers did not look convinced. Sorna panted, face contorted with pain.

'Don't worry,' Nitzel advised. 'Once this is over, she'll have her baby and forget. I've seen it time and time again.'

Perhaps that was true, but why did the gods inflict the agony of childbirth on women?

The answer was simple. There were no gods. No matter how he searched, he could find no proof for the Seven: the Father, his five sons and the Mother. The heretical thoughts terrified Oskane and he kept searching, hoping for a sign.

The pattern of Sorna's breathing changed. Her eyes rolled back in her head and her body arched. Belly stretched under the sheet, hands clutching the pillow beside her head, Sorna gulped a breath and drew her legs up, grunting with effort.

'It's time, baby's coming,' Oskane said.

'I must see this!' King Charald gestured to Etri, who drew back the cover.

Her nightgown had ridden up to her breasts, revealing the swell of her belly stretched tight as a drum. The lips of her vulva bulged outwards. Oskane remembered thinking last time that surely a baby's head could not pass through; he'd been proven wrong. However, according to the midwife, sometimes the baby became wedged and both mother and child died. Fear made Oskane's heart race. A midwife should be present, but Charald would not hear of it. He wanted his son born under the Warrior's patronage.

Trapped between horror and fascination, Oskane could not look away. What happened to the bones of her hips? No wonder women screamed.

Sorna did not scream. She held her breath and bore down with total concentration. The assembled men watched with terrible fascination as a crown of wet, matted hair appeared, then slid back in.

'The head, my king!' Healer Etri announced as proudly as if he was the one producing the child. 'Your son is about to come into the world.'

Sorna gulped another breath, preparing to bear down again.

The infant arrived face down. Etri took the baby's head and turned him, pulling one shoulder through, then the other.

Carried on a tide of blood and fluid, the baby's legs slipped out easily, and Sorna gave a guttural groan of relief. No caul covered the baby's face, which was just as well. The child had to be physically perfect to rule.

The long, ropey cord still pulsed with life as Etri turned the babe around to display his genitals. 'A boy!'

'A boy...' Charald whispered. 'Praise the Seven, a boy!'

'Look at those balls, pouch as big as a peach,' Etri crowed. 'What a man he'll be. And he looks just like you.'

With his little face bruised from the birth and his skin slippery and red, it was hard to tell who the newborn resembled. The babe threw out his arms, screwed up his face and screamed.

'Give him to me,' Charald commanded.

'A moment.' The saw-bones tied off the cord and cut it, then wrapped the babe in a cloth despite his struggles. 'A fine, strong boy. Look how he fights me. Just listen to those cries. Here, my king.'

Charald took the proffered baby, holding his son out towards the Warrior symbol above the bed. 'My heir, Prince Cedon of Chalcedonia, son of Charald, grandson of Cedon. One day he will be King Cedon the Sixth. May the Warrior's fire fill his heart, may the Warrior's guile guide his judgement on the battlefield.' The king lifted his voice addressing the servants by the door. 'Bring us wine!'

They hurried to pour goblets and distribute them.

Oskane glanced to Sorna, lying on the bed in a pool of blood and birthing fluid. There was still the afterbirth, but Healer Etri had left her side to celebrate with the king. Twenty-seven years ago, things had gone wrong at this point. Charald's mother had died three days later of child-bed fever – that, or a broken heart.

'It's starting again. What's happening?' Sorna whimpered, eyes wide with fright. 'Is there another baby?'

Was there another baby? Oskane hoped not, not after last time. He hoped it was just the after-birth.

'Didn't your mother tell you, Sorna?' he asked, then recalled the girl's mother had died giving birth to a stillborn boy seven years ago. 'It's the after-birth.'

Her hand reached for him as she gulped and bore down again. He pushed her hair from her forehead. The exertion of childbirth had made her hair dark at the temples, but the ends were still the colour of honey in sunlight. A sprinkling of freckles stood stark against her pale skin.

With a grunt of relief, she expelled the after-birth. 'That hurt.'

'You must have torn.' Which reminded him – they needed a midwife to sew her up. But Sorna had other thoughts.

'My baby. I want to hold him.' She tried to push herself up the bed, to sit against the headboard. Even as she did this, she adjusted her nightgown and reached for the sheet, wincing. More blood gushed from between her legs. It worried Oskane. The midwife would know what to do.

'Here, let me.' He lifted the sheet, pulling it up and moving a pillow so she could sit comfortably. 'I'll fetch the women now. They'll clean you up. By then, the king should be finished admiring his–'

A roar of outrage made them both stiffen. Everyone feared the king's temper, so violent and unpredictable.

'What's this?' Charald turned, holding the baby out. One little arm had worked loose from the swaddling cloth. Fingers splayed, the newborn reached for something to hold onto and wailed so loudly, Charald had to shout. 'What have you done, Sorna?'

She shrank back, growing even paler. Her mouth opened soundlessly and she shook her head.

'The babe has six fingers!' King Charald declared.

Oskane felt sick.

As Charald strode across the chamber to the end of the bed, everyone looked horrified. Everyone but Nitzel. For a heartbeat his face was unguarded; he was delighted.

'Six fingers!' King Charald thrust the baby forward. 'A filthy Malaunje, a half-blood. This is no son of mine!'

And he threw the wailing baby towards her. Sorna shrieked.

Swaddling cloth trailed the writhing infant as he sailed through the air. Acting on instinct, Oskane lurched forward, catching the newborn before he could hit the headboard.

The baby fell silent.

'There's no Wyrd blood in our family!' Sorna's father insisted, as his two sons reached for their weapons, only to recall they were unarmed. 'You insult our honour!'

'Are you saying there's Wyrd blood in the royal line?' Charald demanded, his skin purpling with fury.

Nitzel, who had also been at Charald's birth, glanced to Oskane. They both knew the truth, a truth Charald had never been told.

'Father,' the younger brother cautioned, putting a hand on the baron's shoulder. Oskane marked his maturity, changing his assessment of Matxin.

'Your daughter cuckolded me!' Charald flung a hand in Sorna's direction.

'No. Never!' Her father spoke over Sorna's denial.

The chamber filled with bellowed accusations and counter-accusations.

Oskane felt a tug on his arm. Sorna reached for her baby. Eyes feverish with intensity, she unpeeled his little furled hand to find... 'Six fingers.' Next she freed a tiny foot. 'Six toes, too.' Terrified, she looked up to Oskane. 'But I never... I've never lain with anyone other than the king.'

Oskane sat on the edge of the bed to get a better look. The babe was a half-blood, no doubt about it – an accursed six-fingered half-blood. Just like Charald's twin, who had been whisked away, never to be spoken of again.

'Before the Seven, I swear this is the king's son,' Sorna insisted.

'I believe you. Sometimes it happens. No one knows why.' Once, Oskane would have said it was the Seven's punishment. 'It happens in the best of families.'

'It's never happened in my family,' Sorna insisted.

'Are you sure? How do you know the babes weren't declared stillborn and taken away?'

That made her pause.

He noticed the king slip outside with the others. What were they up to?

Tears spilled over the young queen's cheeks. 'His eyes... I can't tell. Does he have the T'En eyes?'

Oskane tried to pry the baby's eyelids apart, but his fingers slipped on skin still streaked with blood and birthing fluid. He shuddered, repressing a True-man's natural repugnance for anything to do with Wyrds.

'Are his eyes as dark as old blood?' Sorna whispered.

'Dark blue, I think.' Not that it made a difference. The six fingers and toes were enough to condemn him. Oskane moved so the light from the tall window fell over the baby's face, and then he saw clearly. He met Sorna's sky-blue eyes. 'They will darken to mulberry. He has their eyes.'

Sorna sank against the headboard, arms falling aside so that the baby lay across her body unsupported. The infant was quiet, staring up at the window as if fascinated by the light.

Oskane heard the door open, then close. Charald had returned without Sorna's father and brothers. This was a bad sign. Etri and Nitzel were one step behind the king.

The king radiated determination. 'Stand back, Oska.'

Twenty-seven years ago, he had stood back. Then he had believed in the Seven and the wisdom of men. Now he doubted both. Now he had so much more to lose. He fingered the precious ruby King Charald had given him after the defeat of the barons. As he came slowly to his feet, Oskane felt every one of his forty-seven years.

Sorna gasped and clutched the baby to her chest. 'You can't have him.'

'It's for the best. He will be happier amongst his own kind,' the saw-bones told her.

It was true, but when Oskane glanced to the king, he recognised the grim line of Charald's mouth. The king did not plan to send the child to the Wyrds. Did Etri believe what he was saying, or was his hunger to rise from battlefield saw-bones to the king's personal healer powerful enough to justify killing an innocent newborn?

'We could cut off his extra finger,' Sorna suggested, 'and hide his eyes somehow.'

'Hide his eyes? *How?* You stupid girl!' Charald grimaced, then beckoned the saw-bones.

Etri moved forward, his mouth forming a hard line, and Oskane had his answer. Etri would kill for the king, for ambition.

Desperate, Sorna looked to Oskane.

Chapter Two

'WAIT.'

It was on the tip of Oskane's tongue, then, to tell Charald about his twin but, seeing the king's implacable expression, there was no point.

'Take the brat, Etri,' Charald ordered.

'No. Please...' Sorna hugged the newborn to her breast. She searched the king's face, her eyes widening in horror. 'Surely, you can't mean to kill our baby?'

Charald did not bother to reply.

'Give him to the T'En,' she pleaded. 'No one needs to know he's your son. The T'En–'

'No child of mine is going to serve the Wyrds. Filthy gift-workers, festering in their cankerous city. A pox on King Charald the Peace-maker for giving them that island. King Charald the Weak, I say. Because of him, we're cursed with that Wyrd nest they call the Celestial City – Cesspit City, more like. I wish it would sink beneath the lake.' He paced, working himself up. Oskane recognised the signs. 'For nearly three hundred years, now, the T'En have gathered there, plotting against us, buying up the best farmland and mines in my kingdom, growing ever richer. And all because my ancestor was too weak to destroy them when he had the chance.'

He threw Nitzel and Oskane a filthy look. When he'd first inherited the crown, they had advised him to borrow gold from the T'En to fund his wars. It had been a life-saver, but now that the war was over, he had to pay it back. With interest.

'They say not to look into a T'En's eyes, that they can enslave a True-man and rob him of his will,' Etri said. 'They say their gifts can start fires, bring rain, shrivel a man's–'

'They say a lot of things,' Nitzel snapped. 'But who knows the truth? If their gifts are so powerful, why didn't the T'En defeat us three hundred years ago?'

'They are few, we are many. Even so, it was a battle that neither side won, and the kingdom suffered,' Oskane said. 'Back then, it seemed the king could afford to show mercy. King Charald the–'

'Don't mention his name.' Charald rounded on Oskane.

'If we do not learn from the past, sire, we are condemned to repeat it.' Oskane stiffened, but did not back down; he could not afford to. 'The silverhead T'En are few, but they are powerful.'

'They must have a weakness,' Nitzel insisted. 'Everyone does.'

'If they have a weakness, we are yet to find it.'

'Because we have not looked hard enough.'

'How do we do that, when they turn all True-men out of their island city at dusk every night?'

'We–'

'Enough! You two bicker like old women.' The king pointed to the infant in the young queen's arms. 'I'll see the brat dead before I see him serve the Wyrds!'

'I'll take him,' Oskane heard himself say.

Everyone turned to him.

'I'll take him to study. Why should we hand over our half-blood babies to the T'En?' Oskane found the words falling from his lips as though he'd been planning this for years and, as he spoke, he realised he had. The T'En and their half-blood servants had always held a sick fascination for him. 'Why should our Malaunje grow up to serve them? I've been studying the Wyrd scrolls and–'

King Charald recoiled, making the sign of the Seven to ward off T'En power. 'Unclean –'

'The scrolls were written by True-men,' Oskane protested. While he knew that simple folk believed anything related to Wyrds was tainted by association, he had not expected this reaction from an educated man.

Etri glanced to Nitzel, and Oskane realised the saw-bones was ready to denounce him. When had these two become allies? Nitzel wore an expression of sorrow, but Oskane knew him too well to be fooled. They had been uneasy colleagues for twelve years, and rivals for Charald's trust. Now, Nitzel could see Oskane was destroying himself, and the baron was delighted.

All this flashed through Oskane's mind in a heartbeat. He must not falter. Determined to be understood, he plunged on. 'Nearly three hundred years ago, before King... before the T'En and Malaunje were completely segregated from us, our church scribes kept records of half-blood births. It doesn't happen often, but every now and then a Malaunje baby is born to a True-man and his wife through no fault of their own.' He met Nitzel's eyes. Neither of them was foolish enough to use Charald's twin as an example. 'Back then, the high priest had half-blood spies in the T'En sisterhoods and brotherhoods. And the spies reported that every now and then a half-blood couple would produce a baby with blood that was completely degraded; a full-blood T'En.

'For them, it was – and still is, I imagine – a cause for celebration. The T'En females have trouble falling pregnant and carrying a baby to term, because their blood is so impure. If their kind did not live twice as long as us, there would be even fewer of them. They need full-blood T'En babies born of half-blood parents to boost their numbers.' He met the king's eyes, willing him to understand. 'Don't you see? By giving our half-blood babies to the brotherhoods and sisterhoods, we not only give the T'En Malaunje servants, but we give them half-bloods who could go on to produce more T'En.'

Charald's eyes grew wide with horror. 'Seven save us!'

'I always wondered where those full-blood silverhead abominations came from,' Etri muttered. 'Old hair, young faces, eyes the colour of blood–'

'Rather than give our half-blood babies to the T'En, you're suggesting we kill them?' Nitzel asked.

Sorna whimpered and drew breath to protest.

'Give this one to me,' Oskane said. 'Much better to know your enemy. Much better to study the half-bloods and train them to serve us against the T'En.'

'Of course.' A familiar martial gleam lit the king's ice-blue eyes. 'Train them to become our weapons.'

Oskane had not thought that far ahead – he'd been trying to salvage his family's honour from this setback – but the king's suggestion made sense. 'Sire, if you give me your baby–'

'He's no son of mine. This half-blood is not Prince Cedon.'

'Of course. We can say your son was stillborn.' Like Charald's twin. But what of Sorna's father? Would his cousin agree? He glanced to Sorna.

'Her father is willing to keep his mouth shut,' Charald said, anticipating him. You could say that for the king: he might be quick to anger, but he was not stupid. 'The baron doesn't want his family's name stained by Malaunje blood. He claims the bad blood must have come through the girl's mother. His two sons had a different dam.'

Devastated by this betrayal, Sorna sank down.

Oskane gestured to the newborn. 'I'll rear this half-blood boy and train him to serve the kingdom instead of–'

'We can't have Oskane and the brat near the port and the court, my king,' Nitzel said. 'We can't have the half-blood brat living in one of the Seven's churches, where someone might discover him. He'll have to be sent away, far away.'

Oskane realised he was being banished along with the babe. He wanted to object, but what they said was true. Perhaps he could send the babe away with a trusted servant and visit to make his observations? After all, he did not want to leave Sorna unsupported in Charald's court.

'Where would they go?' Etri asked.

'It must be somewhere people avoid,' Nitzel said.

Oskane knew from his rival's expression that Nitzel already had a suggestion, and was guiding Charald to the idea, so that the king would think it his own. Both he and Nitzel had become adept at this, especially in the last few years when the king had become arrogant with success.

Nitzel's eyes gleamed. 'Somewhere all good True-men and women shun–'

'I have it,' Charald exclaimed. 'Oskane must take the brat somewhere unclean. Everyone avoids those places.'

'Brilliant, sire,' Etri said.

'And not just any unclean place.' Leaning closer, Nitzel lowered his voice. 'If I may, my king, there is an unclean site on one of my estates, far to the north in the highlands. When the villagers discovered it, they fled their homes, but Oskane seems comfortable with the arcane. Send Oskane and the brat there.'

'The highlands?' Sorna repeated, dismayed. 'I'll never see him.'

'The highlands are harsh,' Oskane protested. He had no intention of leaving Port Mirror-on-Sea, and he wasn't going to send the half-blood anywhere near Nitzel's estate. 'How would we survive?'

'You can take a couple of servants,' Charald said. 'As long as they can be trusted to keep their mouths–'

'I can provide trustworthy servants,' Nitzel offered.

Spies and guards. Oskane stiffened. It seemed he was unclean now, because of his research into the Wyrds. 'I have my own servants. I know a place.'

'As long as it's isolated. I'll want reports,' King Charald said. 'Once a year, until the brat is of use to me.'

'And once a year I'll visit,' Sorna said. 'I'll stay for a small moon. See how he's doing.' She smiled down on the newborn and cupped his cheek. He turned instinctively towards her warm palm, seeking a nipple.

'He's hungry,' Oskane observed.

Sorna tugged at the drawstring of her gown to free her breasts.

'What are you thinking, girl? True-women don't feed half-bloods.' King Charald gestured to the high priest. 'Take him now, Oskane.'

Sorna looked up, chin trembling. She did not resist when Oskane took the newborn, although her eyes remained fixed on the babe's face.

The infant writhed in Oskane's arms, little head turning from side to side, seeking sustenance. 'The babe will need a wet-nurse.'

King Charald made an impatient gesture. 'Hire some whore from the docks.'

At this, Sorna made a sound of pain in her throat.

'I'll go and set things in motion.' Oskane's mind raced. He trusted his personal assistant. Franto was absolutely loyal, but he'd need several penitents to provide for the infant's needs.

The baby grizzled. Oskane offered his knuckle to suck on and the infant accepted it.

The other three moved over to the cabinet where Etri had laid out his herbs and oils. Oskane went to leave, but the young queen called him back.

'If I cannot be with him, then I want to give him a keepsake. Pass me my chest.' She pointed to the small chest from the sideboard. When he gave it to her, she opened the lid and took out a silver torc. 'This was my mother's.'

A single, bright blue stone sat in the centre.

'I've never seen the like. What is it?' Oskane asked.

'It's firoza, from beyond the mountains, in the far east. The traveller said it was a protective stone. Keep it safe for him. Keep him safe for me.' Sorna's chin trembled. 'Promise?'

'I will.' Oskane tucked the torque between himself and the baby, so that it was hidden amongst the swaddling clothes.

'Oskane.' The king's tone made them both jump.

Despite his misgivings, Oskane gave Sorna a reassuring smile.

He crossed the chamber to join the king, marvelling at his fall from grace. Last night, when Sorna went into labour, he'd been the king's favourite, the man responsible for introducing Charald to the young queen who was about to present him with a son. By mid-morning, he was as good as banished. Not that he was going to give up his position as high priest; Nitzel did not win that easily. He'd go, see the babe settled, and return to support Sorna and guard his family's interests.

Oskane joined the king. 'I'll send in the women to see to the queen.'

'Not yet.' Charald's gaze flicked to the saw-bones.

In that moment Oskane knew Sorna would not leave the chamber alive. His step faltered.

Not Sorna, not his sweet Sorna.

The king held his gaze, daring him to speak up.

Nitzel watched the confrontation, his eyes gleaming with satisfaction, while Etri studiously measured drops into a goblet of wine.

Oskane swallowed, heart hammering. His cousin, Sorna's father, must have put the family's position and wealth ahead of his daughter's life and cut his losses. Oskane couldn't imagine the brothers doing this. But what was the alternative? Banishment, and their estates confiscated?

There had been a number of confiscations of supposed traitors' estates in the last few years. A portion of every confiscated estate was supposed to be put aside to pay back the T'En, but Oskane did not know if any of the gold had reached them. With every estate that Charald confiscated, he and his supporters grew richer.

The king's need for gold was great. Aside from the repayments to the T'En, there was a grand new palace under construction. It would rival the palaces of the Wyrd city, and it had to be paid for somehow.

Cold fear made Oskane's skin clammy. He could not save Sorna.

Nitzel stepped closer to the king, saying softly, 'Etri assures me she'll just fall asleep, sire. Women die in childbirth every day. No one will be surprised. Don't worry.' He placed a paternal hand on the king's shoulder. 'My daughter will make a good wife. She's already produced two fine True-men sons. And they won't be a nuisance. They'll remain on their father's estate.'

'Your son-in-law is dead?' Oskane asked, surprised.

'Attacked by brigands on the road.'

He'd heard nothing about this. Oskane opened his mouth, then closed it. He'd heard nothing, because it had not happened yet. Pity anyone who stood in Nitzel's way.

'The...' – he stopped to clear his throat – 'the roads are dangerous, since the king disbanded his forces. So many landless men, who know nothing but killing after twelve years of war.'

He glanced to Sorna on the bed, dozing. She was exhausted by the birth. He could not save her, but he could save himself and the boy. If Sorna was not Charald's queen, there was no point him staying in court. In fact, given his family's fall from favour, he would be safer far away from here.

In a way, it was a relief. As high priest of the Father, greatest of the Seven, he was living a lie. He'd always felt a leaning towards the Scholar god, and now he could follow the way of the scholar. In his search for the Wyrds' weakness, he might uncover proof of the gods. At heart, it was the Wyrds who had caused his loss of faith; how could he believe in powerful gods whose existence had to be taken on faith, while Wyrds with real powers existed alongside True-men?

Oskane swallowed. 'Please accept my condolences. If there is anything I can do...' He let it hang and turned to go.

'Actually, there is,' Nitzel said.

Oskane froze. By the time he'd turned around, his face was composed and calm. 'Yes?'

'Stay and give the queen your blessing, high priest.'

'Of course.' Sadistic bastard. Nitzel knew Oskane was fond of his cousin's daughter.

Oskane returned to the bedside. Etri was already there, offering Sorna a deadly paregoric to soothe her.

He wanted to shout a warning and dash it from her lips, but he held his tongue.

As King Charald watched Sorna drink without a flicker of remorse, Oskane was reminded how long and earnestly he and Nitzel had had to argue to convince the boy-king to authorise his bastard brother's execution. *The first time a man kills is always the hardest.* Back then, every death had seemed justified, but it had led to *this*...

'High Priest Oskane.' Sorna smiled. 'Where are the women? I want to bathe.'

'All in good time. Rest now. I'll sit with you until you fall asleep.' *I am a coward*, Oskane thought as he settled his old bones on the chair by her bed. *No, I am a survivor. I must survive to seek revenge on the man who undermined our family.*

Oskane had underestimated Nitzel. He hadn't realised the baron would order the murder of his own son-in-law to further his family.

Sorna's gaze settled on the babe, who had drifted off. She yawned and fought sleep long enough to reach out and touch the newborn. A fond smile lit her face, and her eyes rose to meet Oskane's. 'Thank you.'

He nodded, hardly able to see through his tears. He should never have suggested she would make a good queen; his ambition for the family had killed her.

No, the curse of tainted royal blood had killed her, along with Nitzel's conniving to elevate his daughter as the next queen. Oskane found himself wishing that Charald's marriage to Nitzel's daughter would bring him no sons, bring him nothing but tainted half-bloods.

'Sleepy now,' Sorna said, her voice the merest whisper.

Oskane took her hand and held on until he felt the strength leave her fingers.

Then he stood, and said the words to release her soul. At a council of the Seven, the church scholars had decreed that Malaunje and T'En did not have souls. There had been a debate over the souls of women, and it had been decided that seven of their souls equated to one man's soul. Preposterous.

Obviously the quality of the soul depended on the individual. Some women's souls were particularly pure. Sorna's, for instance. She truly believed, while he...

Oskane was glad he was leaving. Hopefully, in his self-imposed isolation, he would recover his faith. Right now, he felt its lack like an open wound.

'Is it over?' Charald asked.

Oskane turned to face the king and nodded.

'It was her fault,' Charald said. 'All she had to do was produce a healthy True-man son. Was that too much to ask?'

Oskane bit his tongue.

The king returned to Nitzel and Etri, and they put their heads together, speaking in low voices. Feeling his fate hanging in the balance, Oskane moved towards the door.

'Oska,' Charald said.

He froze.

The king gestured to the babe. 'Cover it. If anyone asks, you carry a stillborn.'

Dizzy with relief, Oskane went through the door.

A gaggle of concerned women waited at the end of the corridor. As he strode towards them, they ran to meet him, greeting him with the proper deference and asking after the queen and the baby.

'...for we heard such shouting,' the stout matron said.

'The babe was stillborn.'

They moaned and wrung their hands.

'Poor King Charald.'

Oskane nodded, even though it choked him. 'And, alas, the queen is dead. Please go and see to laying her out. Be...' – his voice broke – 'be kind.'

They rushed past him, carried on cries of dismay.

Mind racing, Oskane left the palace. He wanted to be out of Port Mirror-on-Sea before nightfall.

The Seven had churches in all the major towns, and abbeys throughout the countryside, run by priests and staffed by penitents who wanted to win favour with the gods. The penitents did most of the hard labour on the farms, wineries and mines. He already had a place in mind, a religious retreat, high in the eastern mountains and far to the south. Restoration Retreat was about as far away as he could get from the palace and still be in Chalcedonia.

It had been a copper mine. Over twenty years ago, when he had been the assistant to the last high priest, something had gone very wrong down in the bowels of the mine.

According to the report, the first the priests knew of it had been when three penitents had disappeared, and the only survivor had run screaming from the mine. A perfectly normal man had gone down that morning. He'd come back a lackwit.

Their digging had revealed an unclean site.

The priests declared the mine tainted and everyone fled. The retreat had been closed that very day, and no one had ventured back. Oskane did the sums. He'd been high priest for fifteen years and it had happened nine years before he rose to this position. So, twenty-four years. The old priests who ran the mine were long dead, and the penitents scattered, if they still lived. Nearly twenty-five years... he doubted if anyone other than him even remembered the retreat's existence.

Good. He didn't want Charald deciding to remove him and the lad once Nitzel undermined his belief in their usefulness.

Restoration Retreat was perfect. There had been no reports of more incidents in the area so it was probably a single event site. At any rate, he would have the mine sealed.

In fifteen years – no; he was forgetting, the boy was a half-blood. For all that they grew bigger, they took longer to mature. In seventeen or eighteen years, the boy would be old enough to avenge his mother's murder and help restore the family that his birth had undermined.

And, who knew, he might even prove useful against the T'En, but Oskane had few illusions. The Malaunje he had captured to question had proven fanatically loyal to their masters.

Seventeen years...

Oskane looked forward to the day. He only hoped he lived long enough to see it. By then, he would be sixty-four. Few True-men lived past fifty.

But then, few True-men had the motivation he had.

Chapter Three

THE SCREAMS SUBSIDED.

Irian looked up. All-father Rohaayel came to his feet, eyes fixed on the hastily erected tent where his devotee laboured to birth his son.

In the clearing behind the dunes, the surf drummed on the beach and a seagull called. An afternoon breeze whispered through the pines. The gull called again. Irian winced at its harsh cry and wondered if this was a portent.

Some believed seagulls were messengers of the gods, but his kind didn't believe in gods. The T'En associated seagulls with opportunity. Seagulls were good at making their own luck.

Not that this journey had been lucky.

They'd been delayed, by one thing after another. And then, when they'd finally made their way up the coast, before turning inland for the Celestial City, a fox had startled the horses. The usually placid mare carrying Rohaayel's devotee bolted, charging off into the undergrowth.

And there was not a thing Irian could do to prevent it.

They'd found the devotee only moments later. She had been thrown by her mount, her waters had broken and she'd gone into early labour. Irian looked up through the trees at the late autumn sun. Only mid-morning. The labour could go on all day.

The screaming started again.

Shoulders slumped, Rohaayel sank onto a rock, long silver hair bound in a practical travel-plait. The brotherhood's all-father was absolutely haggard, as if he laboured along with Mariska. Rohaayel never did anything by halves. The ability to ease pain by sharing it was part of the devotee link. The bond between a T'En and his devotee was sacred.

And she had been hurt while under Irian's care. That it had been beyond his control did not matter. In the eyes of the brotherhood, he had failed All-father Rohaayel.

They did not know if Mariska would live, let alone the child. What was worse, the pregnancy had gone past the seven small moons for a Malaunje babe, which meant the child would be born pure T'En. T'En daughters were rare, even rarer if the father was a T'En, so it would be a son.

Irian looked around the clearing. All-father Rohaayel had sunk his head in his hands. No one met Irian's eyes. They all felt his shame.

Their party consisted of two T'En other than himself – All-father Rohaayel and the brotherhood's voice-of-reason, Ardeyne. Then there were the Malaunje, Devotee Mariska and fourteen others, warriors and servants. The only female warrior was in the tent with Rohaayel's devotee, doing her best to help with the birth, but she was trained to kill, not deliver babies.

The screams rose to a desperate, panicked peak.

Irian flinched. The cries carried and the breeze was blowing inland. Their party's impromptu camp was exposed, and he hated it.

The screaming stopped again.

If only the child would be born whole and healthy.

And then what? They'd have to hand him over to one of the sisterhoods to rear. Irian had never fathered a living T'En son. Two boys and a girl, all half-bloods. It was hard enough declaring his newborns fatherless and handing them over to the Malaunje of his own brotherhood. At least half-blood children stayed with their birth-mother. He could not imagine how it felt to give your son to the powerful T'En women, knowing you would not see the child until he turned seventeen.

Unable to sit still, Voice-of-reason Ardeyne sprang to his feet. He paced, his boots sinking into the sandy soil, crushing fallen pine needles; their tangy scent filled the clearing, mingling with the fresh smell of the sea. The power of the gift also filled the clearing. After the accident, the three T'En were on edge, their gifts ready to spring to their defence. The Malaunje warriors responded to this, tension in their every movement.

Rohaayel could have called on his brotherhood link to Irian and Ardeyne to help him shoulder Mariska's pain, but he hadn't. Irian suspected the all-father felt guilty; he should have left his devotee safe in the brotherhood's palace back in the city.

But, if Rohaayel had one fault, it was that he loved too well. Not that Irian would ever say this to him. It was the reason they loved their all-father. Custom decreed it was their duty to die for him but, for Rohaayel, they'd die for love. Few of the brotherhood all-fathers could honestly say the same.

And that was why Irian's failure bit so deep.

The screaming started again. It had been growing hoarser as the morning progressed.

His gift nagged at him, irritating him, until finally he focused and analysed the sensation. The T'En gift was innate and, to a large extent, unconscious, which meant much of their training consisted of learning how to control their reactions. Now he sensed... 'Strangers. Mieren.'

Everyone reached for their weapons.

'True-men, here?' Torekar, the youngest Malaunje warrior, grimaced and spat in contempt. The youth had been hidden at birth and raised by his Mieren parents until the age of eleven. Then, without warning, the villagers turned on his parents, murdering them in their bed. The half-blood boy would have died, but he'd leapt out the attic window and run all the way to the city to claim sanctuary.

'Mieren, *mere men*,' Netaric corrected. He was the most experienced of the Malaunje warriors, and had taken

Torekar under his wing. 'To call them True-men belittles Malaunje and T'En alike.'

Torekar flushed and would have apologised, but one of the servants drew Irian's attention. The man had climbed onto the cart and picked up the reins, and now looked for orders.

Irian shook his head. If the Mieren were on horseback they'd have to ditch the cart. What was he thinking? They could not abandon the devotee.

How many Mieren were out there?

Lowering his shields, Irian allowed his gift to search their surroundings. He sensed two minds, their psychic scents very different from his own kind. They were between his party and the beach.

He beckoned to Torekar and Netaric. Picking his way through the pines, he reached a spot where the trees thinned out and were replaced by chest-high undergrowth. A quick glance told him the two Malaunje warriors were in place, and he signalled them to move forward.

With the devotee so vulnerable, every instinct urged Irian to kill the interlopers. His gift rose, but he banked it and felt for the hilt of his long-knife.

Muffled sounds reached him as the interlopers registered the danger and tried to run.

He forged through the undergrowth. Torekar and Netaric moved ahead, flanking the enemy, closing in on them. Parting chest-high leaves, Irian spotted two Mieren.

Children – a boy and girl, aged five and seven, he guessed, then revised it up to eight and ten. Mieren tended to be smaller on average than his kind. Both had white-blond hair like T'En children, but their eyes were a shallow blue instead of deep mulberry and they did not have the six fingers and toes of his kind.

Those pale blue eyes stared up at him, terrified. While they were distracted, Torekar and Netaric came up behind them and hauled them to their feet, lifting them both off the ground like kittens.

Irian could slit their throats and bury the bodies, and no one would ever know, but it went against his principles to kill children. He was the hand-of-force because of his need to protect and, to his surprise, he found that extended to the young of a race who hated his kind.

He took the boy from Netaric. 'Go back. Tell Ardeyne I need him.'

Both children twisted and kicked, succeeding only in making themselves red-faced and short of breath.

'Let us go,' the girl pleaded in Chalcedonian. 'We heard cries. We came to see if we could help.'

'But you stayed when you saw who it was,' Ardeyne said as he joined them.

The girl had no answer to that. She hung her head.

'They've seen us. We can't let them go. They'll go home and tell their family there's Wyrds camped nearby. Before we know it, the local Mieren will band together and come after us to move us along, or worse. I don't want to have to...' Although Irian spoke T'En and the children would not understand, he could not bring himself to speak of killing them. 'Can you work your gift on their minds?'

Ardeyne hesitated. His gift was a rare manifestation for a noet. Most noets were mind manipulators, who could create illusions in receptive minds, but Ardeyne could do much more, like seeking out specific memories and erasing them.

As the voice-of-reason considered, Irian realised what he was asking. Under the treaty with King Charald the Peace-maker it was forbidden for T'En to use their gifts on unwilling Mieren.

Too bad. This was an emergency. And it was better than death.

'They're young, their minds are impressionable,' Ardeyne said. 'As long as neither of them have innate defences, I should be able to erase the memory. Or at least make them think it was a dream.'

'What if they have defences?' T'En had defences against the gift, even the weakest of Malaunje did, and they spent their childhoods learning to enforce those walls as a matter of self preservation.

'I'll have to break into their minds. I... I don't know if they'll recover.' Ardeyne met Irian's eyes, troubled. 'They could become lackwits.'

The devotee's screams resumed.

'Do what you have to,' Irian ordered.

Ardeyne nodded and raised his hands, and Irian could feel him gathering his gift; his own gift rose in response. He pushed it down. One of them needed to remain alert to danger on this plane.

The voice-of-reason reached for the girl first, cupping her face in his hands – skin-on-skin contact was the most efficient way to conduct power – but she shook her head, trying to dislodge him. Torekar had to hold her firm, pressing her head against his chest.

Meanwhile, the boy writhed and kicked, desperate to go to her aid. Irian had to admire the lad's spirit. He covered his mouth to keep him quiet, and the boy promptly bit him.

This distraction meant he missed observing Ardeyne use his gift. Irian wanted to know how memories could be erased. Not that he would ever be able to do it himself. His gift was basic illusion. He had to be in contact with the recipient, skin-on-skin, and while he worked his power he was vulnerable. It was not much of a weapon. It was just as well he was big for a T'En, and a good tactician, or he would never have risen as high as he had.

In spite of the distraction of the child's bite, he did feel the sudden flare of power as Ardeyne overcame the girl's resistance; the voice-of-reason was sweating despite the sea breeze, and his eyes were closed in fierce concentration.

The boy had stopped wriggling and now wept in frustration, hot tears spilling over the hand Irian had clamped across his mouth.

When Ardeyne finally stepped back, the girl hung limp in Torekar's arms. The voice-of-reason rubbed the back of his neck and took a shaky breath. 'Hopefully, she'll recover. I was as gentle as I could be.'

'Now the boy.' Irian shifted his hand, holding the lad's chin to keep him still.

'You've killed her.' The boy wept tears of fury. 'I'll–'

He broke off in mid-tirade as the voice-of-reason cupped his face. This was Irian's chance to observe Ardeyne's gift. With his hand holding the boy's chin, he would feel the flow of power. Trusting to the strength of his will, Irian lowered his shields, but it was like listening to someone speak a foreign language. No matter how hard he tried, he could not make sense of what Ardeyne was doing. When the voice-of-reason stepped back, leaving the boy limp in Irian's arms, he was none the wiser.

The voice-of-reason was exhausted. Shadows lined his thin face, aging him. Ardeyne's power would take time to recover.

'Take both children to the beach,' Irian told the Malaunje warriors. 'Find a safe spot above high tide and leave them there. When they wake, they'll think they slept the day away.'

Ardeyne looked grim. 'If the girl wakes as a lackwit, our people will be blamed.'

'They blame us for every bit of bad luck that comes their way. For once, we'll deserve it.' He swung his arm under the boy's legs, sweeping him up. So light. So vulnerable. 'Here.' He passed the child to one of the warriors.

Torekar staggered as he turned to go, and it was only the old warrior's quick reactions that saved the girl. Netaric adjusted her weight, while one of his companions lowered Torekar to the sandy soil. The old warrior glanced to Ardeyne, then cursed softly.

Confused, Ardeyne met Irian's eyes.

The realisation hit them both at the same time. Torekar had been holding the girl when Ardeyne's gift flared, overcoming her innate defences. Torekar had trained to reinforce his shields, but only since he'd joined the brotherhood.

The voice-of-reason had imprinted his gift on Torekar.

Ardeyne shook his head, stunned. 'I didn't mean –'

'Take the children,' Irian told the remaining warriors. Rohaayel, Ardeyne and he had been brotherhood leaders less than a year, and they were still making it up as they went along. But one thing was certain – a T'En never revealed weakness. 'We'll see to Torekar.'

Netaric nodded and led the others off.

'I didn't mean to,' Ardeyne whispered. 'I would never force...'

As Irian knelt next to the unconscious youth, he heard his old gift-tutor's voice in his head. *This is what comes of not maintaining the proper distance between T'En and half-bloods. With no power of their own and a sensitivity to the gifts, the Malaunje are vulnerable. If you don't keep your power strictly under control, you'll overcome their shields and imprint your gift on one of them. Then they'll be addicted to your power for life, enslaved against their will.*

'He's just a boy,' Ardeyne said.

Torekar's copper hair was bound in a braid, and he wore the leather vest and breeches of a Malaunje warrior; a hectic flush of colour illuminated his pale cheeks.

'I didn't notice he was the one holding the Mieren girl,' Ardeyne said. 'My concentration was focused on her. I didn't realise when I breached her defences, that I was breaching his. He shouldn't have been here. Why did you bring him?'

'He'd insulted us by calling Mieren True-men. He needed a chance to redeem himself.' In truth, Irian hadn't even thought about it. 'You've made him your devotee.'

'I didn't mean to.'

'I know, but that doesn't change the fact,' Irian said, torn between admiration and annoyance. A hundred years ago, all of the powerful T'En had devotees; even those whose gifts were not strong enough aspired to it. Since then, there had been a philosophical shift away from binding a Malaunje to one of the T'En for life, but... 'It still happens. Some Malaunje choose it.'

'This is not like Rohaayel and his beloved Mariska. I don't even know this youth. What if we can't stand each other?'

'Torekar is an honourable warrior.'

'And I'm a scholar.'

The screaming stopped again. They both glanced back to the clearing.

'I'll give you a hand with him,' Irian said.

'No. He's my responsibility.' But before the voice-of-reason could lift Torekar, the all-father joined them.

'Good, I've caught you alone. Have you told him, Ardeyne?' Rohaayel asked. Then he noticed the unconscious youth. 'What happened?'

'Told me what?' Irian came to his feet slowly.

Rohaayel and Ardeyne were shield-brothers. Only with this bond had they been powerful enough to take down the last all-father and his voice-of-reason. A hand-of-force could expect to die in the service of his brotherhood, so an all-father might go through three or four during his leadership; Rohaayel could not afford a deep bond with Irian. As much as Irian understood all this, he still resented being excluded. The three of them had known each other since they had been returned to the brotherhood, as lads of seventeen. Back then, he'd admired Rohaayel's quicksilver mind and aspired to be like him, but he'd always been the odd man.

Always been scrambling to keep up with the pair of them.

Ardeyne and Rohaayel exchanged a look.

'Tell me what?' Irian repeated.

The youth stirred and sat up. Ardeyne helped him to his feet.

'I'm sorry.' Torekar slurred his words. 'I must have fallen asleep. Apologies, all-father.' He gave the deep obeisance, hands going to his heart to symbolise love, then to his forehead to symbolise duty. He staggered a little as he straightened up. As if that wasn't enough, he reeked of Ardeyne's gift.

Recognising the signs, Rohaayel's eyes widened.

'Go back to the camp and rest,' Irian told Torekar. 'You've had a shock.'

With another apology, the youth left them.

Irian brought his attention back to the two men. 'What was Ardeyne supposed to tell me, Roh?'

'I would have spoken before this,' Rohaayel said. 'I meant to tell you between now and when Mariska went into labour. But the horse...' He did not go on.

He did not need to. Irian felt bad enough. 'So tell me now.'

Rohaayel drew breath to speak.

A newborn wailed.

Rohaayel turned to face the tent. 'My son lives. Mariska...'

Chapter Four

VITTORYXE'S HANDS TIGHTENED on the reins. Her knees pressed into the horse's flanks, causing it to whicker and shift uneasily. Leaning forward, she soothed her mount, her gaze never leaving the far riverbank and the waiting warriors.

The group from All-father Sigorian's brotherhood mirrored her own: five adults – four T'En and one Malaunje – plus the baby. The copper-haired woman carried the infant in a sling across her chest.

This would be the third time Vittoryxe had collected a T'En baby from one of the brotherhoods.

Imoshen the Covenant-maker had written that although you could sometimes trust an individual T'En man, they could never be trusted when they came together, because this triggered a rise in their gifts which could interfere with rational thought.

Much had been written by T'En woman scholars on the danger of the men and how to safeguard oneself from them. While their individual gifts weren't as strong, they were physically stronger and they outnumbered the women four to one. In truth, Vittoryxe suspected if it hadn't been for the women's more powerful gifts, they would have ended up as slaves to the men, like Mieren women.

Unthinkable.

The two T'En men swung from their saddles and jumped to the ground. Vittoryxe's breath caught in her throat. So much strength and barely contained energy. Still, she wouldn't trade physical strength for gift strength.

No, but to be strong in both body *and* gift...

The brotherhood's symbol glinted on the silver arm-torcs around their thick biceps. By the richness of their brocade robes, these two were high ranking, possibly gift-warriors like herself and Egrayne. She thought she caught the flash of silver gift-warrior torcs around their necks. If so, they were not only physically strong, but powerful.

All the more reason to be cautious.

They wore their knee-length robes unlaced, the better to reveal the duelling scars on their chests. Typical – all display and bravado.

Her mouth curled in contempt.

Their only concession to the rigours of travel was the way they bound their long silver hair in plaits. They wore riding boots, and breeches rode low on their lean hips. Jewelled belts held two long-knives, one on each hip. According to the truce with King Charald the Peace-maker, these daggers could be no longer than the distance from index finger-tip to the elbow.

She did not recognise either of the brotherhood warriors, but that was not surprising, since they had chosen to absent themselves from the city and live out their days on a distant estate.

If they had chosen this life. She'd heard rumours that some all-fathers sent ambitious brothers to distant estates to prevent leadership challenges, which meant she must not dismiss these two just because they lived a six-day ride south of the city.

The agreed meeting place for the ceremony was the bridge. Symbolically, it spanned a gulf of four hundred years of mutual distrust between brotherhood and sisterhood, built by ritual, cemented by tradition.

It was unseasonably warm. The bridge's golden sandstone arches glowed in the morning sunlight, and reflected in the smooth surface of the slow-flowing river.

In an attempt to lighten the atmosphere, Vittoryxe pointed. 'Someone should write a poem to the lines of that bridge.'

'Someone probably has,' Egrayne said. She was as tall as a T'En man, broad-shouldered, strong-jawed and popular. For the life of her, Vittoryxe could not figure out why.

Both of the young initiates grinned. They were warriors-in-training who hoped to prove that they had what it took to become elite gift-warriors. Now they shifted in their saddles, communicating their apprehension to their horses.

'Show no fear,' Egrayne told them, dismounting.

This annoyed Vittoryxe, as it gave the impression Egrayne was in charge when in reality they were both trained gift-warriors.

'Don't hold their eyes. They'll see it as a challenge or an invitation,' Vittoryxe told the young initiates. Springing to the ground, she wrapped her reins around a tree branch. 'Think of the brotherhoods as vicious dog packs, each ruled by the strongest and most ruthless of the beasts. The weak become prey, so they can't afford to let an insult pass. Don't give these warriors reason to feel threatened.'

'And don't let your gift defences slip,' Egrayne added.

Vittoryxe hid her annoyance. She'd been getting to that. 'You will have heard that the men crave our gifts, but they also fear them. They might be able to break our necks with their bare hands, but they know we can kill them with a single touch. So don't flaunt your powers.' She held young Kiane and Arodyti's eyes to be sure they were sufficiently impressed. 'Even an accidental slip could be construed as an insult.'

Egrayne nodded. 'Balance in all things.'

Why did she always have to have the last word?

One of the men reached up to help the Malaunje woman dismount. He lowered the woman to the ground, displaying a tenderness Vittoryxe found hard to reconcile with what she knew of them. She'd never forget the way her mother had been murdered. But she mustn't think about that.

'That's the baby's mother?' Arodyti asked.

'Yes,' Vittoryxe said.

'Probably,' Egrayne corrected.

'The Malaunje mother should be present for the ceremony,' Vittoryxe said. 'Sometimes if the woman dies in childbirth, or she's too weak to make the journey, then a close friend stands in for her.'

'Have the brotherhoods ever tried to hide a T'En baby?' Arodyti asked, her wine-dark eyes bright.

She was seventeen and inclined to exaggeration and laughter. What was worse, Vittoryxe had overheard her poking fun at the oldest of the sisters, females who had been born almost a century ago in the High Golden Age. At least Kiane appreciated their sisterhood's proud heritage, with its unbroken line of all-mothers back to Imoshen the Covenant-maker.

'They could claim the infant was stillborn and keep it,' Arodyti said. 'After all, we only have their word.'

'They wouldn't dare!' Vittoryxe felt her heart race and her gift try to rise. 'Four hundred years ago, the all-fathers indulged in a terrible feud. In their greed and ambition, they kidnapped and killed precious T'En boys to weaken rival brotherhoods.

'Horrified by this, Imoshen the Covenant-maker united the all-mothers, took the boys and forced a gift-oath on the surviving all-fathers. Since then, every new all-father gives the same gift-oath, and the brotherhoods have handed over all T'En babies. They know we will safeguard the children and return the boys to them when they're seventeen, old enough to survive the dangers of the brotherhoods. They know they are not fit to raise T'En children.'

'They know...' – dark humour lit Egrayne's mulberry eyes – 'that if one of them breaks his word, the all-mothers will band together and strip the guilty all-father of power. The strongest of their own brothers will then kill him and claim the rank of all-father. We use the ambition of the brotherhood men to keep them in check.'

Both Arodyti and Kiane grinned.

This irritated Vittoryxe. It was supposed to be a solemn and sacred occasion.

Arodyti shifted in the saddle. 'But I don't see—'

'Always questioning,' Vittoryxe snapped. 'It's been this way for nearly four hundred years.'

'It's time,' Egrayne announced.

Vittoryxe took the lead. As she stepped onto the stones of the bridge, a lark sang on the riverbank and the air seemed charged with intensity. She felt as if she was taking part in one of the old sagas. It only confirmed her belief that she was destined for great things. And, all the while, her gift strained to break free.

She'd been eight years old, waiting at the gate of the sisterhood's estate, when her mother had been struck down by the T'En brother. Of course, the other sisters had been swift to execute him, but that hadn't helped her mother, who had bled to death in the courtyard. She mustn't think about her mother.

Two tall T'En men approached, accompanied by the small Malaunje woman and the bundle she cradled in her arms.

Vittoryxe stopped a body-length from them. Egrayne came to stand behind her on her left.

This close, Vittoryxe saw that, yes, both men wore silver torcs around their necks denoting their status as gift-warriors, although neither had the decorative symbols that indicated kills.

'We are here to honour the covenant,' the shorter of the two gift-warriors said. A diagonal scar bisected his cheek, cutting through his top lip to his chin, reminding Vittoryxe of the violence of the brotherhoods.

'We entrust a future brotherhood warrior into your care,' the taller gift-warrior said, as he gave the young mother a nudge.

She undid the sling and parted the cloth to reveal a perfect, naked infant boy, perhaps five days old by the state of the cord.

'A perfectly formed T'En boy,' Vittoryxe acknowledged. She stepped forward before Egrayne could claim the honour and held out her arms.

The young mother looked to be no more than twenty. Tears spilled unheeded down her cheeks. Sometimes the Malaunje mothers looked away at this moment. Sometimes they trembled, and their eyes darted about as if they wanted to run or protest. None did, all were too afraid of the brotherhood warriors.

This young woman said nothing, but her eyes demanded much. Daringly, she met and held Vittoryxe's gaze as she handed the baby over.

Vittoryxe stiffened at the insult. 'By giving him into our sisterhood's care you do the best you can for the child.' Although the words were ceremonial, she sincerely believed them.

The taller of the gift-warriors unrolled a short scroll. He read off the father's name, giving his rank in the brotherhood so that a choice-mother of appropriate stature could be appointed.

Vittoryxe accepted the scroll. 'We swear to protect this child with our lives. We swear to rear him to revere the heritage of the T'Enatuath and protect our Malaunje. His details will be entered into the sisterhood's lineage book.'

The young Malaunje woman swayed and the tall man steadied her.

As soon as he touched her, Vittoryxe sensed the rise of male gift. One or both of the gift-warriors had slipped and lost control. It was only for a heartbeat, but it was enough.

Male power, so different from its female counterpart, registered as sharp and abrasive on Vittoryxe's senses; she'd never liked it, never felt the urge to arrange a tryst with a brotherhood warrior or scholar. That had been her mother's failing, a liking for the men and their gifts; for one man in particular, who thought that two trysts meant he owned her.

Anger fuelled Vittoryxe's gift as it reacted to the threat of the male's. Banking her power, she took a step back.

The tall gift-warrior flushed. So it was he who had slipped. And now he'd been shamed in front of them. His wine-dark eyes glittered with anger, and the line of his jaw flexed as he ground his teeth.

Vittoryxe's heart hammered. She was hampered by the infant. If they resorted to violence, Egrayne would have to hold them off.

While Egrayne was strong and combat-trained, the men were also trained and stronger. Egrayne could take one down, perhaps, but not two. To defeat them, she would have to drag both warriors through to the higher plane, where the female gifts were more powerful.

Vittoryxe felt sickeningly vulnerable.

Her gift rose and slipped her control.

Both men inhaled sharply and the scarred one took an involuntary step forward. The tall one grabbed his companion's arm, while manoeuvring the Malaunje woman behind him.

'Steady...' Egrayne said, moving in front of Vittoryxe. Egrayne's left hand went to her knife hilt, while her right hand gestured for Vittoryxe to stay back.

The two warriors backed up a step.

Vittoryxe did likewise.

Neither side turned their backs on the other, neither relaxed until they were off the bridge.

By the time they reached Arodyti and the others, Vittoryxe's mouth was so dry she couldn't have spoken if she'd wanted to.

The half-blood wet-nurse accepted the baby. She would care for him until they returned to the sisterhood's palace and a suitable choice-mother was appointed.

Vittoryxe's fingers trembled so badly she could barely undo the strap of her saddle bag. Furious with herself, she put the scroll away, fumbled the bag closed and swung her weight into the saddle.

'What happened?' Arodyti asked. 'I thought I caught the scent of male gift.'

'The father lost control for a moment,' Egrayne said, mounting up.

Vittoryxe was surprised. But now that she thought about it, Egrayne's guess was probably correct.

'If he can't control himself,' Vittoryxe snapped, 'he shouldn't have come to the ceremony.'

Egrayne glanced at her, but did not make the obvious rejoinder. Which was strange; after all, Vittoryxe's slip had placed both of them in danger.

She hated losing control. It had nothing to do with witnessing her mother's murder. The brotherhood gift-warrior was to blame; her gift had simply risen in defence.

'She was probably his devotee,' Egrayne added.

'Devotee?' Arodyti asked. 'I thought the T'En weren't supposed to imprint their gift on a Malaunje. If the males are weaker than us, how–'

'Anyone can slip,' Egrayne said. 'The men–'

'The men are weak, but their control is also weak,' Vittoryxe spoke over her. 'Trust a male to slip and enslave a Malaunje.' Even as she said this, envy ate away at her. It was frowned on nowadays to make a devotee, but being powerful enough to sustain one certainly added to a T'En's stature.

'Come on.' Egrayne turned her mount.

Intent on putting distance between themselves and the brotherhood party, they rode off.

The rest of their group waited in a clearing filled with shifting, dappled light. A slight breeze stirred the canopy, sending autumnal leaves swirling down around them.

'It went well?' the oldest of the Malaunje asked.

'As well as can be expected.' Egrayne sounded grim.

Vittoryxe said nothing. She resented the gift-warrior covering for her. What if Egrayne went to Gift-tutor Lealeni and revealed her loss of control? Lealeni was looking for the right gift-warrior to train as her replacement. From gift-tutor it was a short step to sisterhood all-mother, Vittoryxe's true goal.

Her cheeks burned with shame and frustration.

Egrayne would have the opportunity to betray her tonight, but first they would travel east to a sisterhood winery where they had to collect the gift-tutor. In the meantime, Vittoryxe would have to think up a way to prevent Egrayne reporting her slip, as she was certain she would. After all, why should the gift-warrior protect her? Egrayne was just as ambitious as she was.

When the party reached the top of the next rise, Vittoryxe found Egrayne waiting for her. Her stomach lurched. This was it, the confrontation. While the others rode past, Vittoryxe wished she knew of some transgression she could hold over the gift-warrior to ensure her silence.

Egrayne leant forward in the saddle, elbows resting on the pommel as she stared back the way they'd come. With her long nose and strong jaw, she looked androgynous, like a young T'En man. Vittoryxe wondered if she should seduce Egrayne. It was common for an initiate to form a relationship with an adept as she found her way in the sisterhood. As an initiate, Vittoryxe had made sure all her lovers were useful to her, and she'd never had any complaints. Now that she was an adept, she should be looking for a fellow adept, perhaps someone to link up with as shield-sister. If she chose the right shield-sister, it would empower her as they drew on each other's gifts, and improve her chances of rising to the top of the sisterhood.

She glanced to Egrayne again, weighing up her usefulness. The idea held some appeal.

And even as she thought this, Vittoryxe saw a reason for Egrayne protecting her. The big gift-warrior desired her. It explained the brooding silence; the way Egrayne watched her when she thought she wasn't looking.

And to think she'd assumed the big gift-warrior felt threatened by her. This was good, very good.

'We're not being followed,' Egrayne said.

Vittoryxe glanced over her shoulder. The brotherhood party were no longer in sight, lost in the folds of rolling fields. 'Did you expect them to?'

'They're T'En males – all brawn, no brain and full of gift bravado. If one dares another to do something, before you know it, he's gotten himself killed to impress his peers.' She looked up at the sky. 'Not midday yet. We should reach the winery by mid-afternoon. Rather than stay the night, we should collect Lealeni and the lad, and keep going. It's only three days after winter's cusp, and both moons are nearly full so there's plenty of light. I say we keep riding for as long as we can, then make camp for the night. If we're careful not to overtax the horses, we could make it home in five days instead of six or seven.'

'Fair enough.' Vittoryxe agreed. Her lack of gift control niggled at her, and she felt she had to justify herself. 'He shouldn't have slipped. If he hadn't, I wouldn't have lost–'

'Forget it. We all slip sometimes. Your mother's murder–'

'My mother had nothing to do with it. She was weak and foolish.'

'The brotherhood warrior became addicted to your mother's gift. When she turned down his offer to tryst, he killed her because he could not bear the thought of her trysting with another.' Egrayne studied her. 'That was hardly your mother's fault. And because one T'En man went rogue, it does not mean that all–'

'All men crave our gifts and hate us because we are more powerful than them.'

'And we don't crave their gifts?'

'I don't.'

Egrayne raised an eyebrow.

'I don't. I want nothing to do with them.'

'How can you say you don't crave the male gift, if you've never –'

'I'm not going to put myself in harm's way. There were two of them, both gift-warriors and probably shield-brothers. The danger was not in my imagination.'

'No...'

Vittoryxe was reminded how Egrayne had risked her life to protect her.

'Do you aspire to become the hand-of-force?' Vittoryxe's mind raced. If Egrayne filled that role, it would put her out of the running for sisterhood all-mother. 'You'd be excellent. You're as big as a man. You're smart. And you have a way with the young warriors-in-training, both T'En and Malaunje. They admire you. They'd die for you.'

Egrayne gave her a quick look as the colour crept up her pale cheeks.

Without saying a word, the gift-warrior urged her horse to catch up with the others. For a heartbeat, Vittoryxe thought she might have over-played her hand.

'I aspire to survive,' Egrayne called over her shoulder.

Vittoryxe shivered. Egrayne was older than her, and had already fulfilled her gift-warrior vow, risking her life to protect this reality from the higher plane. Vittoryxe had trained, but had not yet made her first kill. Not that she wasn't willing. It was just that predators did not escape the empyrean plane often. When they did, the task of capturing them before they could kill, and dragging them back to the higher plane, was dangerous enough that many gift-warriors had died glorious deaths over the years.

Vittoryxe had no intention of dying, gloriously or otherwise. She was meant for greater things.

Sisterhood all-mother had been her goal since childhood. But now that she thought about it... Maybe even causare.

She whispered the words aloud to see how they felt. 'Causare Vittoryxe. Embodiment of the cause.'

The thing was... they didn't have a cause to fight for.

The T'Enatuath hadn't elected a causare since Imoshen the Negotiator led the brotherhoods and sisterhoods into the final battle against King Charald the Peace-maker.

Back then, it had taken the threat of annihilation before the all-mothers and all-fathers had put aside their rivalries and elected a causare, and Imoshen had stepped down as soon as the treaty was signed.

Still, she was remembered as the greatest all-mother since her namesake, Imoshen the Covenant-maker. Ambition burned in Vittoryxe's chest, stirring her power, forcing her to practise the gift control exercises as if she was still an initiate, and not an adept of four years.

Vittoryxe hung back from the main party, with the excuse that she was protecting the rear. Meanwhile, she dreamed of becoming Causare Vittoryxe.

But this would only happen if she was all-mother of their sisterhood and their people were threatened. She almost wished they were, so she could rise to the occasion, prove herself worthy and secure her place in history.

Chapter Five

'HE LIVES!' ROHAAYEL spun around to hug Ardeyne, pulling Irian into their embrace. 'My son lives!'

Rohaayel's gift brushed against Irian's senses, making colours sharper and scents stronger. He laughed, and suddenly they were all laughing.

The newborn wailed again.

Without another word, Rohaayel ran back to the clearing where the Malaunje had taken a case of the brotherhood's best white off the cart and were pouring drinks to celebrate.

'To the future!' Rohaayel said, lifting his goblet.

Irian drained his wine. He wanted to know what Rohaayel and Ardeyne were hiding from him, but now was not the time to pursue it. Let the all-father celebrate; all too soon, he would have to relinquish his son to a sisterhood.

Rohaayel accepted congratulations, his attention still on the tent. Any moment now, the Malaunje warrior would come out with the child to show him off.

But the tent flap remained closed.

The happy voices gradually faded.

The longer the delay, the more likely something was wrong. A T'En child born of two Malaunje parents had a better chance of being born whole and of sound mind than a T'En babe born of T'En and Malaunje parentage.

The tent flap opened and the warrior appeared. Tiashne seemed shaken. She had killed in defence of their brotherhood. If the sight of the baby had disturbed her, then the news was dire.

Rohaayel headed for the tent. Ardeyne and Irian followed. They were his seconds. With their support, he had won the brotherhood. They would protect his back, even die for him, but they could not protect him from the heartbreak of a deformed son.

Inside the tent, the air was rich with the scent of blood and sweat. Tiashne led them through to the small, private chamber, parting curtains to reveal...

'Mariska.' Rohaayel ran to her side and dropped to his knees. His devotee lay propped up on cushions, with the newborn tucked in the crook of her arm. Exertion had darkened her copper hair, but her eyes blazed with pride and excitement.

The moment Rohaayel touched his devotee, the air in the tent became charged with his gift as Mariska amplified his power. If a T'En was powerful enough to sustain a devotee, then they in turn became more powerful. Of course, if the devotee died, the T'En was diminished, and if the T'En died, the devotee died with them. The high price a Malaunje devotee paid was the reason this kind of relationship had fallen from favour.

'My love,' Rohaayel whispered, kissing Mariska's forehead with great tenderness. He looked up at the Malaunje warrior. 'She came through unscathed. Thank you.' He offered Tiashne his hand to gift-infuse her in gratitude. It was a rare courtesy, a special sign of favour from all-father to brotherhood member, yet the warrior hesitated.

'Roh,' Mariska whispered, her voice raw from screaming. She opened the swaddling cloth to reveal the baby. 'We have a daughter. A perfect, pure T'En girl.'

No one spoke.

They stared at the tiny newborn, all kicking legs and round belly beneath the tied-off cord. There was no mistaking her gender.

It was not unheard of for a T'En man to father a pure T'En female, but it was rare enough that none of them had expected it.

'A girl?' Rohaayel repeated.

A girl would not return to the brotherhood and support him. She would join the ranks of the powerful T'En sisterhoods and help to repress the brotherhoods.

Better she had died, but Irian did not say so.

Ardeyne gestured to Tiashne. 'Leave us, Tia.'

'A girl,' Rohaayel marvelled, as the Malaunje warrior gave the correct obeisance, her hands going to her heart to singnify love, then to her forehead to signify duty, before backing out.

'What will we do now?' Ardeyne asked.

Irian didn't understand what he was asking. It was not as if they had a choice. The gender made no difference. If anything, it made honouring the covenant more imperative. He shuddered at the thought of the righteous indignation of the all-mothers...

'Come,' Rohaayel said. He sprang to his feet. With a final smile for his devotee, he drew them into the outer chamber. 'We go ahead with our plan. Don't you see? This is even better. We say the babe was stillborn and the mother is too ill to move. We–'

'Keep her? Are you mad?' Irian could not believe it. 'What of the covenant? What of your gift-enforced oath? If the all-mothers find out, they'll strip you of your power. Our own brothers would challenge us for the leadership. They'd kill us out of hand.'

But Rohaayel wasn't listening. Instead, he spoke to Ardeyne. 'It's another three days' journey to the headland. We signal the lighthouse to send a boat, as planned. We offer our Malaunje warriors a choice. Either they stay on Lighthouse Isle to protect the brotherhood's investment, or they lower their defences and you erase their memories.'

So this was what they'd been about to tell him. The delays, the journey up the coast road instead of the inland route– it was all part of a larger plan to cheat the sisterhoods of Rohaayel's T'En son.

Only it wasn't a boy.

Irian looked to Ardeyne, hoping the voice-of-reason would live up to his name, but he was actually considering it.

'I don't know, Roh. A female T'En... She's helpless now, but one day she'll be able to kill us with a touch.'

'If she's trained. But if she never receives any gift training, she'll be as ignorant as the first T'En born to Malaunje parents,' Rohaayel said. 'Besides, we won't need to fear her, because she'll be loyal to us. We'll be all she ever knows.'

'I can't believe you are seriously considering this,' Irian muttered. They both ignored him. He forged on. 'This is larger than hiding one child. This breaks the covenant. The all-mothers will have to make an example of us.' The horror of it strangled his voice. 'What you suggest will destroy our brotherhood!'

'No, it will set our brotherhood free.' Rohaayel turned to him, eyes blazing with visionary fervour. 'It will free all the brotherhoods.'

'How? One woman can't stand against the council of all-mothers. They'd unite against her–'

'Of course they would,' Rohaayel said. 'But think about it. Even though they're more powerful, we outnumber the women four to one. Why can't we defeat them?'

'We can't trust the other all-fathers,' Irian said. 'If we lowered our gift defences, the all-fathers would turn on one another. Each would try to strip the others of power in an attempt to make his own brotherhood the greatest–'

'Exactly. The women always work together. That's why they won four hundred years ago. They united, while the all-fathers tore each other apart.'

'If she's untrained, how can she be of use to us?' Ardeyne asked. For once, he was scrambling to keep up. Irian sympathised.

The all-father grinned. 'When she's old enough, but before she can begin to make sense of her gift, I'll send one of our T'En warriors to seduce her. She'll have a sacrare son. He'll–'

'A sacrare male?' Ardeyne said. 'There hasn't been a sacrare male born since before the covenant–'

'Really?' Rohaayel's voice brimmed with bitterness. 'How do we know?'

Ardeyne was truly shocked. 'Are you suggesting the all-mothers would murder–'

'Why not?' Irian answered, even though the question had been addressed to Rohaayel. This was his area of expertise, defensive strategy. 'They choose when they tryst with us, so they know they aren't fertile. If they birthed a sacrare boy, he'd be heir to great power. They couldn't afford to let such a powerful male return to the brotherhoods. He'd rise to become an all-father. He'd be able to...' He broke off as the scope of Rohaayel's vision stole his breath.

'Exactly. My sacrare grandson will unite the brotherhoods and crush the sisterhoods' power once and for all. He will set us free.'

Ardeyne gasped, but Irian saw a flaw. 'T'En women hardly ever carry a healthy baby to term. The chances of two T'En parents producing a healthy child are–'

'...negligible. I know. This is because we no longer make the deep-bonding to allow the gifts to fuse during conception,' Rohaayel said. 'The women don't want to be vulnerable.'

'But she won't know any better,' Ardeyne said, catching fire. 'Brilliant, Roh. She'll accept the deep-bonding because she trusts us. She'll be able to carry the babe to term.'

'A sacrare boy, heir to great gifts, trained intensively from the age of thirteen under our gift-tutor, so that he's ready by the time he is seventeen.'

'So young?' Ardeyne said. 'He won't have full control of his gift.'

'He doesn't need full control. He just needs to be a symbol, to unite the brotherhoods. We'll be there to guide him.'

'Thirty-four years,' Irian said. Seventeen years for the girl to grow up, and another seventeen for the boy. 'Can we hold the brotherhood together for that long?'

'It's not unheard-of for an all-father to rule a brotherhood for thirty years,' Rohaayel said. 'We'll have to invite the strongest of the ambitious males onto our inner circle and let them in on the secret, to win their support.'

'It is possible,' Ardeyne said. 'I swear we can do this.'

'You'll have to kill her right after she gives birth,' Irian said. The other two looked at him in surprise. 'I've read that carrying and birthing a sacrare baby can trigger a maturation of the mother's gift. Even without training, she could become dangerous.'

'Why would she be a danger to us, her beloved father and uncles?' Rohaayel countered. 'If we can get one sacrare warrior from her, maybe we can get more.'

'Roh?' Mariska called from the entrance to the inner chamber. She stood wrapped in a nightgown, beautiful wine-dark eyes ablaze with hope. 'Tell me we're keeping her.'

He strode over, took her face between his hands as if she was made of fine glass and kissed her lips. 'The brotherhood's keeping her. You won't have to give up our baby.'

Tears of relief slid down her cheeks. He kissed them away.

Ardeyne looked across to Irian, confident and proud.

They could do this, Irian realised. They could cheat the all-sisters.

No, it wasn't cheating – it was reclaiming what was theirs. If the all-sisters hadn't been so determined to rob them of their sons, this wouldn't be necessary. With this one daring decision, they would rebuild the very foundations of T'Enatuath society.

'My clever devotee,' Rohaayel crooned.

'What will we call her, Roh?'

'Imoshen,' Irian said.

'What?' Ardeyne baulked. 'But–'

Rohaayel laughed.

And Irian laughed along with him, because this Imoshen would undo all that her namesake had achieved.

Let the sisterhoods chew on that!

Chapter Six

OSKANE'S LAST OFFICIAL act as high priest was to appoint his successor. He handed the decree to his personal assistant, Franto. 'Have six copies made. I will sign them all and apply the official seal. Be sure one copy is kept here with the Father's church. The remaining six are to be sent to the other churches of the Seven.' To circumvent any plans Nitzel had of elevating one of his cronies to the position of high priest of the Father and controlling the power of the Seven's churches.

Small-boned, quick as a sparrow, Franto tilted his head and sent Oskane a wry look. He was already overloaded with preparations to leave the port. 'Anything else?'

'Have you secured the servant I mentioned?' The wet-nurse, but he couldn't say this in front of his replacement, Edorne.

'Not yet, but I will if you let me get on with it.'

Oskane gestured for him to go and Franto scurried out.

'You shouldn't let him speak to you like that, Uncle.'

'I trust him implicitly.'

Edorne did not look convinced.

'You will report to me. I must know what Baron Nitzel and the king are up to.' He leaned forward, dropping his voice even though they were alone. 'Beware Nitzel. He will try to win you over with promises of an alliance, but he is not to be trusted.'

'I'm no fool, Uncle.'

'Which is why I chose you to replace me.' His nephew was smart, but he didn't have nearly thirty years experience of court politics.

'And I am honoured to follow in the footsteps of Oskane the Pious.'

Oskane had the grace to look down. His daily flagellation was common knowledge. Each time he took the holy scourge and punished himself in search of the divine, he dug deeper into the hollow core of a man who could see only human frailty and chance behind events both great and small. And he prayed even harder for a sign from the gods.

Pouring two goblets of wine, he passed one to Edorne. 'To the new high priest.'

Edorne took a sip, then put his cup down, as abstentious as he was fastidious. 'You say you are stepping down from office to carry out a special service for the king?'

'For him and for Chalcedonia.'

'Surely as your successor I should know the nature of this service?'

Oskane drew breath to tell him, only to discover he was reluctant to admit he would be raising a half-blood child, even if that child was the king's unwanted son. Edorne was an educated man, but he had a True-man's natural repugnance for anything Wyrd. 'It would be safer for you if you didn't know.'

'Where you are going?'

'Your reports will be forwarded to me.'

'All this secrecy... is it truly necessary?'

I just saw the queen murdered. What do you think? Oskane raised his glass. 'To Chalcedonia, and the church curbing the worst of the king's excesses.'

Edorne took another sip. 'You can trust me.'

He could. Because Franto had appointed an agent to report on the new high priest.

Oskane put his wine down unfinished. 'I must go.'

'It's mid-afternoon. Surely it would make more sense to leave early tomorrow?'

Oskane shook his head. The longer he stayed, the more chance someone would discover the infant and want to know what he was doing with a newborn. The more chance Nitzel would decide one of his trusted servants was a better choice to train the king's half-blood son. Forcing down his impatience, Oskane gestured to the map of Chalcedonia and the many islands off the coast. 'I have a hankering to live on an island.'

He was going inland and south.

'Very well.' Edorne came to his feet and opened his arms for a parting embrace. 'I will miss you, Uncle.'

Bless him, he meant it. Oskane felt tears burn his eyes and was surprised by the depth of his reaction. As he pulled away from the embrace, he wondered if he was doing the right thing by his nephew. But there was no time for doubts.

When he entered his private chambers, he found a raddled female fingering the rich brocade of his formal robe. The wet-nurse? Was this the best Franto could do? The smell of her made him wrinkle his nose. 'Don't touch that.'

She jumped and snatched her hand back. 'I didn't hear you–'

'Obviously. If the babe wakes, keep him quiet. Sit there and do not move.' He pointed at the velvet stool where he sat each morning while Franto washed and oiled his feet. Surely she was too old to be a mother? 'You are a wet-nurse? You can feed him?'

She nodded and went to unlace her undershirt.

'No need for that,' he said hastily then strode back through the hangings to the outer chamber to find Franto and complain. But his servant had six penitents lined up. There was a cripple, and a boy of seven, and the other four were all over forty. 'These are our servants?'

'You want them to agree to leave the port, leave their families and sign on to serve for seventeen years,' his assistant said. 'This is what you get.'

Oskane sighed and gestured to the penitents. 'Kneel.'

They sank to their knees and lifted their faces. He went to each one and said the words, then stepped back. 'Now sign your names, or make your mark, and your souls will be saved.'

'Even if we die before our times have been served?' one asked. He had a conniving cast to his features, and Oskane didn't want to think what he had done before becoming a penitent.

'That will make no difference.' Because, unless the gods proved otherwise, there was no next world. 'Fetch your bundles and meet us in the courtyard before the next prayer bells.'

They gave the obeisance and left.

Oskane rubbed the bridge of his nose. 'We are packed?'

'Yes. Your clothes—'

'My research papers?'

Franto nodded. 'Everything's ready.'

'Then there's no reason to delay.' The sooner he was out of the port, the sooner he'd feel safe.

The baby gave a tentative cry.

'That...' Oskane searched for the right word to describe the wet-nurse. 'That—'

'...whore was all I could find.'

'You offered gold.'

'Coppers. If I'd offered gold in the street where I found her, I would not have lived long.'

Oskane shuddered. Nothing about this journey was going to plan. 'Does she know about—'

A screech cut him off. Oskane darted towards the hangings, but the whore met him halfway.

She thrust the baby towards him. 'A half-blood? You expect me to suckle a filthy copperhead?'

He had not thought she would be so particular. Seeing her outraged expression, he bit his tongue.

'I'm a True-woman, not some tainted half-blood bitch. Here...' She thrust the baby into his arms. 'Keep your brat, Wyrd-lover!'

Oskane realised what she meant with a start of surprise. 'He's not my child.'

She sent him a withering look and held out her hand, palm up.

He looked at it uncertainly.

She rubbed her finger and thumb together. 'For my silence.'

'Take this.' Franto dropped a small purse into her hand. 'And consider yourself lucky.'

She peered into the purse eagerly. Her face fell. 'The high priest can afford better than this.'

'Would you rather I cut out your tongue to ensure your silence?' Franto asked.

She blanched. She believed him. So did Oskane.

As the whore flounced out, Oskane flushed. Franto had entered the church as a nineteen-year-old penitent. Rather than serving a year and a day to win favour with the gods or absolve his sin, he had chosen to stay. Oskane had never asked why, although he had gathered from things his servant let slip that Franto's background was very different from his own.

The baby wailed in earnest.

They couldn't take him out into the courtyard like this. Oskane offered his knuckle, but the infant rejected it after two sucks with an even more indignant cry.

'Wait here.' Franto disappeared.

Stomach churning, nerves on edge, Oskane paced while the infant writhed and screamed. He tried changing the baby, then re-wrapping him, tucking his arms and legs in tight as the midwife had recommended. That did not help. He felt helpless as he held the small bundle.

Surely the whole church, with its many priests in their little cubicles, must be able to hear the newborn's piercing cries? So much for secrecy. And he still had to get out of the port.

After an age, Franto returned, took the infant from him and offered the babe a rag dipped in a bowl of milky mixture.

The change was instantaneous, from screaming despot to serious suckling. Oskane heaved a sigh of relief, his ears humming in the sudden silence. 'Goat's milk?'

Franto nodded. 'With a little honey and brandy to knock him out.'

Oskane gasped. 'Should you–'

'It's what the mothers used to give their babies to make them sleep while they worked.'

Oskane did not want to ask what kind of work those mothers did, or how Franto knew where to look for whores. 'If you can care for him tonight, we'll find another wet-nurse tomorrow on the road. Some fine healthy farm girl.'

'One night is my limit,' Franto agreed. 'Caring for an infant isn't as simple as slipping into the crypts to steal the Wyrd scrolls.'

'They're safe on the–'

'Everything's ready.'

'Then let's go.'

'As soon as this settles him. I'll hide him in the food basket.'

In the time it took to feed and settle the infant, Oskane wrote one last thing and sealed it with his official seal. It was a confession of his part in hiding the circumstances of King Charald's birth. He would leave it with his agent at Enlightenment Abbey as insurance. On its own, it would not be enough to bring the king down, but it could be used to cast doubts on the legitimacy of Charald's claim to the throne, which meant it could be used to cloud the legitimacy of any heirs he produced through Nitzel's daughter. And it would strengthen his own cousin's claim on the throne.

A little later, they climbed into the cart and tucked the baby under the seat. With the back of the cart a jumble of belongings and penitents, they left by the delivery gate of the Father's great church, where their departure was hidden amidst the comings and goings.

Time had gotten away from them, and the light faded fast as they headed for the port's eastern gate. Franto drove the cart, while Oskane rode beside him, wearing the simple robe of a scholarly priest.

As they rattled down one street and up another, he watched the passers-by, on the lookout for Nitzel's spies or guards, but he couldn't pick them out – in his current mood, everyone appeared suspicious.

He felt out of his element, adrift and vulnerable. He was used to being high priest of the Father's greatest church, leader of the Seven. Now he was just a priest with a handful of servants and a half-blood brat, and he discovered he did not like feeling so powerless.

The jolting of the cart made his bones ache. He was too old to start all over again.

They came to the three-ways. On their right the road went east towards the gate and Chalcedonia. Straight ahead it continued on to the merchant district. On their left the road went down to the docks, where one T'En sisterhood and two brotherhoods had warehouses. If he told Franto to turn left, they could leave the baby on the doorstep of one of those warehouses. He could ride off knowing the boy was safe, find a quiet corner and live out his days without fear of Nitzel plotting against him.

He put his hand on Franto's arm.

The little man hesitated at the entrance to the three-ways. No breeze blew in from the harbour this evening, and the pall from so many chimneys made it hard to see even to the far side of the intersection.

Once he had been driven by ambition, believed in hollow gods and served a king who turned out to be an unpredictable bully. Now, he was an old priest seeking to restore his family's position. He was tired.

Behind them, someone shouted for them to get a move on.

He thought of Sorna, and he found the strength to gesture towards the city gate.

There it was ahead, a dark tunnel behind the guards who stood in the glow of two lanterns, one to each side. Were they in Nitzel's pay?

Apparently not. They waved the cart through.

In the confined space of the gate tunnel, the rattling of the cart's wheels echoed off the walls, obscenely loud. Two shadows detached from the wall and caught the horses' bridles.

Oskane went to cry for help, but the youths pushed back their hoods and he recognised his cousin's sons.

'Uncle Oskane, it is me, Aranxto,' the eldest said.

'Lower your voice.' Oskane beckoned them closer. 'What is it?'

The youths, aged nineteen and seventeen, came to the side of the cart.

'Uncle, I fear for Sorna. Father's heading home tomorrow. I thought you would watch over her,' Aranxto said. 'Then I heard you were also leaving–'

'Aranxto.' If Oskane told the truth, his cousin's sons would get themselves killed, and that wouldn't help Sorna or their family. At least the boys had some spine, unlike their father. 'I'm afraid you two must prepare yourself for the worst. Sorna's dead. I said the words commending her soul to the Mother.'

Aranxto's mouth fell open and he took a step back, shaking his head. The younger one turned to Oskane, frowning intently.

'Take your brother and go home with your father for now,' Oskane told Aranxto.

'But–'

'Go home while you still can. Nitzel's family is rising, and he will seek to destroy ours. Don't play into his hands. We must bide our time. If we move too soon, we lose everything. Do you understand?'

He looked like he might argue, but the younger took his arm, whispering to him.

'Listen to Matxin,' Oskane said. He performed the sign of the Seven, and Aranxto yielded to his authority, backing away.

'But how will we contact you?' Matxin asked.

'I will contact you,' Oskane told them. He nudged Franto, who urged the horses on.

Another moment and they were through.

'Leaving it late to start a journey?' one of the gate guards said as they trundled into the moonlight. Before them stretched the road, a pale ribbon between winter-bare fields.

'Better late than never,' Franto said.

Chapter Seven

VITTORYXE WAS TIRED from the strain of the ceremony on the bridge and a long day in the saddle, but she drove herself on. If Egrayne could walk the camp perimeter before turning in, then so could she. A single Malaunje warrior was on watch by the ford, hidden in the shadow of a tree.

'Good spot,' he said. 'Water and shelter from the wind.'

'We were lucky to find it free of Mieren.' Luck had nothing to do with it. She'd scouted ahead, taking the lead from Egrayne again. The gift-warrior's reaction intrigued her. She couldn't tell if Egrayne resented being bettered or was amused by their rivalry. The sooner they were lovers and she'd won Egrayne's trust, the better.

Lovers let down their guards. Lovers said things... She would find something to hold over the gift-warrior and ensure her silence.

Vittoryxe left the Malaunje and turned uphill. Travelling always unsettled her. It was impossible to keep the proper distance between T'En and Malaunje.

Behind her, the water chattered happily over the shallow ford. Ahead of her, protected from the wind by the deep stream banks, the trees still retained most of their leaves. It was dark beneath the canopy, except where the silvery light of the near-full moons speared through.

Enough leaves had fallen for her boots to stir them as she climbed, making a quiet approach impossible. Good. No one would be able to creep up on them. Vittoryxe reached the spot where Arodyti should have been. Empty.

Where was she? The young initiate fancied herself a warrior, but if she could not follow orders...

'There you are,' Arodyti greeted her, slightly out of breath as she skidded down the slope. She'd come from beyond a fold in the river bank, probably answering a call of nature, but even so...

'You left your post. We have a newborn and a lad struggling with his gift. Your duty–'

'Come, look what I found.'

'I'm not going off on some wild goose chase. I have to check the camp sentries.'

'It's a tree–'

'I've seen trees.'

'Not like this one. Its branches are all twisted. I've never seen anything like it.'

'This is your first time out of the Celestial City. There is much you've never seen.'

'I think–'

'I didn't ask you to think. I asked you to keep watch. Stay at your post.' Vittoryxe headed further up the rise. 'And mind you don't doze off.'

'I wouldn't...'

Vittoryxe ignored her and kept walking. One more sentry. He was perched up a tree, watching the road.

'First sign of approaching Mieren, you warn us,' Vittoryxe said. The thought of sleeping near their ancestral enemy made her uncomfortable. 'We claimed this camp site, and we're not moving.'

She didn't really expect him to see Mieren this close to season's cusp, when the walls between the earthly plane and the higher empyrean plane were at their weakest.

Leaving the sentry, Vittoryxe headed downhill. It was steep here, and she was in a hurry. Her boots slipped in the leaf litter. Before she could fall, a strong hand caught her arm, setting her back on her feet.

'Egrayne.' She reached out to steady herself and let her gift surge so that Egrayne would get a taste of it. 'Thank you.'

The warrior sucked in a breath and stepped back into shadow. Vittoryxe wished she had the raedan gift so she could read her. If she could perceive the nuances of people's feelings, she could manipulate them. Then it would be easy to cajole and threaten her way to become the sisterhood's all-mother. But the last raedan died over two hundred years ago.

'Everything good?' the gift-warrior asked.

'Fine.' She didn't bother to mention Arodyti's tree. Foolish girl. Before this excursion, all the initiate had ever seen were topiary trees in pots and the sculpted trees of the city's park.

Egrayne stifled a yawn. 'I'm for bed.'

'Me too.'

They both clambered down the slope to the spot by the river where two tents had been erected for the T'En. The Malaunje would sleep in the open. Both initiates were on watch; that meant she and Egrayne had the tent to themselves. Perfect.

Already planning her moves, Vittoryxe didn't notice anything as they passed the gift-tutor's tent.

But Egrayne paused, chin lifted eyes narrowed. 'I sense–'

'Male gift?' Vittoryxe opened her senses to confirm it. 'The lad, Graelen.' The one they'd taken from the winery; the one the gift-tutor had been sent to test. 'I sensed it on him when we were riding.'

'He's going to be powerful for a man.' Egrayne was not happy.

'Powerful and physically strong.' Vittoryxe resented the fact that at barely sixteen, the lad was already taller than her. 'Just what the sisterhood needs, a lad who has proven so volatile his choice-mother had to send for the gift-tutor. They'll have to train him hard in gift and body to keep him in line.'

'It's not like he can help it,' Egrayne said.

The T'En's gifts surged in their youth, when they had the least control over it. Gift-empowerers could reach into the youngsters and unlock their gifts smoothly, but they were rare, and the last one had died over ninety years before. This meant all T'En below the age of ninety had been forced to stumble upon the nature of their gifts through trial and error, wasting years before they started training. Empowerment was another high-status gift Vittoryxe would have been happy to possess.

Egrayne gestured to the dark tent. 'He's in with Lealeni. If need be, she can contain his gift for him.'

'He's in with the newborn and the wet-nurse,' Vittoryxe added. 'Hardly ideal.' And this conversation was hardly ideal if she planned seduction. 'Come on.'

She led Egrayne down to their tent and stepped inside.

Egrayne went to light the lamp.

'No.' She caught the gift-warrior's hand, bringing it to her lips, so she could kiss those scarred knuckles. 'You saved my life today.'

Egrayne inhaled sharply.

'You stepped between me and a man in danger of losing control of his gift.'

Egrayne said nothing. The tent was too dark to see her expression.

'I wanted to say how much I admire you.' In Vittoryxe's experience, people loved compliments.

'What are you offering?'

Why did Egrayne have to be so cynical? 'A night's trysting? In each other's arms we could share our gifts, reinforce them. It's a long ride back. We may have need–'

'So you do this to strengthen us both?'

I do it to win your cooperation, but now I'm beginning to wonder if it's worth the trouble. 'That, and...'

Vittoryxe ran her hand up Egrayne's arm, felt goose bumps rise on her skin and the surge of her gift. For all that Egrayne was keeping a cool head, she wanted this.

'The others will know.'

'So what if they sense it when we gift-tryst? Let down your defences.' She reached for Egrayne's long plait and began to unravel it. 'I want to roll naked in your hair. I want to feel your power race over my skin.'

Sensation swamped her as Egrayne let down her gift walls. The depth of the warrior's need surprised Vittoryxe. Triumph and desire made her heart race.

Egrayne pushed the vest over Vittoryxe's shoulders, trapping her arms against her body and baring her breasts. She felt a soft cheek and hot breath on her skin, and knew she could have Egrayne for more than one night, if it suited her.

A scream sounded sharp and clear in the night.

For a heartbeat, Vittoryxe did not understand.

'We're under attack,' Egrayne said. She darted out of the tent, leaving Vittoryxe to straighten her clothing and rein in her gift.

OSKANE DOZED IN the seat. He hadn't had much rest last night, and he'd been on edge all day. Now the rocking of the cart and the gentle plod of the two horses lulled him to sleep. He blinked and took a deep breath.

'You're awake.' Franto spoke softly, so as not to disturb the sleeping penitents. 'The horses are getting tired. We should stop for the night.'

'If I remember correctly, there's a small village over that way.' Now that he was awake, Oskane's mind raced. 'Hopefully, we can collect more penitents at Enlightenment Abbey. It would be good if we could find a former farmer. Restoration Retreat used to be almost self sufficient. We'll need a cow, some chickens and goats. The retreat will no doubt need repairing. A carpenter –'

Angry voices from up ahead made him freeze. Several dogs barked.

Franto halted the horses. 'Could be brigands.'

'The roads are thick with them, but a poor village would not have much worth stealing.' Oskane glanced over his shoulder. There was no room to turn around, and he doubted Franto could make the horses back up in their traces.

More shouts, getting closer. The words were unintelligible, but the anger was clear. They could see nothing beyond a bend in the road.

'Do you have a sword?' one of the penitents asked. 'I used to be a mercenary.'

Oskane jumped with fright. 'We're priests, not men of violence.'

'A staff, then.'

'They will not harm members of the clergy,' Oskane said, hopefully.

His stomach lurched as an angry mob of about a dozen people rounded the bend. The leaping flames of their torches banished the cool silvery light of the two moons. They brandished pitchforks and shovels. Not brigands, then.

His first thought was that they knew about the half-blood infant asleep under his seat, and were going to demand he hand it over to the Wyrds. Then he saw that they drove a young woman before them. The dogs nipped at her bare feet and her calves were revealed by a torn nightgown. She stumbled, almost dropping a weeping infant. There was blood on her nightgown. She lifted despairing eyes and saw the cart.

Recognising the priestly robes, she held out one hand in supplication. Her mouth moved, but between the shouts of the villagers, the barking of the dogs and the whinnying of the frightened horses, he didn't catch what she said.

Seeing the priests, the mob stopped.

'What is this?' Oskane demanded, coming to his feet. 'What have you done to this poor woman?'

One of the villagers gestured with his torch. 'She's a Wyrd-lover.'

'I never–'

'Then where'd the half-blood come from?' another demanded.

She had no answer for that.

'And why'd you keep the copperhead?' The first man bustled forward. He had the shiny patches of many small burns on his brawny forearms; the village blacksmith, Oskane guessed. 'The brat's nearly a year old. She kept it hidden all this time.' He shoved his torch near the crying infant and caught one little hand. 'See, six fingers. Filthy half-blood.'

Franto nudged Oskane, who knew what he meant. This was fortuitous.

'If she loves Wyrds so much, she can go live with them,' a middle-aged woman announced. From her tone it was clear she was relishing the young woman's disgrace. 'We don't want her kind.'

'She can come with us,' Oskane said. 'We're headed south. There's a brotherhood winery down that way. We'll drop her there.'

'They won't take me,' she protested. 'What'll I do?'

The blacksmith stepped away from her. 'You shoulda thought of that before you kept the brat!'

Oskane thought he heard a whimper from the baby under his seat. 'Get on the cart.'

She went to go around the back, but the penitents protested.

'We won't ride with a filthy Wyrd-lover,' one of them said.

Oskane was tempted to tell them they could walk, but he was certain, now, the newborn had woken, and he just wanted to get away. 'Help her up with us, Franto. Our piety will protect us from her taint.'

The cart seat was built for two, but could hold three at a squeeze. Franto put the young mother between them, then took up the reins again. The villagers parted as Franto urged the horses on and the cart rounded the bend.

Oskane could feel the young woman, sitting stiff and reserved beside him. She held her child close to her and hushed the infant with soft words. He heard the penitents muttering amongst themselves. If they refused to share a cart with a half-blood, they certainly wouldn't want to live alongside one. The retreat would have to be segregated. He'd been so intent on getting away that he hadn't given much thought to how he would establish their living arrangements.

Soon they passed through the village, which consisted of six or seven cottages clustered around a mill pond. Chickens fussed as they settled down for the night.

A little way beyond the village, the young woman shifted on the seat. 'Thank you, but you can let us off here.'

'Why?' Oskane asked.

'I'll go, I promise I will. I just need–'

'Your home's near here?'

She nodded and pointed.

Franto turned the cart up the track, and they entered a clearing where a faint light spilled from a simple cottage. The door stood open, half off its hinges.

'Kolst?' the young woman called.

No answer.

'Your husband?' Oskane asked.

She nodded, distracted, as Franto stopped the cart and helped her down. Without another word, she ran into the cottage.

Oskane met Franto's eyes. They both followed her into the cottage, where a single tallow candle burned. The floor was packed earth, but someone had taken the trouble to carve a decorative frieze of the Farmer and the Mother over the mantel, along with the symbol of the Seven. Amidst evidence of a struggle, a young man lay sprawled on a rug made of knotted rags. There was blood in his pale blond hair.

The woman tucked the sleeping infant in a cradle and knelt next to him. 'Kolst, speak to me.'

Oskane nodded to Franto, who knelt and checked the young man's injuries. She looked on anxiously.

Meanwhile, Oskane inspected the cottage. It seemed the villagers had knocked him out and dragged her off. The locals were more forgiving of him. He was a useful member of their community and could take another wife. All he had to do was repudiate this one.

'He'll have a headache when he wakes, but he'll be all right,' Franto said.

'I'll stay with him,' the young woman said. 'We'll leave first thing tomorrow. I promise. We won't give trouble.'

'Where will you go?' Oskane asked, knowing the answer. There was nowhere they could go. All doors would be closed to them, for no True-man would welcome a half-blood, and the Wyrds would not have True-men and -women inside their villa walls.

The young woman's mouth opened, then closed.

'What is your name?' Oskane asked.

'Hiruna.'

'What if I said I know somewhere safe, where you will be able to live and raise your Malaunje child?'

'I'd go there tomorrow.'

'Even if it meant not leaving for seventeen years?'

'Why would I leave my child?'

Oskane nodded. 'We'll take you there. But there is something you must do for me.' And he righted a chair to sit and explain the bargain. 'Are you still feeding your child?'

She nodded, flushing, as if she expected ridicule.

'Franto, bring the baby in.'

While they waited for his servant to return, Hiruna studied him. 'Who are you? You don't speak like the priest who comes to our village.'

'I'm Scholar Oskane. I resigned my position as high priest to the Father, leader of the Seven, to take part in a special mission for the church.' He thought it best not to mention the king yet.

Franto returned with the newborn in the basket. The babe had woken, uttering weak kitten-like cries.

Hiruna plucked him from the basket. 'You poor little thing.' She unwrapped him, spotting his six fingers and toes. 'He's Malaunje and newborn. Less than a day old.' She looked up at Oskane, who said nothing.

Wasting no time, she undid her bodice and freed a breast. The baby turned his face towards her, latching on greedily.

'There, now, isn't that better?' she crooned, then looked up. 'What's his name?'

Oskane had no idea. He saw Franto turn away to hide a smile.

'Sorne. His name is Sorne.'

'Sorne,' she repeated. 'Our son's name is Izteben.'

He nodded and wondered if she realised what she was doing, rearing half-bloods who would one day turn on her.

Because they always did.

'The penitents want to know what's going on,' Franto said.

'We'll stay here tonight. Strip the cottage of anything useful...' – Hiruna looked up as Oskane continued – 'No point leaving your things for the villagers to steal. We leave before dawn.'

Chapter Eight

VITTORYXE FOUND THE camp in uproar. Malaunje ran about shouting, the newborn wailed, and there was no sign of Egrayne.

Over by the fire, Gift-tutor Lealeni was in the midst of a dozen Malaunje warriors lighting torches.

Vittoryxe strode across. 'What is it? What's going on?'

'Graelen's missing,' Lealeni said. 'Last time I looked he was fast asleep.'

'I heard a scream.'

The gift-tutor glanced in the direction of Arodyti's position. 'Egrayne went...'

Vittoryxe was already running. Several of the Malaunje ran with her, bringing torches. At their approach, the trees came alive with leaping shadows.

'Over there.' Seventeen-year-old Frane pointed to a tangle of limbs and a long silver braid amongst the leaves. He bounded off to investigate.

'Wait,' Vittoryxe shouted. Following him up the slope, she scanned the area for threat, but her gaze was drawn back to the body. For an instant, she thought it was Egrayne, then she recognised Arodyti. The initiate had left her post again. It looked like she'd been running back to camp.

What had frightened her?

Frane went to turn Arodyti over, but Vittoryxe stopped the inexperienced warrior with a sharp gesture. She tasted power in the air, like the promise of rain. If Arodyti's gift essence had passed onto the empyrean plane, he would be dragged through with her.

Vittoryxe opened her gift awareness to check. A gentle pulse of power emanated from Arodyti's body; if she had been dragged onto the higher plane, there would be nothing.

'It's all right. Arodyti hasn't passed through,' Vittoryxe managed to whisper. Speaking while she was in this state was incredibly difficult. It was the thing that made her a gift-warrior. Most T'En could not even sustain an awareness of both worlds, let alone communicate.

At her signal Frane turned Arodyti over. Blood, bright with power, seeped from a cut behind her ear. Vittoryxe guessed the young initiate had slipped in the leaf litter and hit her head.

'A simple head wound. Carry her back to the gift-tutor.'

What had the foolish initiate been running from, and where were Egrayne and the lad?

Vittoryxe studied the Malaunje warriors, who appeared as softly glowing forms. 'You.' She pointed to the brightest one, but couldn't tell who it was.

'Roskara,' the warrior said.

'Come with me.' They had to find Egrayne and the lad. 'I can sense wild-power nearby. If I segue to the empyrean plane, watch over my body.'

It was every T'En's greatest fear, leaving their body vulnerable while they worked their gift on the higher plane.

Vittoryxe stumbled up the rise and saw it.

Arodyti's tree.

Wild-power must have surged through here and blighted the tree when it was still a seedling. It glowed, deformed and twisted almost beyond recognition, power pulsing through every branch and twig. What was it doing here? This was not a known weak point between the planes.

It was nearly season's cusp when the walls between the planes were thinnest, but even so, that shouldn't have been enough.

As Vittoryxe plunged down the slope, her boot caught on something soft – a body – and she flew forwards, sprawling in the leaf litter. She tasted dirt, felt grit in her mouth.

Heart thundering, she came to her hands and knees, wiped her mouth, and turned to face the person she'd tripped over. Whoever it was, they appeared to her as a negative space; his, or her, gift essence had segued to the higher plane

Please don't let it be Egrayne.

'Who is it, Roskara?' she asked, fearful of touching the body in case she was pulled through to the empyrean plane.

'The lad.'

She cursed.

At a guess, Graelen had slipped out of the tent and gone for a walk in the moonlight. T'En had a natural affinity for moonlight. It was soothing when the gift troubled them.

She suspected that Graelen had found the tree and been fascinated by its tangled lacework of branches. After that, he must have called his gift, or it had surged beyond his control, creating a breach in the wall between planes.

But that didn't explain why Arodyti had screamed. Had the initiate tried to bring him back herself? No... she'd be beside him, lost on the higher plane.

'I've found Gift-warrior Egrayne,' Roskara called.

Her voice echoed hollowly to Vittoryxe's distorted perception, and she couldn't tell which direction it had come from. 'Don't touch–'

'I know that. I'm not stupid.'

Vittoryxe let the insolence slide, her mind racing. If Egrayne had gone through and failed to return, it meant the big warrior was in trouble. Only one thing for it.

'I'm going after them. Watch over our bodies, Roskara.'

Reaching out into the darkness that was the lad's form, she searched for a patch of bare skin. One touch and she would be dragged through.

Roskara screamed.

Vittoryxe lifted her head. Saw an empyrean predator lumber up the slope. Its form must have been cloaked by the power leaking from the tree. Now that it was on the move, she saw its thick shoulders, its four short legs and sensed its driving hunger. This must be why Arodyti had run to fetch the gift-warriors.

Vittoryxe sprang to her feet.

The predator stopped, massive head swinging from side to side. Out of its natural element, it was confused.

Roskara froze. If she ran, the predator would target her. If she didn't run, it might take her down and devour her essence. It only hesitated now because it could not decide which of them to attack.

Vittoryxe leapt between Roskara and the beast. There was no time to do more than tackle the thing and drag it back to where it belonged.

The passage was instantaneous. One moment she was on the earthly plane, the next, the empyrean. Releasing the stunned beast, she stepped back. The ground fell away behind her and she tumbled down the slope, somersaulting and rolling to her feet.

Here she was powerful, but her gift would attract other predators. She had to kill this one quickly.

Here the very plane itself was hostile to her kind, and hungry for her gift. She could feel the cold leaching up through her feet, stealing her life force, draining her power. Here she existed through the force of her will alone. Her boots were an extension of her and offered no protection from the cold.

An untrained T'En would not last long. Either the predators would tear him apart, or his power would leak away until he slipped into unconsciousness. The lad didn't have enough training to focus his essence and escape, which was why Egrayne had come after him.

She spun around, looking for them. Nowhere in sight.

But Egrayne had been here. Someone had given the empyrean plane form, forcing it to adhere to the layout of their campsite, though there were differences. She saw no trees other than the one misshapen growth, and no stream flowed through the hollow. Only mist gathered down there, cloaking any manner of thing.

The predator had a more substantial form here. She recognised a bane-boar. With her fall their positions had been reversed, and now it held the high ground. Its broad shoulders were as high as her waist and it stood on the crest of the rise, silhouetted against the brooding blue-black clouds.

She'd heard that powerful T'En could bring sunlight to the empyrean plane, but whenever she'd come here, the atmosphere held the menace of the last breathless moment before a summer storm.

The bane-boar lowered its head.

It would charge her, relying on its weight and the steep slope to knock her off her feet. If she fell, she'd die.

She reached for a spear, creating it by the force of her will, drawing on years of training and her innate power. But every act drained her, and too much use of her gift would make her lethargic and vulnerable.

Letting loose a wave of malevolence that would have knocked an untrained T'En to his knees, the beast charged.

She waited, balanced lightly on the balls of her feet. At the last moment, she stepped sideways, letting the bane-boar rumble past her. Quick as thought, she drove the spear into the creature's torso, behind its fore-leg, deep into its chest.

She felt the impact through her whole body; felt the bane-boar's lifeforce surge up the spear and into her.

Before she could reject the tainted power, the spear was ripped from her hands, leaving a raw ache in the centre of her body.

The bane-boar lumbered down the slope, crashing into the tree. At the impact a shiver shot up the tree, racing out to the tip of every torturous, tangled twig.

With a shudder, the bane-boar dropped to its knees, then toppled sideways. She needed to retrieve her spear and absorb it, to heal the wound in her chest, which ached with every breath.

But the tree gave another shudder and she caught her breath as the branches quested blindly until one found the bane-boar; then the tree enveloped the beast. The branches writhed like a pile of maggots devouring a corpse, insidiously single-minded.

Vittoryxe backed up one step, then another, tripping and falling on her backside. A hoarfrost covered the earth. It stung her bare palms as power leached from her.

Sensing a presence behind her, she scrambled to her feet and spun around.

Egrayne and the lad had reached the crest. Untrained, he didn't know how to shield his gift; he burned bright, a beacon to all predators.

In fact, they must have already been attacked. Egrayne was wounded in several places. Power bled freely from her body, weakening her by the moment.

On the empyrean plane, a person's true self could be revealed. In Egrayne, Vittoryxe saw the-way-of-the-warrior. Such purity of purpose – she both hated her and wanted her desperately. Egrayne's gaze slid past her, making Vittoryxe wonder what the gift-warrior sensed in her.

Egrayne gestured to Vittoryxe's chest.

She looked down to discover her wound was weeping power. She shrugged and gestured to the tree. It had settled down now, and there was no sign of the bane-boar. She had the distinct impression that if she ventured too near, the same thing would happen to her. They had to get out of here.

Looking back, she saw Egrayne shove the lad towards her and turn to face something over the rise. Graelen stumbled down the slope, colliding with Vittoryxe.

All that unshielded male power. Delicious. Her first instinct was to feast on him. He was without defences, and she could have drained him in an instant.

But she was covenant-sworn to protect him until he joined a brotherhood. And besides, she feared what would happen to her if she developed a taste for male power.

Egrayne glanced over her shoulder, gesturing for them to keep back.

Something from beyond the rise grabbed the big warrior, wrapping around her calf. Before Vittoryxe could disentangle herself from Graelen, the thing jerked Egrayne off her feet and slammed her onto the ground. In a flash, she was dragged over the rise and out of sight. Graelen shook with fright, shedding power. He would have gone after Egrayne, but Vittoryxe enveloped him in a hug and segued back to the earthly plane before his lack of control could get them both killed.

She regained consciousness to find herself sprawled across him, the pair of them at the centre of a concerned group.

Vittoryxe sat up, head spinning. She felt like she'd been punched in the chest but, when she touched the spot, there was no blood. This time.

'She left Egrayne,' Graelen croaked, voice gathering power. 'She left her to die.'

'You have no idea,' Vittoryxe snapped. She spotted Gift-tutor Lealeni and the initiates, amidst half a dozen Malaunje warriors with torches. Down in the dip, behind the Malaunje, the twisted tree's highest branches stood silhouetted against both full moons. She had a flash of the tree reaching for the bane-boar. 'Get away. Get away from the tree.'

Infected by her fear, the Malaunje clambered up the slope, slipping in leaf litter. Vittoryxe grabbed Graelen's arm and dragged him up the rise, not stopping until they were a safe distance from the twisted tree.

'Why?' Gift-tutor Lealeni asked. She frowned. 'I sense no power coming from the tree.'

'It's sated,' Vittoryxe guessed. When she put her hand to her face, she found frost crystals had rimed her mouth and eyes. Every muscle ached, and her skin stung as if she'd been slapped repeatedly. 'It...' – she glanced to the gathered Malaunje – 'it's a nexus point between the planes. We need to leave a warning.'

'See to the signs before we leave tomorrow,' Lealeni told the oldest of the warriors.

'Are you all right, Vittoryxe?' Arodyti asked. Her head was bound, and she was supported by the other initiate, Kiane. 'What happened to the empyrean predator? I was coming to get you, when I–'

'Gift-warrior Vittoryxe saved me,' Roskara spoke up, from somewhere behind the others. 'She tackled the empyrean beast and dragged it–'

'She left Egrayne behind.' Graelen's voice shook. 'Egrayne saved me from...' He had no words for the horrors he'd seen.

'Of course she did. She swore a gift-bound vow, and so did I.' Vittoryxe turned to Lealeni. 'If anyone killed Egrayne, it's the lad. He opened the nexus point between the planes.' He tried to protest that it was an accident, but she spoke over him. 'He was shedding enough power to attract a dozen predators. Egrayne turned back to give us time to escape.'

Someone made a sound of pain in their throat and Gift-tutor Lealeni stepped aside to reveal Roskara standing guard over Egrayne's body, as she'd been instructed. Judging by her stricken expression, Roskara was carrying a torch for Egrayne.

The big gift-warrior lay neatly on the leaf litter. A fine hoarfrost covered her skin and clothing, and crept outwards, glowing ice crystals decorating leaves and twigs.

'You must go back for her,' Lealeni said.

'What?' Vittoryxe turned to the gift-tutor. It was on the tip of her tongue to point out that Egrayne was already dead. But if she didn't go back, she'd be branded a coward.

'Of course.' Resentment raced through Vittoryxe as she gave a deep obeisance, hands going to her heart and out. 'I live to serve.'

Almost blind with fear and fury, Vittoryxe walked across the slope towards Egrayne. The Malaunje parted, eyes downcast to show respect. Her knees felt rubbery, and a strange rushing sound filled her ears.

One thing was certain, she was not going to die tonight.

Sure, she'd go back, but she would not waste her life on pointless heroics. She'd be in and out again before the predators realised. Egrayne had made her choice. No need for them both to die.

She'd almost reached Egrayne's supine body when, without warning, Roskara crumpled.

The Malaunje warriors and servants gasped. Vittoryxe glanced to the gift-tutor for an explanation, but Lealeni looked stunned.

Vittoryxe was infuriated. Everything must follow the rules. Without rules, they had no certainty. They were scrambling in the dark, blind as ignorant Mieren.

'What's going on?' Graelen asked, his deep voice breathless with fear. 'I don't understand.'

'Egrayne's still alive.' That much Vittoryxe could guess.

'Yes, but she's too weak to make the passage. I've seen this once before, seventy years ago, when I started my training,' Lealeni said. Vittoryxe made a quick calculation. Lealeni must have been barely seventeen. 'Egrayne has anchored herself in Roskara in an attempt to return to this plane.'

Two lives at stake. Vittoryxe looked to Lealeni. The gift-tutor was older, more experienced; she should be the one to attempt this. But Lealeni indicated that Vittoryxe should proceed. Giving her a chance to shine and win stature.

Determination filled Vittoryxe, as she dropped to her knees. She raised her hand, noticing its slight tremor. Before she could touch Egrayne, the gift-warrior sat up. Roskara's head slid down her chest to rest in her lap.

Cries of joy greeted her return.

'Get back,' Lealeni warned, voice shrill. 'It might not be Egrayne.'

Fear speared through Vittoryxe and she lurched back, scrambling to her feet. What was Lealeni thinking? Why hadn't the gift-tutor prepared her properly?

'It's... it's me,' Egrayne croaked. She swallowed, grimacing as if it hurt. Then she looked down at Roskara and wonder filled her face. Gently, she smoothed copper strands from the Malaunje warrior's forehead. 'Roskara?' But she did not stir. Egrayne looked up. 'Lealeni?'

'You've imprinted your gift on Roskara.'

'Devotee?' Vittoryxe repeated, stunned. 'Roskara is Egrayne's devotee now?'

'Of course,' the gift-tutor said. 'What did you expect?'

Egrayne lifted her hands. 'But I didn't mean–'

'You survived against the odds. That's what's important. Too few gift-warriors are born, and we don't want to waste the years of training.'

Vittoryxe hardly heard Lealeni. Envy consumed her. Egrayne had a devotee. Before this, Egrayne's stature was only one step ahead of hers, and now it outstripped hers. Now, more than ever, she needed to seduce Egrayne and find something to hold over her. But the devotee complicated things.

'...and carry Roskara back to camp,' the gift-tutor was saying. She gestured to the Malaunje. 'Leave us. You initiates, take the lad with you.'

By the time the Malaunje had left, Egrayne was also on her feet, swaying slightly.

Tonight, Vittoryxe had banished an empyrean beast and saved a lost lad, but the big warrior's miraculous survival and imprinting of Roskara had robbed Vittoryxe of her glory.

As for Graelen, he refused to leave and the two initiates hesitated, not sure what to do.

'If you won't go, make yourself useful,' Vittoryxe said. She was too angry to touch Egrayne; her defences might not be good enough to hide her true feelings. 'Help her.'

Graelen stepped forward and offered his shoulder for the big warrior to lean on.

At Egrayne's touch, he froze, then sank to his knees. Eyes closed, Egrayne felt his neck, then his jaw and up his cheeks until her fingertips touched his temples. Her eyelids flickered, eyes rolling back in her head.

'What's happening?' Arodyti whispered.

Lealeni opened her mouth but nothing came out.

Both initiates looked to Vittoryxe, who shrugged, torn between fear and irritation. If she ever became gift-tutor, she would study all the treatises until she knew everything there was to know. Impatience made her voice harsh. 'What happened seventy years ago, Lealeni?'

'That time, the gift-warrior didn't come back. An empyrean beast came through. It took over her body. We only managed to kill it because it was trying to control both her body and her devotee's.'

Egrayne let Graelen go. As he pitched forward into the leaf litter, the gift-warrior staggered back a couple of steps, gasping.

Meanwhile, the lad pushed himself up onto his hands and knees. He sat back on his heels and lifted a sleepy face to them, looking younger than his sixteen years. 'What happened?'

'He's a gift-warrior,' Egrayne whispered, voice hoarse. She rubbed her face, hands trembling. 'I sensed the nature of his gift and understood its purpose.'

'Only an empowerer could do that,' Vittoryxe protested. 'Your gift isn't–'

'It is now.' Egrayne showed no doubt. 'I know what I sensed.'

'Sometimes...' Lealeni began slowly, 'sometimes a life-changing event can unlock a new facet of a T'En's gift. I can't wait to tell the all-mother we have a gift-empowerer in our sisterhood.' The gift-tutor's voice rose with excitement. 'The other sisterhoods will have to bring their budding T'En children to us. Egrayne, you–'

The gift-warrior moaned, dropped to her knees and threw up on the leaf litter.

'Help her, Vittoryxe. And Kiane' – the gift-tutor turned to the initiate and gestured to the lad – 'help him. Back to camp, everyone. The sooner we return to the city, the sooner the all-mother can claim stature for our sisterhood!'

Which was all very well for the sisterhood, but no good for her. Vittoryxe hid her resentment as she moved forward to help the gift-warrior... no, *gift-empowerer* to her feet. Egrayne's sudden elevation had completely eclipsed her efforts tonight. An empyrean kill and saving the lad's life should have given her great stature. Just her luck for it to happen the night Egrayne gained a devotee and became an empowerer.

Egrayne was well on her way to becoming the sisterhood's next all-mother. The realisation rocked Vittoryxe. It was so unfair. Why couldn't she develop a new facet to her gift?

How could she compete with an empowerer?

Should she seduce Egrayne and settle for becoming the sisterhood's hand-of-force or voice-of-reason? No, she didn't see why she should have to settle for second best. A surge of anger lent Vittoryxe strength, as she helped Egrayne to her feet.

'You're stronger than you look,' Egrayne muttered.

'You've no idea. Are you alright?'

Egrayne nodded. Then took a couple of unsteady steps. 'My legs don't seem to be working properly.'

'Don't worry, we'll get you home safe.' More's the pity.

Chapter Nine

IRIAN HALTED HIS horse in the jostle at the causeway entrance. It was late afternoon, and Mieren merchants who had ventured into the free quarter to trade were making their way back to the town on the lake's shore.

Although he was glad to be home, he dreaded it. Now they would have to report the infant's death to All-mother Aayelora's sisterhood. His brotherhood had been handing over their T'En newborns to this sisterhood for four hundred years, and the thought of lying to these powerful women made his gut cramp. Even the sight of the city, bathed in the golden glow of the westering sun, could not cheer him.

In front of him, the causeway stretched, a thin ribbon of bridge, wide enough for two carts to pass each other. It was made of the same white limestone as the city walls. To the left, just outside these walls, enterprising merchants from the other six kingdoms had built houses on poles. This was the foreign quarter, and it was connected to the causeway by a bridge.

The causeway ended in the great gates. Each evening when the Mieren were turned out, these gates were closed and secured. Behind them, on the lowest end of the island, the brotherhood formed a barrier to defend the city.

From here he could see their defensive walls, between three and four storeys high. Behind and above the walls were the rooftop gardens, towers and spires of the brotherhoods' palaces.

Further up, the ground rose into the area known as the free quarter. Here there were shops leased by foreign merchants or run by enterprising brotherhoods and sisterhoods, theatres, places to dine and mingle, and the empowerment dome, which had not been used for its true purpose since the last empowerer died.

The free quarter provided a buffer for the sisterhood quarter, which lay behind another wall. On the island's peak, the golden domes and intricate lace-edged towers of the sisterhood palaces shone in the setting sun. All this reflected in the mirror-like surface of the lake.

The sisterhoods dominated the island, just as they dominated the T'Enatuath.

What Rohaayel had set in motion, hiding his female T'En child on Lighthouse Isle, could not be undone, and Irian experienced a heady mix of trepidation and excitement.

He was about to urge his horse onto the causeway, when a woman's voice ordered him to wait. Twisting in the saddle, he saw that a sisterhood party had come up behind them. The speaker was a young, arrogant gift-warrior. She wore a torc of silver with one freshly carved symbol, showing she had recently slain an empyrean beast.

And she was determined to claim precedence.

His instinct was to insist his party cross first, but Voice-of-reason Ardeyne touched his arm. Leaning close, he spoke in a whisper. 'Let them pass. We don't want to attract attention.'

Irian frowned. If he would normally object, then surely letting them pass would be suspicious. But even as he opened his mouth to argue this, Ardeyne gave a gracious gesture and ushered the sisterhood party past, giving them precedence.

The young gift-warrior led her people onto the causeway. Several Malaunje warriors and servants followed. A T'En lad rode by. He flushed when Irian caught him looking, and glanced down.

Irian hid a smile. He could remember being that age; how he'd longed to join his brotherhood and make a name for himself! Those last few years in the sisterhood had grated. Turning seventeen could not come too soon.

A newborn squalled. His heart raced, as he spotted the infant in the arms of a Malaunje wet-nurse. A T'En baby, he guessed, handed over by a brotherhood who, unlike them, had obeyed the covenant.

The T'En infant was the reason the gift-warrior claimed precedence. They flaunted their power.

'I know you,' one of the females said.

He recognised All-mother Aayelora's gift-tutor. For a heartbeat he could not remember her name.

A big gift-warrior rode beside her. This one also had a one-kill symbol on her neck torc.

'Gift-tutor Lealeni,' Ardeyne greeted her.

'All-father Rohaayel, Voice-of-reason Ardeyne, Hand-of-force Irian.' The gift-tutor acknowledged their titles and inclined her head, thanking them with magnificent condescension. She frowned. 'Where is Devotee Mariska? Her pregnancy went beyond seven small moons. She's due to give birth to a T'En infant soon.'

'There was an accident, her horse bolted and she nearly died, gift-tutor. She remained behind to recover,' Ardeyne said, with just the right tone of regret. 'We lost the baby.'

Irian felt the moment stretch. Surely, the gift-tutor would see through their lies, denounce them and turn her gift-warriors on them?

Instead she turned to Rohaayel. 'We grieve for your loss, all-father. I'll let the lineage-keeper know the sad news.'

Irian glanced over his shoulder and saw their all-father hunched in the saddle, as if he'd suffered a blow.

As the sisterhood party rode on, Irian sucked in a ragged breath.

Mieren merchants continued to pour off the causeway, but Irian made no move to cross. Not yet. He'd wait for his hands to stop shaking.

'They believed us,' Ardeyne whispered.

'Why shouldn't they?' Rohaayel countered. 'No brotherhood has dared to flout the covenant for four hundred years. In their arrogance, the sisters would never expect it.'

Ardeyne grinned. 'Especially if we continue to hand over all other T'En infants.'

'Exactly.'

'Come.' Irian turned his mount towards the city. He had to trust Rohaayel's judgement. Their lives and the fate of their brotherhood depended on it.

Glory or destruction.

VITTORYXE HAD UNPACKED and stripped down to her thigh-length undershirt when she heard a cry and pounding footsteps. She took off running down the corridor, bare feet slapping on the slick, cool marble.

A Malaunje servant collided with her at the turn. She steadied the young woman. 'What is it?'

'Trouble with the lads. The new one's fighting–'

'Where?'

'In the training yard.'

'Where's the hand-of-force?'

'With the all-mother. She's gone into labour.'

Vittoryxe cursed and ran down the steps, calling over her shoulder. 'Tell Egrayne I need her.'

She found the youths in the yard. There were seven of them, aged thirteen to sixteen, and the younger ones had wisely backed off to watch the big lads fight. All skill had been forgotten as they rolled on the ground like a couple of brawling Mieren.

It was Graelen and Ashaayel, of course. He was the only one near the big lad's size, and an obvious rival. Cursing the male's instinctive need to dominate, Vittoryxe looked for some way to separate them. She was not going to get between them. Both lads outweighed and out-muscled her and, in their current state, both were just as likely to take a swing at her.

Furious, Vittoryxe strode over to the fountain and filled a bucket, tossing the contents over the two lads.

They came up spluttering, recognised her, and sanity returned.

'Is this how you resolve your differences? Are you no better than Mieren barbarians?' she demanded. The problem was, if they *weren't* ready to resort to violence by the time they returned to the brotherhoods, they would be seen as prey.

Ashaayel ducked his head. But Graelen looked her up and down, his mouth twisting in a smile that reminded her she wore only an undershirt.

Her first instinct was to wipe that insolent smirk off his face, but if she raised her hand to him, he might strike back. Unless she wanted to use her gift on him – she was not going to risk dragging him onto the empyrean plane for this – she could do nothing. Oh, she could have broken down his defences and drained him of his gift, then forced her will on him, at least until his gift recovered, but... she was sworn to protect him.

Graelen grinned.

'What's going on?' Egrayne demanded.

Vittoryxe gestured to the lads. 'More balls than brains, the pair of them.'

Egrayne strode across and casually cuffed both lads across the head. 'Ashaayel, you and Graelen are to clean up the courtyard.' It was a Malaunje task, and an insult to their stature. 'The rest of you, upstairs, bathe.'

The younger lads ran off.

Vittoryxe wanted to tell the empowerer how Graelen had looked at her, like she was powerless. She had never felt so vulnerable and she hated it. She wanted to drive the lad to his knees and make him beg her forgiveness. The force of her anger roused her gift and, for one terrible moment, she feared it would slip her control.

Roskara ran into the courtyard with her weapon drawn, clearly ready to defend Egrayne. The empowerer raised an arm, and her devotee went to her side. They smiled at each other, sharing an intimacy that Vittoryxe found particularly irritating.

As Vittoryxe brought her gift under control, she realised she needed a devotee to add to her stature. She would have to choose the right Malaunje, someone who would be an asset to her, someone ambitious.

'You're all right?' Roskara whispered.

'Vittoryxe had it sorted.'

Ignoring the devotee's grateful look, Vittoryxe gestured to Graelen. She wanted him out of the sisterhood. 'He'd barely walked into the yard before he picked a fight. If this is how he was behaving on his choice-mother's estate, no wonder she sent him away.'

'Grae, Ash, come here,' Egrayne called.

Both lads came over. Graelen's right eye was swollen and Ashaayel had a split lip. Since Ashaayel was not the sort to pick a fight, Vittoryxe had no doubt who had started it.

Egrayne seemed to have come to the same conclusion. 'What do you hope to achieve by causing trouble, Grae?'

He glanced from her to Vittoryxe, resentment clear in his mulberry eyes. 'May I speak freely?'

'Of course.' Egrayne seemed surprised that he would ask.

'I don't belong here. I belong with my brotherhood. I'm ready.'

He's right, Vittoryxe thought. Sometimes, when they sent lads off to become brotherhood initiates, it felt like they were sending lambs to the slaughter. Not this one. He needed to be around other, equally aggressive men who could keep him in line.

'I'll speak with the all-mother,' Egrayne said.

Graelen grinned, and Vittoryxe knew he'd gotten what he wanted.

'Which brotherhood?' she asked.

He blinked.

'Which brotherhood are you bound to?' It would be either Rohaayel's or Sigorian's; their sisterhood had been fostering boys for these two since the covenant. Once, there had been more, but the smallest brotherhoods had been plundered and absorbed by greedy all-fathers.

'Sigorian's brotherhood,' Graelen said proudly.

Vittoryxe glanced to Egrayne. 'That one...' It had a reputation for cruelty and violence, but what was the point of warning him? He had no choice. He'd been born into his brotherhood, he would die in it.

'What?' Graelen asked.

'That brotherhood has a long and proud history,' Egrayne said. 'But I would not rush to leave the safety of–'

'I'm tired of safety. I want to prove myself. I want...' His gaze strayed to Vittoryxe's bare thighs as if he couldn't help himself.

She felt Egrayne bristle at her side, and fought the urge to confront the youth.

'We'll speak with the all-mother,' Vittoryxe said. 'Go upstairs. Get cleaned up.'

Both lads gave obeisance and left.

'We could ask the other sisterhoods,' Vittoryxe suggested, turning to Egrayne. 'See if any of their lads are due to join Sigorian's brotherhood in the near future. It'll be easier for the new initiates if they can back each other up.'

'I'll send word,' Egrayne said.

Vittoryxe had meant the sisterhood as a whole. 'The inner circle should...'

Egrayne looked down, but her devotee was not so modest.

'Gift-empowerer Egrayne is now one of the inner circle.'

Of course she was.

Envy curled through Vittoryxe's body, intimate as a lover.

She congratulated Egrayne and left before she said something she'd regret.

Vittoryxe wanted to rage, but there was no privacy in the chamber she shared with other sisters of her rank. So instead she went to the roof garden and inspected her prize birds. The challenge of breeding them delighted her, and their perfection soothed her. Breeding followed rules. And, if the birds did not breed true, she destroyed the chicks.

But today, the birds did not soothe her. Only working through the exercises to promote balance between body, mind and gift centred her.

THE NEXT DAY, when she was called before the inner circle, Vittoryxe saw Graelen waiting outside the chamber. She had no trouble guessing what this was about. He looked nervous, but hopeful of success. He should have been worried.

Inside the chamber, Egrayne had a place on the inner circle. In this case it was a half-circle, because the sisterhood's voice-of-reason and several others were attending the birth. When All-mother Aayelora fell pregnant at seventy-five, they'd been surprised. No one really expected her to carry the baby to term, but she had. When she had carried the babe past seven small moons, they rejoiced; the infant would be pure T'En. Everyone was hoping for a healthy T'En girl. No one wanted the heartbreak of handing a boy over to a brotherhood at the age of seventeen.

Vittoryxe dropped to her knees, sat on her heels and prepared to argue in favour of sending Graelen to his brotherhood early. She didn't have to.

'You will be pleased to hear another lad of the right age has been located. All-father Sigorian has been notified to expect two new initiates. Graelen will leave us this evening,' Hand-of-force Mefynor said. 'Empowerer Egrayne has informed us of events yesterday and the sisterhood regrets you were subjected to this indignity.'

Vittoryxe flushed. She would rather they did not know that she had been at a loss, even for a moment.

'Gift-tutor Lealeni and Egrayne tell us you made your first empyrean kill and saved the lad's life. Since Graelen's choice-mother is not with us and he lives due to your bravery, you will be given the honour of handing him over to the brotherhood.'

Finally, after striving for so long to have her efforts acknowledged. She scrambled to come up with a suitably humble response. And floundered, because it was about time.

'No, we insist.' Mefynor misinterpreted her reaction. 'Egrayne says the honour should be yours.'

When Vittoryxe sought the empowerer's eyes, Egrayne gave her the slightest of nods. Did she think this crumb made up for the way she'd outshone Vittoryxe on the journey?

Assuming an appropriate expression, Vittoryxe leant forward, placed her hands on the floor, then her forehead on her hands. She forced out the words. 'I am honoured.'

She straightened up.

Hand-of-force Mefynor nodded as if this was to be expected, then lifted her left hand in an elegant signal. Mefynor was a hand-of-force, trained to kill, but she moved with apparently effortless grace, like a T'En of old. Vittoryxe had long admired her and mirrored her.

A baby cried. Vittoryxe looked over to see the wet-nurse, Choris, enter with the T'En infant they'd just collected. He would need a choice-mother...

They could not mean to... she glanced to Mefynor. They did. Her heart sank.

'The inner circle has been impressed with your presence of mind on the journey. To acknowledge your increase in stature, we appoint you choice-mother to this infant.'

Vittoryxe swallowed her protests. Rear a boy? See him every day, knowing that she would have to hand him over to his brotherhood? It was cruel.

But it would do no good to object. The inner circle had spoken.

Besides, this was an honour. It meant she would be given a private chamber. She gave a deep obeisance again.

'I am unworthy,' she said, not meaning a word of it.

As the wet-nurse glided over to join her, Vittoryxe saw the perfect opportunity to raise her stature even further. For at least a year, she and Choris would be sharing the intimacy of caring for the baby boy. She'd test the young Malaunje woman to see if she was smart and resourceful.

See if she was ambitious.

The sisterhood elders would not be happy if she slipped and imprinted her gift on Choris, but they would not condemn her.

Vittoryxe produced a smile. 'I welcome my new choice-son.'

Choris went around behind her, and passed the infant through her legs.

Vittoryxe lifted him up, touched the tip of her left-hand little finger to his forehead and completed the ritual. 'I swear to protect your life with my own. I swear to rear you to revere the heritage of the T'Enatuath and protect our Malaunje.'

'What will you call him?' Mefynor asked.

She considered. Never miss an opportunity to flatter those in power. 'Mefeyne,' she answered, combining both Mefynor and Egrayne's name in masculine form.

'Make a note in the Lineage Book,' Mefynor told the Malaunje scribe.

The baby wriggled and Vittoryxe handed him back to Choris. As she turned to go, eager to take her pick of the private chambers, the door to the all-mother's private chamber flew open.

Narisa, the all-mother's devotee, looked shattered. The birth had drained her and, judging from her expression, it was not good news. The sisterhood's inner circle came to their feet.

'It's a boy,' Mefynor guessed.

Narisa shook her head.

'A girl, stillborn?' Mefynor's voice broke.

Narisa shook her head.

'A geldr?'

She nodded.

There were several soft moans.

'Poor Aayelora,' the gift-tutor said. 'She wanted a girl so badly, she must have attempted to use her gift on the developing baby.'

'Will it live?' Vittoryxe asked. It would be kinder if the babe died, but it was not her place to say this.

'She... he... it,' Narisa corrected herself. 'It looks healthy.'

'Does it seem alert?' Mefynor asked what they were all wondering. More often than not, geldrs grew up to be lackwits.

'It cries and wants to suckle,' Narisa said. 'The all-mother's called it Tancred.'

Vittoryxe's new choice-son chose that moment to wail, and she slipped away, her mind racing. The all-mother would be heartbroken and, with this birth, her stature had been damaged. Most of Aayelora's inner circle were her age or older. They had another ten years at most, and then they would step down. Time for her to gain stature and be ready when things changed.

Her new choice-son – would he never stop yelling? – added to her stature. If she was going to be all-mother, she needed to outshine Egrayne. Which reminded her – it seemed the empowerer had put in a good word for her.

Now that she thought about it, when she became all-mother, Egrayne would make a suitable voice-of-reason.

Chapter Ten

GRAELEN COULD NOT possibly sleep. Not when he knew what was going on outside the brotherhood's palace. The howls and the clash of metal on metal clawed at his nerves. He wished they'd hurry up and kill the banished warrior.

Without a word, Paryx left his bedroll and climbed in next to Graelen. He could feel the other initiate trembling.

'Do you think he was guilty?' Paryx whispered.

Graelen didn't know what to say. If Dekaron wasn't guilty, it meant they could not trust the brotherhood's leaders, and that was a frightening thought.

To think, he'd been so eager to say good-bye to the sisterhood.

Only this evening he'd stood straight and proud as the cloak was taken away to reveal his naked body. By custom, he left the sisterhood as he had entered the world. He lifted his chin, let the gathered sisterhood look upon him. He might have no hair on his chest or chin, but he was no longer a boy. He'd compared himself to the other lads in the bathing chamber and knew he wasn't lacking.

When Gift-warrior Vittoryxe moved behind him to cut his plait he remained perfectly still. The cutting of hair symbolised death. His plait would be returned to his choice-mother. He felt a pang, but quelled it quickly. She'd pushed him away when he turned thirteen and began his basic gift training. He'd hardly seen anything of her these last few years.

She was the past.

Sigorian's brotherhood was his future.

He would win honour, rise in stature and one day become Hand-of-force Graelen. But first, there was another sixteen years' training to complete. He wouldn't become an adept until he was around thirty-three. He would work hard to make his all-father proud.

He hadn't looked back as he stepped through the gate of the sisterhood quarter. Five brotherhood warriors stood there. Their silver adept arm-torcs glinted in the lantern light.

All five of the brotherhood adepts were bigger than him. Scarred and hard-faced, they looked him up and down, made him feel inadequate. His heart thundered.

The sisterhood gate closed behind him, the bolts slid home. For one terrible moment he wanted nothing more than to go back. What had the empowerer said?

Safe. The sisterhood was safe.

He didn't want safe.

He wanted to win his brothers' respect.

Sigorian's warriors stepped apart to reveal another lad about to take his initiate vows. Short hair just brushing his shoulders, the lad stood draped in a cloak, his feet shod in simple sandals. He managed a nervous grin.

Graelen hoped he did not appear as frightened. T'En males respected strength.

One of the adepts handed him a pair of sandals.

He knelt to tie the straps around his ankles. When he straightened up, another wrapped a cloak around his shoulders and guided him to stand beside the other lad. The warriors closed ranks around them.

Without a word, they escorted the two lads down the great road that led all the way to the causeway gates.

In the free quarter, Mieren had already left for the day. Malaunje and T'En alike closed up shop, while eateries and dance halls opened for the night. Music drifted from a courtyard where he heard a poet reciting a saga from the days before the city. The scent of spicy peanut sauce made his stomach cramp. They passed a group of sisterhood scholars, who averted their gaze. Further on, half a dozen warriors from another brotherhood watched Sigorian's men with cold, hard eyes.

Graelen looked straight ahead, past the shoulders of his escort, their long plaits swaying as they strode. His short hair felt strange, brushing his shoulders, tickling his neck. It branded him as new to the brotherhood, vulnerable and untried. He wished the next few years away, wished he had already earned his place and knew who his friends were.

'Paryx,' the other initiate whispered. 'My name's Paryx.'

Graelen studied him. Paryx was not particularly big, but maybe he was quick on his feet. Would he prove a good ally to have in the jostle for brotherhood stature, or would he be a liability?

He decided to take a gamble. 'Graelen.'

'Quiet,' one of the warriors warned. 'We can still turn you away at the brotherhood gates.'

If that happened, no other brotherhood would take them in. A brotherhood reject had nowhere to go, and every Mieren hand would be turned against them.

Paryx sent him a sickly grin.

Show no fear.

He settled for looking grim. At least, he hoped he did.

The road continued on to the causeway gate, but they turned left, entering the brotherhood quarter on the southern side of the island.

Sigorian's palace wasn't the largest, just as his brotherhood wasn't the most powerful. The smallest of the great brotherhoods, it clung to its place in the hierarchy, always looking for ways to grow in power and size, while the larger brotherhoods were always looking for ways to crush it.

As with the other brotherhood palaces, it presented blank walls to the street at ground level, but on the second floor there were windows and balconies. Inside, there were courtyards filled with works of art, courtyards where Malaunje children played and courtyards for weapons practice. Four or five floors above him, Graelen caught a glimpse of palms on the rooftop gardens.

They arrived at a gateway where two warriors in ceremonial dress stood guard. The narrow passage opened into a courtyard. Several Malaunje youths were leading horses away. They cast curious looks over their shoulders.

By now, Graelen's stomach was cramping so badly he was glad he had been too excited to eat. He had to get through this ceremony, make his vows, find a quiet spot and keep his head down until he knew who to trust and how to win stature.

Their escort took them up stairs, along passages, and down the verandah of another courtyard. Graelen tried to commit the route to memory, but after another set of stairs and a walkway between buildings, he was totally turned around.

The adepts left them and they were led into a chamber by an old Malaunje man, possibly a devotee. The first thing that struck Graelen was the impact of the male gift in the confined space. He was accustomed to the female gift, and he found male power abrasive. It made his heart race and his own gift try to rise in response.

Eight high-ranking T'En men turned towards them.

A thin brother frowned. 'Something's come up. Bring them back later.'

The devotee started to herd them towards the door, but one of the brotherhood leaders spoke up. 'No, let the new initiates stay. They should see what happens to those who betray their brotherhood.'

As the devotee led them to one side, Paryx sent Graelen a worried look. Graelen concentrated on trying to make sense of who everyone was. All but one of the brothers wore elaborate, sleeveless gowns of embroidered silk, over bare chests, pleated trousers, jewel-encrusted belts and soft ankle boots. Their long hair was bound with jewelled clasps.

Some wore the slender neck torcs of gift-warriors, others the larger torcs of inner circle brothers. The big one who had told them to stay, and two others, wore the elaborate torcs of the brotherhood triumvirate. Full ceremonial dress for the occasion. He assumed the big warrior was the brotherhood's hand-of-force.

One warrior stood with his bare back to them all. The arc of a triumvirate torc outlined his broad shoulders. He stretched, back muscles rippling. Graelen guessed he was either All-father Sigorian or his voice-of-reason.

Someone whispered to the bare-chested leader. He nodded, and a feeling of gift readiness filled the air. At that moment, two gift-warriors entered with a brother who wore the full-width arm-torcs of an adept. He'd been stripped down to his breeches, but he walked with a defiant step. The brotherhood's inner circle went very still. All chatter stopped and everyone looked to the bare-chested male.

He turned in a very deliberate manner, head tilted. Graelen felt a surge of power. Paryx took a step back. Graelen's own gift flexed; this had to be All-father Sigorian.

Sigorian was not the biggest of men, but every eye went to him. A nasty silvery scar puckered the skin on his chest over his heart. He gestured to the tall, thin triumvirate leader at his side. 'Voice-of-reason Irutz accuses you of spying for a rival brotherhood, Dekaron. What do you say?'

'All-father.' The condemned man dropped to his knees and gave deep obeisance. Raising his head, he lifted both hands in the gesture of supplication. 'I would never–'

'I have three adepts who saw you speak with All-father Chariode's warriors,' the voice-of-reason interrupted.

'About their ships. His brotherhood builds fine ships.'

'Can you prove this?' Sigorian asked, gesturing for him to stand.

Dekaron came to his feet, hesitating. Innocent or not, Graelen couldn't imagine how the accused was supposed to prove what had passed in a conversation.

'Why would I betray our brotherhood?' Dekaron countered. 'What would I gain? I swear I would never–'

'He was heard complaining about the defence roster,' the hand-of-force said.

Dekaron rounded on him. 'I did ten nights straight on the wall without a break. Then I was rostered on ten days straight with no chance to sleep between duties. I ask you...' – he appealed to the rest of the inner circle – 'is that fair?'

'We aren't here to discuss rosters,' the voice-of-reason said. 'He's been fomenting trouble. I say he's All-father Chariode's spy.'

'Spy.' The hand-of-force was firm. Others echoed him.

'I'll drop my defences.' Dekaron had to repeat it to be heard. 'I'll drop my gift-walls and let you taste the truth.'

'Very well,' Sigorian said and nodded to his voice-of-reason, who lifted his hands and flexed them. 'Irutz.'

'No, not him.' The accused looked around, spotted the thin one who had objected when he saw Graelen and Paryx enter. 'The saw-bones.'

'Ceyne?' Sigorian beckoned him.

'Not Ceyne,' the voice-of-reason objected. 'He's been training Dekaron. He's not impartial.'

'And you are?' Dekaron countered.

'Someone else, then?' Sigorian looked around his inner circle.

None would meet his eye.

'See?' Dekaron addressed the all-father, gesturing to the others. 'Even your inner circle is afraid to speak the truth. They know Irutz will accuse them next–'

As he spoke, two warriors moved in behind him. On the hand-of-force's signal one grabbed Dekaron, while the other punched him. The air left Dekaron in a huff and he doubled over.

Graelen's cheeks burned. He had no idea who to believe. It worried him that Dekaron seemed to be speaking sense, but they wouldn't listen.

'Dekaron is trying to plant the seeds of suspicion,' the voice-of-reason said, 'by accusing me to hide his own guilt.'

'What is his punishment, all-father?' the hand-of-force asked.

Sigorian hesitated. 'Someone is fomenting trouble–'

'Turn him out,' the voice-of-reason insisted.

'I'm loyal,' Dekaron insisted, struggling to regain his voice, struggling against the warriors who held him. Graelen felt the surge of Dekaron's gift from the other side of the chamber.

Sigorian studied the accused. The all-father would have to be decisive. If he showed weakness, one of the mid- to high-ranking brothers would make a bid for leadership.

'I withdraw the protection of the brotherhood.' As soon as Sigorian spoke, both warriors stepped away from the accused. 'You are not one of us. Take his arm-torcs.'

'Take them?' Dekaron was so angry he shook. In a fury, he tore the torcs from his biceps and flung them on the floor at Sigorian's feet. 'You're blind. You can't see–'

The hand-of-force didn't let him finish. His warriors dragged Dekaron from the chamber.

Paryx swayed, but Graelen steadied him. 'Show no fear.'

And so it had been. They'd given their vows, sworn allegiance to the brotherhood, and allowed the all-father to establish a shallow link as evidence of their trust.

Now... now they lay on the bedroll, listening to the shouts and clashes as warriors from other brotherhoods hunted Dekaron for sport. The longer it went on, the worse it was.

'Do you think he was guilty?' Paryx whispered again.

Graelen didn't answer.

'I think they were too quick to condemn him. It was as if they wanted to silence him.'

'We don't know that,' Graelen whispered. 'We aren't in a position to judge.' But Dekaron's hearing hadn't felt right to him either.

Mocking laughter echoed in the night. The clash of steel. Running footsteps.

'How much longer?' Paryx whispered.

Graelen couldn't answer.

'Not long,' a voice said from the doorway. A brother stood there, arms folded, leaning against the doorjamb.

Graelen tensed. Had he heard them voice their doubts?

The brother pushed away from the wall and came over to join them. His arm-torcs were almost the thickness of an adept's. 'You gave your vows today. It was a bad day to join Sigorian's brotherhood.'

They came to their knees and gave obeisance. As they raised their heads, running boots echoed from outside the chamber.

'That sounded close,' Paryx whispered. 'Was it inside–'

'The brotherhood walls? Yes,' the stranger said. 'Some of Dekaron's friends did not agree with the judgement. Sigorian's hand-of-force is purging the brotherhood of his supporters. That's why it has gone on so long. They've turned out three more of us.'

Graelen felt sick at the thought.

'As to whether they are guilty or not...' the brother continued. He shrugged. 'You should be careful what you say. You never know who's listening.'

'We didn't–' Paryx began.

'We're loyal,' Graelen insisted.

'You're lost, that's what you are. Out of your depth.'

There was no point denying it.

The brother offered his hand. 'If you need anything, send for me, Kyredeon. Remember my name.'

Paryx went to take his hand, but Graelen did not move and Paryx hesitated.

The brother shrugged and climbed to his feet. 'The offer stands. Meanwhile, watch and learn. Be careful who you trust. There are factions. Not everyone is pleased with Sigorian's leadership.'

He turned to go.

'Why?' Graelen asked. 'Why aren't they happy with the all-father?'

For a heartbeat he thought Kyredeon wouldn't answer, but he said, 'You'll see.'

After he left, Paryx turned to Graelen. 'We should have taken his offer.'

Graelen wasn't so sure. 'Why did he make it? We have no stature. What use are we to him?'

Howls of triumph came from the darkness, carried on the slight breeze.

'One of them's dead,' Paryx said.

Graelen hoped it was Dekaron. Then, at least, his troubles would be over. 'Go to sleep.'

'I can't.'

Graelen stretched out. He didn't object when Paryx stayed on his bedroll.

'What did he mean when he said we'd see?' Paryx whispered.

Graelen didn't want to guess.

They found out when the sound of the hunt faded. Several warriors came to the chamber, smelling of blood and gift violence. They were loud and eager.

And they were not gentle.

OSKANE HAD BEEN living in the mountain retreat six days now, yet he still found the air too thin for his old chest. He sucked in another unsatisfying breath and told himself he'd get used to it; he had to.

He would never get used to the view. It was inspiring. From the window of his study he could see the rolling hills of southern Chalcedonia stretching into the distance.

Eleven days ride north-west lay Port Mirror-on-Sea and King Charald. Surely that was far enough to keep them safe.

With the king married to Lord Nitzel's daughter and another child on the way within the year – if Charald lived up to his boast – Oskane and the king's half-blood son would be forgotten. He hoped.

All he needed was time to raise young Sorne and prepare him to be his weapon. Only one trusted priest at the abbey knew Oskane's true destination. The agent would be passing on messages from Edorne and Franto's spy and, when the time came, would contact young Matxin. And he had the agent in Enlightenment Abbey to ensure he knew what was going on in the world.

Franto peeped around the door. 'It's the wood-worker, Kolst.'

Oskane returned to his desk. 'Show him in.'

The young man had recovered from his injury on the ride here, but he would always have a scar in his hair-line. He was grateful to Oskane for rescuing his wife and child, and eager to prove himself useful.

They were in the process of making two buildings liveable for winter, since True-men could not share the same table as half-bloods. So Kolst and his family would live in the stables, along with the animals.

'The repair of the stable roof is under way,' Kolst said 'I have the penitents working on cutting new shingles. As for the shutters, I did them myself. We'll be safe from the winter winds.'

'Good. Behind the retreat, built into the mountainside, is the entrance to an old copper mine.'

'I don't know anything about mining,' Kolst admitted. 'But I could learn.'

'No need. The mine is played out and useless,' Oskane lied. 'I don't want anyone wandering in and getting lost. You are to block off the entrance.'

'What of the furniture, Scholar Oskane?'

When the retreat's original inhabitants had fled, they'd taken only what they could carry on their backs. But time and the weather had damaged what they'd left behind.

'The copper mine first.' He didn't want anyone discovering that, aside from being tainted, it also contained veins of malachite. The penitents might be tempted to forget their vows of poverty and do some digging of their own.

He could not afford to have them stir up what was hidden in the mine. No one understood why unclean sites appeared. Some blamed the T'En. Sometimes there was a single incident at an unclean site, sometimes repeated incidents. The mine had been undisturbed now for nearly twenty-five years, and it was going to remain that way.

'I wanted to thank you, Scholar Oskane. My Hiruna, she would not give up the half-blood. Usually, she's the sweetest, kindest lass, but it was like a madness took hold of her.'

'I've read of this,' Oskane admitted. 'It's because the minds of women are closer to animals. Like a she-bear, they seek to defend their young. They can't think rationally.' He dismissed Kolst.

Franto sent Oskane a dry look. 'The penitents don't like taking orders from him. They call him Wyrd-lover.'

'He's more use than the lot of them together.' Oskane crossed to a window and looked down onto a courtyard graced by a water-maple, bare now. Winter sunlight warmed the white flagstones and walls. Kolst's son pushed himself to his feet and took his first tentative steps. His mother laughed and clapped as she nursed young Sorne.

She did not seem to mind sullying herself with half-bloods. She and Kolst asked no questions, but they had to wonder – just as the penitents had to wonder – what raising two half-bloods had to do with serving the Seven.

Now that they were here and the gates were closed, he would tell them they served the Seven and the king, by training a weapon to use against the Wyrds. It would be enough to ensure their loyalty. There wasn't a True-man or -woman alive who didn't fear those silver-haired, six-fingered freaks and their half-blood servants.

Someone thumped on the courtyard gates. Oskane glanced to Franto, who took off at a run. From his vantage point, Oskane saw Hiruna pick up her son and retreat to the stables, an infant in each arm.

Franto checked the gate slot, then opened it.

A mounted messenger entered the courtyard and jumped down. Oskane recognised him as the abbey agent's trusted servant. They had not expected to hear from Enlightenment Abbey until spring. This could not be good news.

Franto returned and waited as Oskane read the message.

'It's from your agent back in port,' Oskane said at last. Not content with killing poor little Sorna, Nitzel had manoeuvred to place one of his people as head of the church. 'My nephew is dead. Nitzel's cousin's son is now high priest.'

Franto cursed. 'How? Edorne is... was a young man. Did they poison his food?'

'Apparently he cut himself shaving. The wound festered and he died of bad blood.'

'His razor was painted with poison,' Franto stated. 'It's the only explanation. Just as well the baron doesn't know where we are.'

Oskane nodded, drawing in a deep breath of thin, cold air. Now he had two deaths to avenge. Baron Nitzel had been instrumental in crushing his family. One day, he would see Nitzel's family brought low.

'We hide for now. But Nitzel will live to regret turning on me and mine.'

All depended on his wits, and the infant currently suckling at Hiruna's breast.

'King Charald led an army at the age of fifteen. Let's hope his son is forged from the same steel.'

Chapter Eleven

Year 303

OSKANE FINISHED WRITING his observations of the half-bloods in his journal, then looked up. 'Yes, Franto?'

'The wood-worker is here to see you.'

Oskane closed the journal. 'Show him in.'

In the thirteen years since coming to Restoration Retreat, Kolst's waist had thickened and his fair hair had thinned, revealing the scar he'd received the night Oskane first met him.

'Scholar Oskane,' he said, dipping his head. 'I have a request.'

Oskane gestured for him to proceed.

'Hiruna is with child, and I'd like you to release me and my family. I know we signed on for seventeen years, but I want to go home a few years early. I want Zabier and the new baby to grow up amongst their own kind. I want to see my brother before I die, and make peace with him. I swear on my honour I will not speak of this place.'

'It's not that.' Oskane tilted his head. 'How do you know this new baby will be...'

'A True-man? The gods would not be so cruel. They cursed me with my first child. I was the best woodcarver in the village. I boasted and mocked my older brother. When the gods saw this, they cursed me. I've served my penance. Hiruna's pregnancy was an accident. I'm thirty-five, too old to be bringing a baby into this world. I need to be near my family in case I don't live long enough to raise the new child.' He held out his rough, scarred hands. 'In winter, it's become hard to hold the chisel.'

'What of...' Oskane gestured to the window overlooking the courtyard. Boyish shouts and laughter floated up to them.

'My half-blood son will be fourteen in the spring. Almost a man. You've taught him to read and write alongside Sorne. And they've taught Zabier to read, filling his head with things I know nothing about. I want to take Zabe home to live amongst True-men.'

'Fair enough. But what will you tell your brother? He'll want to know where you've been all these years.'

'I'll... I'll tell them we left Izteben with the Wyrds and I've been working in Navarone, to the south-east.'

'What do you know of Navarone?'

'More than anyone back home.' Kolst grinned. 'Joaken lived there for many years. I've listened to so many of his stories I could describe all the king's mistresses.'

Oskane nodded. Joaken was the penitent who'd been a mercenary. Only three of the penitents still lived – Joaken, the cripple, and the boy, who was now a man of twenty. 'When were you thinking of leaving?'

Kolst brightened. 'Far as we can tell, the baby will come late spring. We'll leave then.'

'Very well. You and your family may go. But...' – Oskane came to his feet – 'if you so much as breathe a word of this place and the two half-bloods, the gods will curse you, your family and your brother's family. All manner of terrible afflictions will rain down upon you!'

Kolst paled. 'I never... I wouldn't.'

'See that you don't.' And Oskane dismissed him before taking his journal through to his bedchamber and placing it with the others in the chest. A journal for each year of Sorne's life. He'd recorded his observations of the boys' development, along with an analysis of the Wyrd scrolls. Oskane had been comparing their theories on the half-bloods with Sorne and Izteben's actual development.

Laughter came through the window, boyish and high, followed by a challenge. Running footsteps. A shriek. The *thwack* of wooden swords.

He went over to the window. Below him on the wall-walk, three boys, one blond and two copper-haired, battled imaginary foes. Sorne led them; his choice-brother, Izteben, was the second in command, and young Zabier acted as their entire army. Sticks were their swords, the exuberance of youth their shields.

From the words Oskane could make out, they were reliving a historical battle, unworried by the fact that they would have been on different sides. Kolst was right, he needed to take Zabier away.

'Regroup!' Sorne yelled. 'There's too many of them.'

He tossed his sword, spear-like, at an imaginary foe and ran for the end of the wall-walk, leaping off it into the courtyard tree. The maple's branches shook with the impact, shedding yellow autumn leaves like drops of pure sunshine.

Lithe and quick, Sorne swung from the upper branches, dropping to land on a lower branch. Izteben followed Sorne, just as agile.

Zabier remained on the wall. He would be nine next spring, so he was more than three years younger than Sorne, but he was also a True-man and would probably never be as big.

'Jump, I'll catch you,' Izteben called.

'You'll do no such thing!' Hiruna came out of the shadows of the stable entrance.

Was Kolst right? Would their next child be a True-man? It took three seasons, the length of six small moons, to produce a True-man, and seven small moons for a half-blood. The problem was it was hard to tell exactly when the child had been conceived. Kolst did not seem to know.

'Tell Zabier to jump and you'll catch him? Of all the foolish things,' Hiruna said. 'You'll get your little brother killed. Come down here this instant.'

The two bigger lads clambered through the tree and dropped to the ground, landing lightly. Zabier had to run along the wall-walk and come down the steps. Oskane envied them their vitality. His bones ached all the time now. And he'd thought he was old at forty-seven.

But he held on, determined to see Nitzel's family suffer and his restored, no matter how long it took.

One thing delighted him. Baron Nitzel's daughter, that producer of True-man sons, had spent several years barren, then managed to birth only one healthy boy. All the infants since had died. His spy reported they'd been born blue.

All this aside, King Charald was happy with his heir and, as grandfather of the future king, Nitzel's influence was secure. So Oskane had work to do if he was going to undermine him.

'Sorne, Izteben?' He leant out the window. 'It's time.'

Everyone turned to look at him.

Hiruna's face tightened; she did not approve.

He'd tried to explain that the half-bloods needed self-discipline and the flagellation was for their own good, but she had a woman's soft heart. She had never known a man like Baron Nitzel, who could order the death of his daughter's husband because the man stood in the way of his ambition for his family.

Hiruna called Zabier, then retreated to the stable, where she lived segregated with the half-bloods. There were no other women, and Oskane liked it that way. Celibacy was good for the soul.

Oskane went through to his study. It was almost winter's cusp but, by his decree, no flames warmed the room. Everyone lived without luxuries. No fires, except on the coldest of winter days, and plain, simple food. Strength came from denial.

Opening the top drawer of his desk, Oskane removed the scourge. It was not his. He would not use something that drew Malaunje blood on his own skin. He took the handle and ran the fine leather strands through his left hand. Each strand ended in a knot to abrade the flagellant's back.

The half-bloods came in, paid him obeisance and removed their shirts without being asked. They stood there, pale-skinned, long copper plaits hanging down their backs. Although they were nearly as tall as him, they did not have the build of men. There was only the promise of muscle on their chests and shoulders.

They looked to him expectantly. A few days short of thirteen years, Sorne had his mother's sweet face, not yet grown into the hard lines of manhood. Izteben's features were more angular, but he had the same vivid colouring. No wonder the first True-men and -women who had birthed half-bloods had protected and nurtured them, unaware of the danger.

But Oskane knew what he was harbouring.

'What are you?' he asked them, just as he had every day since they were five years old.

'Holy warriors,' they answered in unison.

'Whose holy warriors?'

'Your holy warriors, Scholar Oskane.'

'Why do I do this?'

'To make us strong. So we can conquer pain and temptation.'

So they could resist the lure of the T'En gifts.

'Very good.' He gestured. 'Sorne first.'

In a couple of years, Oskane would tell the lad who he really was and what he had been born to achieve. But until then, he would temper him, like a blacksmith tempered metal, pushing it to its limits.

The boy stepped up onto the frame, tucked his plait out of the way, and took hold of the two pegs, presenting his back to Oskane. Multiple fine silver scars ran across his pale shoulders. Izteben went around the other side so he could meet Sorne's eyes. When it was Izteben's turn, Sorne would do the same for him.

'What are you?' Oskane asked.

'I am weak. I am Malaunje. But I will be strong.'

'Where were we up to yesterday?' Oskane asked.

'Charald the Peace-maker had just granted the T'En the island to call their own,' Sorne said.

'Proceed from there.' Oskane lifted the scourge bringing it down across the half-blood's back, across the fine silver lines.

Sorne began to recite Chalcedonian history, his voice jumping a little with each strike.

'Remember you must be strong in mind as well as body,' Oskane told them, speaking over Sorne. 'Remember I do this for you, to armour you.'

When his arm grew tired, he ordered Sorne to step down and Izteben took his place, picking up the recitation where Sorne had finished. Oskane had to change arms. He was getting too old for this.

He tried to ensure their beating was even, but he was tired. That was why he tended to pick Sorne first. The boy must be strong.

When he could do no more, Oskane left the scourge for Franto to clean and leant on the desk. 'Enough for today. Come here.'

He held out his hand, with the ring the king had given him all those years ago. 'Kiss the king's ring and thank me.'

They said the words and kissed the ruby ring. Tears glittered in Izteben eyes, but Sorne was hard-eyed. He had not wept for years. He could solve mathematical riddles under the scourge. He was smart and strove to please. Oskane could not ask for more. Had he been born a Trueman, he would have made a wonderful king.

But there was no point bemoaning what could not be changed. The boys began to get out the inks and papers. They were transcribing the history they'd memorised.

'Let me see yesterday's work.'

'Yes, Scholar Oskane,' they answered dutifully.

He inspected the pages. The lettering was meticulous, just as he'd taught them. But it was the illustration around the edge of the page that stood out. 'Your work, Sorne?'

The boy nodded.

'Very good.' In truth it was beautiful. Oskane didn't know where he got his talent from, for neither Sorna nor Charald had been able to draw. 'Get to work.'

They both settled down at the desk.

It cost him nothing extra to school the carpenter's son, and he figured Sorne would need Izteben's support when Oskane sent him into the Wyrd city. He hadn't considered the gulf this would create between the carpenter and his firstborn. Kolst was right to take his True-man family away.

And considering his hard work, a small payment would be appropriate, something he could use to establish himself back home. He would have to ask Franto to organise it.

If Hiruna's baby was a True-man child.

SORNE RAKED THE old straw. He, Izteben and Zabier slept in a stall in the stable. He didn't mind, not even when the cart came from the abbey and the two cart horses stayed in the far stall.

'Your back's bleeding again,' Izteben said. 'Why is he so hard on you?'

'I'm fine.' Sorne found if he concentrated on other things, he didn't feel the pain. 'The scholar has to make us strong.'

'Take off your shirt.'

Sorne spread fresh straw for their bed. Once this was done to his satisfaction, he pulled the thigh-length shirt over his shoulders and inspected the material. Spots of blood.

'Ma's out in the courtyard doing the washing right now,' Izteben said. 'She'll be upset if she finds out you've been bleeding again, after she treated your back.'

'I'll rinse it at the well,' Sorne said.

As they stepped into the larger courtyard, Sorne looked up and his heart lifted. It was midday, and late autumn sun filtered down through the maple's yellow leaves. Up the high end, near the storerooms, their father was crafting a cabinet for Franto to sell. The awl created sweet smelling wood shavings, which Zabier collected for tinder.

It was a mild day, and the penitents had brought a bench out of the dining hall, setting it against the limestone wall of the main building. They sat, legs stretched out, enjoying the sun as they took their lunch break.

Not far from them was the well, with its pump and white stone basin. Sorne headed over to it; cold water was the best way to get rid of blood. Hopefully, his back would have stopped bleeding by the time their mother saw them.

Sorne bent over to hold his shirt under the tap, and Izteben went around the far side to work the pump. Icy cold water splashed over his hands, soaking the shirt. He began to rub as water flowed over the stone lip and away in the shallow channel, carrying leaves and dirt with it. When they were little, they used to make leaf boats and race them down to the wall where the channel flowed away through a grate.

'Doing women's work now, half-blood?' Joaken sneered, coming to his feet. 'Guess it's not that hard for a pair of copperheads pretty as girls.'

Pendor, the cripple, smirked.

Sorne glanced to their father, but Kolst had gone into the storeroom. They could all hear Hiruna's sweet high singing as she worked.

Following Joaken's lead young Denat spat. 'They're using the True-man's well.'

'It's the only well. What else can we do?' Izteben muttered, leaning over the pump.

'Get out of here, copperheads,' Denat growled, getting to his feet.

Sorne turned, straightening. He was as tall as Denat, but the penitent had the shoulders of a man.

All his life he had avoided the penitents. When he and Izteben were younger, their cold eyes had made him uncomfortable; more recently, it had become a sneer here, a snide remark there. Never anything as overt as this.

'We're done, now,' Sorne said. 'I just had to clean my shirt.'

'What? That shirt?' Denat pointed.

Before Sorne knew he meant to do it, the penitent snatched the wet shirt from him and threw it into the dirty channel. 'Now you can wash it again.' He glanced over his shoulder, inviting the other two to laugh.

The cripple and Joaken obliged him.

'Why, you...' Izteben sprang for him.

Sorne was just as fast, coming between them. He was a little shorter and not as heavily built as his brother.

Denat mocked them. 'Come on, try me.'

'Don't hit him. It means he wins,' Sorne warned.

'Does that mean he loses if we walk away?' Izteben asked.

'Here. What's going on?' Kolst said, coming out of the storeroom with Zabier at his side.

'Nothing,' Joaken replied, but his expression said otherwise, and it was clear he was enjoying himself. 'Nothing that a True-man would object to, unless he was a Wyrd-lover.'

'Izteben, Sorne, go back to the stable,' Kolst ordered. 'Take Zabier.'

'That's right, send the only True-man son you have with the half-bloods. I don't know how you can bear to have them around. I see them watching me with their Wyrd eyes, see them whispering. While we farm and fish, their six-fingered hands stay soft. They think they're better than us, with their reading and book learning.'

'Lunch time.' Hiruna's voice carried sweet and high.

Everyone glanced to her in the stable doorway.

'She's given you two Wyrds and one True-man son. Afraid to try again?' Joaken smirked. 'You should let another man plough her furrow. Maybe you'd get–'

Kolst punched him so hard he flew off his feet and collided with Denat. They both went down.

Sorne felt like cheering.

'Come on, boys,' Kolst said.

Zabier ran to their father's side and they followed him back to the stable. Hiruna looked worried, but Kolst refused to talk about it.

Chapter Twelve

'PULL IN HERE,' Irian said. 'This is the bay.'

The Malaunje rowers bent their backs and the boat surged towards the shadowed beach, riding the low waves. It was late afternoon. The sun was in their eyes as it sank beyond the high end of the island, where the slender lighthouse was almost lost in the glare. That was where the island's Malaunje fisher folk lived, and where Imoshen had spent her childhood.

Somewhere behind the dunes was an abandoned cottage, where the baby would be born – his son, he thought with a thrill, his gift stirring. He pushed it down, reminding himself to be realistic. If the boy was stillborn, as happened so often, no one would be any the wiser, which was why he had suggested bringing his trysting partner to the deserted cottage. When her time came, he would send the cook, who delivered all the island's babies.

For they meant to cheat the sisterhoods once more.

Not cheat. Why should keeping their own children be cheating? Why was it so hard to think of breaking with custom?

Because those customs had four hundred years behind them.

Yet when Karokara's pregnancy progressed past the seven small moons to deliver a Malaunje child, he'd gone straight to Rohaayel and Ardeyne. He'd argued that it was almost thirteen years since they'd hidden Rohaayel's daughter and, in that time, they'd delivered all four T'En boys to the sisterhood. No one would expect them to keep this one. But they had to move quickly, leave early to visit Lighthouse Isle and take Karokara with them.

He looked down to where she sat at his feet, her head resting on his knee. In the belly of the boat she was shielded from the wind; even so, she shivered. He placed his hand on her copper hair and she looked up, wine-dark eyes distant as though she was with him in body but not mind. What went on in her Malaunje head? He resented not knowing. She'd steadfastly maintained her defences.

Did she adore him as much as he adored her, or was he only a means to an end?

'It's time,' Irian said then raised his voice. 'Ship oars.'

The rowers lifted the oars and sat them across their laps. The boat continued to glide towards the beach.

Irian stood, legs braced.

When the hull ground on the sand, he jumped into the shallows, reached up, lifted Karokara in his arms and carried her onto the beach, setting her down on the dry sand. As he did, she leaned against him and he felt his son kick. His gift surged with excitement and she pulled back.

He hid his annoyance and banked his power, then turned to catch the food and stores Ardeyne tossed onto the twilit beach.

Irian waved as they rowed away.

He took Karokara's hand and led her up the slope. The fine white sand shifted under their feet, making it hard going, but she struggled on without complaint.

Where was that cottage? Had his memory played him false? It had been thirteen years since he'd last scouted the brotherhood's island.

They crested another dune to find the empty dwelling just as he remembered, its roof shingles silvered by time. No one lived in the one-bedroom fisherman's cottage now, not since they'd built the stone cottages around the base of the lighthouse.

'Come on.' He drew Karokara down the slope.

He'd been drawn to her laughter and wit, but as the pregnancy progressed, she'd become quieter. When she went past the time to deliver a Malaunje baby, and every day made it more likely the child would be born T'En, she'd begun to mourn the baby in preparation for giving him up to the sisterhood.

It was more than Irian could bear.

When this is over, she'll smile again, he told himself.

Pushing the cottage door open, he expected to find the single room sandy and dilapidated, but it was surprisingly clean. He crossed to the hearth and made up a fire. Someone had left a stack of driftwood. He suspected the fishermen's children had been playing here.

When he had the flames going, he turned to find Karokara stretched out on the blanket. The journey, the excitement, the fear of what would happen if sisterhood gift-warriors caught them... it had all taken its toll.

'You're safe here,' he told her, smoothing the copper strands from her cheek. She wasn't his devotee; he wouldn't do that to her. He would die in the service of his brotherhood, that much was certain, and he didn't want her to die with him. He wanted her to have a long, healthy life.

Her eyes flickered open and she nodded, too tired to speak. As far as they could tell, it would not be her time for another seven or eight days. He watched his son turn inside her belly, the cloth straining. Strange, he'd never felt this possessive about a child before.

Because this time he would be keeping the boy.

'I have to go.' First he laid out the food, blankets and watered wine then lit the lantern. 'I'll visit each day. Don't worry. This will all be over soon.'

'They will not find us here?'

He knew she wasn't referring to the island's Malaunje fisher folk. 'The sisterhood gift-warriors will not find us here.'

'And I'll have him all to myself for five years, just as you promised me?'

'You will have him for five years, I promise,' he said. Five years was what Rohaayel had allowed his devotee. Five years to rear her child, before Mariska returned to him. In those five years, Rohaayel had come to the island often, making excuses to hide his real destination. In Irian's opinion, he'd spent too much time here, but their subterfuges had worked.

No one suspected their secret, because it was unthinkable.

Irian knelt beside Karokara and leant down to kiss her cheek. A rush of love filled him and he felt his power rise, felt her tense against him. The instinct to imprint his gift on her was almost overwhelming. He fought it every day.

'Please,' she whispered.

Please, I'm tired of fighting this, make me your devotee, or, *Please, don't do this?*

Was it only the Malaunje attraction to T'En power, or did she truly love him?

With an effort of will, he controlled his instincts and came to his feet. *If she'd been pure T'En, he would not have to hold back. She could have met him on every level.*

Yes, and even crippled his gift, if she chose. No wonder the males were wary of females.

'You'll be safe here, Karo,' he told her. 'No one comes this way.'

He closed the door, and then set off over the dunes at a jog. He should not have stayed so long. This trip, they were accompanied by the ambitious new gift-tutor and two gift-warriors: all recent additions to the inner circle.

Rohaayel had taken powerful, determined men onto his inner circle and into his confidence, and their triumvirate had been able to retain leadership of the brotherhood. But it did mean, when the new additions learned about Imoshen, they insisted on coming to the island to assess if she was a threat.

Back at summer's cusp, the Scholar Nereon had been new to the inner circle, and had been horrified to discover that instead of maintaining the proper distance, the Malaunje treated Imoshen like one of their own. She worked in the garden, helped haul in the fishing nets and prepared food.

Irian had grown used to how they lived on the island, but he hadn't been aware that she handled uncooked food. He'd taken the cook aside and pointed out how inappropriate this was. T'En might perform the spiced wine ceremony, but they never touched unprepared food, and the proper distance should be maintained. Although Imoshen did not have her gift yet, one day she would and, when she did, an unthinking act could break a Malaunje's defences. Mortified, the cook had been full of apologies. Imoshen was just a child. She'd been with them forever, and she was always offering to help. She had no idea of the proper boundaries between T'En and Malaunje.

'Well, it's time she learnt,' he'd said. 'She's growing up.'

Pity she could not remain a child forever. In a few days, she turned thirteen. If she had been living with a sisterhood, she would have been taken to Egrayne the Empowerer and her gift's true nature discovered, so she could begin her training.

Instead, she was innocent of her gift, and of the rivalry between male and female T'En.

Not that she was simple. Mariska had taught her to read and write, and Ardeyne had selected suitable treatises for her to read. Because he had to find treatises that contained no hint of the true state of affairs between brotherhoods and sisterhoods, he'd resorted to Sagora treatises in the language of True-men. They covered the natural world and philosophy. He'd thought learning another language would slow her down. It had, but not for long.

Rohaayel was so proud of her.

But soon, her gift would stir, and she would begin asking questions. Soon, a lie of omission would not be enough.

*   *   *

IMOSHEN ALMOST CALLED out when she saw Uncle Irian bring the pregnant Malaunje woman ashore, but she was dressed like a half-blood herself, in old breeches and a knitted vest, and she knew he would not approve. Besides, something about his manner made her hesitate.

She'd never seen Irian this way before, protective and proud. Yet when he came out of the cottage, his expression was so forbidding he hardly looked like the uncle she knew and loved.

Intrigued and a little unsettled, she followed him over the dunes for a way to be sure he was heading towards the lighthouse end of the island, before she stopped.

Why had he hidden this stranger in her secret place?

Well, it was not really a secret, as the other children knew about it, but since the others had stopped speaking to her, she thought of it as her retreat. She wasn't sure what she'd done, to make them shun her.

After being shut up all winter in the lighthouse, reading the treatises, she had come out expecting to pick up where they had left off in autumn, but the Malaunje boys and girls of twelve and thirteen she had grown up with had taken on the work of adults.

The change hadn't been as noticeable with the grownups, who had always been busy with work. She'd realised they were shunning her too when she walked into the lighthouse kitchen and the cook had ushered her out, sending her up to her room to wait for the dinner tray.

She hadn't felt so lonely since her mother drowned.

In the past, she'd always looked forward to the half-yearly visits from her father and uncles – when they were here, the world seemed so much richer – but this time she was impatient for company. They would bring more treatises from the Sagoras, and she would finally have someone to talk to.

A seagull cried, and she looked up to see it hovering on the wind.

She could either go back to the lighthouse or go to the cottage. If she went back to the lighthouse, her father and uncles would be there. There had been three extra T'En men in the boat that delivered Irian and the pregnant woman. She loved her father and Uncle Irian and Ardeyne, but she didn't like meeting new T'En men. Scholar Nereon had asked questions, and it didn't seem to matter what she said, he'd made her feel like she'd done something wrong.

She knew what would happen if she went back to the lighthouse. She didn't know what would happen if she went to the cottage.

Propelled by curiosity, she retraced her steps across the dunes, bare feet sliding in the silky, cold sand. Soon she would have to wear boots and stay indoors, and then the days would be interminable, but for the Sagora treatises.

From the top of the dune, she looked down on the cottage. The wind tore the smoke from the chimney and flattened the sharp-edged dune grass, whipping it so that it stung her bare calves.

She was glad when she entered the hollow and approached the cottage. A faint glow came from the only window. Bubbled, distorted glass made it impossible to see inside. She tapped on the door.

No one answered.

Were they deliberately ignoring her? She was so used to this now, she nearly left. But the cottage was her special place and this woman had invaded it – this woman Uncle Irian loved, but had to hide. Why?

She pushed the door open. 'Hello?'

Empty. The stranger must have gone to the outhouse.

The lantern revealed blankets and provisions. A fire burned in the hearth and a pot sat over it. She could smell onions and chicken.

Her stomach rumbled.

She meant to go over to the pot and stir it, but the moment she stepped inside the cottage and shut the door her senses went on alert. Scents suddenly became stronger and sharper, and her heart raced. She had always felt more alive when the T'En men came to visit, but never to this extent.

She inhaled deeply, enjoying the rush of energy that coursed through her body. It felt like when she stood on the cliff tops, daring the wind to pluck her off and blow her away.

Where was it coming from?

Kneeling, she inspected each of the new objects on the floor, handling them, sniffing them; it was on everything and nothing.

Frustrated, she came to her feet and went over to stir the food. If the Malaunje woman wasn't careful, it would burn. Wrapping the edge of the blanket around her hand, she lifted the pot, moving it away from the centre of the fire.

Behind her, the door swung open.

Imoshen turned. 'Your food was—'

The woman's eyes went wide with fear. With a shriek, she turned and made off.

'Wait.' Imoshen ran after her.

She caught up with the heavily pregnant woman before she reached the top of the dune. The poor thing had collapsed in the sand on her knees. She held her hand under her belly, panting.

Imoshen crouched next to her, watching warily, not sure if she should speak in case she distressed her further.

The woman caught her breath and lifted her head to meet Imoshen's eyes. In the moonlight her hair looked black, her eyes enormous. Now that they were close, she looked vaguely familiar.

'I didn't mean to scare you,' Imoshen apologised.

'I wasn't scared, just surprised.'

That was a lie. She'd been terrified. Imoshen didn't know how to respond.

'I should have realised you were Imoshen.'

'I'm sorry.'

'It's all right.' The woman lifted a hand to cup Imoshen's cheek. In that moment, Imoshen realised no one had touched her since summer's cusp, when her father and uncles had visited. She leant into the warm palm, soaking up the sensation.

'Sorry.' The woman removed her hand.

'For what?'

The woman blinked. 'Malaunje and T'En do not touch, skin on skin, unless...'

'Unless?'

'It's just... You look so much like her,' the woman marvelled.

'Who?'

'Your mother.'

'You knew my mother?'

'Knew...' The woman bit her bottom lip and nodded. 'My half-sister. Same mother, different fathers, both T'En.'

'Why did Uncle Irian hide you here...' She realised she didn't know her name.

'Karokara.'

'Why did he hide you here, Aunt Karokara?'

The woman gave her a sharp look. 'T'En don't acknowledge their Malaunje kin.'

'Why ever not?' When Karokara didn't answer, Imoshen wondered if it was a lie. It hadn't felt like a lie, yet... 'My father used to acknowledge my mother.'

'That's different.'

'How?'

Karokara stared at her as if she'd said something extraordinary. Imoshen felt as if she was speaking the same language, but navigating unknown territory. Before she could ask Karokara to explain, the woman winced and bent over her belly.

'Baby's coming,' Imoshen guessed. The summer just gone, she'd seen one of the fishermen's women grow big with child, seen someone come to the kitchen door late one night to get the cook, heard the screams in the night, then watched the excited chatter as the others welcomed the baby to the island. 'Come back to the fire.'

She slid her arms around Karokara and helped her stand. She was nowhere near as tall as her father and uncles, but she was bigger than the cook and the fishermen's wives; as big as some of the Malaunje men.

Another contraction came before they could start walking, another at the base of the dune, and another before they got to the door. This one was worse than any of the others. Karokara doubled over, moaning.

When Karokara could stand again, Imoshen helped her inside. Another contraction came as she tried to lie down on the blanket in front of the fire.

'Baby's coming fast. I'll go get help.'

'Don't leave.' Karokara gripped her arm with surprising strength. 'It's quick because I had a fright.' Her hand tightened and her breathing changed as she went with the pain. When it had passed, she looked up. 'Stay with me.'

Chapter Thirteen

OSKANE LOOKED UP.

Franto stood in the doorway with his evening meal on a tray. He often forgot to eat, so deep was he in his study. Tonight it was the Wyrd scrolls. He had never been able to work out why the T'En had powers, when True-men, the gods' chosen people, had none. If there were no gods, as he feared, then this was just bad luck. But he kept searching for a logical reason, because if he found it, maybe he'd find his faith again.

One heretical priest had put forward the theory that the silverheads were fallen angels, who had defied the Seven and been sent to earth to suffer alongside True-people. He had been excommunicated for his trouble.

Sensible scholars held that the Wyrds were closer to animals, but the logic of this troubled Oskane. If he only knew more about the Wyrds, he might be able to work out where they fitted in, but the old scrolls were full of gaps.

A year ago, his agent from Enlightenment Abbey had captured an adult Malaunje for him to study, but the silly creature had killed itself. If Sorne and Izteben were to infiltrate Cesspit City, they would need to speak the Wyrd's barbaric language, so he'd asked the agent to locate a suitable Malaunje to teach the boys.

Franto cleared his throat.

Oskane looked up to see him in front of the desk with the meal. 'Just put it there.'

His servant slid the tray onto the desk. 'There's been trouble.'

'Between the penitents and the Wyrds?'

Franto nodded.

'It was inevitable. While the boys were little, they looked sweet and innocent. But now that they're as big as full grown True-men... I'm surprised the penitents have put up with them this long. We may have to forbid them from using the main courtyard.'

'Denat threw Sorne's shirt in the mud.'

Oskane shrugged.

'Then Joaken got involved.'

Oskane tensed. 'That man is too quick to resort to violence.'

'Today he got what's coming to him. Kolst knocked him off his feet. Broke his nose.'

Oskane chuckled.

'So MUCH BLOOD,' Imoshen whispered. She wasn't a midwife, but even she knew Karokara had lost too much blood.

The baby mewled and tried to kick the blanket off. Imoshen tucked him in again, fetched the last blanket for Karokara and tried to staunch the bleeding.

During the birth, Imoshen had been totally focused on Karokara, and found herself somehow sharing her pain. Even now, her stomach ached.

At least Karokara was no longer in pain. She seemed to be drifting in and out of sleep. Her eyes would flutter open, then close. Her face was white, lips colourless.

Imoshen glanced to the baby boy. He'd screamed at first, but now he blinked sleepily and sucked his fist. Should she run across the island to fetch the cook? Could she leave Karokara that long? Should she take the baby?

'Pass me Iraayel.' It was the barest whisper as Karokara reached for the baby. 'Is he...'

'Perfect,' Imoshen assured her. As her aunt didn't have the strength to hold him, Imoshen placed him on her chest.

With great effort, Karokara lifted one hand to his head. Tears slid down her face. 'Promise me...'

'Yes?'

Karokara held Imoshen's eyes. 'Promise me you'll look after him.'

'I promise.' Imoshen licked her lips. The baby wriggled and almost slid off his mother's chest. Imoshen moved him to one side, placing him beyond the puddle of blood, then turned back. 'But you'll get better. I'll fetch the cook. She–'

'...shen?' Unable to keep her eyes open, Karokara lifted a hand, blindly seeking her.

'I'm here.' Imoshen took the hand between both of hers. So cold and weak.

'You eased my pain.'

'It didn't help. I'm sorry, I–'

'Don't tell anyone.'

'Tell them what?'

Karokara's eyes flickered open in surprise. 'This was the first time your gift's moved?'

Imoshen didn't understand the question, didn't know what to say.

'Are you a woman yet?'

'No...'

Karokara nodded wearily, lids closing. 'Doesn't always coincide.'

'I don't under–'

'Listen. Hide your gift from the T'En men for as long as possible.'

'Why?'

'Once your gift surfaces, they'll fear you.'

Imoshen tried to pull away.

But the dying woman held on with surprising strength. Karokara forced her eyes open. 'Don't trust them. This island is your prison.'

Shocked, Imoshen broke free and sprang back to her heels. Karokara was raving, like the kitchen lad when he got a fever.

'You're not thinking straight. I'll go fetch the cook. She'll know what to do. I'll take Iraayel with me.' Imoshen scooped up the baby. She'd been kneeling in an ever-growing puddle of blood and her wet breeches clung to her legs. She adjusted the baby, making sure he was well-wrapped, for she could hear the wind keening outside.

Going down on one knee, Imoshen touched her aunt's cheek. 'I'll send help, Karo.'

No response, nothing. An empty husk.

Shock held Imoshen immobile. Fishermen had been lost at sea, and her mother had drowned, but you never saw the bodies. She shuddered.

Dipping into the part of her that had woken tonight, she tried to find a spark of life, but she was exhausted and had nothing left.

So she leant forward to listen to the woman's chest. No heart beat under her ear.

How could life be there one moment and gone the next? Where did it go?

The baby stirred. Imoshen slipped out of the cottage, shut the door and set off for the lighthouse.

'Hold on, Irian.'

He turned to see Ardeyne enter the chamber at the base of the lighthouse. Irian gestured up the steps. 'I'm going to check Imoshen's bedroom. The cook can't find her. She wasn't in the walled garden or...'

The voice-of-reason closed the door and came across to the bottom of the steps. 'I think we need someone new to report on Imoshen.'

Irian came down the steps until they were side by side. 'Why? We have the cook.'

'I want someone who knows what life is like in the city, someone who is closer in age, someone she'll confide in.'

'Ah.' Irian understood. 'Someone she will confess her

first gift stirrings to. That person's loyalty must be beyond question. You want my Karo.'

'She was going to stay here for the next five years anyway. It's not like she's your devotee. Even if the baby is stillborn, she should stay here. Imoshen will trust her and confess her gift stirrings. We can't afford to let Imoshen grow into the full extent of her power. We need to get a sacrare from her before that happens.'

He had already agreed to let Karo have those years with their son. But if there was no son, then he would be five years without her for nothing.

Not for nothing, for the brotherhood. The brotherhood was everything, his duty and his life. 'Of course.'

Ardeyne nodded. 'Go, bring Imoshen down.'

Since it was almost dark now and cold, he guessed Imoshen was reading, so deep in a treatise she hadn't heard the fuss. When he reached the top bedroom, it seemed she hadn't even thought to light a lamp, as there was no light coming from under her door.

Smiling, he thrust the door open. 'Reading in the dark?'

Her room was empty, childhood gifts laid out carefully, precious treatises stacked next to the bed.

Troubled, he headed down the stairs, going straight to the house at the base of the lighthouse where the dining room had been turned over to the T'En. As he approached the door, he heard the cook speaking.

'...I'll send for Imoshen. Dinner won't be ready for a while. We didn't look for you for another–'

Irian thrust open the door. 'Imoshen's not in her room.'

The cook spun around. She was a big woman, with a strong jaw. Sensible, he'd always thought.

'Not in her room?' Rohaayel came to his feet. 'Where could she be?'

'Roaming,' the cook said. 'She's become rather wild since we... we'll look for her.' She bustled towards the door. 'I'll have spiced wine brought in, with bread and cheese. That should hold you 'til dinner's ready.'

'Roaming?' Ardeyne repeated after the cook left.

'Two days before twin full moon,' Gift-tutor Bedettor said. 'If her gift's troubling her, she'll be drawn to the moonlight. If her gift's troubling her already, she'll be powerful as an adult.'

They all went very still.

The two gift-warriors came to their feet. Shield-brothers, they were used to defending each other on the empyrean plane. They were well and truly able to take down an untrained T'En girl. For that matter, any of them were.

In theory.

'Is she a threat?' one of them asked.

Irian felt their power rise and his own gift stirred in response. In defence of Imoshen, which surprised him.

'We saw her at summer's cusp,' Rohaayel said. 'There was no sign of her gift then.'

'We must watch for her hair beginning to darken to silver-grey. It's a sign the gift is maturing.' Like the shield-brothers, Bedettor was new to the inner circle. He had replaced the old gift-tutor, who'd known Imoshen since she was a baby. This was his first visit to the island, and he thought they were underestimating the danger Imoshen presented. 'You haven't tried to test her, have you? The threat of your gifts could trigger hers.'

'No, nothing like that,' Rohaayel insisted. He sought Irian's gaze.

'I'll go see what I can find out.'

'Torekar.' Ardeyne signalled his devotee.

The young Malaunje warrior followed Irian out of the dining room and down the hall into the kitchen. Irian thrust the door open. The Malaunje fell silent immediately. He wasn't wanted here. This was their territory.

He stood in the doorway. 'When did you last see Imoshen?'

'Lunch time,' the cook said, coming towards him. 'She took her meal out in the garden.'

Irian gestured Torekar past. 'He'll help you.'

'Very good.' The cook sent Torekar to join the others, and ushered Irian into the hall. 'Everyone I can spare is out looking for her. Go back to the dining room. She'll be here any moment, full of apology for keeping you waiting.'

Instead of going back to the dining room, Irian went out the front door, out into the night. Clouds scudded across the sky, their edges painted silver by the twin moons' light. Nearly season's cusp and double full moon.

From the island's high point, he could see lanterns bobbing on the path down to the bay, where the fishing boats were kept. More lamps wandered like lost stars across the night-dark fields. When he'd come from the eastern side of the island, he hadn't seen Imoshen. Mind you, he hadn't been looking for her, but if she'd seen him, she would have called out.

He went around the main building, past the row of cottages, threading through the barn and storehouses to look west. All dark.

No... a lantern bobbed on the path to the rocks.

Surely she would not be down there? The cliffs, the rocks, the restless, pounding sea... he took off at a run.

He had to slow down as clouds passed across the moons and he risked losing the path. The lantern bobbed as though the person who carried it knew the path by heart. At length, he came up the rise towards him, a lean lad of sixteen or seventeen who recognised Irian, signalled and kept coming.

Irian tried to remember the lad's name. 'Aric, have you seen her?'

He shook his head. 'Thought she might be on the rocks.'

'On the rocks?'

'She likes to stand there, daring the waves to sweep her away.'

'What?' Not only was she foolhardy but... 'That doesn't sound like Imoshen.'

But there was no reason for him to lie. What if Imoshen had been swept off the rocks? If anything happened to her – Irian's heart lurched – it would tear him apart.

What was he thinking? She was a means to an end.

She was the six-year-old who had sat on his lap and advised him which cards to play with great seriousness.

She was a means to an end.

She was the ten-year-old who had discussed the growing of beans, quoting a Sagora treatise on inherited traits.

She was a means to an end.

His duty was to the brotherhood. He must armour himself against her. Irian swallowed. 'She dares the waves to take her?'

He nodded. 'That, or she wanders on the cliff edge.'

'You know this because...'

'I follow her, to see that she's safe. She's been lonely this summer, since Cook told us we're not to talk to her.' He looked troubled, then a smile tugged at his lips. 'When he thinks no one is looking, she dances on the dunes.'

Irian needed to get this lad off the island.

'Come with me.' He took the lantern and led the way. When he passed the walled garden and entered the quiet lea of the barn, he found half a dozen Malaunje at the kitchen door reporting to the cook.

Torekar jogged over to him. 'No sign of her.'

Irian nodded grimly. What had started out as a curiosity was fast becoming troubling. He returned the lantern to Aric. 'Help them.'

The island was not large, but it was too large to search by night. Where was Imoshen? Had someone warned her against them? Who would do such a thing? Only a small group of Malaunje lived on the island, and only the brotherhood members he approved were allowed to visit.

If she hadn't been warned and she had begun to act strangely, then her gift could be moving. That would complicate things.

When he returned to the dining room, everyone looked up.

'No sign of Imoshen.' She could have been swept off the rocks.

The cook bustled in with her entourage, bringing food to the table. When everything had been laid out, she stood waiting to be dismissed.

'Does Imoshen do this often?' Rohaayel asked.

'Run away at night?' Gift-tutor Bedettor qualified.

The cook lifted her hands. 'How would I know? We sleep down here. She sleeps in the lighthouse. I thought she was in her room all this time. We've done as you ordered, All-father Rohaayel, and maintained the proper distance this summer. It was hard at first. She was so small when her mother went, we'd grown into the habit of treating her like one of us. When we tried to maintain the proper distance, she didn't understand. I told her it was time she grew up, but–'

The door opened behind Irian. Wind swirled in, bringing the scent of the night, moonlight and blood. He turned to find Imoshen standing there.

Her hair was wild and wind-blown, her vest and breeches drenched in blood and her bare feet blue with cold. In her arms she carried a rolled up blanket, and her eyes were wide with shock.

Those haunted eyes went straight to him. 'I'm sorry.' Her teeth chattered so badly she could hardly talk. 'I couldn't save her. The bleeding wouldn't stop. I tried–' The bundle wriggled and wailed.

'Karo?'

'I would have fetched the cook, but there wasn't time...'

Irian thrust past her, running for the door.

IMOSHEN TURNED TO her father and Uncle Ardeyne. The birth had been quick and violent; never had she felt more helpless in her life. 'I did everything I could.'

One of the new T'En males stepped closer to Rohaayel. 'All-father, such an experience could trigger...'

'You're covered in blood,' her father said, his voice rough.

Were they offended? The cook always made sure she was bathed and well dressed when they visited.

Rohaayel gestured to the cook. 'See that a bath is drawn. Take the–'

'No.' Imoshen pressed the baby boy close to her chest. Tonight, she'd fought death and lost. Now she held new life in her arms, and she wasn't giving him up. 'Iraayel stays with me. I promised Karokara.'

'All-father?' the cook asked.

Rohaayel's face was hard, eyes sharp; he didn't look like himself. Tonight, everything was strange. Imoshen felt on edge and she didn't like it. She wanted it to be like it was before the cook told her she had to grow up.

She reached out to Ardeyne. 'Uncle...'

He came over, but instead of taking her hand, he slid an arm around her shoulders, avoiding skin contact. Karokara had been right about that. Why had she never noticed before?

Because they had never distanced themselves from her before.

'Sit here.' He guided her to the chair by the fire and knelt next to her. 'Have you eaten?'

'Don't think I can.' She looked up to see the others watching her with wary eyes. 'Father?'

Rohaayel gestured to the cook. 'Bring what's needed for the baby. Bedettor, come here, see if she's taken a chill.'

'I'm fine. Nothing that a warm bath and rest won't fix.'

But Bedettor knelt next to her. 'Give me your hand.'

It seemed a strange way to see if she had a chill – usually the cook felt her forehead – but Imoshen complied.

His large hands enclosed her hand completely. As soon as he touched her, his eyes took on a faraway look. She didn't like him, and she instinctively raised her defences. She concentrated on the warmth of the fire burning in the grate, how it reminded her of winter evenings, singing and stories.

She yawned. 'Sorry, so tired.'

Bedettor stood. 'There's no sign of... a chill.'

The men visibly relaxed.

'Well, that's that, then. The food's going cold. Can't let it go to waste,' one of the big men said, sitting at the table. The other two joined him, leaving her with Rohaayel and Ardeyne.

'I've missed you,' Imoshen told them softly. 'I want to come home and live in the city, with our brotherhood.'

Her father went very still.

'That's... not a good idea,' Ardeyne said. 'You are the all-father's daughter, and Rohaayel loves you. Rival brotherhoods would threaten you to undermine him.'

So there was a perfectly reasonable explanation for why she lived here on the island.

Just then, the cook returned with blankets and warm water. She spread a blanket on the floor in front of the fire, and held out her hands for the baby. Imoshen knelt and placed him in the blanket. He yelled as she unwrapped him.

They both laughed at his indignant cries. The cook showed her how to bathe him and dress him. When they were done, she produced a milk-sop for him to suck on. Imoshen remained on the floor, near the fire.

'He'll need a wet-nurse,' the cook told the all-father. 'One of the fishermen's wives—'

'I know someone suitable,' Ardeyne said. 'I'll send for her tomorrow.'

Meanwhile, Rohaayel wrapped a blanket around Imoshen's shoulders and sat in the chair beside her. She leaned against his knee.

'Was it terrible?' he asked softly.

She nodded. Tears stung her eyes and she had to swallow before she could speak. 'I couldn't do anything to help.'

'She's no healer, then,' Bedettor said.

The others laughed, and Imoshen wondered how they could be so callous. How was she expected to heal? She had no training, unlike the cook.

'Will Uncle Irian be all right?'

She saw Ardeyne and Rohaayel exchange a glance.

'I'll send Torekar after him,' Ardeyne said. 'At least he hadn't...' He ran down.

'Hadn't what?' Imoshen asked, but no one answered. She felt sick. Karokara was right, they were keeping things from her. But it had to be because they wanted to protect her. They loved her; she knew that for a fact.

Imoshen manufactured a convincing yawn. 'Sorry. So tired. Would you mind if I went straight to bed?'

'Of course not.' Rohaayel kissed her forehead, as he always did. Surely, if he didn't love her, he would not treat her with such tenderness?

'The cook will help you settle the baby,' Rohaayel said. 'Go to bed and don't worry about Irian.'

Imoshen nodded and let her feet take her up to her bedroom, where she found warm water in the small copper tub.

It was hard to stay awake. She felt weary to the point of numbness and couldn't think straight.

The cook took her clothes and she knelt in the tub. There was blood on her thighs. When she wiped it away, more came and her stomach hurt. She knew what that meant. No one had ever told her, but she'd overheard the women speaking. Fear stabbed her.

She looked up at the cook. 'Don't tell. *Please?*'

'You have to grow up. Everyone does.'

'Not tonight. Not this visit. Please.'

The cook gave a reluctant nod.

Later, as the woman tucked the blanket around her and the baby, Imoshen studied that familiar face with its strong no-nonsense jaw. The cook had watched over her after her mother died.

But if what Karokara said was true, the cook was her jailor and everything she believed was a lie. The thought terrified her. Her father and her favourite uncles loved her, of that she had no doubt. She'd known them all her life.

Karokara... she'd known her for one evening.

She was not a prisoner.

Chapter Fourteen

DAWN FOUND IMOSHEN standing at the window with baby Iraayel in her arms, crooning to him. From her bedroom, highest in the lighthouse, she could see right across the island, across the sea to the mainland. Right now the sun was only a pale glow in the east, and the mainland was a blue smudge. After the windy night, the air was still and the sky scrubbed clean of clouds – a new start for a new life.

She was thinking of Irian and Karokara, and how short life is, when the smoke started to rise. Irian must have sat with her all night, and was now burning the abandoned cottage along with her body. The smoke rose, a straight black column in the still dawn air.

He would be back soon. Surely his son would ease his heartbreak.

Imoshen dressed formally, as she always did when the brotherhood came to visit: pleated trousers, knitted undershirt, vest and knee-length robe. She slipped her feet into soft boots and tied the straps around her ankles. She should have done her hair in formal plaits, but she wanted to get downstairs, warm up more goat's milk for the baby and be out front to meet Irian when he returned.

But when she saw him coming up the rise with Ardeyne's friend, Torekar, his face looked so haggard that she doubted if anything would reach him. As he approached, his mouth compressed in a thin line.

She didn't know what to say in the face of such grief. Wordlessly, she held out his infant son, flushed with warm milk.

Irian stared at the baby, his expression unreadable.

She wanted to comfort Irian, and was just about to try when he brushed past her.

Tears streamed down Imoshen's cheeks as she watched him enter the lighthouse. Torekar paused beside her. He went to say something, then shook his head, and followed Irian up the stairs.

IRIAN WALKED INTO the all-father's bedroom without knocking, Torekar close behind him. Rohaayel and Ardeyne were asleep in each other's arms but they woke instantly, alert and wary. Irian had spent the night searching for Karokara's shade on the empyrean plane, without success. Unless she somehow made it to the realm of the dead on her own, she was lost to him forever. From their expressions, he supposed his despair was written on his face.

'You came back,' Rohaayel said.

He had been tempted not to. 'I know my duty.'

Rohaayel glanced to Ardeyne, who went to speak, but Irian beat him to it. 'I am loyal, all-father. I've killed for our brotherhood. Last night I walked the empyrean plane and faced death. It made me confront what I've been denying. I believe we made a mistake with Imoshen.'

'What do you mean?' Ardeyne asked.

Irian knew the all-father could order his death for what he was about to say, but it had to be said.

'Imoshen' – Irian's voice caught; he got himself under control – 'is downstairs weeping for me.'

'Should I go?' Ardeyne's devotee asked.

The voice-of-reason glanced to the all-father.

'He knows all our secrets,' Rohaayel said.

Torekar went over to his bedroll and sat cross-legged. Irian paced.

Rohaayel gestured. 'Go on.'

'When I thought Imoshen had been swept off the rocks, I realised she isn't a threat like a sisterhood gift-warrior,' Irian said. 'She's just Imoshen. *Our* Imoshen.'

Rohaayel looked relieved and Irian knew he felt the same way but Ardeyne looked down, infuriating him. 'What's the matter, Ard?'

'What do you want me to say? That we were young and stupid? That we treated a person like a piece in a game?'

'If we wanted to use her,' Irian said, 'we should never have let ourselves grow this close to her. Now–'

'She had to love us so she would be ready to let down her walls for the initiate that we will send to her,' Ardeyne argued. 'Unless she makes the deep-bonding with him, she won't be able to carry a sacrare child.'

'What are you suggesting, Irian?' Rohaayel asked. 'It's not like we can go back and change the past. Ard's right, we were young and inexperienced. Even so, I wouldn't change a thing. All men should see their children grow up. Four hundred years ago our fore-fathers reared their sons, and we will again. And Imoshen will help us.'

Irian blinked.

Even Ardeyne was surprised. 'You would ask her to support the brotherhoods against the sisterhoods?'

'I would ask her to support our brotherhood against our enemies. You heard her last night. She wants to come home and live with us.'

'It just might work...'

'I hope so,' Irian said. 'Because it gets worse. Her hair is only just beginning to darken to silver at the temples, but I sensed traces of female gift residue in the cottage. Bedettor was right. The birth triggered her gift. She hid this from him. Why would she do that if she trusts us?'

Rohaayel shrugged. 'Bedettor doesn't like her and she knows it. I'm guessing she shielded instinctively.'

'She was also exhausted. Her gift was probably drained,' Ardeyne added. 'This makes it even more imperative that we plant a new agent with Imoshen. I've already sent for

Frayvia. She's twenty-three, but will pass for sixteen. After her baby was stillborn, she served the brotherhood as a wet-nurse. She can win Imoshen's trust, and feed her the right information to show our brotherhood in the best light.'

'That's a lot of responsibility,' Irian said. 'Is she up to it?'

'She's smart and loyal. I trust her.'

Irian was not convinced.

'Tell him,' Rohaayel said.

'She's my Malaunje half-sister,' Ardeyne admitted. 'The big question is not who we should plant as an agent here, but who we should send to seduce Imoshen.'

'He must be near her age, so it seems natural for them to be drawn together,' Rohaayel said.

'And we need to stop our visits, so she feels lonely and misses contact with her fellow T'En,' Irian said.

'He'll have to be someone with a strong gift, or the pair-bonding won't take. I'll ask Bedettor for a list of our strongest young initiates,' Ardeyne said. 'He must be loyal.'

'But he must not be driven by ambition,' Rohaayel said. 'When it comes to how he feels about Imoshen, he must be pure of heart or the deep-bonding won't take.'

'This is impossible,' Irian muttered. 'What were we thinking?

Torekar shifted.

'Speak up,' Ardeyne urged.

The devotee swallowed. 'We Malaunje see the T'En when they think no one is looking. We see them as they really are. If you want someone pure of heart, test them. See what they do when they think no one important is watching.'

Ardeyne grinned. 'Lucky was the day you became my devotee.'

'Very well,' Rohaayel said. 'We can assess the candidates when we get back. Pick one and groom him for his role. He can become a tithe-collector; that'll give him an excuse for coming here.'

* * *

SORNE AND IZTEBEN sat studying by the flickering flame of a candle. Sorne could hear the rain drumming on the shingles. He shivered and winced as his back bled again. According to Oskane, privation made for a stronger will, so there was no fire, even though it was cold and wet.

Shouting, and the creak of the front gate opening, made them all turn to the window. Between the rain and the shutters it was hard to hear, but...

'Someone has arrived.' Sorne sprang to his feet.

'Keep working. I want to see this page finished,' Oskane said, before leaving them.

They waited until they were sure both he and Franto had gone downstairs, then went to the window and opened the shutters a little.

A cart trundled in, the driver's face hidden by a wide leather hat. Water poured off the brim as he nodded to Oskane. The penitents came out. A second person opened the cart and stood in the rain, trying to persuade someone to come out to no avail.

Joaken climbed in and seemed to be struggling with someone half-wrapped in a blanket. A woman cried out in another language, then switched to curse them in Chalcedonian.

Sorne gasped as a long copper plait swung loose from the blanket covering her head.

'A half-blood, like us,' Izteben whispered.

'Not like us,' Sorne corrected, and quoted Oskane. 'She's probably from Cesspit City. She's the enemy.'

But his instinct was to protect her.

Joaken yelped and doubled over.

'She kneed him!' Izteben was delighted.

Despite Oskane's lessons, Sorne felt his heart lift as the she-Wyrd made a run for the wall.

Denat caught her by one arm, swung her around and slammed his fist into her head. Stunned, she dropped and lay on the courtyard flagstones in the rain.

'Quick, get her inside and downstairs,' Oskane ordered.

As the men grabbed her arms and legs and carried her out of view into the building, Sorne fought the urge to run downstairs and save her. He had to remind himself she was the enemy.

'What does Oskane want with her?' Izteben asked, clearly troubled.

'To study her,' Sorne guessed. 'We better get back to work, or...'

Oskane would never lock them up. They were his holy warriors.

They were nothing like the she-Wyrd.

OSKANE SENT THE others away as soon as they tossed her into the cell. 'She cannot hurt you. She's just a half-blood.'

'Are you sure?' the she-Wyrd countered. She grabbed the bars and yelled as the penitents retreated. 'A curse on you and your children. May your cocks shrivel. May you never know a woman's arms again!'

'We are celibate priests,' Oskane told her primly.

'More fool you!'

He flushed.

She eyed him and wiped the blood from her split lip. 'Why do this? I was going about minding my business. Why lock me up here?'

Originally these had been storerooms, dug into the cliff below the ground floor. Only small ventilation windows near the ceiling let in light. Oskane had ordered Kolst to knock out the wall, put in bars and create two cells. The other one was empty.

If the boys were ever to infiltrate the Wyrds, they needed to be able to speak their language. 'You are going to teach the T'En language.'

She laughed.

'Franto, bring the boys down.' He turned back to her. 'How old are you?'

'Why should I tell you?'

She could be anywhere between twenty and fifty. The half-bloods weren't quite as long-lived as the T'En. She wore a rich brocade knee-length robe over a knitted undershirt. Her legs were encased in woollen breeches and she wore well-made boots. For a servant, she was finely dressed.

'What position did you hold in the brotherhood or sisterhood where you served?'

'I'm not going to tell you anything.'

'Oh, I think you will.' He smiled as he heard Sorne's clear voice asking Franto questions and saw her glance anxiously to the stairs at the end of the hall. His servant escorted the two half-blood boys down the passage until they stood opposite the captive. They stared at her and she stared right back at them.

'This is a she-Wyrd from their cesspit of a city. She will be teaching you the T'En language,' Oskane told them. 'Do you have anything you want to ask her?'

Sorne looked away as if he couldn't bear the sight of her. Izteben shook his head and stared past her.

'Very well, Franto, take them away. But leave the lamp.'

His assistant led the boys out.

'Those boys are twelve and thirteen years of age,' Oskane said. 'If you don't cooperate and teach them the T'En language, I will have them killed right here in front of you. Then I will turn my penitents loose on you. They haven't slept with a woman in years. After they are done with you, I'll tell them to throw you off the cliff.'

She shrank back, shaking her head.

'I trust we understand each other now.'

She nodded slowly and he was pleased to see that the fire of defiance no longer burned in her eyes.

'Strip.'

'But you said—'

'Your filthy body doesn't interest me. This is Restoration Retreat. We live a humble life here. You will be dressed accordingly.'

THE NEXT DAY, when Sorne and Izteben were taken down to the she-Wyrd for their first lesson, she looked very different. Gone were her fine clothes. Gone was her long hair. It had been roughly and patchily shorn. She wore a penitent's breeches with a simple thigh-length shirt. She had a bucket for her needs, and a blanket. Other than a slate and nib, she had nothing else.

Sorne was sickened by the sight of her.

Oskane settled himself on his chair and began reading.

Sorne and Izteben sank down cross-legged. The she-Wyrd knelt, placed one hand and then the other on the floor in front of her knees, and pressed her forehead to her hands.

She straightened up. 'Welcome. The trust of student and teacher is sacred. I am at your service.' She picked up the slate and nib. On it were written the words *I am hungry*, then below that a phrase in another language.

'Even the letters are different,' Izteben muttered, dismayed.

'Repeat after me.' The she-Wyrd said the words in T'En, making them repeat the phrase over and over.

The she wrote, *I am cold*, then *I am a prisoner*. When they had memorised these sequences, she pointed out the patterns. Then she wrote *I am a cold, hungry prisoner*, in T'En and asked, 'Do you get my meaning?'

And Sorne did. He glanced over his shoulder, but Oskane was still reading. He didn't want to see the she-Wyrd as a person, but she refused to be beaten down.

And he couldn't help but admire her.

That evening when their mother took over a tray for the she-Wyrd – the penitents had refused to feed her –

Sorne sent Hiruna with an extra blanket and food from his own plate.

After their mother left, Izteben caught his eye. 'I thought you said we must keep our distance.'

'She won't know who sent it.'

Izteben grinned, but said nothing more.

Chapter Fifteen

IMOSHEN WAS NOT sure if she liked this wet-nurse from the city. The girl was a little older than her, sixteen or seventeen perhaps. She came with nothing but a small bundle of clothes and breasts swollen with milk. Her arrival meant Imoshen's father and uncles' departure. Perhaps this was why she resented Frayvia, which was not fair of her.

Now the girl stood on the other side of Imoshen's bedroom.

'I don't want to come between you and the baby,' Frayvia said softly. 'I know I'm only the wet-nurse.'

'I used goat's milk and a rag. He–'

Hearing Imoshen's voice, baby Iraayel snuffled and gave a cry. She was not surprised; he was always hungry.

Frayvia gasped and pressed her hands to her breasts. 'I need to feed him.'

'Sit there.' Imoshen indicated the chair by her desk. 'I'll fetch him.' She picked up the baby and carried him across.

Frayvia had already unlaced her knitted undershirt and freed her breast. Baby Iraayel turned his head, felt the warm skin on his cheek, opened his mouth and captured the nipple.

Frayvia gave a sigh of relief and, for a while, they just watched him.

How far can I trust this girl from the city? Imoshen wondered. Frayvia had been sent to keep an eye on her, that much was certain, but this did not mean that Frayvia was her enemy; her father was only concerned for her.

Even so, she would not reveal her gift. Not that she believed Karokara's warning, but it was wise to be careful.

Anger made Imoshen's stomach churn, for just before the T'En left, the cook had weakened and told the all-father that she was now a woman. She resented having no privacy.

Lucky for her, her gift had only stirred twice since the night Iraayel was born, and she had been alone both times. Both times she had practised repressing it and shielding herself.

They could hear the baby swallowing, over and over.

Frayvia laughed with pure delight, as he gulped down her milk. 'You greedy little thing!'

Imoshen felt a weight lift. A question occurred to her. 'What happened to your own baby?'

Frayvia looked away, eyes shadowed with pain. 'He died.'

'Was he T'En?' She'd heard that it was hard to birth a healthy full-blood babe.

Frayvia shook her head, eyes lowered, but Imoshen could see the glitter of tears half hidden by her lashes.

Imoshen dropped to her knees and slid her arms around Frayvia's shoulders. 'I'm so very sorry.'

The girl looked up, surprised. 'But he was only Malaunje.'

'How can you say that?'

Frayvia flushed, then gulped back a sob. Her mouth worked. 'They... they told me not to fuss. Told me Malaunje girls were more important, and I'd have plenty of chances to produce a girl, or even a T'En. They took him away. I didn't even get to hold him!'

'That's so cruel.'

Frayvia wiped her cheeks. 'That's the way it is.'

'It's not right,' Imoshen said. 'One day, when I live with the brotherhood, I'll change things.'

Frayvia stared at her, then looked down at the baby.

'You don't think it's possible to change things?'

Frayvia shook her head and moved baby Iraayel to the other breast. He burped loudly and they both smiled.

Imoshen watched him feed. 'I have to try to change things. If I think something is wrong, I can't just sit back and let it happen.'

'Oh, Imoshen.'

'HAVE YOU HEARD?' Arodyti asked.

Vittoryxe ignored her for the moment, completing the last of her gift-warrior exercises before stretching. They stood on the palace roof set aside for T'En sisters. Potted palms stirred in the breeze. 'Don't you know it's rude to interrupt a T'En seeking balance?'

The exercises were designed to promote peace and harmony between mind, body and gift. Every adult T'En was supposed to perform them every day. Warriors concentrated on building their strength, while scholars carried out stretches that helped focus the mind.

'Sorry,' Arodyti said, but her eyes sparkled with excitement. 'You'll never believe the news.'

Vittoryxe rolled up her mat and slung it over her shoulder. 'You're carrying on like a new initiate, not someone who will be an adept in three years.'

'Remember Reoden's daughter?'

'Must be a year old soon?'

Arodyti nodded. 'Did you ever wonder why Ree became the all-mother right after giving birth?'

'She's a healer. The best we have.'

'She's also the mother of a sacrare.'

'How could she have a sacrare child?' Vittoryxe demanded, sick with envy. She felt her gift surge and concentrated on banking it. 'She'd have to make the deep-bonding, and no one's done that for four hundred years.'

'Thanks to her healing power, Ree was able to carry the baby to term. She's provided her sisterhood with a daughter who will grow into a powerful adult and win great stature for them. That's why their all-mother stepped down, making Reoden all-mother of the largest sisterhood!'

'Ours is the largest sisterhood,' Vittoryxe corrected. 'It has the longest and most glorious history. More...'

But Arodyti was already darting away to waylay someone else with the news.

Vittoryxe went to check on her birds. Today, even their exquisite forms and fluting songs could not soothe her.

All she had to do was birth a sacrare to become an all-mother. Not only was it next to impossible, but it was not for her. She couldn't bring herself to tryst with a male. Besides, she wasn't a healer. She would never be able to fall pregnant, and carry a healthy child.

Furious with everyone and everything, she headed down to the chambers she shared with her devotee. As she strode into the private chamber, Choris looked up with a guilty start.

Their choice-son, Mefeyne, ducked his head.

Vittoryxe stiffened. Now that he was thirteen, they should be distancing themselves from him, not indulging him. 'What's he doing here?'

'It's not Choris's fault, choice-mother. I cut my hand.'

She took his hand to inspect the injury. It was the merest scratch, and her devotee had pandered to him.

'Don't you understand, Choris? He must go to the brotherhood by the time he is seventeen. He must be hardened up.' She rounded on Mefeyne, trying not to recall the sweet little boy he had been. It helped that he was nearly as tall as her. 'You will thank me for this one day. Go back to the other lads. Don't come here again.'

His chin trembled.

'Go.'

He turned and went.

Choris covered her mouth as if to prevent herself calling out to him. In all other things they saw eye to eye but, when it came to the lad...

Vittoryxe stalked out, her gift raging to be free.

She went straight to Gift-tutor Lealeni, determined to confront her. For years now, the gift-tutor had been promising to name Vittoryxe as her successor, but she had never made the formal announcement.

Reoden was eleven years younger than her, and already led her sisterhood.

Vittoryxe strode into the gift-tutor's training chamber. 'Lealeni?'

There was no sign of her in her private study, and the gift training chamber was empty. Bookshelves stretched along one wall. Vittoryxe was about to leave, when her gift switched to the empyrean plane without warning; the air rippled with distortion.

Something drew her to an aisle between bookshelves.

There Lealeni sat slumped against the shelf, half bent over a fallen initiate. The foolish girl's gift must have surged uncontrollably and torn her from this plane into the next, and the gift-tutor had gone after her.

As Vittoryxe watched, a wound opened up in the side of Lealeni's face, leaking bright power. Another opened on her arm.

She would have to go through to help. Annoyed, because she would gain no stature by risking her life, Vittoryxe knelt to touch the young initiate

Immediately she segued to a twilit hillside. She stood between two rows of heavily laden grape vines. A brooding sky hung low overhead.

There was no sign of Lealeni, and the girl lay on her belly on the icy ground, hands covering her head. Stupid initiate. It was a wonder her gift and life essence hadn't been leached away. At least she was shielding her power. Shielding madly, by the feel of it.

Vittoryxe hauled the girl to her feet.

Sarosune's young face was blank with terror. She was both gifted and smart. Vittoryxe had marked her as a possible future threat. But right now she was barely twenty and out of her depth.

Vittoryxe scanned the hillside for Lealeni, and spotted scuffled ground further up the rise. Each step she took, she expected one of the great predators to spring through the vines and take them down.

Someone had clearly run up this hill, though nothing had followed, which meant the attack could come from above. Vittoryxe looked up, fearing a harrowraven had them in its sights, but the sky was empty.

On the crest of the hill she found disturbed ground. Beyond it, the earth fell away into a natural amphitheatre.

Lealeni was backed up against the wall directly below them, surrounded by the dark forms of a dozen scraelings, sentient shadows. One was dangerous, a dozen were deadly.

Lealeni hadn't sensed Vittoryxe yet, her attention focused on her attackers. She was wounded in several places and bleeding power – irresistible to empyrean beasts.

Scraelings followed big predators eager for their leavings. They had to get out of here before whatever it was came back.

Vittoryxe dropped to her knees and was about to her use her gift to form a rope when she hesitated. If Lealeni died here, no one would be surprised.

And she would become gift-tutor.

The position was hers. *Should* have been hers already.

Sensing the proximity of Vittoryxe's gift, Lealeni looked up. Face pale with fear, she held out a beseeching hand.

Vittoryxe formed the rope and Lealeni caught it. With Sarosune's help, she hauled her up. The scraelings screamed in frustration and charged, but they were too late.

As Lealeni collapsed in Vittoryxe's arms, Sarosune's gift surged on a tide of fear.

Vittoryxe spun around. An omnivulper loped up between the vines towards them, its broad wolfish head lowered in determination.

Vittoryxe felt Lealeni shudder with fear. Quick as thought, she drove her elbow into the gift-tutor's abdomen, sending her reeling backwards into the amphitheatre and the waiting scraelings.

As the omnivulper leapt, Vittoryxe grabbed the girl and segued to the earthly plane, where they returned to their bodies with the juddering impact of a fall.

Gasping, Vittoryxe scrambled to drag them both to safety as Lealeni shuddered in her death throes.

Sarosune shivered, teeth chattering.

'You're safe. You hear me? You're safe.' Vittoryxe shook her.

'What happened to Lealeni?'

'I don't know. She was right behind us.'

A noise made Vittoryxe spin.

Five frightened lads backed off, Mefeyne amongst them. Their gifts surged, driven by fear.

'What're you doing here?' she snapped.

Mefeyne made obeisance. 'We found the three of you unconscious, choice-mother. We didn't know what to do, so I sent for help.'

'You did the right thing not to touch us.'

'The gift-tutor's dying,' Sarosune said, stricken. 'True death, her gift and essence devoured by the beasts.'

Vittoryxe glanced to Lealeni.

The gift-tutor's wounds no longer bled. A white frost covered her, creeping up the wall and across the floor.

'Look,' Vittoryxe told the youngsters, stepping aside so they could see the body. 'This is why we are so hard on you. Even a trained T'En like Gift-tutor Lealeni can—'

Footsteps, voices coming closer.

'Someone said there was trouble.' Egrayne came up behind the lads, accompanied by Arodyti and a younger boy. 'What's going on here?'

In answer, Vittoryxe gestured to Lealeni's still body.

'Lea...' Egrayne whispered.

'The gift-tutor gave her life in the line of duty,' Vittoryxe said. 'She named me her successor.'

No one questioned her announcement.

'Leave us now, boys. We must mourn our lost sister.' Egrayne waited until they had gone then gestured to

Arodyti. 'Aro, take Sarosune away. See that she has something hot and sweet to drink. She's had a shock. We'll investigate this later.'

'It's my fault,' Sarosune whispered. 'I was practising immersion and extraction when–'

'Did you vary your entry points?' Vittoryxe asked.

The girl shook her head.

'That's what did it. You shed power each time. You might as well have lit a beacon.'

A sob escaped Sarosune.

'Enough,' Egrayne said.

'Her lack of thought nearly got us all killed,' Vittoryxe countered. 'I'm gift-tutor now. I say when it is enough.'

Egrayne eyed her thoughtfully, but didn't argue. 'What took Lealeni in the end?'

'We don't know,' Vittoryxe lied. 'She was right behind me when I escaped with Sarosune.'

'There was a vulper,' the young initiate said.

'An omnivulper,' Vittoryxe corrected. 'It was old and smart. It was stalking us.'

'And there were scraelings,' Sarosune added, 'dozens of them. She didn't stand a chance. She saved me by drawing the omnivulper away. Told me to hide.'

'She died serving her sisterhood,' Egrayne said. 'There is no better way to die. Vittoryxe's appointment will have to be recognised by the all-mother's inner circle, but...' They all knew it would be a formality.

'Let me be the first to congratulate you.' Egrayne stepped forward and gave Vittoryxe the formal obeisance of an equal.

Vittoryxe realised that they finally held the same rank. Now only Egrayne stood in her way.

'THERE'S FIVE CANDIDATES waiting in the corridor,' Irian reported. 'How they act when they think no one important can see them will reveal what kind of person they really are.

They've been told we're looking for a new tithe-collector.

'Which is true,' Ardeyne said. 'As far as it goes.'

Rohaayel nodded. 'Send in the tithe-master and his assistant.'

Irian opened the door to the tithe-master's study and beckoned. Tithe-master Ysanyn was an old, mid-ranking adept, who was not privy to their plans for Imoshen. His Malaunje assistant was equally aged.

'When the initiate first enters, I want you to berate your assistant,' Ardeyne told the tithe-master. 'Then tell the initiate to wait and go into your study.'

Ysanyn nodded.

Ardeyne turned to the assistant. 'When you're alone with the initiate, knock the abacus off the desk. The rods have been loosened so the beads will go everywhere. You'll need to repair the abacus between each initiate. We'll be behind the screen observing their unguarded reactions.'

'I don't normally go to this much trouble to select a tithe-collector,' Ysanyn said.

'Indulge me. We're testing a theory,' Rohaayel said.

They retreated to sit behind the screen.

The first three initiates ignored the Malaunje assistant's predicament. The fourth looked contemptuous. The fifth knelt and helped him pick up the beads.

He was still picking up beads when Ysanyn called for him.

'You go,' the assistant told him. 'I'll be alright. Thank you.'

The initiate sprang to his feet, dusted off his pleated trousers and went in for his interview. When it was over, Ysanyn reported. 'Two of the candidates would make good tithe-collectors. Both were smart, with a good head for figures.'

'Which two were they, in order of interview?'

'The second and the fifth.'

Irian saw Ardeyne and Rohaayel exchange looks.

'The fifth one's name was?'

'Reothe.'

'Tell him you've selected him,' Rohaayel said, and then he and Ardeyne walked out.

Ysanyn caught Irian's arm. 'You're not going to tell me what this is about?'

'Sometimes it is better not to know,' Irian said, wondering if Reothe would live to regret the honour they did him; it was not like he could refuse.

A little later, Torekar escorted the young initiate up to the all-father's greeting chamber. Irian waited behind the door, arms folded, watching as Reothe knelt to give his obeisance to the brotherhood's all-father and voice-of-reason.

After Rohaayel had explained about his secret T'En daughter and Reothe had recovered from his surprise, the all-father said, 'We've chosen you to do a great service for our brotherhood. We want you to court Imoshen and make the deep-bonding so that she can carry a healthy sacrare son. With him, we'll unite the brotherhoods and free ourselves from sisterhood domination.'

Reothe remained silent for so long that Irian wondered if he was going to refuse.

'Is there something you don't understand?' Ardeyne asked.

Reothe shook his head.

'Will you accept?' Rohaayel asked.

Reothe glanced over his shoulder; he'd been aware of Irian's presence all along. 'If I refused, I imagine I would become acquainted with the fish.'

Irian grinned. Rumour had it that if an initiate or adept gave him trouble he killed them, tied weights to their body and dropped them in the lake. The fact that people believed him capable of this meant he didn't have to do it.

'If you refused, you would have to lower your defences so that Ardeyne could remove your memory,' Irian said. 'You can refuse. Do you want to?'

Reothe frowned. 'What if she doesn't like me? What if I don't like her?'

'She's kind-hearted and smart,' Rohaayel told him. 'Her idea of a treat is a Sagora treatise on philosophy.'

'Pretty,' Ardeyne assured him. 'She's unaware of the trouble between the sisterhoods and brotherhoods. There's no deception in her.'

Reothe looked to Irian, who remembered finding her on the cliff top, watching the waves crash upon the rocks, the day they left.

'I think she has hidden depths.'

Chapter Sixteen

SORNE TOOK HIS usual chair at the kitchen table with Izteben at his side. Zabier sat opposite. Their mother was so heavily pregnant, now, that she had to sit back from the table.

Seeing he had their attention, Kolst began. 'Your mother is pregnant–'

'We noticed,' Izteben said.

But Kolst didn't smile. He held their eyes until they sobered. 'Your mother is pregnant, and it will be a True-man baby. I'm getting on. If anything happened to me, there would be no one to look after your mother, Zabier and the new baby. We need to go home, where my brother and his family can help us –'

'We'd look after them,' Izteben insisted, and Sorne nodded.

'You're half-bloods. Besides, you won't be here much longer. Scholar Oskane has some grand task planned for you. So, when the baby comes, we'll be heading back to our village.'

'You're leaving?' Izteben whispered.

'But Da–' Zabier protested.

Kolst signalled for silence. 'Zabier needs to meet a suitable wife' – Zabier's laughter interrupted their father, who silenced him with a look and kept speaking – 'and he won't meet one here. Izteben will be fifteen next birthday, a man. I was supporting my mother and brother at eleven.'

'You're really going.' Sorne was stricken.

'We always were. It's just come sooner because of the baby,' Kolst said. He reached over and covered Hiruna's hand. 'I have a responsibility to see that my wife and children are cared for.'

'Can't you stay until Oskane closes the retreat?' Sorne asked.

Kolst glanced to Hiruna. 'If we stay here, Zabier will never fit in back home. That's another thing. No more teaching him to read and write.'

'But–'

Kolst held up his hand. 'All he needs to be able to do is write his name and figure numbers. Anything more, and the other villagers will resent him.'

After dinner, their mother prepared a tray for the she-Wyrd. Sorne offered to take it, but she told him not to worry. Since it was his turn to do the chore, he waited until she'd crossed the courtyard, and then followed. Izteben caught up with him on the stairs. Only the faintest of glows from the passage illuminated their bare toes. Hiruna's worried voice reached them.

'...so there is no way of telling if the babe will be born a True-man or a half-blood?' Hiruna asked.

'Not if you don't know when it was conceived. What will you do if it's a half-blood?'

'I don't even want to think about it. Kolst has his heart set on going home.'

'We can both go home. Set me free,' the she-Wyrd urged. 'I'll take the baby and your boys to my people.'

Izteben would have left their hiding place and confronted the she-Wyrd, but Sorne caught his arm, and a moment later Hiruna found them on the stairs.

'You heard?'

They nodded. Sorne asked, 'Why is Da so sure the baby won't be a half-blood?'

'He's served the church for thirteen years as a penance. He thinks this baby is a sign the gods have forgiven him for being arrogant when he was a young man.'

'What will happen if the baby is a half-blood?' Izteben asked.

Their mother shuddered. 'I don't know.'

'ONLY ONE BROTHERHOOD warrior.' Imoshen shaded her eyes but the distance to the boat, and the glitter of sunlight on the sea, made it impossible to identify the lone T'En. If her father had sent only one of his two seconds, then...

'It will be Hand-of-force Irian,' Frayvia said.

Imoshen chewed her bottom lip. 'My father's never failed to visit before.'

'Perhaps he is ill.'

Baby Iraayel was sitting up now. He waved a chubby hand and sang out. Imoshen smiled and planted a kiss on his dear little neck. He wriggled with delight. This last half year, she had never been happier. Not only did she have Iraayel to love, but Frayvia had proven to be a true friend. Even so, she had been looking forward to seeing her father and uncles.

Shading her eyes, Imoshen stared across the sea. The boat was close enough now for her to see the lone T'En wasn't either of her uncles. Only something serious would keep Irian from seeing his son. 'Not Irian or Ardeyne.'

'You're sure?' Frayvia asked. 'Has this ever happened before?'

Imoshen shook her head.

'I hope...'

'Me too, Fray.'

When the boat drew close, Imoshen asked, 'Do you know this T'En?'

Frayvia shook her head. 'I didn't have much to do with the T'En. My brother made sure of that.'

She hadn't said who her brother was, but Imoshen gathered he was a high-ranking Malaunje. Then it struck her, he might be T'En, which would explain why Frayvia never mentioned his name.

As the boat pulled into the shallows, Imoshen studied the lone T'En. He was more boy than man: long legs, soft cheeks, rather pale. By the way he carefully climbed out of the boat, she concluded he wasn't used to the sea.

The island's Malaunje had gathered on the beach and now hung back, whispering. She detected an undertone of worry.

As the lone T'En came up the beach towards her, Imoshen set off to meet him. 'Who are you, and where is my father?' Then she recalled her manners. 'Welcome to Lighthouse Isle. May your stay restore your balance. Is something wrong with the all-father?'

He hid a smile. Did he think her gauche? Imoshen bristled.

'Is Voice-of-reason Ardeyne safe?' Frayvia asked, adding quickly, 'and Hand-of-force Irian?'

'They're well.' He gave Imoshen the formal obeisance of equals – no one had ever bothered before – then removed a message from under his vest. 'But it was not safe for them to leave the city.'

Imoshen passed Iraayel to Frayvia before accepting the message. The moment she touched it, she sensed the youth's gift. The message contained no more information than she already knew. It was written in formal language, and addressed to the cook, which made it most unsatisfying.

He stepped closer, lowered his voice and explained kindly, 'In case I was killed on the road and the message discovered, it's made out to the cook to keep your identity–'

'...hidden. I'm not stupid,' she told him, and stepped back. Why couldn't he keep his gift reined in?

'I'm to stay to check the catch and the island's tithes. They said you might send a message with me when I return but it would have to be written as if you were the cook.'

She rolled her eyes. 'How old are you?'

He drew himself up. 'Eighteen.'

A youth then, not much older than her. It seemed she was no longer important to All-father Rohaayel, otherwise why would he send an errand boy?

Imoshen sighed. 'I suppose you'd better come up to the lighthouse. Cook will get you something to eat and I'll show you to your room.'

She turned to find the gathered Malaunje waiting. Of course, they wanted to know what was going on.

'Brotherhood business has prevented All-father Rohaayel's visit,' Imoshen announced. 'Bring your tithes to...' She glanced to the T'En errand boy. 'What's your name?'

'Initiate Reothe, tithe-collector for Tithe-master Ysanyn.'

As Imoshen led him towards the lighthouse, a Malaunje followed with his travelling kit. She recognised him as Netaric, a regular visitor, one who might know more – if she could just get him alone for a moment.

Once inside, Frayvia took Iraayel upstairs for his nap while Imoshen showed Reothe into his bedchamber.

Netaric put his things down. 'Will that be all, Initiate Reothe?'

'Find me a study so that I can collect the tithes and check the catch records.'

Netaric nodded and left.

Imoshen went to follow him.

'Imoshen?' Reothe called after her.

Why was he staring at her like that? 'What is it?'

'They didn't tell me you were beautiful.' He flushed, and she felt his gift surge.

Immediately she raised her defences. When her father called her lovely, she'd always assumed that he was biased because he loved her. Reothe's observation surprised her. It also confused her, because she couldn't see the relevance. Perhaps this was how they talked in the city.

She gave the obeisance of equals, as he had done earlier, and tried to formulate a polite reply. 'Thank you. You are very beautiful, too. I have work to do now. If you need anything, Cook can be of assistance.'

And she left him, running downstairs after Netaric. Through the door to the kitchen, she could see him chatting to the cook. Imoshen hung back, eavesdropping on their conversation.

'...don't be worried. All-father Rohaayel is the smartest of the lot. Now tell me how you've been.'

'This initiate, what is he to the all-father? Isn't he a bit young to be entrusted with this task?'

'He is, but the all-father's taken a shine to him. He's clever and gifted, and I know he'll go far. I've missed you, Melli. Come here and give me a kiss before the others get back.'

The cook laughed like a girl, and there was no more useful conversation.

Sighing, Imoshen turned to find Reothe watching her from the end of the hall. Her face grew hot; she gestured to him to hold his tongue as she approached.

'You were listening at the door.'

'How else am I going to find out what the Malaunje are saying? Now come along and I'll find you a suitable study.'

She opened a door and stepped into a dusty room. 'I'll have a table and chair brought up here. That way the Malaunje won't have to give up one of their rooms in the big house.'

'T'En don't usually worry about inconveniencing Malaunje.'

'They would if they could hear what the Malaunje think of them.'

He stared at her blankly for a moment.

'What now?' she asked.

'The things you say... I don't know what to make of you.'

Imoshen laughed. 'Then it's just as well you don't have to make anything of me.' He might be from the city and her father might be grooming him for greatness, but she wasn't impressed.

'So, you have all the answers, do you?'

'How could I, when I don't have all the questions?'

He laughed at that.

She grinned. Now things were getting interesting.

SORNE ALWAYS LOVED fishing. The moment Oskane declared it a rest day, he had taken off with Izteben and Zabier. That afternoon, they returned with five fine trout. The air was warm, with the promise of the summer to come, the mountainsides green and the shadow of their family's imminent break-up made every moment precious.

'Wait 'til I show Da the fish I caught,' Zabier crowed. He ran on ahead and pushed open the kitchen door.

There was no sign of their mother, and nothing cooking on the stove for dinner. A baby's cry made them run to the door to their parent's bedroom.

Hiruna sat up in bed with a newborn at her breast. 'You have a little sister.'

Zabier ran to the bed and threw his arms around their mother. 'I don't want to go. Can't we stay here?'

The baby was all wrapped up, and Sorne couldn't make out if it had six fingers or the Wyrd eyes. 'Is it a half-blood or...?'

'Half-blood,' Hiruna said, voice raw as if she'd been weeping.

'Good.' Zabier hugged her. 'That means we can stay.'

But Sorne knew there was no easy answer.

OSKANE OPENED THE report from his port agent and read it swiftly. King Charald's queen had delivered another blue baby. Good. So far the king still had only one heir, in Cedon. The lad was three and a half years younger than his half-brother Sorne, which made him around Zabier's age.

Next he read Matxin's report. His cousin's youngest son had inherited the barony after the elder brother took a wound that turned septic. Matxin was always urging Oskane to make his move, but Oskane would not be rushed. Both half-bloods needed to be fluent in T'En before they could blend in to the Malaunje of Cesspit City. From his research about the brotherhoods and sisterhoods, he was leaning towards using the boys to assassinate key leaders, then plant incriminating evidence so the T'En would turn on each other. This would weaken them and make them easier to conquer. According to his sources, the king's debt to the T'En was mounting. The day Oskane came to Charald with a way to defeat the Wyrds would be the day his family was restored.

There was a knock at the door.

'Come in.'

Franto opened the door for Kolst. Oskane had heard the birthing screams and, from the carpenter's troubled expression, knew the news was not good.

'I don't understand,' Kolst said. 'Why are the gods punishing me like this?'

Oskane had no answer. The more he looked for answers, the more questions he found.

Kolst ran his hands through his receding hair. 'Hiruna won't part with the babe. It's like a madness with her. As long as she keeps it, we can't go home.' He turned to Oskane. 'Do you have need of another half-blood?'

'I plan to send the boys out in a few years. The child won't be ready. She should give it to the Wyrds as soon as possible. The longer she holds onto it, the harder it will be for her to give it up,' Oskane said. He'd never really understood why Kolst put up with Hiruna. The man could have held a position of respect in his village. 'She's your wife. By law, she has to do what you say. You've been more than fair. Most men would have repudiated her when she produced the first half-blood and taken another wife. Most men would leave the babe with the Wyrds, take their wife and son, and go home.'

'It's Zabier I worry about,' Kolst confessed. 'The way he follows Sorne and Izteben around, he might as well be a half-blood.'

'You have a responsibility to your True-man son,' Oskane agreed. 'I've put aside a sum to help you establish yourself when you do get home.'

Kolst looked up, and Oskane could see the longing in his eyes.

'What will you do?'

'I don't know.'

IMOSHEN FOUND FRAYVIA dozing with baby Iraayel in her arms. She took the sleeping infant and placed him in his cradle, before turning back to her friend. The room was lit by moonlight, turning Frayvia's hair and eyes black.

'I know they sent you to spy on me,' Imoshen said. 'I know you owe your loyalty to the all-father, but even more to Ardeyne, your brother.'

Frayvia gasped. Imoshen's guess was correct.

'Now, will you answer my questions truthfully?'

'When I can. I took a vow to serve the all-father.'

'Fair enough.' Imoshen sat on the bed under the window, so that she was in shadow, but she could see Frayvia's face. 'Why have they sent Reothe and not come themselves?'

'I don't know.'

'Why can I sense Reothe's gift so much more strongly than I could sense the all-father's and his seconds'? They have to be more powerful than him. He's only an initiate. Is it because my gift has grown this last half year?'

When she and Frayvia had not spoken of her gift, she'd gathered that it was a private thing, like the kisses Netaric and the cook had stolen when no one was looking.

'If we speak of your gift, I must mention it in my report,' Frayvia said at last.

Imoshen shrugged. 'If my gift did not rise, that would be remarkable.'

'I'm guessing the growth of your gift has made you more sensitive to theirs. I can show you the mental walls we Malaunje build to retain our integrity. As for this Reothe, he may simply be young and powerful. The gift surges erratically, until the T'En learns to control it. I know this, because they warned me against you and your gift. I haven't been accustomed to the male gift. They warned me that your gift could manifest powerfully and I had to get away from you if that happened.'

'So this Reothe is just unskilled?'

She nodded. 'Or he may be trying to lure you. The male and female gifts are very different, yet they attract each other.'

Imoshen nodded her understanding. This was why she was irrationally drawn to him, and now that she knew, she could work on developing her defences. 'Thank you. I don't want you to feel torn by conflicting loyalties. I know my father is only trying to protect me.'

Frayvia hesitated, then nodded before disrobing and climbing into bed.

Imoshen slipped in beside her. Now that she was forewarned, she could have a little fun with Reothe. It would serve him right.

Now that she was forewarned, she wouldn't mention how sometimes the world took a side-step and she saw things that weren't there. She wouldn't mention that sometimes she had nightmares where she was on her beloved island but it was subtly different. There were hungry beasts after her and even the sea was her enemy.

No, she wouldn't mention any of those things, particularly as the nightmares happened when she was awake.

IMOSHEN WENT LOOKING for Reothe. During the three days he had been on the island, she had been testing him to see if he could keep up with her. She might not know much about the city, but she had read Sagora treatises and had no trouble following them. While she might surprise him, he was never left stranded.

Now she had a message to give him for her father.

She found Reothe wandering along the cliff edge. He was dressed for travel, reminding her that he went back to a world she had little knowledge of.

Up here on the cliffs, the wind was fierce, masking her approach. A smile tugged at her lips as she came up behind him. 'This is one of my favourite places.'

He jumped and she caught his arm to steady him. Skin to skin, she felt his gift surge. It had been involuntary on his part, she was sure of that now.

'Do you like the sea?'

'I find it... fascinating. But threatening.'

'Only a fool wouldn't respect the sea. It doesn't care for you or me. It could suck us under and kill us in a matter of moments.'

Great waves rolled in from the west, expending their power on the jumble of rocks far below in magnificent fountains of spray. She studied Reothe as he watched the sea. He seemed more aloof than usual today.

'Dangerous and untamed,' he said. 'Yet this is your favourite place.'

'One of my favourites.'

'Which is your absolute favourite?'

'Would you like to see it?'

He nodded.

'Come on.' She drew him down the cliff path, which was a challenge in itself, especially on windy days, to the huge jagged rocks that led like a giant's stepping stones down to the sea.

Jumping a gap that was as wide as she was tall, she landed on the flat-topped rock that was her favourite. He joined her.

In front of them, the sea smashed into the rocks in a fury of foam and spray; a fine mist hung in the air.

'This is my favourite place,' Imoshen said. 'Here, you know you're alive. Every sixth or seventh wave is bigger than the rest. The trick is to recognise it before it hits.'

A gleaming green-blue wave rolled towards them, shattering around the rocks below.

Reothe's gift surged and she rode his exhilaration.

'You're testing me, Imoshen.'

She rolled her eyes.

The next wave gleamed large, sullen and inevitable.

'I can't figure you out.'

'Watch the sea, not me.'

He glanced that way. Swore. And fled.

They both jumped the gap and scrambled up the rocks just in time.

White water boiled over where they'd been before, shooting up in a sheet of spray that drenched them both.

As the sea retreated, Imoshen leapt to her feet, threw back her head and laughed.

He grabbed her shoulders. 'You're mad. Absolutely mad.'

She brushed his hands off, before her gift slipped out of her control. 'If you can't take it, don't come back.'

And she ran up the path, leaving him behind.

SORNE COULDN'T CONCENTRATE on his studies. For three nights in a row, Kolst and Hiruna had argued. It always began softly and ended up with Kolst berating her for being selfish. The baby was better off with its own kind. Think of Zabier. And then the tears would start and the baby would scream. No one got any sleep.

Now, as the *thunk, thunk* of the axe came from beyond the storeroom, where the penitents were chopping wood, he felt himself almost dozing off.

Zabier ran into the study. 'Da needs you. Come quick.'

They looked to Oskane, who gestured for them to go.

The storeroom where Kolst kept his tools was empty, but they could hear raised voices from the patch of ground beyond.

'...a man should be king in his own home.' Joaken's voice held contempt. His broken nose was a reminder of their last run-in. 'Yet, she leads you around by your prick. You're a ball-less wonder, Kolst. A ball-less Wyrd-lover!'

Through the door they could see their father confronting Joaken, while Denat and the cripple stood back, grinning. Kolst looked past Joaken's shoulder to them.

The moment their father was distracted, Joaken pulled a knife and went for him.

Sorne shouted a warning and charged Joaken, but it was too far. Time seemed to slow. He saw Kolst deflect Joaken's knife. Kolst was younger, but Joaken was a trained killer. The pair of them grappled, tripping over the chopping block.

Joaken landed on top of Kolst. But the time Sorne and Izteben reached them, blood was pooling under the wood-worker. They pulled Joaken off him, rolling him aside to kneel beside their father. He lay still, pale blue eyes staring up at the sky.

'Da.' Zabier threw his arms around Kolst, who blinked.

Sorne was so relieved he felt dizzy. They helped their father to sit up.

'What's going on here?' Oskane demanded as he arrived with his assistant. 'Well?'

'Joaken pulled a knife on Da. He...' Sorne gestured to the ex-mercenary and fell silent. The knife hilt protruded from Joaken's belly. The penitent panted, bleeding profusely. Denat and the cripple stared in shock.

'Franto.' Oskane gestured to the wounded man.

As Franto knelt over the stricken penitent, Izteben and Sorne helped their father to his feet. Kolst swayed as if drunk and had to lean on the chopping block.

Franto reported softly to Oskane.

'I've killed him, haven't I?' Kolst demanded. He was pale; blood covered his belly and thighs.

Hiruna came through the storeroom. She gave a cry of horror and ran towards him.

Kolst held her off. 'I've killed a man, all because you won't listen to reason.' His hands shook and his voice cracked. 'That's it. We're going.'

Hiruna took a step back, shaking her head.

Sorne's mouth went dry with fear. Was he the only one who saw the flaw in their father's logic? Nothing was Hiruna's fault. They were all victims of the divide between True-men and Wyrds.

Kolst beckoned. 'Zabier, come here. Help your mother pack.'

'No.' Hiruna looked desperate. 'You can't ask me to give up my baby daughter.'

'She's a Wyrd. She belongs with her own people.' Kolst made an impatient gesture. 'I'm leaving today. Right now.'

Hiruna stared at Kolst. 'You're in shock. You're not thinking clearly.'

'For once, I *am* thinking clearly. I should never–'

'I'm not leaving Ma.' Zabier threw his arms around Hiruna.

Kolst looked to Oskane.

'You have to, son,' the scholar said. 'Your father's word is law.'

'Ma?' Zabier lifted his face to Hiruna, who appeared stricken.

'She has no say,' Oskane told him. 'Do as your father tells you.'

A rushing filled Sorne's head. Everything seemed unreal. Before dusk, Joaken was dead, their father and brother were gone and it was like a light had gone out in their mother.

Chapter Seventeen

Year 307

OSKANE MENTALLY REVIEWED his list as he travelled. Almost seventeen years of studying the scrolls and observing the half-blood boys grow up, and four years of careful questioning of the she-Wyrd, and this was what he had come up with. The females were more powerful than the males, and they all needed touch to use their gifts. He'd discarded the instances of mass hallucinations and gift use without touch because they could not be verified.

Nothing had been found to protect True-men from the Wyrds' power, although some men seemed to have natural resistance. Oskane suspected it came down to a person's will and self-belief. He opened his travelling kit and fingered the malachite Franto had found when one of the boards covering the entrance to the mine had fallen down in a strong wind. Trust his assistant to go poking around in there. At the discovery of semi-precious stones, the street urchin in Franto had surfaced and he'd wanted to dig up more to guard against a rainy day. Oskane stopped him when he had enough to test his theory.

If a man believed that malachite could protect him, Oskane suspected it would; belief was a powerful thing.

The cart came to a stop. As Oskane climbed down, he took a deep breath. It was good to leave the mountains. At least you could get a decent chestful of air here.

His agent met him and took his bag.

'You have her? A full-blood Wyrd?' Oskane asked. 'A T'En?'

'The silverhead's locked in the cellar.' He gestured to the abbey's burnt-out mill house. 'You were right. She did not suspect the child who led her to us.'

'Because the child did not suspect.'

'I'd no idea it would be so easy,' the agent said.

'Only because you followed my instructions. If she hadn't been concentrating on the child, she would have anticipated the blow to the back of her head.'

The agent chuckled. 'My, but she was furious when she woke up chained to the cellar wall.'

'She's chained? So much for the stories of Wyrds manipulating metal,' Oskane said. 'And the volunteers?'

'Six of them. All healthy young penitents.'

Oskane nodded and entered the burnt-out building. The roof had collapsed, letting in dusty shafts of sunlight.

Six young hopeful faces turned to Oskane. He repressed a feeling of regret. There was a good chance some or all of them would die.

'The king thanks you for taking part. If you ever speak of what passes here today, the Father will turn His face from you. You will be buried in unsanctified ground and your soul will never know peace.'

They looked suitably frightened.

'The Wyrds have grown arrogant and powerful, and the king has asked me to discover their weakness. I have been studying the Wyrd scrolls, and I have found that most of what you've heard about Wyrd power is a myth. They cannot bend metal with their will alone. They cannot control fire or the weather. And they cannot take over a True-man's mind if his faith is strong. You will all wear these.' He produced the malachite pendants from his bag. 'This rare stone will protect you from their gift. After it is all over, I will purify you, so you don't need to worry about being tainted.'

They nodded and stepped forward, one by one, to receive their pendant and blessing. Which would do precisely nothing, other than armouring them with the idea that it would.

'You and you, come with me.' He selected two men at random and led them into the basement.

The sight of the Wyrd warrior chained to the cellar wall thrilled him. She glared across the dim cellar, lit by a single lantern hanging over the stairs.

Oskane dipped into his bag and handed the two penitents gloves. 'You'll wear these. You will not touch her flesh. You will not look into her eyes.' He had several knives: one made of silver, another of gold, and a third of bronze. He even had a malachite knife. He selected the silver knife. 'One of you will hold her still, while the other cuts off her little fingers.'

The captive's eyes widened. 'What is wrong with you people?'

He hadn't realised she spoke Chalcedonian; not all of them did.

'Ignore her. Her voice holds no power. That is another myth.' It was wonderful to see ignorance defeated by knowledge.

The first two penitents crossed the cellar. One of them forced the woman's arm against the wall. Her eyes darted about in panic and, although he couldn't sense it, Oskane knew her gift would be rising.

'Eh.' The one holding her arm turned his face away. 'Fair makes me teeth ache.'

So he was sensitive to Wyrd power; some True-men were.

'Hurry up. I can't take much more of this.'

The other one was having trouble holding her hand still. Finally, he had the fingers splayed against the wall and started sawing at her little finger. Blood ran down her arm and the wall. She writhed and jerked, shrieking at them in her heathen language.

All of which proved Oskane's theory. If she had any real power, she would not put up with this treatment. All these years, it had been the True-man's fear of Wyrds that had held them back.

The two penitents cursed as they fought to keep her still. The one with the knife slipped and the blade slashed his companion's arm.

'Watch what you're feckin' doing,' the bloodied man cursed.

Then his eyes rolled back in his head and he reached clumsily for his companion's knife.

'Don't give it to him, you idiot!' Oskane yelled.

Too late. The possessed penitent slid the knife up into the other man's ribs, then turned towards Oskane

Oskane looked past the penitent to the Wyrd. She was focusing inward as she controlled the man. Darting forward, Oskane took the knife away from the possessed penitent, who stood there stupidly.

The agent, who had stumbled down the steps behind them to see what all the shouting was about, turned to Oskane. 'I thought you said she couldn't–'

'Her blood mingled with his, giving her power over him.' Why was he surrounded by fools? 'Tie him to the wall.' Oskane needed to know if she could control more than one man at a time.

But before he could be bound, the possessed penitent tackled the agent. The two men rolled across the floor. Oskane watched the silverhead; she was completely still, eyes closed. All her concentration was on the man she controlled, and he realised how vulnerable she now was. He'd read of this, silverheads lying unconscious or frozen in place while they worked their gifts, protected by half-bloods or other T'En.

There was the sound of a rib cracking and then something soft being punctured. The agent came to his feet, a little unsteady.

'Why did you have to kill him?' Oskane had wanted to cause the possessed man pain, to see if the Wyrd felt it too.

'The malachite didn't protect him,' the agent said, as he held up the pendant.

'Of course not,' the Wyrd said. 'There's no power in it.'

'The power is in the idea. The man clearly had a weak mind,' Oskane said. 'Get the bodies out of here, sluice away the blood and send the next two down.'

The next two men put on their gloves, took a knife each and came at her from the sides. She couldn't watch both.

This time she didn't let them get near.

With surprising speed, she kicked the first one under the chin, driving his head back. Oskane heard the click as his neck broke. The second man got in a single strike, pulled the knife out and turned to see if his partner was all right. Grasping her shackles, the woman lifted her legs, caught him around the waist with her thighs and squeezed.

'You should have chained her legs as well,' Oskane told the agent.

'I didn't think it mattered,' he said and went to help the penitent, who had lost his grip on the knife and was struggling to breathe.

'No. Leave him.' Oskane noted the way the penitent pried at her legs, gasping. Would she lose strength from blood loss before he passed out? No. The man laboured to breathe, then dropped.

'She crushed his ribs,' the agent said.

Yes, but she'd used her strength, not her gift. It appeared the Wyrd powers were not useful in a direct physical confrontation.

Oskane's agent dragged the body away. All the while, the silverhead gasped, flinching as her rapid breathing tugged on the wound in her side; she was failing. One attempt to use her gift on them. One attempt to use her strength. What did she had left?

'What do you want from me?' she gasped.

'You specifically? Nothing.' Oskane knew the extent of her gift now. If she was reduced to bargaining, she had nothing in reserve. 'But I will take your hair and your little sixth fingers for trophies.' He wanted to test Sorne, to see if he could sense residual power.

The agent brought down the next two penitents. Their eyes darted about the dim cellar.

Oskane gave them the gloves and the knives. 'Kill her.'

'You are an evil man,' she told Oskane.

The penitents eyed her warily.

'She cannot hurt you. If she had any power, do you think she would be manacled in a cellar, bleeding, at my mercy?'

Seeing the sense in this, they looked to each other and drove their knives up under her ribs.

She sent Oskane a look of triumph and...

Disappeared.

Her clothing dropped to the ground. At the same time the two penitents fell like sacks of grain and a sharp smell filled the cellar, reminding Oskane of the sea.

'That was most unexpected.'

The agent ran to check both penitents. 'Dead. But I thought they were safe if they didn't touch her skin.'

'They were covered in her blood.'

'If she could get away at any time, why didn't she do it sooner? Why stay here and let us torture her?'

'Because she didn't get away.' Oskane was certain of this. 'She's dead. Wherever she went, it was a last resort, and she chose to go there to cheat me of my prizes. But today has not been a total loss. I've proven several theories. Next time, kill the silverhead from a distance and don't approach until you are certain it's dead, then send me the trophies.'

When he got back to the retreat, he wrote up his observations. He should have taken her clothing. It would have been imbued with gift power. Never mind; his agent would send him suitable T'En artefacts.

If he could teach Sorne to resist their lure, the lad would be able to enter the city. But it might take years for the boys to work their way into positions of trust where they could carry out assassinations. Oskane was tired of waiting.

He needed something concrete to take to Charald, and soon. Besides, after seeing the full-blood take over the penitent, Oskane did not know if the two half-bloods would come out of the city as his spies, or the Wyrd's double agents.

He'd give them a year. If they had nothing by then, he'd go to Charald with the 'discovery' that Wyrd power was mostly bluff. Avoid the eyes, avoid touch, wear a talisman. Malachite would be as good as any.

There were many more half-bloods in Cesspit City than T'En, and only the adult T'En had innate power. The Mieren vastly outnumbered Wyrds. If they lost ten thousand True-men to the T'En gifts, those men died martyrs and it was worth the sacrifice to take the city and wipe out the Wyrds.

SORNE FOLLOWED FRANTO into the courtyard when the cart arrived. Oskane's assistant welcomed the carter, then called for Denat to come and unload. He was the last of the penitents, and he avoided work whereever possible.

Sorne called through the stable door. 'Cart's here.'

'Cart's here,' little Valendia repeated in a sing-song voice as she trotted after Izteben. At three and a half, her head was a mass of red-gold curls that had yet to darken to copper, but the distinctive eyes and six fingers revealed her tainted blood.

'Wait, Dia,' their mother warned. She picked up the toddler and watched from the doorway. When Kolst had taken Zabier, something in Hiruna had died. She was less trusting, and never let Valendia out of her sight.

'It's just the cart, Ma,' Sorne said. 'With the same driver as always. He's not going to take Valendia.'

'Zabier will be thirteen next spring. Almost a man,' Hiruna said. Sorne and Izteben exchanged looks. Where had that come from?

'I think of him every day.'

Franto called again for Denat but there was no sign of him.

'Go help Franto unload,' Hiruna urged. 'He'll do himself an injury, if he's not careful.'

Sorne and Izteben crossed the courtyard.

'Have you seen Denat?' Franto asked them.

They shook their heads, shouldered a sack of flour each and took them inside.

As Sorne returned to the cart, he saw the driver hand Franto a carved chest. A word was exchanged and Franto turned to look up to the third floor window, where Scholar Oskane was watching. The scholar beckoned eagerly.

Sorne had to get a look inside that chest.

OSKANE TUGGED HIS gloves on, pressing down between each finger to ensure a neat fit. Then he spread out the bloodstained robe; brocade edged with semi-precious stones. Such an arrogant display of wealth. Typical of the T'En.

According to his Enlightenment Abbey agent, a full-blood female had worn it. She'd been old and frail, and had fallen behind the rest of the party, accompanied only by an equally elderly half-blood.

They'd thought themselves safe, had discovered otherwise when they'd taken arrows in their backs.

There were stories of T'En catching arrows in flight, but that was three hundred years ago during battle, and Oskane suspected such tales were grand exaggerations.

Oskane took the small knife from his waist and sliced off a silver button, tucking it into his vest pocket before thinking better of it and wrapping it in a kerchief. He refolded the robe and placed it on his bed.

Next he picked up the silver braid. It was almost as long as he was tall. The T'En wore their hair long in elaborate styles, as a sign of status.

He hesitated for a heartbeat, then removed one glove and ran his hand over the plait. It felt like silk, fine, soft and slippery. He'd always wondered what their hair would feel like.

During the great war between the True-men and the Wyrds, the barons strung these trophy plaits from their banners. As a boy, he'd stared up at their family's banner in his cousin's hall and wondered about the four silver plaits, each thick as a man's wrist. Four dead T'En.

Oskane put the T'En artefacts away, hid the chest under his bed and removed the gloves. He lifted the leather to his face and sniffed. Nothing. But, if his research was correct, a half-blood would be able to sense the residue of the gift on things worn or used daily by T'En. That was why he wore gloves while handling their artefacts.

Walking into his office, Oskane found Sorne and Izteben waiting for him, bare-chested. Aged just seventeen and nearly eighteen respectively, they were both half a head taller than him, but their chins were smooth and soft as a girl's and there was no hair on their chests. It was strange the way Wyrds matured. It made him uncomfortable.

'What are you?' he asked them.

'Holy warriors,' they answered in unison, voices deep and melodic.

'Whose holy warriors?'

'Your holy warriors, Scholar Oskane.'

'Why do I do this?'

'To make us strong. So we can conquer pain and temptation.'

And today he would find out if they could sense T'En power. 'Very good.' He gestured. 'Sorne first.'

Sorne stepped over to the frame and took a hold of the pegs, arms spread, broad back ready. Oskane handed Izteben the scourge. 'Proceed.'

The older youth stepped back, raised his arm and struck, accurately and hard. They both knew that if he didn't, Oskane would send for Denat, who would enjoy scourging them.

While Izteben attended to Sorne, Oskane leant on the edge of his desk. He was sixty-four and he thought he'd been old at forty-seven. He could wait no longer. Lucky for him, Nitzel still lived to feel Oskane's revenge.

Izteben changed places with Sorne and the scourging continued.

This winter, Oskane would have Hiruna make up clothing based on the Wyrd designs he had seen; he'd send the two half-bloods to Cesspit City in the spring. He allowed himself a pleasant daydream, where King Charald begged his forgiveness while Nitzel looked on.

'Scholar Oskane?' Sorne had finished. 'Do you want me to work on your portrait today?'

'Not today.' Oskane held out his hand, and they both kissed the ruby ring. 'You can go, Izteben.'

The older youth glanced to Sorne, who gave the slightest nod of his head.

Oskane went around his desk and sat down. 'Come here. Sit.'

Sorne obeyed.

Oskane knew he really should tell the half-blood the truth of his birth and his mother's murder, but he found himself delaying. He wasn't convinced that the boy had the maturity to deal with the facts yet. He would tell Sorne the truth in the spring, before he sent them both out. That way they would be fired up with righteous anger.

Dipping into his pocket, Oskane retrieved the silver button. The thought that it could be contaminated with a residue of Wyrd power revolted him. With meticulous care, he unrolled it from his kerchief and placed the artefact on his desk. It sat there on the polished wood, catching the light. He gestured. 'Pick it up. Tell me what you feel.'

Sorne reached out, then hesitated. 'What am I supposed to feel?'

'I don't want to lead you.'

The youth nodded. He picked up the button and frowned. 'I feel nothing.'

'Are you sure? The trader said it came from one of the T'En, and should contain some residue of her gift.'

'I can sense nothing. Perhaps the trader lied.' Sorne returned the silver button. 'After all, you only have the trader's word that this button came from one of the T'En.'

That would be true, if it *had* come from a trader, but it had come from his agent and he had the bloodied T'En garment and plait as proof of the man's veracity.

Oskane frowned. If Sorne could not sense the T'En gift, then it meant either he had not developed this ability yet, or his awareness was weak.

Did Sorne even have the natural gift defences Oskane had read about? Without them, he would be easily enslaved by the T'En.

'Have I disappointed you, Scholar Oskane?' Sorne asked.

'A little, but perhaps it is too soon. You should be able to feel the gift residue.'

'I could try again.'

Oskane waved him away. It was probably his youth, but there was only one way to be sure. 'That's all for today.'

Dismissed, Sorne collected his shirt, made the obeisance of student to tutor and left.

After wrapping the button, Oskane followed him out. Franto was not at his desk. He knew that his assistant's stomach had been giving him trouble for a while now. He only hoped it wasn't a sign of something serious.

Oskane descended the stairs, heading for the cellar. For the past four years, the boys had taken T'En language lessons from the captive every day. In that time, Oskane's eyes had become so bad he could only read for a short while before they went blurry, his knees had seized up and his hair had gone completely white.

He pulled up a chair and sat facing the cell. 'I have something to show you.' He tossed her the silver button.

The half-blood caught it and lifted it to the weak shaft of light falling through the bars of the high window. She cupped her hands around it and breathed in deeply. Her eyes closed and she swayed.

'So you can sense the gift residue.'

Her dark eyes flashed with anger. 'Where did you get this?'

'At what age did you first become receptive to the T'En gifts?'

'I've been around them all my life. It's like asking me when I could first hear.'

'Can you tell if this button came from a male or female?'

'A female. The male gift is rank and offensive, to those of us who grew up accustomed to female power. Will I see the boys today?'

'Not today.'

He thought she would ask why, but she cast him a sly look. 'Will you bring me more T'En things?'

'Perhaps.' This was interesting. She'd never asked for anything before. The taste of gift power must have awakened a dormant craving, as theorised in the scrolls. 'What can you give me in exchange?'

'Nothing. I've given you too much already.'

But they both knew she would weaken.

IMOSHEN WAS TRULY happy. She hadn't realised how lonely she'd been since her mother had drowned, but now with her choice-son, Iraayel, Frayvia and Reothe... Just thinking of Reothe made her smile. Her hand slid down over her belly and the baby kicked. Yes, she was very lucky.

She finished pruning the peach tree for the winter, then straightened up, arching her tired back. Something tugged at her awareness. She followed the thread of worry to its source, which was...

Her link with Iraayel; he was in trouble. Her first thought was the sea.

The baby gave a sharp kick.

She placed the clippers on the stone beside the peach tree and hurried out of the walled garden. She'd left Iraayel napping, while Frayvia wrote her report for the all-father. Reothe sailed for the mainland tomorrow.

Where could her choice-son be?

She forced down her fear and opened her gift senses. The link with her choice-son drew her across the high ground beside the lighthouse, down past the fields, towards the trees. Beyond them lay the dunes and the sea.

Breaking into a run, Imoshen headed across the winter-bare fields and into the trees. She placed one hand under her belly to support the weight, and let her instincts guide her.

'Iraayel?'

The answering cry caused her to look up, to find the four year-old clinging to a tree trunk above her head. 'Stay there. I'm coming up.'

She might be heavily pregnant, but there was nothing wrong with her arms and legs. She reached Iraayel, and he threw his arms around her.

'Don't be angry,' he pleaded.

'I could never be angry with you.' It was true. She loved him so much it terrified her. 'Now we just have to get down.'

Iraayel relaxed, trusting in her.

As she neared the ground, Reothe arrived. They'd slept in each other's arms last night, which meant the link was fresh and intense. He'd sensed her worry for Iraayel.

Reothe took Iraayel from her, setting him gently on his feet. Then he reached for her. 'You should have waited for me.'

'We managed.'

'Imoshen...'

The four year-old tugged on Reothe's arm. 'I climbed the tree.'

Imoshen took Iraayel's chin in her hand. 'Promise me you won't go climbing trees again. Not until you're bigger, anyway.'

'I promise.' Iraayel's face brightened. 'Did you see how high I climbed?'

'Too high, I'll wager,' Reothe said and caught her eye.

'I'll miss you,' Imoshen said. It just slipped out.

'I'll be back before midwinter for the birth.'

They both felt the baby kick.

He grinned. 'Energetic little boy.'

'Busy little girl.'

He laughed then grew serious. 'Last time I saw the all-father, he said he would come for the birth.'

'Rohaayel?' She hadn't seen her father for four years. 'Irian and Ardeyne, too?'

He nodded.

Her heart rose, her gift surged, and she felt the baby wriggle in response.

Reothe took her hand, and they headed back for the lighthouse. As they stepped out of the trees, they saw Frayvia in the fields, searching for them. They signalled, and she ran across the stubble to join them.

'You're all right, Imoshen?'

'I'm fine. Iraayel got stuck up a tree.' Imoshen laughed. 'There's good news. Reothe says the all-father will visit when the baby's born. Maybe then we can all go live with the brotherhood in the city.'

She caught Frayvia exchanging a look with Reothe, and a chill settled around her heart.

They were not in league against her. They loved her. She was imagining things.

Imoshen slid her arm around Frayvia's shoulders. 'You'll see, everything will work out. The baby will be born healthy. Reothe will be so proud, and my father will be a grandfather. We're really very lucky.'

Chapter Eighteen

SORNE'S HEART HAMMERED with the enormity of what he was about to do. He had never lied to Scholar Oskane before, but it had been the way his tutor had placed the silver button on the desk with barely concealed repugnance that prompted the lie.

At first Sorne did not want to touch the thing. Then, when he did and he felt the sensation, he did not want to admit it, did not want to associate himself with the power Oskane so clearly despised. As if he could deny his tainted blood.

Until this day, he'd been able to tell himself he might look like a Malaunje, but he wasn't corrupted. Feeling that odd reverberation of gift residue in the button had stripped him of his illusion.

He hated the button. Wanted to destroy it and everything associated with it.

Wanted to hold it and savour the sensation.

Yesterday, the chest had arrived, and today Oskane had tested him with the button. What else did the chest contain?

He had to know.

Sorne slipped past Franto's empty chair, into the study.

There was no sign of the chest in here, which left Oskane's private chamber. It was just as austere as the study, containing a low bed, the symbol of the seven True-man gods, a large chest for his tutor's robes and his tutor's scourge.

Sorne remembered being shown the vile thing when he was five and wanted to know why he and his brother had to be beaten. They had been told that only through pain and denial could a man find true strength.

But, if that was so, why did he still feel drawn to the Wyrd's power? Sorne dropped his shirt on the bed and opened the large chest. The blankets, night-shirts and simple white robes of a priestly scholar lay within, neatly folded. He moved them to one side, looking for the smaller chest, and discovered something wrapped in fine wool. It felt heavy, round and flat. He unwrapped it, keeping the wool between the metal and his bare fingers, as Oskane had done with the ring.

A silver torc set with a bright blue stone lay in his hands. Should he touch it? As much as he wanted to feel the rush of power, he feared it. Yet he had to know if this object contained gift residue. Teeth clenched, he touched the tip of one finger to the silver. Nothing. Nothing from the stone, either. He felt like laughing.

Replacing the torc, he checked the chest one last time. As he did so, Oskane's journals caught his eye. The scholar started a new one every year. He selected last year's and opened it at the first page.

This is the boy's seventeenth year and already he is taller than me...

He flicked through pages at random, skimming words.

...I have searched and even here, in Restoration Retreat, I can find no evidence. All I have left is this hollow ache and the conviction that it is all lies. There are no gods watching over us. Is it better to be happy and believe a lie, or to suffer knowing the truth?

...today I dreamed of Sorna as she was on her wedding day, so happy and innocent. But then she turned on him and denounced him as her murderer...

...Good news, another dead baby. How Nitzel must be gnashing his teeth. If he is not careful, Charald will do away with his daughter and take another wife, one who can give him living sons. He's done it before...

Closing the journal, Sorne opened the most recent one. Here there were only a couple of pages of writing.

...today the chest arrived. I'll test Sorne. If, as I suspect, Wyrd power proves addictive for half-bloods, then I must find some way to armour him against it, for I very much fear what will happen when I send him to the Wyrds. He must be ready by spring.

Then I will tell him the truth, most importantly Nitzel's part in his mother's murder. If Nitzel hadn't had his own son-in-law murdered, his daughter would not have been free to marry Charald. Sorne needs to know who his enemies are. He needs to know he's King Charald's son and that it is his destiny to bring down the Wyrds and crush Nitzel. Only then can he redeem himself in his father's eyes, and only then will Sorna's murder be avenged...

Sorne blinked, unable to believe the magnitude of Oskane's betrayal. The very foundation of his life was a lie. Grey moths fluttered in his vision. He couldn't get enough air.

He sank to his knees by the bed, forehead on the cold wooden floor. For a couple of heartbeats, he concentrated on breathing.

Oskane had lied to him. His mother was not his mother... but Hiruna loved him, for all that he was not her true son.

As Sorne's vision cleared, he realised he was staring at the small chest, tucked neatly under Oskane's bed.

Spurred by anger, he dragged it out, flipped it open and pulled out the first thing he laid his hand on. A gown made of magnificent brocade, glinting with gold and flashing stones, stained by blood... his hand registered power in the dried blood. He wanted to bring it to his face and rub it on his skin, but he was not a slave to sensation. He put the gown aside, to discover a long silver braid curled in the bottom of the chest.

The moment he touched it, he felt the power. His senses sharpened and his heart raced.

Then he heard voices, Franto and Oskane in the outer chamber. No time to waste.

He dropped the braid on his shirt. The journal was at his feet. He grabbed it and returned it to the big chest.

The voices came closer.

Refolding the bloodstained robe, he placed it in the chest, which he shoved under the bed. Sorne rolled the plait up in his shirt and flung it out the window to fall onto the wall-walk below. He swung his leg over the window sill, lowered himself and let go...

He rolled with the impact. It jarred his teeth and every bone in his body but, when he came to his feet, he was unhurt. And there was the silver plait on the ground next to him, along with his shirt.

Quick as thought, he snatched up the braid and wound it three times around his waist, before throwing his shirt over the top. He sprang off the wall-walk and into the tree, then climbed down into the courtyard.

His mother was standing in the stable doorway. She beckoned him with a smile.

No, Hiruna wasn't his mother. Sorna was his mother, and Baron Nitzel had ordered her death so his daughter could marry the king.

'Come, Sorne. I must treat your back,' Hiruna said.

He could not bear to be near her, knowing she'd lied to him all his life. Rushing through the storerooms, he ran out the back and onto the hillside.

Dimly, he heard Izteben calling him.

He kept going up the old winding path until he came to the sealed mine, and there he leaned against the boards, unable to see for tears.

Furious, he wiped his face and turned to confront Izteben, who'd just caught up with him. 'Did you know?'

'Know what? What's wrong? Did he scourge you again, after I left? Why is he so hard on you?'

Of course Oskane was harder on him. He was the king's unwanted half-blood son. But he didn't say that, he wasn't ready to explain. He wanted time to think things through.

If Oskane had lied to him about this, what else had he lied about?

'He did scourge you.' Izteben leaped to his own conclusion. 'I swear he enjoys it. One day I'll turn that lash on him and... Seriously, Sorne, what happened up there? You look...' – he struggled for words – 'stunned.'

'You'll always be honest with me. Won't you?'

'Of course, we're brothers.'

And it was as simple as that. They mightn't be related, but they were brothers. Sorne sank to the ground, his back to the boards.

Izteben came over and dropped down beside him.

There was a creak and a soft *thud*, and they turned to see that one of the boards had fallen away into the darkness of the mine.

Izteben came onto his knees to inspect the damage. 'Not rotten. Looks like it's been propped in place.' He turned to Sorne. 'Someone's been going down the mine.'

'Has to be Denat. Oskane's knees are too bad. Franto's belly is his main preoccupation. And Ma–'

'Hides herself away.' Izteben nodded to himself. 'What does Denat want with an old mine? He's allergic to hard work.'

Sorne grinned. 'One way to find out.'

'We're not going down there. It's dangerous.'

'How do we know that?' All his life, he had blindly accepted everything Scholar Oskane told him. No more. From now on, he would discover his own truths.

'It was boarded up. Of course it's dangerous.' Izteben shook his head. 'What's gotten into you today? We should tell Oskane.'

'Why tell Oskane, when we can catch Denat ourselves?' Sorne could feel the Wyrd plait around his waist infusing his body with impatient energy. 'Only the other day you were complaining that nothing ever happens.'

'It would be good to surprise Denat,' Izteben admitted. He grinned. 'All right. But if we're going down, we'll need lanterns.'

'And something to mark our path. String would do. Maybe some rope.' Sorne brushed past him. 'Come on. Everything we need is in the storerooms.'

Together they walked down the path. Sorne threw open the storeroom door and they collected what they needed.

Soon, they were back at the mine entrance with their supplies. The last thing Sorne had grabbed was a crowbar. He used it now to pry another plank of wood loose from the entrance.

They bent double and stepped inside. Outside it had been mid-afternoon and sunny, if cool. Inside, aside from the single shaft of sunlight, it was dim.

As soon as Sorne lit the lantern, the entrance of the mine was revealed.

'I'd no idea it was so big,' Izteben said.

Sorne looked up. It was larger inside than the boarded-up entrance had led him to expect. Instead of gradually sloping downwards, the tunnel before them rose at a gentle incline. A small cart stood near them. 'The penitents would have dragged the copper out in these.'

Ahead, there was only darkness.

Izteben looked to him. 'How will we know which way he went?'

Sorne took the lantern and held it low, searching the uneven floor. 'Boot prints. Coming and going. Denat's been here many times.'

'But why?'

'Maybe the mine is not played out.'

'Then why board it up?'

Sorne shrugged. He could feel the power in the plait tugging at him, urging him on. 'Come on.'

'SEND HIM IN,' Oskane said.

Oskane steepled his fingers as Franto ushered Denat in. The penitent had asked to speak to him, which was convenient, as Franto had complained again.

'You've been with us since you were a lad of seven, and you've served us well.' Behind Denat, Oskane saw Franto raise one eyebrow. 'But Franto tells me you've been shirking your duties and disobeying–'

'Disobeying? Don't talk to me about disobeying. I just saw those half-bloods you're so fond of break open the old mine and go down.'

'What?' Oskane sprang to his feet.

Denat nodded. 'Reckon they plan to steal from the church.'

'When did they go down?' Oskane asked. What if they went too deep? What if they disturbed the unclean site? All his work rearing them would be wasted.

'Just now. I come straight here to tell you.'

'Quick, there's still time.' Oskane brushed past Denat. Franto fell into step with him. 'If we go after them right away, we can bring them back before...'

'THERE'S MORE HERE.' Sorne pointed to another section of wall, where there were fresh pick marks. He held his lantern higher. The stone gleamed.

Izteben dug out a chunk with the little hammer. 'Hmmm, pretty. Could be worth something. Do you think this is what Denat was after?'

Sorne was sure of it, but he also wondered why the mine had been boarded up if it was not played out. Oskane was hiding something, and that infuriated him.

'We should go back and show Oskane.' Izteben glanced over his shoulder. 'Why did we come so deep?'

'Just a little further.' Sorne was determined to discover what Oskane was trying to hide.

They went on. There were carts sitting abandoned, some with rocks still in them, which was curious. Eventually the path narrowed and became more roughly hewn.

'That's it, we're out of string,' Izteben announced, sounding relieved.

Sorne felt a pang of guilt. They should go back. But he'd been fooled all his life, and he wasn't going to let anyone fool him again.

'Through this gap.' It was twice as tall as him and only a little wider. At the top, it leaned to one side like a drunken man.

'I don't know,' Izteben muttered. 'We can already prove what Denat's been up to.'

Sorne pushed through the gap and Izteben followed him, as he knew he would. A large empty cavern opened up before them. They stood on a broad ledge looking down at the floor, which sloped away from them in shallow undulations.

'That's it, nothing,' Sorne said, going right to the edge of the ledge. His disappointed voice echoed across the chamber and back again. On the last echo, the air inside the cavern condensed, pressing in on his ears. A rushing filled his head.

Izteben looked up in wonder. 'What is it?' His voice sounded flat and thin, and his breath misted. 'Look at that. Why is it so cold all of a sudden?'

Light didn't seem to go as far. There was no sound but their rapid breathing. As Sorne listened, the plait around his waist seemed to throb in time to his heartbeat.

'Sorne?' Izteben jerked his arm. 'Let's go.'

'Don't tell me–' He turned to brush off the restraining hand and lost his footing, falling from the ledge. His back stung with the impact as he felt his wounds open up. The lantern clattered across the floor, shockingly loud in the confined space. It came to rest not far from him, its wick still mercifully alight.

Before his shirt could dry and stick to the open wounds, Sorne pulled it off.

'What's that around your waist?' Izteben asked. 'It looks like plaited hair, T'En hair.' His voice grew tight with envy. 'Was that what Oskane wanted to show you?'

Sorne felt blood trickle down his back. He reached over his shoulder, flicking it off. The moment he did this, the air became too thick to breathe, and the far corner where the lantern lay grew dim.

Izteben cursed and dropped to his knees, offering his hand. 'Quick, Sorne.'

The darkness spread towards them, rippling across the floor.

Fear leant Sorne strength as he lunged for Izteben's hand and pulled himself onto the ledge.

As Sorne surged to his feet, the plait came undone, unwinding from around his waist, and he caught one end.

'What's going on here?' Oskane demanded, Franto at this side.

Sorne spun around for one last look. As he did so, the braid swung out in his hand like a whip and something caught the other end. There was nothing that he could see, but the plait was pulled taut between them.

'Drop it,' Izteben urged.

A jolt, like the slap of a winter gale, travelled down the braid. It stung his hand, flinging him onto his back.

He felt his head collide with stone.

The last thing he saw was the braid hanging in mid-air, glowing and writhing as if alive. A flash of light seared his eyes. And then he knew nothing.

Chapter Nineteen

SORNE WAS BEING rattled apart. A tall man with white hair led him up a slope. The man pointed to an army; leading them was a king with a battle-scarred face, his features obscured by a crested helmet. The king was wearing full armour and stood on a rise, highlighted against a sky filled with blue-black storm clouds. Pipers prepared to play a victory march. The bags produced strange, almost animalistic sounds as they filled with air. A shout of triumph rose from the battlefield, making Sorne's heart swell with joy, and he glanced to his grim-faced guide, who turned towards him, revealing the other side of his face. There was no eye on that side, the skin was smooth. The white-haired man gestured, pointing to the scene below.

They weren't storm clouds behind the king. It was the smoke of a burning city; the harbour beyond was littered with ships ablaze.

Sorne woke with a jolt.

He wanted the dream back. He wanted to be there with the warrior king, alive in that moment, sharing in the triumph. A moan of frustration escaped him.

'Sorne, are you all right?' Scholar Oskane leaned over him and he realised he lay in a mining cart.

Izteben put the handles down then came back to him. 'You're awake. You were so cold and pale.'

'I'm fine. I...' He winced as he felt the lump on the back of his head and his hand came away sticky. He sat up. 'Did I fall? Where's my shirt?' As soon as he said it, he remembered. A white flash filled his vision, and as it cleared he saw... the burning city, tattered standards, the warrior king.

Sorne held out his hand and Izteben helped him climb out of the cart.

'How could you?' Oskane demanded. 'How could you come down here when you knew it wasn't safe?'

'We wanted to find out what Denat was doing in the mine,' Izteben said. He dipped into his pocket and produced the stone. 'He's been digging out–'

'Green-eye stone,' Franto said.

'Malachite,' Oskane corrected. The two of them shared a look that told Sorne he'd been right, they'd been withholding information about the mine. The realisation angered him.

He shouldn't be surprised. They'd been lying to him all his life. He blinked, and white light filled his vision again, clearing to reveal the... 'Burning city. Pipers playing, the one-eyed man–'

'The unclean site has stripped him of his wits,' Franto muttered, dismayed.

'There's nothing wrong with my wits,' Sorne insisted. 'I saw...'

'What did you see, Sorne?' Oskane asked.

'A dream...' Embarrassed, he shrugged and went to walk off.

Oskane stopped him. 'I'll tell you what I saw. I saw the T'En braid glow and revolve in the air. The records of unclean sites have never mentioned this before. Something extraordinary happened. What did you *see*?'

'A warrior king on a battlefield. A grim, one-eyed man showed me a conquering king.'

Oskane's eyes widened. 'Did the king have a scar here on his chin?' He pointed to the side of his mouth.

'How did you–'

'It was King Charald!' Oskane turned to Franto. 'It was Charald, and the boy's never seen him.' He clasped Sorne's free hand in both of his. 'What else did you see?'

'A burning city. Pipers prepared to play but, as they warmed up, their instruments sounded like wounded beasts. Everyone cheered. I felt it here.' Sorne put his hand over his heart.

'The pipers... he's never heard them warm up, Franto. It must have been a vision sent by the gods,' Oskane marvelled. 'To think... all this time they were testing my faith while I looked for a sign. Here it is. And a battle won! But what battle? Where, Sorne?'

'I don't know.'

'Could you draw what you saw?'

'I could try.'

OSKANE'S HANDS SHOOK with excitement as he gave Sorne the paper, brushes and coloured inks to draw his vision. While Sorne worked, Oskane plucked a book of the Seven from the shelf and showed him an illustration of the Warrior god. 'Did the one-eyed man look like this?'

Sorne frowned. 'He looked grim, and sort of familiar.'

Aware of Izteben watching him, Oskane closed the book and paced. His mind raced. He'd scourged himself every day for forty years, yet the gods manifested for the half-bloods. A lesser man than he would feel resentful. He was grateful he'd lived long enough to see this. 'When the T'En plait glowed and writhed on the air, it was a visible manifestation of the gods.'

'I don't understand,' Izteben said. 'Why did the Warrior god want the T'En plait?'

It was a good question. Oskane paced, his mind racing. 'The T'En deny the existence of the gods. They think they are as good as gods themselves, thanks to their gifts. But their very existence is an insult to the Seven. For hundreds of years, scholars have been trying to work out why the T'En have power that should belong to...'

He stopped as a thought struck him. 'What if their power was originally *stolen* from the gods? The gods

would seek to recover it. They'd look for ways to...'
Everything fell into place. 'The unclean sites! Our
people had been shunning them for hundreds of years
because they disappeared or went mad when they
ventured into them. Of course True-men lose their wits
when confronted with the Seven. Their minds cannot
encompass the magnificence of the gods. But this time,
purely by chance, the half-bloods offered the gods what
they wanted. When Sorne gave them the T'En artefact,
he returned a portion of their stolen power, so they
rewarded him with a vision.'

A wave of relief made Oskane feel light-headed. All his
life he had been searching for answers and now, finally, it
all made sense. He turned around to find Sorne studying
his drawing. 'Have you finished?'

'It doesn't do it justice. I felt like I was really there, filled
with wonder, joy and triumph. The sky was black with
smoke from the burning port. The banners snapped in the
wind. I could almost see the symbol on the city flag.'

'Let me see.' Oskane accepted the drawing, which was
crudely done, though the king in his armour was instantly
recognisable. 'We have no enemies in Chalcedonia other
than... Could it be the Wyrd city?'

Sorne frowned. 'I could see a bay and the sea beyond.
There were ships burning.'

'Not their city, then.' That was disappointing.

'I'll work on it some more. The more I draw, the more it
comes back to me.'

'Yes, you do that.' Oskane returned the drawing,
dismissed Izteben and stepped into the outer chamber. 'Did
you find Denat, Franto?'

'His things are gone. He must have run away when he
sent us into the mine.'

'Sly little thief,' Oskane muttered. Yesterday this would
have been a tragedy. Today it was only an inconvenience.
'He's stolen from the church, and he knows too much.
Find Denat and kill him. Bring the malachite back here.'

Franto nodded. It was not the first time he had killed in the service of the Seven.

'I'll send a message to the king, to meet me at Enlightenment Abbey.'

SORNE WAS HUNGRY. The smell of onions and mushrooms frying made his stomach rumble. It was full dark, and he'd been drawing by the light of the lamp for what felt like ages. He sat back to look at his work.

'Finished?' Scholar Oskane asked.

'For now. More may come back to me.' Sorne wondered how much he had filled in from his imagination. 'May I go now? I'm hungry.'

'Yes, go.'

He came to his feet and offered obeisance before heading for the door.

'And Sorne?'

'Yes, scholar?'

'Was the braid all that you stole from my bed chamber?'

Sorne blushed. 'Yes, scholar.'

Oskane's eyes narrowed. 'Very well. But if I find you have been into my things again, I'll... I'll bring Valendia in here and scourge her.'

'But she's innocent.'

'Then you had better make sure you're innocent, too. Do you understand me?'

'Yes, scholar.' Sorne kept his eyes lowered to hide the hatred that burned in him.

Over in the stable, his mother... Hiruna would have something set aside for him, but he didn't go across the courtyard. Instead, he headed down to the she-Wyrd's cell. The light of the two moons pierced the small, high windows.

In a dark corner, he could just make out the gleam of her eyes. He found he was angry with her and didn't know why. Maybe it was because she'd been warning him for years not to trust Oskane, and now she'd been proven right.

'Is it true the T'En have no gods?' he asked

'The T'Enatuath, that's what we call ourselves, the full-bloods and the half-bloods, and yes. We have no gods.'

'The True-men believe in the Seven.'

'If one man believes something crazy, he is crazy. If ten thousand men believe it, then it must be true?'

'Of course not, but how can you be sure there are no gods?'

'When a True-man sees something he doesn't understand, he sees the gods at work, but everything follows laws, even if we don't understand them yet.'

'Who made the laws?'

'You think like a True-man.'

'What do you know of unclean sites?'

'Why do you ask?'

'There's one here, deep in the mine. It's why the retreat was abandoned. Back when we first came here, Scholar Oskane ordered the entrance boarded up to hide it.'

The Wyrd woman left her bedding and crept over to the bars. Her hair was loose on her shoulders, down to her thighs again. She wore a thin shift, and her arms were pale in the moonlight. She smelled different tonight. Sweet. 'If I tell you what I know, can you get me another button?'

'He showed you the button?' Sorne was shocked and surprised she would admit to craving T'En power.

'He gave it to me.'

'What do the T'En say about unclean places?'

'You'll get me another button?'

'If I can. If I touch his things again he threatened to use the lash on...' Sorne still found it hard to believe.

'On Valendia.'

'How did you know?'

'When I first came here, he threatened to kill you and Izteben, if I didn't teach you the T'En language.'

'But...'

'He never meant it. I know that now, although I would not be surprised if he has ordered the deaths of others.' She gripped the bars. 'You know you are as much a prisoner as I am.'

He shook his head. 'I'm valued. I have visions.'

She snorted. 'Only the T'En have visions, and only a very select few. Sometimes a seer or a scryer isn't born for a hundred years or more.'

'About the unclean sites...'

'Stay away from them. They'll be your death. There are predators–'

'I survived.' But he had sensed something... a predator, or an angry god? 'There was something powerful down there.'

'I'd like to know how you survived. Only gift-warriors dare to tackle empyrean beasts.'

'Another T'En word I don't know.'

She sighed. 'What I tell you now, I tell you to save your life, foolish boy. There is this plane, the world you see about you every day, and there is another world that lies alongside it, the empyrean plane. In places, unclean places as the Mieren call them, the walls are weak. At certain times of the year, like season's cusp, the walls grow even weaker.

'Terrible beasts roam the empyrean plane. The T'En protect us from these predators. If the beasts break through, they cannot stay long, but in the little time they have they can wreak havoc, devouring the life force of any man, woman or child they find. I've heard some can feast on a person's wits and leave them a simpleton. Only T'En gift-warriors can protect–'

'If that is true, why did the creature devour the T'En plait?'

She went very still, then looked up. 'You killed a T'En? You wicked, wicked boy!'

'I killed no one.' Although, now that he thought about it, *someone* had killed a T'En to get the blood-stained robe and the braid. 'Where did you think the button came from?'

She did not answer.

'The plait glowed and writhed in the air as if something was playing with it,' Sorne said. 'Why would a beast do that?'

'Why do cats play with mice before killing them?'

'Why was there a flash of light?'

'It was the surge of power as the beast was dragged back into its realm.'

'Why did I have a vision after the light blinded me?'

'You? A vision?' She laughed.

He found he was on his feet. 'You're weak. You're addicted to T'En power.' Contempt filled him. 'I'm not like you. I'm never going to be a victim. I'll be powerful.'

And he strode off.

Her voice carried after him. 'Don't go down there again. Not if you want to live.'

He went back to the stable, where Hiruna berated him. 'What were you thinking, going down that mine? You could have gotten your brother killed.'

He hugged her.

'What was that for?'

For treating me like I'm your son. 'I'm hungry.'

Chapter Twenty

IRIAN STUDIED THE big T'En male as he went through his combat sequence.

'Should we offer him a place on the inner circle?' Ardeyne asked. They stood on the balcony overlooking the weapons training courtyard. 'With both Nereon and Araze dead, there's room for Mefusun, and we have passed over him before.'

'For good reason,' Irian said. 'He's powerful and ambitious, but his thinking is far too rigid. Mefusun is paranoid about T'En females. I would not be comfortable with him on our inner circle.'

'If we pass over him this time, it will be seen as an insult. We'd need to honour him in some other way.'

'We could send him to manage one of the brotherhood estates.'

'He'd see it as banishment from the city.'

'He'd be ruler of his own domain,' Irian said, but Ardeyne was right. Nereon and Araze's deaths were inconvenient. Nereon couldn't help his sudden illness, but Araze should have known better than to duel at his age.

'I'll talk it over with Roh.' Ardeyne left him.

Gripping the rail, Irian watched the mid- to high-ranking brotherhood warriors. Juggling powerful, ambitious men was a challenge. Sometimes there was no easy answer.

A little later, Ardeyne's devotee came looking for the voice-of-reason.

'He's with Roh. What is it?'

'Reothe's back.'

A thrill of excitement ran through Irian, rousing his gift. The sacrare boy would be born soon and, through him, they would unite the brotherhoods. Truly, Rohaayel was a visionary, the greatest all-father in the history of the T'Enatuath.

'Go tell Roh and Ard. I'll bring Reothe up after he's made his report to the tithe-master.'

The devotee left. Irian couldn't wait, and went to meet Reothe on the stairs.

Looking at the initiate, you could not tell he had made the deep-bonding, but it must have changed him. Trysting with a T'En female was unforgettable. The first time, it had taken Irian three days to come back to earth. Trysting, while sharing the intimacy of the deep-bonding... how he envied the youth.

'Hand-of-force.' Reothe was surprised to see him on the stairs and made obeisance, acknowledging Irian's higher rank.

'Reothe.' Glancing around, he lowered his voice. 'The sacrare is...'

'Well. If his kicks are anything to go by.'

'She suspects nothing?'

'Not a thing. In fact, after she has the baby, she wants to come live with our brotherhood.' Reothe frowned. 'We can't keep lying to her. There has to be a better way.'

'There is a better way for the T'Enatuath. That's why we're dismantling the covenant.' He held Reothe's eyes. They could not afford doubts. 'I know it's hard, but we have to stay strong. Imoshen will thank us, one day.'

Reothe nodded. 'It's just... it doesn't feel right to lie.'

Irian gave a wry smile. 'The higher you rise, the more you come to realise honesty is a luxury. Go make your report to Tithe-master Ysanyn. We'll be waiting for you on the roof.'

The youth nodded and left him.

He hadn't told Reothe, but they were going to bring the gift-tutor with them. If the birth of a sacrare could trigger the development of a female's gift, then they might need Bedettor's advice.

'Hand-of-force?' The leader of Irian's Malaunje agents came up the stairs.

Netaric was no longer a warrior, but he knew everyone, and Irian trusted his judgement. 'What is it?'

'Down in the Malaunje quarters, there is whisper of Imoshen. Someone must have let something slip.'

'How much do they know?'

'Rumours of a secret lover, a daughter, a T'En girl hidden from the sisterhoods and kept locked in a tower.'

Irian cursed. 'I'll tell Roh. Your people–'

'Are denying it, but they're worried. They fear the sisterhoods' wrath if it's true.'

'Tell them the all-father would never...' He was about to say Rohaayel would never put his brotherhood at risk, but he had done just that for an ideal. 'Tell them it's nonsense. Quash the rumour.'

Netaric nodded and went down the stairs, while Irian went up. When he stepped out into the silvery winter sunshine on the rooftop garden, he spotted Rohaayel and Ardeyne. They had finished their balance exercises and were dressing warmly.

Irian jogged over. 'We could have a problem.' He told them Netaric's news and his orders.

'It's just a rumour,' Ardeyne said. 'Like the story of the village high in the mountains where Malaunje live free of Mieren and T'En. No one will believe it.'

'Ard's right,' Rohaayel said. 'What we've done is unthinkable.'

'Maybe we shouldn't go to Lighthouse Isle for the birth,' Irian said.

'We've said we're going south for the winter. If we change our plans it'll look suspicious. No, we stick to the plan.'

The next day they rode out with the gift-tutor, Reothe and four Malaunje servants.

*   *   *

IMOSHEN MARVELLED AS she held her newborn in her arms. The birth had happened so fast, there hadn't been time to get the cook. Her son was early and... 'So small.'

A fierce instinct to protect her child surged through her, rousing her gift. With it came rush of power, sweeping through her body and mind with such intensity it was painful.

She was still reeling when a sound made her look over to Frayvia, who was watching her with the baby. Her gift rose and she realised a pall of sorrow hung over her friend. 'Why are you so sad?'

'I'm not,' Frayvia lied. 'I'm happy for you.'

Imoshen's gift surged again. Her friend was torn apart inside. Why had she never seen it before?

'I should tell the cook she missed the birth, and bring Iraayel in to meet his choice-brother,' Frayvia said.

'No, wait. I'd like to clean up first.' Imoshen looked down at the sleeping infant. 'You said T'En babies take a full year for their gift to mature. Do you think he'll be alright?'

'He was early, but not too early.'

Imoshen could read the conviction in Frayvia. It felt so natural, it took her a moment to realise her gift had flexed again. She had never had this depth of insight before.

'Why are you staring at me?' Frayvia asked, fear hiding behind a smile.

Frayvia feared her?

'I would never hurt you.'

Frayvia gasped and took a step back, colliding with Reothe.

'Reothe?' Imoshen sat up, wincing with pain. 'I thought you—'

'We just arrived. When I heard you were in labour, I ran up from the boat. The cook told me you wouldn't deliver until tomorrow morning but...' With a laugh, he brushed past Frayvia and dropped to his knees by the bed, where he cupped the tiny head of his son in his palm. The new part of her gift enabled her to sense a wave of protective wonder fill him. 'Oh, Imoshen...' He looked up at her. 'What did you call him?'

'I haven't named him yet. I thought Reo-something. Reonyx or Reomyr, perhaps.'

He smiled and she sensed his love: a bright and shining shield. 'Reoshen?'

She laughed, then winced.

'You're hurt?'

'A bit. The birth happened quickly. I was torn.'

He flinched and she felt his pain for her. Everything was so raw; her body, her emotions, her gift... she was overwhelmed.

'The all-father and his seconds are probably downstairs by now.' Frayvia stood in the doorway, radiating angry resentment.

'Yes,' Reothe said, and in that one word, Imoshen glimpsed a world of regret and guilt. 'The gift-tutor's with them.'

Imoshen reached for his hand. 'Why is Fray angry with you, and why do you feel guilty?'

His mouth dropped open and she read his dismay. Touch made it so much clearer.

He looked down to their joined hands. 'You're a raedan, able to read emotions. They said there was a chance your gift would mature. That's why they brought the gift-tutor with them.' He glanced over his shoulder to the door and she saw him make a decision.

As he took her shoulders in his hands, a sick dread filled Imoshen; she already knew what he was going to say. Karokara had tried to warn her. *You're a prisoner...*

'I love you,' Reothe said. 'I have from the day you took me down to the rocks and nearly drowned me. But I haven't been entirely honest with you. This island is your prison.'

Imoshen hadn't wanted to see. A moan escaped her.

'I'm sorry.' He hugged her, pressing his lips to hers, then pulled back. Tears slipped down his cheeks. 'I'm sorry. I would never have lied to you, but it's for a great cause. They plan to use our sacrare son to unite the brotherhoods and free us from the covenant.'

'What covenant?'

Frayvia made an impatient gesture. 'You'll have to tell her everything now.'

OSKANE CURSED. KING Charald had refused to meet him at Enlightenment Abbey. He smoothed out the paper, passing it to Franto. 'I can read between the lines. He listens to Nitzel, who tells him I am delusional.'

'That's easily disproved.' Having read the reply, Franto folded it and returned it to the packet. 'Tell them to come here.'

'But it's unclean.'

'Not any more. Now it is a doorway to the gods.'

'They'll refuse outright. The taint–'

'There is *no taint*.'

'But they will think there is. That's why I wanted to meet them in the abbey. I was going to tell them in person when I showed them the drawing of Sorne's vision!'

'Anyone can do a drawing. Much better to set up a demonstration. Have the half-bloods make another offering. Stage another vision, one that favours your cause.'

'The vision was real.'

'As you say,' Franto agreed. 'But that doesn't mean the half-blood can't have a vision that suits your purposes.'

'Ask him to lie for me?' Oskane shook his head. 'I don't want to put the idea of lying into his head. He and Izteben are innocent of deception.'

'They'll need to lie convincingly when you send them into the Wyrd city.'

'I'm not sending them, now. I know' – he shrugged – 'seventeen years of training for just that purpose. But why waste them as spies, when I can use them to communicate with the gods? Through them I can regain leadership over all seven churches. With the power of the church behind me, and Charald listening to my advice, I can restore my family's fortunes.'

'Only if you can convince Charald to come here.' Franto's face lit up. 'We have the bag of malachite Denat tried to steal. I could slip into the palace and bribe my way in to see the king, then plead your case.'

Oskane shook his head. 'I don't want you appearing before Charald and Nitzel as a supplicant. I want them to come to me.'

'Then negotiate from a position of power. Promise them a vision from the Warrior if they come here, to the holy site!'

'Holy site, that's very good. And you're absolutely right. The Warrior is Charald's patron god, he won't be able to resist.'

Oskane was halfway though the message when a noise from the courtyard interrupted him. 'What is that commotion?'

Franto went to the window and opened the shutters.

'The half-bloods have opened the gate to someone. It's...'

'Zabier!' Izteben's cry reached them. 'Ma, it's Zabier.'

'Zabier and Kolst?' Oskane came to his feet.

'No sign of Kolst. Just the lad. How old is he now?'

'Thirteen next spring, same age as Prince Cedon.' Oskane looked down through the maple tree's bare branches to see Sorne hugging Zabier, lifting him right off his feet.

'Scholar Oskane!' Zabier spotted them. 'Master Franto. I've come home.'

'Zabier!' Hiruna ran out of the stables, leaving Valendia to trot along behind her. She threw her arms around her son and kissed him, weeping.

Franto wiped his eyes and Oskane cleared his throat. He frowned. 'If Kolst did not bring the lad, how–'

'He found his way back to us, Ma,' Izteben said.

'All the way on his own,' Sorne said proudly.

Oskane stepped away from the window. 'If a boy of twelve can find us...'

'Then Nitzel's agents could find us,' Franto conceded.

'We'll be safer in plain sight, negotiating from a position of power. They must come here.' Oskane sat down to finish writing his reply. 'Send the boy up.'

A few moments later, Zabier entered.

Oskane put his nib down. 'You have returned. What happened?'

'Da used the gold you gave him to build a fine house for the family and improve his brother's business.' Zabier licked his lips nervously. 'It was a mistake going back. Da fought with Uncle. When Da turned up drowned in the millpond, Uncle blamed it on drink, but he hardly ever drank. Uncle treated me like a servant. My cousin teased me because I could read and write. I had a big fight with him and he said I'd end up floating face-down in the millpond like Da. So I came back.'

'Very wise,' Oskane said. 'The church is a good career for a smart lad. You could go far, but you'll have to work hard at your studies.'

'I don't mind as long as I can be with my family.'

'It's decided then. Off you go.'

Franto stepped into the study and closed the door. 'You need to tell the half-bloods there's been a change in plan.'

'The goal was always to crush Nitzel and restore my family's fortune. Spying on the Wyrds was only a means to an end.'

'Then you need to make it clear they will be serving the church and king in a new, more important capacity.'

SINCE ZABIER'S RETURN, Sorne had smiled so much his face hurt.

'...I always meant to return,' Zabier was saying as they ate. 'So I marked all the important places in my mind.'

Hiruna laughed and pressed a kiss to his forehead. 'My clever, clever boy!'

'Clever boy!' Valendia repeated.

'Oh, Ma,' Zabier whispered. 'I've missed you all.'

After she'd put Valendia to bed, Hiruna took Zabier with her to cook the meal for the scholar and his assistant.

As Izteben watched them leave, he said, 'I can't believe it, Zabe has seen more of the world than we have. Our clever little brother.'

Sorne felt a pang of remorse. He hadn't been able to bring himself to tell Izteben they weren't really brothers. There had never been the right moment, and it didn't seem to matter since they were as good as brothers anyway.

'This is my chance to read the latest messages,' Sorne said. After he'd discovered the truth about himself, he'd made it his business to read all the messages from Oskane's agents, dating right back to when they first came to the retreat. He knew his uncle, Matxin, was eager to restore the family's fortune, and he knew the king saw threat everywhere. If it wasn't his barons fomenting revolt, it was the rulers of neighbouring kingdoms after his throne.

Sorne took a needle and thread from Hiruna's sewing basket. 'I promised the she-Wyrd a new silver button. The last one's gift residue is worn out. Keep watch for me?'

As they crept across the courtyard, they could hear Hiruna happily singing to herself as she cooked. Oskane and Franto sat chatting by the fire.

Sorne left Izteben to keep watch, then slipped up the stairs to the scholar's chambers. He went straight to the packet of messages on the desk, next to a letter in Oskane's hand addressed to King Charald.

Sorne made himself study the messages first. He knew the different agents' hand writing. There was one in the Seven's church in Port Mirror-on-Sea who had a spy at the palace. He reported on the doings of Baron Nitzel, the ins and out of court politics and the rivalry between the churches. There was one at Enlightenment Abbey, who collected reports from churches and abbeys all over Chalcedonia, and there was Baron Matxin, his mother's brother. And tonight there was a message from King Charald himself. Sorne opened it. To think, his real father had held this paper.

Charald refused to meet at Enlightenment Abbey. Disappointment stung Sorne. The king's excuses were flimsy. It was winter, he had pressing duties and the other kingdoms bordering the Secluded Sea were plotting against him.

Next Sorne read Oskane's letter addressed to King Charald.

In it, Oskane claimed unclean places were really pathways to the gods – holy sites. And he took credit for Sorne and Izteben's discovery. There was the mention of a vision from Charald's mentor god, the Warrior. What's more, Oskane had offered the king a chance to see the holy site, and to attend a ceremony where Sorne had another vision.

His stomach clenched with fear. Last time, they had been lucky to escape with their lives.

According to the she-Wyrd, only T'En could have visions, but when Sorne had described in detail how it had happened, she no longer sounded so sure. Which reminded him...

Placing the letter on the desk, he slipped into the scholar's bedchamber. He took the chest out from under the bed and unpacked the robe, then went over to the fire to see more clearly. Knowing now that what he felt was the residue of a murdered T'En, his skin crawled with a mixture of revulsion and longing.

But he hadn't spent years under the scourge for nothing. He concentrated on his task. It was the work of a moment to remove a fresh button and sew the old one in its place. Now Oskane would never know.

An owl called, then called again.

Moving swiftly, Sorne put the robe back into the chest and slipped out.

Oskane's voice echoed up the stairwell as he spoke to Franto.

Sorne couldn't go down. He couldn't go back, either; while he could jump to the wall-walk, the open shutter would betray him. Sorne leant the back of his head against the wall, cursing under his breath.

Right above him, he saw the cross beams of the roof, hidden in shadows.

Climbing onto the banister, he reached up, caught hold of the beam and managed to hook his legs over it. He swung his weight onto it, then crept out over the stairwell until he was above the landing between the second and third floors.

Not a moment too soon. Oskane and Franto passed under him.

'...we'll save the bag of malachite for an emergency,' Oskane was saying.

Sorne held his breath, but neither of them looked up. They passed into Franto's chamber and closed the door.

Carefully, he lowered himself back onto the landing and hurried down the stairs.

As he stepped out into the moonlight, Izteben grabbed him and shook him. 'I was worried sick!'

Sorne laughed as if he hadn't nearly been caught, and they went down to see the she-Wyrd, who was waiting for them.

'I managed to get–'

She snatched the silver button from his outstretched hand and ran into the darkest corner.

Izteben gave a bark of laughter. 'We risked the scholar's ire for that.'

'I thank you for the gift-infused token,' the she-Wyrd whispered from the shadows. Her voice sounded richer, and Sorne could already detect a change in her scent. He felt nothing but contempt.

'The king is going to come here and I'm going to win him over with a vision,' he told her. 'I'm going to be a messenger of the gods. Did you hear? Iztében and I are going to serve the king.'

Still no reaction.

'Come on.' He turned on his heel and strode towards the stairs.

'Even if the Mieren believe you are messengers of their gods,' she called after them, 'in their eyes you will always be filthy Wyrds!'

Chapter Twenty-One

IMOSHEN HELD HER newborn so that his head lay on her chest, close to her heart. She still found it hard to believe he was real, had to keep checking that he was breathing. Reothe stretched out beside her as they talked about the gifts, what life was really like in the city and how Rohaayel would make a better life for everyone. She'd felt angry and betrayed at first. But now, from what Reothe told her about T'Enatuath society, she saw that they were all trapped, Malaunje and T'En, male and female.

Frayvia sat on the end of the bed with Iraayel in her arms. He'd been fascinated by the newborn, but when the baby did nothing other than sleep, he'd lost interest.

Now he sat up. 'I'm hungry.'

'Me too.' Reothe swung his legs off the bed and held out his arms. Iraayel jumped off the bed, and Reothe caught him, swung him around then set him on his feet, laughing.

Imoshen smiled up at them. She felt raw and fragile, but she was happy.

'I'll tell the all-father the good news.' Reothe grinned. 'You'll be swamped with visitors.'

'Give us a few moments to clean up,' Frayvia said.

Reothe took Iraayel's hand and left.

IRIAN WARMED HIS hands at the fire, while Torekar poured wine.

Rohaayel accepted his glass. 'To our sacrare.'

The others echoed his toast.

Irian put his goblet down. 'Reothe's taking a long time. I'll check on him.'

'Tell him a watched pot never boils,' Ardeyne said.

'He's made the deep-bonding with her. I'm guessing he'll be tempted to ease her pain by sharing it,' Bedettor said. 'We might not see him all night.'

Irian smiled as he headed for the door. It opened to reveal Mefusun, who strode in on a wave of threatening male gift.

Irian backed up swiftly, glancing to Ardeyne. The voice-of-reason took a step closer to Rohaayel, as Bedettor and the devotee joined them.

Another seven men followed Mefusun into the dining chamber. They spread out across the far side of the room, cutting off the door to the hall and lighthouse. Even from this side of the room, Irian could feel their aggressive power. He assessed the odds. Eight against five, and one of his men was the Malaunje, Torekar.

'What are you doing here, Mefusun?' Rohaayel asked.

'Twice now, I've been passed over. So I asked myself, why doesn't the all-father offer me a place on his inner circle? Then I heard the merest whisper of a T'En female, hidden in a tower. Impossible, I thought. But–'

'You didn't follow us out of the city,' Irian said. He'd made sure.

'No. We were waiting across the bay, and sure enough, you took a boat to the island. I'm guessing you have her shut in the lighthouse.' His brows drew down. 'What were you thinking? She'll turn on you, turn on us all.'

Irian felt the gift power rise another notch. It became hard to think.

'She's loyal to the brotherhood. We're all she's ever known,' Rohaayel said. He took a seat at the table, helping himself to a chunk of cheese, gesturing with the little cheese knife. 'There was no need for this, Mefusun. We were going to invite you onto the inner circle when we got back. Then we would have explained the whole plan. Wine?'

When Mefusun declined, Rohaayel poured himself a glass and leant back in his chair. Irian could sense no gift aggression coming from Rohaayel, and admired his control.

Mefusun's supporters looked uncertain.

Ardeyne followed Rohaayel's lead and took a seat. Bedettor and Torekar sat down. Irian forced himself to sit casually on one end of the table and swing a booted foot. As Torekar poured him more wine, Mefusun's supporters exchanged looks.

'Imoshen thinks she is one of us,' Rohaayel said. 'She's taken Initate Reothe for the deep-bonding. She's going to give us a sacrare son to unite the brotherhoods.'

'A sacrare could unite the brotherhoods, but you can't trust her, or her bond-partner. He's been corrupted by his addiction to her gift. And birthing a sacrare will make her more powerful,' Mefusun said. 'After the birth, you'll have to kill her, and him, too. The sacrare is what's important.'

'I agree.' Rohaayel lifted the wine. 'To the sacrare.'

IMOSHEN HAD JUST finished dressing, when Reothe thrust the door open. He came in on a wave of roused gift. Her power surged and she read him – betrayal, disbelief, fear and... determination.

'What?' Imoshen reached for her newborn. Iraayel ran to her and threw his arms around her.

'We have to go right now. I was in the hall, I just...' He shook his head. 'I would never have believed it, but I heard them plotting to kill us and take the sacrare.'

'No,' Frayvia cried. 'That was never the plan.'

'They toasted to its success.' Tears glittered in Reothe's eyes. 'Back in the city, Irian told me honesty was a luxury.'

He believed what he'd said; Imoshen could feel it. 'Grab some warm clothes, Fray. We must get down to the boats.'

Iraayel whimpered. Imoshen sat him on the bed next to the baby. 'Be big and look after Reoshen for me.'

Frayvia threw some things in a bag, while Reothe watched the lighthouse steps.

'We're lucky, they think you're still in labour. The cook expected the birth to take all night,' he said. 'Ready?'

Was she ready to leave her home? She had to be. Imoshen summoned a smile for Iraayel, who was watching her anxiously. 'Time for an adventure. You must do everything we tell you.'

He nodded solemnly.

She made a sling from a blanket and tucked the baby into it, planting a kiss on the newborn's head. Lucky for them, he had just been fed and was sleeping.

Frayvia took Iraayel's hand.

'I'll go first,' Reothe said. 'Keep your gift tightly reined, Imoshen. If they sense it, they'll come after us.'

He went down the stairs, and they followed him.

At the base of the lighthouse, he opened the door to the hall. They could hear the clatter of dishes and excited chatter from the Malaunje in the kitchen. From the dining room, they could hear deep voices.

Reothe drew back. 'It's clear to the front door.'

In a rush, they went down the passage and out the front door. No snow had fallen yet, but the cold was biting. It was not long until midwinter and the night was dark – the small moon was new, the big moon waning – but Imoshen knew every path and every rock on this part of the island.

They reached the cliff edge and the steps to the beach without trouble, and ran down to the beach. The tide was on the way in. Some of the boats had been pulled up onto the sand. Others were moored out in deeper water. They made straight for a six-man rowboat, which lay with its nose on the sand. Reothe swung Iraayel into it then reached for Frayvia, but she'd already scrambled aboard. Before Imoshen could protest, he lifted her into the boat and began to shove it into the shallows.

'Here, you,' someone yelled.

Imoshen saw three Malaunje warriors come running across the sand towards them. 'Hurry, Reothe.'

She darted back to grab the closest oar. The water was thigh-deep on Reothe now.

Their attackers ran through the shallows, sending plumes of water to each side. One of them grabbed Reothe. He shoved the boat out into deeper water, then let go.

Reothe and his attacker grappled. The second warrior tried to haul Iraayel out of the boat, while the third went for Frayvia. Imoshen swung the oar at the man clutching Iraayel, striking the Malaunje across the head. He released her. Bringing the oar around, Imoshen tackled the other one.

Reothe escaped his attacker and headed for the boat. The warrior tackled him, and they collided with the boat. It rocked alarmingly. One of the warriors tried to spring into the boat and Imoshen swung the oar again.

The world tipped.

Shockingly cold water closed over her. She didn't know which way was up. Something clipped her head. She lost all sense of direction.

Mercifully, her face broke the surface and she gasped a breath. She couldn't feel the sea bed under her feet. Frayvia waved. Iraayel clung to her.

Imoshen pulled the baby out of his sling, lifting his face above water. Someone grabbed her, ducking her under. She couldn't fight back, not without dropping Reoshen. She twisted and turned.

They let her go and she struggled to the surface, weighed down by clothes and the baby. Kicking out, she made for Frayvia. She heard splashes behind her, and knew Reothe was still struggling.

Ahead of her, Frayvia seemed even further away. She felt the current take her, sweeping her away from the bay as it had taken Frayvia and Iraayel.

So cold... they had to get out of the water.

In desperation, she made for one of the moored boats. She lifted Reoshen over the side of the dingy and let him roll down into the nose of the boat. Without him in her arms, she was able to kick up, lift her weight over the boat's side and slither in.

Shaking with cold, she settled the baby in a coil of rope, hauled in the anchor, grabbed two oars and...

Felt Reothe die.

Felt it like a light going out.

But she had to save Frayvia and Iraayel. She put her back into working the oars.

In a few moments she came alongside them. Tucking the oars into the boat, she took Iraayel from Frayvia and lifted him over the side. He shivered violently as she lowered him into the bow of the boat. 'Don't move.'

The boat rocked as she dragged Frayvia in.

As soon as they were both safe, she crawled to the nose where Reoshen lay. She unwrapped him, bent her head over his tiny chest to listen and...

Heard nothing.

GRAELEN AND PARYX stepped aside to let several high-ranking adepts past. Although they were also adepts, they were only in their first year and had a long way to go to win status and respect.

Paryx waited until the five T'En men were out of sight before whispering to Graelen. 'That's the brotherhood's tithe-master and his collectors. I've heard he robs the estates so Sigorian can build the new wing of the palace. All to impress the other all-fathers.'

'Kyredeon says bluffing the other brotherhoods is better than shedding blood on this plane, or power on the empyrean plane.' In the seventeen years since he'd joined Sigorian's brotherhood, Graelen had learned who to avoid, who to trust, and how to keep out of trouble and, for the most part, he succeeded.

They passed a Malaunje lamplighter before climbing to the old part of the palace, where the low-ranking adepts and initiates lived.

Kyredeon beckoned to them from the balcony shadows.

In the years since he had first offered them advice, Kyredeon had risen to be one of the most influential men in the brotherhood. He had managed to gather a group of dissatisfied adepts and young initiates around him, all without drawing Sigorian's notice.

'Kyredeon,' Graelen greeted him with the abbreviated obeisance of a low-ranking adept.

'Grae, Paryx.' Kyredeon gave them both a quick nod.

This close, Graelen could feel Kyredeon's barely contained gift, and he was reminded of his first night in the brotherhood. That night, seven males had been killed, purged because Sigorian perceived them as a threat. 'Is something wrong?'

'I need a favour.'

'Name it.' Brotherhood life consisted of a web of obligation, and they both owed Kyredeon.

'Every evening, the new hand-of-force meets his Malaunje lover on the new rooftop garden. They tryst, then go their separate ways. When Fraysun goes up there, follow him and bolt the door. Let him spend a night on the roof in the cold and damp. You heard what he did to Ekanyn?'

They nodded. Ekanyn was higher-ranked than they; if he could be publically humiliated, then what protection did they have?

'Do this and you win Ekanyn's gratitude.'

Paryx glanced to Graelen. It seemed simple enough, and the new hand-of-force would not know who to blame.

'We'll do it,' Graelen said.

'Good.' Kyredeon glanced over his shoulder as several Malaunje servants came along the balcony, carrying dinner trays. 'Go now. He'll leave as soon as he's eaten.'

They would miss their meal, but it would be worth it. They'd repay a debt to Kyredeon and Ekanyn would be beholden to them.

Graelen and Paryx made their way to the new part of the palace.

'What's the remodelling in aid of?' Paryx whispered. 'Does Sigorian feel threatened?'

Graelen signalled for silence and pulled him into the shadows. A moment later, the brotherhood's new hand-of-force strode past. He was alone

They waited. No lover came.

'Looks like his lover's stood him up,' Paryx whispered.

'Then we better shut the door before he realises.' Graelen slipped out of the shadows, closed the door and slid the bolts.

'That's it then,' Paryx said. 'We can go back.'

On their way back to their quarters, they passed the bathing chamber, where Graelen heard Kyredeon's voice.

'I'll just let him know there was no lover,' Graelen said, slipping silently into the chamber.

Only a few lamps were still lit, their light gleaming on the wet tiles; he smelled scented oils and bath salts. He peered through the steam, but could not see the adept he sought. Then Kyredeon's voice came again, and Graelen sensed the rise of the gift, redolent with danger. He backed up. He didn't want trouble.

'...you two have the advantage of being shield-brothers. You have the mid-ranking adepts behind you. I can bring my supporters in. You must challenge the all-father tonight, before the new hand-of-force can make good on his threat to you. I've ensured that when Sigorian summons Fraysun, he won't answer...'

Graelen's mind raced. If the all-father got wind of this, he'd kill them.

'...their triumvirate will be weakened,' Kyredeon was saying. 'You'll have the advantage.'

'What have you been up to, Kyredeon?' Ekanyn asked.

'Ensuring you'll win.'

'But what do you get out of this?'

'Let me guess,' Hariode, Ekanyn's shield-brother, said. 'He wants to be hand-of-force.'

'That's right,' Kyredeon agreed. 'Divide all-father and voice-of-reason between the pair of you. I'll take hand-of-force.'

'Done.'

'Done.'

Graelen backed silently out onto the verandah.

'You've gone white,' Paryx said. 'What's wrong?'

'Come with me.' They sped back to the new part of the palace. When they reached the deserted upper floor, Graelen explained. 'So we have to make sure Fraysun doesn't leave the roof.'

But they found the door open and the roof top deserted.

'His lover must have come after all,' Paryx whispered. 'Now what'll we do?'

Graelen cursed. Unless they acted swiftly, Kyredeon's challenge would fail and all his supporters would be purged. 'Come with me.'

IRIAN LIFTED HIS wine glass. 'To the sacrare, and the end of the covenant.'

Rohaayel, Ardeyne and the others played along, raising their glasses.

One of the kitchen hands opened the door, backing in with a tray. He looked surprised to see more T'En men, and he stiffened as he felt the gift readiness on the air.

'Tell cook there'll be another eight for dinner,' Rohaayel said. 'And bring more glasses.'

'And more wine,' Irian added, feigning bonhomie.

Still Mefusun did not let down his guard.

'Irian, what do you think of Rohdeyne, for the sacrare's name?' Rohaayel asked.

'Why not Bedian?' Bedettor suggested.

'He's my grandson, I get first naming rights,' Rohaayel said. 'Isn't that right, Mefusun?'

The kitchen hand returned with a tray of goblets and more wine. As he left, Rohaayel came to his feet and gestured to Torekar. 'Pour wine for everyone.'

Mefusun came over to the table with his supporters and accepted the wine.

Irian had already decided who he would kill first.

'To this glorious day and our brotherhood.' Rohaayel met Irian's eyes and he knew this was the moment.

Dropping his goblet, Irian pulled his long-knives. His gift surged, heightening his senses. Time slowed; he anticipated strikes before they came. He gutted one warrior, cut another's throat, felt something slam into his back, staggered, but kept moving. Lost one knife in someone's ribs, then lost the other when a blow broke his arm.

He saw Bedettor get his throat cut before he could segue to the higher plane with his two attackers, then drag them along anyway, ripping their shades from their bodies. There was no yelling, just grunts and thuds, gasps of pain. He saw Torekar go down, trying to save Ardeyne.

He saw Rohaayel stagger as his shield-brother died.

Mefusun leapt for the all-father, who ducked. One-handed, Irian caught Mefusun by his hair and slammed his face onto the table top, until he stopped moving.

That was the last of them.

Irian looked across the bloody chamber to Rohaayel, who was clutching his side. Blood seeped between his fingers. A whimper made Irian turn. The cook, and several of the kitchen hands, stood terrified in the doorway.

'Cook, go check on Imoshen and Reothe,' Rohaayel ordered. 'Did Mefusun bring any Malaunje with him?'

'There were some,' one of the kitchen hands said.

'Tell them they have the option of renewing their oaths to me or dying with Mefusun,' Rohaayel said.

Irian could not believe they'd both survived. By wiping out Mefusun and all his supporters, they'd purged the brotherhood of aspirants for the leadership. They could rebuild the inner circle.

'Burn the bodies of the traitors,' Rohaayel ordered. 'Our dead will be properly honoured.'

As they followed his orders, Rohaayel came over to Irian. He moved with care, grimacing in pain. Irian couldn't seem to get his breath. When he inhaled his back hurt. A cough surprised him and blood bubbled out of his mouth.

'Roh?' He reached for the all-father as he toppled forward. Rohaayel caught him, staggering with his weight. Irian must have blacked out; the next thing he knew, he was propped up in a chair in front of the fire.

'...she's not there,' the cook told Rohaayel. 'None of them are. She can't have gone far with a newborn. I've sent the lads out looking for her.'

'Roh.' Irian wanted to ask after his son, who he hadn't seen since he was born, but he couldn't catch his breath. He coughed again. Bright blood poured from his mouth.

The all-father came over and caught his hand. 'Don't worry. They'll find Imoshen. She's probably hiding. Very wise.'

'I'm sorry,' Irian whispered. 'I failed you.'

'No...' Rohaayel shook his head, tears in his eyes.

One of the kitchen hands came running in with a soggy travelling bundle. He reported to the cook, who looked worried.

'What is it?' Rohaayel asked, rising to his feet.

The cook came over with the wet bundle. 'They found this down in the shallows. It's Imoshen's blanket. There's three dead Malaunje, an overturned boat, a missing boat and...' Her mouth worked as her voice broke. 'Reothe's body.'

'What are you saying?' Rohaayel whispered.

'She tried to sail away. The boat tipped over. She drowned.'

'But there's no body,' Rohaayel insisted.

The cook shook her head. 'The current...'

'The missing boat–'

'Could have broken its moorings and been taken by the current.'

'The baby?'

'No sign of him, or Frayvia or Iraayel. No sign of Imoshen.'

Rohaayel swayed and Irian lost feeling in his legs.

Lost. Everything, lost...

Chapter Twenty-Two

As GRAELEN SEARCHED for Fraysun, his mind raced. He hadn't seen the hand-of-force on his way up here, which meant he must have gone down the other steps.

Several moments later they spotted him halfway along the corridor, only two doors from the all-father's chamber.

'Hand-of-force?' Graelen called.

Fraysun turned. 'Grae?'

'I was down below.' He gulped a breath. 'Near the boat-house gate. I heard voices and caught the scent of gift-working.'

'Near the boat-house gate?'

Graelen nodded. 'I didn't recognise the voices.'

'You think they're from another brotherhood?'

Fraysun glanced to Paryx, who said nothing. He was trying to catch his breath. His surging gift betrayed his fear, which fitted in with Graelen's story.

The hand-of-force glanced over his shoulder. 'We need—'

'There's only two of them. But they could let more in.'

'We can't have that. Come on.' Fraysun brushed past them and ran down the corridor.

Graelen grabbed Paryx, dragging him along in his wake.

The hand-of-force led them down several stairs and across a deserted courtyard, through the oldest part of the brotherhood's palace to the boat-house, which was built into the lake wall.

Fraysun stopped at the entrance to the boat-house, the power of his gift radiating from his skin. 'I can't hear anything.'

'They were right there.'

Fraysun put his back to them and peered around the corner. Driven by fear, Graelen pulled his knife, caught Fraysun around the neck and slid the blade between his ribs. Graelen felt reality waver as the warrior's shade nearly dragged him onto the higher plane. Then the big warrior tipped forward, collapsing on the stone.

Paryx moaned.

'Come on. We have to see this through.'

They carried the body to the nearest rowboat, dropped it in, and washed the blood from the stones where Fraysun had been slain. They tied weights around Fraysun's body, then climbed into the boat.

After they dumped the body in the lake, they left the rowboat where they'd found it. By this time, Paryx was shaking.

Graelen took his arm. 'No one will suspect what we've done. No one saw us lead Fraysun away.'

Paryx turned terrified eyed to him. 'What if Kyredeon fails?'

'Kyredeon had better win.'

As they made their way through the palace, they heard celebrating.

'What does it mean?' Paryx whispered.

'One of the triumvirates has lost and one has won. We better get upstairs and clean up.'

Then Graelen caught a name. 'All-father Ekanyn!'

He grinned and dragged Paryx into the young adepts' chamber, where they stripped, throwing their bloodied garments into the fireplace.

By the time they blended into the general celebration, there was wine and singing and trysting going on in every chamber and stairwell.

Athamyr found them drinking and singing with the other young adepts. 'Hand-of-force Kyredeon wants to speak with you two.'

They followed him to what had been Fraysun's quarters. Malaunje were busy stripping it and moving furniture.

Kyredeon led them into his private chamber. 'What happened?'

'We killed Fraysun and dumped his body in the lake,' Paryx blurted. 'Graelen killed him. I—'

'Really?' Kyredeon's eyes narrowed. 'Why would you do that?'

'To ensure he could not interfere with the challenge,' Graelen said.

'How did you know about the challenge?'

'I went back to speak with you and heard you making the pact with Ekanyn and Hariode.'

'So you killed yourself a hand-of-force?' Kyredeon said. 'Why?'

Because I was terrified. 'To win stature. To win a place in the new inner circle.'

This made Kyredeon laugh.

'I had no idea you two were so ambitious.' For a heartbeat, Graelen saw Kyredeon's friendly mask slip as naked cunning lit his eyes; then he grinned. 'Very enterprising of you, but we don't put adepts still wet behind the ears in the all-father's inner circle.'

'You'll tell the all-father how we served him,' Graelen said. 'We'll need protection. Fraysun's shade may come after us.'

'I doubt it. The empyrean beasts have had a feast tonight. Ekanyn and Hariode saw to that. They killed the all-father, his second and all the inner circle. Now I have to purge the brotherhood of Sigorian's remaining supporters.' Kyredeon glanced to Paryx. 'You two killed yourself a hand-of-force. Let's see if you are strong enough to survive his revenge.'

Outside, Paryx maintained his calm until they reached the steps to their quarters, then he slumped against the wall gasping.

'Just breathe slowly,' Graelen told him.

'You could have gotten us both killed. What if he'd taken offence to our initiative?'

'He would have taken offence if he knew Fraysun's lover had let him go. I saved our lives. We've won so much stature we'll never be at the beck and call of the high-ranking adepts again.'

'If we survive Fraysun's shade.'

'He may not come for us. Tell you what... I'll watch your back, you watch mine.'

IMOSHEN HELD REOSHEN'S still form. No breath. No heartbeat.

Dead...

He could not be dead. She couldn't lose them both in one night. Not Reothe and their son.

A wave of fury engulfed her and she felt that odd sensation as the world shifted. She saw Iraayel at the other end of the boat, his life force dulled by cold and shock. She saw Frayvia, also exhausted.

In her newborn there was nothing. He did not register on her sight. But she would not give up. She tucked him in the wet wrappings and mentally prepared herself.

Reothe had spoken of the empyrean plane and its predators, and how the essence of the dead had to traverse it to reach death's realm. She'd go after Reoshen, catch him and bring him back.

The thought of entering the higher plane terrified her.

Even so, she flung herself through.

Now she stood on a beach in the late afternoon. A wintry silver sunlight filled the sky. The dunes stretched before her, dune grass waving in the wind.

Over the rise, she'd find the cottage. It was where she'd found Karokara and taken Iraayel home with her. Surely that was a good sign?

She ran up the dune and looked down into the next hollow.

The cottage was not there. Only a scorched square remained. That's right; Irian had burned it.

If the cottage was not here, then where should she look for Reoshen?

She already knew the answer. He was so small and defenceless, and he had no sense of himself. His essence would have dissipated.

She turned around...

And spotted Frayvia kneeling on the beach. A thousand tiny crabs converged on her.

Forgetting that she had no voice here, Imoshen tried to shout a warning. She felt the world shiver and knew she'd done something dangerous. She should go back, but not without Frayvia.

Running down the slope, she charged across the beach, deliberately stamping on the crabs, cracking their shells. With each step she took, they scattered.

Frayvia lifted her head, terrified. She was already starting to dissipate.

Imoshen swept her arms around her, had to pin Frayvia with her gift to...

Segue back to the boat.

Her body burned as if with a fever. Frayvia clung to her. Iraayel crawled over to join them. She held them both in her arms and felt them grow warm as she shook.

As for Reoshen, there was nothing she could do. She'd failed him.

GRAELEN WOKE TO a new brotherhood leadership. He rolled over and found Paryx next to him. They'd known each other half their lives now. Barring accidents, assassination, murder and Mieren, they had perhaps another seventy years ahead of them.

Paryx grinned and Graelen knew if he asked, Paryx would become his shield-brother, but he also knew that, after yesterday, Paryx would be a liability.

'What?' his trysting-partner asked.

'Today, Kyredeon is hand-of-force, and he'll acknowledge our stature. From the screams last night, I'd say he's purged half the top-ranking initiates. We'll never have to live in fear again.'

Cerazim, an adept of three years' experience, came in and sat cross-legged on his bedroll. He looked shaken.

Graelen sat up, the covers pooling in his lap. 'What's going on?'

'We have a new all-father.' Cerazim said.

Graelen shrugged. 'So?'

'Not Ekanyn. He and Hariode are dead. While they were recovering from the leadership challenge, Kyredeon took Farodytor for his shield-brother and killed them both. He's the new all-father. Athamyr is his hand-of-force.'

Paryx sat up slowly. 'That's... Is that legitimate?'

'Yes, barely,' Cerazim said. 'The all-father and his voice-of-reason must be ready to defend their leadership at all times.'

'But they'd only just defeated Sigorian,' Paryx said. 'Their gifts were drained.'

And they weren't expecting their own hand-of-force to turn on them. What's more, Graelen knew Kyredeon had urged Ekanyn and Hariode to take the gamble and make the challenge.

It seemed Graelen and Paryx had attracted the attention of a very dangerous man.

'All-father Kyredeon has called everyone to the main courtyard.' Cerazim came to his feet. 'Coming?'

'In a moment,' Graelen said.

As soon as Cerazim left, Paryx turned to Graelen. 'Kyredeon thinks we're ambitious. He thinks we're a threat. What do we do?'

'We give him no reason to doubt our loyalty.' Graelen stood and reached for his breeches. 'Starting with being on time for his speech.'

IMOSHEN WOKE WITH a sense of urgency. Every muscle in her body ached, and she was barely warm. Frayvia lay on one side of her and Iraayel on the other. He wriggled against her, triggering a wave of love for him, but she had the feeling that when she came fully awake she would regret it.

'I'm hungry,' Iraayel said.

She remembered the last time he'd said those words, back in her room after the birth.

Her eyes snapped open. The three of them lay in the belly of a rowboat. It was listing to one side; they must have run aground. Anyone could find them here.

Frayvia jerked awake. 'What is it?'

'Get up.' Imoshen crept to the side of the boat and peered along the beach in both directions. Deserted. Even so... 'We have to hide. Quick, up the beach, behind those rocks.'

Frayvia climbed out and lifted Iraayel onto the hard sand. She took his hand, and they stumbled up the beach towards the outcrop.

Imoshen collected Reoshen, holding the tiny bundle against her body as she headed up the beach. Behind a row of rocks and wind-twisted trees was a marsh. Birds called and circled in the grey winter's dawn.

Frayvia bent double, her hand pressed to her chest. 'I hurt here. Hurt so bad...' She raised pain-filled eyes to Imoshen. 'Am I dying?'

An impossible ache filled Imoshen's chest. She looked down to the bundle in her arms.

Frayvia's mouth opened in a silent gasp, then she dropped to her knees, making a keening sound. Iraayel threw his arms around her.

Imoshen sank to her knees beside Frayvia and Iraayel. Nothing felt real.

After a while, Frayvia caught her breath and lifted her head. She stared at Imoshen. 'I remember there were hundreds of tiny crabs trying to eat me. Am I going mad?'

'That was on the higher plane.'

Horrified, Frayvia shook her head.

'I went looking for Reoshen, took you with me by mistake. I'm sorry.'

Frayvia's lips parted in a silent O.

'I couldn't save him. I failed him.' Imoshen sat with the dead newborn across her lap. Hot tears poured down her cheeks. She didn't know if she could ever get up again.

Iraayel patted her face, weeping with her, trying to soothe her.

Frayvia wrapped her arms around them both and held on. How long they sat there, Imoshen didn't know. After a while, she heard a dog bark. Where there were dogs, there were people. And this was the mainland; they would be Mieren people, hostile to her kind.

She lifted her head, numb but determined. 'We go to the city. We go to...' She'd been going to say *the brotherhood*, but she knew better now. While she fed the newborn yesterday, Reothe – it hurt to think of him – had told her about the armed truce between the brotherhoods and the sisterhoods, and what the all-father had planned to do with their sacrare child.

He had wanted her to absolve him of guilt, and she had. He'd been as much a victim of the all-father's machinations as her. She was glad they'd had their time together, even if there was an open wound inside her where Reothe had belonged, and another where the baby had grown under her heart.

Frayvia pulled back, rubbing her chest. 'It aches...'

'It does,' Imoshen agreed. 'But why do you feel my pain?'

Frayvia's eyes widened, then she hit her forehead with the heel of her hand. 'Of course.'

Iraayel laughed once, bright and clear. 'Silly Fray.'

'Of course what?' Imoshen prompted.

'You dragged me onto the empyrean plane. You have no training, it's a wonder we survived.'

'I've been there before,' Imoshen admitted.

'You never told me.'

'I didn't want to compromise your loyalty, so I didn't tell you about it. At times, the world shifted, and I'd see the other place super-imposed over this one.'

'You're a natural gift-warrior.'

Imoshen caught herself rubbing her chest. Frayvia was doing the same. 'You're doing it again. Feeling what I feel.'

'Because we're linked. Your gift breached my walls. I'm your devotee, tied to your gift for life.'

'Oh, Fray...' Yesterday, Reothe had explained the relationship between Ardeyne and Torekar. How it was frowned upon. 'I'm so sorry. I didn't mean–'

Frayvia shook her head, brushing this aside. 'We'll have to bind your breasts to stop the milk. Are they swollen and sore?'

Imoshen shook her head. 'After I came back to this plane, my skin was hot and I burned with a fever. I kept us warm. Now I feel hollow, like my gift is used up.'

'I'm not surprised.' Frayvia nodded to herself. 'Don't worry. It will come back.'

'It has to, if I am to keep you two safe. We're surrounded by Mieren. We'll go to the sisterhoods.'

Frayvia nodded. 'To the city.'

'Is it far?' Imoshen asked.

'Days and days.'

'Then we had better start walking.' Imoshen came to her feet.

Frayvia took Iraayel's hand.

'We have breakfast now?' he asked.

'Soon,' Frayvia said. She glanced to the dead baby in Imoshen's arms.

'I know. I can't carry him forever. But I have to find somewhere safe to...'

She would find somewhere safe to leave him. And, with him, she would leave her illusions. All her life so far had been a lie. She had been partner to her own delusion. Her weakness had caused Reoshen's death.

From this day forward, she would look on the world with absolute honesty, and use everything in her power to protect those she loved.

Chapter Twenty-Three

'THE CELESTIAL CITY...'

Imoshen had to admit, it was every bit as beautiful as the poets claimed. A city of white stone, domes and spires, reflected in the perfect stillness of the lake.

A bird called. The trees above her were covered in a mist of green buds. It was almost spring cusp. Her stomach rumbled; she could smell the breakfast Frayvia was cooking and hear Iraayel's soft chatter.

Through the last part of winter they'd walked halfway across Chalcedonia, sleeping in barns and stealing food. It was the worst time of year to be travelling. Imoshen had become adept at calming farm dogs, and she'd discovered how hard it was to create an illusion in Mieren minds. She'd been called a *filthy Wyrd* and she'd seen, firsthand, how much the Mieren feared her kind.

Today they walked into the city to claim sanctuary. All they had to do was get through the Mieren town built on the lake's shore and across the causeway.

'There you are.' Frayvia was sharing the pot of oats with Iraayel. 'We saved you some.'

Imoshen sat by the fire and waited her turn. They all ate out of the one pot, and they would leave it behind today. She would be glad to finally eat something other than warm, soggy oats.

Frayvia handed her the pot. 'You can't use your gift once we reach the city. You must keep it tightly reined. To do otherwise will be taken as an insult and a sign of poor control. And you must not cast illusions. Only men have that ability.'

'But –'

Frayvia shook her head.

'But Reothe showed me how he did illusions. It was a game we played.'

'A dangerous game. We must blend in.'

Imoshen nodded. She could sense Frayvia's fear through their link.

'We'll go in early, before the T'En are about,' Frayvia said. 'Their Malaunje servants will be opening businesses in the free quarter, but they will not stop us if we act as though we know what we're doing. All-mother Aayelora leads the oldest and most powerful of the sisterhoods. She can protect us.'

Iraayel looked up. 'We go home now?'

'Yes, we go to our new home now,' Imoshen said.

'VITTORYXE, COME QUICKLY!' It was Egrayne's devotee. She must have completely forgotten herself, or she would have used Vittoryxe's full title in front of her pupils.

'What is it?' the T'En boys asked, wide-eyed with curiosity.

'You will sit here and practice your focusing exercises,' Vittoryxe told them. She gave them all a hard stare, including her new choice-son. Bedutz was not quite five, but she was training him early. She'd made the mistake of letting her last choice-son get too close, and it had almost broken her heart to send him to the brotherhood at winter's cusp.

She would not make the same mistake again.

'Gift-tutor Vittoryxe?' Egrayne's devotee prompted, remembering to use her title this time.

'I'm coming.' Vittoryxe looked around the training chamber. Who should she leave in charge? Arodyti was the most gifted, but she didn't take the exercises seriously enough. 'Kiane, you're in charge while I'm gone.'

The adept bustled over and listened intently as Vittoryxe explained the lessons she had planned for today. Vittoryxe was inclined to think, when she became all-mother, she would name Kiane the next gift-tutor.

Egrayne's devotee shifted her weight from foot to foot, radiating impatience. Vittoryxe delayed deliberately, leaving only when she considered she'd made Roskara pay for forgetting her title.

Outside in the corridor, Roskara could not contain her excitement. 'You'll never guess what's happened!'

'Then you'll have to tell me.'

The sarcasm went straight over Roskara's head. 'A lost sister just walked into the palace asking to see the all-mother.'

'Lost sister? What lost sister?' Vittoryxe ran through the T'En who had gone missing over the last ten to fifteen years. Just last winter they'd lost one of the inner circle, along with her devotee, on the road back to the city. 'Is it old–'

'It's no one we know. She's young. She's come with a Malaunje and her choice-son.'

'If she's from another sisterhood, why did she come to us?'

'I don't know anything more about her. Egrayne sent me to fetch you.'

Vittoryxe swept into the all-mother's greeting chamber to find the rest of the inner circle facing a slight T'En female. Her hair had been shorn in mourning. The stranger did not look old enough to be an initiate, let alone a choice-mother. She was accompanied by a young Malaunje woman and a boy about the same age as Vittoryxe's new choice-son. They stood in filthy clothes that were little more than rags. Vittoryxe could not believe her eyes. How dare they appear before the all-mother of the greatest sisterhood in such a state?

As Vittoryxe took her place beside the sisterhood's hand-of-force, she wished she'd had time to fetch Choris, so her devotee could add to her stature. At least she stood only one remove from the all-mother, the same as Egrayne, who had taken up her position beside Aayelora's voice-of-reason. Of all the sisterhood, only Egrayne presented a real threat to Vittoryxe's ambition.

So she made sure all eyes were on her as she gestured to the bedraggled T'En initiate. 'Who is this, and why did she come to us?'

The all-mother gestured to the stranger. 'Go on.'

The lost sister made the correct obeisance, with a brotherhood flourish. Seeing this, a ripple of unease passed through the inner circle.

'I am Imoshen. This is my devotee, Frayvia.' She reached around, drawing the Malaunje woman to stand at her side. At least the Malaunje knew better and tried to hang back. As though unaware of the insult she'd offered the inner circle, the stranger continued. 'And this is my choice-son, Iraayel. All-mother Aayelora, I come to you to claim sanctuary.'

'You should go to your own all-mother,' Vittoryxe told her, ignoring her ridiculous claim that the Malaunje was her devotee. As a ploy for stature, it was laughable. If this troublemaker had such a powerful gift, she would have lived in the city and Vittoryxe would know her by sight, if not by name. As it was, Vittoryxe could not sense her gift at all; she was clearly weak, as well as a malcontent. 'We cannot interfere with the way your all-mother runs her sisterhood. If you have a complaint, take it to your sisterhood's inner circle.'

The malcontent flushed. 'I have no all-mother. I was raised by a brotherhood.'

'Impossible!' Vittoryxe snapped. 'That would mean an all-father broke the covenant.'

Imoshen – how dare she use that honoured name – nodded.

A hush fell over the inner circle, then...

'Raised by a brotherhood?'

'A T'En girl, born to a T'En man?'

'It's not impossible, just rare. Why, I remember–'

'How dare they hide a T'En girl baby!'

'Which all-father broke the covenant?' the hand-of-force demanded. Everyone fell silent. 'Who dared to break the covenant?'

Imoshen lifted troubled eyes, to the inner circle. 'All-father Rohaayel.'

'But...' The hand-of-force was stunned. 'But he is one of the more reasonable all-fathers.'

'I suppose that's why he thought he could get away it,' the voice-of-reason whispered.

'True,' Egrayne agreed. 'If he dared to do this, and kept her hidden for...' – she gestured to the female – 'How old are you?'

'Seventeen.'

'And you have a choice-son?' Vittoryxe was horrified. 'That should never have been allowed. Choice-mothers must be adepts. They must be carefully selected for–'

'There is something more important at stake, gift-tutor.' Egrayne cut through her tirade.

Vittoryxe fell silent, stomach churning.

'If what Imoshen says is true, and we have no reason to doubt her, then news of Rohaayel's daring will spread throughout the brotherhoods. It makes the all-mother council look weak. He broke the covenant and got away with it.'

'We have his gift-enforced vow. He will pay,' Aayelora insisted. 'I'll send for the all-mothers right now.' She turned to her devotee, who was one step behind her, and whispered instructions.

'We must crush Rohaayel,' Vittoryxe said. 'He must be made an example of before all the brotherhood leaders. We can't appear weak. The only thing the men respect is power. To be weak is to be a victim, and T'En women are *never* victims.'

At her words, the inner circle turned to look at Imoshen. She was a victim. Her bedraggled appearance confirmed it. The girl was a liability – proof that T'En men could contain and suppress women. Raised by a brotherhood, she had been exposed to their gift since birth...

'She's corrupted.' Vittoryxe's mind raced. 'If what she says is true and she's been raised by a covenant-breaking brotherhood, she'll be addicted to the male gift. We should turn her out.'

'We can't turn her out,' Egrayne argued. 'She'd be at the mercy of the men, or the Mieren.'

'Egrayne's right,' the hand-of-force agreed. 'If the men have power over one T'En woman, they have power over all of us.'

'We can't have her amongst us,' Vittoryxe insisted. 'She's corrupted.'

'You can't turn Imoshen out.' The bedraggled Malaunje dared to speak without permission. 'She's a raedan.'

'Raedan?' the all-mother repeated. A raedan would greatly add to their sisterhood's stature. Vittoryxe could hear the ambition in the all-mother's voice. 'The last one died over two hundred years ago.'

Vittoryxe's stomach curdled with jealousy. Then she saw the flaw in this ridiculous claim. 'Rubbish, a raedan would have been able to read her captors' emotions. She would have known the brotherhood was lying to her.'

'I didn't see their deception because I grew up with it. It was normal,' Imoshen said. 'Besides, my raedan gift didn't surface until after I gave birth to the sacrare.'

'You birthed a sacrare?' Vittoryxe wanted to laugh. 'Next you'll be claiming you have more than one gift.' She was so angry her body shook and her gift surged. 'Where is this sacrare?'

'He...' Imoshen's chin trembled as she fought back tears. 'He died.'

'Stillborn, of course.' Vittoryxe was relieved. 'Now, if you had birthed a healthy sacrare–'

'He was perfect.' Imoshen's temper flashed. 'Absolutely perfect. His father and I shared the deep-bonding. When the brotherhood came to kill us, his father gave his life so that we could escape the island, but the boat tipped. I...' She faltered and fell silent.

If the sisterhood accepted Imoshen, Vittoryxe would never be all-mother. She could not compete with a raedan who had birthed a sacrare. She had to destroy Imoshen's credibility.

'You heard her.' The words spilled from Vittoryxe. 'She admits to sharing the deep-bonding with a male. No matter how powerful she is, no matter how useful her raedan gift is... we can never trust her. I am your gift-tutor. Her gift has been polluted. She's not one of us!'

'ONE, TWO, THREE,' Sorne said.

On *three*, Izteben stood up with Sorne's foot in his hand, propelling him straight up the wall. Sorne caught the windowsill and pulled himself up. Lucky for them, the scholar had left his shutters open. Once inside Oskane's chamber, he signalled Izteben, who would watch the courtyard.

In a couple of days it would be spring cusp, and the walls between this plane and the next would grow weak. Before then, King Charald would arrive with a T'En artefact to offer to the gods. The king expected a visitation from the Warrior god: at the very least a flash of blinding light, at best a vision to guide him.

King Charald had been fighting wars since he was fifteen. He was belligerent, paranoid and deeply religious. Sorne intended to prove to the king that he had been wrong to discard his half-blood son. To do this, he needed to know which southern kingdom the king feared most. He needed to read the agents' latest reports and catch up on Oskane's plans for him and Izteben.

Chalcedonia's neighbouring kingdoms were constantly on the verge of war. They clustered around the Secluded Sea like piglets around a sow's belly. To the east, a huge semi-circle of mountains protected the kingdoms from invasion, which meant they concentrated all their enmity on each other.

Any sign of weakness in a neighbouring kingdom was an invitation to strike. The royal families had intermarried so many times that any of the kings could prove a claim to rule another.

Two kingdoms had the advantage of natural defences. Mountains protected Chalcedonia from the other five kingdoms on the mainland, and Ivernia was an island – actually, two islands – to the west.

The rulers of the other kingdoms resented King Charald, and were waiting for him to die. At forty-four, he did not have many years left in him. His only son would be thirteen soon, and the kingdoms with suitable brides were vying to offer a marriage alliance.

Any one of the six kingdoms could build a fleet and sail their army across the Secluded Sea to attack Chalcedonia. All Sorne had to do was pick the kingdom the king most feared and King Charald's wrath would descend upon them. The thought was electrifying.

He found what he was looking for in a message from his uncle, Matxin. A moment later, a mountain hawk called twice, then called again once more.

Sorne swung his legs over the sill and dropped to the ground.

Izteben steadied him. 'The king is coming!'

They ran to the wall. Far below, on the steep switch-back road, a party of horsemen plodded uphill, followed by the familiar cart from Enlightenment Abbey.

'So, did you find anything useful?' Izteben asked.

'Baron Matxin writes that the ruler of Khitan would happily see King Charald dead. He offered Matxin an alliance and mercenaries to take the throne from Charald.'

'From the king? But he's the king!'

'Matxin's claim to the Chalcedonian throne is almost as good as Charald's. That's why Charald's first wife was

Matxin's sister,' Sorne explained. It was on the tip of his tongue to add that Queen Sorna had been his mother, but he lost his nerve.

'So you'll tell King Charald it was Khitan he conquered in your vision?' Izteben asked.

'I'll take my cues from the king and Oskane.'

'The king... here!' Izteben gave a shiver of excitement. Then he gestured to Sorne's hair. 'Every time I see that white streak in your hair...'

Sorne reached around to the back of his head. The streak grew from the place where he'd hit his head when they went down the mine.

'What if the T'En artefact doesn't appease the god?' Izteben asked. While Izteben accepted that the thing they'd seen in the mine was one of the Seven, he refused to believe Sorne had had a vision. As he put it, Sorne was the brother he'd known all his life. Something as marvellous as a vision could not happen to him.

'The she-Wyrd says the... gods' – *beasts* was what she'd said – 'are always hungry for T'En or Malaunje blood. So we have to be very careful. I'll keep well back and throw the artefact towards it.'

'And then you'll have your vision. It needs to be a useful vision for us. How does sending the king across the Secluded Sea to wage a war undermine Baron Nitzel?'

'The king takes the army, leaving Nitzel as regent. Cedon won't be fifteen for another two years. Oskane returns to the court. Next thing you know, Nitzel catches a chill and dies.'

'Murder?' Izteben baulked.

'Nitzel poisoned Oskane's nephew.' *And my mother.* Every chance he missed to say it made it harder.

'What is it, boys?' Franto called from the courtyard. Izteben's brother was with him again. Since Zabier's return, Oskane's assistant had been training him. Sorne suspected the True-men were trying to separate Zabier from them. Or maybe they saw his potential, and were giving him a chance of a higher station in life, one that did not include living with half-bloods.

'King Charald is coming,' Izteben called.

Zabier and Franto headed for the steps, where the boy easily outdistanced the old man.

Zabier leant over the wall-walk. 'There's twenty riders and a closed cart.'

Franto puffed as he reached the wall-walk and leant over to have a look. 'Hmm, even with the cart in tow, the king rides. If he can spend all day in the saddle, he's doing well for a man of forty-four. Come along, boys. We'll get you cleaned up.' He nudged Zabier. 'Let Hiruna know the king is arriving.'

Sorne looked up to see Scholar Oskane watching them from his study. Surely now the scholar would reveal his true identity? With his royal father at the gate, how could he not?

Chapter Twenty-Four

OSKANE HEARD THE excited shouts. The king's arrival must be imminent. A mixture of satisfaction and trepidation filled him; the moment had arrived. Sorne's ability to seek out the Seven made all the years of scourging and disciplined study worthwhile.

Oskane went to the window of his office. 'Franto, prepare to welcome the king,' he called. 'Send Sorne up here.'

The season's delay had been well-spent. He'd ordered material: serviceable cotton for the servants, good brocade for himself and plain black for the two holy warriors.

Going into his private chamber, Oskane stripped. Then he opened the chest, dressing in his new white breeches and a calf-length undershirt. He draped the brocade robe over his shoulders, and settled the stiff cap on his head. Immediately, he stood taller. Strange how clothes made a man feel the part.

'Scholar Oskane?' Sorne spoke from the study.

'In here.' Oskane unpacked the two sets of breeches and thigh-length shirts. 'Put yours on. Braid your hair and wear this cap.' It was an acolyte's cap and would hide his hair colour, but he could do nothing about the Wyrd eyes and extra fingers. 'There's a set for Izteben as well.'

Sorne did as he was told, tying the cap under his chin. Oskane tried to look at him as if for the first time, but he knew the youth too well. 'Before you go, I have something important to tell you.'

Sorne raised his face to Oskane, mulberry eyes glistening with excitement.

'You are not the son of a carpenter. You are King Charald's half-blood son,' Oskane said, then waited for Sorne to react.

The youth nodded. 'The Warrior told me.'

'What?' Oskane's knees went weak and he sat on the bed. 'You knew? Why didn't you say something?'

Sorne shrugged. 'The Warrior showed me a silver neck band.' He held up his hands. 'About so big, with a blue stone in the centre. He said it would be given to me when the time was right.'

'And so it shall.' Oskane went to the chest, found Sorna's torc and unwrapped it.

'That's it,' Sorne said, as if pleased to be proven right.

'Wear it,' Oskane told him. 'It was your real mother's. You've heard me mention Baron Nitzel?'

Sorne nodded, concentrating on trying to do the catch behind his neck.

'Turn around.' Oskane fastened the torc, then turned the youth around to face him. Sorne was half a head taller; easily as tall as his father. 'This will be hard to hear, lad. Your mother was murdered by Baron Nitzel. He–'

The gate opened, horses entered, hooves clomping on the paving. Men called for the stable boys.

Oskane had meant to say more, but he'd run out of time. 'Tomorrow evening, we will go down the mine. The vision you have there will decide our futures. If we are to take revenge on the man who killed your mother, we must go back to court, and to do that, we must impress King Charald. Do you understand me? Nothing can go wrong.'

Sorne nodded and picked up Izteben's clothes.

'Very well.' Oskane escorted him out of the bedroom.

And there was the carpenter's son. From his stunned expression, he'd overheard everything. His gaze went to the torc around Sorne's neck, visible evidence of the gulf between them.

'Get dressed,' Oskane said, but neither half-blood moved.

Oskane took the clothes from Sorne's unresisting hands. Izteben accepted them automatically. 'Go get dressed.'

The deep voices of King Charald and his men echoed up from the courtyard.

Izteben turned on his heel and left.

Sorne would have followed, but Oskane caught his arm.

'Let him go. You are about to start a new stage of your life. Time to leave the past behind. Come, the king is waiting.'

And he led Sorne down the stairs, going as fast as his bad knees allowed.

As they stepped out into the sunshine, Oskane looked across to see around twenty men unloading their saddle bags. About a dozen were men-at-arms, the rest influential barons, no doubt warned by Nitzel to beware of trickery.

But this time, Nitzel would be the one who backed down.

The biggest of the True-men turned around. Seventeen years... Charald had aged well.

'Oska!' The king strode towards him, grinning. His smiles had always been charming; it was his temper you had to watch. 'When did you get so old and ugly?'

'My king.' Tears stung his eyes and he blinked them away. 'You look as fit as ever.'

Charald laughed and pulled him into a hug.

As the king drew back, he looked past Oskane to Sorne.

'That's him?' Charald whispered. 'The Warrior's voice?'

Oskane glanced over his shoulder and saw the half-blood hastily lower his eyes, as he'd been taught. 'Sorne, this is–'

'...the half-blood you've been training all these years?' a familiar, hated voice asked.

Oskane turned to see Baron Nitzel approaching.

But this time, Oskane had the upperhand. He smiled, relishing the chance to confront his old rival.

'Prince Cedon, come along.' Nitzel beckoned a skinny youth with pale hair and equally pale eyes. The king's heir was shorter than Zabier and slighter of build. He swaggered over, draped in finery even more ornate than the king's.

Oskane felt Sorne stiffen beside him; he should have warned him the prince might come.

'So this is the half-blood who has visions from the Seven,' Nitzel said, mocking laughter in his eyes. Clearly, he thought Oskane had hoodwinked the king.

'The Warrior has spoken,' Oskane said with dignity. 'As you will see–'

'Oh, we will see, all right.' Nitzel's gaze rested on Sorne for a moment. 'We will all see how things really are.'

'Enough, Nitzel,' the king growled. 'So this is Restoration Retreat.' Charald spotted Hiruna with Izteben beside her and Valendia in her arms, watching from the open stable door. 'What's this? I didn't expect an entire nest of half-bloods.'

'Strange company you keep,' Nitzel said.

Oskane flushed. 'Someone had to look after the boy's needs.'

'Who is this half-blood, Father? And why is he dressed like a dark priest?' Cedon seemed tired as he joined the king. Next to Charald, it was clear Cedon took after Nitzel – small and slight, with none of the energy that drew every eye to the king. In his over-elaborate clothing, he seemed ridiculous. He looked Sorne up and down, then dismissed him. 'You promised me a vision of the future, Father.'

'And you shall have one. Tomorrow.' Charald put his arm around the prince, who fitted neatly under his shoulder. 'But right now we will see an illustration of the first vision. Come, Oskane, show us the drawing.'

The scholar led Nitzel, Cedon and the king up the steps.

As Sorne followed them, he was aware of his choice-family watching from the far side of the courtyard, separated from him by the king's powerful barons and their men-at-arms. He might be Malaunje, but he wasn't an outcast. Oskane needed him to win over the king and defeat Nitzel.

'So this is the vision?' Charald was saying, when Sorne entered Oskane's study. The scholar had pinned the drawing to the wall.

Charald, Nitzel, Oskane and Sorne's half-brother – the skinny, pompous little runt – crowded around to inspect the drawing.

'That's definitely me,' Charald said. 'There's my scar.'

'He wears a helmet with cheek-guards.' Nitzel pointed out. 'Almost the only thing we can clearly see is his scarred chin.'

'The Warrior sent this vision, so that the half-blood could be his voice,' Oskane stated. 'He sent it in a flash of power that stunned the half-blood, and when he woke up, this is what he'd seen.'

'You saw this flash of power, too?' Nitzel asked.

'Yes, as you will see for yourselves, tomorrow night when the Warrior returns.'

'*If* the Warrior returns,' Nitzel countered.

Charald laughed. 'It's been seventeen years, yet you two still bicker like old women.' He tapped his finger on the drawing. 'It's definitely a port. Do you recognise it, Nitzel?'

'It could be any number of ports along the Secluded Sea.'

'You say my men were cheering?' Charald asked. But he asked Oskane, not Sorne. No one had so much as glanced in Sorne's direction since he entered the room.

'They cheered in triumph, my king,' Oskane confirmed. 'They cheered you, while the port and the harbour burned.'

Charald rubbed the scar on his chin. 'I wish I knew which kingdom–'

'It's not much of a drawing,' Cedon sneered. 'In the palace, the paintings look so real, you could walk into them.'

Sorne bristled.

'This is a simple ink illustration, my prince. It was not drawn by a trained artist,' Oskane said.

'What, the half-blood drew it?' Nitzel asked.

I'm right here. But Sorne did not speak.

'The Warrior's-voice,' Oskane said, applying enough emphasis to make it a title.

'How do you know the half-blood didn't draw something he'd already seen?' Nitzel continued.

Oskane stiffened. 'He has never left this retreat.'

'You could have described it to him.'

'Enough.' The king sounded bored. 'We'll know tomorrow evening, one way or the other.' He turned to Oskane. 'I could do with some wine, and bread and cheese, to hold me until dinner.'

'This way.'

Oskane led them past Sorne without acknowledging him.

Not one of them looked at him. Not even Cedon, who only came up to his chin. Sorne's top lip curled in contempt. If Nitzel was anything to go by, Cedon would not grow any bigger. Not that it mattered; his opinion of himself was big enough.

Sorne waited until they had entered the dining room, then went down the stairs and across the empty courtyard to the stable.

The travellers' horses filled all the available stalls. He and Izteben would be sleeping in the hayloft. He could smell Hiruna's delicious potato and leek soup but, when he entered the kitchen, he saw that it was Izteben serving up yesterday's soup and bread to Valendia.

'Where's...' Even as he asked, Sorne knew. Hiruna and Zabier would be serving the visitors' food. Franto had taught her to make some fancy dishes for this occasion.

Silently, Izteben put a bowl on the table in front of Sorne.

Izteben sat opposite, mulberry eyes stormy in the candle light. 'I can't believe you've known all along.'

'I didn't. I found out the day we went down the mine but, with everything that happened...' he shrugged.

'So you've been laughing at me all this time? Slumming it with the wood-worker's son!'

'Izteben...'

'Izteben...' Valendia echoed. She looked from him to Sorne and her bottom lip trembled.

Sorne pulled her onto his lap and pretended to eat her dinner. She protested and took the spoon, feeding herself.

He looked up to Izteben, who gave him a reluctant smile.

'I always wondered why Oskane was so hard on you,' he said. 'It never seemed fair.'

'I don't think much of life is fair. I think the deck has been stacked against us half-bloods, and we have to make our own luck.' Sorne felt his face grow hot. 'I was there as they looked at the drawing of my vision. Not one of them spoke to me. It was like I didn't exist.'

'If you're the king's eldest son, Nitzel must wish you didn't exist.'

'A half-blood? I'm no threat.' Sorne dipped his bread in the soup. Plain fare but hearty, unlike what would be served in the dining room tonight. 'They're trying to come between us and Zabier. Oskane and Franto, I mean.'

'I know.'

'They're grooming him to serve the church.'

Izteben shrugged. 'What does it matter? We won't be staying here. Oskane will be powerful again and Zabier will be coming with us. He could have stayed in the village with father's brother, but he chose to come back, so now he has to make his way in the world. According to Oskane, the church is powerful and independent of the king.'

Izteben stood and made up a plate of food for the she-Wyrd. 'Do you want to go, or...'

'I'll go.' Sorne slid off the seat, setting Valendia in his place.

He crossed the courtyard under the maple tree. Through the windows he could see the king and his barons eating and drinking, while Hiruna and Zabier ran about, bringing more wine and taking away plates.

Watching the high table, Sorne felt sick with jealousy. He should have been there. He was the king's son, and Oskane's relative by blood.

Instead, he went down the dark steps to the cellars.

The she-Wyrd was waiting for him at the bars of her cell. 'So the king is dancing to the priest's tune now?'

He slid the tray under her door.

'Do you have my button?'

'I didn't get a chance to make the swap. Besides, I think the gift residue is fading.'

'Depends how the artefact is kept.' She pulled the tray closer and dipped the bread in the soup. 'A lead-lined chest will keep it fresh for years. Silver's good at absorbing power.'

He watched her eat, meticulous, tidy. How could she bear being imprisoned?

She looked up. 'So, you're going to perform for this True-man king, summon a god and have a vision?'

'I'm going to be powerful.' He leaned one shoulder against the wall, arms folded across his chest. 'I'm never going to be a prisoner.'

'You've been a prisoner since the day you were born.'

'We've been through this before. Am I a prisoner if I know they're lying to me? Who imprisons who, if I use the lies for my own ends?'

A chair scraped overhead and a man shouted something, followed by rowdy laughter; the she-Wyrd flinched.

'Are you done?'

She slid the tray towards him. As he reached under the bars, she caught his hand. 'Find the key. Let me out tonight.'

He broke free, annoyed at himself for letting her touch him. 'I can't. They'd know who did it.'

'Free me tonight and I'll take you, your brother and your sister to the T'En. These True-men are using you.'

He turned to go.

'It isn't safe,' she called after him. 'Don't risk your life for nothing.'

But it wasn't nothing. It was a chance to win the king's trust and respect; it was a chance to impress his father.

Chapter Twenty-Five

'FINALLY, SOME FOOD,' Imoshen said, as several Malaunje entered bearing trays. The day seemed to have gone on forever. She was tired, weary beyond belief and worried. The longer the all-mothers debated, the less likely it seemed that they would offer sanctuary.

The Malaunje placed the food on the low table. When Imoshen thanked them, they gave her an odd look and backed out.

'I don't think I was supposed to thank them,' Imoshen said, as she prodded some pretty tarts. She nibbled one before deciding it was safe to give to Iraayel.

'In the brotherhood, the T'En rarely thanked the Malaunje. It was as if we were invisible,' Frayvia said. 'I think they're just curious about you. Everyone will have heard by now. Even the brotherhoods.'

'I thought there was a state of armed truce between the males and females.'

'There is, but the Malaunje mingle. Things are overheard at festivals and ceremonies. And in the free quarter, there are sisterhood shops just around the corner from brotherhood businesses. Messages are passed.'

Imoshen could hardly eat, but she made sure Iraayel had a good meal. They were used to going to bed with the sun, and Iraayel was tired, so they curled up in front of the fire and sang him to sleep.

'Do you think the all-mother council is finished yet?' Imoshen whispered. 'That gift-tutor doesn't like me. She's afraid of me, and I don't know why.'

'You mustn't use your raedan gift on her. If you do and she senses it, she could challenge you to a duel.'

'They duel?'

Frayvia nodded. 'If one T'En insults another's stature, the one who was insulted will challenge the other to a duel.'

'What kind of duel?'

'Either on the empyrean plane or on this plane. You've no gift training and you've never been taught to defend yourself with long-knives. You mustn't do anything to insult the gift-tutor, or anyone else, for that matter. Promise me?'

'I wouldn't set out to insult anyone. But how do I know what they'll find insulting? Even you don't know how they do things in the sisterhoods. I'll keep my head down and observe them.'

More time passed and no one sent for them. Warmed by the fire, Imoshen fought sleep. 'Do you think All-mother Aayelora will give us sanctuary?'

'Not if the gift-tutor has anything to say about it.'

Imoshen hugged Frayvia. 'I'm so glad I didn't lose you.'

'I beg your pardon. The all-mother...'

They came out of the embrace to find a Malaunje behind them. He looked away as though embarrassed.

Frayvia shrugged off Imoshen's arm, whispering, 'We must maintain proper distance.'

Imoshen wanted to argue, but she came to her feet. 'My apologies. You were saying?'

'You have been summoned to the all-mother council.'

Imoshen swallowed and glanced to Frayvia. 'Stay with Iraayel. He'll be frightened if he wakes and I'm not here. Hopefully, I'll be back soon with good news.'

The council chamber was so beautiful it stole her breath. A row of arched windows looked out onto a terraced garden, where lights flickered in fanciful topiary trees.

Inside the long chamber, scented candles and mirrors lit the assembled women. At a quick count, there were around thirty of them, all beautifully dressed in silks and brocades. Gleaming stones flashed when they gestured. Their hair was piled in elaborate styles, fixed with jewelled combs.

With so many powerful gifted women present, the room was filled with tension: Imoshen's own gift stirred. Focusing, she forced down her power, just as she had been doing ever since they arrived in the city.

'So many all-mothers—'

'There are six sisterhoods. The all-mothers have come with their seconds,' Egrayne told her, 'and their gift-tutors, since the matters under discussion included your addiction to the male gift. Some brought their sisterhood historians, too.'

Imoshen didn't like being described as an addict, but she kept quiet. She looked up at the tall T'En. 'I remember you from Aayelora's inner circle. You aren't the gift-tutor, or her voice-of-reason, or hand-of-force. Are you a historian?'

'No. I'm the T'Enatuath's empowerer.'

'I don't know what that means.'

'It means I can reach into a child of thirteen or fourteen and identify their gift and help focus it, so that they can begin studying right away, instead of wasting years while they try to work out what kind of gift they have. You say you are a raedan?'

'That's what Reothe and Frayvia said.'

'Then be prepared, they may ask me to confirm it. Or they may ask you to prove it.'

'Imoshen of no sisterhood, step forward,' Gift-tutor Vittoryxe said.

Imoshen walked across the marble floor, all too aware of the ragged state of her clothes.

The women whispered and pointed, and she could feel them judging her, feel their gifts battering against her defences.

'Stand here,' Egrayne said, before stepping behind her.

Imoshen faced the gathering of powerful all-mothers and their sisters. These were the women Rohaayel had planned to defeat, using her sacrare son. She had to impress them enough to offer her sanctuary, but not so much that they found her dangerous.

'Your presence here means the covenant that has stood for four hundred years has been broken,' All-mother Aayelora said. 'You come asking for sanctuary. You come after escaping brotherhood warriors sent to kill you. You come claiming to be a raedan. You come claiming to have birthed a healthy sacrare. Do you deny any of this?'

Imoshen shook her head, then in the interests of honesty, she added. 'I don't claim the last two things. Others described me as a raedan. And I had a sacrare boy – that is a fact. I had him for less than a day, but he was p–perfect.' Tears blurred her vision.

The women whispered. Imoshen blinked and studied their faces. The instinct to draw on her gift was overpowering. Her gift rose and she saw fear, disbelief and jealousy. Mostly, she saw fear. Fear of change, she guessed.

'No respect...'

'What do you expect of a brotherhood-raised...'

'She has no idea.'

In one woman's face she saw sympathy, and Imoshen held her eyes as she spoke in her own defence. 'I've done nothing wrong. The wrong was done to me.'

'It doesn't matter,' Gift-tutor Vittoryxe said. 'She–'

Aayelora held up her hand for silence. 'We have our doubts about you, Imoshen. Not that you were wronged, but that it would be safe to take you into our sisterhoods. We cannot turn you out, but we do not know if we can accept you.'

Imoshen blinked. Was the all-mother saying they would rather kill her than let her go? Her gift leapt to defend her. A rush of power made her heart race and skin itch. She heard Egrayne's soft intake of breath behind her.

'Is she truly a raedan?' one of the women asked. 'Have the T'Enatuath's empowerer test her claim.'

Was her raedan gift the only thing that stood between her and execution?

Imoshen felt Egrayne approach her from behind. 'Do you agree to this?'

'What choice do I have?'

'Then kneel and lower your defences.'

Imoshen knelt. The only person she had ever lowered her defences for was Reothe, and she struggled to do it now, with so many hostile women judging her. Egrayne placed large, warm hands on her neck. Fingers slipped up her cheeks to her temples. The gathering looked on in silence.

Imoshen felt trapped.

'Drop your walls,' Egrayne urged.

'I can't.'

Egrayne raised her voice. 'Her shields are too powerful. She must prove her raedan ability by reading some of us.'

Imoshen's knees felt weak as she tried to stand. Egrayne hauled her to her feet.

'That's no test,' Gift-tutor Vittoryxe said. 'I could guess how we are all feeling. Worried, angry–'

'Frightened of change,' Imoshen said. It was so much easier not to fight her instincts. She saw Vittoryxe flinch. 'Why do you feel guilty? I don't understand.'

'I don't. That's nonsense.'

She was lying. Imoshen searched the faces of the sisterhoods' most powerful T'En women and came back to the one who felt sympathy for her. This sister wanted to...

'Heal me. You think I have been injured by the brotherhood, and you want to heal me.'

'It's true,' she acknowledged. She smiled. There was no fear in her, which was refreshing.

'Imoshen could have heard that Reoden is a healer,' Vittoryxe argued.

'Is she? That makes sense,' Imoshen said to herself.

Her gaze settled on All-mother Aayelora. Like the others, she was worried, but also determined to make the right decision. Beneath this there was a bone-deep sadness that

Imoshen recognised, because the same sadness was inside her. But there was also a curious sense of shame.

'What is it? What do you see in our all-mother?' Egrayne asked, from just behind her.

'It makes no sense,' Imoshen said. 'A sadness walks alongside her. I thought it meant she had lost a child, like I have. But there is also shame, as if she did something wrong–'

The sisters gasped.

'She could have heard about the geldr,' Vittoryxe said.

Imoshen looked over her shoulder to Egrayne. 'What's a geldr?'

'She's a raedan,' Egrayne announced. 'There can be no doubt.'

'Then she is useful to us,' Healer Reoden said. 'Too useful to waste.'

'But how do we know we can trust her?' a sister asked.

'She must prove her loyalty,' another insisted.

'We must call the brotherhood leaders to account. Call an all-council. The all-father who broke the covenant must be punished.'

'That's how she must prove her loyalty,' Vittoryxe said, and all Imoshen could read from her was a vicious triumph. The gift-tutor wanted her to fail. 'Imoshen must be the one to punish him.'

'Me?' She took a step back. Kill her own father? 'But–'

'You say the wrong was done to you. You must administer the punishment. You must prove your loyalty,' Vittoryxe said. 'You kill him. Or we execute you, your devotee and your choice-son.'

Imoshen reeled. So much vitriol. She found it hard to think. 'Does Gift-tutor Vittoryxe speak for the all-mothers?'

There was whispering and All-mother Aayelora received several nods.

'In this case, yes,' Aayelora said. 'You must prove your loyalty by executing Rohaayel the Covenant-breaker.'

'Well?' Vittoryxe prodded. 'Can you do this?'

Imoshen had to keep her family safe, no matter what. She lifted her head. 'I can do it.'

Chapter Twenty-Six

THEY BATHED AND dressed her in fine silks, painted her face, pinned jewels in her hair, and dabbed scent behind her ears and between her breasts. All the while, she felt as if she was being prepared as a sacrifice.

The sisterhood leaders were using her. If she failed to kill the covenant-breaking all-father, they would punish those she loved. She had been used by her brotherhood, and now the sisters were using her.

The all-mother's devotee regarded her critically. 'There, you look presentable.'

'Thank you, Narisa.'

'You haven't even looked at yourself yet.'

Imoshen took a deep breath. Until she came here, she had only ever caught glimpses of herself in a window, or reflected in water. Last night when she looked in a real polished mirror it was almost too painful to bear. Her gift stripped her of all illusion. She saw failure, wilful blindness, and the naive trust that led to her infant son's death...

Now she looked at her reflection and tried to contain her gift. But try as she might, she could only catch a glimpse of the line of her chin, the arch of one eyebrow and the way the jewels lay at the base of her throat, before she had to look away to Egrayne behind her.

'Lovely, thank you. I'd like to see Frayvia and Iraayel, in case...'

'Of course.' Egrayne led her down a passage to a terrace. 'They're in the hot-house.'

Imoshen found the two people she loved most in the world picking flowers on the terrace. When she stepped inside the hot-house, the air smelled fecund and rich.

'Iraayel.'

He ran to her, and she dropped to her knees for a hug. Holding him hurt, because Reoshen was missing, but it only made her hold on tighter.

He pulled back. 'You smell sweet, like the flowers.'

She kissed his forehead. Had Irian ever been a dear little boy like this, once? She mustn't think of him, or of Ardeyne and Rohaayel. Mustn't think of them as anything but the covenant-breaking all-father and his seconds, men she must kill if she wanted sanctuary for her family.

After all, they had used her and lied to her.

Coming to her feet, she took Frayvia in her arms and kissed both her cheeks, then her lips. 'Don't cry.'

'It's not fair. How can they make you do this?'

'The *how* is easy. They hold you and Iraayel hostage. The *why* of it's the thing. That gift-tutor set out to destroy me, using the sisterhood leaders and their fear of the T'En males. But...' – Imoshen shrugged – 'it would probably have come to this anyway.' She held Frayvia's eyes. 'If I die...'

Frayvia tried to pull away.

'No, listen. If I die attempting this, I don't want you to die. Is there some way we can sever our link?'

Frayvia shook her head. 'I don't think so. The T'En devotee bond is supposed to be for life. A T'En might survive their devotee's death, but–'

'I need you to live to watch over Iraayel.'

'Time to go, Imoshen,' Egrayne called.

'Promise me?'

Frayvia nodded.

Imoshen leant down to Iraayel. 'Be good for Fray.'

He smiled. 'I'm always good.' And he pulled a flower out from behind his back. 'A pretty flower for a pretty lady.'

Imoshen took it, tears stinging her eyes. Her gift rode just below the surface of her skin, enhancing emotions and scents. She tucked the flower in the shoulder strap of her bodice, where she could smell it with each breath.

Then she left them.

Egrayne saw the flower. 'Gardenia.'

'Is that what it is? We grew marigolds amongst the vegetables to keep away the pests.' Imoshen sensed Egrayne's discomfort and made a note not to talk about her past.

If she survived.

Ahead, she could see Vittoryxe and two gift-warriors waiting for her at the terrace doors. She stopped. 'Will they kill Frayvia and Iraayel, if I fail?'

'Your devotee will die with you. The boy...' Egrayne hesitated. 'They'll kill him.'

Imoshen studied the tall gift-empowerer. 'You lie to me so that I will fight for my life, to save him. Why do you care if I live or die?'

Egrayne blinked, and then a slow smile made her face come alive. 'I forget you're a raedan...' – her eyes narrowed – 'who just used her gift on me without my permission. I could challenge you to a duel for that.'

Imoshen laughed. 'I have enough challenges without making an enemy of you. I already have an enemy in the gift-tutor.'

Egrayne did not deny this. She shook her head. 'I must admit, I don't understand you, Imoshen.'

'Then we are even.' Imoshen discovered she liked Egrayne. 'I don't understand why T'En women fear the men.'

'Because they seek to destroy us.'

'Because you fear them. It's a circular argument, don't you see?'

'Don't listen to her, Egrayne,' Vittoryxe warned as she strode towards them, radiating determination. 'I'll take over from here.'

'You're not coming?' Imoshen asked Egrayne.

The tall gift-empowerer shook her head and Imoshen sensed her withdrawing; she didn't like the gift-tutor either.

'The all-council is only attended by the leaders of the brotherhoods and sisterhoods.' Vittoryxe was dismissive. 'Come along now.'

'I think Egrayne should come, too,' Imoshen protested. Vittoryxe stiffened. 'After all, she is the T'Enatuath's gift-empowerer, she can vouch for my gift.' Imoshen caught a glimmer of amusement in Egrayne's dark eyes.

'You're right,' Vittoryxe said, as if the words tasted bad on her tongue. 'The more members of our all-mother's inner circle attend the council, the more it raises her stature.'

By the time they reached the doors, Vittoryxe had started lecturing her.

'The male gift is the problem, Imoshen. Until they are thirteen or fourteen, they are not much different from us. Then it floods their minds, making them irrational and prone to violence. One male is not so bad, but in a group...' She shook her head. 'Their gifts trigger each other, rising in a spiral of aggression. It clouds their minds. They cannot be trusted. Certainly not with precious T'En children. That's why the covenant exists.'

Imoshen bit her tongue. As Reothe had explained it, Rohaayel wanted the brotherhoods to reclaim their boy children. She didn't know what to believe any more, but she clung to one fact: her father had planned to kill her and steal her child.

She had to protect Frayvia and Iraayel. She must not falter.

Time seemed to behave strangely as her gift surged. One moment they were in the sisterhood quarter, meeting up with the other five all-mothers and their seconds, walking along avenues bathed in afternoon sun. Then they were through the gate and on the wide road that ran down to the causeway. Then they were approaching an elegant domed building.

Inside, it was huge. The dome soared, seeming to float above the windows encircling its base. Mosaics of great events were edged with thousands of tiny gold tiles, glittering in the morning sun.

In the centre was an empty marble floor, surrounded by rising tiers of seats. One side was filled with all-fathers and their seconds. The men outnumbered the women and, for the first time, Imoshen felt that frisson of fear that all the female T'En must feel when confronted by the sheer physicality of the males.

They wore neck torcs denoting their stature and their brotherhood affiliations, and went bare-chested, the better to show off duelling scars. Pleated breeches rode low on their hips, with wide, jewelled belts.

Even from this side of the dome, she could feel the force of the men's combined gifts. It promised violence and left a bad taste on her tongue. This wasn't an aspect of male gift she was used to, and she stepped back, her own power rising in response.

She had to remind herself that Reothe's gift had never felt like this. A challenge, yes, but never a threat. In fact, she had never felt threatened by her father and her uncles, either. Yet they had betrayed her.

No time for emotion. Focus.

Behind her, the seats filled as the all-mothers and their seconds filed in. They were as richly dressed as the men and just as nervous, their gifts primed for use.

'Stand here,' Vittoryxe told Imoshen, before stepping back, just behind her.

Imoshen glanced over her other shoulder to find Egrayne leaning on the waist-high balustrade. The empowerer gave her a reassuring nod. Imoshen had thought she'd requested Egrayne's presence to bring Vittoryxe down a peg, but now she understood she needed a friendly face.

Searching the women, she found another friendly face, Healer Reoden who, she now knew, was the all-mother of a great sisterhood.

The sisterhood leaders whispered, silver-haired heads inclined, jewelled combs catching the light. One by one, they fell silent and looked past her. Imoshen turned to see the silhouettes of broad-shouldered men as they entered the corridor on the far side of the dome.

When they stepped into the light, she counted seven T'En men, none of whom she recognised. They parted to reveal Rohaayel wearing only breeches, no torc of office. She winced; it hurt her to see him like this. She still loved him, which made his betrayal all the worse.

Where were Irian and Ardeyne?

Dead. Only death would keep them from their all-father's side. Loyal Irian, clever Ardeyne...

The high-ranking males shifted in their seats, muttering. Imoshen felt their gifts rise and sensed their anger, fuelled by fear. Her gift surged as she read them. Rohaayel was one of their own. He might have been a rival, but he was still an all-father. He had done what they had not dared to do, and now he was going to pay.

Vittoryxe stepped forward to stand beside her, unrolling a scroll and clearing her throat. 'You have heard the rumours. The all-mothers have called this all-council to determine the truth and punish the transgressors. Standing beside me is Imoshen the Raedan, who came to All-mother Aayelora seeking sanctuary. She was stolen and imprisoned by Rohaayel the Covenant-breaker.'

Vittoryxe rolled up the scroll and stepped back, and Imoshen felt the gift-tutor's satisfaction.

All-mother Aayelora descended the steps. 'Imoshen, is this the all-father who broke the covenant and kept you captive for seventeen years?'

Imoshen went to answer, but one of the men who had escorted Rohaayel spoke up.

'He was the all-father of our brotherhood until yesterday, when we received the all-mothers' summons and learned how he broke the covenant. He admitted guilt and stepped down. I am the new all-father. We knew nothing of his plans. He was working alone with his two seconds, who are dead. We deliver him for punishment.'

'Does he speak the truth?' Aayelora asked.

Imoshen hesitated. None of these men were familiar. What had happened to the old inner circle?

'Imoshen?' the all-mother prompted. 'Did they know their all-father had broken the covenant?'

'I don't recognise them.'

'If you are the brotherhood's new all-father, step forward, give your covenant vow and be acknowledged by the sisterhoods,' All-mother Aayelora said.

He crossed the dome's floor then knelt.

Aayelora touched his forehead with the little finger of her left hand. As she gathered her gift, Imoshen felt the men's gifts respond as if to a threat.

'Four hundred years ago, the all-father of your brotherhood gave his vow to the all-mother of our sisterhood. Now you renew this vow. Drop your defences,' Aayelora commanded.

The rest of all-fathers looked away, and Imoshen sensed their anger and disgust. She could feel the power of Aayelora's gift as she breached the new all-father's defences.

Imoshen felt someone watching her, and met Rohaayel's gaze.

This is why I kept you, he seemed to be saying, *to free us from this slavery. This demeans us all, male and female.*

It was true, but she hardened her heart against him. She must not fail Iraayel and Frayvia.

Aayelora released the new all-father. He swayed on his knees and his inner circle helped him to his seat.

'I would speak,' Rohaayel said.

'Why?' Aayelora bristled. 'Imoshen is living proof of your guilt.'

'It's true that I broke the covenant, but I believe–'

'There can be no excuse!' Vittoryxe shouted him down.

'She's right,' another woman said. 'Pronounce sentence, Aayelora.'

'Make an example of him.'

Driven by anger and fear, the women's gifts gathered. Imoshen inhaled sharply; her nostrils stung with the rush of power.

The all-fathers and their seconds did not respond. They sat in icy, determined silence. This struck Imoshen as odd. Surely, they would protest the execution of a fellow all-father.

'Imoshen?' Rohaayel reached out to her.

'Prove your loyalty. Kill him, or die trying.' Vittoryxe shoved her in the small of the back.

Imoshen staggered forward, off balance. Her hands landed on Rohaayel's bare chest. The shock of his gift made hers rise in response. Instinctively, she segued to the empyrean plane, taking him with her.

To Lighthouse Isle.

But this wasn't her home. She recognised the island as Rohaayel's mind, and the white tower as the source of his gift.

She had to destroy it to protect herself.

She ran up the rise to the base of the lighthouse, where she found a locked door. The first of his defences.

Desperate, she slammed her shoulder into the wood. To her amazement, the tower swayed and began to topple. Of course, his two seconds were dead, and the link to his inner circle had been severed. His gift was crippled.

The tower tumbled, falling over the edge of the cliff. Jumbled white stones now formed a path to the rocks below, where the waves broke.

A storm brewed, blue-black thunder clouds gathering. The wind drove the waves, piling them high, and great showers of white spray shot up, raining down on the rubble. Where the spray hit, the white stones sizzled and dissolved, as the empyrean plane devoured Rohaayel's gift.

She caught a glimpse of him lying, defenceless, on her favourite rock near the thundering waves.

She had to save him. Instinct drove her to run down the stone path, jumping jagged gaps until she had almost reached him.

Then she stopped. What was she doing?

Rohaayel lay amidst the broken stones of his tower. A wave rolled in and swirled around the rock, sending up a shower of spray. When droplets landed on her forearms they stung like embers.

The sea was the manifestation of the empyrean plane, and it would devour him. That was how it should be. But still she hesitated.

He stirred and lifted his head, saw her there.

Sensing a threat behind her, she turned to see more men appear on the cliff edge, ten in all. A gift-warrior from each of the other brotherhoods...

It was an ambush. That explained the all-fathers' determined silence. The brotherhoods were not going to let the sisterhoods execute one of their own all-fathers without exacting vengeance.

She glanced to Rohaayel. He was as surprised as she was. The gift-warriors ran towards her, jumping over the rubble.

Trapped, she leaped and landed on the same flat-topped rock, not far from Rohaayel. Three of her ambushers caught her up, and she backed away, glancing towards the sea.

A wave, glistening with menace, rolled towards them. She could feel its hunger in the marrow of her bones. Now she knew why she'd been attracted to these rocks, when her gift began to stir, why she had dreamed of them over and over, and why she had dared the sea to take her. It had all been practice for working her gift on the empyrean plane.

As a fourth gift-warrior closed in on her, Rohaayel reared to his feet. He formed a blade and stabbed one, then another. The third saw what was happening and turned to him. They fought, as a fourth came after Imoshen.

She backed up and glanced over her shoulder. Directly behind her was a rock that was drowned by each crashing wave, but could be used as a bridge to another, higher rock and safety. She would have to time her jump so as not to be swept away.

Wounded now, Rohaayel grabbed both the gift-warriors and threw himself into the sea. White foam closed over them. A cry of protest died on her lips.

Spray showered Imoshen, stinging her exposed skin.

She glanced to her left. The remained six gift-warriors were ready to make the leap to her rock. To her right, she saw the glistening crest of a monstrous wave coming towards them, large enough to sweep them all to their deaths.

Confident they had her, the gift-warriors leapt onto the flat-topped rock with her. She turned and fled, jumping to the lower stone. Three of the men followed her.

She backed up, timing her escape. They were too intent on her to realise the danger. She hesitated as if terrified, keeping their focus on her.

At the last possible moment, she leapt for the higher rock, scrambling madly to gain enough height. The wave smashed into the rocks behind her like a thunderclap of power. Stinging droplets scoured her back.

Shaking with fright and pain, she turned to look down.

All of the males had been swept away, devoured by the sea.

Stunned, exhausted and in pain, Imoshen huddled on the rock, hugging her knees. The gardenia Iraayel had given her pressed against her cheek, reminding her of him. And her love for him gave her the strength to segue back to the earthly plane...

...where she felt soft petals, rich with perfume, on her cheek. Opening her eyes, she found herself in the empowerment dome. Her breath misted in front of her face.

A chill silence hung on the air. No one moved as she uncurled and came slowly to her feet. A white hoarfrost covered the marble where she stood. Rohaayel's body lay where it had fallen, frozen solid. He'd saved her life.

He'd loved her in the end.

Tears stung her eyes, and she shivered. The little burns all over her back and forearms stung.

Directly across from where she stood, the all-fathers and their seconds stared at her. No one spoke. Ten all-fathers, ten voices-of-reason... and ten dead hands-of-force. Frozen solid, their bodies slumped in their seats. Proof of the ambush.

Imoshen glanced over her shoulder to find that the all-mothers and their seconds had united behind her, coming to their feet. She felt a wave of female gift power gather and knew all their lives hung in the balance.

Rohaayel's body shattered, breaking into clear shards of ice, which swiftly melted. A heartbeat later the gift-warriors' bodies shattered and melted.

As if this was a signal, the brotherhood leaders stood and filed out of the dome, never turning their backs on the women.

When all the brotherhoods had left the building, the sisterhood leaders descended from the tiers.

Imoshen shuddered with cold. Egrayne took the robe off her own back and slid it around Imoshen's shoulders.

'Are you all right?' Reoden asked. She ran her hands over Imoshen, healing the burns. The cessation of pain was a balm, but it was her motivation that did more to heal Imoshen. Reoden's actions sprang from compassion.

'They ambushed her,' Egrayne said.

'They had to, or appear weak. But she survived,' Vittoryxe said, and the look she gave Imoshen was not much different from the one the brotherhoods had given her as they'd left. 'She killed the old all-father *and* ten gift-warriors. That's–'

'Rohaayel...' Imoshen voice cracked. If Rohaayel hadn't killed the first four, she would not have survived. He'd saved her. In the end, he'd loved her. Tears stung her eyes. 'He–'

'He paid the price.' Vittoryxe spoke with vicious conviction. 'And, with your display of power, none of the all-fathers will dare break the covenant.'

Imoshen felt sick. A wretched wave of dizziness swamped her senses, and she reached out to Egrayne, who caught her as the world went away.

Chapter Twenty-Seven

SORNE TENSED. IT was some kind of test; he could tell by the way Nitzel watched him.

'Put it here,' Nitzel ordered. The barons' men placed the dining table under the maple tree. It was almost dusk and the courtyard was blanketed by shadow. Hiruna and Zabier brought out lanterns, hanging them from the lower branches of the tree. It all looked quite festive.

Sorne leaned in close to Oskane. 'What's going on?'

'I'm not sure.'

Izteben watched from the stable door with little Valendia.

'Put the chairs here,' Nitzel ordered.

Three chairs were lined up, one each for the king, the prince and the prince's grandfather. As they took their seats, the barons' men carried out seven identical small chests and set them on the table.

'Ah.' Oskane sounded relieved. 'It's the T'En artefacts. Although why there are so many, I don't know. He'll ask you to pick one to take down for the offering.'

'Pick one? Why?' But, even as he asked, Sorne knew the answer. He needed to choose the artefact with the most T'En gift residue. By doing so he would confirm that his half-blood made him sensitive to T'En power.

As if there was any doubt.

Last night, Sorne had climbed the maple outside the king's chamber and had listened at the open window as Nitzel and the king discussed the threats the other kingdoms represented. He knew who Charald most feared amongst his own barons, and which kingdom the king most wanted the gods to tell him to conquer. In fact, it was a pity they needed to go down to the unclean place at all now, but it was necessary. He needed the flash of light to convince them it was the gods speaking.

'Sorne?' Oskane nudged him. 'It's time.'

'Time for the half-blood to choose the artefact,' Nitzel announced, and everyone fell silent. 'Only those with tainted blood can sense the residue of T'En gift.'

Sorne stepped forward. He rolled up the long sleeves of his knitted undershirt and opened the first chest. A T'En plait. He took it out. The watchers whispered and pointed.

Only the faintest residue of power remained. Useless.

He rolled it up and put it back.

In the second chest he found a gleaming skull, the jaw wired shut. It had rubies for eyes and it made the watchers gasp with horror, but it was completely devoid of power. He guessed it dated from King Charald the Peace-maker's time.

The third chest contained a small vest. It must have belonged to a child. He heard Hiruna's soft gasp at the dried blood. Old, flaky. Powerless. He was glad. He didn't want to think about the child who had died, many years ago, wearing this vest.

The fourth chest contained bones. His gut tightened. Two sets of sixth finger bones. They used to take them from T'En on the battlefield and string them on chains, to wear as talismans around their necks.

These bones held little residue.

The fifth chest contained another plait. This one was both silver and copper, the T'En and Malaunje hair inter-woven. He didn't want to know why their killer had ordered this done. His hands trembled as he returned it. It brought home to him how vulnerable he was, unless he proved himself useful to the king.

The sixth chest contained a pair of six-fingered gloves made of white kid-leather. They were fine and soft as skin, and the backs of the hands were covered in tiny seed-pearls set in a swirling design. The gloves made the watchers murmur in appreciation, but they held no power.

The last chest contained a silver arm-torc. This artefact was fresh, fresher even than the ones Oskane had stashed under his bed. There was a design on the silver armband – a snake swallowed its tail, forming a circle.

Sorne held up the armband, showing it to the king, but he was really looking past the king's chair to Izteben. 'This is the offering.'

Charald sprang out of his chair. 'Let's be off, then.'

'Bring the lanterns,' Nitzel ordered. 'I want plenty of light.'

Clearly, he still thought they were going to stage some sort of trickery. Sorne smiled grimly and sought Izteben's eyes. His choice-brother's smile mirrored his own.

Prince Cedon watched all these preparations, eyes glittering with fear and excitement. Nitzel looked sceptical. The barons each took a lantern. They laughed too loud and fingered the hilts of their swords. Not that a sword would do them much good where they were going.

Sorne's hands trembled as he returned the arm-torc to the chest. Another pair of hands reached across the table to take the box; he looked up to meet Izteben's eyes.

'You didn't think I'd let you go down there alone, did you?'

For a moment, Sorne was so relieved he could not speak. Then he recovered his voice. 'We throw it and run.'

Izteben grinned. 'Better yet. Get that plait, tie the arm band to the end.'

'Good idea.' He went back to the first chest and removed the braid. It was easily longer than he was tall. The original owner must have been a giant.

The end was tied off with leather strips, which he used to attach the armband. Then he returned the armband to the chest and wound the plait around it. He could feel gift residue coming from the chest itself, which was lined with silver.

'Everyone ready?' King Charald raised his voice.

Sorne and Izteben hurried over to walk behind Oskane. They fell into step together as the party set off. Sorne looked over his shoulder and saw Hiruna's worried face. She had Valendia in her arms and was holding Zabier to prevent him from following.

Gift residue clung to Sorne's hands and heightened his senses. The night felt strange and unreal, but everything around him seemed sharply defined. He noticed wild flowers growing in the cracks of the stone steps, their petals closed for the night; he heard the birds singing as they settled in the branches above.

And he dreaded going down into the mine. Last time, they'd only escaped due to luck.

The entrance had been widened, and a proper door attached. They stepped through and milled about.

'The half-bloods lead the way,' Oskane said. He gave Izteben a lantern. Sorne followed, carrying the chest.

Eventually the tunnel narrowed, and Sorne's mouth went dry as he recognised the odd-shaped gap that he and Izteben had squeezed through.

'Through there is a cavern,' he said. 'That's the place where the walls between us and the gods are thinnest. There's a shelf on the other side. It will take six or seven people, no more.'

'Go on,' Oskane urged.

As he and Izteben went through the gap and into the cavern, Sorne's heart hammered. He wondered if you could die of fright alone.

'The old lantern's still here from last time,' Izteben said.

Behind him, Sorne could hear the barons coming through the gap and shuffling forward to make room for more.

'I remember the air feeling thick, making it hard to hear,' Izteben whispered.

Sorne nodded. 'And then a darkness, in that corner.' He pointed to where the lantern lay on its side.

'Well?' Nitzel's belligerent voice carried to the far side of the chamber.

'Go on,' Oskane urged. 'Call on the gods.'

Sorne swallowed and glanced to Izteben. They would have to climb down. Crouching on the edge of the steep rock, Sorne lowered his weight to the cavern floor, a body-length below. Izteben followed him down.

Sorne opened the chest and unrolled the braid, hanging it across his arm with the silver arm-torc tied to the end.

'We seek the Seven,' Oskane said, his voice echoing across the cavern. 'We seek enlightenment, Father. Your wisdom, Scholar, Your guidance, Warrior.'

Nothing happened.

Izteben nudged Sorne, who swung the plait out and let go. The metal of the arm-torc flashed as it sailed through the air. It clattered to the floor and rolled to a stop.

Nothing happened.

'When will it start?' Cedon asked. 'Have we come all this way for nothing?'

'Who knows?' Nitzel said, but he sounded pleased.

Sorne frowned. What had they forgotten? He'd fallen, scraped his back and...

'You were bleeding,' Izteben said, following the same train of thought. 'Cut your finger and flick blood in that direction.'

'I'll do more than that.' Sorne rewound the braid. He took out his knife and nicked his finger, rubbing blood on the silver torc. Immediately, he felt his senses sharpen; the air seemed thicker, sounds magnified. 'It's working.'

'Your neck.' Izteben gestured.

Sorne looked down at his mother's torc. A glow came from the blue stone.

At the same moment, Cedon said, 'It's getting dark in the corner. I thought the god appeared in a flash of light?'

Izteben glanced to the gathering darkness and began to edge back towards the entrance. 'Throw the offering, Sorne. *Throw it!*'

Sorne flung the silver torc away from him.

Something caught it before it could land on the stone. The plait stretched taut between Sorne and the unseen thing.

'Look at that!' Cedon marvelled.

'Praise the Seven!' Oskane sounded delighted.

The king laughed. 'Well, I'll be–'

Something else snatched the braid from Sorne's hands and it was pulled taut between two unseen forces.

'Seven bless us, there's two of them!' Oskane cried.

'I can't see the gods,' Cedon complained. 'Why can't I see them?'

'You can see how much they despise the Wyrds,' Oskane said. 'See how they fight over who gets the offering. See how the silver arm-torc glows.'

Sorne felt the steep stone ledge at his back.

One end of the braid dropped and the darkness rushed towards them.

'Jump!' he cried, throwing the chest towards the beast. Not waiting to see if it was satisfied, he turned to give Izteben a boost.

A flash of white burned his eyes, and a sudden wind drove him into stone. Men cried out. Cedon screamed. King Charald roared.

We poked the hornet's next. What do they expect? Sorne thought, as he blacked out.

'IT'S JUST HORRIBLE,' Imoshen muttered. She and Frayvia sat in the window seat, heads together, whispering. Thankfully, Iraayel slept nearby, unaware of the violence. The night air was filled with shouting, the clash of metal on metal and the breaking of glass from the brotherhood quarter.

'It's to be expected,' Frayvia said. 'The all-fathers blame Rohaayel's brotherhood, they're fighting over it, strongest takes all.'

Imoshen shuddered. 'I don't like this place. Nothing is what I expected. There's–'

'There's nowhere else to go.'

'We had no choice, I know, but... I don't understand why I had to kill Rohaayel. Why the sisterhoods are so afraid of the brotherhoods. I don't understand why our people are locked in war like this. There has to be a better way.'

Frayvia hugged her. 'My poor, idealistic Imoshen.'

'I can't afford to be idealistic. There's you and Iraayel to think of.' She chewed on her bottom lip. 'When I gave my vows to All-mother Aayelora tonight, Vittoryxe was not happy.'

'As long as you keep out of her way.'

'I can't. She's the gift-tutor. I suspect she is going to pick holes in everything I do. According to her, a T'En can only have one gift, but I know that's not true.'

'Imoshen, she's a gift-tutor with thirty or forty years of experience. Listen to her. Work out how to win her over. The sisterhoods have given us sanctuary. Be grateful for that. I am.'

Imoshen nodded but, in truth, she was numb.

'Look,' Frayvia whispered, as flames and sparks lifted high into the night sky above the brotherhood quarter. 'Rohaayel's palace is burning.'

'I'm sorry. Here I am thinking only of me. Did you have family there?'

Frayvia shrugged. 'There was Ardeyne, but he's gone now and I was never close to him. There were others, friends...'

'Will they be safe?'

'They're Malaunje. Not important enough to be in danger.'

'I don't understand how you can say that.'

'I know.' Frayvia kissed her cheek and stood up, offering her hand. 'Come to bed.'

LIGHTS DANCED OVER Sorne's head.

When they settled down and resolved themselves into lanterns strung from the branches of the maple tree, he knew where he was. Nearby, he heard several voices arguing.

'...no, a True-man cannot see the gods. They are too magnificent for our minds to comprehend,' Oskane was saying.

'Then the light is...' This was Charald.

'All that our minds can cope with. The half-bloods are closer to animals, and so they pass out when the gods plant visions in their minds.'

'Are you sure it's safe?' Nitzel asked.

'Of course, it's not safe,' Oskane snapped. He was clearly enjoying himself. 'If you think contacting the gods is safe, you're a fool. They are so far above us, we–'

'I wasn't scared,' Cedon boasted. 'Not for one moment.'

Liar, Sorne thought. Cedon had been terrified, just like the rest of them.

'Where's Izteben?' He tried to sit up, winced and dropped back. The moment his eyes closed he saw a ship's deck, the king, a boy...

'He's right here, safe,' Hiruna said. Sorne opened his eyes to see her leaning over him with a damp cloth. 'You cut your forehead.'

'The other half-blood's awake now,' one of the barons announced.

Sorne struggled to sit up, and Izteben helped him. Hiruna had bandaged his choice-brother's head, and now she began to bandage Sorne's, watched by the king, the prince, the barons and Oskane. It seemed the scholar had risen in stature, for he now sat on the king's left. Behind the four chairs, the barons' men watched. They were subdued, stunned.

When Sorne closed his eyes, he saw the deck again, saw the king hug the small boy.

'Enough, woman, get out of the way and let him tell us his vision,' the king commanded.

Hiruna ignored him.

Sorne glanced to Izteben. 'You all right?'

'Seeing double. Something slammed me into the wall.'

'From what they're saying, you're both lucky to be alive,' Hiruna whispered. She tied off the bandage and stepped back.

Sorne was having trouble focusing, and the glow from the lanterns fractured into streamers of light. Each time he blinked he was back on... 'the deck.'

'What did he say?' Charald demanded. 'Speak up, boy.'

'This is not just any half-blood boy,' Oskane said. 'He speaks for the Warrior.'

Sorne felt a bone-deep satisfaction. Now the king had acknowledged him and was finally talking to him. 'I saw a ship's deck. King Charald was with a boy–'

'Prince Cedon!' Charald announced.

It hadn't been the prince. It had been another boy, much younger. But now was not the time to quibble.

'What were we doing, Warrior's-voice?' the king asked, finally using his new title.

'You hugged him,' Sorne said. 'You seemed pleased, as though something momentous had just happened.'

'A victory,' Charald stated and jumped to his feet. 'That's it. We're meant to sail down the coast and attack –' he broke off. 'Did you see which kingdom I'd conquered?'

'I saw the moons,' Sorne lied. 'Crescent moons with–'

'Khitan. I knew it!' Charald told his barons.

Sorne sought Oskane's eyes; the scholar was pleased. They would be welcomed back to court, and Oskane would see his family restored to its former position of influence.

The king paced. 'It's spring cusp. The barons could summon their men and set sail before the next small moon, the sooner the better.' Charald turned to Oskane. 'Pack your bags, old man. I hope you don't get seasick.'

Oskane's face dropped and his mouth gaped.

'Nitzel.' The king beckoned him. 'I appoint you regent to rule for Cedon until I return.'

'But, father...'

'Now listen to me, Cedon.' Charald pulled his son to his feet. 'I was crowned on the battlefield and handed a kingdom in chaos when I was fifteen. Oskane and Nitzel helped me hold onto it. Don't ignore good counsel.'

'But I want to come with you and fight.'

'Someone must stay to rule the kingdom.'

'And he will do that, with my advice, King Charald,' Nitzel said. 'I am honoured.'

And pleased, very pleased, Sorne could tell.

'But...' Oskane began.

'The half-blood, I know,' Charald said. 'We'll take the Warrior's-voice with us. He was born under the sign of the Warrior, and the Warrior has claimed him.'

'There were two gods in the cavern, King Charald,' Izteben said.

Everyone fell silent as the king turned to the other half-blood, the son of a poor carpenter, who had dared to address him without permission.

Sorne didn't know what Izteben was up to, but he trusted him.

'When the Warrior gave Sorne a vision, the Father sent me a vision.' This from Izteben, who did not believe in visions. 'The Father is angry with True-men. He hasn't been worshipped as he should have been. I saw Scholar Oskane returned to his place as high priest of the Father's church, ruling over all the other churches as the Father rules over his home. I saw unclean places accorded their proper reverence as holy sites. I saw the Seven honoured with offerings of T'En artefacts presented by the six-fingered hands of copper-haired half-bloods.'

Sorne looked down to hide his amusement. Clever, clever Izteben.

'The Father has spoken through this half-blood,' Oskane announced. 'So it shall be.'

While the king and his barons discussed this new turn of events, Izteben's eyes gleamed with triumph. He edged closer to Sorne to whisper, 'Now we both speak for the gods. You'll sail with the king and I'll go to the Father's church in port with High Priest Oskane.'

The king and his men ordered chairs brought out, and their evening meal was served under the maple tree. There was talk of logistics, ships, men, and supplies, all embellished with eager boasting and copious drinking. And later, after Hiruna returned to the stable with Zabier, there was more drinking, bawdy songs and shouting. Hiruna sent Sorne to check that their door was barred.

They went to their beds, but it was hard to sleep, what with all the noise. It was only as the retreat fell silent that Sorne remembered the she-Wyrd, locked in her cell. Now that her usefulness was over, he had a terrible feeling she would be killed.

Throwing back the covers, he crept to the ladder and climbed down. The horses stirred in their stalls.

'What are you doing?' Izteben whispered, following him down.

'Freeing the she-Wyrd.'

'Oskane will know it was us.'

'I don't think he'll be too worried. He's been restored to high priest.'

'Wait,' Zabier whispered, eyes bright, hair tousled. 'I'm coming with you. I know where Franto keeps the key to the cell.'

'Tell us and we'll get it,' Izteben said.

'Oh, no. I missed out on the mine. I want to be part of this.'

'Very well,' Sorne said.

Zabier jumped off the last rung. 'Let's go.'

'Wait.' Sorne caught Izteben's arm. 'The she-Wyrd will need shoes, a knife, some food...'

'My shoes will fit her,' Hiruna said.

The three of them jumped and turned, to find her watching from the doorway of the kitchen.

'Did you think I wouldn't notice? Come here.' She put a hamper on the kitchen table and packed a set of clothes, her winter shoes, fresh bread, smoked meat, some cheese and preserves. Lastly she added a knife, a cup and a bowl, flint and a candle stub.

Hiruna spoke softly as she worked. 'This reminds me of the night we didn't run in time. Kolst wanted to stay, thought his brother would protect us. The villagers knocked him down and dragged me out of my home. You were just a baby, Izteben. I thought we were going to die.' She shuddered. 'Then Scholar Oskane saved us...'

'Why aren't all True-men and -women like you?' Sorne asked.

'How do you know more of them aren't?' she countered. 'Maybe they're afraid to be known as Wyrd-lovers.'

Sorne shook his head. 'Even the penitents despised us.'

She shrugged and handed him the travelling kit. 'Don't get caught.'

Both moons were full and bright, casting the shadow of the maple onto the courtyard stones. The door to the main building opened on oiled hinges. Sorne could hear the barons' men snoring in the dining room.

Izteben signalled for Sorne to wait, and went up the steps with Zabier.

Moments later, Izteben and Zabier slipped back down the steps, looking very pleased with themselves. Sorne led the way to the cellar, where they were shocked to see the door to the she-Wyrd's cell standing wide open.

'She must have escaped already.' Izteben sounded relieved.

Sorne had a bad feeling. 'Hold this.' He gave the hamper to Zabier and crept along until he came to the cell. It was hard to make out much in the darkness. Sorne lit a candle.

The she-Wyrd lay near the far wall in a pool of blood. Her gown had been shoved up to reveal her body, and there was something wrong with her face...

'Go wait at the stairs, Zabier,' Sorne said. For once, their little brother didn't argue. Sorne could hear him weeping softly.

Torn between pity and contempt, Sorne made himself study the body. Her eyes had been gouged out, her hair hacked off and the little fingers on both hands were missing.

Izteben retched. Sorne fought the same reaction.

In the retreat, there were no women other than their mother and the she-Wyrd, but when Joaken and the other penitents had been alive, they'd boasted of the women they'd known, and they hadn't worried who overheard. Sorne and Izteben knew what had happened here.

Guilt hit him. 'She asked me to free her last night. But I...'

'Why didn't you?' Izteben asked, his voice thick with emotion.

'Yesterday, we weren't important. Tonight...' Tonight he'd felt powerful. Now he saw this for the illusion that it was. If True-men could do this to someone who was no threat to them, what would they do to half-breeds who dared...

'It's not decent.' Izteben picked up her blanket. 'We should cover—'

'Don't.' Panic made Sorne's voice sharp. 'They mustn't know we've been here.'

Izteben looked confused. 'We're the gods' messengers. The king himself listens to us.'

Sorne licked dry lips. 'Who do you think condoned this? Why do you think Ma had me check the stable door was barred?'

Izteben looked shocked.

Sorne licked his thumb and finger and pinched the candle flame. 'We should go.'

They sent Zabier to bed while they replaced the key in Franto's chamber. When they returned to the stables, Hiruna was waiting for them.

'We were too late,' Izteben said, returning the hamper. 'How can someone do that to another person?'

'I'm sorry.' Hiruna did not seem surprised. 'I'm sorry you had to see that.'

'She was weak,' Sorne said.

'No.' Hiruna's eyes glittered. 'She was strong. She could have killed herself, but she chose to stay and help you boys, even after I told her Oskane wouldn't kill you.'

'And look what it got her,' Sorne said, voice thick with anger. 'She died in the end.'

'Everyone dies. It's how you live that's important.'

'Oh, Ma.' Izteben hugged her. She sobbed softly. 'Don't worry. We'll look after you.'

'I know that.' She summoned a smile. 'It's just... Tomorrow we leave. Everything is changing.'

'For the better,' Sorne insisted.

But on the morrow, he discovered the covered cart was being put to a new use.

Sorne had known there were not enough horses for them all to ride. He'd expected to walk. He hadn't anticipated...

'The half-bloods will ride in the cart, out of sight,' Franto said, flipping the cover back.

'Much more comfortable than walking.' Hiruna climbed up, then held out her arms for Izteben to pass Valendia.

'And Zabier?' Sorne asked Franto.

'Zabier will be serving Scholar Oskane.' Franto made an impatient gesture. 'Be realistic, Sorne. The king cannot be seen to be travelling with half-bloods.'

Heat filled Sorne's face. 'Not even–'

'Come on.' Izteben slung an arm round his shoulder and drew him away from Franto. 'Now is not the time for this.'

He was right. Sorne felt he should insist they bury the she-Wyrd, but he was a coward. His face burned with shame as he climbed into the cart. Izteben sat next to him. Morning sunlight came through the gaps in the canvas. They could hear the men joking and grumbling as they mounted up. Yesterday those same men had cowered in fright, while he and Izteben stood between them and death.

'One day, all of Chalcedonia will look up to us,' Sorne said. 'We will stand between the True-men and their gods.'

Chapter Twenty-Eight

'MAKE IMOSHEN A provisional-adept?' Vittoryxe repeated. 'She hasn't even covered the basics of gift control, or gift hierarchy, or the theories behind gift power. She might be seventeen, but she's not even an initiate, let alone a provisional-adept.'

The all-mother glanced to her voice-of-reason, but it was Egrayne who spoke. 'She executed Rohaayel and ten gift-warriors–'

'How?' Vittoryxe fumed. 'That's what I'd like to know.'

Egrayne shrugged. 'If Imoshen doesn't have provisional-adept status, what does it say about us? None of us have been tested like this.'

'If I give her provisional-adept status, what does it say about the twenty years of training everyone else goes through?'

'We aren't belittling the work you do training the lads for entry into the brotherhoods,' the all-mother said. 'Or the way you mentor our girl-children. But...'

'But Imoshen has already proven she has the power and the control,' Egrayne said.

'She has no sense of history, and she doesn't appreciate the power she has.'

'Then teach her these things,' the all-mother said. 'That's why we suggested provisional-adept status.'

'After all, Vittoryxe,' Egrayne said. 'You don't have to give her full adept status until she turns thirty-three and takes on adult duties in the sisterhood.'

Vittoryxe could see the sisterhood's inner circle was determined. If she had no choice, then she was going to pull Imoshen up on every little mistake. The brotherhood-raised sister was going to rue the day she tried to side-step the hierarchy and accepted the rise in status. Vittoryxe smiled. 'So be it.'

'Send her in,' the all-mother told her devotee.

Vittoryxe moved aside as Imoshen entered and made obeisance.

Dropping gracefully to her knees, Imoshen sat on her heels. 'You sent for me, all-mother.'

'Gift-tutor Vittoryxe has something to say.'

Imoshen looked up expectantly.

'I have decided to accord you provisional-adept status.'

Imoshen nodded. No surprise or delight, and no gratitude.

Egrayne cleared her throat. 'Imoshen, you have killed adepts on the empyrean plane. Only another adept can do that. We T'En train for twenty years to become adepts. We are according you a very great honour.'

Colour raced up Imoshen's throat and over her cheeks. She leant forward to put her hands on the floor and press her forehead to her hands. Then she lifted her head. 'Forgive me. I don't know your ways. Forgive me, gift-tutor, I'll work very hard to be worthy of this honour.'

'See that you do.' Either Imoshen was a conniving schemer, who had her eye on the role of all-mother, or she really was completely unaware, but Vittoryxe did not believe *that* for a heartbeat.

Imoshen was a real threat to Vittoryxe's plans to become all-mother and, should the opportunity arise, causare.

Certainly, Vittoryxe would train Imoshen, but she'd also test her. The girl was definitely powerful, but power was only a tool. Lack of knowledge was Imoshen's weakness. It would be a simple thing for her to have an accident on the higher plane.

It was sad, but it happened and, considering Imoshen's lack of formal training, no one would be surprised.

'WHAT DID THEY say?' Frayvia asked, as soon as Imoshen returned to their chambers.

Iraayel ran over to show her his puzzle then climbed into her lap as they all sat in the window seat. Outside, birds wheeled in the brilliant blue spring sky, circling one of the city's white towers.

'I've been given provisional-adept status.'

'So why aren't you happy?'

'The gift-tutor is furious.'

'You read her?'

'I didn't mean to. Don't worry, she didn't notice.'

Unaware of the undercurrents of their conversation, the four-year-old pulled the wooden horse apart and began slotting it back together.

'It's not surprising the gift-tutor is annoyed,' Frayvia said. 'You have no formal training.'

'She's also very determined.'

'To do what?'

'That's just it. I don't know.'

'I did it.' Iraayel held up the horse.

'Well done.' Imoshen hugged him. 'My clever boy.'

'You are a threat to the gift-tutor because you have no training. Vittoryxe is a teacher, and the trust between student and teacher is sacred.' Frayvia smiled. 'Work hard and show proper respect, and you'll win her over.'

'IT'S STILL DANGEROUS,' Oskane said. He gestured to his private office. 'Just because we are back in Port Mirror-on-Sea and I'm high priest of the Father's church, it doesn't mean we are safe.'

'That's why I don't want to leave you,' Franto insisted.

'I won't be alone. You've been training Zabier.'

'He's only just turned thirteen.'

'He's smart and loyal. Also I have Matxin. He's my blood kin and equally determined to bring Nitzel down. You are going with Charald to advise Sorne. Your job is to keep him out of trouble. Don't worry, Charald expects to be back by winter. Now send Matxin in.'

As Franto left the high priest's office, Oskane adjusted the folds of his formal robe. He had not seen his cousin's son in seventeen years. Now Matxin was a middle-aged man of thirty-four, with children of his own.

The baron strode in, still covered in the dust of the road. He gave a perfunctory bow and kissed Oskane's ring.

'So Sorna's half-blood boy has the king dancing to his tune now,' he said.

'The Warrior speaks through him. Praise the Seven that I lived to see this.'

Matxin cast him a swift look. 'I see... But what of the Wyrds? Charald still owes them a fortune. If they were to call in the debt, they could beggar the kingdom, and leave us ripe for invasion.'

'Then we're lucky there's been fighting in Cesspit City,' Oskane said. It was three days by fast rider from the Wyrd city to the port. News of the fighting had arrived before the king's party. 'Did you hear? At least one of their palaces has burned. As long as they're busy fighting amongst themselves–'

'We're safe. Yes, but your half-blood sent Charald to war against the one king who offered to help me take the throne. What was he thinking, Uncle?'

'Sorne is the Warrior's-voice. He was only repeating what the Warrior god told him.'

'Of course... What of Nitzel? He murdered my sister and sent my father home with his tail between his legs. I've spent the last seventeen years keeping my head down, while Nitzel lined his pockets, placing his supporters and relatives in positions of power. I must see him brought low.'

'And you shall. But–'

'This summer is the perfect opportunity. While the king and his war barons are conquering Khitan, Nitzel will be alone with the prince – an old man and a boy of thirteen. I have supporters, men who are tired of Charald's taxes and temper.'

'I'm glad to hear it, and I'm sure they will come in useful. But first we must consolidate our hold on the church. Next to the king, it is the most powerful body in Chalcedonia. In a way, it is more powerful, because kings come and go, but the church lives on. I'll win over the–'

'Just how will you do that, Uncle? There are whispers in certain quarters. True-men and -women do not take kindly to half-bloods interfering with their gods, advising the king and claiming the title of Warrior's-voice!'

'Charald is taking Sorne with him. I'm sending Franto to make sure the half-blood causes no trouble.'

'But there's more, aren't there? You brought a nest of Wyrds with you, and one of them claims to be the Father's-voice. What if he gets cocky?'

'I have his mother and sister to ensure his cooperation.'

A grim smile split Matxin's face. 'That should do it. But I don't think branding yourself as a Wyrd-lover is going to help our family's cause.'

Feeling battered, Oskane sat down. 'This summer's cusp, the Father's-voice will make an offering to the gods. I've already invited the leaders of the other churches. Believe me, after this you will not doubt me, or the Seven, again.'

'I see. What I don't see is why we need the half-bloods.'

'We...' But he was too tired to explain. Oskane rang the bell. Zabier opened the door. 'Where's Franto?'

The lad hesitated, and Oskane guessed Franto's stomach was troubling him again.

He gestured to Zabier. 'Matxin, this is the other brother, born a True-man. He'll take you to see the half-bloods. They'll tell you how they contact the gods.'

Matxin nodded and left with the lad.

Oskane felt exhausted, lightheaded and short of breath. There was a dull nagging pain in his left arm. The pain eased and Oskane managed to catch his breath. Now that he was back in port, in a position of power, he hardly had the energy to enjoy it.

'A GILDED CAGE.' The chambers they had been given were more sumptuous than anything Sorne had ever seen. Leaded windows looked out across the rooftops to the port beyond. 'That's what this is, a gilded cage. And we're prisoners.'

Valendia whimpered. Hiruna picked her up and went through to the sleeping quarters. Meanwhile, Izteben stretched out on a padded chair by the fireplace.

'What's the matter with you?' Sorne stood over him. 'You used to be the one who'd get all fired up.'

'If you recall, I used to get fired up because Oskane was being unfair to you. Now you're about to sail off with the king to lay waste to the unsuspecting innocents of Khitan.'

Sorne had the grace to blush. 'I had to send him somewhere, and if it hadn't been Khitan it would be some other kingdom.'

'So the secret is to tell people what they want to hear? Very wise. I'll remember that, because I have to stay here and serve Oskane's greater plan. Look around you. We're living like kings. We're half-bloods, Sorne. If we weren't here, we'd be serving the Wyrds in the Celestial City.'

The door opened, and they both turned to see Zabier enter with a well-dressed stranger. The man was travel-worn, and something about him was vaguely familiar.

'This is Baron Matxin,' Zabier said. 'Scholar Osk... High Priest Oskane sent him, so you could explain how you speak to the gods.'

Zabier introduced Sorne and Izteben, and they made their bows.

Matxin took a seat by the fire. 'Come here and sit down, so I can get a good look at you.'

He gestured to the hearth in front of the fireplace, and they knelt like students before the teacher.

'Between us, Oskane and I seek to restore our family fortunes,' Matxin said. 'Baron Nitzel is responsible for the murder of my sister, Queen Sorna.'

'We know,' Sorne said.

'Did you know that after Prince Cedon, I am next in line to the throne?'

Sorne nodded. 'We know who you are, and what Scholar Oskane wants to do.'

'Good,' Matxin said. 'Now Oskane has made the mistake of believing his own lies. He thinks you speak to the gods.'

'But we do,' Izteben protested, and Zabier nodded.

Matxin's sharp eyes noted Sorne's lack of reaction.

'And the visions, are they real?' the baron asked. 'Come now, you can tell me the truth.'

'The visions are real,' Zabier insisted.

Izteben looked down.

Sorne shrugged. 'I saw the things I described, but whether they are visions from the gods...'

'Just as I thought. This summer's cusp, Oskane is going to have Izteben contact the gods in front of the church leaders to prove he's speaking the truth. If this fails, we lose everything, and you will be–'

'Sent to the Wyrds,' Izteben said.

Matxin shook his head. 'Oh, no. Executed, at the very least. You dared to trick the True-men. They'll be furious.'

'We're not tricking them,' Sorne said. 'We did contact beings of great power.'

'They are the gods,' Izteben insisted. 'Whatever the she-Wyrd might have said.'

Matxin's sharp eyes fixed on Sorne. 'What did the she-Wyrd say?'

Sorne told him how, according to the Wyrds, there was a higher plane filled with predators that craved the T'En gift, and blood.

'Blood?' Matxin repeated.

Sorne nodded. 'Both times I bled. The first was an

accident, the second was deliberate. This time I won't be here, so Izteben will have to do it alone.'

'I can help him,' Zabier insisted.

'I'm not worried,' Izteben said. 'As long as we are on a holy site at season's cusp, I can contact the gods.'

'But he must have something that's imbued with gift residue,' Sorne said. 'Or...'

'Or?' Matxin prompted.

'Or the gods will take me,' Izteben said. 'Once I call them, they must have their offering.'

'I see.' Matxin nodded. 'That's why, when True-men venture into unclean places, they disappear or lose their wits.'

'Oskane said it was because the gods were too magnificent for them to gaze upon,' Izteben said.

Sorne sought Matxin's eyes. The baron was under no illusions.

Matxin came to his feet. 'I see I don't need to worry.'

Sorne sprang up. 'I sail with the king in a matter of days. Please, Uncle, look after my family.'

Matxin looked down, and for a moment, Sorne thought he would refuse to acknowledge their relationship. But he nodded.

After he left, Zabier paused at the door. 'This evening, I'm going down into the crypts again. It's amazing, the tunnels go on forever. Do you want to come?'

Sorne grinned. 'I've had enough of dark tunnels to last me a lifetime.'

Zabier laughed and left.

'See,' Izteben said. 'We do have supporters. Once I've proven we can contact the gods, we'll be safe.'

Sorne let out a sigh of relief. 'And I'll be back by winter.'

Five days later, Sorne packed his travelling bag and said his goodbyes to Hiruna and Valendia.

'Don't worry,' he told them, seeing their tears. 'King Charald is certain he'll have Khitan conquered by winter.'

'I wish I was going with you,' Izteben said. 'You get to sail across the Secluded Sea and ride with King Charald's army.'

Sorne had to admit the idea was appealing. 'By the time I get back, you'll have impressed the church officials, and will be well on your way to winning the respect of True-men for half-bloods.'

'I hope to,' Izteben said. 'Meanwhile, you'll win the respect of the king and his barons for the half-bloods.'

They both grinned.

Chapter Twenty-Nine

VITTORYXE LEANED AGAINST the door jamb, pleased with the way her students were attending to their studies. Not one head rose from the long tables under the windows. She prided herself on keeping a tight rein in the training chamber. It used to annoy her, the way the last gift-tutor permitted nonsense and play.

Gift power was dangerous, not something to be treated lightly.

Seeing Imoshen leave her seat and wander through the tall shelves of scrolls and books irritated Vittoryxe. Surely the girl couldn't have finished the set texts already?

One season had passed, and it would be summer's cusp in a few days. Vittoryxe had to admit, Imoshen worked hard. But what was she up to now?

Threading her way through the shelves, she came up behind Imoshen who was reaching for a book. 'Don't waste your time with *The Theories of Scytheon*, Imoshen. He's been discredited.'

'Then why is his book here?'

Why did she have to question everything? 'Did you finish the texts I set you?'

Imoshen nodded. 'That's what made me look up Scytheon.'

'He wasn't mentioned.'

'No, but his student Edune was, so I read about him and that made me look up Scytheon.'

'You can't have read the works of Edune. At least, you can't possibly have taken them all in.'

Imoshen looked away.

Vittoryxe expelled her breath in a huff of annoyance. 'Come with me.'

She led Imoshen into her private chamber and gestured for her to kneel on the carpet in front of the empty fireplace. If Imoshen was reading Edune, then she was dabbling in adept-level theory, which would provide a plausible explanation for her over-reaching herself and getting into trouble. But first, Vittoryxe needed to test the limits of Imoshen's knowledge. 'Do you have any questions?'

'Well...' She folded her hands in her lap and paused to collect her thoughts. 'If each T'En only has one gift, then how could Egrayne have been a gift-warrior, when she is now the empowerer?'

'A gift-warrior is able to perceive power on this plane and manipulate it on the higher plane. A near-death experience on the higher plane triggered the further development of Egrayne's original gift. An empowerer perceives the different types of power nascent within the young T'En. Opening the child to his or her power is a form of power manipulation. You see, it is another step up the ladder.' A very big step.

Imoshen nodded. 'So I couldn't be both a gift-warrior and a raedan?'

'Exactly.'

Imoshen nodded. 'The common male gift is mind manipulation. And females can't have this gift, because it is rare for male and female gifts to overlap?'

'It almost never happens. If they do share a common gift, the gift is expressed differently. For instance, in females the gift of seeing the future appears in a scryer, who can search for specific events. In males, the gift of seeing the future appears in a seer, who has visions that he can't direct.' Vittoryxe gestured. 'Now, prove you understand Edune's theories. Tell me what he said in your own words.'

'It was more what he didn't say that interested me. We have these gifts that are more powerful on the higher plane. But to gift-work on that plane is dangerous, because it attracts the predators. On this plane, most gifts require touch to be effective. The power of the gift is innate and it builds up, like water pouring into a cup. The gift must be used or the cup overflows.'

Vittoryxe nodded. 'Right so far.'

'If we do segue to the higher plane, our bodies are vulnerable, and we must be defended on this plane. It seems to me that the main purpose of our gifts on this plane is to make us aware of other T'En, and whether they are a threat. Other than that, they are not actually very useful. In theory, the gifts surface to protect us, but in reality the gift is protecting itself, because if we die, it ceases to exist. To me, the gifts seem to be almost parasitic.'

'You're quoting Scytheon and he's discredited,' Vittoryxe snapped. 'Do you think me a fool? You couldn't have come up with that on your own.'

Imoshen's mouth opened in dismay. 'I haven't read Scytheon's—'

'I'm not interested in your lies and excuses.' Vittoryxe studied her. Without the training, it was hard to distinguish between the higher plane and a construct that a gift-tutor had created for training purposes. Vittoryxe had created several constructs, where she trained her students in safety.

If she told Imoshen that she was taking her to one of these, but actually took her to the higher plane, the girl would not be able to detect the difference and would not be on her guard. When Imoshen got herself killed, Vittoryxe could claim Imoshen had lost control, segued to the higher plane and been devoured before she could find her.

'Tomorrow, I'll take you into my higher plane construct and show you the different predators. Read the relevant descriptions.'

'Yes, gift-tutor.'

* * *

IMOSHEN KNEW IT wasn't a normal training day when she arrived and found the chamber empty. It was mid-afternoon, and shafts of sunlight streamed through the tall windows, reaching deep into the aisles between bookshelves. Dust motes hung on the golden light.

She'd been studying nonstop since she arrived, but the more Imoshen read, the less she understood.

People tended not to talk about their gifts, almost as if it was private, like sex.

That was the other thing; the attraction between male and female gifts. When she and Reothe had made the deep-bonding, it had seemed perfectly natural.

It had been a good thing. Wonderful.

Yet Vittoryxe seemed certain the bonding had addicted Imoshen to the male version of the gift; that she was flawed.

'There you are. Come through to my study,' Vittoryxe said.

Imoshen read the gift-tutor. Vittoryxe was so very determined she was having trouble controlling her gift.

They took up their positions, kneeling in front of the empty fireplace.

Imoshen wiped her hands on her thighs. 'Why don't our kind make the deep-bonding anymore?'

Vittoryxe's mouth twitched as if she'd said something crude.

'I don't mean any disrespect. But if men are drawn to female power and vice-versa, then it seems to me that bonding is a natural part of gift-working.'

'T'En men cannot be trusted. Look what they did to you.'

Heat raced up Imoshen's cheeks and her gift surged, prickling over her skin. She'd never revealed how her father died to save her, and she wasn't going to reveal it to Vittoryxe. But this was about bonding, and Reothe deserved his due. 'My bond-partner died to protect me. Not all T'En men are the same.'

'And one of my mother's lovers murdered her. So don't talk about things you don't understand.' Vittoryxe's eyes glittered with anger. She rolled up her sleeve jerkily, and raised her left arm. 'Now, lower your shields.'

Imoshen swallowed and mimicked her. With their hands linked, skin touching from elbow to palm, Imoshen tried to lower her walls. Ever since she'd started training, she'd found this particularly difficult, and today she had to make several attempts. Vittoryxe grew more impatient each time.

Finally, Imoshen managed to establish a link and the gift-tutor took control, segueing to the higher plane construct.

Vittoryxe's construct was like her: bleak and hard-edged. They stood in a town square on a cloudy day. Buildings three and four storeys high lined the square. A row of trees at each end cast shadows that seemed too deep for the dull day. It was bitterly cold, and Imoshen sensed a storm about to break. Fear made her stomach clench, and she had to remind herself that this place was only a construct.

Imoshen looked around for any sign of empyrean beasts, but they were alone. Behind them was a fountain, with a statue of a woman astride a horse, her long hair covering her body like a cloak. The fountain was dry and edged with lichen.

Imoshen felt her gift stir and the fountain sprang to life, clear water sparkling in a sudden shaft of sunlight. Joy filled her. If this had not been a construct, she wouldn't have attempted such a thing, for fear of attracting predators.

When she took the gift-tutor's arm to show her the fountain, Vittoryxe's skin felt like cool smooth leather, alive with an undercurrent of power.

Before she could point to the fountain, a screech tore through the air. Sound behaved differently here. The cry rippled over Imoshen's skin. It registered as waves of pain, reverberating in her ears. She'd read of the harrowraven's cry and how it triggered fear in those who heard it.

Above them, a harrowraven circled and Imoshen's hand tightened instinctively on the gift-tutor's arm. Just as the empyrean bird dived towards them, Imoshen saw three scraelings creep out from the shadows of the trees.

Vittoryxe focused her gift to form a spear and hurled it towards the harrowraven. The spear caught the bird mid-chest and the creature dropped, falling amongst the scraelings, which tore it to pieces.

As Vittoryxe recalled the spear, her gaze travelled past Imoshen's shoulder and she stiffened.

Imoshen turned to see a T'En man walking towards them, long hair loose on his shoulders, broad chest bare, breeches worn low on his lean hips. What was she supposed to learn from this?

She glanced to Vittoryxe, but the gift-tutor had gone utterly still. Then, to Imoshen's amazement, Vittoryxe shrank, becoming a child of seven or eight.

The man sauntered towards them, a half smile on his lips. There was something about him that made Imoshen uneasy. She glanced to Vittoryxe for a sign, but the child was frozen in terror.

Imoshen's instinct was to protect the little girl, but when she took her arm, the child's flesh burned like cold fire. As if from a great distance, she heard a keening cry. Even though she did not move, the little girl wept as if her heart was breaking. Imoshen knew the feeling. She still experienced it whenever she was reminded of Reothe and her dead son. The pain nearly brought her to her knees.

It was more than she could bear. Gathering her mental resources, she focused and segued back to the earthly plane, taking Vittoryxe with her.

Blinking, she found Vittoryxe had collapsed beside her and curled into a ball. A hoarfrost covered them both.

'Gift-tutor?' Imoshen touched her arm. The instant she did, she heard the wailing child again, and felt the little girl's outrage.

Something was very wrong.

Imoshen ran out into the corridor, where she grabbed a boy in his mid-teens. 'Fetch Egrayne, quickly.'

He took off at a run.

Returning to Vittoryxe, Imoshen called on her gift and looked into the empyrean world. The gift-tutor's power pulsed within her, but very faintly. Imoshen guessed Vittoryxe was lost in the mind of the child she had been, the child Imoshen had seen in the construct.

Unsure of what to do, she took Vittoryxe's hand and tried to reach the gift-tutor.

The grief of the child was terrible.

It swamped Imoshen's defences, triggering her own grief. The loss of her son hit her all over again, and then the grief went deeper still until she returned to the five-year-old child she had been when she lost her mother.

That child had no defences. Her grief went beyond tears, to a place where there was no hope. Nothing but this.

And it went on forever...

'Imoshen?'

Someone reached out to her.

'Imoshen?'

She opened her eyes, found Egrayne and...

'All-mother Ceriane?' Imoshen blinked, and the gift-wright squeezed her fingers.

'She recognises us.' Egrayne sounded relieved.

'I'll work on Vittoryxe,' the gift-wright said. 'You see to Imoshen.'

Egrayne pulled Imoshen to her feet and drew her over to a chair by the fire. Others had come in, among them the all-mother and Vittoryxe's devotee, who seemed dazed.

'What happened, Imoshen?' Egrayne asked, kneeling by her side.

'We... we went to the empyrean plane... No, it was a construct, but it felt so real.' Her power was drained and her mind felt sluggish. 'The gift-tutor was going to show me empyrean predators. We saw a harrowraven and some scraelings. Then a T'En male came towards us. At first I thought he was part of the lesson. But Vittoryxe went very still and then she changed form, becoming a little girl. I didn't like the way the man felt. He smiled, but...'

'Are you sure it was a construct and not the empyrean plane proper?' Egrayne radiated intensity.

'That's what Vittoryxe said. But it felt real.'

Egrayne squeezed her hand and came to her feet. Gift-wright Ceriane had been working on Vittoryxe, using the devotee to assist her. When the gift-tutor stirred, Devotee Choris came out of her daze and wept with relief.

Meanwhile, Egrayne whispered to All-mother Aayelora.

Imoshen came to her feet. 'Is Vittoryxe all right?'

Egrayne and Aayelora looked to the gift-wright, who joined them.

'Imoshen saved the gift-tutor's life,' Ceriane said. They all turned to look at Vittoryxe. She appeared shattered.

Imoshen was reminded of the desolate child within the woman, and knew nothing would ever satisfy that child. The thought filled her with a deep sadness.

The devotee helped Vittoryxe into the fireside chair and stayed with her, watching her closely.

Meanwhile, the gift-wright, the all-mother and the empowerer spoke softly. Imoshen caught snatches of their conversation.

'...a male. Don't know who he was.'

'But it was supposed to be a construct.'

'...Vittoryxe must have decided to test her with the real thing, meaning to pull her out if she got into trouble.'

'...what if it wasn't one of our people?' Ceriane said. 'What if the T'En man –'

'Was a predator that could take on any form?' Egrayne suggested.

'You mean it plucked the memory of her mother's murderer from her mind?' Aayelora asked. 'That would explain Vittoryxe's reaction. As a child, she had no defences. She was only eight when her mother was killed in front of her.'

'The perfect predator,' Egrayne said. 'Using our deepest fears to disarm us.'

'I don't remember seeing that predator on the study list,' Imoshen said.

The three women turned to face her. They exchanged looks.

'You don't know all the predators of the empyrean plane,' Imoshen guessed. 'The list is a work in progress, isn't it?'

Egrayne nodded and took Imoshen aside. 'There's much we don't know about the plane, and how our gifts manifest there. Many T'En have died to provide the knowledge we currently have, but there is more to learn.'

'Not according to Vittoryxe.'

A wry smile tugged at the big empowerer's lips.

Imoshen warmed to her. She wanted Egrayne to think well of her, but... 'It's my fault we were attacked. I thought we were in a construct, not the empyrean. I would never have flaunted my power, if I'd known.'

Egrayne brushed this aside. 'You did well to recognise the danger, bring her back and hold her until the gift-wright could save her.'

Imoshen shrugged. She didn't feel as if she'd done well.

Devotee Choris whispered to Vittoryxe, who called Imoshen over.

'I hear I have you to thank for my survival. I am in your debt.'

'Oh, no. It's nothing,' Imoshen insisted, embarrassed. 'I'm just glad we both made it out.'

The all-mother's devotee arrived with a tray of glasses. The rich scent of warm spiced wine filled the chamber, and Imoshen felt herself begin to relax.

When everybody had a glass, the all-mother raised her own. 'To Imoshen's quick thinking.'

They echoed her toast. Vittoryxe grimaced.

'No,' Imoshen said quickly. 'To a lucky escape, for both of us. All I did was run.'

'True,' Egrayne said. 'But the important thing is that you didn't panic and leave Vittoryxe behind.'

Imoshen noticed the empowerer and the gift-tutor share a look. Would she ever understand the T'En women? At least one good thing would come of this.

She and Vittoryxe had survived a common threat; now they could be friends.

Chapter Thirty

'WEAR THE CLOAK, pull the hood down, keep your hands hidden and follow me,' Franto ordered.

Sorne resented the way they made him hide his hair, eyes and fingers, but he knew the war barons didn't like him. Whenever they discussed strategy with the king, he had to go into the alcove at the back of the royal tent.

He'd been waiting all spring to see the fall of Port Khitan, so he put on the cloak.

When they'd first arrived in port, he had to stay on the ship, and had only been allowed on deck at night. Through the tiny window of his cabin, he'd seen the blockade of the harbour and heard the strange language of the locals. He'd seen the camp fires of the besieging army on the hills outside of the port, and heard the distant roar of battle as Charald assaulted the port walls. It had fascinated him, until he became frustrated with being cooped up.

Then he'd badgered Franto to speak to the king. Finally, he'd been transported to the royal tent on the hillside overlooking the port. From there he could watch as the constant assault wore down the Khitite defences, and listen in to the king discussing strategy with his barons. At night he was allowed out to wander through the camp, cloaked and hooded.

Leaving the tent now, he found the king and his barons in full armour. With their banners unfurled and their war horses saddled, they were ready for the ceremonial entrance into the captured port. As pipers prepared to play a triumph, the bags produced those strange sounds he'd heard in his first vision.

Behind the king, buildings burned and pillars of dark smoke obscured the twilit sky. Sorne gasped as he recognised the scene. 'Look, Franto. It's my vision come to life.'

The little man nodded, but he had only ever seen the drawing. He hadn't seen it like this, in vivid colour, with the banners snapping and the pipers playing.

The king mounted his war horse and everyone cheered. Sorne felt the surge of elation he'd felt during the vision, and he waited for the king to beckon him and acknowledge his part in all this.

'Word has just come through,' Franto said. 'The port has fallen, but the Khitite king must have been smuggled out. The palace is deserted. Charald's going down to claim the port and the palace, but he'll have to chase the king and his court across Khitan. This is summer's cusp and it'll be hot, dusty and uncomfortable on the plains.'

'But we'll be home for winter,' Sorne said. Tonight was his triumph, the confirmation of his power, and it would be Izteben's night too. For tonight, his brother made the offering before all the church officials. One day, half-bloods would be valued and respected by True-men.

King Charald rose in the stirrups and signalled; the men-at-arms cheered. Then the pipers played a triumph, as the king entered the port with his barons.

While Sorne remained behind, the unwanted half-blood. Disappointment and shame burned in him.

And he vowed, one day, he would make the king acknowledge him. One day, Charald and his war barons would dance to his tune.

'BRING A CUSHION,' Matxin ordered.

Oskane sank onto it with relief. He felt light-headed and his heart hammered in his chest. It was the climb that had done it, but he needed the right place to stage the ceremony and this tainted site – *holy* site, he reminded himself – was perfect, a natural amphitheatre to which seats and a stage had been added.

It had served this purpose for a Wyrd sisterhood's winery over a hundred years ago. But one season's cusp, under the light of the double full moon, a salacious play was disrupted when the gods had struck down the Wyrds.

The sisterhood had packed up and left the estate. Since then, the winery's vines had gone wild, choked with brambles. Over on the next hilltop, the sisterhood's villa had fallen into disrepair. The tiled roof had collapsed and trees now grew through the mosaic floor.

In the last few days, Baron Matxin had cleared a path up to the amphitheatre. Now Oskane sat in the front row, where he had a good view of the stage. Behind him were the leaders of the Seven's churches. On his left were two dozen nobles: the prince, Nitzel, his two sons and many supporters who would bear witness to the reclamation of this holy site.

Oskane could hear Prince Cedon boasting, telling everyone what would happen based on what he had witnessed in the mine. Since the king sailed, the prince had been surrounded by sycophants, and his head was swollen with their flattery.

'Are you alright, Uncle?' Matxin asked. His help had been invaluable, taking on much of the preparation that his assistant would have seen to himself. Oskane was surprised how much he missed Franto. 'I can get you some wine, if you need it.'

'I'm fine.' He wasn't. He felt terrible. 'See that Izteben and Zabier are ready.'

Yesterday, Izteben had selected a suitable sacrifice, a long silver braid. Now the chest was brought down and placed on a stool covered with red velvet.

Izteben wore the simple breeches and thigh-length shirt of a lowly acolyte, in black rather than white. His hair was bound in one long plait and he wore a cap tied under his chin. But nothing could disguise his half-blood eyes and six fingers. By contrast, Zabier stood by him, dressed in white. His hair fell in rippling waves down his back, golden in the torchlight.

'...and then a flash of light filled the cavern,' Prince Cedon was saying. He stood in front of the nobles, holding forth. 'Everyone screamed but me. I wasn't afraid. I–'

'You should move further back, my prince,' Matxin said. 'If you are lucky, the vision may be about you. The half-blood and the carpenter's son are nearly ready.'

'To do what?' Cedon sneered. 'Throw a bauble at the gods?'

The nobles laughed obligingly.

'Cedon,' Nitzel called. 'Come here.'

'I'm a prince, born of kings. The gods should be speaking to me, not some half-blood peasant.' Cedon brushed his grandfather's restraining hands aside. 'Here, let me perform the ceremony.'

Matxin turned to Oskane, lifting his hands helplessly.

'We seek the Seven,' Cedon called, as he strode into the amphitheatre. 'We seek enlightenment, Father. Your wisdom, Scholar. Your guidance, Warrior.' He picked up the knife and gestured to Izteben to provide the blood.

Izteben glanced over his shoulder to Oskane.

'Go on.' He gestured wearily. His arm hurt and he felt cold. He needed to lie down and just wanted the ceremony to be over.

Cedon smiled as he sliced Izteben's palm deeper than he needed to. The half-blood flinched, but said nothing. Cedon dipped the knife in the blood and flicked it across the stage. Immediately the air grew heavy and oppressive. Zabier gasped, his breath condensing as mist.

Everyone went silent with anticipation.

Nothing happened.

Someone whispered and there was a giggle.

'Give me the chest, quickly.' Izteben reached for it.

Cedon snatched it from him and pulled out the braid. 'Hold out your hand.'

Izteben did as he was told. Oskane was close enough to see Izteben whisper something to Cedon – telling him to hurry, by the look of it.

Cedon dipped the end of the plait in Izteben's bloody palm and flicked the braid out. It hardly reached the full extent of its length before it was caught by the invisible god. The prince laughed and wound the plait around his hand, tugging on it, taunting the god.

'Cedon!' Oskane lurched to his feet. Pain shot through his chest and down his arm.

'See.' Cedon turned back to the audience. 'It's simple. We don't need half-bloods. The secret is the T'En ar...'

The god jerked the prince off his feet. He clutched Zabier as he flew backwards. Izteben darted after him, pulled Zabier free and shoved him to safety. Both Izteben and Cedon were lifted into the air.

'No!' Nitzel leaped to his feet.

Zabier would have gone to help, but...

A blinding light illuminated the amphitheatre.

Zabier was flung back into Oskane. They tumbled onto the stone steps. Spots of light danced in Oskane's vision; each breath was agony. Screams filled his ears. His chest felt like a giant hand was pressing down upon it.

Zabier was out cold. Oskane could hear men shouting, metal striking metal, and the soft thunk of weapons striking unprotected flesh.

Oskane shoved the lad off him and reached out. 'Matxin?'

But Matxin lunged to grab Nitzel. Moving with surprising speed, the old baron twisted free and made a run for it. He tripped over Zabier and fell across Oskane.

The impact almost made Oskane pass out.

Matxin leant forward, caught Nitzel by what was left of his hair and spoke so that only the three of them could hear.

'Yesterday, I replaced the sacrificial plait with one that had no gift residue, and I primed your stupid grandson with talk of how unfair it was that a carpenter's son, a half-blood at that, had the honour of communicating with the gods. Everything that happened here tonight, happened because I planned it. I've waited half my life for this day; now don't you wish you'd let my sister live?'

And he snapped Nitzel's neck.

'See, that is how it is done, Uncle.' Matxin calmly knelt and looked into Oskane's face. His eyes widened. 'You look terrible.'

Oskane caught his arm. 'I'm sick, I need–'

'I don't think anything but a god's intervention is going to help now, Uncle. At least you lived long enough to see Sorna avenged and Nitzel's line ended. None of his blood will leave this place alive.'

'Izteben...'

'Taken. But he served his purpose. You lost sight of it, Uncle. You lived with Wyrds so long you forgot True-men would never accept them as the gods' messengers.'

Matxin sprang to his feet. Nearby, a woman sobbed uncontrollably.

'Someone shut her up!' Matxin ordered. The woman fell silent abruptly. 'The rest of you, sit down and be quiet.'

Oskane was having trouble seeing, but he identified the bodies of Nitzel's supporters sprawled on the steps. Their spilled blood looked black in the moonlight. The terrified church leaders returned to their seats as directed, while a score of men-at-arms awaited Matxin's next order.

'Tonight you saw the gods in action,' Matxin said, his voice echoing around the amphitheatre. 'You saw them claim a half-blood as their sacrifice. You saw them take the unworthy prince and strike down his grandfather. The gods have chosen me to rule Chalcedonia. My first promise? No more unfair taxes.'

His men cheered but it was not a happy sound. It held the eager edge of greed and ambition.

'No more gold squandered on a palace to rival the Wyrd palaces.'

More cheers.

Zabier groaned.

'The gods spared this boy's life.' Matxin leant down and helped him to his feet. Sweet-faced, biddable Zabier. The baron leant close. 'What was that? You've had a vision? Praise be the Seven!' He turned to the watchers. 'This is the Father's-voice.'

His supporters cheered again.

Matxin knelt beside Oskane, who could no longer feel his legs or his hands.

'We need your ring, Uncle, as a sign that the leadership of the church passes to the lad,' he whispered. 'I'm sure you understand.'

Oskane could not have stopped him.

Matxin raised his voice. 'What was that, Uncle?' Pause. 'Why, thank you.'

He stood, holding up the ruby ring. 'My uncle, High Priest Oskane, gives his blessing to High Priest Father's-voice Zabier, along with his ring.'

And Matxin's supporters cheered once more. But the sound faded as a wave of numbness travelled up Oskane's body. He had time for one last thought – *I'm dying...*

PART TWO

Chapter Thirty-One

Year 308

SORNE FELT HELPLESS. 'Can I get you anything?'

'What do you think?' Franto snapped. His body might have betrayed him, but his mind was as keen as ever. 'There's a lump under my ribs and it's going to kill me.'

It was true. The king's healer, Baron Etri, had examined Franto and shaken his head.

Dying was one thing, dying by degrees in agony...

For three days now, Franto hadn't eaten. He'd had the shakes and a high fever, and had vomited repeatedly.

And for the past three days they'd been camped below the Khitan ruler's summer palace in the foothills of the mountains, waiting for him to surrender; he had nowhere else to run.

Franto grimaced and groaned in pain. His breath came in short, sharp gasps and his skin shone with sweat. Sorne wished he could do something, but Baron Etri had run out of pain relief. In fact, he'd run out of most of his medical supplies when the flux had swept through the camp.

Now Sorne hardly ever left Franto's side. They ate only food they had personally washed and prepared according to Franto's strict instructions. They were just as scrupulous in their ablutions and, when Sorne did venture out, he went hooded, with his mouth and nose covered. But none of this would help the little True-Man. He was close to death now.

If this was what happened when you became old, Sorne never wanted to grow old. He would be eighteen this winter's cusp and he'd much rather die on the battlefield than in a camp tent, bathed in sweat and reeking of illness.

He'd seen glorious triumph when King Charald claimed Port Khitan; he'd been there to see them raise the symbol of the Seven above the Khitite gods. On that day, Charald had insisted Sorne personally thank the Warrior god for the vision that prompted all this. The rest of the time he'd travelled in a closed cart.

Franto shuddered.

'Wine,' Sorne suggested. 'Lots of wine...'

'There is one thing you could give me. A knife with a keen edge.'

Sorne flinched. Franto had always been fair and, from a purely selfish point of view, Sorne did not want to lose him. He didn't see how he would manage without Franto's advice.

But Sorne couldn't bear to see him suffer anymore.

Going to his chest, he retrieved the ceremonial dagger Oskane had given him. He examined the edge and decided there was no need to get out the whetstone. Returning to Franto's side, he placed the knife in the old man's hand and closed his fingers around it. 'You can't get much sharper than this.'

Franto spoke in a rush. 'I'm sorry I won't be here to help you. Beware the king when he gets in one of his states. It's not natural to go days with almost no sleep. When he's like that, his temper is dangerous. The moment he's crossed, he'll turn vicious.'

'I've seen it... well, heard it.' They'd both been in the back of the king's tent when a messenger had arrived with the news that Baron Uldarvo had failed to cut off the Khitite king's retreat to his summer palace.

'Tell Oskane I was faithful to the last. Now, go see if there is a message from him.'

That seemed unlikely, and Sorne was about to say so, when he realised what Franto was doing. 'Which god do you want your soul entrusted to?'

The little man's mouth twisted with contempt. 'We both know there are no gods.'

'Then why serve...'

He shook his head and waved Sorne off.

Blinded by tears, Sorne wrapped a scarf around his lower face, then threw his hooded cloak over his shoulders.

'And Sorne?'

'Yes?'

'Charald likes warring. It makes him feel powerful because underneath, he secretly fears he is not worthy.'

Sorne blinked. The king not worthy?

'When Charald crushes an enemy, he feels like a god,' Franto whispered. 'Remember this and you have the key to him. Now go.'

Sorne made his way out into the night. Above him, the summer palace perched on the end of a high spur.

Meanwhile, the army was like a plague of rats, devouring everything in its path. The longer they remained in one place, the further they had to range to find food and the more men came down with the bloody flux. He'd heard the men talking. They worried they would not live to sail home this winter.

Home... He missed Izteben and Zabier, missed Hiruna's singing and little Valendia's cheeky smile.

Nearing the king's tent, he heard men arguing.

'I won't do it,' one of the night-watchmen said. 'You saw what the king did to the baron's messenger.'

'Someone has to tell Charald.'

'Tell the king what?' Sorne asked.

They turned to Sorne with relief, which made him distinctly uneasy.

'Warrior's-voice.' One of the men acknowledged his status, though he still made the sign to ward off Wyrd power.

Sorne spotted a brass cylinder, the sort that contained news from Chalcedonia; bad news, no doubt. Nitzel's death? Had Oskane struck already? Sorne felt a stab of disappointment. He resented being here in Khitan while events unfolded back home. 'You have a message for the king?'

'I do, Warrior's-voice.'

'I'll deliver it.'

The man handed it over to him. This must be very bad news, indeed. But knowledge was power. Sorne returned to his side of the royal tent.

'Franto?' he called.

The little True-man had climbed out of his bedroll and dressed himself in his simple white robe before taking his life. He lay on the carpet on his side. There was surprisingly little blood; he was as efficient in death as he had been in life.

Sorne let his breath out slowly. He was on his own now.

With some trepidation, he sat cross-legged next to Franto's body and took off the cylinder's cap, to find two scrolls inside. One had the royal seal and one was addressed to him in Zabier's handwriting. This he opened first, wondering why Izteben hadn't written.

Because, as Zabier wrote, Izteben had been claimed by the gods.

Anger sliced through Sorne like a blade. Heart hammering, he forced himself to read the message again from the beginning.

So much to take in... Baron Nitzel and Prince Cedon dead. All of Nitzel's sons dead. Sorne's uncle, Matxin, the new king; Oskane dying after handing Zabier the ring and naming him the next high priest and Father's-voice.

How had the offering gone so wrong? Izteben knew the danger. He read Zabier's message again, but could find no reason for the ceremony to fail.

Hot rage rolled through Sorne, swelled in his throat threatening to choke him. Tears of angry loss scalded his cheeks.

When he could think again, Sorne glanced to the other message. Perhaps he could glean more from it. He held a knife in the flame, then slid it under the wax seal and unrolled the scroll, to find an official proclamation.

King Matxin of Chalcedonia had decreed Charald's rule illegal, and the eight barons who'd sailed with him traitors. Their sons or younger brothers had been offered the choice of banishment, or swearing allegiance to him. It did not say, but Sorne suspected they'd chosen the latter.

The document went on to explain that only untainted True-men could rule Chalcedonia, and since Charald had shared the womb with a half-blood twin he was tainted. As proof of this, the Father's church held the official signed confession of former High Priest Oskane, who had been present at Charald's birth. So Oskane had always intended to bring Charald down along with Baron Nitzel.

Sorne swore softly. Chalcedonia must be buzzing with the news. No wonder the messenger did not want to be present when the king read this.

But Oskane's sudden death left Sorne in a difficult position. He was stranded halfway across the known world, with a dethroned king and a flux-ravaged army with no support, no supplies and nowhere to call home.

'Seven save us,' Sorne whispered, then heard what he'd said. No one was going to save him. When the king got the news, he would want to know why the gods hadn't foreseen it. He may even come to the conclusion that Sorne was not the Warrior's-voice, and his patron god had deserted him.

Panic made Sorne's stomach churn.

The king would want to sail right back to Chalcedonia and retake his kingdom.

Oskane had handed Matxin the throne.

It was Sorne's duty to give his uncle time to consolidate his rule. But how?

By convincing Charald this was all part of the Warrior god's plan. Why would the Warrior make Charald suffer in this way?

Oskane had assumed the gods were testing him. The Warrior could be testing Charald. Four more mainland kingdoms lay between them and Chalcedonia. Sorne could claim that this was a sign from the Warrior, and Charald's duty was to conquer the heathen kingdoms. Only then would the Warrior consider him worthy to rule Chalcedonia.

This would require another vision, so he could do nothing until season's cusp. In the meantime, Charald could consolidate his hold on Khitan, which would give them time to find a suitable place for the offering.

Sorne's loyalty was to his uncle, not to King Charald, the father who had repudiated him. He could not return home until Charald got himself killed in battle. The king was old, nearly forty-five. Few True-men lived past fifty. Charald would not live to see Chalcedonia again.

As Sorne considered the enormity of the plans he was about to set in motion, he stared at Franto's slack face. 'You picked a fine time to die.'

Which gave him an idea.

He melted the underside of the wax seal and resealed the royal decree, returning it to the message cylinder, before burning the message from Zabier.

Slinging the message cylinder over his shoulder, Sorne carried Franto's body through to the king's chamber and arranged him on the carpet in front of the king's favourite chair, as though he had delivered the message then killed himself.

Sorne placed the brass cylinder in front of Franto.

Then he retreated to his alcove, put out the lamp, stripped naked and lay down on his bedroll to wait. His mind raced as he listened for Charald's return.

A little later, the king and his barons enter the tent. He heard Charald's exclamation of surprise, followed by his curses, calling on the Seven. Then the king called for the Warrior's-voice.

Sorne rolled out of bed, tugged on a pair of breeches and was lacing them up as he answered the king's summons.

'What's this?' Charald pointed to Franto and the brass cylinder.

'Dead?' Sorne dropped to his knees to examine Franto. He looked up, pretending to be devastated. 'He killed himself. His stomach was giving him trouble, but... why would he...' Sorne's gaze fell on the message cylinder. 'Seven save us. What could it say?' Very gingerly, he picked up the cylinder and offered it to the king.

'You gave it to Franto to read?' the king asked.

Sorne nodded. 'I thought it might contain a message from High Priest Oskane. When Franto read it, he wept, then sent me to bed. That's all I know.'

Charald eyed the message cylinder, then gestured for Baron Etri to take it. 'Read it.'

The baron took out the proclamation. 'Where is the message from Oskane? How do you know it was from him?'

'It had the Father's seal. What's left of the message is in there. Franto burned it.' Sorne shrugged. 'I thought it strange, but...'

Charald sank into his chair. 'What does the decree say, Etri?'

The baron opened it, went very pale, then lifted his head. 'I think you had better read it yourself, sire.'

'Permission to take Franto's body?' Sorne asked.

The king dismissed him with a wave.

Sorne carried Franto into their alcove and laid him out on his bedroll. Then he knelt by the body and waited.

The king's rage, when it exploded, was truly terrifying. His shouts thundered, carrying across the camp. Wood splintered, glass smashed.

The first time he'd heard the king in a temper, Sorne had felt fear. Now, after Franto's explanation, Sorne felt contempt. Rage achieved nothing.

The barons joined the king in cursing Matxin's betrayal and heaping scorn upon Nitzel for his failure to protect Prince Cedon.

Sorne thought he'd escaped the worst of it, when Charald began bellowing for him. He entered the tent, and two of the barons grabbed him and dragged him in front of the king.

They tossed Sorne onto the carpet. Charald pulled him to his feet, shaking him like a dog. They were the same height, but the king was heavily muscled and Sorne had yet to fill out.

Charald's hands closed on his throat. 'How can this be?' Foam flecked the king's mouth, spraying Sorne's face. 'The Warrior promised me victory!'

Sorne caught the hands on his throat and held on, struggling to suck in a breath. 'You had victory in port–'

'And, while my back was turned, I lost my son and my kingdom! Why is the Warrior doing this? What have I done? Those lies... how could Oskane write them?'

'I don't know what you're talking about.'

'It's just as well he's dead. I'd have his balls for–'

'He's dead? Scholar Oskane's dead?' Sorne wasn't supposed to know this yet. He held onto the hands at his throat, in the hope he would live long enough to make the offer that would send the king out to conquer the kingdoms of the Secluded Sea. 'No wonder Franto wept.'

The king's eyes narrowed. 'I'm here because of you, half-blood. You sent me–'

'The Warrior sent you here. I bear the Warrior's mark.' He had another streak of white hair growing from the scar on his forehead. 'You stood in the presence of the gods. You were blinded by the flash of light.'

Charald released him, and Sorne crumpled to his knees.

'Why is the Warrior doing this?' Charald paced, rubbing his face. 'I've done everything he wanted and now–'

'Perhaps the Warrior is warring with the Father?' Baron Norholtz suggested. 'You left the Father's-voice in Chalcedonia.'

Sorne looked up, surprised by help from this quarter. From Norholtz's expression, it was a genuine suggestion.

'That's right,' Baron Etri said. 'A son sometimes fights with his father. Have the half-blood make an offering. Ask the Warrior what he wants of you.'

Which was exactly what Sorne wanted to suggest. He lowered his eyes to hide his relief.

The king strode back to stand over him. 'You'll summon the Warrior for me.'

'As soon as your men find me a holy site.'

'A holy site? Do they even have them, this far south?'

There was silence, then Baron Norholtz ventured a reply. 'They have what they claim are holy sites, but whether they are truly pathways to the gods... Only the Warrior's-voice could tell you.'

Charald brushed this aside. 'We'll find a holy site and make a sacrifice to call the gods.' He returned to stand over Sorne. 'The Warrior will grant you a vision.'

Sorne nodded and came to his feet, although he kept his head bowed. 'As you say, sire. At the season's cusp, when the walls are weakest, I will be able to reach the one-eyed Warrior god. Until then–'

'Your pardon, my king?' One of the night watch pushed the tent flap aside.

'What is it now?' Charald turned on him.

'There's a delegation from the Khitite ruler. They just arrived.'

Charald sent a triumphant look to his barons. 'Now we talk terms.'

'Accept what he offers,' Baron Etri urged softly. 'As soon as news reaches him, he'll know we're stranded here.'

Charald grimaced and flung himself into his chair. 'Show him in.'

The barons ranged themselves behind him, and Sorne moved to one side.

Three men entered. One wore rich brocade, decorated with the geometric patterns popular in Khitite clothing and architecture. His black hair was oiled and sleek. To Sorne, it seemed too black for a man of his age. Rings covered his fingers. The other two wore simpler garments, and each carried an ornate chest.

'King Charald the Great,' the leader said, giving him the Khitite bow. 'His Majesty King Idan has sent me to negotiate. As a token of his sincerity, he offers these gifts.'

The two servants went on bent knee to present the two small chests.

With a flourish the Khitite gestured. 'The first is filled with precious jewels.'

Charald inspected the gems. 'I have whole chambers filled with such stones at home.'

Sorne hid a smile.

'Secondly, the orb of power.'

The servant opened the second chest. Charald leant forward to look.

Sorne stepped in. 'Allow me, your majesty. I will ascertain the orb's authenticity.'

He rolled up his sleeves and went to take it out of the chest. A tingle of awareness told him it did indeed hold power, but when he removed the glass ball from its bed of silk nothing happened.

The orb's power was unlike anything he had encountered before. Curious, he touched the orb with his other hand and the moment his fingers made contact he felt the power flow through him. The orb glowed with an inner radiance.

Sorne returned the orb to its chest. 'It is indeed pretty, your majesty. But it is nothing compared to the objects of power we have back home.'

King Charald smiled and Sorne enjoyed his approval, before remembering this man did not deserve his loyalty.

The next morning, they accepted King Idan's surrender and took his eldest son hostage, before the Khitite king realised all but four of Charald's barons had deserted him in the night.

Chapter Thirty-Two

IMOSHEN FELT SICK with dread. Ever since she'd escaped from Lighthouse Isle, she couldn't bear to be apart from her choice-son. Logically, she knew he was safe in the sisterhood palace, playing with Egrayne's choice-daughter Saffazi, but even so, her heart raced. She couldn't help but envision a terrible accident befalling him.

'What is it?' Reoden asked. 'Do you need to go back?'

Imoshen shook her head. This was the first time she'd been out of the sisterhood quarter, out of the palace even, since the all-council where she'd...

But she mustn't think about that.

Nearly half a year, locked away. For someone who was used to wandering her island, it was unbearable.

It was autumn cusp, the air was warm and the stones under her feet held the heat of the day. Sweet-scented flowers tumbled from shopfront pots and over balconies, mingling with the aroma of rich food being prepared in the eateries for this evening's celebrations in the free quarter. Soon the Mieren shopkeepers would pack up for the day and hurry out the causeway gate.

And all she could think about was getting back to her choice-son.

Reoden pulled her into an alleyway between shops. Imoshen looked up at the sisterhood leader: beautiful, exotic and powerful. Her gift stirred.

'I can feel your heart racing, Imoshen,' Reoden said. 'What's wrong?'

'Nothing, I...'

Two brotherhood warriors tackled another group. It was play fighting, but the sudden surge of their gifts made Imoshen gasp. When had she become this timid creature?

'Imoshen?'

She should never have come here.

'Imoshen?'

She despised herself.

Reoden kissed her.

It was so unexpected that her gift broke free and she sensed the nature of Reoden's healing gift, so pure and powerful. Lips incredibly soft, skin like hot satin. Who would have thought a kiss could be this perfect?

Reoden pulled back and Imoshen saw colour race up her cheeks as she fought to rein in her gift.

'Come on,' the healer said. 'If we don't hurry, they'll be closed.'

'Where are you taking me?' And what had just happened?

'You'll see.' There was laughter in Reoden's voice; she sounded young and happy. This wasn't the face she showed the other leaders of the sisterhoods.

Imoshen felt privileged, and a languid warmth flowed through her body. Her feet barely touched the ground. Since arriving in the city, she'd observed the T'En sisters. She knew that it was common practice for an adept to take an initiate for a lover and guide her as she settled into the sisterhood, like Arodyti and Sarosune. Sometimes they became shield-sisters when the initiate finished her training. But she and Reoden were from different sisterhoods. Was it even possible for them to be lovers?

In the street, they passed T'En and Malaunje alike, some hurrying to complete their business before the shops closed, others already off to celebrate, dressed in their finery, and a few Mieren wearing the distinctive short red mantles that proclaimed they had a licence to be in the city.

'Here we are.' Reoden pulled her around a corner and covered her eyes.

Imoshen could feel the healer at her back. The warmth of Reoden's body, the sensation of her gift barely leashed, made Imoshen's heart race.

'Are you ready?' the healer whispered, breath brushing Imoshen's ear.

She removed her hands.

Imoshen blinked. Before them was a single-storey shopfront. What was so special about this place? Then Imoshen recognised the scroll and the nib: the symbol of the Sagoras.

'They have a shop here? I can buy treatises? Learn anything I want?'

The healer laughed. 'Come inside, before they close up.'

As they ran across the street, a young shop assistant stepped out of the door to lower the shutters. He, or she, wore traditional Sagora clothing, a long-sleeved gown and hood with a fine mesh veil that revealed only the mouth and chin. The Sagoras were notoriously private.

Imoshen and Reoden entered the shop. By the glow of a single lamp, Imoshen saw maps, diagrams of plants and animals, cunningly constructed models and cleverly wrought puzzles in both wood and metal. This must be where Ardeyne used to purchase the treatises for her.

That thought brought a halt to her joy, but instead of sadness she felt anger. Such a waste.

A man came out of the shop's backroom. Like the young assistant, he wore the Sagora costume, but the slight stubble visible beneath the veil revealed his gender. He spoke Chalcedonian with an accent. 'I'm sorry, we are closed for today.'

Imoshen could not leave without getting one thing to take home and treasure. She wanted to understand why the problems between the brotherhoods and sisterhoods existed and the closest she could think of was... 'Do you have any treatises on military history?'

'No, but I can order something in for you.'

'Do that, but...' Imoshen desperately wanted to take something home with her now. She'd had to leave all her wonderful treatises back on Lighthouse Isle. And she remembered one she'd been reading. 'Do you have Felesoi's treatise on the passing-on of traits in plants?' In her excitement she couldn't remember the exact title and her Chalcedonian was a little rusty.

'That one I do have.' He smiled as he turned away and searched several small drawers. He retrieved the treatise with a flourish, placed it on the counter and named a price.

Only then did Imoshen realise she had no way of paying.

'Let me,' Reoden said, stepping forward and producing some coins. 'Think of it as a welcome home gift.'

'Thank you.' Imoshen blushed.

She accepted the treatise and they were escorted out

'We should get back,' Reoden said. 'The free quarter can get rather... wild during celebrations.'

'Thank you for taking me to the Sagoras,' Imoshen said, touched that Reoden should remember a chance remark.

'Not everyone sees scholarly works as a treat.'

Imoshen smiled. As they crossed the street, she memorised the shop's location.

They were on the main road, heading for the sisterhood quarter, when she felt the approach of aggressive male gifts. Tension gathered in Reoden's body and Imoshen's mouth went dry.

'Keep walking. Don't meet their eyes. They'll see it as a threat,' the healer said softly, then raised her voice. 'Are you pleased with your purchase?'

'Oh, yes, I had no idea the Sagoras had a shop here...' But her senses were trained on the five T'En men walking towards them. Gift-warriors, armed with long-knives, armoured with hate; so much anger and violence seethed within them.

It was only when she and Reoden entered the sisterhood gate that she felt Reoden relax and ceased her chatter.

'That...' Reoden sagged against a wall. She took a moment to catch her breath before hurrying Imoshen on.

'I've never sensed that much animosity before. I shouldn't have taken you into the free quarter. It's too soon. I'm sorry, Imoshen. You were right to be nervous.' Reoden summoned a smile. 'Don't worry. One day you'll be able to walk the streets without fear.'

'Would they attack me?'

'No... No, that would be an attack on the sisterhoods.'

But Reoden's hesitation gave her away. She wasn't certain.

As they reached the steps of Aayelora's palace, the healer went to place a kiss on Imoshen's cheek, then hesitated. Both of them could feel it, this thing that surged between them. There would be no more casual kisses.

Reoden cupped Imoshen's cheek, looked into her eyes and was gone.

Imoshen hurried up the steps palace and ran straight into Vittoryxe.

'Where have you been? I've looked everywhere.' Her gaze fell to the scroll Imoshen held to her breast. 'What's that, a treatise?'

'A Sagora–'

'Mieren knowledge? I don't know why you bother. Their perception of the world cannot match ours. They have nothing to teach us.'

Imoshen's gift surged and she saw a closed loop. Vittoryxe could not be reached.

The gift-tutor stiffened. 'Did you just–'

'I'm sorry, my gift slipped my control. I had a fright in the free quarter, some brothers–'

'Who? Which brotherhood?'

'I didn't notice.'

Vittoryxe shook her head, a malicious gleam in her eyes. 'A raedan with so little control? You'll never earn full adept status. Go.'

Grateful for her escape, Imoshen hurried away.

'If you know what's good for you,' Vittoryxe called after her, 'you'll stay in the palace, where you're safe.'

She wasn't safe here. Vittoryxe was just waiting for a chance to discredit her. She'd thought, when she helped the gift-tutor escape the attack on the higher plane, that they could be friends. But the near-death experience seemed only to have sharpened Vittoryxe's animosity.

Imoshen had barely reached her chamber, when a Malaunje came with the news that Reoden wanted to see her.

Excited and curious, she followed them down to a small greeting chamber on the ground floor. It was dark, and a single lamp had been lit.

Reoden turned to face her as she entered. 'Close the door, Imoshen.'

The healer's tone made her stomach clench.

'Don't look so worried.' Reoden sighed. 'You aren't used to our ways. I thought I had better be plain with you. It was wrong of me to kiss you. You weren't prepared, and know nothing of casual trysting.' There was nothing casual about the way Imoshen felt. 'There is a gulf between us. You're too young for me.'

Imoshen understood. 'You don't want to be associated with me. I'm hated by the brotherhoods and an inconvenience to the sisterhoods.'

Reoden flushed. 'You know nothing of life in the city. I lead a great sisterhood. I must think of them.'

Imoshen nodded. Her instinct was to fight for what could have been, but they would see each other all the time and... 'I don't want to lose you as a friend.'

'Oh, Imoshen, I will always be your friend.' Reoden crossed the chamber, went to hug her, then hesitated. She took one of her hands. 'And we will see each other all the time. You do understand, don't you?'

She nodded but, as Reoden left, she felt betrayed. She hated this place, with its restrictions and barriers.

'What did the healer want?' Frayvia asked when she returned to their chambers.

'Where's Iraayel?'

'With Arodyti and Sarosune. They took him up to the roof garden to show him the glow worms.'

'Glow worms? This, I must see. Come on.'

So she joined the gift-warriors and her choice-son on the roof. As Iraayel and Frayvia marvelled, Imoshen buried the girl who grew up wild on the island. That girl couldn't survive here, and there was no other place for her. She would have to reinvent herself.

VITTORYXE SEETHED.

Imoshen had seen her at her most vulnerable, and it infuriated her. Knowing that Imoshen had saved her life only added to her frustration. If Imoshen had acknowledged the debt and allowed her to work it off, Vittoryxe could have put it behind her. But Imoshen had dismissed it, so the obligation could never be erased.

Just as Imoshen could not be removed. Not when Egrayne suspected Vittoryxe's part in the last gift-tutor's death. The empowerer had no proof, or she would have laid an accusation, but the message was clear: there could be no more accidents.

Which left Vittoryxe with Imoshen, the raedan. The wildcard.

Imoshen... None of the others could see how ambitious the girl was, how she turned every event to her advantage.

Like now.

There she sat under the awning between the two sisterhood leaders. If Imoshen hadn't been a raedan, they would not bother to cultivate her. If she hadn't been so powerful, they wouldn't bother to groom her for leadership. If she hadn't had a choice-son around the same age as Healer Reoden's two children, she wouldn't be sitting there with them right now. The healer said something. All-mother Aayelora laughed, but Imoshen hardly smiled.

Did she even know what an honour it was for her choice-son to associate with the healer's daughter? Lyronyxe was a sacrare, born of two pure T'En parents. Sacrares were rare. They were hard to carry and birth. More often than not, they were stillborn. They were heir to great gifts, a boon to their sisterhood.

Lyronyxe was the reason the healer had won the leadership of her sisterhood at such a young age. And it was only Reoden's healing gift that allowed her to produce a healthy sacrare.

Vittoryxe was so angry she had trouble controlling her gift. Power prickled across her skin. All around her the half-bloods worked, tending the flowerbeds and clipping topiary trees. Their copper hair shone in the sun as they studiously ignored her.

'Choice-mother?'

Vittoryxe looked down on her own choice-son. Why had the inner circle saddled her with another boy child?

'May I go play with the other children?'

It was on the top of her tongue to refuse Bedutz, but if Imoshen's child could play with a sacrare, then so could he. 'Yes. Go on.'

He ran off happily.

The two all-mothers waved, beckoning Vittoryxe. So as not to appear too eager, she turned to her devotee and pretended to inspect her latest acquisition – a bird, with fine tail feathers. She hoped this trait would breed true. 'Take him to the aviary and place him in the cage next to the others, so they can get used to him.'

Choris nodded and took the bird away.

Only then did Vittoryxe wander over and join the T'En females under the awning.

As she crossed the rooftop garden, the children ran past her, playing hide and seek amongst the flowering pots and citrus trees. Iraayel brushed against a cumquat tree, scattering fruit in his wake.

'Watch where you're going!' Vittoryxe snapped. 'Honestly...'

'Vittoryxe.' Reoden smiled. 'I was just telling Imoshen, her lack of energy doesn't arise from a physical illness, but an injury to her gift.'

'It's nothing. Don't trouble yourself,' Imoshen said quickly.

She was pretending to be humble, but for some reason, only Vittoryxe could see this. 'Of course Imoshen's gift is injured. She made the deep-bonding with a male who was then murdered. It's a wonder she didn't die with him. The loss of her sacrare son will have damaged her power, too.'

'Have you heard about the new king of the True-men?' Reoden asked.

'What new king?' All-mother Aayelora sat up.

'It's a terrible thing,' Reoden said. 'The old king sailed away to make war and, the moment his back was turned, his cousin murdered his heir and claimed the throne. The new king shut the murdered boy's mother up in an abbey dedicated to their goddess, the Mother.'

'Vittoryxe, why didn't I hear of this?' Aayelora asked.

'Mieren squabbles are no concern of ours. And King Matxin didn't murder his cousin's son,' Vittoryxe said. She savoured the chance to prove that she was better informed. 'King Matxin says the gods killed the boy. Apparently, they decided to hold one of their barbaric rituals in a place we had clearly marked as being dangerous, and there was a breach between the planes. The boy was taken.'

'How awful,' Imoshen said. 'The Mieren have no protection from empyrean predators. Why would they–'

'Because they're arrogant, and think they know better,' Vittoryxe snapped.

Imoshen blushed.

One of the children wailed and Imoshen jumped to her feet to check on them.

'That's what Malaunje are for,' Vittoryxe called after her, but she didn't seem to hear her. With a shrug, Vittoryxe glanced to the two all-mothers. 'She has no decorum. Have you seen the way she treats her devotee? No concept of the proper distance between T'En and Malaunje.'

'I'm surprised that nobody informed me about the new king,' Aayelora said.

'Personally, I don't care how many of the Mieren kill each other off, as long as they leave us alone.' Vittoryxe said. 'In fact, the more the Mieren fight amongst themselves the better.'

She spotted Imoshen weaving through the potted plants with three children clustered around her while she carried the fourth child, who sobbed in her arms.

'Mama, come see.' Lyronyxe beckoned the healer.

Imoshen entered the shadow of the awning and sat down with the child on her lap, turning him around. It was Bedutz.

'He fell and cut his knee on the edge of a pot,' Imoshen said.

'Here, let me...' Reoden knelt at Imoshen's feet.

'No.' Vittoryxe was determined not to let Imoshen interfere with how she raised her choice-son. 'He fell because he was being careless. He must suffer or he won't be careful next time. Bedutz, come to me.'

He slid off Imoshen's lap and went to her, trying to hold back his tears. Vittoryxe took his hand and stalked off.

She'd only gone a few steps when she turned back. 'If you ask me, all-mother, it's not the Mieren we need to worry about. It's the brotherhoods. Imoshen executed one of their all-fathers and survived an ambush by their hands-of-force. The men fear her, and what they fear, they seek to destroy.'

'You could just as easily argue that they respect strength,' Egrayne said, coming up behind her.

'Safi!' Iraayel darted past Vittoryxe to hug Egrayne's choice-daughter. Like Lyronyxe, she was a little older than the others and always leading them into trouble. Sure enough, the sacrare and Reoden's choice-son ran over to join them. The children huddled together, whispering and giggling, before breaking apart and running off. The garden rang with their laughter.

Vittoryxe felt Bedutz tug on her hand, his injury forgotten. She kept a tight hold on him.

'The good news is that the brotherhoods are feuding,' Egrayne said. 'All-father Chariode won the assets and survivors of the disgraced brotherhood, beating off three of the other all-fathers. There's been two assassinations since spring that I know of.'

'That's terrible,' Imoshen said.

'No, it's good,' Vittoryxe corrected. 'There will be retaliations. As long as the men are fighting amongst themselves, they aren't plotting another brotherhood uprising.'

Imoshen went pale. 'There was an uprising?'

Vittoryxe smiled. The more Imoshen opened her mouth, the more she revealed her ignorance of the sisterhood's proud history.

Surely the others must realise she wasn't suitable to be all-mother. It wasn't enough just to be a raedan.

Vittoryxe had been busy, planting seeds of doubt in the minds of all the mid- to high-ranking sisters, while shoring up support for her own claim to the position. One day Vittoryxe would be all-mother, which meant if their people ever needed a causare to unite the T'Enatuath, she would be in the running. Then it would be a matter of making sure the vote went her way.

'Instead of wasting your time reading Sagora treatises, Imoshen, you should study the T'Enatuath's history.' Satisfied that she had made her point, Vittoryxe left.

And the very next day, she found Imoshen near the aviary, reading a treatise on the origin of the T'Enatuath.

'That's just an educated guess. No one really knows where we came from,' Vittoryxe told her.

'I thought I should start from the beginning and work my way through. I need to understand why we have brotherhoods and sisterhoods.'

'Because it's the only safe way for adult T'En to live,' Vittoryxe said as she inspected the plumage of one of her birds.

'This is your new one?' Imoshen came over. 'He's very beautiful.'

Vittoryxe was not entirely comfortable having Imoshen this close to her prized birds.

'How do you know their traits will breed true?'

'Some do, some don't.'

'You must have been doing this a long time.'

'Since I came here,' Vittoryxe said. 'It was right after I saw my choice-mother murdered by a brotherhood warrior. The sisters thought it best if I had a complete change, so they sent me to the city. My new choice-mother gave me a pair of nightingales. I've been breeding birds ever since.'

'I'm sorry. I didn't mean to stir up painful memories.'

'I feel nothing,' Vittoryxe said, determined to make it true.

Imoshen sighed. Vittoryxe wished she would go away.

'I'd like to help,' Imoshen offered.

Vittoryxe hesitated. She wanted someone to admire the birds and her knowledge of them, but she did not want to share something this precious with Imoshen.

'I'm fascinated by how the traits come down through the generations.'

Vittoryxe sniffed. 'Very well.'

Chapter Thirty-Three

Year 316

'COME WITH US.'

Imoshen looked up to see Arodyti and Sarosune in their finery, eyes and lips painted, silks parting to reveal glimpses of pale skin, jewelled sandals flashing as they swept into her chamber. She could feel the overflow of their gifts from here.

'Is it that time of year again?' Imoshen teased.

'You've never been and you promised us last time.'

Imoshen gestured to her bird breeding chart. 'I'm working.'

Moving in a cloud of subtle scent, enhanced by her gift, Sarosune came over to see what she was doing. 'Oh... Vittoryxe and her birds. She works you too hard.'

Imoshen looked down. Vittoryxe wasn't to blame, although she would give the gift-tutor a copy of the charts. She'd created the charts for the Sagoras and was waiting to hear back from them as to whether her theories on inherited traits matched up with theirs. Venerable Felesoi had been most interested.

'Reading about a festival and taking part in it are two different things.' Arodyti rested her elbows on the desk. Imoshen's gaze slid to the dip of her breasts, a delicate curving shadow. 'You've never attended a spring cusp brotherhood display. You can help us pick our trysting partners for midsummer.'

Imoshen felt her face grow hot.

Arodyti laughed and kissed her cheek. 'You're priceless.'

Imoshen shrugged. 'It's just... it doesn't seem decent, inspecting the men like wares in a shop.'

'If we don't go watch the displays, how will we know which ones we want?' Sarosune countered. She wrinkled her nose. 'We don't want the all-mother wasting her time negotiating a tryst for us, only to discover we don't fancy the man she picks.'

Imoshen laughed, put the chart away and came to her feet. 'I'll just tell my devotee.'

'And wear something nice,' Sarosune called as she walked out.

'The men will be looking at us, too.' Arodyti said. 'They give their all-father a list and the all-mother compares it to our list.' She laughed at Imoshen's expression. 'Each person's stature and the nature of his or her gift must be taken into account.'

After eight years in the city, Imoshen had come to understand the workings of the sisterhood. Egrayne formed the link between the elders of the inner circle and the next generation. Of the younger sisters, Arodyti and Sarosune were her closest friends

She and the healer Reoden had fashioned a friendship that was too important to Imoshen to jeopardise. And she'd even overcome Vittoryxe's hostility.

In her private chamber, Imoshen found Frayvia playing cards with Iraayel. He would turn thirteen this winter's cusp, and then he would move his bedroll in with the rest of the lads training to take their place in the brotherhoods. She didn't want to send him to live with the lads; didn't want to send him to Chariode's brotherhood, when he turned seventeen. The day they'd arrived in the city, it had all seemed so far away. Now...

'I claim the sisterhood,' Iraayel announced, placing his cards in a line one by one. 'I have the all-mother, voice-of-reason, hand-of-force, an empowerer and even a wildcard raedan!'

'That beats me.' Frayvia put her cards down. 'All I have is a pair of shield-sisters, the gift-tutor and three gift-warriors.'

Summoning a smile, Imoshen interrupted. 'I'm going out for a little while, down to the free quarter with Arodyti and Sarosune.'

'Can I come?' Iraayel put his cards down. 'I'm tired of being shut in the palace.'

'We'll all go to the empowerment celebration tomorrow,' Imoshen said.

'That's right, Lyronyxe is being empowered. I wonder what her gift will be. Sardeon told her she'd be a wind-wender, because she's full of hot air.'

Frayvia rolled her eyes. 'Brothers.'

Imoshen planted a kiss on her devotee's forehead and tugged affectionately on Iraayel's plait, which had grown past his knees. When he left the sisterhood she would have to cut it, to symbolise that he was dead to her.

Anguish, sharp and savage, made her gift surge.

Frayvia felt it. 'Imoshen?'

'It's nothing.' She slipped out to rejoin the shield-sisters.

'You took so long I thought you'd changed your mind and put on something silky,' Sarosune teased. 'But here you are, still in the same boring clothes... the absent-minded scholar.'

'At least wear your raedan torc,' Arodyti urged.

'I'm not sure where my torc is.'

'Oh, Imoshen.' Sarosune rolled her eyes. 'You're hopeless.'

'She doesn't care about stature, Saro.' Arodyti shook her head and threaded her arm through Imoshen's. 'Sometimes, you say the most shocking things.'

'You love it.'

Arodyti laughed. 'Yes, I do, and that's why I will never be welcomed into the inner circle.'

'No serious talk today. I forbid it.' Sarosune took Imoshen's other arm. 'Come on.'

As they left the sisterhood quarter, they were surrounded by T'En women, laughing and talking. It was the last day of spring and the air was warm with the promise of summer.

The vivid colours of the sisters' silks and satins contrasted brightly with the city's white stones. The boulevard stretched out before them, all the way to causeway gate, which was closed today. No Mieren were allowed in for the next two days.

Up ahead, Imoshen could hear the deep voices of the men, and the sounds of drums and pipes made her heart race.

Sarosune shivered with excitement. 'You should see them dance!'

In the park, each of the brotherhoods had staked out an area for themselves. Some played music, some performed poetry, others danced or practised their balance and combat exercises.

The impact of so many T'En men with their gifts barely contained was overpowering. Imoshen opened her gift awareness and saw that while there was some aggression in the air, the men were mainly focusing their gifts on bravado and display, honed with the keen edge of desire.

'There's so many of them. And they're all so... hungry.'

'Yes. Isn't it wonderful!' Sarosune spun happily on her toes. Her trousers swirled out provocatively, revealing the curve of her calves.

Several brothers responded by inviting her to hear them sing, or watch them dance. Imoshen tensed.

'Don't worry.' Arodyti squeezed Imoshen's arm, while Sarosune darted on ahead. 'They won't touch us without our permission. They wouldn't dare.'

Gradually, Imoshen became entranced by the displays. Some of the men wore elaborate costumes. Their faces painted and their long hair dressed with jewels, they gestured elegantly as they recited poetry. Their words conjured up tragic pasts and brilliant futures. Others wore only breeches, their hair bound in the warrior's braid as they practised their balance and strength exercises, moving into the long-knife patterns, blades flashing. Their athleticism and daring took Imoshen's breath away.

'See!' Sarosune breathed. They'd paused to watch two shield-brothers. 'Live blades.'

'Live blades?' Imoshen asked.

'Not blunt practice blades.'

'Oh... Such precision and trust,' Imoshen said. This close to Sarosune and Arodyti, she could feel the shield-sisters' gifts riding their excitement.

The men responded with teasing and bantering. They offered glimpses of their gifts, laden with promise. Imoshen smiled. She hadn't let down her guard and played like this since Lighthouse Isle and Reothe. The pain of the memory made everything sharp and bright.

A group of women, beautiful as birds, swept past, their high sweet voices carrying over the din.

'...Rutz's new play is about to start,' one said. 'I swear he is the greatest living playwright.'

'Come on.' Arodyti urged. 'We can't miss this.'

'Will Rutz be there?' Imoshen asked. She'd seen two of his plays in a free quarter theatre.

'Probably, not that we'll know. Rutz is not his real name.'

'Why doesn't he use his real name? Doesn't he want stature?'

'They say his plays are so good he's more than a word-smith,' Arodyti said, eyes sparkling. 'They say he is able to imbue spoken words with the power to sway people. With a gift like that, he could win himself a brotherhood, maybe even enslave the other all-fathers. If his identity got out, it could cost him his life.'

'Hush, it's starting.'

As Imoshen sat on the grass with Arodyti and Sarosune, she hugged her knees and studied the audience's reaction to the play. It was about the handing over of a T'En baby, born of a Malaunje mother. The man playing the mother did a brilliant job. The audience laughed, but Imoshen found it difficult to join in. Didn't they realise the play was a tragedy?

She looked away from the stage, and noticed a commotion at the edge of the park. The crowd parted to let a group of brothers through; shouts and laughter followed them.

Such was the disturbance that the musicians faltered and the actors fell silent. One of the new arrivals climbed onto the stage and unrolled a banner, waving it above his head.

'Would you look at that?' Arodyti gasped. 'That's All-father Hueryx's banner, taken from his brotherhood's palace tower.'

Imoshen had heard of banner-stealing, but couldn't see the point.

'It's not easy to take another brotherhood's banner,' Arodyti told her. 'They have to slip in, hide, make their way to the tower, grab the banner and get out again without hurting anyone. If they get caught, the other brotherhood beats them and throws them in the lake.' She laughed at Imoshen's expression. 'A broken nose, maybe a broken bone and a ducking – worth it, for the stature.'

Another brother joined the first on the stage, displaying All-father Chariode's banner to more cheers. Two more arrived with brotherhood banners, then another and another.

'That's six out of nine banners. I don't believe it!' Sarosune sprang to her feet. 'I've never seen this many banners.'

'I don't think it's individual brothers making a play for stature,' Arodyti said as she drew Imoshen to her feet. 'This is an all-father, claiming stature for his brotherhood.'

'But which one?' Sarosune asked.

'We'll know when we see the last two banners.'

'All-father Paragian!' The shout went up as two more men mounted the stage. 'Paragian!'

Imoshen shook her head. After eight years of study, she believed she understood the customs of the T'Enatuath. Then something like this happened.

Would she always feel like an outsider?

* * *

BUILDINGS STILL BURNED. Sorne ignored the piteous moans of the injured, the weeping of mothers searching for children, and the cries of men looking for their wives and daughters among the raped and murdered. If he didn't, he would go mad. A conquering army expected certain rewards, and King Charald was generous to his followers.

Sorne strode through the capital of Navarone, the final kingdom to fall to King Charald. After winning Khitan only to lose Chalcedonia, the king had started out with just four loyal barons and an army depleted by the flux; now he ruled all the mainland kingdoms of the Secluded Sea, except Chalcedonia.

Sorne was alone, having left his holy-swords taking a census of Navarone's largest temple. He'd discovered leadership was mostly a matter of rewarding those who worked hard. The chance of advancement made men eager to serve him, and he did not favour noble over commoner.

Stepping around the rubble of a collapsed shop front, he ducked past an overturned vintner's cart.

The softest of sounds made him glance behind him in time to see a blow coming his way. He ducked, and the cudgel took him on the shoulder.

With no time to go for his sword, Sorne grabbed the cudgel and twisted. Something snapped in his attacker's wrist. The man swore and lost his grip on the weapon.

The scarred, middle-aged man backed up, calling for his companions.

Sorne tossed the cudgel away and drew his sword.

His new attackers were a pair of skinny, poorly-dressed youths, armed with nasty little knives. He recognised the type. Poor and desperate, they were more comfortable slitting the throats of drunks than facing an armed man.

As King Charald's personal advisor, messenger of the Warrior god, Sorne had fought off two assassination attempts in the first year. This was without any combat training, and he still bore the scars of both encounters. His holy-swords were supposed to come between him and assassins, but he wasn't the type to leave anything to chance, so he'd taken training in both armed and unarmed combat.

Now he eased into a swordsman's stance.

The youths cast the middle-aged thug a quick look, turned and fled. The older thug spat and backed off.

Sorne's hand trembled slightly as he sheathed his sword. He felt his shoulder gingerly. Broken collar bone. Again.

Breathing carefully, he cradled his bad arm against his chest and headed for the palace, where he would take some of the Khitite soothing powders. Not that he would admit to using them. The king used nothing for his wounds, and despised men who did.

Something about Sorne's encounter with the thugs troubled him. It took him a few moments before he realised that, although they had all dressed like men of Navarone and the middle-aged thug had spoken Ronish, he had sworn in Chalcedonian. This was no random attack. Sorne suspected either his uncle, King Matxin, or one of the king's supporters was behind it.

Keeping to the middle of the streets, Sorne finally reached the palace square. He paused at the steps of the palace, to shake the ash and dust from his robes.

'King Charald is looking for you, Warrior's-voice.' It was the son of the deposed Khitite king. Eight years ago, young Idan had been a hostage; now he was fifteen and loyal to King Charald. Baron Etri – *King Etri*, Sorne reminded himself – had married Idan's sister, and their son was heir to the throne. According to rumour, Etri wore his hair oiled and was now more Khitite than Chalcedonian.

'I warn you, the king's in one of his moods,' Idan added.

Sorne nodded and gestured. 'Over that way three blocks, there's a wagon of wine barrels. See if you can find a cart. I'll split them with you.' Idan nodded and took off. For a prince, he had the soul of a merchant, and war was all about turning a profit.

Sorne entered the palace. He stepped over smashed glass, and dodged men removing bodies before making his way up the grand staircase. The buzz of activity told him where Charald was. How a man of fifty-two had so much energy, Sorne didn't know.

He entered the chamber to find Charald dealing with the necessities of a conquered city. Judging by his rapid speech and hectic colour, the king was in one of his states. When he was like this, he needed very little sleep, and his temper could flare up at the slightest thing.

King Charald was ordering his men to put out the fires, clear the streets, make sure there was clean water, and get the markets up and running as soon as possible.

Seeing Charald would be busy for a while, Sorne went through to the balcony. If the king's mania became too bad, he would slip Charald some of the soothing powder. He'd been doing it for a while now.

From the balcony, Sorne looked out across the port to the docks. Down by the wharfs the warehouses were still burning, and out on the bay ships were ablaze. In the last eight years, he'd seen his vision repeated over and over, accompanied by the pipers playing the triumph. Now he hated the sound.

Back in Khitan, he'd been a naive boy of seventeen. Shielded from the world, he'd wanted power, believing it would make True-men respect him. And he'd thought he owed Oskane and Uncle Matxin his loyalty. To that end, he'd turned Charald loose upon the kingdoms of the Secluded Sea. Tens of thousands had died, and Charald had forged an empire, rewarding each of his faithful barons with a conquered kingdom.

Now, with the fall of Navarone, Charald had the might of five kingdoms behind him, and Sorne's plan to buy his uncle time to consolidate his hold on the Chalcedonian throne had backfired spectacularly. King Matxin would be quaking in his bed.

Sorne hadn't heard from Zabier since Khitan, but the Father's-voice had often been mentioned in reports from

Charald's loyal spies. It appeared Zabier held much the same position in Chalcedonia as Sorne did here.

Meanwhile, as King Charald's prestige rose, so did Sorne's. He hadn't been called a half-blood for years, at least not in his hearing. He was the Warrior's-voice, advisor to the king, leader of the holy-swords. But soon, Charald would return to Chalcedonia, and Sorne needed to decide which king deserved his loyalty.

The uncle he hardly knew, or the father who had denied him at birth? Once he had admired Charald's tactical brilliance, but now he knew him for the flawed human being he was. As for his uncle, they called him a despot, but they were Charald's spies.

'There you are.' The king joined him, followed by a servant who filled two goblets before retiring. 'To Navarone, last to fall.'

'To Navarone,' Sorne repeated. He leant against the railing so that he didn't tower over King Charald. Hopefully, now that he was twenty-five, he'd stop growing.

'You're white as a sheet and you're favouring that arm again,' Charald observed. 'What happened?'

'Three thugs thought they'd take my head and hands back to King Matxin. I convinced them otherwise.'

'For a priest, you're mighty handy with a sword.' Charald laughed.

Sorne grinned. 'What will you do, now that Navarone is yours?'

'Reclaim Chalcedonia and crown myself High King of the Secluded Sea. I've proven myself worthy, and the Warrior has rewarded me with victory after victory. Matxin put his trust in the Father, and look what it got him!' Charald laughed with malicious delight. 'They tell me he has the honey-piss. The saw-bones have to keep taking slices off his rotting leg. Soon they'll get to his balls and that'll be the end of him. They say his daughter is so old and plain, no baron will marry her, and his son is so busy whoring, gambling and drinking that the barons have started preying on each other.'

Sorne watched as Charald paced, unable to stand still.

'When I sail home, the son will turn tail and run, and the people will welcome me. I'll take my pick of the barons' daughters and plant an heir in my new wife's belly.' Charald reached down and adjusted himself, aroused by the prospect. 'You must make an offering and seek guidance from the Warrior.'

'I would...' Sorne hid a smile. The king was an odd mix of superstition and practicality. 'But the gift residue has worn off the remaining T'En artefacts.' He didn't mention the orb of power. Only a fool would use a tool he didn't understand when dealing with hungry empyrean beasts.

He'd half expected Charald's temper to flare up – they hadn't had an episode for a while now – but the king was watching a man ride across the square. The rider arrived at the palace steps.

'What news?' Charald asked, leaning over the balcony.

The recent assassination attempt prompted Sorne to add, 'Is King Matxin dead?'

'No. It's his son. Killed in a duel. Stuck his prick in the wrong man's wife. Just got the news from a merchant ship's captain. Happened ten days ago.'

'It's a sign from the Warrior!' Charald told Sorne. He called down to the rider. 'Send the ship's captain to me.'

The man rode away.

'To Chalcedonia.' The king drained his glass. 'I'll sail as soon as I can load the ships.'

'Who will you leave to rule Navarone?' Sorne asked. 'It must be someone you trust to guard your flank.'

Charald put his glass down. 'How would you like to be king?'

For one impossible moment, Sorne actually considered it. He'd watched Charald's barons wrestle with various problems in Khitan, Maygharia, Dace and Welcai. With their experiences to draw on, he could...

What was he thinking? While True-men might fear him and respect him, they would never bow to a half-blood king. When Sorne opened his mouth to refuse, Charald's reaction cut him off. The king clutched his belly and roared with laughter.

Cold fury solidified inside Sorne. He had to force himself to produce a rueful smile.

'Ah...' Charald caught his breath and wiped his face. 'That was priceless. I had you for a moment, there.' He adjusted his belt. 'Send in Nitzel's grandsons.'

When King Matxin came to power, Charald's queen had retired to one of the Mother's abbeys. But first she had pleaded for the lives of her two sons from her original marriage. They had been young men of nineteen and twenty-one at the time. Matxin had confiscated their family's estates and banished the brothers.

The two brothers had promptly sailed for Khitan and offered their services to King Charald. The elder had proven himself a good leader on the battlefield, and had earned the title of war baron. The younger was loyal to his brother, but he opposite in nature. Inclined to be impetuous, he was popular with the young men.

'Right away, my king.' Sorne bowed and left the balcony. He told the servants to send in Baron Dantzel and Nitzane, then went down the corridor.

As soon as he entered his own chamber, he let his guard down. He wanted to break something and roar with rage. He wanted to strangle King Charald and wipe that stupid grin off his face.

He did nothing, as a cold sweat of fury and pain soaked him. This was his answer. Charald did not deserve his loyalty.

But Charald was undefeated, and his uncle was dying.

Nursing his broken collar bone, Sorne stripped and strapped his shoulder. The pain was a constant nagging ache.

He hesitated. He could take one of the soothing powders, or...

After making sure his door was bolted, he opened the chest containing the last T'En artefact, a neck torc. He'd told Charald the gift residue was all used up, but it was a lie.

Stretching out on the bed, he held the artefact to his chest, and let its gentle warmth ease his pain.

Chapter Thirty-Four

ARMS FOLDED, GRAELEN leaned against the verandah, watching the procession. The sisterhoods had come down from the island's peak, into the free quarter, for Empowerment Day. After the ceremony, the T'En children would have free run of the park, and their excitement was palpable.

While Graelen had not fathered a T'En child himself, some of the brotherhood's men had, and they leant over the balcony, watching for their choice-sons. Sweet voices and innocent laughter filled the air.

Graelen felt nothing.

It was the only way to survive in Kyredeon's brotherhood. Any emotion was a sign of weakness, and the all-father would use it as a lever. In the years since he'd become all-father, Kyredeon had called on Graelen and Paryx several times, ordering them to perform tasks even his own hand-of-force wasn't aware of.

They'd carried out the assassination that had almost destabilised Chariode's brotherhood, and they'd planted the rumours which led to the suicide of another brotherhood's gift-tutor and the rise of All-father Hueryx. But Kyredeon had not gained from this, as Hueryx had proven more than a match for him.

Being all-father of his brotherhood was not enough for Kyredeon. He had his sights on becoming leader of the greatest brotherhood, and to do this, he had to weaken the other all-fathers. Eventually, one of the brotherhoods would falter, and he would step in to acquire their wealth and remaining warriors, which would make him the most powerful of all the brotherhood leaders.

Now Kyredeon wanted Graelen and Paryx to abduct and murder an all-father's devotee. They'd spent most of the winter observing Paragian and his devotee, looking for a pattern and a chance to strike. It had to be silent and it had to be in secret. And, according to Kyredeon, it had to be done. He believed the all-father was so much in love with his devotee, her death would destroy him and leave his brotherhood ripe for take over.

Graelen did not mind killing a warrior, with blood on his hands, to remove a threat to their brotherhood but killing an innocent was another thing entirely.

Paryx leant close to Graelen. 'Time's running out. What will we tell him?'

The thin T'En warrior had never been strong in gift, mind or body, and the strain of being Kyredeon's assassin was wearing him down; he laughed too loud and drank too much. It had earned him something of a reputation.

Paryx's troubled eyes flicked towards the all-father and his two seconds. 'He expects an answer today.'

'He'll have his answer.' Graelen would think of something. 'Trust me. Watch the procession.'

Below them, T'En youngsters were passing on their way to being empowered. All six of the sisterhoods were represented, and each child was accompanied by his or her choice-mother, brothers and sisters. The sisterhoods' leaders, inner circles and gift-warriors were also in attendance. Everyone wore their finest, including the Malaunje, who carried refreshments for the celebration in the park afterwards. Amongst the sisters were groups of T'En youths. The lads stuck together, teasing each other and showing off.

To be so young...

Graelen spotted Egrayne the empowerer and, not far from her, the gift-warrior who had saved his life just before he joined the brotherhood.

Back then, he hadn't realised how easily the gift-warrior could have drained him. She'd saved his life, and the very next day he had insulted her. He'd been impatient to leave the sisterhood and start his adult life. When Egrayne had announced he was a gift-warrior, he'd thought his future would be filled with honour and glory, not the assassination of innocents. A deep and abiding anger ignited his gift, and the young initiates edged away from him.

When had he become someone to fear?

Once the procession had passed, there was a rush to get down to the park. Graelen followed Paryx and the others.

'...oldest original building and the envy of the other all-fathers,' Paryx was telling a young initiate. 'The theatre was built during the first ten years of settlement. Many a famous play has opened here, to great acclaim.'

In the throng of brothers heading down to the park, Graelen felt the jostle of gifts empowered by excitement, but the potential for violence was also there.

They passed the empowerment dome, its doors firmly closed. The only adult males who'd been allowed in today were fathers who had been invited to witness their sons' empowerment.

Graelen saw Paragian ahead of them, an arm around his devotee, laughing with his inner circle. Why couldn't Kyredeon be more like him?

The thought shocked him. His brotherhood was his life; he'd given his vow. If Kyredeon suspected a brother of treason, the all-father would be within his rights to have his hand-of-force execute him.

They came to the street bordering the park, which was the largest open space in the city. Some lucky fathers of empowered youngsters would be invited into the park to spend the afternoon with their children. If there was any drunkenness or violence, the sisterhood gift-warriors would eject the men responsible, and they would never be invited back.

Already the brotherhoods were pouring into the buildings overlooking the park, to claim their places on the verandahs.

Several dozen Malaunje stood at the entrance to the park, holding formal invitations to join a sisterhood for the afternoon. One approached All-father Paragian.

He consulted his devotee, then sent her off with an escort.

'There,' Kyredeon said, startling Graelen. 'That is the kind of moment you were supposed to watch for.'

'We could not know Paragian would be invited–'

'His son's choice-mother is the healer, Reoden. She has a daughter about a year older who is being empowered today. The healer sees the best in everyone, so she invited Paragian to join her. You should know all this, and should have anticipated her actions. You're no use to me if you can't think for yourself.'

'You're right,' Graelen acknowledged. 'But I'm not a master strategist like you.'

Kyredeon gave him a sharp look.

'All-father, the dome's doors have just opened. You won't believe what I –' Hand-of-force Athamyr broke off when he saw Graelen.

'Go on,' Kyredeon said.

'Reoden's daughter is a sacrare. The empowerer–'

'A sacrare?' Graelen repeated. 'Why didn't the healer announce it when the child was born?'

'She must have told the all-mothers. They weren't surprised,' Athamyr said. 'The empowerer said the girl would be a gift-wright.'

'Not surprising, considering her mother's a healer.' Kyredeon's eyes narrowed thoughtfully. 'A sacrare has the potential for great power. If the girl will be able to heal gifts, then she'll also be able to destroy them. She'll be even more deadly than Imoshen the All-father-killer. Who was the father?'

'He wasn't invited.'

Kyredeon nodded and gestured to the stairs. 'You go ahead. I'll be up in a moment.'

Athamyr hesitated as if he would like to argue, then nodded and left.

'Do you want me to follow the devotee?' Graelen asked.

'Forget Paragian,' Kyredeon said. 'Think. Why did the healer hide the identity of the sacrare's father?'

'Reoden must feel something for him. He's not just a casual trysting partner.'

'Exactly. I want to know who he is. I want you and Paryx to abduct the sacrare. Reoden will contact the father.'

Graelen swallowed. 'What will knowing the father's identity achieve?'

'When you know what someone wants, you can control them.'

Graelen nodded. But the more he thought about it, the more he didn't like it. 'Abducting the sacrare girl... that's poking a nest of snakes. The all-mothers will strike back.'

'They would if they knew who to strike. Besides...' Kyredeon shrugged. 'We won't hurt her. We'll let her go in the free quarter. Make it look like someone took her in a misguided attempt to claim stature. But in the meantime, we will have flushed out the sacrare's father.'

IMOSHEN HID HER excitement, keeping her gift tightly reined. She'd never been backstage in the brotherhood's theatre before. After five days of festivities, the celebrations were winding down, and Rutz's latest play had been performed for the last time tonight. She'd watched it herself two nights ago, and now she wanted to confront the playwright and ask him if he knew he'd written a tragedy. If he was aware of it, then it meant that one other person could see their society's flaws. And she would have someone to talk to.

Imoshen had snuck backstage after the curtain had fallen for the final time. Dressed as a Malaunje woman, she waited to take the costumes to be laundered.

Imoshen the All-father-killer could not go many places in the free quarter without being recognised and remarked upon. Imariska, the Malaunje washer woman, could go just about anywhere. To most T'En, the half-bloods were invisible.

Frayvia had made the disguise for her, and though it was convincing, Imoshen was afraid that it would be her gift that would give her away. She would have to use it to identify Rutz, but she was hoping, in all the excitement, one brief flash of her power would go unnoticed.

As she gathered discarded costumes, she listened in on the actors' conversations but she didn't spot anyone likely to be Rutz.

Disappointed, Imoshen took the last washing basket out to the cart, where the real washerwoman waited to do her job.

'Was it as thrilling as you thought it would be?' the woman asked, amused.

'They're smelly and they shout a lot.'

The woman laughed and flicked the reins, carting the laundry away.

But Imoshen had not given up. She waited outside the theatre as the actors and stagehands left. Several of them talked of meeting at a late-night eatery to celebrate the play's success. Surely Rutz would go to that?

She waited a little longer, just in case Rutz had stayed behind, and was about to step out of the shadows when two T'En men arrived. They opened the stage door and slipped inside.

Thinking one of them had to be Rutz, Imoshen followed. Inside the theatre, a few high windows let in the moonlight, but for the most part Imoshen had to find her way in darkness. The men she was following were so quiet that she lost track of them. They were not in the auditorium, so she made her way through the wings and into the backstage area, hoping to search the dressing rooms. At the far end of the corridor she thought she saw a glow. Was that smoke? Had someone left a candle burning, or knocked over a lamp?

She ran down the passage, to find the largest dressing room alight. Her gift rose, responding to the threat. Grabbing a discarded cloak, she covered her face with one arm, and tried to beat out the flames, but soon realised it was futile.

The facade of the building was stone, but the rest was dry, old wood. The theatre would go up like a bonfire. She had to find Rutz and his shield-brother to warn them.

Even with her sleeve over her face, she struggled to get enough air as she ran up the stairs. The auditorium was also ablaze and she realised that this was no accident. The men she'd been following must have set the fire.

Imoshen fled for the stage door, burning curtains falling around her and flaming cinders raining down. Her gift tried to rise. Her wig caught fire; she tore it off and kept running.

The stage door refused to open. In desperation she retraced her steps through the stage wings towards the auditorium and the front door, but a piece of burning scenery toppled, driving her back. She was trapped.

Her gift surged, turning her inside-out, and she fell to her knees, stomach heaving.

Dashing tears from her eyes, she lifted her head.

'Imoshen?'

'Frayvia?' She blinked, finding herself naked in her devotee's bedchamber.

Frayvia sat up, revealing a Malaunje male on the other side of her bed. Imoshen recognised her devotee's casual trysting partner. Frayvia sent him off with a kiss and the admonishment to say nothing, as Imoshen tried to make sense of what had just happened to her.

'You're covered in soot and you smell of smoke,' Frayvia said as soon as they were alone. 'Where have you been?'

'The theatre burned down.'

'That's terrible. How many were killed?'

'None. I was the last one out. I'm sorry, I lost your hair. The wig caught fire.'

'Forget the wig. I'm just glad you're safe. You're in such a state, how did you get into the sisterhood palace without being noticed?'

'Just lucky, I guess.' Imoshen came to her feet. She was all right now, but tired, as if she had pushed her gift to its limits.

'Where are your clothes? Did they get burned?'

'They're gone.'

'You threw them out? Good. Come to the bathing chamber.'

As Imoshen followed Frayvia, she felt tiny burns all along her forearms and neck. No point denying it; her gift had taken over and saved her. It had brought her back here, to Frayvia, because she was linked to her devotee.

How much time had passed? While Frayvia ran her bath, Imoshen padded to the window and opened it. Below her, in the free quarter, the theatre was well alight. Someone had finally raised the alarm, and she heard shouts.

'Imoshen, what are you doing?' Frayvia beckoned. 'Come here and clean up. If someone comes in and finds you like this, there will be questions.'

Imoshen sank into the tub, wincing at the burns. Frayvia dropped her gown and climbed in with her. As her devotee began soaping her body, Imoshen said, 'I can do this, you know.'

Frayvia ignored her. 'Your hair smells of smoke. Lean back.'

She relaxed as Frayvia's competent fingers went to work. So tired...

'I dreamed I was shut in a burning building,' Frayvia told her. 'I woke and there you were. I knew no good would come of gallivanting around in disguise. Rinse.'

Imoshen did as she was told, and Frayvia began to comb her hair.

'This was an attack on Kyredeon,' Imoshen said. 'His brotherhood owns the theatre. Someone hated him enough to destroy a piece of the T'Enatuath's heritage.'

'Better a building than a person.'

'It's a warning.'

Frayvia struggled to hold back a yawn and failed. 'Don't know why I'm so tired.'

'You're very good to me.' Imoshen kissed her cheek. 'I don't deserve you.'

Her devotee sniffed.

GRAELEN HAD NEVER seen Kyredeon so angry.

He paced, spitting out his words. 'One of the oldest building in the city, burned to the ground. Three adjoining buildings damaged. Chariode's eatery will have to be demolished. It was deliberate, I know it was, but I can't prove it. The all-fathers are claiming it was negligence on our part that started the fire. Three brotherhoods claiming compensation. We'll be beggared.'

Paryx gave Graelen a worried look.

'What do you want us to do?' Graelen asked.

'Mingle in the free quarter, get drunk with other brotherhoods. Keep your ears open. Someone won't be able to resist boasting. One of my enemies did this to cripple my stature. I want to know who and, when I do, I will geld him. I'll assassinate his lovers and I'll see his brotherhood ruined. He'll rue the day he attacked me.'

Graelen nodded.

'Get drunk in the free quarter,' Paryx grinned. 'Wish all my duties were—'

He gave a grunt of surprise as Kyredeon grabbed him and slammed him up against the wall.

Paryx gulped.

Kyredeon let his gift rise on a wave of anger. 'I could break your walls, drain you and hand you over to my followers for their entertainment.'

Paryx shuddered and dropped his eyes.

Kyredeon released him. 'Get out.'

As Graelen stepped towards the door Kyredeon added, 'And don't forget the sacrare. I want to know when she's unguarded.'

'She's never unguarded. Reoden hardly ever lets her venture into the free quarter.'

'Nevertheless, keep watching. Everyone makes mistakes.'

When they were alone, Paryx turned to Graelen. 'What's this about the sacrare? Why didn't you tell me? Don't you trust me?'

Graelen rubbed his face in frustration. 'Kyredeon wants us to abduct the sacrare and release her, to gain stature.'

Paryx shrugged. 'So, what's the problem?'

Graelen said nothing. Once, Paryx had been cautious, but now his thinking was sloppy, and so was his gift control. In fact...

'Open your gift to me.'

Paryx frowned, anger hardening his mouth. 'Isn't it a little late for that? Once, we could have been shield-brothers. Once, we could have lived with honour. Now...' He pulled away from Graelen.

But not before Graelen caught a glimpse of his gift. He was no gift-wright, but... 'There's something wrong with–'

Paryx thrust Graelen away with trembling hands. His gift was corrupted, fouled by the turmoil in his mind. 'I'm not like you. I can't go on like this. Always afraid, always on edge.'

'We can't leave. We know too many of Kyredeon's secrets.'

'Oh, yes. And whose fault is that?' Paryx turned on his heel and strode off.

Graelen exhaled slowly. He didn't know what to do, so he did the one thing he was good at; he did his duty.

'YOU'RE LATE.'

'Sorry. I was finishing this.' Imoshen handed Vittoryxe the latest breeding chart.

The gift-tutor took it, looked it over and put it aside. 'I don't know why you bother to make up such detailed charts.'

'What are we doing today?'

They worked side by side in silence for a while, before Imoshen said, 'I read about an unusual gift-working, and now I can't remember where I read it.'

'Hmmm?' Vittoryxe was distracted, making notes on her new acquisition's measurements and distinguishing markings. 'What was it?'

'It spoke of the T'En using the gift to move from one place to another instantaneously.'

'Impossible.'

Impossible, like it was impossible for T'En to have more than one gift? But Imoshen held her tongue.

Vittoryxe finished her notes. 'Put the bird back and get out the next one.'

Imoshen obeyed her. She was good with the birds. They responded to her confidence. She could feel the racing heart of the tiny creature through her fingertips. 'What exquisite colouring. That blue is so vivid it hurts my eyes.'

'There *is* transposition... Your description of the passage was so poor, I didn't recognise it at first,' the gift-tutor said. 'According to the legend, some T'En were able to slip into the higher plane and come back to this one in another place. Of course, it drained their gift and risked their lives. Taking your physical body onto the empyrean place is like inviting the beasts to a feast. It had to be instantaneous, to avoid detection, and they needed to be linked to someone on this plane to reach their destination.'

'Like a devotee or a shield-sister?'

Vittoryxe nodded. 'Something like that. Open his wings.'

'So where did I read about transposition? I can't remember.'

'Look in the first records of the oral stories. But don't put any stock in it. They're myths. Now hold that bird still.'

* * *

GRAELEN SLIPPED BETWEEN the tall shelves and hid behind a chart depicting the flow of blood around the body. From here, he could see the shop's front door. Sure enough, the two T'En women entered and went over to the counter. Since the first day of spring, he'd been following Reoden whenever she entered the free quarter and, when he saw her with Imoshen the All-father-killer, he'd anticipated their destination.

As he'd hoped, the two T'En women did not guard their tongues in front of the foreign shopkeeper, who could not understand them.

'...for years, making charts of the gift-tutor's birds and their breeding traits,' Imoshen was telling the healer. 'I send them to a Sagora scholar, to see if...' She broke off as the Sagora shopkeeper came out to serve them.

Imoshen said a greeting in the Sagora's tongue, before switching to Chalcedonian. 'Do you have a reply from Venerable Felesoi?'

'Not this time. I'm expecting another shipment by midsummer. You could come back then.'

She thanked him, then took Reoden's arm and headed for the door.

Without warning, Imoshen stopped, gave a little cry of delight and ran towards where Graelen was hiding. He only just managed to fight the instinct to reach for his gift. Imoshen hadn't spotted him. It was an odd brass instrument, constructed of circles within circles and decorated with intricate markings, that had captured her interest.

'Look Ree, an astrolabe.' Her face lit up. He could not reconcile Imoshen the cold killer with this Imoshen. 'I've always wanted one.'

'Really? What does it do?'

'You use it to work out the paths of the planets and stars.'

'Yes.' The healer's voice was dry. 'I can see how that would come in useful.'

Imoshen laughed, and the look she sent Reoden was pure affection. They were more than friends, more than casual trysting partners; secret lovers? What would Kyredeon give to know this? Maybe he could trade the knowledge to get Kyredeon to send him and Paryx to live in peace on a distant estate. So far, he'd had no luck discovering which all-father was responsible for torching the theatre.

Imoshen switched to Chalcedonian. 'How much is the astrolabe?'

'It's on order for a brotherhood sea captain.'

'Oh...'

'Imoshen, if you want it so badly you could order one,' Reoden told her.

'It probably costs a small fortune.'

'Imoshen,' the healer chided. 'Your sisterhood can afford a dozen astrolabes.'

'Yes, but they'd think I was being frivolous. No one would understand why I want it. They think Mieren knowledge is worthless.' She switched languages again. 'When is the captain due to pick it up?'

'Any day now,' the Sagora said.

'I know!' Imoshen's expression cleared. 'I'll bring Iraayel down to have a look at it. He'll be fascinated.'

'Really?' Reoden sounded dubious. 'You sure he wouldn't rather be fitted for his first long-knives?'

Imoshen rolled her eyes, slid her arm through Reoden's and thanked the shopkeeper.

Before they could leave, however, the shop door opened and a brotherhood warrior came in. Graelen didn't know him by sight, but going by the symbol on his arm-torc, he was one of All-father Chariode's.

The man gave Imoshen and Reoden a brief nod and they stepped aside, revealing the astrolabe.

'Good, it's arrived.'

Imoshen's face fell. Neither she nor Reoden spoke while the sea captain paid for his purchase and left.

'There's one T'En who doesn't think Mieren knowledge is worthless,' Reoden said.

Imoshen didn't respond.

'Cheer up.' Reoden guided her towards the door. 'I know. Let's give the children something to look forward to. Lyronyxe has been studying so hard, she needs a break. She loves going out on the lake. We can–'

The closing door cut them off.

Graelen exhaled slowly. A lake outing was the perfect opportunity. The all-mothers kept their barges in the boat-house next to the causeway gate. All he and Paryx had to do was watch the sisterhood-gate for the party accompanying the sacrare, then lie in wait for them in the boat-house.

But that would mean confronting the healer and the all-father-killer, both powerful T'En women. He had to come up with a way to separate them from the rest of the party.

An injury... The healer would stop to help someone in need, and if it was a messy injury, she wouldn't want the children to see the blood.

Graelen waited until the shopkeeper retreated to the backroom of his shop before he returned to the brotherhood's palace.

Kyredeon saw him right away.

'...so all we have to do is wait for the day they go out on the lake to stage the abduction.' Kyredeon nodded, almost dismissively. 'Very good. But it won't be you. I'm sending you to the Mieren port. It's in chaos. They say King Charald is due back, and King Matxin is dying. I want you to observe and report.'

It was so unexpected, Graelen didn't know what to say. He settled on practicalities. 'We don't have a warehouse in port. Where will I stay?'

'I'll negotiate with Chariode. I've just paid him compensation for the fire damage to his building. He'll be receptive. You'll leave tomorrow. Now, go find Paryx and tell him how to set up the abduction.'

Graelen nodded and continued. 'You want me to observe the Mieren. What exactly are you looking for?'

'Change brings opportunity. Make a note of everything that goes on.' Kyredeon held his eyes. 'We are still the size of a great brotherhood, but I've had to barter away some of our wealth to compensate the all-fathers. We need an advantage. We could all too easily slip to the stature of a lesser brotherhood.'

The great brotherhoods would be watching them for any sign of weakness, seeking an opportunity to absorb them. If that happened, all the high-ranking brothers would be executed. Graelen amongst them.

Chapter Thirty-Five

A BITTER-SWEET SATISFACTION filled Sorne. Here he was, returning to Chalcedonia on the flagship of a conquering army, as the personal advisor to King Charald.

Eight years ago, when they'd let him out of the tent to witness the surrender of Khitan, he'd had to hide his identity under a cloak. Now, his head was bare and he lowered his eyes for no one. How he wished Izteben had lived to see this.

Izteben had planned to elevate the half-bloods to a position of not just acceptance, but respect. Looking back, his brother had been a better man than him, thinking of all the half-bloods rather than trying to win power just for himself. It would be interesting to see what Zabier had achieved in their brother's memory.

Sorne grinned. Little Zabier, the Father's-voice. Not so little Zabier now. Zabier would have just turned twenty-one, and Valendia would be nearly twelve. As for Hiruna, he hoped she still lived. He needed to see the woman who had reared him as if he was her own son.

If Charald's spies could smuggle reports to the king, Zabier could have found some way to send word to him. Surely his brother did not think he was an enemy?

Looking out over Port Mirror-on-Sea, it was clear the populace did not see King Charald as the enemy. Not only were the wharves packed with well-wishers, but every balcony and rooftop was crowded with cheering people.

They had sailed through the headlands last night and anchored across the bay, to give Matxin time to send a delegation. The Father's-voice had sent an elderly priest with the news that after a great suffering, King Matxin had died six days previously, and his daughter was ready to talk terms with King Charald.

Matxin's death left Sorne rudderless. It had all seemed so simple when he was growing up; serve Oskane to defeat the devious Wyrds, then serve Oskane to defeat the devious baron who had ordered his mother's death. Do all this while winning respect for himself as a half-blood. After Oskane's death, he'd thought his duty was to buy King Matxin time to consolidate his hold on Chalcedonia.

Now...

As they approached the docks, the crowd cheered wildly.

'They love you, sire,' Nitzane said. 'There'll be no need of a sword to conquer Chalcedonia. She'll lift her skirts for you.'

Charald threw back his head and gave a deep belly laugh.

'There's Baron Matxin's banner.' Nitzane pointed to the wharf. 'The white stag on the greensward. Looks like the usurper's daughter has sent a welcoming committee.'

Sorne spotted the banner, but the delegation seemed to consist of a dozen white-robed priests.

'I bet the barons who swore fealty to Matxin are wishing they'd stayed loyal. I wonder who Matxin gave my family's estates to. Do you know if—'

'Don't worry, I'll restore your barony with all its lands and more besides,' Charald assured him. 'I reward loyalty, just as I punish treason. I'll confiscate the traitorous barons' estates and reward my followers.'

Sorne expected no less. Among Charald's new war barons were common men who had risen through ruthless leadership on the battlefield, and foreign nobles who had turned against their own people when they realised Charald could not be beaten.

As the flagship made fast to the pier, Charald turned to Sorne, saying, 'Go meet the delegation. Tell them King Charald, High King of the Secluded Sea, will be waiting in the throne room. They have my terms. Bring back their answer.'

'What of Matxin's daughter, Marantza?' Sorne asked. If she was twenty-one now, she must have been thirteen when her father had seized the crown. Like him, she'd had no say in her fate.

'She's of royal blood,' Nitzane warned. 'If you don't marry her yourself or execute her, the deposed barons will rally behind her. It won't matter how plain she is, one of them will marry her, plant a babe in her belly and declare himself regent.'

'So you think I should marry the plain cow?' Charald asked.

Nitzane floundered. Sorne hid a smile.

Charald gestured to Sorne. 'Do you think I should marry her?'

'Marantza is loved by the people. Executing her would not be a popular move.'

'So I must make sure she can't be used against me.' Charald shrugged. 'Tell the advisors Matxin's daughter must be handed over along with their reply.'

'As you say, my king.' Now Sorne knew his duty; save his cousin, Marantza. He called his holy-swords and strode down the gangplank with them at his heels. Unlike the war barons and their men-at-arms, Sorne's holy-swords wore simple priestly vestments of black breeches and ankle-length robes.

On the docks, the crowd parted for them. They whispered and pointed to his mulberry eyes and his hair, which had gone white. He heard his title. It pleased him to discover even the common folk had heard of the Warrior's-voice.

He made for the delegation of tightly packed priests. With their fair hair loose on their shoulders, shining in the sun, they were a stark contrast to his holy-swords.

Sorne approached and gave an abbreviated bow. 'Who's in charge here?'

A skinny old man stepped forward; his head barely reached the middle of Sorne's chest. 'I am Utzen, assistant to the Father's-voice.'

Zabier had his own Franto? The thought amused Sorne, but he didn't let it show. 'I have a message for the advisors of Marantza, daughter of King Matxin, from King Charald, High King of the Secluded Sea. Take me to them. I am Sorne, the Warrior's-voice, advisor to the High King.'

And didn't it feel good.

Sorne followed the Father's priests up through the labyrinth of streets to a flat-topped hill, where the Seven's churches and the king's palace formed the sides of an octagonal plaza.

Unlike the rest of the city, which had grown every which way, this area had been meticulously planned. Charald had boasted that he built a palace to outshine the Wyrd's palaces. He'd chosen the highest point of the city, where the churches had always stood. The Seven's priests had had no choice but to accommodate the king as he pulled buildings down to realise his vision of a grand, tree-lined plaza. Each of the churches tried to outdo each other with their magnificent entrances and elaborate facades, but none matched the palace.

Sorne strode up the steps and into the grand entrance.

The place was deserted. Torn wall hangings clung to the stonework; cracked plinths held the remnants of shattered statues. It was clear to Sorne that there had been a panic and servants had fled with whatever they could carry.

The old priest led him into an ante-chamber and stopped in front of a bronze door, its panels covered in bas-relief carvings. He glanced at Sorne's sword, but did not suggest he remove it.

Sorne gestured to his men. 'See that my holy-swords are given drink and food.' He beckoned the captain. 'This may take a while.'

'Do you want a scribe?' The captain was new to the post. Serving the Warrior's-voice as one of his holy-swords was to be envied. For all that they were called the holy-swords and stood between Sorne and assassins, any sensible assassin avoided attacking him when they were present. Most of the time they acted as tithe-collectors. They took a census of conquered churches, collected half the wealth and distributed the tithe to set up new churches. Every time this happened, Sorne selected seven of the holy-swords to head the churches, so their numbers were always changing. Sorne was no fool, he knew some of the gold stuck to their fingers, but he tolerated it, as it made his holy-swords eager to please him.

'No. I don't want a scribe.' Not when he planned to act in Marantza's best interests and not King Charald's. He pushed open the doors and let himself in before the old priest could announce him.

He'd expected a grand greeting chamber with opulent hangings to impress the visitors. This chamber had the look of a private sitting room. There were low couches by the empty grate, and a table covered in half-eaten delicacies. But his gaze went straight to the woman who had her back to the balcony doors.

Sorne turned to the priest. 'I asked to speak with the king's advisors.'

'They've fled.' Her voice was low and slightly husky. 'Everyone has, including the servants, so you will just have to speak with me.'

She opened the shutters and light flooded the chamber, momentarily blinding him. After so many assassination attempts, he stepped back into the shadows instinctively.

'You can go, Utzen,' she told the old priest.

As she turned to face him, Sorne assessed her. She was not plain, so much as no-nonsense and determined. She was tall for a Mieren woman, and didn't defer to men. He had expected panic and trembling – she had enough reason to fear for her future – but instead, she met his eyes, waiting.

'Marantza?'

'Yes. And you are...'

'Sorne.' He was a little surprised that his uncle had not told her who he was eight years ago. It seemed, other than Charald and Zabier, no one knew he was the king's half-blood son. 'Sorne, the Warrior's-voice, advisor to High King Charald.'

'So it is true, he keeps a white-haired half-blood by his side. Has the king spent so much time with foreigners he has forgotten Chalcedonian ways?'

Sorne ignored this. 'Have you read the terms of surrender?'

'Hand over the palace, city and kingdom, and the barons who supported my father.' She shrugged. 'It is within my power to hand over the palace and city, but as for the kingdom and the barons... Charald will have to claim the kingdom piece by piece. Most of the barons have packed up their families and their wealth and fled to Ivernia. A few have retired to their estates, in the belief Charald will not bother with them. The more martial have ridden over the pass into Navarone. They hope to turn Charald's puppet-king against him.'

It was a masterly assessment of the situation, and franker than Sorne had expected. 'What do you plan to do?'

She gave him a sharp look, as if she hadn't expected this question. 'I'm going to retire to the Mother's abbey. Since my father let Charald's queen do this, I...' She ran down, seeing his expression.

'She was Baron Nitzel's daughter. You are the granddaughter of King Charald's aunt. Until he has a child, you are his heir. You'd never reach the abbey.'

She digested this in silence, then lifted her head. 'I see. Does he plan to marry me?'

'That, or have you killed.' Sorne watched her reaction. She did not seem surprised; she had been testing him, then. 'You could retire to the Father's church and claim sanctuary. Our spies tell us you are well-liked, the dutiful daughter who nursed her dying father. King Charald could drag you out of the Father's church and kill you in the plaza, but it would turn the people against him.'

Her gaze flicked to the screen in the corner, then back to him. 'Why are you telling me this?'

'Because you haven't run off to join the rebel barons,' Sorne said, strolling around the room as if he was inspecting the paintings. 'Because you were just a child when your father seized the throne. Because you didn't ask to be born of royal blood, any more than I asked to be born a half-blood.' He stopped, struck by a thought. 'Do you want to hold onto the throne? After all, your father spent seventeen years plotting to seize it and eight years trying to hold it.'

She laughed. 'Will you think poorly of me if I say no? I don't want the throne or revenge. I saw what revenge did to my father. It ate him up inside and killed him long before his body died. After King Charald ordered Aunt Sorna's death, my father vowed—'

'Charald ordered her death?' This was not the story Oskane had told him. 'I thought Baron Nitzel murdered her.'

'Nitzel offered his daughter to Charald because she had already produced two True-men sons. The king had Sorna killed so he could marry again.' She studied him. 'After Aunt Sorna died and our family was shamed, my father could never be happy. Chalcedonia wasn't enough, especially when Charald went on to conquer all the other mainland kingdoms. It didn't matter how many offerings the Father's-voice made, my father—'

Sorne had reached the screen. Flinging it aside, he dragged the spy out, pinned his arm up behind his shoulders and drove him to his knees. 'And who is this, Marantza? An assassin?'

'Hardly. It's the Father's-voice.'

'Let me up, Sorne.' His captive sounded disgruntled.

'Zabier?' Sorne released his hold and helped the priest rise, so he could study his face. Last time he'd seen his brother, Zabier had been a boy of thirteen. This was a man, with Hiruna's jaw and Kolst's eyes. 'Zabier, it is you!'

He pulled him into a hug.

'What's going on, Father's-voice?' Marantza asked. 'Why is this half-blood—'

'I'm his brother,' Sorne said, voice thick with emotion. He pulled back to feast his eyes on Zabier. 'That's a mighty fancy robe for a carpenter's son. I guess it comes with being the Father's-voice.' Sorne felt a grin pull at his lips. 'Ah, but it's good to see you. How are Valendia and Hiruna?'

'Who are these people, Father's-voice?' Marantza asked. 'And why didn't you tell me Charald's priest was your brother?'

'Choice-brother,' Zabier corrected. 'My mother was paid to be his wet-nurse.'

VITTORYXE SMILED AND toasted All-mother Aayelora, but inside she fumed as everyone remarked how well Aayelora looked and how sharp she was for someone celebrating her hundredth birthday.

When Aayelora gave birth to the geldr, Vittoryxe had thought she would step down, but no; she held onto the sisterhood. Ten years ago, just before the all-mother turned ninety, Vittoryxe had gone to all the high-ranking sisters who owed her favours and gently reminded them of their obligations, but the all-mother hadn't stepped down.

Vittoryxe had never imagined Aayelora would still be their all-mother at a hundred years of age.

The all-mothers of the other sisterhoods and their inner circles had come to the rooftop garden party to celebrate. As Vittoryxe drifted from group to group, accepting congratulations on behalf of her sisterhood and all-mother, she cursed her luck. Here she was, all-mother-in-waiting to the oldest all-mother on record.

Laughter drew her behind the refreshment tent, where she found her choice-son up to no good with Imoshen's and Egrayne's choice-children. All three gave a guilty jump.

'Bedutz, go down stairs.'

His face fell, but he didn't argue. He would turn thirteen this year. Time to send him to live with the lads. Time to harden him up.

'As for you two...' She turned on Saffazi and Iraayel.

'Your pardon, gift-tutor,' Saffazi said. The words were appropriate, but there was laughter in her eyes.

Saffazi and Iraayel ran off before she could chastise them. Egrayne's choice-daughter was older than the boys, and the empowerer should be weaning Saffazi from her childhood friends. No point in growing fond of the lads you grew up with. Not when they were going to become brotherhood warriors.

Vittoryxe returned to Aayelora's side, because surely she would announce her successor and step down tonight.

She didn't.

Chapter Thirty-Six

SORNE FLINCHED. 'WHY would you say that?'

'Because it's true. Father told me when we left the retreat.'

'You came back to us. Why have you turned against me now?'

Zabier took a step away, bristling. 'Why did you turn against me? I wrote, pleading for you to come back. I was only thirteen, trying to protect mother and Valendia, trapped in the city while King Matxin purged the kingdom of Charald's supporters. There were executions in the plaza. The king wanted me to have visions and name his enemies. He gave me the lists of names and told me to say the Father had spoken. I didn't know what to do. You never replied–'

'I never got your messages.' He understood why Charald would have kept them from him, but that didn't mean he liked it. 'I thought you'd rejected me because I'd stayed with King Charald. I'm sorry, Zabier.'

'Zabier died eight years ago, when Izteben died.' His features hardened, brows drawing together, and he fingered a ring, which Sorne recognised as Oskane's. 'I became the Father's-voice. I had to, to survive. I've done things...' His gaze slid away from Sorne and he went to stand beside Marantza. 'I'm here to lend my support to King Matxin's daughter.'

'If you want to help Marantza, you'll smuggle her out of the palace and give her sanctuary in the Father's church. Oskane used to say, next to the king, the high priest was the most powerful man in the kingdom. In fact, he's more powerful, in some ways, because the church endures, while kings come and go.'

Marantza eyed him suspiciously. 'Why should I take your advice? Your loyalty is to King Charald.'

'It doesn't matter who my loyalty is to. These are the facts. King Charald is going to march in here and purge the kingdom of Matxin's supporters. He'll do it whether you live or die, Marantza. He'll do it whether you are the Father's-voice, Zabier, or whether some other priest takes the post. I'm trying to save your lives. Is that so hard to believe?' He glanced around the chamber, spotting a door on the far side. 'Where does that lead?'

'To my bedchamber,' Marantza said.

'Is there another exit from your chamber? Because I have a dozen holy-swords in the antechamber who will report my actions, if I let you go out that way.'

'We can get out through my bedchamber,' Marantza said.

'I'll give her sanctuary,' Zabier said.

Sorne noted the way he took her arm. So that's how it was. That was going to be inconvenient for Zabier; priests were supposed to be celibate. This had never bothered Sorne, as he seemed to be numb to the desires of the flesh.

'Zabier, you'll need to find a disguise for Marantza. Do you have another priestly robe?'

'I can get one.'

'Do it. Leave now. Go straight to the Father's church. From there you'll both be in a better position to negotiate. Charald will need the support of the Seven's churches to hunt down the rebel barons.'

Marantza and Zabier glanced to each other.

'Go,' Sorne said. 'I'll buy you the time you need.'

Sorne waited while they slipped out the door. When he felt that enough time had passed, he went to find the king. Charald was on the balcony of the throne room, sipping wine with Nitzane.

'There you are. Pour yourself a glass,' Charald said.

Sorne joined him, as the king gestured to the wharves. 'My war barons are unloading their men-at-arms. In another day, this palace will be crowded with them, wanting their rewards, and with local nobility eager to prove their loyalty, along with the port's merchants trying to insinuate themselves into my good graces. I already have a list of requests for audiences. At least I don't have to put out fires and restore the water supply.' He tossed down his wine and put his back to the balcony, resting his elbows on the rail. 'Well, Warrior's-voice? How cooperative are they going to be?'

'Matxin's daughter cedes you the palace and the city. She has sought sanctuary in the Father's church, under the protection of the Father's-voice.'

'Has she just?' Charald muttered.

'As a sign of good faith, she revealed what the Chalcedonian barons are up to.' And he repeated what Marantza had told him.

Charald grimaced. 'So, I have to go around mopping up resistance before I can truly reclaim my kingdom?'

'You have a city full of men-at-arms bristling for a fight. Send your war barons out to claim their estates.'

'And what of my family's estates?' Nitzane asked.

Charald grimaced. 'You've ridden on your brother's coat tails ever since you came to me. Now it's time to prove you can lead men. A baron who can't support me in battle is a liability.'

'Of course, sire.' Nitzane said, quickly. 'What of this Marantza? What will you do about her?'

'What do you suggest I do?'

Nitzane opened his mouth then closed it.

Charald looked to Sorne. He had been doing this since they set sail, playing them off against each other.

Sorne was not going to oblige. 'You know what you have to do, my king.'

'What if she's plain as a pikestaff and I can't get it up?'

'From what I've heard, that's never been a problem for you,' Sorne said.

Charald laughed.

Sorne went to leave.

'Wait. There's something else.' Charald looked pointedly at Nitzane until he left them. As soon as he was out of hearing, the king snorted. 'Old Nitzel would be turning in his grave. I guess the pup will grow into a wolf one day. Or at least a fox.'

Sorne said nothing. Nitzane was two years older than him. He'd been impulsive and careless for as long as Sorne had known him.

Charald studied Sorne. 'Are you loyal to me?'

'Have I ever given you reason to doubt me?'

'No... There's something preventing me marrying Matxin's brat to secure the crown.'

Sorne waited.

'I'm still married!'

Sorne blinked.

'Yes, you and everyone else have forgotten, but I'm still married to Nitzel's daughter. Matxin let her retire to one of the Mother's abbeys where, as far as I know, she still lives.'

'You want me to go and find out if she lives?'

'I want you to go and make sure she doesn't. I need a message from the abbess offering her sympathies on the death of my second wife, so that I can marry my third.'

'I see.' Sorne looked down. He had been the instrument of the deaths of tens of thousands of mothers and their children, throughout the kingdoms of the Secluded Sea, but he had never killed a woman or child with his own hands.

'Is there a problem?' Charald asked.

'Do I leave before or after I've brokered this marriage?'

Charald barked a laugh. 'You're sharp, I'll give you that. It's a pity...'

He broke off and turned away, to look out over the port.

Sorne hesitated, not sure if he was dismissed. It had been a while since the king had had one of his irrational rages. They were unpredictable, but they were inevitable and they were getting worse. Perhaps it would be wise to complete his service and retire. But could he live without the thrill of wielding power? More to the point, would Charald let him? And if he did, where would he go?

'Back in Restoration Retreat you had a vision,' Charald said. 'You saw me on the deck of a ship with a boy. But my son died.'

'It wasn't Prince Cedon. It was a much younger boy.'

'You let me believe it was Cedon.'

'I was seventeen.' He lifted his hands, palms up. 'You were the king.'

Charald nodded to himself.

Sorne was anxious to visit the Father's church and see his family. 'Am I dismissed?'

'Yes, go.'

GRAELEN CURSED HIS luck. He'd arrived the very day King Charald's fleet returned, and the streets were packed with Mieren. Between the locals, who ignored him and his Malaunje servants, and the foreign barons and their men, who stared openly at his party, it took the better part of the morning to thread through the packed streets. It didn't help that he wasn't used to riding and, after four days in the saddle, every step the horse took was agony for him.

To reach the docks and Chariode's warehouse, they still had to traverse the wealthy part of the port. The quickest way was through the royal plaza. It was here that Charald had built his new palace, surrounded by the seven churches of the Mieren gods.

It was only the third time Graelen had been in a Mieren town, and the previous two times he had only been passing through. The weight of so many unguarded minds was punishing, but he had expected that.

What he hadn't expected was to see one of his own kind dressed in priestly robes, leading six Mieren in the same attire across the plaza. It was only as the male passed that Graelen noticed the coppery streaks at the end of his braid. Malaunje. What had he been doing, for his hair to go completely white?

'Who was that, Harosel?' Graelen twisted in the saddle to speak to the Malaunje veteran who acted as his guide and bodyguard whenever he left the city.

'I've no idea.'

'Ask around when we get to Chariode's.'

Later that evening the veteran returned, and they retired to Graelen's chamber. From here, Graelen could see the ships floating on the bay, lanterns reflected in the sea. It would be quite lovely if it wasn't for... 'What is that horrible smell? Fish?'

'Seaweed. It's low tide.' The veteran smiled, then sobered. 'The white-haired Malaunje goes by the title of the Warrior's-voice.'

'But he's one of us.'

'When King Charald came back from conquering the Secluded Sea, he had the Warrior's-voice with him.'

'Isn't the Warrior one of the Mieren gods?'

Harosel nodded. 'Apparently this half-blood has visions from the Warrior.'

'Impossible.'

'He tells the king what he sees, then the king acts on his advice. As a consequence, Charald has conquered the Secluded Sea.'

A Malaunje serving a Mieren king as his advisor. Graelen would have said it was impossible. As far as he knew, their kind did not live outside of Chalcedonia.

'There's more,' Harosel said. 'Apparently there's a Mieren who calls himself the Father's-voice. He served King Matxin. He came to power the night Matxin stole the throne from Charald.'

'Don't tell me he has visions, too?'

Harosel nodded. 'Although Matxin's dead and Charald's back on the throne. Guess which one has better visions?'

'They can't have visions.'

'The Mieren believe they do. And guess where they do it?' He didn't wait for Graelen to reply. 'At holy sites.'

'Holy—'

'Places where the walls between the planes are weak.'

Graelen swore softly. 'Where did you learn all this?'

'Mieren taverns and whorehouses, mostly from off-duty palace guards.'

'They let half-bloods in?'

'Not on your life, but my hair's going white, so I'm easy to miss. I keep my eyes lowered, not that these places are brightly lit, and my hands under the table. I listen and I ask the occasional question.'

'What would happen if they realised?'

'What do you think?'

'A beating?'

'At the very least.'

'Ask around. See what more you can learn.'

Harosel nodded and left him alone.

To think, he'd believed this trip would be a waste of time.

SORNE FELT LIGHT as air as he told his holy-swords to wait and followed the priest. The Father's church was beautifully designed, but the deeper he went into the labyrinth the older the buildings became, dating back hundreds of years.

Now that little Zabier was high priest of the Seven, he ranked alongside the king's barons. In fact, Oskane would have said he ranked above them, since he was independent, with the vast power of the church behind him. Theoretically, as the Warrior's-voice with the king's trust, Sorne's power rivalled Zabier's. Perhaps they could finally realise Izteben's dream for the half-bloods.

Right now, the priest was taking Sorne to see the Father's-voice, but all Sorne could think of was his family.

He wanted to hug Hiruna and laugh at her tears of joy. Would Valendia recognise him? He'd sailed just before she turned four, and all he could remember was red-gold curls, dimples and a little voice that repeated everything he said.

Now that he thought about it, he wanted time alone with Zabier, to ask how Izteben had died. Why had Izteben succumbed so easily, when he'd survived eight years of interactions with the higher plane?

At last they came to the high priest's chambers. Zabier's assistant, Utzen, looked up from his desk, and then gestured for Sorne to go into the next chamber.

Sorne was ready to confront Zabier about Izteben, but he didn't see the Father's-voice, he saw the boy who had crossed Chalcedonia to come home.

Zabier cleared his throat. 'I take it you want to ask about Izteben's death.'

'You were only thirteen. Izteben knew what he was doing. I mourn our brother's loss, but I don't hold you responsible.'

Sorne wanted to grab him by the shoulders and hug him as if they were boys again, but the desk stood between them; that and eight years. He'd spent those years warring. He suspected Zabier had spent them politicking.

Zabier looked down. When he lifted his head again, he was the Father's-voice. 'Come.'

He led Sorne into the next chamber, to a sturdy wooden door, which he unlocked.

'So they aren't in the same apartment?'

'That was eight years ago,' Zabier said as he opened the door to reveal a narrow stair. 'Valendia needed to be able to run around in the open air.'

Sorne followed his brother up a narrow staircase to another door, which Zabier opened.

The room ran along under the roof. Dormer windows looked out over a courtyard on his right. On his left, tall doors with many panes of glass opened onto a rooftop garden. One of the doors was open, and he could hear music; some sort of pipes. In the sunshine he caught a glimpse of an old woman in a chair with her feet up, her legs covered by a blanket, and a youth with long copper hair playing a small set of pipes.

Where were Hiruna and Valendia?

Zabier led him through the main room and onto the tiled balcony. There were raised flowerbeds and vegetable patches. Hiruna had clearly used her time in exile productively.

'Sorne?' Hiruna threw off the blanket and put her feet down. He'd known she was over forty, but seeing her like this stunned him. Her hair was nearly white and she'd lost several teeth, yet her blue eyes were as bright as ever, and brimming with tears.

He knelt beside her chair and she threw her arms around him.

He'd come home. In her embrace, everything he'd done or left undone was forgiven, and he felt he could still redeem himself. But she was so frail in his arms, her flesh soft over the bones, her skin fine as silk. He had a sense of her fragility, and an urge to protect her.

'Back by winter,' she chided, pulling away. 'Eight years later...' Then she hugged him again. 'Oh, but it's good to see you.' As she drew away to study him, her gaze slipped to his hair. 'So the white streaks overtook the copper?'

He nodded, unable to speak.

'Ma?' The voice sounded tentative.

Hiruna glanced behind him. 'Say hello to your sister, Sorne. Dia's been waiting all day to see you.'

He came to his feet and turned to the youth. Gone was the plump three year-old with red-gold curls. Valendia was almost as tall as Zabier now, and took his breath away. Had he and Izteben been like this, pale-skinned with such dark brows and lashes, such red lips and rich copper hair?

Valendia smiled, shy yet hopeful. 'The song was for you. Did you like it?' She showed him the pipes. 'Zabier gave them to me.'

So innocent, so eager to please. He and Izteben had been five and almost six when the scourging had started. A flash of rage shot through Sorne. How could Oskane have done that to them? They'd trusted him, believed everything he told them, and all the while they'd just been his tools in his private feud with Nitzel.

Valendia's eyes widened. She looked past him to Hiruna and Zabier.

Sorne found his voice. 'It was wonderful.'

She beamed. 'I made the music sound happy. But I can make sad music, too.' She gestured to a larger, instrument that consisted of a pipe and a bag very like the ones the martial pipers carried. 'Would you like to hear–'

'That's enough music for now,' Zabier said. He came over to hug Valendia. His hand cupped her cheek fondly. 'Now run and fetch the treats.'

She darted off, her ankles showing, and Sorne realised her breeches were about a hand's span too short. She must have had a growth spurt.

'She plays more than one instrument?'

'She plays several. The music carries across the courtyards, but I don't have the heart to take them away from her,' Zabier said.

'She's a credit to her teacher.'

'She doesn't have a teacher. She's self-taught.'

'Amazing.'

'Isn't it?' Hiruna agreed. 'Neither Kolst nor I had any music in us.'

'You used to sing all the time,' Sorne told her fondly.

'Yes, but I could never play an instrument.'

'Dia grew up listening to the church choirs rehearse.' Zabier gestured to the courtyard beyond, which was hidden behind a screen. As if on cue, Sorne heard voices rise in a three-part harmony. 'She was always pestering me to let her join the singers, so I gave her the first set of pipes.'

Just then Valendia returned with a tray of custard tarts; they'd been his favourites. He glanced across to Hiruna and she nodded with a smile.

As Valendia darted off to get the watered wine, Zabier set the table and Sorne went over to Hiruna, moving her chair closer so she could join them.

'Doesn't Valendia have any friends?' he whispered.

'How could she?' Hiruna's mouth tightened. 'She's not allowed to show her face beyond these rooms.'

Sorne held her chair as she settled herself, then took a seat. Valendia offered drinks and served the food, always watching Zabier for approval.

'Why does Valendia have no friends?' Sorne asked. 'She needs company. When we were growing up, we three had each other.'

And there it was between them, Izteben's ghost.

'It's all very well for you. You've been away. You don't know what it was like here,' Zabier said. 'I've done the best I can. Valendia can read and write. She knows her history and she's safe, from Wyrds *and* True-men.'

'But what's going to happen to her? She can't spend her whole life a prisoner.'

Hiruna covered her mouth and looked across the table to Zabier.

'You weren't here. You've got no right to criticise.' Zabier put down his wine glass, restrained anger in his precise movements. Remembering the eager child Zabier had been, Sorne did not recognise the man he had become. 'Chalcedonia is not a good place for half-bloods.'

'It's all right,' Valendia said quickly, fixing on Sorne with desperate hope. 'When you go away again, I'll go with you.'

Into war? Into the path of assassins? Sorne put his glass down. 'Out of the question. I –'

'You can't be bothered with me.' Valendia sprang to her feet. 'I'm a burden on Ma and Zabier. No one wants me.' And she ran inside.

Sorne heard a distant door slam.

Zabier pushed his plate aside. 'I knew it was a mistake to bring you here. We were getting along just fine until you turned up. You've got no right, no right at all!'

And Zabier stalked from the table.

Sorne looked across to Hiruna; tears slid down her cheeks. This wasn't what he'd wanted.

'Don't...' – he went to her, knelt and put his arms around her shoulders – 'don't cry, Ma. I didn't mean to spoil things.' He felt like he was twelve again. 'I'm sorry.'

'You said what had to be said.' She pulled back and patted his arm. 'I don't know what's going to become of Valendia. I'm sick, Sorne. I have the wasting illness. There are lumps.' She gestured to her breast.

He didn't want to hear this.

'Sorne, are you coming?' Zabier called from the doorway.

'Don't tell Zabier or Dia,' Hiruna whispered.

'Don't worry, Ma.'

'She's not your mother, Sorne.' Zabier must have read his lips. 'And Valendia is not your sister. Come, we're keeping the king's daughter waiting.'

Hiruna squeezed Sorne's arm and sent him off with his head reeling.

He followed Zabier out of the secret apartment where his family was imprisoned and down to one of the church's formal greeting chambers. There was no sign of Marantza.

'Wait here,' Zabier told him.

So much for keeping her waiting. Sorne looked out on a courtyard where penitents clipped hedges into a knee-high maze. It seemed to negate the whole purpose.

Nothing made sense today.

Aware that he was not in the right frame of mind to start the negotiations, he was about to request they reschedule when Marantza entered, escorted by the Father's-voice.

'I have been giving what you said a lot of thought,' Marantza said. 'And I see that I have three choices.'

'Really, what's the third?'

'Set sail and never come back. But this is my home, and I don't want to leave.'

'So you'll marry King Charald?'

'Tell the king I cannot marry when our land is full of strife and war. When Chalcedonia is at peace he can court me.'

Sorne hid a smile. Had his little brother come up with this, or was it Marantza's idea? Charald would hear what he wanted to hear in this answer. It wasn't quite the response Sorne needed, but it would buy them all some time.

'I will convey your words.' He gave his bow and left.

Six of his holy-swords waited to escort him across the plaza back to the palace. He just wanted to make his report to Charald, find his chamber and think through what had happened today. There was an underlying hostility in Zabier that puzzled him. Hiruna's illness saddened him, and as for Valendia... she had no experience of the world, or of people. She was a total innocent. How would she survive, in a world filled with ambitious, conniving men?

As he put his foot on the top of the broad sweep of stairs to the royal plaza, something made Sorne look up. A half-blood stood on the steps to the Warrior's church, staring at him. Sorne was so surprised, he came to a sudden stop, and the holy-swords almost ran into him.

The man was a warrior, by the way he carried himself. His clothing was rich and there was pride in his stance, reminding Sorne of the she-Wyrd. Here, in the True-men's port, the Wyrds might be amongst enemies, but some of them were clearly not afraid.

And they'd set someone to watch him.

He kept walking as though the Malaunje warrior's presence meant nothing to him, but it had surprised him. Now that he thought about it, returning to Chalcedonia in service to the king as the Warrior's-voice meant he was bound to attract the attention of the Wyrds. After all, he was a Malaunje walking amongst True-men, and he wielded power.

He'd proven the she-Wyrd wrong. A flash of memory came to him – the she-Wyrd lying dead on the floor, limbs splayed, eyes gouged out...

He almost staggered. He'd left the she-Wyrd to die.

She'd asked him to save her and he'd refused.

At seventeen, he hadn't understood the consequences of leaving her in the cell. She'd been raped and murdered, and her body mutilated by the barons. And then he'd sailed off with the king and the barons, tacitly condoning her murder. Stunned and sickened by the memory, Sorne was hardly aware of his surroundings.

He had never even asked her name. It had been easier to think of her as *the she-Wyrd* than to acknowledge her humanity. He was a coward. And this came as a surprise to him.

Chapter Thirty-Seven

VITTORYXE COULDN'T UNDERSTAND why the Sagoras had sent her the treatise. She'd never had anything to do with Venerable Felesoi, and she wasn't interested in their thoughts on inheritable traits. She almost threw it out, but something caught her attention.

Why was there a whole section on her birds?

'Imoshen!' Her gift surged, and she let it.

She stalked into the all-mother's greeting chamber to find Egrayne with Aayelora. The two were always together. It only confirmed her fear that Egrayne would be named the next all-mother.

'Look at this!' Vittoryxe thrust the treatise under the all-mother's nose. 'Look what that... that sorry excuse for a sister has done now. She's taken my prize birds and fifty years of breeding and given everything I've learnt to the Sagoras!'

Aayelora looked sufficiently horrified. 'Send for Imoshen.'

Egrayne took the treatise to examine it.

Vittoryxe paced. She didn't know when she had last been so angry. There was a rushing in her head and she let her gift ride her body; she could feel it pulsing just below her skin.

Imoshen arrived, slightly out of breath. 'Sorry, we were about to take the children out on the lake.' She glanced to Vittoryxe, and the smile left her lips. 'Is something wrong? Is someone hurt?'

'You are what's wrong.' Vittoryxe stalked towards her. 'How dare you pretend to befriend me to steal fifty years of knowledge and give it to the Sagoras!'

Imoshen went white as a sheet and took a step back.

'You thought I wouldn't find out. That's it, isn't it? You thought you'd claim all my work—'

'No, I told them it was your work.'

'Your name is on here, Vittoryxe, credited with supplying the charts,' Egrayne said. 'And your name is above Imoshen's as author of the section on the birds.'

'What?' She was associated with Mieren scholars? She would be the laughing stock of the T'En, her stature ruined. 'How dare you use my name? I didn't write any of it.'

'At first I was just interested in your bird breeding. But it wasn't structured, so I drew up the charts. You said they made the links easier for you to see. Remember, we discussed the patterns? Then I wrote to the Sagoras to see if our insights matched theirs, and then they wrote back and—'

'I didn't give you permission to send anything to the Sagoras!' Vittoryxe could not believe Imoshen had done this. That said, she could see a positive side. After this, no one would trust Imoshen's judgement; the other sisters would shun her. It would be such a blow to her stature, she would never recover. And the stupid girl had done it all herself. Vittoryxe could hear other sisters arriving, hear them whispering. She felt like laughing, but she had to play the victim. 'You befriended me to get access to my birds. You never told me you were sending my work to the Sagoras.'

'I never told you' – bright spots of colour blazed in Imoshen's cheeks – 'because when I mentioned the Venerable Felesoi's work on inherited traits, you wouldn't look at it. You said Mieren knowledge was worthless.'

'So you went behind my back? You betrayed me!'

Imoshen flushed.

'Did you send the work to the Sagoras without Vittoryxe's permission?' the all-mother asked.

'Yes.'

The gathered inner circle sisters murmured in shock and disapproval. Tears glittered in Imoshen's eyes. Vittoryxe had no sympathy; the stupid girl deserved everything she got.

'I did it, and I would do it again, because knowledge should not be hidden.' Imoshen's voice shook, but she did not falter. 'Every piece of knowledge builds on what has gone before. The Sagoras are beginning to understand inheritable traits in people, and when they do, they'll share this information. The treatise they write will save lives. There are indications the bleeding disease is an inherited trait–'

'In Mieren?' Vittoryxe let scorn drip from her voice, she could not be happier. 'Who cares what happens to Mieren? They don't care about us.'

'How can you be so short-sighted?' Imoshen appeared shocked. 'If we understand inheritable traits, we'll understand why some Mieren parents produce Malaunje babies. We'll understand why T'En women have trouble carrying T'En babies to term. One day, we could choose whether we have boys or girls, Malaunje or T'En. T'En females could carry sacrare babies without fear of deformities.'

Imoshen looked around the inner circle. No one made a sound.

'Don't you see?' she appealed to them. 'That's why it's important that knowledge isn't hidden.'

'Oh, Imoshen,' Egrayne whispered.

'She went behind my back. My stature has been insulted,' Vittoryxe insisted. 'I demand satisfaction.'

'You're challenging me to a duel?' Imoshen asked, stunned.

'I could,' Vittoryxe said. But she wouldn't. She wasn't going to get herself killed. She wanted to make Imoshen suffer. 'All-mother, inner circle, do you agree this sister has insulted my stature?'

'What do you have to say in your defence, Imoshen?' All-mother Aayelora asked.

'Of the charge that I did not tell Vittoryxe what I was doing? I admit guilt. Of the charge that I shared knowledge so that everyone would benefit? I admit guilt.' She gestured to Vittoryxe. 'If it will make the gift-tutor happy, I will clean her bird cages for the next year.'

This was a Malaunje job, and it was exactly what Vittoryxe was going to demand, but to have Imoshen offer to do it made her hesitate. How could Imoshen not feel the blow to her stature?

'Are we all agreed Imoshen must make amends to Vittoryxe?' the all-mother asked.

The inner circle agreed.

'Then choose the means for Imoshen to make amends,' Aayelora told Vittoryxe.

Imoshen accepted this without argument. Vittoryxe found it so frustrating she could scream.

'There's no need for Imoshen to clean my bird cages,' Vittoryxe said. 'I don't want her near my birds. To make amends, Imoshen must promise not to send any more messages to Venerable Felesoi.'

Imoshen's gasp was everything Vittoryxe had hoped for.

'There,' the all-mother sounded relieved. 'That seems fair. Imoshen, do we have your word?'

Imoshen looked from her to Vittoryxe; she seemed shocked and disappointed. Vittoryxe was delighted. She felt Imoshen's gift surge, and knew the silly girl was reading her. She didn't care.

The fight seemed to go out of Imoshen. 'I give my oath I will not contact Venerable Felesoi about Vittoryxe's birds.'

AS IMOSHEN WALKED down the boulevard with Reoden, Vittoryxe's accusations kept replaying in her mind. Why couldn't the others see how important the Sagoras' research was?

Their children ran on ahead, escorted by Reoden's hand-of-force, her sisterhood's scryer and a gift-warrior.

Two Malaunje followed with food and blankets. Imoshen carried some hand-reels; she planned to teach Reoden's children to fish. Iraayel already knew how.

She didn't see why T'En were prohibited from preparing food. It was one of those customs that made no sense to her. What if they had to fend for themselves? Today she found the restrictions on T'En particularly irritating.

The sound of laughter made her look up. Iraayel and Reoden's choice-son, Sardeon, were teasing Lyronyxe. The boys had both turned twelve last winter's cusp, but they were already taller than Lyronyxe, who had turned thirteen just after midwinter.

Her sacrare son would have been eight. It still hurt to think of him; it always would.

'You're very quiet today,' Reoden said.

'Do you think knowledge should be shared?'

Reoden blinked then laughed. 'I never know what you're going to say next. Why so serious? Look around you. Isn't it a glorious day?'

Shop doorways stood open, flowering plants hung from balconies, the sweet smell of baking reached them as the eateries prepared for the day's mid-morning rush, while T'En, Malaunje and the occasional Mieren in their distinctive red half-capes passed by.

Reoden linked arms with her.

The youngsters were at the next cross-street. Imoshen frowned. 'Wait for us, Iraayel.'

When they caught up, Reoden's hand-of-force grimaced.

'A day on the barge, drifting across the lake... I am going to be so bored.'

'Think of it as a well-deserved break,' Reoden said.

A loud clatter and a short sharp scream startled everyone on the street. It seemed to have come from a brotherhood eatery. Imoshen caught a glimpse of a courtyard, tables under a blossoming tree in the sunshine.

'Someone's hurt,' Reoden said. 'I must–'

A Malaunje girl of about ten came running out. There was blood on the front of her work apron. 'Someone help! Ma's hurt and my brother–'

Reoden turned to her hand-of-force. 'Take the children to the boat-house. I'll be down soon.'

Imoshen gestured for Iraayel to go with the others and took the girl by the shoulders, escorting her inside the eatery. When they reached the courtyard, she saw the stairs from the balcony had collapsed.

Shattered crockery littered the courtyard. Two people were injured. At a glance, there seemed to be broken bones, cuts and bruising. The youth was sitting up, holding a wound on his forearm closed. The mother wasn't moving. Reoden went to the mother first.

Imoshen sat the child down, checked her over for injuries, found none, then lifted the girl's chin. 'You aren't hurt. Everything is going to be all right. Do you understand?'

The child nodded.

Imoshen went to help the healer. 'What can I do?'

'I don't know. What can you do?'

'I have basic healing training.'

While they stopped the bleeding and strapped broken bones, Imoshen could feel the healer's gift. With each touch, Reoden encouraged flesh and bone to knit. When the T'En brother who ran the eatery turned up, they were almost done.

'You should keep your premises in better repair, if you value your Malaunje,' Reoden told him.

He bristled, but did not protest, and took over organising the removal of the injured.

Imoshen lifted her head. The emergency was over, yet her stomach churned with fear and her gift surged.

'Something's wrong!' Reoden said, rising swiftly.

'Iraayel.' Imoshen found herself on her feet, heading for the door. Out in the street, everything seemed normal, but she still felt sick with horror.

She kicked off her sandals and ran towards the boat-house. Barefoot, her feet slapping on the warm stones, she kept pace with Reoden.

They'd left the free quarter now, and were in the last stretch before the causeway gate; brotherhood buildings stood on either side.

Imoshen spotted Iraayel leaving the boat-house. He seemed to be following a T'En warrior, making for the brotherhood quarters on her left. Imoshen put on a burst of speed to try and cut him off.

The brotherhood warrior saw her and sped up.

He just made it through the brotherhood gate ahead of her, and she followed. Iraayel caught up with her as the warrior darted into the second palace down the street.

Imoshen skidded to a halt. T'En women did not go into the brotherhood quarter uninvited, let alone into a palace. Stepping back, she looked up to the symbol over the gate. The eye of the seer. 'Kyredeon's brotherhood.'

By now a dozen or so men, both Malaunje and T'En, were watching them. They carried themselves like warriors, and Imoshen's gift surged, responding to their threat.

'Just turn around and walk away slowly,' Imoshen whispered to Iraayel.

He nodded and they backed away.

'What happened?' Imoshen asked as they stepped out of the brotherhood quarter onto the boulevard.

'They attacked us. They took the gift-warriors down first, then the old sister. The Malaunje tried to defend us, but there were too many of them.'

'But you're all right? You, Lyronyxe and Sardeon are all right?'

Iraayel shook his head. His face crumpled and he gulped back a sob.

Imoshen's stomach twisted with horror. She broke into a run and threw open the boat-house door.

Through the arch to the lake, sunlight glistened on the water. Inside the boat-house it was dim. Barges and rowboats rocked gently. She saw broken picnic baskets and scattered food. The sickening smell of spilled blood mingled with the stink of gift aggression. Imoshen staggered.

A noise made her turn. Lyronyxe lay still, covered in blood, a boathook protruding from her chest. One glance told Imoshen they'd been too late to save her.

Not far from the sacrare, Sardeon lay sprawled, as if he'd been running towards her. He was bleeding from the back of his head. Reoden knelt beside him.

Imoshen sank next to her. 'He's–'

'Unconscious. He'll come round.'

Imoshen glanced to Lyronyxe.

Reoden shook her head.

Imoshen's raedan gift left her with no defences. In that instant, she felt what Reoden felt. It hit her like a blow and she curled up.

'Ma?' Iraayel came to her side.

She shielded to shut out Reoden's pain.

'I'm fine,' she whispered, coming to her feet.

Reoden had already moved off to see to the others. Imoshen went to the door. Outside, a crowd had gathered, and she gestured to three of the Malaunje. 'Come here. See to the wounded.'

'What is it?' an elderly brotherhood scholar asked.

'There's been a tragedy. The sacrare–' Her voice broke.

Imoshen recognised a T'En youth who had been sent to the brotherhoods only last winter. 'Tamaron, go up to the sisterhood quarter and tell them I need a dozen gift-warriors, the healer's voice-of-reason and two dozen Malaunje with stretchers and healing kits.'

He took off.

'Can we help?' the elderly scholar asked.

She considered. 'It might be better if no brotherhood men come in. In fact, make sure you stand well back from the sisterhood gift-warriors when they arrive.'

With that, she went inside. Now Reoden was kneeling next to the two injured Malaunje. Imoshen could feel the healer's gift as she worked on them.

Imoshen was so grateful Iraayel was unhurt, and that made her feel guilty. She searched for him and found him standing over a brotherhood warrior. The man's stomach was covered in blood, but the wound wasn't bleeding; Reoden had already worked on him. He blinked in shock.

'What happened here?' Imoshen asked.

The blankness left his eyes. She saw panic rise and felt the surge of his gift. There was something wrong with it.

She pulled Iraayel away. 'Don't go near him.'

'They didn't expect to die,' Iraayel said.

'What?'

'They didn't cut their hair.' He pointed to the three dead brotherhood warriors. 'They didn't expect to die.'

She shook her head and went to check on the sisterhood scryer. One of the Malaunje held a bloody cloth to her face. With so many injured, Reoden was concentrating on the life-threatening wounds first and then going only so far as to begin the healing process.

The scryer raised stricken eyes to Imoshen. 'How's Lyronyxe?'

Imoshen shook her head.

The scryer moaned, and Imoshen rubbed her back. There was silence, but for the whimpers of the injured, the soft lap of the lakewater and the distant call of birds.

'I failed her,' the scryer whispered.

'We all failed her.'

Next, Imoshen checked on Reoden's hand-of-force. Dead. The other gift-warrior, Cerafeoni, was unconscious. She had a crushed cheekbone; she'd probably lose the eye.

Iraayel was helping Sardeon to sit up. Sardeon thrust his hands aside and crawled to Lyronyxe's body. A high keening noise came from him as lay beside her, his head pressed to hers.

Tears stung Imoshen's eyes.

Iraayel went to draw Sardeon away, but Imoshen caught his arm. 'Let him mourn.'

Iraayel gestured to Lyronyxe. 'The brotherhood warriors were waiting for us. They grabbed her. She got away, tried to run. Fell. That was when the other brotherhood warrior fled and I chased him.'

'You chased an adult male warrior? What were you going to do if you caught him?'

A laugh escaped Iraayel and turned into a sob. He wept in her arms.

Moments later, Imoshen heard voices. Reoden's voice-of-reason entered the boathouse along with several sisterhood gift-warriors and Malaunje, with healing kits and stretchers.

'We have three dead brotherhood warriors and one injured,' Imoshen said, releasing Iraayel, who turned away to compose himself. 'Take the dead outside.' She pointed to the brotherhood warrior Reoden had healed. 'Don't go near that one. There's something wrong with his gift.'

'No, no!' A female voice, close to panic. 'Don't touch me.'

It was Cerafeoni, backing away from the healer.

'Heal the sacrare,' the gift-warrior insisted. 'Don't help me, help her.'

'I can't,' Reoden said in a flat voice, reaching for the gift-warrior.

'No.' Cerafeoni backed up until her shoulders hit the wall.

Reoden looked lost.

'Ree!' Her voice-of-reason, Nerazime, pushed through the crowd to join them. 'Oh, Ree.'

As Nerazime reached Reoden, the healer went down, legs crumpling.

Nerazime caught her.

'She's exhausted herself,' Imoshen said.

'Some help here,' Nerazime called.

Imoshen could feel the anger brewing as the sisterhood gift-warriors took in what had happened; their surging gifts made the hairs on her arms rise.

'There will be no unsanctioned reprisals,' Imoshen said.

'You're not our all-mother,' one of them snapped.

'No, but your all-mother chose to heal the wounded brotherhood warrior. Respect her wishes. When we have clearer heads, we will discuss this.'

They looked to their voice-of-reason. Nerazime nodded.

Imoshen stepped out into the sunshine, blinking. Colour had washed out of everything. Emotion had washed out of everything. Nothing felt real.

Mieren were being herded through the causeway gate. They shuffled in a long line of short red half-capes, whispering and pointing.

The gathered T'En and Malaunje stood in solemn groups and watched as the injured were taken to the sisterhood quarter.

Everyone avoided the dead brotherhood warriors and the all-father and his seconds who stood over them. She was reminded that one of the attackers had gotten away.

Her gift flexed as she approached them, and she read Kyredeon. He was angry and disgusted... not shocked and horrified as he should be.

'These were your men. They–' she began.

'They were acting under their own initiative,' he said. 'They thought to win stature. I would never have sanctioned the killing of the healer's sacrare.'

'There will be an all-council,' Imoshen said, because if there wasn't, there would be chaos. 'You will bring the warrior Reoden has healed, and the one we chased back to your sisterhood.'

'They were acting alone,' Kyredeon repeated. 'They–'

'Their fate will be decided at the all-council. Do you understand? This is why the covenant exists. When stature is put ahead of the lives of children, the sisterhoods must intervene.'

For a heartbeat, grief and anger threatened to overwhelm her gift control. She had to walk away.

Inside the boat-house, it was much less crowded now.

Iraayel came over and took her hand, drawing her towards Reoden's children. 'There's something wrong with Sardeon. He's unconscious again.'

Imoshen's heart sank. Ree mustn't lose both children. She sank to her knees beside Sardeon. He was completely still, barely breathing. A wave of sadness swept through her and her vision shifted to include the empyrean plane. She saw her choice-son's nascent gift stirring within him. Sardeon registered as having no gift, but she remembered Reoden saying his gift was starting to develop. There should be...

Realisation came to her. Sardeon was so attached to Lyronyxe, he'd segued to the empyrean plane.

'Sard?' Iraayel reached out to touch him.

'Don't, you'll be dragged through to the higher plane, too.' Imoshen struggled to form words. One thing was clear. Sardeon had no training. If she didn't go after him, he'd be devoured by empyrean beasts. It was a wonder he hadn't been killed already. She had no choice. She had to go now. 'Stand back. Don't let anyone near. I'm going after him.'

Imoshen placed her hand on the boy's forehead. The shift was instantaneous.

Under Sardeon's untrained gift, the empyrean plane had taken the form of a nightmare, all vague shapes and shadows. He stood not far from her and she was surprised that he was shielding his gift. It had to be instinctive.

Imoshen sensed his urgency as he searched for something. She lunged and caught him, and they segued back to the earthly plane.

One child saved.

One child lost.

Lost forever, because Lyronyxe's shade would have been confused by the violent death. Without training, she would have had no defence from the empyrean beasts. She would have needed an escort to reach death's realm.

This was what Sardeon had tried to do. At risk to his own life, he had gone after Lyronyxe to see her safely across.

Brave boy.

Chapter Thirty-Eight

'ARE YOU ALL right?'

Imoshen looked up and realised she'd been ignoring her devotee as Frayvia unpinned her hair, freeing it from the formal style.

She summoned a smile. 'Ree says Sardeon is subdued. Not surprising, since he saw his choice-sister murdered. Despite being lost on the empyrean plane, he seems to have all his wits. We've been lucky.'

'I'm glad, but you know very well I'm not talking about Reoden's choice-son.' Frayvia gently pushed Imoshen's hair to one side and undid the clasp of the raedan torc.

Imoshen was glad to be rid of it. She resented the weight of it on her neck and shoulders.

'Stand.' Frayvia stepped back.

Imoshen rose and her devotee steadied her as she slipped her feet free of her jewelled sandals. 'I can undress myself.'

'Indulge me.' Her devotee slid the calf-length brocade robe off her shoulders. 'Was it horrible?'

'Kyredeon strangled them slowly while we looked on. What do you think?'

Frayvia hung the robe without comment.

'I'm sorry, Fray,' Imoshen whispered as her devotee came back.

Frayvia gave a little shake of her head and began undoing the clasps of Imoshen's fitted vest.

Words spilled from Imoshen's lips. 'The brotherhood leaders chose the punishment. I think it was meant to punish Kyredeon as much as those he executed. We...

the sisterhood voted for death, but not there in the empowerment dome. We didn't want it sullied.'

Frayvia nodded as she finished undoing the clasps and slid the vest off Imoshen's shoulders.

'We all filed out of the dome and watched from the steps while Kyredeon led them both down to the street. They knelt facing us, and he went around behind them. He killed the initiate first, the one Iraayel and I chased back to the brotherhood's palace. But before he started, they acknowledged their fault, absolving their brotherhood and its leader of blame. They claimed it was all their idea to make a bid for stature, claimed they only meant to abduct the sacrare, to prove they could. The idiots...' Imoshen's voice faltered. She had wept so much these last four days, she felt utterly drained. 'It's all so stupid, such a waste... I don't know how Ree can bear it.'

Frayvia hugged her. Imoshen clasped her devotee's hands and they stood there for a while, saying nothing. Frayvia's hands went to Imoshen's waist, loosening the ties that held up her silky pleated trousers.

'And the other one, the one Reoden healed... The one with the corrupt gift—'

'Paryx,' Imoshen said. 'The gift-wright confirmed his mind and gift were both unstable. There was a chance she could have healed him with time, but he was to be executed. He wept softly, but died bravely in the end.'

Frayvia began to plait Imoshen's hair.

'It reminds me...' Imoshen began.

'Of our sacrare's death. I know.'

'When will it stop?'

'When we are dead and can no longer feel pain.'

'Oh, Fray, you are such a cynic.' Imoshen took her shoulders in her hands. 'You know I love you... but I meant, when will the feud between the sisterhoods and brotherhoods stop? I used to think it was cruel to take the T'En children away from their fathers. I believed Rohaayel was trying to do the right thing when he kept me, even though he did wrong by me. Now, I think we need to protect the children from the men. Yet, he...' She shook her head, unable to go on.

'I can feel how much it hurts you to remember. Don't keep it bundled up inside you. Turmoil will corrupt your gift. That's what a devotee is for.'

'Don't say that.' Imoshen felt fresh tears slide down her cheeks. 'You are so much more to me.'

'So tell me.'

'I'm not the great all-father-killer. At the end, when we were both on the empyrean plane and I was ambushed by the brotherhoods' gift-warriors, Rohaayel dragged several of them to their deaths to save me.'

'Oh, Imoshen.'

SORNE WRAPPED THE instrument in a length of material from Khitan. It was a deep purple silk embroidered with silver thread in swirling patterns. He'd bought it eight years ago, and he'd kept it all this time. The instrument was from Maygharia. It had a wooden base, inset with metal bars of different lengths. Its name translated to *thumb-player*. He'd tried it, and the notes rang out clear and pure; Valendia would be delighted.

As he crossed the plaza, he looked for the half-blood spy the Wyrds had planted on him, but couldn't spot the man. Either the spy was hiding, or he had better things to do than follow the Warrior's-voice around. Sorne had timed his visit so that Zabier would be busy.

Assistant Utzen waved him through, and Sorne unlocked the narrow door. He found Valendia alone on the balcony, picking grubs off the vegetables.

'Where's Mother?'

She gave a little jump, then laughed, her gaze going straight to the object in his arms 'Sleeping. She's not feeling well today. What is that?'

'A gift for you. Well, two gifts really.' He put it on the table, unwinding the material with a flourish. 'First, there's silk from Khitan to make you a beautiful robe.'

'Lovely.' She ran her hand over the fabric, but her attention was on the instrument.

Sorne grinned and showed her how to play it. 'And this. It's called a thumb-player, from Maygharia.'

'But it's not my birthday until after summer's cusp.'

Sorne shrugged. 'I couldn't wait. You hold it like this, and play it with both thumbs.'

She began to experiment with the sounds, tilting her head and listening. Within a few moments, she had a simple tune, something he remembered Hiruna singing as she rocked Valendia's cradle.

'Do you miss not having friends your own age, Dia?'

'I've never had any, so I don't know, do I?'

He smiled, content to sit and watch her. 'What would make you happy?'

'I am happy.'

But what would become of her?

'Listen to this.' Her eyes sparkled. 'It's little mice, running across the floor.' And she produced a string of notes.

'So it is.' He laughed.

'Oh...' She put the instrument down and came over to sit in his lap. Pulling his arms around her, she tucked her head into the crook of his neck.

A little surprised, he pressed his lips to her head. 'What's wrong?'

'Nothing. I just... Since you came back, you've felt like a stranger to me. But just then, when you laughed, I remembered you and Izteben together. And it made me sad inside, because we can never go back.' She lifted her head, magenta eyes gleaming with tears. 'We were happy there, weren't we?'

He nodded, unable to speak. Despite Oskane's scourging and the penitents, he'd been happy.

'Why aren't we happy here? It seems like I've waited all my life for you to come home, and now–'

'What are you doing?' Zabier demanded. He strode onto the balcony, grabbed Valendia's arm and pulled her to her feet. 'Go inside.'

'Why? What did I do wrong?'

'You didn't do anything wrong,' Sorne told her.

Zabier glared at him. 'Don't contradict me. I'm her brother.'

'Why are you angry with Sorne all the time?' Valendia asked. 'We've waited so long for our brother to come home, and now–'

Zabier shook with frustration. 'He's not our brother.'

'Of course he is.' She glanced to Sorne for confirmation. He shrugged. 'Technically–'

'He's not family. You shouldn't sit on his lap.'

'Why are you being horrible?'

'Zabier,' Sorne protested. 'You're making something out of nothing. I think of Valendia as my sister. She's not twelve yet. As if I'd–'

'She was in your lap, in your arms.'

'She was sad.'

Zabier rolled his eyes.

Sorne drew himself up. 'I'm a priest. We're–'

'Celibate?' Zabier rounded on him. 'We all know what priests get up to. This secret love-nest was built for the high priest's mistress.'

'Oskane would never–'

'Not Oskane. The previous high priest.'

'I just want to know one thing,' Valendia said, chin trembling as she fought her tears. 'If Sorne isn't our brother, then who is he?'

'You are my family,' Sorne told her. They were all he had in the world. 'You and Hiruna will always be–'

'He's the king's unwanted half-blood son. Mother was paid to be his wet-nurse.'

Sorne winced. 'Zabier...'

Valendia turned betrayed eyes, not on Sorne, but on Zabier. 'How can you be so mean?'

He lifted his hands. 'I'm the one who's kept you safe all these years. He comes back, and in no time you're crawling all over–'

Valendia fled inside.

'Why did you do that?' Sorne rounded on Zabier.

'I have to protect her. You saw what they did to the she-Wyrd. Dia's all legs right now, but in another year she's going to be beautiful. If I put her out on the street, how long do you think she'd last?'

Sorne had no illusions about that. 'But–'

'She's a half-blood female, and she's going to be a beauty. There are powerful men out there who would abduct her and lock her away for their own entertainment. You haven't been here for years, and before that you lived in a mountain retreat. You don't know what goes on. She's *my* sister, not yours. I'll decide what's best for her.'

'And Hiruna?'

'Of course.'

'Then hire a healer. She has the wasting illness.' And he walked away, vowing to visit only when Zabier was busy.

IMOSHEN HID BEHIND the verandah post as she watched Iraayel practice his martial exercises – precision, strength, speed and total concentration. He wouldn't be thirteen until winter's cusp, but he had asked to train with the adolescent boys and he was swiftly catching up.

Fifteen days had passed since the sacrare's murder. For the first two days, Iraayel had taken to his bed and refused to eat. On the third day, he had risen as usual and gone about his lessons. That was when she'd discovered she could no longer read him. Some people were impervious to her gift, and now he was one of them. She'd been grateful, because she thought he was recovering.

Now this...

'I can't read him. But you're right, Fray, there's an unnatural energy and focus to him,' Imoshen admitted.

'He's studying weapons training with the application of a youth about to go into the brotherhood.'

'As if he knows his life depends on it.'

'Iraayel saw the brotherhood warriors in action. He saw Reoden's hand-of-force die trying to protect the children.'

Her devotee nodded. Tears made her eyes glisten. 'His childhood is over.'

'I hate it. I wish we'd never come here. This place corrupts. I swear, if I stay here, I'll–'

'Hush. Don't let anyone hear you. Besides, where else could we go? Mieren hate us.'

'Not all the Mieren. The Sagoras...' Imoshen broke off. She grabbed her devotee and kissed her.

'What's that for?' A fond smile tugged at Frayvia's lips.

'How would you like to live with the Sagoras?'

Frayvia considered it. 'They're very secretive, and they live segregated lives. I don't think they let anyone in–'

'To the walled section where they live, no. But they welcome students to the Halls of Learning. They're teachers and searchers of knowledge. If I applied to study with them, I could take you and Iraayel with me.'

Frayvia frowned, deep in thought. 'We'd still have to come back when you finished your studies.'

'Not if I kept studying.' Imoshen hugged her and nodded to the courtyard, where her choice-son worked himself to the point of exhaustion. 'If Iraayel was studying, I wouldn't have to hand him over to his brotherhood when he turns seventeen.'

'You can't break the covenant, Imoshen.'

'I wouldn't break it, just side-step it. He could give Chariode his oath of loyalty, but continue to study.' A great weight lifted from her. 'That's it. I'm going to ask the all-mother if I can study with the Sagoras.'

'I don't know, Imoshen, after Vittoryxe and the birds–'

'She'll be glad to get rid of me!'

*   *   *

GRAELEN PACED. USED to roaming the city, he found the confines of port life frustrating.

Someone gave the Malaunje knock on the door.

'Come in.'

A pretty young Malaunje woman entered, bringing with her the smell of apple and cinnamon tarts baking. 'Adept Dragomyr invites you to the rooftop garden for refreshments.'

He found Dragomyr reclining on a couch, while his devotee prepared spiced wine. Graelen passed potted flowers and vegetables, and pruned fruit trees. The sea breeze stirred the cherry blossoms, sending petals across the paving.

After giving the obeisance of a visiting adept to a higher-ranking adept, he said, 'Your rooftop garden does your brotherhood credit.'

'Yes, you would not know we'd had such a dry summer last year. We're hoping for spring rains.' Dragomyr did not rise to greet him, instead waving him lazily into a chair. 'What have you learnt about this Warrior's-voice?'

'Not much more,' Graelen admitted. When Kyredeon had negotiated for him to stay in Chariode's port warehouse, part of the agreement meant he had to share information. Kyredeon had made it clear he was to share only enough to ensure Chariode's future cooperation. Kyredeon still hadn't forgiven Chariode for winning Rohaayel's brotherhood ahead of him. 'The Warrior's-voice spent the last eight years with King Charald, but no one knows where he came from before that.'

'Our kind are not welcome in the ports of the Secluded Sea,' Dragomyr said. 'We trade, but to stay overnight ashore we have to get special permission, so we usually organise meetings on our ships' decks.'

'Then he must be from Chalcedonia.'

'Unless he was sold by Mieren parents as a slave for the entertainment of some rich noble.'

'That happens?' Graelen was shocked.

Dragomyr closed his fan with a snap and regarded him thoughtfully. The adept had captained a trading vessel until he was injured. With the loss of his leg, he'd retired to run the brotherhood's trade from Port Mirror-on-Sea. He was very old now and very fat, due to the excellence of his personal cook, but his mind was as sharp as ever. 'They say the half-blood has visions sent by the Warrior god. How can this be?'

'He holds ceremonies at what he calls holy sites.' Graelen was sure that Dragomyr knew this, and was testing him. 'He breaks the walls between the planes and absorbs the power that is shed as a result.'

'His hair is white but his face is young. What does this tell us?' Dragomyr asked, reminding Graelen of his old gift-tutor. 'I see you don't know. Not surprising, since most of the devotees you see would have grown old with their T'En. Ysadore, come here.'

His devotee poured them each a glass of spiced wine.

Graelen savoured it and complimented the adept.

'Yes, Ysadore is very talented.' Dragomyr gestured with the fan. 'Did you notice his hair is nearly white, like your Harosel? How old is your servant?'

'Sixty, no... I think he's closer to seventy.'

Dragomyr nodded. 'Ysadore is forty. He became my devotee in the raid where I lost my leg. It's fifteen years since we left the ship, and in that time his hair has gone completely white. It's because of the strength of my gift. I don't say this to boast. I say this because you are young and have not seen as much of the world as I have. As a child, I knew T'En who grew up in the height of the High Golden Age. In those days, how fast a devotee's hair went white was a sign of the extent of their T'En's gift.'

'Why had I never heard this?'

'Some things are not said. They are understood.'

'You're saying this Warrior's-voice has been steeping himself in power.'

'Exactly, which brings us back to the *how*. How does he break the walls in the first place?'

'Sometimes they break on their own.'

Dragomyr nodded, then yawned behind his fan. 'Set your Harosel to find this out. You are dismissed.' Seeing Graelen's expression, he smiled sweetly. 'Eccentricity is the privilege of great age.'

Graelen hid a smile as he gave the correct obeisance and left. Downstairs in his chamber, he found Harosel waiting to report what he had learnt the night before.

He finished with, '...the locals are grumbling about the barons' men. They drink, they fight and they accost the women.'

'Not surprising; they spent the last eight years killing, raping and stealing,' Graelen said. 'Ask around. See if you can find out how the Warrior's-voice breaches the walls between the planes.'

'Only high church officials and nobility are present at these ceremonies. What I hear is all speculation.' Harosel shrugged. 'The Mieren don't like it that King Charald has a half-blood advisor. They're saying the Warrior's-voice has ideas above his station. They're saying the Father's-voice is a True-man and has visions, so why does the king need a half-blood?'

'It would be remarkable if they didn't say that.'

Harosel went to leave, but hesitated at the door.

'What?'

'I was speaking with the warehouse Malaunje. They've only had one half-blood infant handed in to them in the last ten years. Lysania's choice-daughter. For such a large port, that seems strange.'

'There's another brotherhood and a sisterhood in port. Perhaps the infants have been delivered to them.'

Harosel nodded and left.

Graelen knew he should report to Kyredeon, but he had no solid news, only speculation.

*   *   *

VITTORYXE WAITED UNTIL Imoshen left before speaking up. 'Send her to study with the Sagoras. She's a liability to us.'

The all-mother glanced to Egrayne. Why was she looking to her? Egrayne wasn't the sisterhood's voice-of-reason.

No, but the sisterhood's voice-of-reason was failing and, when she died, there was a good chance the all-mother would die with her. They were shield-sisters, gift-linked. The day was coming when the sisterhood would have to elect a new leader and, thanks to Imoshen's rash behaviour, the choice would be between Egrayne and Vittoryxe.

Egrayne lifted her big hands in a shrug. 'We can't let her leave the sisterhood–'

'She'd still be part of the sisterhood. It would be no different from her going to live out on an estate,' Vittoryxe argued.

The all-mother looked to Egrayne, and Vittoryxe knew she would recommend the empowerer for the next voice-of-reason. Excitement raced through Vittoryxe; this meant Aayelora would name her the next all-mother.

Just then the all-mother's geldr came running in, chased by the devotee. With the reasoning power of a five-year-old but the body of a full-grown adult, he was dangerous. In a fit of temper, he could break bones or even kill.

Vittoryxe grimaced and stepped aside as the geldr tried to hide behind the all-mother. Tancred might be a neuter, but Vittoryxe always thought of him as male. He was big and strong, and useless – the all-mother should have suffocated him at birth.

He made Aayelora look ridiculous, hiding behind her smaller frame and giggling. The all-mother's devotee apologised profusely and lured Tancred out of hiding, then out of the chamber, with the promise of sugared fruit.

As soon as she was all-mother, Vittoryxe would have him locked up somewhere down below in the crypts. Fed once a day, he would soon waste away and die.

'Kyredeon lost wealth and stature when his theatre burned. I hear rumours his brotherhood is in trouble. The all-fathers are manoeuvring for power,' Egrayne said. 'As long as Imoshen the All-father-killer remains in the city, no all-father will risk crossing the all-mothers.'

'So what do you suggest?' Aayelora asked.

'Tell Imoshen she may study with the Sagoras, but not until she can speak their language fluently,' Egrayne said. 'From what I hear, they don't even use the same alphabet. Tell her you could only negotiate a lesson every ten days. That should slow her down, and who knows what will happen in the meantime?'

The all-mother nodded. 'Send for Imoshen.'

IMOSHEN RETURNED TO her chamber at a run. She had to learn the Sagoras' language, then they could leave. 'Frayvia, guess what?'

The chamber was dim, illuminated by beams of golden, late afternoon sunlight, which filtered through the patterned screen. A shadow detached itself from the darkness – long, elegant legs, hair cut so short she could see the line of the beautiful throat, and a body clad in silk so fine it was almost transparent. Imoshen sensed the familiar gift, with its enticing power.

'Ree...' Imoshen swallowed. 'What are you doing here? Where's—'

'I sent your devotee away.'

Imoshen closed the door after her, and leant against it. Her gift surged. She sensed the healer's desire, but underneath that was desperation and determination. Imoshen was out of her depth. 'Ree...'

Reoden came closer. 'Your gift draws me, Imoshen. I can feel it on my skin.'

'Why are you here?'

'You know why.'

'Why now?'

'All the others, they offer platitudes or they avoid me. You know what I've been through. You only ever offered me the truth, and I turned you down.'

'You were right to turn me down. I wasn't ready.'

'Are you ready now?'

'I am, but I'm not sure you are.'

For answer, Reoden kissed her. 'Make me forget.'

'You would use me to forget?'

'Yes. Isn't it awful?'

'Only if I say no.'

Chapter Thirty-Nine

A SENSE OF purpose filled Imoshen as she tried on the Sagora style clothing. She pulled the hood into place, and lowered the net over her face so that only her mouth and chin were visible. The world appeared blurry. Why would anyone limit their vision like this?

Because they valued privacy. It had taken delicate negotiation to organise her language lessons, and part of the stipulation was that she would honour Sagorian customs.

'Hold still while I get the length right.' Frayvia knelt to pin in the hem. 'There. How does it feel?'

'It's a little odd having sleeves that cover my hands, but I'll get used to it.'

'Now try the Mieren half-cape.'

Imoshen swung the red half-cape around her shoulders to complete her costume. She studied herself in the mirror.

'If I keep my gift tightly reined, no one will know I'm T'En. In fact...' She turned this way and that. 'Unless I speak, they won't know my gender either.'

The thought of such freedom gave her a thrill.

'Take it off and I'll finish the hem. You'll be ready for tomorrow.'

Imoshen removed the Mieren half-cape, and Frayvia smiled.

'What?'

'You're the only T'En I know who would like to be invisible.' Frayvia accepted the costume and went over to sit by the lamp to finish pinning the hem. 'You want to hide. Meanwhile, there's a white-haired Malaunje walking around Port Mirror-on-Sea, bold as brass, calling himself the Warrior's-voice.'

'I know.' Imoshen sat beside her. 'No one knows what to make of it. They say he has visions and advises the king. Egrayne has asked our people in port to find out more about him, but he's so deeply immersed in the Mieren world it's proving dangerous for our informants. What do the Malaunje say? Are they tempted to leave the city and try their luck in the church? No more T'En to answer to, no more fear of gift addiction?'

Frayvia looked up sharply; there must have been talk. 'Only fools would think that. This Warrior's-voice – I don't know who he is, or where he came from, but I do know this. He'll come to a bad end.'

Imoshen suspected she was right.

GRAELEN WATCHED AS a stream of priests wearing the dark robes of the holy-swords left the palace, carrying travelling kits. There was no sign of the Warrior's-voice amongst them. It was hard to tell Mieren apart, especially when they wore identical robes and tied their hair back the same way. They entered the Warrior's church and did not come out while he waited.

For the last nine days, Graelen had walked to the plaza to watch for the Warrior's-voice. He'd seen the white-haired Malaunje cross from the palace to the Father's church at around the same time each day and stay for at least one prayer bell, before returning to the palace. There was an intense rivalry between the two churches. Before this, the Father's high priest had always been the king's advisor. Now a half-blood from the Warrior's church advised him, even though there was a True-man who claimed to have visions.

What was the Warrior's-voice doing in the Father's church? Why hadn't he moved his personal belongings into the Warrior's church, when his holy-swords had moved there?

Here he came now, crossing the plaza. He glanced over, as if he sensed Graelen's presence, but he didn't break his stride.

Rather than wait around for him to come back out, Graelen headed to the docks. Harosel had said he might have information for him today.

As one of the war barons rode by, followed by a column of men-at-arms, Graelen stepped into a doorway. King Charald had been rewarding his war barons. This was the third baron to ride off at the head of a long line of men-at-arms to claim his estate and flush out Charald's enemies.

As soon as the baron passed, Graelen stepped down onto the street. It was amazing how the Mieren could watch him, without actually meeting his eyes. He'd learned to maintain his mental shields so that their unguarded minds no longer gave him a headache.

Was that Harosel coming this way? The veteran looked grim, and Graelen increased his pace. When they met at a crossroad, Harosel led him into a dim alleyway, where Mieren children played in the puddles.

A grubby child looked up. 'Wyrds!'

The children disappeared into the rickety buildings that rose three and four storeys high. The lane was not wide enough for Graelen to walk with his arms outstretched. Harosel glanced up and down the alley.

Graelen didn't need to be a raedan to read his anger. 'What is it?'

'The Warrior's-voice is sacrificing half-blood children.'

'What? Impossible. Are you sure?'

'No. But I went to Paragian's warehouse. They've had half the usual number of Malaunje infants delivered. So I went to the sisterhood warehouse and their numbers are down, too.'

'I see.'

'Mieren parents can't keep their half-blood children. If they do, other Mieren turn on them. They have to hand them over.'

Graelen nodded. 'The Warrior's-voice makes sacrifices to gain power from the higher plane. He has no innate power of his own, so he has to break the walls somehow. The beasts of the higher plane are hungry for the life force of Mieren. If they have a choice, they prefer the gift-enforced essence of T'En. Half-bloods aren't quite as tasty, but...' Graelen shuddered, sickened. It was all making horrible sense. Outrage made his heart race and his gift surge. 'The Warrior's-voice does have pure white hair. He must have been immersing himself in stolen power, paid for with the blood of innocents.'

'The numbers have been down for years, more so in the last five.'

'He only just arrived.'

'There's the Father's-voice. And now there's two of them, competing for the king's ear.'

Graelen cursed. He'd sworn an oath to use his gift to protect half-bloods. If, as he suspected, this white-haired Malaunje had been sold to someone down south and 'rescued' by the king, or hidden by the church as a baby and reared to serve the king, then he had never heard of the oath. He knew only what the Mieren had told him of his own kind. Fed lies since he was old enough to listen, it wasn't surprising he'd been convinced by the church of the justice of their claims.

Even so, how could he sacrifice his own kind? Infants, at that. Contempt filled Graelen. 'This has to be stopped.'

'If it is happening,' Harosel agreed.

'You brought this to my attention. What're you—'

'All I'm saying is, we need to be sure before we execute him.'

'You're right. It's time we questioned this Warrior's-voice.'

* * *

SAFE IN THE knowledge that no one would recognize her in the guise of a Sagora, Imoshen slipped out into a lane and then onto the causeway boulevard, where she mingled with the passing trade as she made her way down to the gate.

This was the same gate she had entered eight years ago, seeking sanctuary, and when she stepped through it this time, a wonderful sense of freedom filled her. It came as a shock to realise how much she hated the Celestial City.

Look what it had made her do to Rohaayel before it would accept her; look what it had done to generous, kind-hearted Reoden; look what was happening to Iraayel, as the boy she loved disappeared behind a shield of determination and martial prowess.

At the arched bridge to the foreign quarter, she found a Sagora servant waiting to escort her to their residence. The buildings of the foreign quarter were owned by banks and great merchant families whose influence spanned kingdoms. The first of these houses had been built on stilts in a shallow part of the lake almost two hundred years ago. As more and more premises were built, walkways and bridges had been added, linking the buildings.

At last they came to the Sagoras' premises. Three storeys above them, the scroll and the nib symbolised the Sagoras' quest for knowledge. Conviction filled Imoshen; this was where she belonged.

The servant showed her where to hang her Mieren half-cloak, then led her through a courtyard to a chamber. 'Merchant Mercai will be with you presently.'

The servant left her in a wood-panelled chamber, where every shelf was packed with books, curios and intricate brass machinery, all glowing in the late afternoon sun.

Merchant Mercai entered, giving the Sagora bow, and she mirrored him. He sat cross-legged on a cushion on a raised platform. Imoshen felt somewhat intimidated as he looked down on her.

'While we are here we have no names, no titles. You are *student* and I am *teacher*. You speak only Sagorese during the lesson.' He indicated she was to sit.

Imoshen took out her nib and paper and prepared to make notes.

Nothing happened.

She waited.

Normally, her gift enabled her to read the subtle nuances of expression and movement. The Sagorese style of dress left nothing for her power to work on. She felt blind.

The servant showed someone else into the chamber. They wore the traditional Sagora costume but Imoshen sensed the male gift. Her stomach tightened with fear and her power tried to rise. She forced it down. No attempt had been made on her life since she executed Rohaayel, but every time she went into the free quarter she sensed the animosity of the T'En men. They would never forgive her.

The T'En man bowed to Merchant Mercai, settled himself cross-legged and took out a nib and ink.

Of course, if he was wearing the Sagorian costume, he was just another student. Imoshen almost laughed with relief.

Then a wave of annoyance swept through her; she didn't want to share her teacher. Lessons with the gift-tutor had taught her how frustrating learning could be when other students took too long to understand. She was not going to put up with that here. She would study hard, and too bad if he couldn't keep up.

As the lesson progressed, Imoshen opened her mind, absorbing every scrap of information, adding to the framework of grammar she had created to learn Chalcedonian. As she laid down each new piece of information, she ran over it three times to be sure it was firm.

Despite her misgivings, the student kept up with her every step of the way. She felt alive, exhilarated by the challenge, and truly awake for the first time in years. How could she have forgotten her love of learning?

A chime sounded somewhere out in the courtyard, bringing Imoshen back to the real world with a jolt.

Merchant Mercai switched to Chalcedonian. 'Soon, the Mieren bell will ring. A servant will escort you to the city gates before they close.'

Imoshen came to her knees to give obeisance and spoke in Sagorese. 'Student-she thanks teacher.'

'Student-he thanks teacher. May the light of knowledge burn more brightly every day.'

Once the teacher had departed, Imoshen came to her feet and turned to her fellow student. 'You know more Sagorese than you let on. Just how many languages do you know?'

'Four, fluently. There's another four or five I can get by in.'

Why would he need to know so many languages? Only the sisterhood's sea captain, Iriane, knew... He must be a ship's captain.

As they turned to go, Imoshen noticed an astrolabe on a shelf. She could not resist going over to examine it... so cunningly wrought.

A six-fingered hand stopped the outer circle turning. 'This is a tool, not a toy. An astrolabe reveals the path of the stars.' He proceeded to explain exactly how the planets moved. Imoshen bit her tongue.

And watched him talk. At first she was annoyed but, as the explanation went into more detail, she came to appreciate his depth of knowledge.

'Sorry.' He gave a rueful grin. 'I forget not everyone is interested in the paths of the planets.'

Imoshen shrugged. 'It's no surprise to find an astrolabe here. The Sagoras came from across the Endless Ocean. They must have an excellent understanding of the stars and planets to have navigated this far. No one else has sailed from beyond the eastern horizon in over three hundred years.'

'You knew what it was?'

'Yes, but you explained it so well, I didn't have the heart to stop you,' Imoshen told him sweetly, and walked out into the courtyard.

One part of her wanted to rush home so she could go over what she'd learnt. Another part of her wanted to bait him. It was invigorating.

They'd reached the foyer, where her Mieren cloak hung. There was no Mieren cloak for him. He was too tall to pass for a True-man. Seeing her cloak reminded Imoshen of her life outside these lessons; she didn't want him walking her back to the free quarter. If he knew which sisterhood shop she changed in, he might guess she was Imoshen the hated All-father-killer. And that would be the end of her fun.

'I've thought of something I must ask the teacher,' she said. 'You go without me.'

'Until next lesson, then...?' He paused, waiting for her to give her name.

Instead, she gave the Sagora obeisance. 'Student-she bids farewell to student-he.'

He smiled slowly.

Imoshen waited to be sure that he had gone and wasn't lurking nearby before she donned the Mieren half-cloak. She only just made it back to the sisterhood's shop in time.

As she changed into her own clothes, she remembered the ship's captain who had bought the astrolabe from the Sagoras' shop, back in early spring. Only All-fathers Chariode and Paragian had trading fleets, so it would not be hard to find out his identity. But she didn't want to.

GRAELEN WATCHED THE comings and goings in the plaza. Today, when the Warrior's-voice went to the Father's church, they would take him for questioning. Harosel was already in place.

The half-blood would then be taken to a wine cellar. Below the earth, surrounded by thick walls, they could question this betrayer of his own kind without fear of being interrupted. Graelen was ready to slit the half-blood's throat himself.

Shouting, and the steady thud of many booted feet, echoed across the plaza. The local Mieren hurried out of the way as a long column of men-at-arms, walking four abreast, entered the plaza. In the lead rode their captain. It appeared another baron was heading off to claim his estates.

As Graelen watched, the white-haired Malaunje came out of the palace, accompanied by the king and one of his barons. They said their farewells on the steps. The baron looked grim as he strode down the stairs with the Warrior's-voice by his side, followed by a foreign Mieren youth in dark priestly robes, carrying two travelling kits. He strapped them onto their horses' saddles as the three of them mounted up.

Graelen glanced to Harosel, who shrugged. They hadn't anticipated this. Why was the half-blood accompanying one of the barons?

Graelen left his hiding place and met Harosel, as the baron and his men-at-arms marched past.

Graelen studied the baron's banner. 'Any idea who–'

'The newly restored Baron Nitzane. His father's estate was confiscated when Matxin seized the throne. He's the grandson of Baron Nitzel. Since his banner carries both symbols, I expect the king has returned his father's estates and his grandfather's as well. He'll be on his way to reclaim them.'

'Why does he have the Warrior's-voice with him?'

'No idea. Should we follow? Take the half-blood on the road?'

'From amidst two hundred men-at-arms?' Graelen grinned. 'No. He'll be back. He serves the king.'

'And if he doesn't come back? Maybe the king's rewarding him with an estate and title, too?'

Graelen snorted. 'A half-blood?'

'Look what this half-blood does for the king. He receives visions, Grae.'

Graelen let the use of his familiar name slide. 'At what price?'

They both stared at the half-blood as he passed.

'Give me a day with him,' Harosel muttered, voice thick with anger. 'I'll get everything he knows out of him.'

'Give me a few moments. I'll break his walls,' Graelen said. 'He won't be sacrificing any more Malaunje after that. He won't be much good for anything.'

Chapter Forty

SORNE STUDIED THE stronghold. A solid stone structure, built on the hilltop above a bend of a river, it was not a castle he would want to be laying siege to. From where he sat, astride his horse, he could see people scurrying about in the small, walled township clustered around the base of the hill. Having spent the last eight years at Charald's side, Sorne was skilled in assessing defences and planning attack strategies. 'The gate to the township is open, as is the gate to the castle itself. They know we're here, so–'

'It's hard to march two hundred men across the countryside without the locals noticing,' Nitzane said. He'd been furious when King Charald sent the Warrior's-voice with him, and he hadn't missed a chance to snipe at Sorne. He didn't know that Sorne had been sent to discover if Charald's second wife had died, and kill her if she hadn't. Had Nitzane given his mother a moment's thought, these last eight years?

Idan shifted in his saddle, irritably. The Khitite prince had sworn the holy-sword's oath when they had arrived in port and had been a faithful companion ever since.

The captain of the men-at-arms said nothing. He was a veteran and had served Nitzane's older brother, who now ruled Navarone. Sorne gathered that he'd fled with the brothers when they were banished, and now he wanted to return home; probably had family on Nitzane's estate.

'I think the baron who held his estate under Matxin has fled,' Sorne said. 'He will have taken his family and faithful retainers. What we can see are probably the original farmers, townsfolk and retainers, who served your grandfather and would no doubt welcome you back.'

'I don't see why we had to come here first,' Nitzane said. 'This isn't my home. I would rather have reclaimed my father's estate.'

Sorne urged his horse closer to Nitzane. 'If you look west to the sea, and follow the curve of the river, you will see the Mother's abbey.'

Nitzane frowned and glanced quickly to Sorne, who nodded once. Sorne did not particularly like Nitzane, but he thought the man deserved to know what Charald had in mind for his mother.

'You two stay here, I want to get a closer look,' Nitzane said. 'Come with me, Warrior's-voice.'

They rode on a little until they were out of hearing, then Nitzane brought his horse around to face Sorne. 'I knew my mother retired to one of the Mother's abbeys. It's this one, isn't it? Charald has sent you to find out if she still lives.'

'He's sent me to make sure she's dead.'

Nitzane grimaced. 'Go ahead. You have my blessing.'

Sorne was shocked.

'What do I care for the mother who abandoned my brother and me to marry King Charald? I swear my father's body was still warm the day she married the king!'

'It's not like she had much choice. Your grandfather had her husband murdered. He held you two boys as surety of her good behaviour–'

Nitzane's riding crop flashed out. 'You lie!'

'I had it from Oskane.' Sorne felt a sting and blood trickled down his cheek.

'He lied.'

'I read it in his journal, his private journal.'

'Ha! I have you now.' Nitzane urged his horse back towards the others, calling over his shoulder. 'Charald gave me Oskane's journals. The Father's-voice has had them all these years, and Oskane left them to the king.'

Sorne's horse caught up with Nitzane's. 'Why would the king give you—'

'Because he can't be bothered reading them. According to Oskane, no True-man knew more about the Wyrds than he did. The king thinks there might be something useful in them. I have them on the supply cart, so you can show me the passage and prove your allegations.'

When they joined the others, Idan and Ballendin stared at Sorne's bleeding cheek, but said nothing.

'What's your assessment of the keep, Captain Ballendin?' Nitzane asked. 'Should we just ride in?'

'We have two hundred men. You'd be lucky if there's four hundred people in the town and castle, and most of them will be old folks, women and children. The gates are open and no one's going to stop us.'

So they rode right up to the township's wall, through the gate and up the rise towards the castle. Sorne cast an assessing eye over the buildings. Some were of a reasonable size, but they had been allowed to fall into disrepair. The baron who'd taken this estate had milked it dry.

Thin-faced, nervous people watched from doorways; women held skinny children at their sides. They whispered and pointed to the banner, which incorporated their old lord's standard.

'It's Baron Nitzel's grandson come home,' Captain Ballendin announced. 'Baron Nitzane.'

Nitzane smiled. By the time the party reached the castle gate, the locals were cheering.

'I don't think there'll be a feast tonight unless we supply the food,' Captain Ballendin told Nitzane.

'Go ahead, organise it. There's something else I must do.' Once they were in the castle courtyard, Nitzane dismounted. A skinny boy ran forward to take his horse.

Nitzane beckoned Sorne, and together they pulled the old chest off the cart. When Sorne saw the elaborately carved chest, he recalled climbing into Oskane's bedchamber to read the scholar's journals and his agents' messages.

They carried the chest into the castle, where the wife of the original castle-keep greeted them. She showed them to the baron's private chambers, which had been stripped of everything that could be loaded onto a cart.

Sorne and Nitzane placed the chest in front of the empty fireplace. Sorne opened the shutters, letting in a shaft of sunlight.

'There.' Nitzane opened the chest with a flourish. It gave a terrible creak. 'I swear this has not been opened since the day Oskane died. Now prove you speak the truth. If you've been lying to me, I'll have my men hang you from the rafters.'

Sorne spotted the journals under a pile of scrolls. 'Who would have thought the old scholar had so many scrolls?'

'You're saying you can't find it?'

'Nothing of the kind.' Sorne removed the scrolls by the handful. As he did so, he read the tags. For the most part they were treatises on the Wyrds, dating from before King Charald the Peace-maker's time. He'd often seen Oskane going through these scrolls and questioning the she-Wyrd, making careful notes from her responses.

Below the scrolls he found the journals. Maybe they would tell him why Izteben had died. But first he had to satisfy Nitzane.

Sorne found the relevant journal and flicked through the pages. His mother's name leapt out at him. He and Nitzane had a lot in common; both Sorne's mother and Nitzane's father had been killed so that Charald could take Nitzane's mother for his second wife. Now Charald wanted to do away with this wife so he could marry again.

'Have you found it?' Nitzane asked.

'Did you know, Charald ordered my mother killed, so he could marry yours?'

'That... that would make you Queen Sorna's son.' Nitzane's eyes widened. He grimaced. 'You were a newborn, I was less than two years old. How can we ever know the truth? You tell me my own grandfather ordered my father's murder, so my mother could marry Charald. Prove it.'

'Here it is.' Sorne read the passage. '*Then I will tell him the truth, most importantly Nitzel's part in his mother's murder. If Nitzel hadn't had his own son-in-law murdered, his daughter would not have been free to marry Charald. Sorne needs to know who his enemies are.*'

Nitzane turned away abruptly and went over to the window. He stood looking down into the courtyard, three floors below. Sorne could hear the shouts of the men as they unloaded the carts.

'Oskane wrote this just before I turned seventeen,' Sorne said. 'He planned to use me to take vengeance on your grandfather. We both lost our mothers because of Charald's need for an heir and Nitzel's ambition for his grandson to be the next king.'

'I couldn't stand Cedon. Only met him twice, but both times he was a spoilt brat,' Nitzane admitted, his voice raw.

Sorne closed the journal and repacked the chest. 'Do you want me to look after these? There's dozens of dry dusty scrolls—'

'Seven save me, yes. Take them away.'

Sorne shut the chest and came to his feet, dusting off his hands. 'I have to ride out to the abbey tomorrow. See if your mother still lives. It has been eight years and no one's heard from her. Do you want to come with me?'

Nitzane swung around to face him. 'Why are you doing this?'

Sorne shrugged. 'You can see your mother. I can't.

Nitzane's brows drew together and he strode towards Sorne. 'I won't let you—'

'If I meant to kill her, would I have told you?'

The chamber door flew open and they turned as Captain Ballendin entered, Idan in his arms. For a moment Sorne could not make sense of what he was seeing. Why was the front of Idan's chest wet? Why was there blood on his lips?

'The Khitite prince is dying,' Ballendin gasped, out of breath.

'No!' Sorne had known the youth since he was a boy of seven. 'Have you called the saw-bones?'

'Aye, he's on his way. But Idan was asking for you.'

'How did it happen?' Nitzane demanded.

'We were setting up the hall for the feast. He was joking around and sat in the baron's chair, *your* chair. It had been rigged. His weight triggered a crossbow. The bolt—'

Nitzane cursed.

'Warrior's-voice?' Idan's eyes opened and he reached for Sorne.

'I'm here.' Sorne took his hand.

'The king has my gold,' Idan said, between gasps. Blood ran from the side of his mouth. 'I want my sister to have it. You'll give it to her?'

'I will,' Sorne said.

'Tell my mother...' His body jerked in a spasm; blood frothed from his lips. In another heartbeat, he was dead.

'By the Mother,' Nitzane whispered. He picked up his cloak and swung it over his shoulders. 'I'm going to the abbey.'

'Now?' Captain Ballendin asked. 'It'll be dark by the time you get there.'

Nitzane walked out.

Ballendin tried to pass Idan's body to Sorne.

'No, I have to go to the abbey too.' Before Nitzane could warn his mother and complicate Sorne's plan.

'What's at the...' Ballendin asked, then his eyes widened. 'The queen still lives?'

'We don't know. Are you loyal to Nitzane?' Sorne asked.

'I followed him and his brother across the Secluded Sea because I promised their mother I'd look after them.'

'Then come with us.'

'What about...' Ballendin glanced down to the youth in his arms.

For a moment Sorne didn't know what to do. Then he had an idea. 'Bring him.'

They went down to the stables, where Nitzane was waiting for his mount to be saddled. The horse had been ridden all day and was reluctant to leave its warm stall.

'Harness a cart,' Sorne said. He caught Nitzane's eye, hoping the baron would play along. 'We're taking the Khitite prince's body to the Mother's abbey, to lay him to rest. The queen is buried there. Royalty should be buried with royalty.'

He'd committed himself now. He hoped the abbess would cooperate.

It was dark by the time they reached the gates of the abbey. Sorne jumped down and rang the bell. He glanced back to the cart. Captain Ballendin held the reins, while Nitzane stared fixedly ahead.

A slot opened in the gate. 'We're closed, come back tomorrow.'

'Since when does the Mother turn her sons away?' Sorne asked.

'Since her sons rode in here eight years ago, took all the young pretty novices and rode off with them.'

Sorne raised the lantern so she could see mulberry eyes. 'I'm the Warrior's-voice. Open up.'

'We don't accept Wyrds here.'

'I'm King Charald's advisor. Open in the name of the king.'

The slot closed and they heard worried whispers, then scurrying steps. Sorne was about to ring the bell again when the gate finally opened. He walked in ahead of the cart.

Four women in priestly white stood in the entrance to the courtyard. Looking around, Sorne had an impression of decay. Weeds grew in the cracks between the paving stones, and creepers crawled over the buildings.

'Who else is here?' he asked.

'There are just the five of us,' the gate-keeper said, coming up behind him. 'The baron taxed the abbey until we could no longer afford to feed ourselves, let alone anyone else.'

'Who is in charge?' Sorne asked.

'I'm the abbess,' the smallest and oldest of the women said. 'We heard King Charald had returned, but–'

Looking grim and determined, Nitzane jumped down from the cart. 'I'm looking for the queen.'

'King Charald's second wife died two winters ago,' the abbess said.

Nitzane groaned and sank to sit on the mounting block. Sorne put a hand on his shoulder.

'You keep telling them that,' Captain Ballendin climbed down from the cart. 'We'll all be safe and happy.'

'Ballendin?' The gate-keeper sounded stunned. 'What are you doing here?'

'Reporting on your sons, my lady. Charald rewarded your eldest son with the kingdom of Navarone. And Nitzane, here, has had his father's title and estates returned, along with his grandfather's. He's now the most powerful baron in Chalcedonia.'

The gate-keeper turned to Nitzane. 'Is really you, my little Zane?'

Sorne grinned as Nitzane jumped to his feet.

Leaving the three of them together, he went over to the old abbess. 'Do you have a nun who was buried in the last eight years?'

'We have several, why?'

'King Charald wishes to remarry, so the queen must be dead. We need to establish a royal crypt here. Baron Nitzane will make a generous donation to ensure there is a suitable stone carved. And' – Sorne gestured to the cart – 'I have the body of Idan, prince of Khitan. Royalty should be buried with royalty.'

'We don't lay foreigners to rest in our sacred grounds.'

'He swore to serve the Warrior. He's a faithful servant of the Seven. I will make a generous donation to ensure a suitable stone is carved.'

'In that case...'

It took the better part of the night to prepare the crypt and lay Idan to rest alongside the nun, who would henceforth be known as the queen.

Burying young Idan was hard for Sorne. He wept unashamedly as the crypt was sealed.

The next morning, they shared the same meagre fare as the nuns, then hitched up the horses and turned their noses toward the castle. The abbess gave him a message of condolence addressed to the king, informing him that his queen had died two years earlier.

Sorne took the reins while Nitzane's mother hugged him one last time.

'Good-bye, my little Zane.'

As the cart trundled out the gate, Sorne asked, 'Zane?'

'My brother's pet name for me. I misjudged you, Sorne. Consider me your friend.'

Chapter Forty-One

WHEN SORNE RETURNED with the news of Idan's death, as well as the queen's, King Charald was pleased. Eight years had passed since the king had taken Idan hostage to ensure the cooperation of the Khitite royal family. In that time, the boy had grown into a man, and allied himself with Chalcedonia.

'If one of the royal hostages had to die, then Idan's the best one to lose,' he told Sorne, who hoped his face did not betray his true feelings. 'Idan's father is dead, his sister adores Etri and they have three children. Etri's hold on Khitan is secure, and I trust him. He has the other royal hostages in his care. Just as well we didn't lose the Maygharian prince. Norholtz is having problems. The man always was a pious prick with no head for strategy.' Charald cast Sorne an assessing look.

'Idan said you were minding his gold.'

Charald laughed. 'Yes, the lad had a way of making coin breed.'

'He wanted me to take it to his sister.'

'I'll send it to Khitan.'

'I promised him I would do it.'

'I have all my barons out claiming their estates, and it's summer's cusp now. Do you think it's too soon to wed Matxin's filly? I need to get a son by her before the year is out. I've heard the whispers. They say I'm getting on, that I've won an empire and made myself high king for nothing, since it will all die with me.'

Sorne knew he should reassure Charald, but tonight he could not bring himself to speak the platitudes. He made his excuses and left.

When he returned to his chamber, Sorne unpacked Oskane's journals and scrolls, along with a bag of malachite he'd found in the chest.

Although the scrolls were probably full of interesting information on Wyrds, he went straight to Oskane's last journal. It started on his seventeenth birthday, just after winter's cusp, and went through to summer's cusp, when Oskane had died. If something had gone wrong in the preparation for the ceremony that killed Izteben, perhaps he'd find it here.

Oskane's last few entries made it clear that Matxin had been a great help to him. He also wrote of the pride he took in Zabier. The scholar's plans for Baron Nitzel's downfall did not correlate in the slightest with what had unfolded that evening. Clearly, it had been a terrible accident, and there were forces on the higher plane that could not be appeased with a T'En artefact.

Sometimes it didn't matter what you did, things were beyond your control.

Flicking through the pages reminded Sorne how happy he'd been in the retreat. When Zabier returned to them, Hiruna had become her usual sunny self. Catching glimpses of his family through Oskane's journal was painful.

Then he came to the morning they'd set off for the port. Meticulous as always, Oskane had recorded the she-Wyrd's passing.

...woke up this morning and found the barons had saved Franto the trouble of killing the she-Wyrd. This evening, when we made camp, they showed me their trophies. Norholtz has one little sixth finger and Etri the other. Bazajaun and Ferminzto divided the hair between them. Roitz took the eyes. I don't know what he thought he could do with them.

Sorne closed the journal with a snap. Until tonight, he had not understood how Oskane could beat them every day, yet continue to tutor them and take pride in their work.

It was clear there was something missing in the man.

Sorne returned the journals to his chest and hid them under oddities he'd collected in his travels, before concealing the chest under his bed.

That night, sleep was a long time coming. He tossed and turned, troubled by what he had read. If he was any kind of man, he would hunt down the five barons mentioned in Oskane's journal.

Norholtz, Etri and Roitz had remained loyal to Charald, and now ruled Maygharia, Khitan and Welcai respectively. The other two had returned to Chalcedonia and sworn allegiance to King Matxin. Sorne could find out where they were now, if they still lived.

The next morning, as he headed across the plaza, he saw that parts of it had been roped off, and performers were entertaining the crowds. A group of jugglers blocked his path to the Father's church, so he took a side street.

'Warrior's-voice?' A pretty Malaunje woman approached him. 'Will you help me?'

He didn't know her... but he remembered Zabier's saying how pretty Malaunje women were taken off the streets. Imagine if it were Valendia? 'If I can.'

'Come quickly.' She took his hand, weaving through the crowds.

'Wait, where are you taking me?'

'Please?' She looked up at him, wine-dark eyes wide with fright. And he remembered the she-Wyrd asking him to set her free. He'd failed her... maybe he could atone by helping this woman.

She tugged on his hand and he followed.

'THEY'RE COMING.' HAROSEL ran lightly down the wine cellar steps and moved into the shadows. The cellar was long and deep, with huge barrels stacked all the way to the vaulted ceiling.

Graelen's gift surged, and he reined it in as he checked that the infant was still sleeping safely in her basket under the table. She was a necessary part of his plan.

The Warrior's-voice had been away from the city for almost a whole small moon, giving Graelen a chance to refine his original plan. As much as he would like to dispense justice, he needed more information first. If the churches were sacrificing half-bloods, he wanted to know where, when and who.

While spying for Kyredeon, he had discovered that information freely given was more likely to be the truth, and nothing loosened a tongue more than a pretty girl in trouble – in this case, a pretty girl with a baby. If the Warrior's-voice was sacrificing infants to feed an addiction to power, he would want the child and give himself away.

Lysania drew the white-haired Malaunje down the steps.

Hidden in the cellar were Graelen's four Malaunje, plus two of Chariode's, who were there to ensure Lysania and her daughter came to no harm. They all knew of Graelen's suspicions, and – once the white-haired Malaunje's guilt was confirmed – were ready to execute him on the spot.

The half-blood seemed to sense this; he looked around, uneasily. The Warrior's-voice was armed with a sword, worn low on his right hip for left-handed use. Yet, according to the treaty with King Charald the Peace-maker, Wyrds were not allowed to carry swords.

'You said you would help me,' Lysania pleaded. 'I need–'

At the sound of her voice, her choice-daughter gave a tentative cry. Lysania ran over to pick up her baby, crooning softly.

'Boy or girl?' the white-haired Malaunje asked, clearly interested in the infant. Graelen felt his gift surge, and knew his Malaunje warriors would be getting edgy.

'Girl. Tamoria.' Lysania settled the baby on her hip. The infant studied the white-haired Malaunje with frank curiosity. 'She's almost a year old. She's the reason I came to you.'

'I don't know how I can help you.'

This was not the reaction Graelen had expected.

Lifting a hand, the half-blood went to touch the baby, but Lysania drew back.

'If you two are in danger, you'd be safer with your own kind.'

'They want to take her away from me,' Lysania improvised.

'Why would they do that? I know True-women have to give up their half-blood babies to the Wy... T'Enatuath, but–'

One of the Malaunje shifted impatiently. The Warrior's-voice thrust Lysania and the child behind him, drawing his sword. He handled the weapon with confidence.

'Were you followed?'

'I don't know.' Lysania glanced to where Graelen was hiding, clearly desperate.

The Warrior's-voice was ready to protect her, and the last thing Graelen wanted was a dead Malaunje on his hands. Focusing his gift, Graelen prepared to overcome the half-blood's untrained defences. All he had to do was slip into his mind and trick him into revealing what he knew.

Gesturing for Lysania to step away, Graelen glided silently into her place and went to touch the half-blood's neck. But before he could turn...

SORNE FELT A gathering of power that was both terrifying and exhilarating. He'd been on edge ever since he entered the wine cellar, and now he realised he'd been lured into a trap.

He turned, raising his weapon, to find a T'En warrior behind him. Well-dressed, scarred forehead, crooked knuckles on his left hand suggesting broken bones in the past. A fighter, then. Older than him, not an initiate; an adept.

Seeing the warrior was unarmed, Sorne hesitated. Then he realised the T'En didn't need a blade, not when they had their gift.

Sorne swung his weapon, but before he could land a blow, someone grabbed his arm from behind and twisted. The sword hilt flew from his fingers and the blade clattered to the floor. A second assailant pinned his other arm and a third grabbed him around the waist.

Sorne turned so swiftly, the one holding his arm lost his grip and was flung up against a wine barrel. The air was driven from the young Malaunje's chest, with a crack that sounded like ribs breaking.

The attacker who had Sorne around the waist lost his grip as Sorne drove his elbow into his throat and he went down.

The third attacker tried to grab Sorne, who swung his leg out, kicking the man behind the knees and sending him to the floor.

Sorne backed up. Three Malaunje staggered between him and the T'En adept, whose gaze flicked to something behind Sorne. He turned and failed to duck in time as a fist drove into his head, over one eye.

He reeled and staggered, bent over double. Someone grabbed him from behind. Sorne reached down, caught one of his attacker's knees and straightened up. The man went over backwards, clipping a wine barrel.

Two of the attackers caught his arms and two more moved in on him. Their eyes blazed with anger, and their blows were driven by vicious determination. He didn't understand what he'd done to earn their hatred. A fist slammed into his belly. He doubled over, and someone grabbed his hair. A knee slammed into his face, hitting his mouth.

The two men restraining him hauled him upright.

Still reeling, he sucked in a desperate breath. As one of his attackers went to punch him again, the T'En adept caught the man's arm in mid-strike.

'Get Lysania out of here,' the adept ordered, shoving the warrior away.

This close, Sorne felt the force of the adept's power. Like the heat of an open fire, it could so easily burn him up.

As soon as the adept become involved, Sorne had felt his attackers relax their grip on his arms. He dropped, stepped back between them, and grabbed the backs of their necks as they staggered, driving them in together. Their heads met with a satisfying *thunk*.

Sorne backed off, heading for the steps.

Someone grabbed him from behind, pinning his arms at his side. Sorne threw his head back, heard the crunch of his attacker's nose. That one let him go, but at least three of them pounced on him, driving him to his knees on the cold stone floor of the cellar. The sheer weight of numbers kept him down.

'We have him,' one of them reported.

'You sure?' the adept asked. 'There's one of him and only five of you!'

'You said not to hurt him.'

They spoke T'En, and apparently didn't expect Sorne to understand.

At a signal from the T'En warrior, they lifted him to his feet, but kept him pinned between them.

The young woman and her infant were gone. Two injured half-bloods were a little unsteady on their feet, but that left three relatively uninjured Malaunje and the adept, who had not raised a sweat while Sorne staggered and bled.

Anger curled through Sorne; he could feel the tug of the adept's gift from a body-length away. Resisting the lure of power was what Oskane had spent years preparing him for. Sorne no longer felt a duty to Oskane, but that didn't mean these Wyrds were his brothers.

'I am Adept Graelen of Kyredeon's Brotherhood.' The full-blood spoke Chalcedonian. 'And you are going to answer my questions.'

Sorne lifted his chin and glared, the effect slightly spoilt by the way blood kept dripping into his right eye.

In truth, his mouth was so swollen, he didn't know if he could speak.

'We could rough him up some more,' the one with broken nose offered in the T'En language.

'Because that's worked well so far.' Graelen grimaced, then returned his attention to Sorne. Lifting the lamp, he switched back to Chalcedonian. 'Just who are you, Warrior's-voice?'

'You must know who I am, since you sent the woman to lure me down here.' Sorne was pleased to find his words were only slightly slurred.

'Show some respect,' Broken-nose barked, kicking the back of his knees and driving him back to the floor.

The adept crouched in front of him and tore his robe open, exposing his chest.

'Make sure your hands do not touch bare flesh,' Graelen told the Malaunje who held Sorne captive.

Panic welled up in Sorne and he jerked back, to no effect. His heart convulsed as if a fist squeezed it, once, twice. He wondered if he could die of fright.

Graelen closed his eyes. Sorne felt his gift gather like the threat of a thunderstorm. He inhaled sharply. The power seemed to have a taste and, as it hit the back of his tongue, it terrified him. Because he wanted it.

Oskane had been right to despise him.

The thought centred him. Pure, cold fury coalesced in his core.

The adept rubbed his hands together, before placing his left hand over Sorne's heart. Where flesh touched flesh, it burned, but not as much as the cold fire of Sorne's anger.

The adept frowned and moved his hand, pressing the fingertips of both hands to Sorne's temples. Power beat on Sorne's awareness and he went away to...

The scourging frame. His back burned anew with each strike. The only thing that kept him from crying out was a deep, cold anger, that and the way Izteben held his eyes. If he faltered, Izteben would spring to his defence, prompting Oskane to beat his brother even more harshly.

So he had to be strong.

Had to hold on...

It stopped and the end of the pain was so abrupt that he toppled forward.

Chapter Forty-Two

GRAELEN CAUGHT THE captive as he fell. The torn robe slipped from his shoulders to reveal his back, which was a mass of silver scars. Bright beads of blood clung to the deepest ridges.

'That scarring is old,' Harosel said. 'Must have happened when he was a child, yet it's bleeding.'

'Go,' Graelen said.

The Malaunje hesitated.

'Go. Leave us.'

Graelen placed the unconscious captive belly down on the cold stone floor. He took a strip of material from the torn robe and wiped the blood from his captive's back, using wine as a cleanser. The skin had been scoured so many times it was hard, like a carapace.

The thought of someone doing this to a child infuriated him.

Next he poured two cups of wine and watched as the Warrior's-voice regained consciousness.

'Wine?' Graelen offered.

No response.

He put the cup halfway between them and went to sit, with his back to a barrel.

The white-haired Malaunje wouldn't look at him.

'You didn't break,' Graelen said.

He looked up swiftly, then away.

'No, really, I couldn't break your walls. Who made such a mess of your back? Was it the Mieren?'

No response.

'At least have some wine. You need it.'

The Warrior's-voice glanced to the cup, and Graelen realised he was exhausted. Moving slowly to appear less threatening, Graelen crept over on his knees, picked up the cup and handed it to the half-blood, who took it in both hands and drained it.

Now that Graelen was close, he could see several more scars on the captive's chest. He gestured to them. 'What did they do to you?'

'They tried to assassinate me. And failed.' He said it with pride.

'How many times?'

He shrugged. 'I was... *am* King Charald's advisor. They thought if they could kill me, they'd weaken him.' The half-blood cast him a thoughtful glance. Graelen wasn't used to being so frankly assessed by a Malaunje. 'You sent the others away. Why?'

'I thought we'd start again. I am Graelen, an adept from Kyredeon's Brotherhood. I'm investigating something and I need your help, Warrior's-voice.'

'Sorne.'

'What?'

'My name is Sorne.'

'Very well, Sorne. We lured you down here because we've heard rumours of Mieren sacrificing Malaunje infants–'

'What?' He came to his knees, horrified. 'Impossible.'

'It's not impossible, that's the problem. In recent years, we've had less than half the usual number of Malaunje babies delivered to us.'

'Coincidence.'

'Both here and at the Celestial City?'

'How many years do your records go back? How do you know this is unusual? It could be part of some sort of cycle.'

'Good point. If that was all it was. But then there's you. You receive visions at places the Mieren have begun to call *holy sites*. We know these are sites where the walls between the planes are weak. The king boasts of your visions, but the fact remains that only T'En have visions, and then only seers or scryers. Your hair has gone completely white, yet you're... How old?'

'Twenty-five.'

Graelen nodded. 'Only Malaunje who have been in contact with great power go white so young. I've been told that to get these visions you make offerings–'

'Of T'En artefacts that True-men bring to me. I would never...' Sorne shuddered. 'That's why your men beat me?'

Graelen nodded.

He shuffled forward on his knees, determined to defend himself. 'I find the artefact with the most residual power. I use my own blood to lure a creature. It breaks the walls between the earthly plane and the higher plane. When the creature takes the sacrifice and returns to its proper place, power is shed. The power hits me, knocks me out. I wake with a vision. That's all.'

'*That's all?* You risk death, for what? A jolt of power and a vision?'

Sorne met his eye with cold determination. 'I risk death for respect. True-men despise half-bloods. The only thing they respect is power. The visions give me power, power over them.' His lips twisted in contempt. 'They believe the creatures of the higher plane are their gods.'

Graelen swore softly, amazed at Sorne's daring.

'I admit the power behind the Warrior's-voice is based on a lie,' Sorne said. 'But it is not based on...' He shuddered. 'I would never–'

'What of the Father's-voice? He...' Graelen noticed Sorne was already shaking his head. 'Hear me out. The Father's-voice has been making offerings and having visions for the last eight years, ever since King Matxin came into power.'

'No.' Sorne staggered to his feet, and Graelen rose to steady him. Sorne brushed his hand away. 'The Father's-voice is my brother, Zabier. He would never–'

'You've been away for the last eight years. How do you know what–'

'I know what kind of man Zabier is. When he was a boy, his father took him away from us to live with True-men. Zabier was only twelve when he made his way back. He chose us over True-men. He's still doing it. For the last eight years, he's protected our half-blood sister. He loves Valendia. How could he sacrifice other half-blood children?'

'So the rumours are –'

'Horrible lies.'

'Perhaps,' Graelen conceded. 'But you have shown others how to break the walls between the planes. Children are missing. It's possible that other True-men have seen what you can do, and–'

Sorne cursed. 'I never meant... I never thought True-men would... The first time we broke the walls it was an accident. We–'

'We? You and Zabier?'

'No. My brother Izteben and I discovered we could open the walls between the planes. The gods and their visions seemed like a way to gain the respect of True-men.'

'Where's Izteben now? Perhaps he–'

'Izteben died the night Matxin came to power. The higher plane took him.'

'And you kept doing it?' Graelen wanted to shake him. 'Do you have a death wish?'

'I didn't have any choice. I was King Charald's captive vision maker. I was alone in the middle of his army.'

'In Khitan?'

Sorne nodded.

'So you've no more idea what's been going on with the Mieren priests these last eight years than I have?'

'No. But if they are sacrificing innocent half-blood children to the creatures of the higher plane, then it's my fault. I led them to believe these creatures were gods. I'll see what I can find out.'

'Good.' It was suddenly very important to Graelen that he bind Sorne to him in some way. 'If you hear who is doing this, you must tell me.'

'How?'

Graelen thought quickly.

'I can't be seen to associate with Wyrds,' Sorne said.

'But you're a Malaunje.'

Sorne shook his head. 'I'm the Warrior's-voice, blessed by True-man gods. I have to distance myself from ordinary Wyrds.'

'He could come here,' Harosel said from the shadows. 'Leave a message–'

Graelen stiffened. 'I thought I sent you away.'

'I came back.' Harosel stepped into the lamp light. He carried a bundle, which he deposited on the table and began to unroll. 'I've brought clean clothes. It would be dangerous for the Warrior's-voice to walk through the port bloodied and beaten.'

'I wasn't beaten,' Sorne said.

Graelen hid a smile, but all he said was, 'Thank you, Harosel.'

SORNE REMOVED HIS sword belt with its empty sheath, and his ruined robe dropped to the floor. He reached for the robe that Harosel had offered him, a plain dark garment that was enough like a priest's robe to pass at first glance.

'You can't go out like that,' the T'En adept objected, gesturing to his face. 'You're covered in blood. Harosel, fetch some warm water and a cloth.'

Sorne bristled on Harosel's behalf, but the Malaunje went off without complaint. Graelen ordered him and the other half-bloods around with an arrogance that clearly came from long practice.

The adept both fascinated and repelled Sorne. Graelen's gift poured from him in waves. Maybe Sorne's defences had withstood a direct assault, but he was not sure he could withstand the gradual attrition of the constant tug of T'En power.

The adept retrieved Sorne's sword and handed it to him.

'You know we *Wyrds* are not allowed to carry swords. The treaty allows us only our long-knives. How is that you are allowed to go around armed?'

Sorne sheathed his weapon. 'After I fought off the first assassin without training, the king appointed the holy-swords to protect me. They weren't there when the second assassin came after me. That was when I asked for lessons, and Charald agreed.'

'Charald?' Graelen raised an eyebrow. 'A half-blood who calls the king by his first name?'

Sorne shrugged. 'They told me things about Wyrds when I was growing up. I don't know what to believe.'

'Ask.'

'Can you catch an arrow in flight?'

Graelen laughed. 'I offer to tell you our secrets, and that's what you ask. No, I cannot catch an arrow in flight. At least, I've never had to.'

The adept made him feel young and ignorant.

'Where did you grow up, Sorne? Why didn't your Mieren parents give you to us? Who beat you until your back turned into a carapace of scars?' Graelen's eyes widened. 'They beat you to make you strong enough to resist T'En power. I'm right, aren't I?'

Sorne looked away, not sure what he should admit to.

'You don't have to say anything. I understand duty and loyalty. Although I don't think you owe the Mieren anything.'

'Why does it anger you, that they did this to me?'

Graelen drew breath, hesitated, then answered. 'I took an oath. All T'En swear to protect the Malaunje with our lives. That's why I'm trying to find out if the rumour about the sacrifice is true.'

Just then Harosel returned and put a bowl on the table. Graelen took the cloth from the water, wrung it and lifted it to Sorne's face.

He brushed the hand aside. 'I can–'

'Really? Without a mirror?'

He had a point. Sorne grimaced and folded his arms. 'Go on.'

'Here...' Harosel objected. 'That's not–'

'What?' Graelen asked in T'En.

'He doesn't show you proper respect.'

'And you do?'

Harosel flushed.

'Wait outside,' Graelen told him, then switched to Chalcedonian. 'You can follow the Warrior's-voice and make sure he gets back safely.'

'I've crossed the port before,' Sorne said.

'And fought off assassins, I know. But now you are my spy, it's in my interests to protect you. Sit.'

Sorne sat on the table.

As Graelen began sponging the blood from his brow, it was almost more than Sorne could bear. Very few people touched him, and the gift made it hard for him to think. His body reacted and when the adept turned to rinse the cloth, he put his hands in his lap.

'There's blood all through your hair. You can't go amongst Mieren showing any sign of weakness. Take out your hair.'

Sorne did as he was told. Graelen cleaned the blood from his face and hair, then his throat and shoulder. When the adept got to his mouth and swollen lips, Sorne closed his eyes and concentrated on the sensation.

It hurt, but only a little. He'd learnt to bear pain, but he'd never learnt how to cope with pleasure.

With a start, he realised he'd reached a point where he was happy to sit there and feel the adept's gift beat against his skin like the fire of an open forge.

It was a subtle assault.

He caught Graelen's hand. 'Don't use your gift on me.'

'I'm not. You must be sensitive to the power.'

Sorne frowned, not sure if he was speaking the truth.

'Your hair is completely white. You've been stealing power from the empyrean plane for years. You're a gift addict, whether you like it or not.'

Sorne flushed, furious, because he knew it was true. Yes, the king wanted him to experience visions, but he wanted it too.

'Are you done?' Sorne brushed the adept's hand aside and stood up, forcing him to step back.

Turning away, Sorne pulled the robe over his head before the adept could notice his arousal. And to think he'd been so proud of his self control. He buckled on his sword belt, fingers slowing as he felt the tug on his hair. He jerked away from the adept. 'I can plait my own hair.' He quickly bound his hair and then turned around. 'Now, will I do?'

'There's swelling around your eyebrow and your mouth is a little uneven, but yes.'

'Good, I'll ask around, see what I can learn. If I hear anything, I'll leave a message here.'

'And I'll meet you the next day.'

'I'll leave a message. There's no need—'

'Only True-men think it's a crime for men to be lovers. We live in brotherhoods and sisterhoods. What do you think happens?'

Sorne could not look at him. He hurried up the steps.

'Who would have thought King Charald had a secret family of half-bloods,' Graelen remarked.

Sorne stopped halfway up. 'You're provoking me to test your guess.'

'Is it working?'

He felt a smile tug at his swollen lips. 'They're my choice-family. I'm—'

'Queen Sorna's son.'

Sorne nodded, not surprised he'd guessed. 'Charald had my mother murdered so he could marry again, and sent me away.'

'Why do you serve him?'

'I don't serve him. I serve myself. It just happens to have aligned with what he wants.'

'What's going to happen when you want something different?'

He didn't have an answer for that.

Chapter Forty-Three

SORNE WAS RELIEVED. No one gave him a second glance in the street. He was vaguely aware of Harosel following. When he reached the steps to the Father's church, he glanced over his shoulder, but the half-blood had disappeared.

Turning away, Sorne focused on the tasks ahead of him. He wanted to warn Marantza that Charald would not wait much longer but, as he was so late, he went to see his family first.

He was relieved to find them on the terrace. They were safe, but for how much longer if what Graelen feared was true? Perhaps he should take Valendia to Graelen and... what? Hand her over to T'En warriors whose gifts would bind her to them?

At the same time, they would die to protect her.

If she remained here, what would happen to her when Hiruna died? That was something to worry about another day, hopefully many years from now.

When Hiruna saw him, instead of her ready smile, she frowned and shook her head. Valendia noticed Hiruna's expression, stopped playing her pipes and turned around.

'You're late.' Zabier glowered and came to his feet. 'I don't know why you bothered coming at all.'

'It's all right,' Valendia said. 'I don't mind.'

He glanced to the table, saw the special treats and realised...

'You forgot her birthday.' Zabier spat the words. 'You expect to walk in here and pick up after all these years, and Mother lets you. She trusts you with... How do you get people to trust you, Sorne? And since when do priests wear swords? Since when does a half-blood flout the laws of Chalcedonia? You and Nitzane, with his two baronies, walk into my church like you have the right to—'

'Enough, Zabier,' Hiruna said. 'Sorne, what's wrong with your face?'

He lifted a hand to his mouth. If he told the truth, he would worry Hiruna, yet, if he lied and said it had been an accident at weapons practice, he would infuriate Zabier. He could not win. 'It's nothing, Ma. I'll go now. I'm sorry, Valendia.'

'It's all right.' The twelve-year-old did not meet his eyes.

'No, it's not,' Zabier snapped. 'If he's been drinking and brawling, he shouldn't have come here.'

'I don't drink,' Sorne protested.

'Dia, I want to lie down.' Hiruna lifted a hand.

Sorne went to help her.

'That's right,' Zabier sneered. 'Play the dutiful son when it doesn't cost you anything.'

Sorne bit back a retort, waiting until Hiruna and Valendia had left the balcony before turning on the man his brother had become. It was on the tip of his tongue to ask him what had happened to the Zabier he knew, but that would only get his back up, and Sorne had already made a mess of things today. Better to state the facts.

'I'm late because there was an attempt on my life. I carry a sword because of the assassination attempts.'

'You shouldn't have come.'

'You're right. And I wouldn't have come, but I need to see Marantza. She's still protected by the church, isn't she?'

'What do you want to see her about?'

'King Charald intends to marry her sooner than any of us anticipated.'

'I'll tell her. She trusts me.'

As the Fathers-voice, he was the equivalent of a king inside the church's walls – a king who could be voted down and replaced at any moment, a king whose protection of a half-blood sister made him vulnerable, especially if Graelen's suspicions were true. 'There's a rumour half-bloods are being sacrificed.'

'Who said this? Who's spreading this disgusting rumour?' Zabier was so angry, he shook. 'Tell me. Tell me and I'll have them silenced.'

Sorne took a step back. The force of Zabier's reaction satisfied him. If the head of the Seven's churches knew nothing, then this was just a vicious rumour, unless... 'Are any of the other churches making—'

'Only the Father's-voice speaks directly to the gods, until you came back.'

Ah, that explained Zabier's resentment. His return had stirred up the old rivalry between the two biggest churches. But... 'What if there was some hidden group, eager for power?'

Zabier was shaking his head before Sorne had finished. 'That first demonstration of power when Izteben and the prince died scared them off.'

As far as Zabier knew, Sorne thought.

Graelen would have to follow the rumours to their source and track them down.

Sorne took his leave and returned to the palace. By now it was nearly dusk, and his body ached with every step. He wanted nothing more than to take a hot bath, then crawl into bed, with a T'En artefact pressed to his chest. After sleeping with it, he would wake refreshed and revitalised.

And to think, he used to scorn the she-Wyrd for her addiction.

Shame curdled his belly; Graelen must despise him.

Charald's palace had been built to imitate the great Wyrd palaces, and the best chambers had hot running water. Since Idan's death, he had no servant, so he lit a lamp, prepared the bath and stripped.

He was dozing in the sunken tub when he heard a furtive noise. Assassins, here?

He pulled himself out of the tub and reached for his sword. Still dripping, he crossed the tiles, making for his bedchamber.

There he found two figures in the shadows on the far side of his bed. He circled the bed, blade ready.

'Sorne?'

'Nitzane? Who's with you?'

'Do you normally greet visitors naked with a blade?' Marantza asked.

The laughter in her voice made him feel ridiculous.

'Get dressed, Sorne,' Nitzane said, but his voice also held laughter. 'You're offending my wife.'

Wife? 'What are you two doing here and when did you...' Decide to infuriate King Charald by uniting the wealthiest baron with his heir? Sorne turned away, dried himself and dressed.

While he did this, Nitzane lit a lamp and tried to justify his actions. 'After I learnt what Charald did to my mother, I got to thinking. He's used people all his life in the pursuit of power. Why should he use Marantza? So I returned to port and–'

'Came to see me,' she said, keeping her gaze on a point somewhere above Sorne's shoulder as he laced up his breeches. 'I told Zane *no* last night, and again this morning, but–'

'She didn't want to marry Charald, a man who's nearly old enough to be her grandfather, so she settled for me,' Nitzane said with a fond smile. Sorne wanted to shake him. 'We were married this afternoon in the Mother's church.'

And by the way they reached for each other it was a love match. Could two people fall in love so quickly?

All he could think was poor Zabier, no wonder his brother had been angry. He must have suspected Nitzane was up to something, but he was hardly in a position to offer Marantza an alternative.

'Why come to me?'

'We want you to smooth things over with Charald,' Nitzane said.

Sorne backed up a step. 'No, thank you. I–'

Someone hammered at his door.

'Just a moment,' Sorne called.

'King Charald demands your presence, Warrior's-voice,' a man announced.

'The Father's-voice must have discovered I'm missing,' Marantza whispered. 'He usually has his evening meal with me.'

Sorne finished dressing and then tossed a robe to Marantza. 'Put this on. You're tall enough to pass for a man. Stay here until I've led him away. Nitzane, where are your men-at-arms?'

'I've thirty trusted men with Ballendin, waiting on a ship to sail to my estate down the coast.'

'Good. Make your way to the wharves. I'll do what I can to buy you time.'

'Warrior's-voice?' the escort prompted.

Sorne strode to the door, thrust it open and stepped out as he finished plaiting his wet hair. 'What's this all about? I was bathing.'

'The Father's-voice is here. The Lady Marantza has been abducted and...' – the young guard lowered his voice – 'the king is livid.'

Sorne understood. The king was in a rage. Sure enough, when he approached the chamber, Sorne found a dozen terrified servants huddled in the corridor. None dared go inside, but neither did they want to leave and miss all the excitement.

Sorne mentally prepared himself. He had been dealing with these outbursts for eight years now. When he entered the chamber, he found the Father's-voice standing to one side of the entrance, staring straight ahead with a strained expression while the king raged.

Zabier looked pale, as if he wished himself anywhere but here. The remains of a meal was splattered across the wall, and broken crockery lay scattered across the floor.

'You?' The king pounced on Sorne, thrusting a finger in his face. 'Why didn't you warn me about this?'

'You haven't requested a vision, since we arrived–'

'I want a vision now. Ask the Warrior where they've taken her.'

Sorne played for time. 'You know we must wait until season's cusp.'

'This priest tells me he can reach the gods anytime.' Charald stabbed a finger at Zabier.

'There's a holy site, very powerful, one day's ride from here to the east,' Zabier said.

'Then, by all means, let us go there,' Sorne said, his mind racing. Inland was good, it would give Nitzane and Marantza time to set sail. But, unless they wanted civil war, he would have to find a way to reconcile Charald to the idea of their marriage by having a vision that told him... what? All he could think of was Graelen's warning. Would this be the time he poked the beast and it turned on him? 'We can arrange the offering as soon as I have a suitable artefact. Do you have T'En artefacts, Father's-voice?'

'It may take several days to find a suitable one.'

All the better.

As Zabier bowed and left, it was clear he was happy to escape. Sorne followed him to the door, calling for more food. A meal would settle the king, combined with a little alcohol and a soothing powder.

While Charald held forth on Marantza's parentage, Sorne poured some wine, slipped the powder from his robe, unfolded the paper and tipped the contents into the goblet. He had been gradually increasing the dosage, as the king seemed to have built up a resistance to it. The powder took a moment to dissolve, and when Sorne turned around he found Charald had settled himself at the table.

Charald accepted the wine and tossed it back. 'More.'

'You know...' Sorne said, as he poured a second one. 'The Warrior moves in mysterious ways. What if this was meant to happen–'

'My wife abducted?'

'She is not your wife, sire. She's your heir. But if her abductors killed her, you would be free to marry where you chose.'

'And if they didn't kill her, they would feel justified in claiming the throne.'

'Not if you already had a wife and an heir on the way.'

'Ignore Marantza's claim on the throne?'

'The stronger your claim is, the weaker hers appears by comparison. A son–'

'Yes, a son.' He grimaced. 'I've had no luck with sons.'

The blood rushed in Sorne's ears, but the king seemed to have forgotten he was Charald's eldest and only surviving son. Somehow, he found his voice. 'There is still my vision of you on the ship's deck with a small boy to consider.'

'That's right!' The king looked delighted. 'A wife and a baby boy within a year would stop the tongues wagging. I'm almost fifty-three, but look at Oskane, he was still scheming at seventy-two. I could have another twenty years in me. Time to secure the kingdom and the empire for my heir.'

Servants arrived with food, and he welcomed them. As they set the table, Sorne's stomach rumbled; he'd barely eaten all day. Behind him, he heard servants scurrying about as they cleaned up the broken crockery and spilt food.

'Sit down.' Charald gestured to the chair on his right. 'Tell me about the barons' daughters. I like them short and plump, with thighs a man can grab a hold of.'

Sorne reached for a chicken leg.

'This isn't the war tent.' Charald slapped his hand with the flat of his knife. 'In the palace, you know your place. Now talk.'

Sorne swallowed down his anger with his hunger, wiped his fingers on the edge of his robe and gathered his wits. 'The southern barons who followed you back to Chalcedonia are either foreign nobles or mercenaries who have made good. They may have daughters of a suitable age, but–'

'You're right. I want noble blood, old blood. What about the Chalcedonian barons who came crawling to lick my boots?'

'I'll make a list of suitable girls. You could invite those barons to witness the Warrior's offering. Once they see you have the most powerful of the Seven gods on your side–'

'Do that. Excellent.' Charald wiped the grease off his mouth with the back of his hand and tore off a chicken leg. He tossed it to Sorne, who caught it. 'They're afraid of you. Think you have some sort of hold over me. But they don't understand, Oskane trained you well. Eat up.'

Sorne forced himself to take a bite of chicken.

'You know...' The king tore the meat off another chicken leg and threw the bone onto the table. 'I think they did me a favour, abducting that bean-pole of a woman. Sour-faced bitch was always looking down her nose at me.'

Chapter Forty-Four

IMOSHEN KEPT HER head lowered and her gift under tight rein as she passed through the causeway gate. Warriors from Kyredeon's brotherhood were rostered on the gate today. Their brotherhood symbol was the eye of foresight. Back when Kyredeon's brotherhood was first formed, the all-father had been a seer. But none of the brotherhoods had produced a seer for hundreds of years. Now only Reoden's sisterhood had a scryer, the female version of the gift. Poor Lysitzi felt so guilty about not foreseeing the sacrare's death, she would not let Reoden heal her face.

The Mieren cloak made Imoshen all but invisible to the gift-warriors on the gate. Feeling lighter of heart, she went down the causeway. She'd just crossed the arched bridge to the foreign quarter when student-he hailed her in Sagorese.

Imoshen gave him the Sagora obeisance and they walked on in silence. Even though this was only their fifth lesson, her instinct was to trust him.

'Were you in the city when the sacrare was killed?' she asked softly in T'En.

'Yes. Such a waste.' He shook his head.

Reoden's exact words. Her heart warmed to him. Of course, it could all be an act, designed to win her confidence, but if it was, she couldn't see the point. He did not know who she was.

He glanced to her, only his mouth and jaw visible. 'Why do you ask?'

'The sacrare debacle is why I took up Sagorese. I want to study on Ivernia.'

'And your all-mother has approved this?'

'She said I must learn their language first.'

'That's why you study so hard. But what does studying with the Sagoras have to do with the girl's death?'

Imoshen hesitated. They'd come to the centre of another arched bridge, where she could see straight down the canal to the lake and the shore beyond. It was late afternoon, nearing midsummer. Sunlight danced on the water, reflecting on the buildings, creating shimmering patterns of light.

Beautiful, but it was still the Celestial City and all that entailed.

'What did you think of Rutz's latest play?' she asked.

'I don't see the connection.'

'Answer the question.'

'What did *you* think of it?'

'I saw it three times.'

'So you liked it?'

'It made me cry every time.'

'But it was billed as a comedy,' he protested, with a smile.

'It was a tragedy masquerading as a satire.'

He said nothing, which disappointed her.

'So you want to leave the city and study with the Sagoras because you can't stand the restrictions of T'Enatuath society?'

Imoshen smiled with relief. 'Yes.'

'You agree with Rutz? The restrictions reinforce the problems they are meant to alleviate?'

Imoshen nodded.

'So your answer is to run away.'

She flushed. 'I am only one person. What can I do?'

'Rutz is only one person. He writes plays.'

'And people laugh at them. They don't see what he is satirising.'

'You did.'

'But I am only one person.'

'Change starts with one person.'

'Tell that to All-father Rohaayel!' And she walked off. Tears stung her eyes and she fought back a sob. Horror filled her. She must not cry here, in front of a T'En man, not after what she'd said about Rohaayel. She should never have brought up his name.

By the time she reached the Sagoras' premises, she'd regained her self-control.

He caught up with her in the foyer.

'Rohaayel broke the covenant,' he said. 'He hid a female child. He knew the risks he was taking. He went about change the wrong way.'

'There is a right way?'

He hesitated.

'By writing plays that go over people's heads?' Imoshen prodded.

Feeling she had made her point, she went through the courtyard and took her place as student-she. But it was a hollow victory, because she *did* want to change things. These were her people, whether she liked it or not. When Iraayel grew up, he had to live amongst them. If she had another child... The thought shocked her.

She had no chance of another child. The sisterhood would never give her one. And she wasn't going to take a Malaunje male for a lover, not when she risked having to give up her baby if it was born a half-blood. In the eight years she had been here, no T'En man had ever asked to tryst with her on midsummer's day. The brotherhoods feared and hated her. She was a symbol of T'En female oppression. To the sisterhoods, she was a symbol of T'En male aggression.

She would never fit in, and she didn't want to. She should leave. But, as the lesson progressed, she realised that the Imoshen who had lived on Lighthouse Isle would never have run away.

That Imoshen would never have given up, and she was still that Imoshen. A shiver passed over her body, rousing her gift. Even though he sat across from her, she felt student-he react, his power rising in answer to hers.

It was as if she had been asleep for eight and a half years, and was finally waking up. A strange euphoria filled her.

It was still there when the lesson ended, and they made their way to the foyer.

'You seemed distracted today, student-she. I'm sorry if I offended you.'

'No. What you said was true. It is cowardly to run away from the city.'

'Your... your honesty is disarming.'

Imoshen thought about it. 'If we are not honest with ourselves, then we do ourselves and others a disservice.'

He gestured to her Mieren cloak. 'Says student-she, who denies her identity and her race.'

They forced me to become this person. To save my choice-son and my devotee, they forced me to execute my father. Now the brotherhoods hate me. But she didn't say this. Instead, she took her Mieren cloak from the hook and settled it on her shoulders.

Then she turned to him. 'When we are out there, the city and everything that it entails gets in the way. When we are here, it is you and me. Is that enough for now?'

Even as the words left her mouth, she realised she was asking much more than the promise he would not try to find out who she was.

She saw him swallow and felt his gift surge. Instead of the fear she had come to associate with men's gifts, she felt drawn to his power and to him. Perhaps Vittoryxe was right. Perhaps she was addicted to the male gift.

'You are as secretive as the Sagoras, student-she. But...' He reached out to fasten the clasp of the Mieren cloak under her chin.

She brushed his hands away. 'I can do up my own–'

'Of course you can.' He pulled her close and kissed her.

Imoshen's gift surged. She let it, felt the moment it meshed with his, felt him ignite.

Shaken, he let her go and stepped back. He took another step and his shoulders hit the wall. He seemed as surprised as she was.

He left her without a word.

SORNE LEFT THE message in the wine cellar, along with the borrowed robe, then made his way back to the palace. He had timed the message's delivery so that he could not meet the adept tomorrow.

Tomorrow they would ride out to the holy site, where he would perform for King Charald's barons and the church leaders. To think, after eight years of this, he had to prove himself all over again. He might die tomorrow night, but if he didn't...

With this offering, he would be more powerful than any other priest in all of Chalcedonia, even the Father's-voice, since Zabier's visions weren't real.

His brother was barely speaking to him. He had taken it as a personal insult that Hiruna had told Sorne about her illness and not him. Valendia had retreated into her music. The only truly happy person was King Charald; it turned out one of the barons had a daughter of marriageable age, and she was just his type.

Sorne felt sorry for the girl, who would not be sixteen until midsummer. She and her father had been invited to the ceremony. Charald had made it clear he expected Sorne to get the Warrior's blessing for what he intended to do.

An altercation made Sorne look up.

At the next intersection, the driver of a carriage was arguing with a carter about right of way. As Sorne stepped around the carriage, someone came out of a shop's doorway, grabbed him and bundled him into the vehicle.

He recognised the adept's gift even before the door closed and the carriage started moving, rattling over the cobbles.

'So the Father's-voice knows nothing of these sacrifices?' Graelen said, gesturing with the message Sorne had left. 'And you ride off to put yourself in harm's way tomorrow.'

'Using a T'En artefact.'

'Is it a braid, like this?' The adept gestured to his own hair, his eyes glittered with anger. 'Do you see any T'En walking around with short hair? Or is it a pendant made of little finger bones?'

'I didn't kill the T'En these artefacts came from. Some of them are hundreds of years old.'

'But the ones with the most gift residue are recent, aren't they? No, you don't kill or rob a T'En to get the artefact, but someone does.'

'I've done what I said I would. Only the Father's-voice speaks with the gods, and Zabier was deeply offended when I asked about the sacrifices. It's just a rumour, like the terrible things they told me about Wyrds, when I was growing up. Unless there's a splinter group of priests ambitious for power.'

The carriage came to a stop. Sorne tried for the door.

Graelen caught his hand, crushing it on the handle. 'I'm not done with you yet.'

Short of drawing his sword in the confines of the carriage, there was not a lot Sorne could do. He did not want to head-butt the adept.

'So you'll risk death to impress King Charald's barons. I hear one of them ran off with his wife-to-be.'

Sorne winced. If the adept had heard it, then likely the king would know the truth soon. 'Charald has his eye on another baron's daughter.'

'What will this make, queen number three? And if he tires of her, will you murder her, like you killed the second queen? Was that revenge for your own mother?'

'Your spies don't know everything.'

'I know you went to the Mother's abbey and came back with proof of a woman's death.'

'She isn't dead.' Sorne stopped trying to turn the handle and sat back. Graelen let him go. 'Baron Nitzane was reunited with his mother. A nameless nun lies buried in the queen's grave. So the king is free to marry where he chooses. And tomorrow night, Charald expects the Warrior to send me a vision supporting his choice of wife.'

'Can't you just say you've had a vision? Do you have to through this whole—'

'Offering? Yes. They want to see the artefact glow and disappear in a flash of light.'

'There are beasts on the empyrean plane so powerful a braid with residual gift essence is not going to satisfy them.'

'I know.'

'Yet you do it anyway.'

Sorne did not speak.

'Do you have a powerful T'En artefact?'

'I have three to choose from. They're all of equal strength. I'll make the one I select more enticing by rubbing my blood on it. That helps to...' He sat up. 'What are you doing?'

The adept produced a silver chain, holding a heavy silver disk. Without answering, he grasped the disk in his hands, closed his eyes and concentrated. Sorne could feel the build-up of power.

Sounds became strange and distorted, and scents grew more powerful... His skin prickled.

'There.' The adept exhaled and opened his eyes. 'That should do it.' Graelen hung the chain around Sorne's neck, tucking the silver disk inside his robe. 'Use that. It's freshly gift-infused. Plenty of power.'

Sorne could feel the power leaching into his skin, making him feel invincible. Was this how the T'En felt all the time? No wonder they were so arrogant. 'Why help me?'

'You know why.'

'I'm not a tame Malaunje.'

The adept smiled. 'Exactly.'

At that moment, the carriage ground to a stop. Sorne didn't know whether he was disappointed or relieved.

The door swung open, revealing Harosel. Sorne could see a courtyard behind him.

'It's safe to get out here,' Harosel said. 'You're only one block from the palace.'

Sorne touched his chest, where the silver disk sat, pulsing with power. He tried to speak, but his mouth was too dry.

Graelen nodded and Sorne stepped out of the carriage. Harosel took his arm and led him to the end of the lane. 'That way.'

'Who... who is he?'

'Graelen? He's the brotherhood's greatest assassin.'

Sorne's head filled with white noise.

He found he was walking across the plaza, passing True-men and -women with no memory of leaving the lane.

An assassin. Twice, the adept could have killed him.

But he didn't want to kill him; he wanted to rob him of his freedom.

When Sorne entered the palace, he heard shouting from the king's greeting chamber and saw Zabier walking swiftly towards him.

'He knows it was Nitzane who took Marantza,' Zabier reported. 'They've been sighted at one of his estates.'

Sorne glanced down the corridor. A servant hastily backed out of the room, followed by a tray that flew through the air and hit the wall with a *clang*. Sorne grimaced and turned to Zabier. 'Are you sure you don't want to take part in the ceremony tomorrow? All the church leaders and the barons, old and new, will be there. I don't mind sharing the stage with the Father's-voice.'

'No. You do it. The church officials have to see the Warrior's-voice in action. Have you decided which artefact to use?'

It was on the tip of his tongue to say he did not need one but the addict in him surfaced and he found himself saying, 'The matching silver arm-torcs.'

'Good choice. I'll have them packed.'

'Did you find out where Barons Bazajaun and Ferminzto went?'

'They're in Navarone, stirring up trouble. Why?'

He was about to tell him they had taken trophies from the she-Wyrd's body, all those years ago, but a female servant ran past them, weeping.

'I should go,' Sorne said. It was the longest conversation he'd had with Zabier since he'd missed Valendia's birthday. 'How's Mother?'

'She's fine. The healer says he can cure her. It'll be expensive, but I can manage. He's started her on a potion of crushed mother-of-pearl and gold dust in white wine.'

'Are you sure he knows what he's doing?'

Zabier bristled. 'He's the best healer in all of Chalcedonia.'

'I thought the Wyrds had a healer in—'

'No Cesspit City Wyrd is touching her. She's my mother and I'll take care of her.'

Several servants spotted Sorne and came running.

'You're needed.' Zabier slipped away as the servants all but dragged Sorne down the corridor and shoved him into the king's chamber.

'The ungrateful...' King Charald stopped mid-tirade, spotting Sorne in the doorway. 'Did you hear about Nitzane?'

'A masterly stroke, sire,' Sorne said. 'By encouraging the baron to run off with Marantza, you've kept her from the enemy barons and freed yourself from the duty of marrying that bean-pole of a woman. Now, all you have to do is plant a baby in the belly of Baron Janzten's daughter and...'

'Janzten thinks she's too young for me.'

Sorne thought so too, but he wasn't foolish enough to say it. 'Have you eaten, sire? Call the barons in, toast Nitzane and Marantza, make it clear they've done exactly what you wanted them to do.'

'Good idea. Organise it. Then come back here. Norholtz is having trouble with the Maygharians. I should send you there to advise him. You have a fine head for strategy.'

It was the closest the king had come to praising Sorne, but he didn't want to leave Chalcedonia, not when he'd only just come home.

Chapter Forty-Five

SORNE CLIMBED THE path that circled the pinnacle, followed by Captain Aintzo and three of his holy-swords. The spire of black rock was the height of a six-storey tower; each turn of the path took them another storey higher.

Eight years ago, while crossing Chalcedonia, Sorne had peeped out of the closed-cart and seen this pinnacle, or one similar: great spires of rock that rose out of the rich, rolling countryside. Straight and tall, it was almost as if they were constructed, rather than natural. When the sun struck the sheer rock, they shone like black glass. Trees and bushes clung to the crevices. Some of the pinnacles were unclimbable. On this one, stairs had been cut, following the natural crevices or carved into the sheer rock. He was lucky he didn't suffer from a fear of falling.

According to Zabier, it was possible to reach the gods on the pinnacle's flat top any time of the year. That did not reassure Sorne; he touched his mother's torc, where it lay just below the hollow of his throat. The blue stone's glow would tell him when empyrean beasts were present. Under his robe, over the centre of his breastbone, lay the silver disk. He had placed a vest between it and his skin, because he wanted the power to last. Even so, he could still feel it pulsing softly. Every time he thought of it, he felt a mixture of longing and self-contempt.

One thing was clear; deliberate gift-infusion was much more powerful than residual gift essence.

He was puffing slightly when he reached the top of the pinnacle. It was almost flat, with a dip on the far side.

From up here, he could see the sun setting far away beyond the sea. But it wasn't until he went right to the edge that he could see the field below the pinnacle, where Charald had pitched their tents. They would spend the night there, drinking and celebrating his betrothal.

As Sorne watched, another baron rode in with a party of followers. His men began unloading the carts while he and his good wife made their way to see the king. Even from up here, Sorne recognised Marantza's tall frame, and he was glad to see that Charald had taken his advice and invited them to the ceremony, which had been delayed to allow them to travel.

'Where do we set up, Warrior's-voice?'

Sorne returned to his holy-swords. 'Put the table here, about halfway. The barons and officials will stand back there.'

He had chosen these four True-men because they had been with him when he had his last vision and knew what to expect. Tonight he would impress the barons and church leaders, and consolidate his place in Chalcedonia as King Charald's advisor. He wished Izteben could be here.

Reminded of how his brother had died, Sorne ran through the process of the ritual one last time. He drew the knife Oskane had given him. 'I'll prick my skin and rub blood on the sacrifice. Where is it?'

'Here.' Captain Aintzo opened the small, lead-lined chest to reveal two silver arm-torcs. They had been tied together on the end of a long silk scarf.

Sorne could feel their residual gift essence. It was weak compared with the silver disk, but once he added his blood it would be enough.

'Good, put the chest here.' Sorne indicated the table. 'When I feel the Warrior's presence, I'll make the offering. Don't get between me and the god. His touch will send you mad, or he may take you in place of the offering. Am I clear?'

They all looked suitably solemn. He wondered if he should add anything more to impress them with the danger of the ritual, but they already seemed tense enough. He glanced at the setting sun, trying to judge how long they had until full dark.

'You go down and start escorting them up. I'll stay here and meditate.'

He needed time to come up with a suitable vision that would reconcile Baron Janzten with the idea of giving his daughter to King Charald. As far as Charald was concerned, he didn't see why winning the king's favour wasn't enough for Janzten. There were half a dozen barons who would have happily pimped their daughters as the king's mistress, let alone his wife, to win Charald's favour.

Sorne shook his head. Charald just happened to have taken a fancy to the daughter of the one principled baron in Chalcedonia.

As he sat and contemplated his vision, he thought of Izteben and whether Chalcedonia would have been different had he lived.

What had Sorne achieved?

He'd been behind the conquering of five kingdoms and the reclamation of a sixth. He personally held a position of power, but Valendia had spent her childhood hidden from the sight of True-men, and his kind were no closer to being accepted. He could not change men's hearts and minds unless they wanted to change.

Izteben was right, to effect true change you first needed to attain power, but if you became too powerful it could promote more fear.

Sorne was no closer to a solution, when he heard voices. His holy-swords were escorting the barons and church leaders up the stairs. Sorne retreated to the top of the pinnacle and readied himself. As the dignitaries kept arriving, he grew uneasy. There were so many of them. What if the empyrean beast charged him and people scattered? They could fall to their deaths. He spotted Zabier and tried to get his attention, but the Father's-voice was distracted by one of the arrivals and didn't see him.

More and more people arrived, shuffling forward until these in the front row reached his table. A southern baron went to pick up his ceremonial knife and Sorne hastily retrieved it. He beckoned Captain Aintzo, who appeared as nervous as he felt. 'Watch the table. I'll be back in a moment.'

Sorne wanted to cancel the offering and stage it in a safer place, or at least with fewer people. If he could get the Father's-voice to back him, the king might agree. Finding King Charald wasn't hard; his big voice boomed out. It was getting through the crowd who were gathered around him that was a struggle. Sorne discovered Baron Janzten and his daughter, Jaraile, with the king, as well as Nitzane and Marantza, but no sign of Zabier. There he was, several rows back, trying to get to the front.

Charald caught sight of Sorne. 'Here's the Warrior's-voice. Are we ready to start?' He nudged Jaraile's father. 'After this, Janzten, you will never doubt I have the Warrior's favour.' And he pulled Jaraile close to plant a kiss on her lips.

'Sire–'

'That's pretty,' Jaraile said. She reached up to Sorne's throat where his mother's torc was glowing, which meant...

Sorne spun around, thrusting through the crowd. What was going on? He had not even started the ceremony.

Captain Aintzo stood next to the table with two of Sorne's holy-swords. The third had taken a bowl down to the far end and appeared to be dipping a brush in it and sprinkling the contents on the ground.

This wasn't part of the ceremony.

As Sorne watched in disbelief, the liquid hit the ground and sizzled, and a growing darkness blotted out the evening stars behind the holy-sword.

'Get out of there,' Sorne called. He felt the build-up of power and knew he was running out of time. 'Quick, give me the offering.' Raising his voice, Sorne shouted over the chatter of the gathered crowd. 'Warrior, Greatest of the Seven, I seek your guidance...'

Sorne broke off as one of the holy-swords yelped in fright. Sorne spun around to see the man with the bowl had spilled its contents on his robe. That was not wine. That was blood; Malaunje blood, he guessed. Where had it come from?

The holy-sword's body jerked as he was lifted off the ground. He writhed once, twice, then went still and winked out of existence.

'Quick.' Sorne thrust his hand out to his captain. 'Give me the offering, Aintzo!'

The two remaining holy-swords grabbed his arms, pulling him around to face the captain.

Aintzo picked up Sorne's ceremonial dagger. 'A Trueman should be the Warrior's-voice, not some tainted halfblood. Hold him.'

Sorne gasped in pain as Aintzo drove the knife into his belly.

'Now throw him to the god.'

Sorne gasped and bent double as he felt the blood run through his fingers. Aintzo turned to face the crowd. Some looked on in horror, but many were pleased to see Sorne brought down.

'Warrior, Greatest of the Seven, I seek your guidance for King Charald, High King of the Secluded Sea...' Aintzo began, holding the bloodied knife above his head.

Desperate, Sorne let himself become a dead weight as his captors dragged him backwards. He twisted to the right, slapping his bloodied hand in his captor's face. The holysword let him go and pulled back. Darkness took him, lifting the man off his feet. He writhed in desperation, then disappeared.

The remaining holy-sword dropped Sorne's arm and backed away.

Sorne smeared blood on his skin, then thrust him towards the darkness. Ignoring the man's shrill scream, Sorne stumbled up the slope towards Aintzo and the table. Surely it had not been this steep before.

Aintzo turned and raised the knife. But Sorne wasn't attacking him, he wanted the T'En artefact. He snatched it before the captain could strike him. Something caught him around the waist, lifting him off his feet. The chest flew open and the arm-torcs tumbled out. They stopped tumbling in mid-air.

Aintzo screamed as the empyrean beast snatched him, too. Sorne felt a bone-numbing chill enter his body through the belly wound. He felt himself weakening and knew the beast was feeding on his life force. The world no longer looked real; the crowd appeared as beacons of warmth. He was cold. So cold...

He'd pushed his luck too far, Graelen was right. Graelen!

His muscles felt sluggish as he reached up inside his robe. The moment his bare hand closed on the silver disk, warmth ran down his arm, giving him strength. He snapped the chain and threw the disk over his left shoulder towards the beast.

It had barely left his fingers when there was a flash so bright it burned.

Something slapped the side of his face and he was flung towards the edge of the pinnacle.

He barely had time to think, *so this is how it feels to die*, before he collided with the stone and the whiteness expanded to fill his mind.

SORNE WOKE TO weeping and wailing. The world swung above him: stars, tree branches, more stars... he was being carried on a cloak, almost at a run. The top half of a tent flashed past. He was in the camp. There was Nitzane's new standard.

'Can you hear me?' Marantza asked, leaning over him. She searched his face, her expression anxious.

He tried to speak, but his throat felt raw. Swallowing was agony.

'Don't worry. We've got you,' Nitzane said, leaning over him on the other side. They entered a tent and someone lit a lamp.

They deposited him on a bedroll. Marantza knelt beside him and picked up a knife, and he wondered why they'd bothered to save him if they were going to cut this throat. But she began cutting his clothing off.

'Get some watered wine,' she called over her shoulder. 'And honey and yoghurt.'

It seemed a strange combination. He had to turn his head to see her as he tried to tell her his stomach wound was the most pressing problem. He felt cold, as if he would never get warm again.

'He's trying to speak,' Nitzane said.

Sorne swallowed and winced.

Someone produced a bowl of honey. Marantza stirred it into a bowl of yoghurt, then told a servant to feed him. After the first mouthful, the pain in his throat eased.

Sorne became aware of men shouting outside the tent.

'You've been badly burned,' she told him.

'Cold,' he croaked.

She and Nitzane exchanged looks.

'I'm going to sponge the burns clean and cover them with honey,' Marantza explained. She spoke slowly and clearly, as if he was stupid.

'Knife wound,' he managed to gasp, gesturing to his stomach.

Someone had taken his left arm. He could feel them bathing it, and turned his head to look. A livid red mark ran down the inside of his arm to the elbow.

'Better check the knife wound,' Nitzane said. 'No point bathing the burns if he bleeds to death.'

'I'm not stupid,' Marantza snapped. 'That's the first thing I checked. The bleeding's stopped. See.' She flicked his robe back.

Sorne heard King Charald shouting, something about the Warrior and being High King. His exact words were lost in the din.

Marantza and Nitzane looked at his stomach wound, then up to each other, their faces carefully neutral. Before Sorne could ask what was wrong, a servant came running in.

'The king's in a rage. The barons are saying the Warrior has turned against him. Charald's demanding the Warrior's-voice reveal his vision.'

They all looked to Sorne.

'Help me up.'

'You can't–' Marantza began.

'He has to,' Nitzane told her, even as he helped haul Sorne to his feet.

The robe dropped around his waist. He couldn't see out of his left eye. He kept a hand pressed to his belly wound, not sure if he could walk. Blood covered his breeches, which were only held up by his hand. 'Can't go like this.'

'Strip him,' Marantza ordered.

He steadied himself on her shoulders as Nitzane and the servants peeled off his clothes. Lifting his feet so they could take off his boots was a challenge. Looking down he saw the white puckered skin of the belly wound, which hung open but did not bleed. He'd seen such wounds on dead men and that frightened him more than the thought of being blind in one eye.

'I can't get the torc off,' Nitzane said. 'The metal's melted.'

'Don't worry about that,' Marantza told him. 'Find him some breeches. We–'

'Here he is!' a man-at-arms announced from the tent's entrance. 'I've found him. He's with Baron Nitzane.'

'Send him out here,' someone called.

'Send out the Warrior's-voice!' King Charald. 'Send him out now.'

'Why are they hiding him?' someone demanded.

'He's dead.'

'Living but a lackwit, like the captain of the holy-swords!'

The whole tent swayed and one wall came apart as blades cut through the fabric.

Nitzane went to protest, but Sorne stopped him. 'Get back. Don't put yourself in danger for me.'

Nitzane pulled Marantza aside.

One wall of the tent dropped away to reveal King Charald standing there with his sword drawn, blood dripping from the blade.

A hush fell over the crowd as they saw the Warrior's-voice standing there naked, a bloodless wound on his belly.

Charald raised his sword and advanced on Sorne, bringing the tip to his throat. 'They're saying the Warrior has abandoned you and that I am no longer in his favour because of it. What do you say to that?'

'The Warrior...' Sorne's voice cracked. He despised them. His own holy-swords had turned on him. King Charald was ready to turn on him. Tears clouded his good eye, blurring his vision. He didn't care what they thought. He was tired of lying. 'The Warrior is nothing but a blood-hungry beast. It can never be satisfied. The Warrior is the beast in all of you. You are the Warrior.'

'You hear that?' Charald demanded, raising his sword over his head. 'The Warrior is in me!'

Sorne blinked and searched for his brother. Where was Zabier? Had he been killed on the pinnacle?

'And the vision. What did the Warrior show you, that I must do?' Charald pressed eagerly.

'He showed me...' Sorne prepared to lie, but his vision faded and he saw... a half-blood woman and children weeping... 'Women and children laughing.' Being loaded into a cart as they clung to each other. 'Climbing into carts.' Wearing rags. 'Waving banners.' As they were delivered to a silver-haired she-Wyrd at some kind of... 'Ceremony. The woman vows to–'

'To take the man for her husband!' Charald finished for him. 'It's my wedding. You hear that, Janzten? The Warrior god blesses this union. Bring her to me now.'

Men ran off to find Janzten's daughter. Sorne swayed and the world went grey.

He pitched forward, and the king only just caught him.

'Get him out of here. Take him back to my tent,' Charald ordered.

Then Sorne was being lifted and carried, as he heard the king call for the Father's-voice to officiate the wedding.

Chapter Forty-Six

IT WAS NINE days since Sorne had nearly died, and he still marvelled at his escape. He'd used up the residual gift essence in his last T'En artefact, but he felt no guilt. It was due to the artefact's power that his burns had healed as well as they had. The skin on the left side of his face, across his forehead, eye and cheekbone, looked like it had melted and reset. He was missing that eye, a chunk of hair and most of his left ear. It was a face of nightmares.

But it was the stomach wound that confounded everyone. It did not bleed, yet it did not heal. A part of him was dead, and he believed that he deserved it. He'd turned King Charald loose on the kingdoms of the Secluded Sea. He'd been a naive youth, who did not know the horror of war, but that was no excuse. With tens of thousands dead, he could never atone for what he'd done.

So he accepted the constant pain as his punishment.

Today was the first time he would leave the palace since he'd returned, half out of his mind with pain. For three days, he had been feverish from the burns. Marantza and Nitzane had stayed by his side, but they had sailed for their estate yesterday. Since then, no one had checked in on him, or even remembered to bring him food.

The palace was in upheaval due to the king's new queen. With the celebrations in the port still going strong, it was a good time to slip out and find Graelen, and tell him of his vision: half-bloods being herded into a cart by True-men. He didn't understand what the T'En woman was doing in the vision; maybe Graelen could make sense of it.

He strapped his stomach wound, dressed, then pulled his hood over his head, not because he was ashamed of being a half-blood, but because the sight of his burns was enough to scare small children.

Someone knocked on his door.

Six palace guards stood outside, along with Baron Janzten. He was nearly the king's age, and had lost all his sons to the wars. Jaraile was his only surviving child. Sorne had been recuperating in the back of the king's tent on their wedding night; he knew what she'd been through. Shame held him silent. The baron had every reason to despise him.

'I bring a message from the king.' Jantzen opened a scroll. 'Sorne the half-blood, formerly the Warrior's-voice, you are to take this chest' – the baron nodded and two guards stepped forward with a heavy chest, dumping it at his feet – 'to King Etri of Khitan, along with the king's sincere condolences on the death of the queen's brother, Prince Idan.'

Sorne drew breath, but Jantzen kept speaking.

'When you have done this, you are to go to King Norholtz of Maygharia and provide what assistance you can to help him quell the uprising.' Jantzen rolled up the scroll and offered it to Sorne. 'A ship is waiting to transport you.'

Sorne accepted the scroll. He recognised the king's handwriting and seal; it was all in order. Events that night on the pinnacle were still a little unclear, but he'd thought he'd saved the king from embarrassment and redeemed himself. It seemed the king remembered things differently. He didn't mind resigning his position as the Warrior's-voice. He didn't mind stepping away from a god he'd never believed in. And he didn't mind taking the chest to Khitan; this was a duty he had sworn to do. It was the service in Maygharia under Norholtz that dismayed him. The crushing of the uprising could take a year or two, and it could claim his life.

If he had a couple of days in port, maybe he could salvage the situation. 'Very well. Give me a couple of days to–'

'We are to escort you now.'

'Right now?'

Baron Janzten nodded. He looked grim but satisfied.

So this was his new enemy at court. The father of the queen had been poisoning Charald against him.

Sorne's mind raced. He was being sent to serve two of the barons who had raped, murdered and mutilated the she-Wyrd. It seemed his duty was clear.

'I can barely move. I need help.' To ensure their cooperation, Sorne flicked the hood back, revealing his face. The baron and the palace guard gasped and looked away. 'I don't have much to pack.'

The palace guards strode into his chambers. There was his chest of curios, within which he had hidden the Wyrd scrolls and Oskane's journals, and there was his clothing and personal items. It was the work of a few moments to pack these into another chest. He took the Khitite orb of power with him, on the off chance he would find a use for it, and slipped the rest of his soothing powders into his pocket.

He rejoined Janzten at the door, pulling his hood into place. 'There is one thing. If I may, baron, I'd like to say goodbye to the Father's-voice. He is...' He wanted to see Hiruna and Valendia, but no one knew of their existence.

'I know what he is to you,' Janzten said with distaste. True-men did not speak of their half-blood kin. 'Very well.'

They crossed the plaza under a cloudless sky. It was almost midday, and fiercely hot. While travelling through the countryside with Nitzane, Sorne had heard the people complain of a poor harvest last year. It looked like they hadn't had the rains they needed this year either, but it would be even hotter and drier on the plains of Khitan.

Sorne searched the crowd for Harosel or any of Graelen's Malaunje; no luck.

By the time he'd crossed the plaza, he'd come to a decision. Who knew what lay ahead of him? He could not take Oskane's journals and the Wyrd scrolls with him and risk losing them.

At the Father's church, they left the guards to wait, while Janzten took him through to the Father's private chamber. Sorne carried the chest, not trusting the men-at-arms with it. Zabier's assistant was used to seeing him and waved him through, studiously avoiding his gaze.

Sorne turned to the baron. 'I give my word, I will return before the next prayer bell.'

'You seem to think I value your word,' Janzten said, but indicated he was to go ahead.

The high priest's study was empty.

Torn between relief and disappointment, Sorne unlocked the secret door and plodded up the narrow stairs. By the time he reached the top he was trembling and had to put the chest down; he hated being so weak. The door to the balcony was open, but he could see only one person out on the terrace.

Valendia, bent over the thumb-player.

Remembering how he looked now, he hesitated.

She glanced up and saw his outline in the shadow of the doorway. 'Sorne?'

'Don't come too close.' He stepped back. 'Where's Mother?'

'Sleeping. The healer visited this morning.'

'Good.'

'Zabier said you were hurt.'

'You don't want to see.'

She followed him into the shadows, reaching for him, and he let her push the hood back.

'Oh, Sorne,' she whispered.

'It isn't important.' He took her hand. 'Listen, I know my return has not been...' What could he say? It had been a disaster for them. 'Now I'm being sent away again, on a mission for the king. I don't know how long I'll be. There's something I need you to do.'

'Anything.'

Was he ever so young?

He showed her his burned left hand. 'Can you write a message for me?'

She nodded and they went through to the kitchen, where she prepared her writing things. Sorne was reminded of teaching Zabier his letters at another kitchen table. 'This is a message for Adept Graelen of Kyredeon's brotherhood.'

'A Wyrd?'

Sorne nodded. 'Give it to Zabier to deliver, and tell him it's important.' He dictated quickly, recounting his vision of Wyrds being herded onto the cart, and added a final line – *Your gift saved my life.* Then he had her seal it and address it to Graelen.

'Remember his name, Valendia. If you are ever in trouble and you must escape from True-men, you can go to him. He'll take care of you.'

'But they wouldn't accept Mother.'

The bells began to ring.

He took the key from his pocket and placed it in her hand, curling her fingers over it. 'This is the key to the door at the bottom of the stairs. If you have to run away, use it and take the chest. Wear a hood and make your way down to the Wyrds at the wharves or to the Celestial City.'

'What chest?'

'The one by the door.' He gestured to it. 'It has important documents in it.'

She held his eyes, looking years older than her age. 'According to your vision, bad times are coming for our kind.'

'It could be just one cartload of our people. It could happen in fifty years time, for all I know. I have to go now.'

He came to his feet, already weary and all too aware of the long journey ahead of him. Would he ever find a place to call home?

Valendia threw her arms around him and held him tight.

'Dia, I don't know how long I'll be away, but if I survive, I'll come back, I swear. I'll find you, whereever you are. You might not be my blood kin, but you are all the family I have. Now, you know what to do?'

'The key, the chest, the adept.'

'Yes.' He kissed her forehead and left, pulling the door closed behind him without looking back. If he did, it would undo him.

The walk to the wharves was almost more than he could manage. He was shaking by the time they reached the ship. Janzten offered his arm and escorted him to his cabin. As the guard deposited his clothing chest, he wondered sourly if the captain had orders to throw him overboard, once they were at sea. Right now, he was too exhausted to care.

When he sank onto the bunk, the baron turned to go.

'I'm sorry,' Sorne said. 'Sorry it was your Jaraile the king wanted.'

Janzten studied him from the doorway. 'I believe you are, but it doesn't change things between us.'

'What Charald wants, he gets. No one could have stopped him. You must watch out for his rages.'

Janzten released the door handle. 'I've heard about the king's rages.'

'The king gets into such a state he hardly sleeps for days on end. Anything could trigger a rage. The smallest thing. There's no reasoning with him, when he's like that.'

'Why are you telling me this?'

Sorne emptied his pocket, tipping the contents onto the bed beside him: a dozen little packets of folded paper, each one sealed with a drop of wax.

'Soothing powders,' Sorne said. 'When Charald gets overwrought, slip one or two into his wine. It will help calm him down. It also acts as a pain killer.'

'This is some kind of trick.'

'Pick one and I'll take it, right now, to prove that it's not poison.' Sorne poured himself a glass of wine. 'Put the powder in there.'

Grimly, Janzten followed his instructions.

Sorne swirled the wine, then swallowed it all. 'Take the rest. I can get more in Khitan.'

But not T'En artefacts. They were rare and very expensive where he was going. Although he had the orb of power, it was not T'En power, and did not soothe his craving. He would be sweating and in pain by this evening. So be it. He did not want to live his life a slave to need, he would conquer the cravings.

Janzten gathered the powders, slipping them into the draw-string pouch. 'Why are you helping us?'

Sorne could hardly keep his eyes open. 'My mother was Queen Sorna. The king had her murdered after she birthed me. She was the same age as your Jaraile. I wish your daughter a happier life.'

GRAELEN HAD BEEN consumed with worry since he heard about the disastrous ceremony nine days ago. Now he hid behind a column in the entrance to the Warrior's church, waiting for the evening ceremony to begin. T'En and Wyrds weren't allowed into Mieren places of worship, but he was well hidden and he should be able to see Sorne from here. Rumours of the Warrior's vengeance on the pinnacle were still travelling across the city.

'They say he's been left a lackwit,' someone muttered, as they passed by.

'If he was a lackwit, he wouldn't be conducting this ceremony,' the companion said.

'True,' a third said. 'But he could still do it, if he was merely horribly deformed.'

'Come on, or we'll be right up the back and miss everything.'

The three of them hurried inside.

Trusting to the curiosity of the Mieren, Graelen slipped just inside the entrance. He had no trouble seeing across the sea of heads. A hush fell over the crowd as a dark-robed priest was escorted in by two priests wearing white. He was too short and plump.

The Warrior's-voice put back his hood. A Mieren.

Had Sorne lost his position?

Graelen left the church and the plaza, making his way to the wine cellar near the port. No message. He was almost at Chariode's warehouse when he spotted Harosel, returning from the Celestial City.

The veteran Malaunje dismounted and walked with him.

'What did Kyredeon say?' Graelen asked. 'Does he want me to look further into the rumours?'

'He consulted the saw-bones. Ceyne says he has records going back three hundred years, and there have been other times when the numbers of half-blood infants dropped.'

'Then it is cyclical. Sorne was right,' Graelen said. Harosel seemed strangely reticent.

'What's wrong?'

The veteran met his eyes and shook his head. They entered the warehouse and took the horse across to the stable. Once Harosel had made sure that none of Chariode's people were around, he took a message from inside his vest. 'You've been recalled.'

'But–'

'Kyredeon needs you. Paryx botched the sacrare's abduction. She died and he's been executed. The brotherhood's suffered a severe loss of stature. Kyredeon fears one of the all-fathers will make a move on him.'

'Paryx dead.' Graelen felt no grief, only relief, which saddened him. But he didn't want to leave the port yet. 'Nine days ago, Sorne's own holy-swords tried to throw him to the beasts of the higher plane. He was alive when they brought him back, but...'

'I'll ask around.' Harosel began to unsaddle his mount. 'We can delay a few days. No more.'

After three days, Harosel returned with the news Sorne had been sent to Khitan on a mission for the king.

'He's already sailed?' Graelen found it hard to believe.

'After Khitan, he goes to Maygharia. It looks like he became an embarrassment and the king sent him away.'

'But he was alive and well?'

Harosel hesitated. 'They say he was horribly burned.'

Graelen went to the window. Ships sat on the sparkling sea or were nestled into the quay, where Mieren bustled about, loading and unloading. Sorne hadn't left a message for him, which surprised him. 'Did he say anything to you, the last time you saw him?'

'Nothing out of the ordinary.' Harosel shrugged. 'He did ask what you did in the brotherhood.'

A feeling of foreboding settled on Graelen. 'And you told him what, exactly?'

'I told him you're our greatest assassin.'

Recalling the assassins' scars on Sorne's body, Graelen sank onto the window seat.

'It's nothing but the truth.' Harosel shrugged. 'Do you want me to check the wine cellar one more time?'

'No. There will be no message.' Graelen came to his feet. 'We return to the brotherhood.'

Back to Kyredeon and his paranoia.

Four days later, he led his Malaunje into the Celestial City. As they rode through the causeway gate, a Sagora stepped aside to give them precedence.

IMOSHEN KEPT HER head lowered and her gift under tight rein as a grim-looking gift-warrior from Kyredeon's brotherhood rode past her, through the causeway gate.

'Who's that?' someone whispered behind her.

Imoshen glanced over her shoulder, spotting two Malaunje warriors: a veteran and a youth, from All-father Hueryx's brotherhood. The veteran didn't answer until the gift-warrior and his Malaunje had passed by.

'One of Kyredeon's killers. If you see him or any of his Malaunje watching our high-ranking T'En, let me know. Or any of our devotees, for that matter. Kyredeon's not above using them as weapons to get to us.'

Imoshen's stomach churned. The brotherhoods had still not forgiven her for executing Rohaayel. If Kyredeon suspected she felt something for a T'En man...

Deep in thought, she hurried along the causeway. After what had happened at the last lesson, she had been tempted not to come today. Yet nothing could have kept her away.

It was an unusually overcast and muggy summer day; clouds hung so low over the lake that they brushed the pinnacle of the highest sisterhood tower, and the air felt heavy with foreboding. Her gift responded, surging as it sought to break free of her control.

A scattering of heavy rain droplets hit the hot stone of the arched bridge to the foreign quarter. She recognised the signs. Soon the heavens would open. She could not wait for him here; she sped down the far side of the bridge and made for the Sagora's house.

A hand caught her arm, stopping her in mid-flight. Her captor used her own momentum to swing her into the shadows of a building's portico, where she collided with his chest. The instant he grabbed her, her gift surfaced.

Recognising his power, she let down her defences. Her senses were heightened, and everything beyond the shadowed portico became unreal. Her heart beat a rapid tattoo. Imoshen knew her gift was on the verge of something momentous, but she managed to rein it in. Like a spoilt child it lashed at her, impatient with her control.

'What was that?' he whispered.

'Nothing...' But she'd promised herself, since she had to lie about her identity, she would lie to him about nothing else. 'I don't know what it was. My gift tried to slip its constraints.'

There was so much more to this than the gift-tutor had let on. Was Vittoryxe wilfully blind, or was it that she simply did not know, having shut herself away from male company?

'Where are you?' he asked. 'Your body is here, but your mind–'

'Sorry.' She stepped back. At that moment, the heavens opened. Sheets of rain poured down, drumming on the stone, slapping the canal water. She had to lean close to him to be heard. 'I'm sorry, I can't–'

'Don't.' He gestured from himself to her. 'This is very rare. Don't you feel the way our–'

'I'm not ruled by my gift, or my body. I can't be.' She wanted to see his eyes, but that would mean revealing herself, and she was afraid that if he knew her true identity, he would despise her. She caught his hands in hers, lifting them to her lips to kiss. 'I have people depending on me. I have to think of them.' *And you. It's safer, if no one ever knows how I feel about you.* To start something now, when he did not know her true identity, was dishonest.

She let his hands drop and stepped back. 'It's for the best.'

'Don't make decisions for me, student-she.'

Tears stung her eyes. She gave the Sagora bow and spoke Sagorese. 'Student-she apologises to student-he.'

At that moment, darkness filled the doorway. They both turned towards the threat, gifts rising.

But it was only the Sagora servant, standing under a sheet of canvas. The hem of her gown was sopping wet.

'Merchant Mercai sent me.' She gestured.

As Imoshen stepped forward, he caught her arm and whispered. 'You're wrong. Life's too short to be cautious.'

Then they were making their way to their lesson.

Imoshen was preoccupied when she returned to the sisterhood that evening, and it took her a while to realise Frayvia was subdued.

'Something's wrong. Tell me.'

'You haven't heard?'

'I've been at my lesson all afternoon. It's bad news, isn't it?'

Frayvia shrugged. 'I said he would come to a bad end, and he has.'

'Who?'

'The Warrior's-voice. Something went horribly wrong at a ceremony. Several Mieren died, and he's been banished. Well, sent south, but it amounts to the same thing.'

'I'm sorry.'

Chapter Forty-Seven

Year 317

MORE THAN A year later, and student-he still had the ability to make Imoshen question herself. Despite this, she always arrived early and waited for him, on the arched bridge near the Sagoras' building.

During the last lesson, they had circled back to their old argument. She was torn between wanting to leave to study on Ivernia, taking Iraayel with her – not that she had told student-he about her choice-son – and wanting to stay and change things in the Celestial City, but she was not a brilliant playwright like Rutz. What could she do to change the way people thought?

Tragic as it was, it seemed the sacrare's murder had done much to foster good relations between the brotherhoods and sisterhoods. That first midsummer after her death, there had been no trystings. Since then, the brotherhood leaders had set out to win the all-mothers' trust.

But Imoshen had had a glimpse of the worst of brotherhood life, and time was running out for Iraayel. In three years, he would be handed over to Chariode's brotherhood.

But Imoshen didn't want to declare Iraayel dead to her. She did not want to see him grow callous and cruel like Kyredeon's killer. And that was what he'd have to do to survive. He was her choice-son, and the brotherhood would be twice as hard on him.

She should take him to study with the Sagoras.

Only yesterday, Egrayne had helpfully pointed out that, once he joined his brotherhood, Iraayel would be subject to his all-father, and might not be allowed to remain with the Sagoras.

'You are far away today,' student-he said.

She jumped with fright and her gift surged. It was on the tip of her tongue to confess her worries over Iraayel, but that would mean revealing her identity and she was afraid if he knew she was Imoshen the All-father-killer, he would despise her.

'Is something wrong?'

Yes, I've been lying to you all this time and now I regret it. 'No.' Imoshen tried to come up with something to distract him. 'You know more languages than I do. Does it strike you that the structure of Sagorese is too logical?'

'Too logical?' His lips twitched.

Her heart rose. 'With T'En and Chalcedonian, there are as many exceptions as there are rules. But in Sagorese, once you know the rules–'

'Just be grateful it is logical.'

'Oh, I am.'

'Do you still plan to run away to live with the Sagoras?'

She wanted to tell him the truth, wanted it so badly she couldn't bear it if he turned away from her. 'We're here.'

'High King Charald!'

'To High King Charald!' the deep voices of Norholtz's war barons echoed. And Sorne raised his goblet in response to King Norholtz's toast to celebrate the successful suppression of the Maygharian uprising.

More than a year had passed since Baron Janzten had bundled him onto a ship and sent him south to King Etri of Khitan. During that time, Sorne had come to terms with King Charald's actions. After the debacle on the pinnacle, the king had to claw back control. He'd known Sorne was not at fault, but others could not see that.

So, while appearing to banish him, the king had actually rewarded him. Charald could not acknowledge his first-born half-blood son, but it was clear he trusted Sorne. He'd made him his agent.

Sorne was effectively the king's voice abroad and, as an extension of that power, it was he who controlled Norholtz's war barons. Twenty days ago, he'd sent a message to Charald reporting the successful suppression of the uprising.

The musicians struck up a Chalcedonian air, and the dancing began. This was Norholtz's problem. The customs, beliefs and language of Maygharia made Norholtz uneasy. Unlike Etri, Norholtz had clung to Chalcedonian ways.

Sorne studied the feasting hall as he drank his wine. The barons danced with their Maygharian wives, but the servants, all locals, were sullen and downcast. Against Sorne's advice, four days ago, Norholtz had made an example of the uprising's two leaders and their entire families, executing them publicly. Instead of subduing the populace, it had forged resentment into hatred. That hatred was now directed at Sorne and Norholtz. Force may have secured this kingdom, but it had not secured the minds of its populace. King Norholtz had bought himself a few years' peace at most. And as for his wife...

Sorne leaned back to look at her. She sat on the king's left, ignored and isolated, while Norholtz tapped his foot in time to the music and talked of his boyhood in Chalcedonia to one of his aides. He was almost fifty, and had never been the same since taking a leg wound in the first battle for Maygharia.

There was only one child, a boy of five, and, judging from their separate bedrooms, there would be no more. Although Norholtz had taken the vanquished king's daughter to wife, he had never taken her into his heart, and the queen did not love him. Right now, her eyes followed a servant who moved like a warrior. The next uprising could be closer than anyone guessed.

Hand in his pocket, Sorne rubbed the silver-mounted trophy Etri had made from the she-Wyrd's little finger. When he'd arrived in Khitan, Sorne had delivered the news of Idan's death and his chest of gold. Then he'd lingered, intending to execute Etri in such a way that his death would be considered an accident, but not before explaining to the True-man why he had to die.

The she-Wyrd's undignified, mutilated body still haunted Sorne's dreams.

But then he'd experienced life in Etri's court. Philosophers and scholars were welcome at the king's table, along with painters and poets. His wife, Idan's sister, hosted discussions, debating with the king and the scholars. Their three children listened and learned.

Sorne could not bring himself to avenge the she-Wyrd.

Troubled, he had stayed his hand while he wrestled with the conflict between his duty and his instincts. It wasn't until Hiruna came to him in a dream that he understood.

Even now, he could see her clear as day, hanging out the washing in the courtyard at Restoration Retreat, while Valendia played at her feet.

'Etri took part in the she-Wyrd's murder. He murdered my mother on Charald's orders. But I can't–'

'Kill him? Of course not,' she'd said brusquely. 'He's turned his life around. And, if you asked her, the she-Wyrd wouldn't want you to kill him. If we can't atone for the past, what point is there going on?'

'But...'

'Do you want to end up like Oskane, eaten away by revenge? He never could appreciate my two beautiful half-blood boys.'

'I failed her, Ma. She asked me to free her, but I...' Tears stung his eyes.

'So this is about you, trying to atone?' Hiruna had asked. 'What did the she-Wyrd do for you boys?'

'She taught us the T'En language.'

'No, what did she really do?' Hiruna saw he did not understand and picked up Valendia, balancing the toddler on her hip. 'She tried to repair the damage Oskane had done. He made you hate your half-blood.'

'Don't hate your half-blood,' Valendia said.

And he'd woken with the conviction that if he could find a woman like Hiruna to share his life, he would be happy; but no woman had wanted him before he was burned, and now they turned away or looked on him with pity.

There was one more thing he had to do in Maygharia. After that...

He had been expecting King Charald to send new orders, and a message addressed to Norholtz had come from Chalcedonia this evening just as they were entering the feasting hall.

Sorne wanted to return to his bedchamber and seek oblivion in sleep. The pain of his unnatural stomach wound was a constant reminder of his failings.

He could sit still no longer. Leaning closer to the king, he said, 'If you will excuse me...'

Norholtz nodded and waved him off.

But Sorne did not go straight to his chamber. Instead, he went to Norholtz's private chambers. The guard nodded to Sorne. As the king's agent, he had free run of the palace. The scroll with the king's seal was waiting to be read. It was the work of a moment to slide a hot knife under the wax.

It seemed to Sorne he had been reading messages meant for others most of his life and turning that information to his advantage. Tonight he learnt that Charald had an heir: a baby boy, born in the spring, named Cedon.

Sorne was looking forward to returning to Chalcedonia and seeing his family again. He had served the king well. Surely enough time had passed for Charald to welcome him back? But the last paragraph of the message destroyed his illusions.

On the other matter, it would be convenient if the half-blood suffered a fatal accident while returning to Chalcedonia; during the voyage would be best. At sea, he will not be able to escape his assassins.

The king wanted him dead. Charald didn't need Sorne's visions, not when he had his kingdom and his heir. He didn't need the political embarrassment of a half-blood advisor who was really his son. Sorne flushed. He'd been a fool to think Chalcedonians could overlook his tainted blood. The king was nothing if not ruthless.

Hands shaking, Sorne resealed the message. Behind him the door opened and he looked up, surprised to see... 'Queen Ariama.'

When she didn't ask him what he was doing in Norholtz's private chamber, he made no excuse.

She was barely twenty-one, yet she'd seen her kingdom fall and her father executed, and had been forced to marry a man she despised.

'You were kind to my son when his father mocked him.'

'Ayghar is a clever boy with an enquiring mind.' Nothing like his rigid father. Sorne liked children, but he doubted if he would have any of his own. Soon it would be winter's cusp, and he would be twenty-seven. The age Charald had been when Sorne was born.

Tears of anger glistened in the queen's eyes. 'Norholtz plans to send Ayghar to Chalcedonia. Please talk to him. My son is all I have, and he needs to grow up here, in the kingdom he will one day rule.'

'He needs to be Maygharian, not Chalcedonian.'

'Exactly.' Smiling in relief, she came over to Sorne. 'I thought you would understand, when you tried to convince the king not to execute those women and children.'

'I failed.' He was tired of the killing. Tired of trying to prove his worth. 'Now that the uprising is crushed, he won't listen to me.'

'He's never listened to me. It seems that none of the Chalcedonian men value their wives as they should.'

Sorne's belly ached. The pain was always worse when he felt low. 'It is the way of their people.'

'It is not the Maygharian way. Since Norholtz became king, he has made new laws. Widows cannot inherit their husband's properties or run their family businesses. Everything must go to the eldest son.' Anger made her voice thin and hard. 'A woman must do what her husband, father, brother or son tell her. Women cannot sign legal documents, and it is illegal to teach girls to read and write.'

'Chalcedonian ways.' Sorne was tired of serving True-men who did not value him. Time for them to learn their mistake. 'Norholtz is an old man. He will not live forever. When Charald conquered your country, he sent your brother to Khitan as hostage to ensure your cooperation. If Norholtz died, would you bring your brother back?'

'Why would I do that? He was a gambler and a drunkard when he left and, from what I've heard, he's worse now. I was the one being groomed to rule.'

Sorne nodded. 'If Norholtz died of a heart attack tonight, what would you do?'

'I wouldn't send my son to Chalcedonia.'

'The palace is full of Norholtz's barons. They are ambitious, ruthless men. How would you stop one of them from marching his men into the palace, declaring himself king and marrying you?'

Her eyes narrowed as she considered this. 'The palace is full of my loyal servants. The city is full of loyal Maygharians. Behind every baron is a Maygharian woman, who is the equivalent of a servant in her own home. I would set them all free.'

'So you would make a pre-emptive strike, and kill the barons in their beds?'

She laughed, but her answer was serious. 'Some could not be reasoned with, I know this already. Others... would swear allegiance to me.'

'Norholtz will never understand your people, Ariama. His unjust laws chafe at them every day and the brutal suppression of this uprising has hardened their resolve to be rid of him.

'If he learns about your lover he'll have the man hung, drawn and quartered. He'll have you executed and your son will grow up in Chalcedonia. Ayghar won't even remember you.'

She went very pale. 'Are you threatening me?'

'If I can spot your lover, someone else will. Even if you hide him, what do you think will happen if the next uprising is organised by someone else and they succeed? Will you be returned to the throne your family has held for two hundred years, or will you be executed, because you aided and abetted Norholtz?'

'Why are you saying this?'

'You came to me for help. Sometimes we have to help ourselves. All the barons are staying in the palace tonight. They have only a few trusted men with them. Their captains and the men-at-arms have ridden back to their estates. Men without leaders are sheep.'

The door swung open and Norholtz limped in. When he saw the queen with Sorne, a spasm of anger crossed his face. For a heartbeat, Sorne thought Norholtz would accuse him of trying to seduce his wife.

'What are you doing, woman, whingeing to the half-blood? Go back to your room. My mind is made up. The prince will grow up in Chalcedonia. Maybe they can make a man of him. The Warrior knows I can't.'

The queen glared at him, turned on her heel and walked out.

'Stupid woman...' Norholtz muttered, sinking into his chair with a grateful sigh. 'Filling my son's head with ridiculous ideas. Why are you here, king's agent?'

'A message arrived from King Charald.' Sorne was curious to see Norholtz's reaction. 'Does it contain my new orders?'

Norholtz picked up the scroll, broke the royal seal and brought the candle closer to read. When he got to the end, he frowned and Sorne saw his shoulders tense.

'Bad news?'

'What? No...' Norholtz rolled up the message and shoved it in a drawer. 'Doesn't concern you.'

Well, that was no surprise.

'Before I left Khitan, King Etri gave me a gift.' Sorne pulled a chain from his pocket. On the end swung the she-Wyrd's sixth finger bones, set in silver.

'He gave you that?' Norholtz seemed surprised. 'Did he say where it had come from?'

Sorne placed the chain with its gruesome trophy on the desk. 'He said that you had the matching finger. You know I collect T'En artefacts—'

'You want to add it to your collection.' Norholtz sounded relieved. He bent down to open a drawer and put a small draw-string bag on the desk.

'That's it?'

Norholtz tipped out the three little bones that made up the sixth finger. 'I never got them mounted. Filthy things. Should have thrown them away years ago. You're welcome to them.'

'Thank you.' Sorne slipped the chain and trophy into the draw-string bag. He tucked it in his pocket, then pressed the tip of his knife to Norholtz's neck.

'This is about the she-Wyrd, isn't it? But... but Etri lives. Why kill me and leave him alive?' Norholtz asked, incensed.

'The she-Wyrd was a sensible woman. She wouldn't want me to kill a man who genuinely regretted his past and was trying to atone.'

'Etri? He's forgotten what it is to be Chalcedonian.'

'Yes, he's a true Khitite.' Sorne could hear footsteps in the corridor. 'His three children love him and he listens to his wife. You should have listened to yours.'

The door opened and the Maygharian queen entered, followed by half a dozen palace servants, including her lover. They all carried bloody weapons.

'What's this?' Norholtz demanded.

'This is me, doing what I should have done years ago,' Ariama said, and signalled to the servants.

Ignoring Norholtz's protests, they dragged him out.

Sorne took Charald's message, set it alight and dropped it in the empty fireplace.

'I suppose Charald will send another war general like you,' Ariama said.

'There is no one quite like me. If you have a mind to do me a favour, you could let the king think I am dead.' Sorne watched the message burn. 'King Etri of Khitan bears no love for Charald, so don't expect trouble from him. King Roitz of Welcai is having trouble with his barons. Navarone is also rife with insurrection. That only leaves the kingdom of Dace. Even if King Dakon remains loyal to Charald, he'll be too busy watching his borders to bother you.'

'COME ON.' EGRAYNE took Imoshen's arm and drew her across the crowded theatre foyer. The empowerer gestured to the ceiling fresco. 'Kyredeon's outdone himself rebuilding the theatre. Must have cost a fortune!'

For the grand reopening, they'd staged Rutz's latest play. It was a curious piece about an all-father who woke up one morning to discover his gift had changed his gender and he was now female. The ensuing complications with his shield-brother and inner circle had kept the audience on the edge of their seats. Imoshen had laughed so much she'd cried, and was looking forward to discussing the play with student-he.

But she wasn't used to crowds; the eager gifts and animated chatter of excited T'En made her head spin. She planted her feet and looked for Iraayel. When Egrayne learned that Imoshen had arranged to take her choice-son to the theatre for his birthday, she had invited her choice-daughter to keep Iraayel company. Not to be outdone, Vittoryxe had invited her own choice-son, Bedutz. Since

All-mother Aayelora and her inner circle were already going, Imoshen had ended up as part of their group.

Everyone who was anyone was here tonight.

All around them, T'En drank wine and talked about the play they'd just seen at the top of their voices, while watching everyone else, sharp eyes glittering.

'I don't...' Imoshen glanced over her shoulder, searching for Iraayel, Saffazi and Bedutz. There they were, with the sisterhood's hand-of-force. Mefynor spotted Imoshen and Egrayne, and herded the three youngsters over to join them.

'What's the hold-up?' the sisterhood's hand-of-force asked.

'All-father Chariode and some of his inner circle are just over there.' Egrayne indicated with her fan. 'Iraayel will be going to serve him in a few years. Imoshen should meet him. It would put her mind at rest.'

'Egrayne's right. Chariode is one of the more reasonable all-fathers.' Mefynor gestured to Iraayel who, having heard his name, was listening unashamedly into their conversation. 'It would be good for Iraayel to meet him, too.'

'Besides, Rutz belongs to Chariode's brotherhood,' Vittoryxe said, as the rest of the inner circle joined them. 'We should compliment the all-father, since we can't compliment the playwright.'

'Perhaps he'll tell us who Rutz is,' Saffazi said. She had a fragile beauty, behind which lay a will of steel.

'It's decided, then,' Egrayne announced. Imoshen's gift surged and she knew Egrayne had planned this all along. The gift-empowerer was just trying to help, but Imoshen didn't like being backed into a corner.

All-father Chariode and his inner circle were holding court as everyone came over to congratulate them on the success of the play. And, she suspected, to see if they could identify Rutz.

Chariode's Malaunje served wine, while more half-bloods played elegant music composed for the play. The crowd eased a little as several groups left to visit the eateries and make a night of it.

'All-father Chariode,' Aayelora said, making obeisance.

'All-mother Aayelora.' He returned the obeisance with just the right degree of deference for her advanced age. All-fathers tended to be younger than their female counterparts, as so few of them had the chance to grow old.

'We came to congratulate your brotherhood on the success of Rutz's latest piece,' the all-mother said.

Imoshen had to admit the T'En men did look fine. In their formal robes, with their elaborate torcs of office on their shoulders, thick silver brotherhood bands gleaming on their biceps and jewelled pins glinting in their hair, they reminded her of the paintings of the High Golden Age.

Of course, none of them met her eyes. She was Imoshen the All-father-killer and, other than student-he, she had not had a casual conversation with a T'En man since Lighthouse Isle.

'Also, I want to introduce you to a lad Egrayne has identified as a powerful gift-warrior in the making.' Aayelora gestured to Imoshen's choice-son. 'Iraayel will be seventeen three years from today, when he will join your brotherhood.'

Imoshen saw Iraayel's shoulders tense as the five closest men turned to inspect him. To reassure him, she placed her hand on his back.

'Iraayel...' Chariode said. It was clear he did not know the name. When Rohaayel's brotherhood was absorbed into Chariode's, the T'En boys would have been the last thing on the all-father's mind. Chariode would have been concentrating on containing the rivalry caused by integrating so many powerful men into the ranks of his warriors and scholars. 'From Rohaayel's brotherhood?'

'Yes. Hand-of-force Irian's son.' Vittoryxe spoke as if she was being helpful, but was clearly making sure they knew the boy was the son of a disgraced, covenant-breaking father. Imoshen didn't have to read her to know her motivation.

Saffazi and Bedutz flushed in sympathy with Iraayel.

Anger made Imoshen's gift hard to control, but she hung back and said nothing. As far as she could tell Chariode and his inner circle had not connected Iraayel to her.

'A potential gift-warrior?' Chariode studied Iraayel. 'So tell me, Iraayel, what would you like to do when you join us?'

'I... I don't know. Does Rutz do more than write plays?'

'Why?' Chariode laughed. 'Are you going to compete with him? Do we have an aspiring playwright here?'

'No. No, I...' Iraayel flushed, glancing to Saffazi and Bedutz.

Imoshen wanted to protect him, but held her tongue. Hearing their all-father's laughter, two more of his inner circle came over.

Chariode took pity on Iraayel. 'Work hard for your gift-tutor, but don't neglect your other studies.'

'I do work hard,' Iraayel said. 'I'd like to go to Ivernia one day.'

Imoshen glanced to him. Had Frayvia let slip their plans to her son?

'Then you'll want to be a sea captain, like Ardonyx, here,' Chariode said, apparently not realising Iraayel meant he wanted to study with the Sagoras. The all-father beckoned the captain, who had only just joined them. 'He's our greatest explorer. What made you decide to go to sea, Ardonyx?'

'I didn't. I was a terrible student, who drove my teachers to distraction,' he said, his voice so familiar Imoshen's heart lurched. Ardonyx was student-he. All other sounds retreated. Her gift surged, and she had to fight to repress it. She needed to get out of here. 'I kept asking my tutors why this, why that, and always they had the same answer.'

'What was their answer?' Iraayel asked, intrigued.

'Things are the way they are because that's the way it has always been. Finally, they sent me to sea. They thought it would knock some sense into me.'

'Did it work?' one of Chariode's inner circle asked.

'No...' Ardonyx shook his head with mock sorrow. 'I'm still asking why.'

Imoshen read him. He *was* Rutz. His plays were his way of expressing his frustration, at a society he had compared with so many others, and found wanting.

Ardonyx grew very still, and she felt his power questing for hers.

Imoshen knew she had to make obeisance and slip away before everything unravelled but, at that moment, Egrayne put a hand on the small of her back, urging her forward.

'Chariode, this is Iraayel's choice-mother, Imoshen.'

Seven high-ranking T'En men focused on Imoshen, and she wanted to sink through the floor. The instant she spoke, student-he would recognise her voice. But she had no choice; she had to thank Chariode. The moment seemed to last forever.

Egrayne nudged her.

Imoshen gave the obeisance of obligation. 'All-father Chariode, as Iraayel's choice-mother, I thank you for accepting him into your brotherhood.'

She kept her gaze on Chariode, but sensed Ardonyx stiffen. He'd recognised her. Meanwhile, Chariode's inner circle watched their all-father, waiting to take their cue from him.

'Imoshen...'...*the All-father-killer.* Chariode didn't say the words. He didn't need to; they all heard them.

'I hope...' Imoshen's voice faltered. 'I hope you can ignore the identity of Iraayel's choice-mother and accept him for the potential gift-warrior he is.'

At that moment Ardonyx took a step back, and her gaze flew to him. His eyes gleamed with pain and anger. She'd lied to him, hurt him. Certainly, he'd had a secret, but it was something to be proud of, whilst her secret...

Ardonyx gave the all-mother an abrupt bow and walked away.

No one spoke.

Imoshen felt Iraayel's dismay, and she sensed his struggle to contain his newly-risen gift.

'What does this mean?' Saffazi asked, bristling on Iraayel's behalf.

'It means,' Chariode said, 'that due to his choice-mother, Iraayel will have to work twice as hard to gain stature in the brotherhood.'

'That's not fair,' Saffazi protested.

'Life is rarely fair.' Chariode made his obeisance to the all-mother and walked off with his inner circle.

And, when Imoshen went to her next Sagorese lesson, there was no sign of student-he. Through judicious questioning of the sisterhood's sea captain, who had recently returned from an unsuccessful voyage to find a way through the northern ice floes, Imoshen learnt that Captain Ardonyx had left the city to sail south.

Chapter Forty-Eight

Year 318

'NEXT,' VITTORYXE CALLED. The requests for midsummer trystings were flowing in. Personally, she didn't see what all the fuss was about. But she had the responsibility of making up the list, and she would do a good job.

Each individual T'En male's gift, stature and brotherhood had to be assessed before he could be added to the list, and half a dozen high-ranking sisters waited with her to discuss each request. Among these sisters were Imoshen and Arodyti. It had been Egrayne's suggestion, and Vittoryxe didn't see what they could add to the discussion. Arodyti was like a cat on heat; she and her shield-sister asked for several different males each year. Vittoryxe suspected the pair of them regularly slipped out to the free quarter to indulge in illicit trystings. As for Imoshen, she might pretend disinterest in T'En males, but Vittoryxe knew better. Imoshen had grown up in contact with their gift; she was flawed.

The sea captain, Iriane, strode in. 'Captain Ardonyx is back.'

Vittoryxe looked up at the sisterhood's famous sea captain. 'So you want to tryst with this Ardonyx.'

'What? No. I want to mount another expedition.'

'What does he have to do with this?' Vittoryxe asked.

'He's the greatest of the brotherhood sea captains, a brilliant navigator.' Iriane spoke as if everyone should know this. 'He's been scouting a southern route to the far east. If he finds one, Chariode's brotherhood will negotiate an exclusive trading agreement with–'

'So you want to make another voyage north?' All-mother Aayelora said, and looked to Egrayne; always Egrayne. Vittoryxe had seen this as confirmation Egrayne would be named the next voice-of-reason, and she would be the next all-mother, but the longer Aayelora delayed, the more it undermined her conviction.

Egrayne sat forward. 'Iriane, last time you tried to find a way through the ice floes, you lost two toes to frostbite and–'

'I'll be better prepared this time.' She shifted her attention to the all-mother. 'Ardonyx has been back four days already, and I only just heard. I need your approval, Aayelora. I need to find a northern passage ahead of him, if our sisterhood is going to have an exclusive trade agreement.'

As Vittoryxe waited for the all-mother to respond, she noticed Imoshen quietly coming to her feet. 'Where are you going? We haven't finished yet.'

'It's nearly time for my language lesson. I thought–'

'Imoshen can go,' the all-mother said. 'And Iriane, you can have your expedition. We'll finish this tomorrow.'

Annoyance flashed through Vittoryxe. She should have been the one to call an end to it.

'Right, that's it for today,' she said, reclaiming control, and then she went one better. 'Tonight the sisterhood will hold a farewell dinner for Iriane and her crew.'

IMOSHEN'S HEART RACED – he was back. There was a chance he might not come to the Sagorese lesson but, if he did, she would be ready for him.

'Imoshen?' Egrayne called.

Controlling her impatience, Imoshen waited at the top of the grand staircase.

'Did you notice the all-mother?' Egrayne asked.

Imoshen thought back. 'She seemed tired.'

Egrayne nodded. 'And she's forgetting things. They all remark on how well she is for her age, but she's failing, Imoshen. She should have stepped down years ago. She didn't because she couldn't hand the leadership over to the wrong person.'

'But you'd be a wonderful all-mother,' Imoshen protested, and she meant it.

'Vittoryxe thinks she'd make a wonderful all-mother, and she's spent the last thirty years shoring up allegiances with the high-ranking sisters to ensure she'll have the numbers. There's no point Aayelora naming a new all-mother if Vittoryxe forces a vote; and, if the vote doesn't go the way she wants, she could offer challenge.'

'I thought only brotherhoods–'

'It happens if a sister puts personal ambition above the good of the sisterhood.'

Imoshen winced.

'Exactly. Vittoryxe believes she has the best interests of the sisterhood at heart, but–'

'If she did, she would accept you as all-mother. What will you do?'

Egrayne studied her. 'I've been waiting for you to grow into your gift. You're a raedan. With that skill, you could make our sisterhood the most powerful...' She ran down because Imoshen was already shaking her head.

'I don't want to lead the sisterhood. The sisters don't like me. Vittoryxe has seen to that. And the brotherhoods *hate* me.'

'They respect strength and power. Vittoryxe does not have as many friends as she thinks she does. Certainly, if she became all-mother, the sisters would defer to her, but they would be relieved if she didn't.'

'You're serious.' Imoshen stared at her. 'I can't do this.'

'You'd have me to advise you, and your choice of hand-of-force.'

Even as she shook her head, one part of Imoshen was already planning the changes she would make. Of course, she could not implement them right away, but this would be a chance to gradually bring the sisterhood into a new age, the *Age of Enlightenment*, as she and Ardonyx called it.

Oh, but she wanted to see him; *needed* to see him.

'If Vittoryxe could call on the votes to beat you, she'd beat me.'

'Not if you birthed a sacrare girl, who would grow up to make our sisterhood more powerful than any other. When Reoden had her sacrare daughter, the old all-mother stepped down. You've already given birth to a healthy sacrare boy. So your chances of carrying one to term are better than average. I've made a list of the suitable males who have asked to tryst with you.'

'I thought no one ever asked.'

'That's what we told you, because Vittoryxe said–'

'...that I would become addicted to the male's power if I trysted with a male.'

Egrayne nodded. 'So the all-mother turned down all requests.' She passed Imoshen the list. 'Take a look. Pick two or three to tryst with. If you do have a sacrare from the midsummer trystings, we don't want a male claiming stature because of it.'

'Besides, if it was a boy, the sisterhood would have to hand him over in seventeen years, and his brotherhood would...' Imoshen read Egrayne. 'You couldn't kill–'

'We can't give the brotherhoods a weapon to use against us. You'd better have a girl.'

'There's no way of ensuring a girl,' Imoshen protested.

'Don't mention this to Vittoryxe. Come back to me with at least three trysting partners for midsummer.'

Imoshen looked down at the list, then up. 'I'll think about it.'

She turned to go, but Egrayne caught her arm. 'Your sisterhood needs you.'

'I understand. I really do.' They could not go on like this, living in fear of the men. There had to be a better way.

Imoshen left the palace and made her way to the sisterhood jewellery shop in the free quarter to get changed.

During the time that Ardonyx had been away, Imoshen had realised two things. The first was that she loved him, and without him life was flat and grey. The second was that he had been right – she could not live her life in fear. If she believed there were injustices, she had to try to redress them.

And she had a chance of achieving this as all-mother of the most powerful sisterhood, but only if one of the brotherhoods cooperated and set an example for the others. If Ardonyx was all-father of a powerful brotherhood... Her heart raced; together, they could change things for the better.

There was no sign of Ardonyx on the arched bridge. She waited, but he did not come. Head down, she made her way to the lesson, but a hand caught her arm, pulling her into the same shadowed portico as last time. Her gift recognised him and broke free of her control for a heartbeat.

He pushed the hood and veil back so that she could see his face. 'Imoshen...'

'I'm sorry.' The words poured out of her. She pushed back her own hood and veil. 'I should have told–'

'You couldn't. I wouldn't have–'

'Then later I didn't say anything, because I didn't want to risk losing you. You were right, I can't live in fear.'

'Then say it.'

This was too intimate. Too powerful. She couldn't speak. Her gift surged and he swayed towards her. She reached out and brushed aside his robe to find bare flesh.

Everything was in alignment, her gift, her body and her mind. She was ready for this. Her power built.

'What is that?' he whispered. 'I can feel...'

'The deep-bonding.' In this state, it was hard to speak. 'It's all or nothing.'

He covered her hand with his, and went to lower his defences.

'Wait.' She wanted to set her gift free, but... 'Bonding with me will complicate things for you. You'll have to hide it from your own brotherhood. If the news gets out, it'll make you a target for men like Kyredeon.'

'He's not my all-father. Chariode's brotherhood is strong.'

'I don't want to put you in danger.'

'It's all or nothing.'

She smiled. 'If we do this, there's no going back.'

'There never was any going back.'

Imoshen allowed her gift to meld with his.

Sorne hobbled into King Roitz's hunting camp, carrying a bundle of firewood on his back. The servants were busy preparing for the midsummer feast. With his head down and the scarred side of his face turned towards them, the men-at-arms did not look too closely; they were too busy watching each other for the first sign of betrayal.

After spending the better part of a year making his way across the kingdom, Sorne had confirmed the rumours. Roitz could not trust his own barons. He'd executed two in the last three years and confiscated their estates. King Roitz went in fear of the men he had once commanded, and had taken to consulting seers and oracles. His last oracle had been executed by the king's two Khitite bodyguards when she failed to predict an assassination attempt.

Sorne adjusted his protruding stomach. Tucked into the padding around his waist was the orb of power he'd acquired in Khitan all those years ago. It would not glow until it touched both of his hands. It was part of his oracle disguise.

No one in Welcai associated the scarred, white-haired, half-blind cripple – he'd adopted a limp – with King

Charald's advisor, the Warrior's-voice. If he kept his hands hidden and the hood shaded his good eye, no one realised he was a half-blood.

In the days immediately after leaving Maygharia, Sorne had been sorely tempted to sail back to Chalcedonia and confront Charald, but he'd set himself a duty and he'd come to appreciate anonymity. Norholtz had died in the uprising, killed by his Maygharian queen and, as far as Charald knew, Sorne had perished with him.

So he no longer had to fear assassins.

Leaving his firewood with the rest of the pile, Sorne leaned on his staff and followed his nose to the cooking fire. The king had invited his five surviving barons to go hunting with him and celebrate the midsummer feast. Tonight there would be much drinking and roistering. The cook took pity on Sorne and gave him a chunk of bread to eat while the venison roasted.

As he sat by the fire, he listened to the servants talk and learnt that the camp was teetering on the edge of violence. Roitz and his barons had agreed to bring no more than fifteen men-at-arms each to the midsummer feast, but they'd made sure all their servants were sturdy young men, able to wield a knife or a cudgel.

Sorne wandered through the camp, chewing on his bread. All around him, men-at-arms drank and boasted while eyeing each other, their hands never far from their weapons. Spotting Roitz's banner, Sorne fed his bread to a horse and hobbled over to the tent.

'The king will want to see me,' he said, speaking Chalcedonian with a Khitite accent.

'And who might you be?' a man-at-arms asked. A veteran of the wars, he was older than Sorne and missing most of the fingers on his left hand.

'A seer.'

'Wait here.' The veteran went into the tent.

'What's in store for me?' his young companion asked.

'Give me your hand.'

Sorne accepted the proffered hand and leant forward to sniff the palm. 'There was a scarred man.' Everyone over fifteen was scarred around here. 'He touched his sword hilt when he met your eyes today.'

'How'd you know?'

Because it was a common mannerism. 'He'll come after you before dawn.'

The youth swore and pulled his hand back.

'The king will see you now,' the veteran told Sorne. 'But I warn you, if one of the barons has paid you to stab him, the king's bodyguards will gut you, slowly.'

Sorne lifted his bandaged hands. 'I'm unarmed and crippled.'

As he went inside, he heard the youth telling the veteran what the seer had said, and hid a smile. The camp was tinder ready for the flame.

Two sturdy Khitites stood in the shadows behind the king. Roitz had known Sorne when he served King Charald but the former baron didn't recognise the broken man before him now.

Tilting his head so that the lamplight fell on his scarred eye socket, Sorne studied King Roitz. Drink, fear and constant worry had aged him. His eyes kept darting about the tent, and the slightest noise made him jump.

'You're certainly ugly enough to be a seer,' Roitz said. He had started roistering early; two pretty girls went to serve him wine, but he pushed them both aside. 'What can you tell me?'

'Give me your hand.'

Sorne made a performance of kneeling, groaning as though his body ached. Tonight was one of his better nights, his belly hardly pained him. He accepted the king's hand, bent low and sniffed. One of the girls made a disgusted noise.

'I see... a cell with bars, lit only by moonlight. I see a captive woman with copper hair and wine-dark eyes...'

The king pulled his hand back, swearing softly under his breath. Roitz licked his lips. 'What about this woman?'

Sorne held out his hand again. He did not speak until the king's hand lay in his. Then he swayed and moaned. 'There are several men, four... maybe five. They laugh when they see she cannot get away. They take turns with her. One of them, I cannot see his face, puts his hands around her throat and strangles her.'

'Ferminzto,' Roitz whispered. 'What about her? What is she to me? All this happened more than a decade ago.'

'She is here, tonight.'

'What?' Roitz jerked back.

The girls both gave squeals of fright and darted away to crouch in the shadows. The Khitites shifted from foot to foot, infected by the king's fear.

'What's she doing here?' Roitz asked.

Sorne tilted his head, as if listening. Then he shrugged. 'Makes no sense. She has no eyes, yet she says she came to watch you die.'

'The barons are coming to kill me.' Roitz lurched to his feet, turning to the Khitites. 'Go quickly, out the back. Rouse my men.'

They hesitated, glancing to Sorne, who slid both his hands inside his robe, cupped the orb and held it at chest height. As it began to glow through his vest material, he began to babble in T'En. Crying for help and cursing... as he imagined the she-Wyrd would have done.

The girls wailed and fled from the tent. The Khitites drew their weapons and followed them, leaving Roitz alone.

Roitz sank to his knees, moaning.

After a moment, Sorne heard shouting, and then the clash of metal on metal, as seething tension erupted in violence. He let the orb slip down into its padded pocket and flicked back his hood. 'Why did you take her eyes, baron?'

Roitz lifted his head, took one good look at Sorne, then gasped, clutched his chest and pitched over. He jerked twice, then lay still.

Sorne checked, but there was no pulse.

Satisfied, he replaced his hood, picked up his staff and hobbled out the back of the tent.

IMOSHEN PEERED THROUGH the gap in the awning. A dozen lantern-lit, richly-decorated barges floated on the dark lake, while music and laughter drifted across the water. 'It's beautiful.'

'You've never been out on the lake on midsummer's night?' Ardonyx asked as he ran a hand down her bare thigh.

'You know I haven't.' She shivered and felt him harden against her buttocks. The melding of their gifts enhanced and shared every sensation. It was intoxicating, and rather overwhelming.

This was only the third time they had managed to escape alone together. Yet, tomorrow... 'I can't believe you're going to sail off tomorrow.'

'Strictly speaking, I am going to ride off. I can't set sail until I reach–'

She thumped him. They wrestled, laughing softly. She let her gift rise and felt the moment his responded. He sensed her sorrow.

'I have to go,' he said. 'Blame your sisterhood. I can't risk Captain Iriane making it through the northern passage before me–'

'How long will you be away?'

'No more than two years.'

'Two years?' She could not bear it. Not when the bonding was so fresh and intense. To make matters worse, in two years' time, her choice-son would be seventeen, just before winter's cusp.

She hadn't told Ardonyx of Egrayne's plan to make her all-mother, hadn't suggested he become all-father. 'If you find the southern passage, you'll return with so much stature you could become all-father.'

'If I wanted to paint a target on my back.' He shrugged. 'Besides, Chariode is honourable. What kind of man would I be if I swore loyalty to him, then undercut him?'

Imoshen had to admit he was right. If he could kill to satisfy ambition, he wouldn't be the man she loved. 'I want to change the way we live, but I'm not talented like Rutz.'

'Rutz, that silly dreamer?' He cupped her cheek. 'You are Imoshen the All-father-killer. You've already changed the way we live.'

'For the worse.' Tears stung her eyes. 'And not by choice.'

He kissed her. 'I wasn't here when the all-mothers made your sanctuary conditional on killing Rohaayel. When I came back, it was all the brotherhoods could talk of, that and the injustice of the covenant, the way it divides us.'

'I bet they talked of how they hated me.'

'Many did,' he conceded. 'But the thinkers could see the underlying problem. Four hundred years of custom had made us blind to it. The wrong had to be exposed before we could begin to devise ways to fix it.'

'The day Kyredeon's warriors killed the healer's sacrare daughter, I was so angry, I felt the covenant was justified.'

'Her death shamed us all. We should not have to live in fear, not the sisters and children, not the brothers.'

'It's been years since Rohaayel died, and we're still divided.'

'These things take time.'

'You...' Imoshen smiled and propped herself on one elbow. 'Who would have thought? Rutz, the biting satirist, is secretly an optimist.'

He laughed.

'So, is it true?' she asked. 'Is Rutz more than a wordsmith, capable of crafting a clever rhyme? Can he imbue words with power?'

Ardonyx rolled his eyes. 'If Rutz could imbue words with power, do you think he'd be a lowly sea captain? He could rule the T'Enatuath, the world even.'

'Only a madman would want that.'

He threw back his head and laughed.

Imoshen watched in wonder, as happiness formed a bright ball in the centre of her chest. She savoured the moment; it would have to last a long time. Tonight, when she went back to the palace, she would memory-share with her devotee, while everything was fresh in her mind. That way, it would be preserved.

Frayvia was covering for her tonight. Egrayne did not know Imoshen was out of palace. The list of suitable T'En men for trysting had been returned with no names selected. Ardonyx hadn't been on the list. She was glad. She didn't want anyone suspecting they shared the deep-bonding.

Ardonyx was an optimist, but she...

'Where have you gone, Imoshen?'

'I'm right here, with you.' For tonight. 'Student-she is going to miss student-he.'

He took her hand, placing it over his heart and opened the link again. 'Student-he loves student-she far more than he should.'

She laughed and he silenced her with a kiss, but she suspected he was right.

Chapter Forty-Nine

Year 319

SORNE CURSED. IT had taken almost a year to get to this point, but it had taken only a moment of overconfidence to undo everything.

He'd travelled through the kingdom of Dace into Navarone, where he'd searched for news of Barons Bazajaun and Ferminzto. They'd fled Chalcedonia, when Charald returned as High King of the Secluded Sea. Taking their families and loyal men-at-arms, they'd crossed the pass into Navarone.

When Nitzane's brother, King Dantzel, turned down their offer to help him conquer Chalcedonia, the barons had taken to the foothills of the Navarone Mountains. Like all landless men, they'd faced a choice: serve other men or serve themselves. They'd become bandits, which meant he had to follow the trail of their raids. No one had heard of a bandit leader called Ferminzto, but Bazajaun was well known. Sorne tracked his band of men until he finally wandered into their camp, late one evening in early summer.

There'd been sentries, but they hadn't bothered to stop a blind, lame beggar. Eyes bandaged, back bent as he leant on his staff, Sorne picked his way through the tents. With its fierce women, quick-fingered children, scrawny goats, raucous chickens and mangy dogs, the camp was a roving village.

After leaving Roitz's hunting camp, Sorne had earned his way by telling futures, never staying long enough to be proven a fraud. The ploy had served him well, and he planned to use it again.

Bazajaun the Bandit led the most successful of the fugitive barons' bands. The locals described him as cunning, capable of executing daring raids on estates and merchant caravans. He was also described as ruthless, often using cruelty to prevent the locals from betraying his band's whereabouts to the king's men.

The last time Bazajaun had seen him, Sorne had been a half-blood youth of seventeen, skin soft as a girl's. He approached the bandit leader's tent, confident he wouldn't be recognised, and that his ruse would get him close to the baron. Every man was curious about his future. Time spent in Bazajaun's company would reveal his weakness. Every man had one. He'd exploit Bazajaun's, learn where he kept the she-Wyrd's hair and...

There it was. Sickened, Sorne stared at the bandit's banner. The she-wyrd's hair hung long and thick, glinting copper as it stirred in the breeze. His gut clenched with sorrow and anger. He could grab the hair and be off, escaping across the foothills of the Navarone Mountains. But, after seeing what Bazajaun's men did to the last merchant caravan, Sorne had decided to kill the baron, then retrieve the trophy, before going in search of Ferminzto.

He limped over to three men, who were sitting under the tent's awning, deep in conversation. They were scarred, dirty and dressed in stolen finery. None of them reminded him of the baron.

As they picked through a chicken carcass, they tried to outdo each other, telling crude jokes in Chalcedonian, laughing too loud and draining their wine. Their high spirits reminded him of naughty boys who had escaped their tutor for the day.

'Tell your fortune?' he offered as he hobbled up.

The one with a broken nose spat at him.

He persevered. 'Tell the noble bandit's fortune?'

'If you value your hide, fortune teller, you'll piss off,' the skinny one said.

He was about to go when someone rode up behind him, jumped down from the horse and tossed the reins to one of the children who had run to meet him. As the new arrival strode past, Sorne caught a quick glimpse of a slender youth with long golden hair and striking features.

'What did I tell you?' The youth cuffed one of the men over the head. 'Leave no survivors.'

'We left no one alive.' The fear in the men's faces seemed absurd, considering the pretty youth's slight frame.

The youth grabbed the big man's shoulders, tilting the chair off balance. The man clung to the chair's arms.

'Then why are there fifty of the king's men making camp in the valley below us?' The youth shoved the chair and the man went over backwards.

The other two exchanged looks. Broken-nose stabbed a finger at Sorne. 'He led them here.'

'Yeah,' the skinny one said. 'It was the seer, Bazajaun.'

Bazajaun? This was not the baron.

The youth strolled over to Sorne, who was bent almost double, so that he had to look up at him. Most Chalcedonians had the kind of blond hair that turned the colour of dirty straw when they grew up. The youth's hair was actually golden and the angles of his face were so perfect, he looked like a statue.

'The seer?' the youth asked.

Either Baron Bazajaun had died and this was his son, or the youth was using his name and his banner. Sorne was about to go into his spiel when, quick as a cat, the youth snatched the bandage off his head.

The moment he saw Sorne's good eye, he caught a handful of his hair, jerking painfully. 'A half-blood. He's King Charald's spy!'

There was a fraction of a heartbeat, when Sorne could have broken his hold, dropped the youth and tried to escape, but he was in the middle of the bandits' camp, so he played up his weakness, and pleaded innocence.

The other three scrambled over, seeming glad their leader's attention had been diverted.

He should have taken the she-Wyrd's hair when he had the chance. Now...

They stripped him and found his orb of power, but nothing else, since he'd hidden his travelling pack in a rock crevice just off the path.

They hadn't been gentle and, by the time they finished, at least one of his ribs was cracked, his mouth was bleeding and his good eye was so swollen he could barely see out of it. The dead wound in his stomach ached with a cold malignancy. Sorne let his body go limp as Skinny and Broken-nose held him between them.

The youth gestured to the tent. 'Take him in there. And start moving the camp. We haven't used the giant's navel for a while. Lead the others up there.'

'You don't have time to play with him,' Broken-nose warned. 'We have to–'

'I know what we have to do.' The youth unhooked the lamp and led them into the tent.

The tent had been erected around a tree that had been cut off at about head height. The youth stood, tossing the glass ball from hand to hand, as Skinny bound Sorne to the trunk. With ropes around his shoulders and chest, thighs and knees, his genitals were exposed and his hands were free from the elbow down.

'Wha...' Skinny gagged as he spotted the open wound on Sorne's stomach.

Even a veteran like Broken-nose was revolted. 'That... that–'

'That's no ordinary wound. Bring that lamp closer.' The youth used the tip of his knife to prod the dead white skin, watching for Sorne's reaction. 'The wound is open, but it does not heal. The skin is dead, but it does not decay. Does it hurt, half-blood? How did it happen?'

'I played with power one too many times.'

The bandits drew back, making the sign to ward off evil.

But their leader was clearly fascinated; a sly smile lit his lovely face. 'You can't be all that powerful. Here you are, my prisoner!'

A wagon trundled past, followed by barking dogs, and a voice yelled for someone to hurry up and finish packing.

'You'll have to kill him quick,' Broken-nose said.

The youth turned towards them. 'Have I ever given you reason to think I'm stupid?'

Broken-nose cleared his throat. 'We'll pack up camp.'

As the two bandits left, Sorne wondered how the youth could have men twice his age terrified.

'I didn't lead the king's men here, you know,' Sorne said.

'Of course not.' The youth tossed the orb of power from hand to hand. 'But you are a spy, and a Wyrd spy at that.' He walked around Sorne. 'A Wyrd spy with a wound that does not heal, covered in scars. This burn...' He gestured to Sorne's face, then tugged at the hair that grew from the right side of Sorne's head. 'White, not silver; you're a half-blood.'

'Where is Baron Bazajaun?'

'Clearly, I am Baron Bazajaun. And just as clearly, you're talking about my father. He was weak. We wouldn't have survived the first winter, if I hadn't taken over.'

'How old were you when you gained the leadership?'

'Thirteen.'

That made him around sixteen now. Sorne didn't know how he'd done it.

Young Baron Bazajaun laughed. The sound made Sorne's skin prickle. There was something very, very wrong with him.

'I know who you are,' Bazajaun announced. 'You're the Warrior's-voice!'

Sorne tried to hide his surprise.

'I'm right. I knew it,' Bazajaun crowed, then leant closer. 'They said you had visions. Is it true?'

Sorne nodded slowly, mind racing. 'I saw things. Not all of them have come true yet.'

'Did you see me?'

'No... but then, I never looked for you. Do you want me to?'

He laughed. 'Oh, no. You don't get around me that easily. You're being boring now, like the rest of them. The longer you prove interesting, the longer I'll keep you alive. Shall I tell you my game?' He tossed the orb from hand to hand. 'I ask you questions, and if I don't like your answers, I cut off bits of you. I could take my knife and see how deep that dead wound goes.' He watched Sorne's face as he spoke. 'Or I could go a little lower...'

The youth's gaze fell below Sorne's waist, and Sorne felt his balls try to crawl up into his body.

'Why would I care? My cock doesn't crow. It hasn't been able to crow since I took the stomach wound. It's useless.'

'Really?' The youth shoved the orb inside his vest and drew his knife. He grabbed Sorne's prick. 'Why don't we just cut it–'

'Don't! Don't...' Sorne cried in horror.

Satisfied, the youth let him go and put the dagger away. He retrieved the orb and began to play with it again.

'See,' the youth said. 'I'm much better at playing this game than you are. Why are you here, Warrior's-voice?'

'Don't call me that.' Sorne hated the person who'd been the Warrior's-voice.

'Why not?'

'I'm not the Warrior's-voice anymore. I'm...' Who was he, and how could he appeal to this mad youth? 'I'm on a sacred mission to right an old wrong. I came here tonight to retrieve something your father stole.'

'Good answer.' A smile made the youth beautiful. He tilted his head thoughtfully, then cast Sorne a triumphant glance and ducked out of the tent.

A few moments passed. Sorne could hear shouts, thumps, horses, creaking wheels, dogs barking.

The youth returned, with the banner, which he leaned against the wall. Taking his knife, he removed the long tail of copper hair. 'You're after this. Why?'

'To right a wrong. She asked me to let her go, but I was arrogant. She died because of me.'

'What do you mean to do with it?'

'Return it to her, so she can rest in peace.'

'So you can rest in peace, you mean.'

A blush crept up Sorne's cheeks.

The boy saw he was right. 'Too easy. You're starting to bore me.'

'No. You're trying to trick me,' Sorne said, desperate to divert him. 'The hair's the right length and colour. But it's too thick for half a head. So it can't be my she-Wyrd's hair. Bazajaun divided her hair with Ferminzto.'

'You're right. They did divide it, but I won Ferminzto's half from him.'

'I bet you did.' Sorne had to keep the youth talking. 'What happened to him?'

'He was weak.'

'Is everyone weak?'

'Pretty much.'

'You think you're smart, don't you?'

'I know I'm smart.' He grinned. 'Smarter than you. You're the one tied up with his cock and balls hanging in the breeze.'

Sorne fought panic. If he could just work out his tormentor's weakness... The youth was smart and focused, but had no empathy. It was like looking in a mirror at what he might have become, had Oskane succeeded in his indoctrination.

'You're interesting,' the youth said. 'You have a high tolerance for pain. I could make you last days. But we have to move tonight, thanks to King Dantzel.'

'You could just give me the hair and let me go.'

'Oh, I like you. I really do.'

He was going to kill him soon. Sorne could see the excitement glittering in the youth's eyes. Fear made

Sorne's mind race. He glanced around the tent, looking for inspiration. No weapons, nothing within reach.

The youth tossed the orb from hand to hand, enjoying his desperation.

'You shouldn't let it come in contact with your naked skin,' Sorne told him. 'It'll make you sick.'

'Sick? In what way? It's just a glass ball. You can't trick me with your fake visions from the gods.'

'There are no gods.'

'Now that's unusual. Very few people will admit it, even if they think it.'

'No gods. But the visions were real.'

'Father and Ferminzto swore they saw you interact with the gods. They saw strange lights, and objects disappearing.'

'The light was a byproduct of the power shed when I opened the walls between this plane and the empyrean plane. The offerings disappeared when they were taken across. But the creatures that did this were not gods. They were beasts, nothing but hungry predators.'

'Says who?'

'The Wyrds. The T'En scholars.'

'Oh, I have to keep you.' He gave Sorne a sly look. 'Maybe I could just cut the back of your heels, and then you'd hobble for the rest of your life. You wouldn't be able to escape.'

'You don't want me to save you from the orb? It may have tainted you already.'

'You mean this piece of pretty glass?'

'It's called the orb of power.'

His tormentor tilted the glass ball this way and that. 'I see no power.'

'Keep it next to your skin and all your golden hair will fall out.'

'No.'

'Yes.'

'Prove it.'

Sorne lifted both his hands, palm up. 'Watch.'

The youth placed the orb in his hands.

It began to glow, growing in brilliance.

'See?' Sorne said, triumphantly.

'What is it?'

'Trapped inside it is...' – he had no idea, and no one had ever been able to tell him – 'one of the beasts from the higher plane.' It was as good an explanation as any.

The youth leaned over the orb and peered into the light, just as Sorne hoped he would.

Sorne lowered the glass ball ever so slightly, drawing him in, then lifted it suddenly with great force, smashing the thick glass ball into the youth's face. The baron fell back just as Broken-nose entered the tent.

'Clever half-blood.' Broken-nose came over and crouched, to touch the youth's throat. 'He's dead.'

And now Broken-nose would kill him. Sorne cursed his bad luck.

'The little fecker's dead.' Broken-nose shook his head in wonder, then sprang to his feet. 'I could kiss you.' He took another look at Sorne. 'Maybe not.'

Someone called from outside.

'Hold on,' he yelled and grabbed Bazajaun's banner. 'Time for a new baron.'

As Sorne watched, he went to walk out. 'What about me? I killed him for you. Just cut me free. That's all I ask.'

Broken-nose laughed, grabbed the lamp and left him in darkness. Sorne waited, hoping he could convince someone to let him go, but no one came to take the tent down.

The following day, fifty of King Dantzel's men arrived in camp. They peered into the tent with great caution, as if used to finding traps. When all they found was Sorne and the body, one of them called for the captain.

This man studied Sorne, grimacing in distaste. Next, he examined the fallen youth. 'Pretty as a girl. What a waste.'

'That's Bazajaun. I killed him.'

The captain snorted. 'That's not Bazajaun. The baron's a full grown man with a broken nose. That's just some poor boy.'

'That poor boy tied me up and was going to cut off my prick.' Sorne couldn't repress a shudder. 'A man with a broken nose took Bazajaun's banner. He's calling himself the baron now. But he'll be easier to catch than the real Bazajaun. I know where they're going.' Sorne hoped they had taken the youth's advice and gone to the giant's navel.

'Untie him,' the captain ordered. 'We'll take him with us.'

One of them went around behind Sorne, while the other one dragged the youth's body to one side.

The orb rolled away from him.

'That's mine,' Sorne said.

The captain picked up the she-Wyrd's hair.

'That's mine, too,' Sorne said.

'You're mighty pushy for a hideous half-blood who's tied to a pole, standing in a circle of his own piss,' the captain said.

Sorne ignored this. 'I'm a personal friend of King Dantzel. He'll reward you for delivering me safely.'

They released him, and he tried to take a step, but fell to his knees. No one helped him as he rubbed the blood back into his feet and legs. At least he was alive and intact.

Chapter Fifty

VITTORYXE PUSHED PAST the heavily pregnant Imoshen. It was midsummer's night of the year 319 and All-mother Aayelora lay dying.

At last.

The sisterhood's high-ranking members had been called to hear the all-mother name her successor. Now they were waiting for Egrayne to let them into her bedchamber.

Last year, around winter's cusp, their old voice-of-reason had died. Egrayne had taken on the role, allaying Vittoryxe's fear that the empowerer would oppose her for all-mother.

Frustrated by the delay, Vittoryxe strode along the length of the chamber, past a row of windows. From here, she looked out over the other sisterhood palaces, down to the lake where revellers celebrated on barges: singing, drinking and trysting as they had done for three hundred years. Vittoryxe could feel the pages of history turning, presenting her with a blank page to write her name as the new all-mother.

Turning on her heel, she almost collided again with Imoshen, who walked with her hands on her lower back, pregnant belly swaying in front of her. Imoshen seemed preoccupied, and didn't even apologise for getting in the way.

Vittoryxe glared at her, but she didn't notice.

When Imoshen had made it past the seven small moons it took to deliver a Malaunje baby, Vittoryxe had cursed her. Trust Imoshen to carry a T'En baby.

The door to the all-mother's private rooms opened, and Egrayne ushered them into the all-mother's bedchamber. Most of Aayelora's inner circle were dead; only old Tiasarone still lived. Vittoryxe had already picked her new inner circle. She was stuck with Egrayne as her voice-of-reason, but she would name Kiane her hand-of-force. The old hand-of-force, Mefynor, was almost eighty and ready to step down.

Egrayne stood on the far side of the bed, with Arodyti and her shield-sister, Sarosune. Imoshen stood with them. Her eyes were closed, and she appeared to be distracted. Typical. She didn't appreciate the solemnity of the occasion. How could she, when she wasn't really one of them? Their sisterhood should never have accepted her.

Egrayne had propped Aayelora up on pillows, so that she could make her announcement. Through a closed door to the next chamber, they could hear the geldr sobbing; he might be simple, but he knew his mother was dying.

When Vittoryxe was named all-mother, she would get rid of the embarrassment.

'Come closer,' the all-mother said, her voice not much more than a whisper. She'd held the reins of the sisterhood for almost fifty years. No brotherhood leader had ever survived that long. Few sisterhood leaders could equal her.

Vittoryxe made sure she wore a suitably humble expression as she shuffled closer to the bed.

Imoshen swayed, and the two shield-sisters reached out to steady her; trust her to make a play for attention.

Egrayne offered the all-mother her hand, opening her gift so the old T'En woman could draw enough strength to make her announcement.

'The last years of our sisterhood have been turbulent, with the execution of All-father Rohaayel the Covenant-breaker and the murder of the healer's sacrare daughter. Hopefully, you will see some peace now. I'm tired, and happy to go to death's realm. Hand-of-force Mefynor is ready to step down. The new all-mother will want to appoint her own hand-of-force, so I will not name one. Our sisterhood is lucky to have a strong voice-of-reason in Egrayne, who is also a gift-empowerer. Our sisterhood is lucky to have a well-read gift-tutor in Vittoryxe. As the new all-mother, I name...'

Vittoryxe squared her shoulders.

'...Imoshen, who–'

'Imoshen? But she's not even an adept,' Vittoryxe protested.

'She carries a sacrare child,' Egrayne said.

'She what?' Vittoryxe wanted to laugh. 'No. She took a Malaunje lover. The inner circle never approved a T'En tryst for her.' But when she glanced at Imoshen, she knew it was true. Imoshen was addicted to the male gift; she would never have settled for a Malaunje lover. 'Who is it? Who is the father?'

'She kept his name secret to protect him.'

'She hasn't birthed the babe yet. It could be deformed, for all we know–'

The sisters cut her off, protesting, and she knew she had pushed too far.

'Imoshen has already birthed one healthy sacrare,' Egrayne said. 'If our all-mother wishes to name her the next all-mother, that is her right.'

No one protested. Vittoryxe glanced around to her supporters, half of them would not meet her eyes. 'Are you all blind? She was raised by a covenant-breaking brotherhood. She doesn't value our proud tradition. She–'

Imoshen bent double with a groan, holding her belly.

'What? No, you can't be serious...' Vittoryxe was beside herself.

'She's been in labour since sunset,' Egrayne said, dropping Aayelora's hand. 'Quickly, get her up on the bed in the next room.'

Arodyti and Sarosune helped Imoshen from the chamber, and the rest of the inner circle followed in her wake.

Left alone with the dying all-mother, Vittoryxe knelt on the bed and grabbed Aayelora's shoulders, shaking her.

'What's wrong with you? *Imoshen?*' She was so angry she could feel her gift crawling across her skin like a thousand burning ants. 'She's a gift addict! She'll ruin the sisterhood! What were you thinking?'

But the old all-mother had no answer. She was dead.

Vittoryxe thrust Aayelora aside in disgust and stalked into the next chamber.

The moment she entered, she felt the pressure of the sisters' gifts. But above that, she felt Imoshen's gift, and it repelled her. All she could see was a row of backs as the sisters crowded around the bed.

'Open your gift to us, Imoshen,' Egrayne urged. 'We can help you bear the pain.'

'Too late for that,' old Tiasarone said. 'One more push, and the baby will be here.'

'She can't be ready to deliver,' Vittoryxe protested. 'She was walking around just before.'

A baby cried, proving her wrong.

'It's a girl,' Egrayne said, delighted.

Vittoryxe rolled her eyes. 'Of course it is.'

But no one heard her, they were all congratulating Imoshen, the sisterhood's new all-mother.

KING DANTZEL WAS not exactly pleased to see Sorne, but he gave him a chamber and invited him to tonight's feast to celebrate the destruction of Baron Bazajaun's bandits.

No servants came near Sorne, either too busy organising the feast, or reluctant to be associated with the disfigured half-blood. That suited him just fine.

He had washed the she-Wyrd's hair and spread it on the window ledge in the sun, and now he waited for it to dry. A flock of birds circled the castle towers.

Mad Bazajaun had been right; he was trying to atone. Sorne would take the trophies home to Restoration Retreat, where he would bury them and make his peace with the she-Wyrd.

It would not be so easy to atone for the path he had set King Charald on, when Matxin seized the throne. In fact, he could see no way to atone for the conquest of five kingdoms. Maygharia and Welcai had already reverted to their original dynasties, but that did not restore the lives of those slain in the conflict.

Sorne just wanted to go home, and even as he thought this, he realised home was where Hiruna was – Hiruna and Valendia. His vision had told him something bad was going to happen to the half-bloods. At least he'd warned Graelen. He should go home and make sure his mother and sister were safe.

Charald believed Sorne was dead, but the scars that made him invisible here would draw attention in Charald's port city.

As soon as the she-Wyrd's hair was dry, he plaited it neatly, wrapped it and stored it in his travelling kit. He needed to think, and headed downstairs to take a walk. Through a doorway he saw a balcony bathed in the light of the setting sun and a familiar voice reached him, carried on the evening breeze.

Baron Nitzane, here?

Well, why not? Dantzel was the baron's brother. Sorne moved through the chamber, towards the open doors. It would be good to see Marantza and Nitzane again. He smiled to see Nitzane with his small son, who looked to be about two.

'I'm so sorry. Such a terrible accident,' Dantzel said. 'He must miss his mother.'

'The bridge didn't just collapse.'

Marantza dead? Sorne's feet slowed. He'd had no idea. But then he'd been gone for three years. He shouldn't disturb them.

Nitzane grabbed his brother's arm. 'It was murder, made to look like an accident. Her carriage was found washed up on a river bend. Our son was supposed to be with her, but he came down with measles and she'd left him at home. It was Charald.'

'Are you mad?' Dantzel drew him towards the door.

Sorne couldn't reach the hallway door in time. He darted back and bumped a sideboard. An apple jumped off a plate. He caught it, knelt and crawled under a table.

Dantzel closed both doors. 'There, now we're safe, Zane. What makes you think–'

'She was Charald's heir.' Nitzane put the small boy down.

'He has an heir, a son, almost the same age as yours.'

'Prince Cedon? He's a cripple, born with a club foot. An imperfect man cannot sit the throne, and Charald's queen just birthed a blue baby. It's the same thing that happened with our mother. Every baby after her first one died. Charald will have no more children.'

Silence stretched. Small feet trotted by the table.

'Why are you here, Zane?'

'You know why I'm here. I want justice. My son is the rightful heir to Chalcedonia.'

'I can't betray Charald. He gave me this kingdom.'

'Out of guilt. I wrote you how he had our father killed so he could marry our mother.'

'No... I never got your message.'

Nitzane swore softly.

A friendly little face peered under the table at Sorne. Luckily it was dim and his good side was towards the small boy. Sorne held his finger to his lips. The toddler grinned and climbed under to join him.

'There's more. When Charald returned to Chalcedonia, he sent Sorne, the Warrior's-voice, to kill our mother so he could marry again.'

'The Warrior's-voice is here, in the palace.'

'What? Charald said he was dead, killed in the Maygharian uprising two winters ago.'

The little boy grew restless. He wanted to play. Sorne undid his boot straps, freed the lace, and made it wriggle across the polished wood. The toddler giggled and tried to grab it. The two brothers kept speaking.

'The Warrior's-voice is very much alive and on some private mission for the king, I suspect,' Dantzel said. 'He was the one who guided my captain to Bazajaun's camp. Now you're telling me he killed our mother?'

'What? No, she's alive. And now that I think about it, this makes Charald's club-footed heir illegitimate!'

'But Charald doesn't know that,' King Dantzel reminded him. 'And if he did, Mother wouldn't be safe. You must go back to Chalcedonia and arrange for her to come to me.'

'If I go back to Chalcedonia, I'll fear for my son's life. Charald killed his mother. He would not hesitate to kill my boy. I...' Nitzane broke off. 'Where has he gone?' Footsteps. 'Martzane, where are you?'

The little boy giggled.

'He's hiding,' King Dantzel said. 'My boy was the same, at that age. In fact, he still likes playing hide and seek. Look, Zane, you can leave your son here. I'll raise him with my children, but I won't attack Charald.'

'Then you might as well kill my boy, because Charald will. He can't afford to let him live.' Anger made Nitzane's voice shake.

The little boy responded to his father's emotion with a whimper.

Nitzane heard him. 'Martzane, are you all right? Where are you?'

Sorne held up the apple, rolling it from hand to hand. He offered it to the child, who reached out. Before the boy could grab it, he rolled the apple out from under the table across the floor and the toddler went after it.

'There he is.' Nitzane sounded relieved. 'What's he got?'

'An apple... and a boot strap.'

Sorne looked down. Sure enough, the child had taken his boot strap.

'Where would he–'

'I have to go back to Chalcedonia,' Nitzane said. 'If the king suspected I knew he was behind Marantza's murder, he'd accuse me of treason and confiscate my estates.'

'You can leave Martzane here. He'll be safe. Charald is an old man. He must be nearly sixty. He'll take a fall off his horse, or eat something that disagrees with him, and then your troubles will be over.'

'Careful, brother. It sounds like you think the king's death would be a good idea. Speak of it to no one. Not even your wife. You know how women gossip.'

'Ginnie doesn't gossip.'

They were heading for the door. Sorne started to relax.

'Whatever you do, don't say a word in front of Sorne,' Nitzane warned. 'He's been good to my family, but...' Their voices faded.

Sorne breathed a sigh of relief and climbed out from under the table. His knees felt weak. After a moment, he checked the hall. When it was empty, he headed back to his chamber. All the while, his loose boot slid around on his foot.

At the top of the stairs, Nitzane called his name. 'Sorne, is that you?'

He turned, hoping the length of his breeches hid the missing bootlace, which was still there in little Martzane's hand.

'Who else?' Sorne asked.

A servant hurried by, lighting the lamps.

Nitzane studied him. 'I'm sorry we couldn't do more about the scarring.'

Sorne shrugged and wiggled his fingers. 'I'm alive and I have the use of my hand.'

Martzane grinned at him and reached out for him.

'He likes you.' Nitzane smiled. 'What are you doing here? Charald told everyone you were dead.'

Sorne wanted to tell him the truth, but that wouldn't help either of them right now. 'I must dress for dinner.'

'Got you on some secret mission, has he?' Nitzane shrugged. 'We can catch up tomorrow.'

Sorne nodded. Tomorrow he would ride for Chalcedonia, visit Restoration Retreat, then head across country to the port, where he would have to hide his identity. Even as he thought this, he realised he could buy his way back into the king's good graces by revealing the brothers' treason.

But he wouldn't. His sympathies were with Nitzane.

And besides, Charald would thank him in one breath and turn on him in the next.

Chapter Fifty-One

TOBAZIM'S GIFT WAS unusual. He had the ability to perceive the weights and stresses involved in building. And his gift demanded to be used. It had driven him to examine the collapsed Mieren bridge. He hadn't expected Baron Nitzane to welcome his interference, but he had expected the Mieren to reply. First Nitzane hadn't responded when Tobazim inspected the bridge and sent him a message about the cause of its collapse. Then the baron hadn't made any move to rebuild the bridge, or to authorise Tobazim to repair it. ·

Tobazim understood the man was heartbroken; his wife had died when her carriage plunged into the river last winter. But since then, everyone, Mieren and T'Enatuath alike, who lived south of the bridge had to detour out of their way to use the Westborough Bridge. Nitzane was a baron and he had responsibilities to his people.

Tobazim had waited until spring and, when there was still no contact from the baron and no sign of the bridge being repaired, he could stand it no longer. His gift drove him to design a new bridge. He'd always thought the old one was in the wrong place. This was the fourth summer of poor rainfall and the river was running low, but he'd allowed for flood.

Now he studied the stone supports and the first graceful arch, which had been completed today. He was pleased with the way he'd built up the road so that it flowed smoothly onto the bridge.

'Admiring your handiwork?' Learon grinned and slung an arm around Tobazim's shoulders. They'd grown up as choice-brothers, and had remained fast friends during their initiate years. Now they were both adepts and wanted to go to the Celestial City to win stature.

'The bridge will be strong and serve its purpose, but it doesn't compare to the all-father's new theatre,' Tobazim admitted. 'I've heard the ceiling soars four storeys in the air–'

'Here comes Gift-tutor Nerasun.' Learon nudged him. 'Ask him now. Ask if we can go to the city.'

They'd asked this time last year, just before they became adepts, but the retired gift-warrior who ran the brotherhood winery had refused them.

At ninety-two, Nerasun had lived in the city during the High Golden Age. For some reason, he'd come out to the brotherhood's winery thirty-five years ago and never returned.

'Gift-tutor Nerasun.' Tobazim made obeisance. 'Everything is on schedule. When the bridge is complete, Learon and I were hoping we could–'

'Serve our brotherhood in the city?' Nerasun shook his head with a rueful smile. 'Why are the young always eager to leave? Is life so boring in the country?'

Learon looked to Tobazim, who tried to explain. 'Now that we are adepts...'

Nerasun took pity on them. 'You want to chase stature, I know, but... You've been raised on tales of the High Golden Age. Life in the city may not be what you expect. So many T'En, so many powerful gifts packed in together. The overflow affects even the strongest-willed men, driving them to–'

'We've been trained to shield against other T'En,' Learon said. 'And I've mastered every form of combat, armed and unarmed. I want to be the all-father's hand-of-force one day, and I can't do that here.'

Tobazim thought his choice-brother had a good chance. Learon was a head taller than him, and he wasn't short. To his frustration, his choice-brother had only to watch someone do an action to mimic it perfectly. It was impossible to play any sort of physical game against him without losing. Tobazim suspected his skill was tied to his gift.

'And you, Tobazim?' their old gift-tutor asked.

'I must build. My head is full of ideas and my gift drives me...'

Nerasun sighed. 'When the bridge is finished—'

Learon hugged him, lifting him off his feet.

Nerasun laughed and straightened his robe. 'When you do get to the city, look up Adept Kithkarne. He's an old friend of mine. He'll help you settle in. But there is a task I need you to do. The sisters have a lad who will turn seventeen soon. Athlyn's his name.'

'You want us to go to Silverlode Mine to collect him?' Tobazim tried to keep his voice neutral. They had not been back since they left, seventeen years ago. They might catch a glimpse of their old choice-mother. Might even get a chance to speak to her. 'What, just the two of us?'

'The air is thinner up there and the road steep. Old bones...' Nerasun shrugged. Their old gift-tutor climbed back into the cart. 'I hope All-father Kyredeon appreciates you two.'

IMOSHEN SMILED AS her choice-son settled the baby. Iraayel would be sixteen this winter's cusp. All being well, Ardonyx would be back by summer next year, maybe sooner.

Frayvia leant close to whisper. 'Reoden's here.'

Imoshen turned with a smile.

'A perfect little girl. How clever of you.' Reoden kissed Imoshen's cheek.

'Yes, very clever.' They both knew it was pure chance.

'They tell me you didn't let the sisters share the pain.'

'It wasn't as bad as the first time.' Imoshen shrugged. 'Vittoryxe is furious, by the way.'

'Vittoryxe is always furious.'

Imoshen laughed and the baby stirred.

Iraayel looked up. 'Did you see that? She likes it when you laugh. She smiled.'

'She's five days old,' Reoden said. 'It wasn't a smile, it was wind.'

'He's besotted with her,' Imoshen whispered. She glanced behind Reoden. 'You didn't bring Sardeon? We haven't seen him in ages, not since right after...' She didn't want to talk about the sacrare's death today.

A shadow moved over Reoden.

Imoshen drew the healer away. 'Is there something wrong with Sardeon because of the time he spent on the empyrean plane?'

'The gift-wright is working with him.'

'Oh, Ree, I'm so sorry. Will he be –'

'We don't know. Can I hold her?'

'Of course.' Imoshen collected the baby from Iraayel and sent him back to the lads. The sisters didn't approve of how much time he spent with her and the new baby. They thought he should keep his distance. No point getting attached to a little choice-sister he would not see grow up. A choice-sister who would not even remember him. Tears stung her eyes.

'Imoshen, what's wrong?'

She shook her head. 'I cry at the slightest thing.'

'It happens when the milk comes in. Makes us soft-hearted.' Reoden took the baby from her. 'What did you call her?'

'Umaleni.'

'*Joy so powerful it brings tears.* How appropriate.' Reoden slid an arm around Imoshen's shoulders. 'I've been thinking, and I'm sorry I wasn't more help to you when you first arrived here. You'd lost your little boy, and all we thought about was how to teach the brotherhoods a lesson.'

Imoshen nodded. She'd been thinking of Reoshen a lot lately. 'He would have been eleven this midwinter. But he didn't even live one day. When I had to leave him, I cut off my hair and wrapped him up in it like a shawl. That's how I buried him.' She wiped the tears from her cheeks. 'I've never told anyone else.'

'Oh, Imoshen. Things are going to get better now. You'll see.'

'All-mother?' It was Egrayne.

'You go,' Reoden said. 'I'll sing the baby to sleep.'

Imoshen kissed her cheek and joined Egrayne at the door. She hadn't wanted to move into the all-mother's chambers, but people were constantly coming to see her and she needed a proper greeting chamber, so she'd shifted her things in this morning.

From the nursery, they went through to her private chamber, where Frayvia was playing a game with Tancred. Poor thing, they'd told him his mother was gone, but he kept forgetting and looking for her.

Egrayne led her down a short hall, past her study, to the all-mother's greeting chamber, where a dozen of the top-ranking sisters waited to see her.

'What now?'

'You must appoint a hand-of-force, name your inner circle and accept their formal oaths. Then you must accept the formal oaths of the sisterhood. Then you must see the all-fathers of the brotherhoods who owe our sisterhood their covenant oath. They must renew their oaths to the sisterhood.'

'They aren't going to like that.' Imoshen's head was spinning and the sisters watched her expectantly.

'We've already waited four days,' Egrayne said, standing in pride of place on her left. 'Name your hand-of-force.'

That was easy. 'Arodyti, will you be my hand-of-force?'

Sarosune hugged her shield-sister. As Arodyti stepped forward, there were tears in her eyes.

'Name your inner circle, All-mother Imoshen,' Egrayne said.

Careful to accord Vittoryxe the honour due a gift-tutor, Imoshen named her first. She included old Tiasarone and Arodyti's shield-sister. All in all, she tried to balance Vittoryxe's supporters with those she knew to be neutral or supportive of Egrayne.

When this was done, everyone but the new inner circle left, and Egrayne handed her a sword.

'But T'En aren't allowed to carry–'

'It was Imoshen the Covenant-maker's sword,' Tiasarone told her. 'We were never going to hand it over to the Mieren.'

'She must have been as tall as Egrayne,' Imoshen said.

'She was a mighty warrior,' Arodyti agreed.

'Our inner circle gives their oaths of loyalty on this sword,' Egrayne said. 'Then it is locked away again.'

GRAELEN SENSED HE was being followed. Nothing would raise a warrior's stature faster than killing the brotherhood's assassin. When he reached the stairwell, he stepped to one side and reined in his gift.

Footsteps. Two sets. A whisper.

Just let them try to knife him, let them try. He wanted to crack heads, spill blood and let his gift exult.

Clearly, he'd spent too long in the city, walking Kyredeon's palace corridors, listening for rumours against the all-father; too long walking the brotherhood quarter, on alert for plots against him; and too long wandering the free quarter, watching the sisterhood gift-warriors for threat.

On a good day, he could convince the all-father that he had allayed all suspicion. But the bad days far outnumbered the good days.

If he didn't get out of the city soon, his gift would corrupt like poor Paryx and...

Here they came; two against one. He would kill the first one through the door, then he'd take his time with the other one.

He grabbed the first brother and slammed him up against the wall, knife to his throat. The elderly T'En gasped and blinked.

'Tithe-master Kithkarne!' Graelen stopped his blade. 'I'm so sorry.'

'Then let him go,' Ceyne said. The saw-bones was the only one of Kyredeon's inner circle Graelen trusted.

'Sorry,' he repeated, releasing the tithe-master. An explanation seemed in order. 'I thought you were following me.'

'We were.' Ceyne's voice was very dry. 'Kithkarne wants to speak with you.'

Graelen could not imagine why. The work he did for Kyredeon was on the shady side of brotherhood business. Both of these brothers owed their stature to the upright nature of their work.

'I think Kithkarne is feeling a little faint,' Ceyne said. 'We'd better take him to my chambers.'

Graelen helped the old tithe-master as they made their way through the palace corridors.

Once there, Ceyne shut the doors and Graelen turned to Kithkarne. 'You wanted to talk to me?'

The old tithe-master nodded. He did look shaken.

'Here.' Ceyne offered him a drink of something in a glass no bigger than his thumb. The liquid was cloudy and white.

Kithkarne took it and tossed back the contents. His eyes watered.

Graelen grinned. 'What is it?'

Ceyne poured two more, offering one to him. 'A restorative.'

'Looked like it nearly restored Kithkarne to death's realm.' He sniffed and then took a sip. It burned right down to his toes. He coughed. 'A... anise?'

'Yes, and sweet fennel and medicinal herbs. Thank you for coming. Kithkarne has found something, and wants you to go with him when he reports to Kyredeon.'

'The all-father's not in a good mood right now. Imoshen gave birth to a sacrare. She's been made all-mother and Kyredeon has to renew his covenant oath this afternoon.'

'She'll be even more powerful,' Ceyne whispered.

Graelen nodded. 'And no one knows who the sacrare's father is. As far as I've been able to discover, she never leaves the sisterhood quarter except to visit the Sagoras' shop, or attend jewellery-making classes in her sisterhood's shop.' Frustration ate at him. 'The infant was born on midsummer's day, which means it must have been conceived on or around midsummer last year. But none of the all-fathers have ever been successful in requesting a tryst with her.'

'What does it matter who the father is?' the tithe-master asked.

Graelen glanced to the saw-bones, to see if Kithkarne was serious.

'He's very good with numbers,' Ceyne said. *But clearly not with politics.*

'I'm much better with history than numbers,' Kithkarne said. 'That's how I put it all together.'

Graelen turned to Ceyne, lost.

'Start from the beginning,' the saw-bones advised, gesturing to the seats by the fireplace.

Kithkarne dropped into one with a sigh of relief.

'As you know, the burning of the theatre nearly crippled our brotherhood. The compensation payments to the other brotherhoods cost us valuable assets. Then there was the building of the new theatre.'

'It's the envy of all the other brotherhoods,' Graelen said. 'The marvel of the age.'

'It cost an arm and a leg, and for what? Stature?' Kithkarne shrugged. 'That's why I was so excited when I found the old debt.'

'What debt?'

'Start again, Kith,' Ceyne advised. 'Start when Kyredeon became all-father.'

'He purged every high-ranking brother. I only survived because I was living out at Vanillin-Oak Winery. He executed Sigorian's tithe-master and all his tithe-collectors. When they couldn't find anyone who knew how to make the counts add up, they sent for me. I told him I was a historian, not a mathematician, but he handed it all over to me, with two assistants who had never done more than add up a row of numbers. It was absurd.' The old scholar shook his head. 'For the first few years, I had to make it up as I went along. Sigorian's tithe-master had made some risky investments, backing Mieren ventures through intermediaries. I had no idea where the gold had gone, or when it was supposed to be paid back—'

'No one's blaming you,' Ceyne assured him.

'Kyredeon will,' Graelen corrected.

'The counts were a mess. That's why I didn't find it until now. My new assistant – the silly lad's all thumbs – knocked over a cabinet. While I was tidying up the mess I found this.' He pulled a folded sheet of thick vellum from inside his vest.

Graelen accepted it and opened it up. The writing was Chalcedonian and very faded. 'This must be forty or fifty years old.'

'Over forty. King Charald was only fifteen. That's his signature. The other two are Baron Nitzel and a priest called Oskane, who went on to become high priest.'

'So the Mieren king borrowed some gold.'

'Over forty years ago, that was a very large sum. Without it, he would have lost the kingdom. The barons revolted. His father died on the battlefield. The lad was a natural strategist. Why, in his first battle—'

Ceyne cleared his throat. 'We don't need a history lesson, Kith. Get to the interesting bit.'

'That *was* interesting.' But he shrugged and went on. 'The boy-king's advisors told him to sign this document. The gold we loaned him saved his kingdom. As far as I've been able to trace, he made a few payments on the loan, about twenty to twenty-five years ago, then nothing. No payments for over twenty years now.'

'And in all that time, the debt has been gathering interest,' Ceyne said. 'Show him your calculation, Kith.'

With a dramatic flourish, the tithe collector pulled out another sheet of paper and handed it to Graelen.

'But it's huge!'

'Charald, High King of the Secluded Sea, owes our brotherhood gold to the value of a kingdom,' Ceyne said, replenishing their drinks.

The tithe-master raised his glass. 'To a clumsy boy who knocked over a cabinet. If he hadn't, I would never have found this.'

'The Mieren king will never pay up,' Graelen said.

'No, he won't,' Kithkarne agreed. 'We don't expect him to. If we tried to get that much out of him, he'd be better off slitting our throats. No, we just want him to acknowledge the debt then I can negotiate a sum that will put our brotherhood in the clear and help us to re-establish ourselves.'

'You want to go to King Charald's palace?'

The tithe-master nodded. 'I want you to go with me to see Kyredeon and explain it all, and then you can come with me to the port to see the king. I'll need an escort as befits the representative of a great brotherhood. Charald doesn't need to know we're nearly destitute.'

Graelen's head reeled.

Ceyne squeezed his shoulder. 'It's good news, Grae. Kyredeon will be delighted. As long as he doesn't get greedy, we can save the brotherhood. This comes just in time, as Chariode and Hueryx have both caught wind that we're in trouble.'

'Yes.' The tithe-master bristled. 'They're trying to squeeze us out of ventures, and calling up loans to force us to declare our brotherhood insolvent.'

Graelen finally understood Kyredeon's paranoia. 'Right.' He came to his feet. 'We'll go see Kyredeon.'

And he would get out of the city before his gift corrupted.

Chapter Fifty-Two

SORNE FORCED OPEN the gate of Restoration Retreat. The place been empty since they'd left, in the spring eleven years ago. Now it was midday and a summer breeze stirred the leaves of the maple. He could remember the tree: winter-bare, full of spring buds and glowing yellow in autumn.

He looked around. There was the water pump where the penitents had bullied him and Izteben. That was the day Kolst punched Joaken. Back then, he and Izteben had thought they were brothers.

So many ghosts.

Time to lay one to rest.

Sorne went through the store rooms to the small graveyard where the penitents had been buried. The symbol of the Seven had been carved onto rocks and placed over each grave. He counted the grave-markers, but didn't find one for the she-Wyrd.

Of course not. She had no soul, according to the church.

Anger gnawed at him. He thought he'd come to terms with everything, but there it was – anger with Oskane for scourging them, and anger with himself for not being the man he should have been. He had a horrible feeling they had just ridden out that morning and left the she-Wyrd...

Sorne forced open the door to the main building. A feeling of dread settled on him as he went down to the cellar.

To his relief, time, insects and rodents had removed everything but her bones. She lay much as he remembered, sprawled on her back. Some of her bones had been gnawed.

His legs gave way and he sat abruptly.

Sobs shook him.

He wept for her, for Izteben, for the boy he'd been. And for Zabier, because he could not love the man he had become.

When he was done, he felt weary, but better.

He was not going to leave her bones here, but he didn't want to bury her with the True-men who had imprisoned her. So he laid out his blanket and gathered her remains, adding the trophies: her little finger bones and her hair. The last had remained virtually unchanged; rich copper waves.

It reminded him of Valendia. She would have just turned fifteen – he had to make sure she was safe.

Tying off the bundle of the she-Wyrd's remains, he left the cell. There was one more thing he wanted to do.

He went through the stable into the little kitchen Kolst had built for Hiruna. The table and chairs remained, and the cabinet. As he recalled Hiruna bustling about the kitchen, singing and laughing, it came to him that this was what he wanted for himself. Someone so loyal, they would defy convention for him. He wanted what Kolst had thrown away.

But who would have him?

The pain burned in his belly. For the first time since he'd recovered, he wondered how long before the wound killed him; if not directly, then indirectly, because he could not stand the pain and the remorse any longer.

As he left the stable, he looked up at Oskane's window. The priest had been a vindictive old man, who'd used people for his own ends. Sorne was glad he was nothing like him. Nothing like his father, either.

He was glad he'd been born a half-blood, otherwise he would have been the heir his father wanted, and then what would his life have been? One long battle after another, to stop ambitious men from stealing his throne.

He felt better. Coming here had settled more than the she-Wyrd's ghost. Time to lay her to rest.

There was a field, bordered by a stream, where he and his brothers used to go trout-fishing. In the spring the field was covered in wild flowers. That's where he went now. He chose a hollow, laid her out on the grass, covered her with the blanket then piled rocks on top.

Standing there under the open sky surrounded by mountain peaks, he felt satisfied. The she-Wyrd was free now.

The urge to see Hiruna and Valendia returned, stronger than ever. Sorne grabbed his travelling kit and set off.

TRAVELLING AS A blind cripple, Sorne accepted a ride with a farmer and his son, who were heading to market. Four piglets squealed in the back of the cart, as if aware their lives were going to be cut short. The smell was powerful, but at least he was headed in the right direction.

All afternoon he'd listened to the farmer's complaints. After four years of drought, if they did not get good spring rains, their farms would be nothing but dirt and brown stubble.

The six year-old pointed to green fields on a distant hill. 'What about there, Da?'

'Wyrds.' The farmer spat. 'They stole the best land. You can bet their wells don't run dry. Feckin' Wyrds.'

'Feckin' Wyrds,' the boy repeated.

Sorne made sure his sleeves covered his hands. Upon reaching the town, the farmer picked a prime spot in the crowded market field and Sorne was about to thank them and slip away when he heard shouting and jeering. The farmer stood in the cart, to see over the crowd.

'What is it, Da?'

'Stay here.' He tapped Sorne on the shoulder. 'Stay with m'boy.'

Sorne nodded. He was happy to wait. He didn't like the tone of the crowd, but the disturbance was all over pretty quickly and the farmer returned, dusting off his hands.

'What was it, Da?'

'Bit o' trouble with a local Wyrd. Here, jump down, lad. Make up the beds.' The farmer thrust some blankets into the boy's hands and drew Sorne away a little. 'Caught one of them copperheads walkin' down the main road, bold as anythin'. Sent him on his way.' He chuckled. 'That's if he can swim.'

Sorne thanked the farmer for the ride and headed off. He just wanted to get out of the field, with its many True-men and -women.

He heard the babble of a stream and felt his way down the bank. Once he was out of sight, he lowered the blind-man's bandage. There was just enough moonlight to make out the water, moving quite fast. No sign of the beaten half-blood. He'd either climbed out or been swept along. Sorne picked his way downstream until he came to a bend and found a dark shape snagged on a fallen trunk.

He waded out into the freezing water and grabbed the injured man, dragging him back to the edge. Sorne's stomach wound protested when he lifted the man onto the bank.

The half-blood's mouth was swollen, and he moaned as he regained consciousness. Seeing someone was crouching over him, he said, 'They've taken my purse. I don't have anything of value.'

'Except for your life. If you lie here wet all night, you'll catch a chill. Come on.'

Sorne struggled to his feet and helped him upright. More pain in his gut.

The man gasped and clutched his side. 'Why are you helping me?'

For answer, Sorne slid the bandage off his right hand and revealed his six fingers. 'Which way is home?'

The half-blood pointed up the bank, then shook his head. 'Better not use the road. I don't know what's wrong with them. I've been passing through here for thirty years and never had any trouble.'

'It's the drought. They say the Wyrds stole the best land and their wells never run dry.'

'If this drought keeps up, all the wells will run dry.'

Sorne slid his arm under the man's shoulder. They went along the stream bank, slipping in the long grass, staggering, struggling over fallen trees. The injured half-blood stopped to rest, and his breathing sounded bad; Sorne wondered if he would have to carry the man. 'How much farther?'

'Up the bank and across the road, to the Twin Oaks.'

'Can you make it?'

'I have to, don't I?' He reached for Sorne, who pulled him upright, but passed out before he could take another step.

When Sorne lifted the man across his shoulders, his stomach felt like it was tearing open. Would the wound start bleeding again? All the healers he had consulted had taken one look at the ragged, bloodless tear and backed off.

Somehow he made it up the bank, across the road and down the lane under the twin oaks. Adjusting the man's weight, he kept going. Eyes on the ground in front of him, he almost walked into a metal gate set in sandstone walls. Hoping someone was waiting for the man's return, Sorne called out in T'En.

A pool of lantern light fell over him. He spotted two Malaunje, one with a lantern, and an armed T'En woman. A gift-warrior? Sorne turned, so they could see the man he carried.

'Open the gate,' the gift-warrior ordered. 'It's Bedore.'

She stood back as the two Malaunje took the injured man from Sorne. His legs shook with relief.

'What happened?' the gift-warrior asked.

'The Mieren beat him, stole everything and threw him in the river.'

'You speak strangely.'

Sorne felt her gift rise. It was different from Graelen's but he still had to fight to resist the attraction. 'I'm not from around here.'

The gift-warrior grabbed him, swung him off his feet and slammed the gate shut. Before he could recover his balance, she'd thrust him up against the wall. The back of his head hit stone, and his teeth bit down on his tongue.

She held a knife to his throat. 'Which brotherhood are you from?' The knife point dug deeper. 'Which all-father sent you?'

He struggled to draw breath. The pain in his belly...

Sorne came around lying on his back in a tiny room. He could smell roast beef and hear voices arguing. He was naked under a rough blanket, and his head hurt.

'...looked suspicious, with that hood,' the warrior was saying. He could just see her in the doorway. 'How was I to know he was a cripple?'

'Well, Bedore says the stranger dragged him from the river and helped him back here. We must at least give him shelter for the night.' This was an older, richer voice. 'If you've injured him and his all-father protests, we'll have to pay compensation.'

'His injuries look old. Did you see that wound on his belly?' Her horror and disgust came across clearly.

Sorne forced himself up on one elbow, swung his legs to the floor and looked for his clothes. He saw them on a chair, along with his poor-man's bundle, which held the torc and orb. He didn't know what the sisterhood would do if they discovered he used to be the Warrior's-voice. He had to get out of here.

'Oh, no you don't.' A plump T'En woman entered. She placed her hands on his bare shoulders and pushed him back onto the bed. It did not take much effort on her part. He could not sense her gift at all.

'I'm fine.' He brushed at her hands.

'Is that what you call it? I'm the herbalist. I'm here to look you over.'

He held the blanket to his chest.

She eyed him thoughtfully before turning to her companion. 'Go away, Karyxe.'

'I'll be just outside, if you need me.' She shut the door.

'I'm fine,' Sorne told the herbalist. 'Food and sleep will see me right.'

'Karyxe tells me there's a wound on your stomach.'

'It's old.'

'Then it won't hurt to let me see.'

He realised he wasn't going to win this argument and released the blanket. She examined the wound, and he watched her face, ready for revulsion.

She frowned. 'This should have been seen to when it first happened. If one of the sisters treated her devotee like you've been treated...' She shook her head. 'Well, it just wouldn't happen.'

He didn't answer. He wasn't sure what she was talking about.

'Too loyal for your own good.' She examined him further, clucking over his old scars and burns. 'It's a wonder you're still walking, but you're right. There's nothing I can do for you. The sisterhood offers you food and shelter for tonight and longer, if you need it.'

Sorne shook his head.

'Have it your way.' She came to her feet and dusted off her hands. 'But I will say this. It's a disgrace, the way they've treated you. And as for sending you out to spy... Yes, I saw your blind-man's costume. Consider this. The Mieren roughed up Bedore just for being a half-blood. If they catch you spying, they'll string you up.'

The Malaunje brought him hot food, and took his clothes away to be laundered.

They next morning, he had a hearty breakfast and dressed in clean clothes. When he reached the gate, they gave him a well-made leather travelling kit, packed with a clean blanket and food for the journey.

He set off, aware that a lot of what Oskane had told him about his own people was an outright lie. The new leather travelling kit was too good for his disguise, but his old poor-man's bundle was literally falling apart. So he put it inside the new bag and rubbed dirt on the leather, until it looked grimy.

Restored, he set off for Port Mirror-on-Sea.

Chapter Fifty-Three

TOBAZIM WONDERED IF he had looked so young the day he left the sisterhood's estate to start his life with the brotherhood. It did not help that Athlyn was a particularly pretty youth. At almost seventeen, he could have passed for a girl, although certainly not naked, as he was now.

Learon handed him clothes, boots and cloak. It was late summer, but the nights were cold in the mountains.

While Athlyn dressed, Tobazim studied the front of Silverlode Retreat. It looked much the same as it had during his childhood. The sandstone glowed in the midday sun. Several white-haired T'En children peered down curiously from the walkway above the defensive wall. He could remember doing the same, and wishing he was grown up. But, when the day came for his choice-mother to declare him dead to her, he had not wanted to go.

He'd been afraid his non-martial gift would make him a target in the brotherhood. Sensing this, his choice-mother had had taken him aside.

It's easy to kill and destroy, she'd told him, holding his ink-stained fingers in her hands. *It is much harder to build and grow. The things you build will live on after you. Take pride in that.*

Not long after he'd arrived in the brotherhood winery, he'd found a silver nib in his bedroll with no explanation for how it got there. But he knew his mother had asked one of the brotherhood Malaunje to give it to him, as a sign of her faith in him.

Now the children parted, as she appeared on the wall-walk. He waved and shaded his eyes.

'Look at you, Tobazim,' his choice-mother said. 'All grown up.'

The sound of her voice was enough to make him smile.

'Not as big as me,' Learon boasted. Coming up behind Tobazim, he caught him in a headlock and knuckled his head as if they were twelve. The children laughed.

'I doubt there are many as big as you, Learon.' There was love in their choice-mother's voice.

Learon released him. Tobazim straightened his clothes and brushed hair from his eyes.

'Watch over Athlyn for me,' she said. 'He's a good boy.'

They glanced to the youth, who was sitting on the mounting block, tying his boot straps.

'I'll check his mount's stirrups,' Learon said, heading off with a wave to their choice-mother.

'We would watch over him,' Tobazim said, 'but after we deliver Athlyn, we're going to the city.'

'That's... Things have not been good in the city. An all-father broke his covenant oath, and the healer's sacrare daughter was killed.'

'We heard.' He glanced over his shoulder. Learon was waiting, holding the horses' reins. Athlyn sat in the saddle.

'I heard about your bridge.'

'It's going to stand for hundreds of years.' He couldn't keep the pride from his voice.

She smiled. 'When you reach the city, be careful of Kyredeon. The all-mothers don't trust him.'

'He executed the two brothers who killed the sacrare. He knew nothing of their plans.'

'Of course.'

It was obvious that she believed the worst of All-father Kyredeon. Tobazim was disappointed.

'I'll look for your name,' she said.

'And I'll keep your silver nib safe.'

*   *   *

GRAELEN INSPECTED THE Mieren king's greeting chamber.
It was as fine as anything in the Celestial City – marble
floor, frescoed ceiling, intricate screens over the windows.

'Built in the last thirty years,' Kithkarne whispered.
They were both very aware of the Mieren guard on the
door. 'This is where the king's gold went, instead of
repaying us.'

Graelen glanced to the door. The Mieren guard met his
eyes, then looked away quickly. They thought T'En could
overcome their will and enslave them with a glance.

Kithkarne settled in a chair and placed the leather
folder holding his notes on the table. He looked pale.
They'd carried him in a cart and taken it slowly, making
the journey in six days instead of four, but the old brother
had still found it taxing. Then, this morning, they'd had
to wait for an hour in the grand hall with everyone else
who wanted to have an audience with the king, before a
servant led them to this chamber.

Graelen's stomach rumbled. It was lunchtime, now, and
he could smell food cooking somewhere in the palace. He
hoped the king would see them soon.

They were kept waiting all day, and by dusk he was
starving. A servant arrived to say the king been delayed
and wouldn't be able to see them. Four guards waited to
escort them from the palace.

Infuriated, Graelen had to help Kithkarne to rise.

The old male winced as he bent to collect his folder.
With dignity, he straightened up and informed the
servant, 'You can tell King Charald we will come every
day, until he sees us.'

They returned to Chariode's warehouse, where
Dragomyr was intensely curious as to why they wanted
to see the Mieren king.

*   *   *

ZABIER ENTERED THE queen's private chamber on a wave of delicious anticipation. It seemed he was fated to fall in love with unattainable women.

Strictly speaking, since priests were meant to be celibate, all women were unattainable for him. But the last king's daughter – poor Marantza, who had died so tragically – and the new king's wife were unattainable for almost all men. Why couldn't he settle for some poor girl who would be grateful for a roof over her head and food in her belly, in exchange for certain favours?

No, he had to desire Queen Jaraile. Not desire... *love*.

Whoever had decreed that priests should be celibate was a fool. Men were not meant to go without a woman's touch. The more he tried not to think of it, the harder it became. Lucky for him, the priestly robe could have been designed specifically to hide his indiscretion.

Poor Jaraile. In late winter, the queen had lost her newborn and her father within a day and, ever since then, she'd turned to him for advice. Here she came now, slipping into the chamber almost at a run.

She was a small woman, with soft curves and slightly protruding front teeth that made her top lip beg to be kissed; he found her mouth fascinating.

'Father's-voice, thank you for coming.' She hurried over to him, carried on the whisper of silk and the scent of jasmine. 'I'm at my wit's end. I don't know what to do.'

'Tell me. I'm sure I can help.' It would be Charald, curse him. Ever since poor Jaraile delivered the blue baby son, his rages had been getting worse. At least when her father was alive, the baron could calm the king. Since Jantzen's sudden death, it had been left up to the queen and himself, and they didn't have the knack. 'Is the king in a rage?' Again.

'No, but he soon will be. I've just come back from visiting the Mother's church. You know how I pray every day that she'll give me a healthy baby...'

Zabier nodded. *He'd* give her a healthy baby. There was something wrong with Charald's seed. All those blue babies his last queen had produced, and now Jaraile.

'...coming back to the palace, I overheard some milliner apprentices talking.' She clutched his arm, hands trembling. 'They know about Prince Cedon's club foot. If apprentices know, everyone must know. The king...'

Naturally, the king wanted to keep his son's deformity quiet. He'd been consulting healers to see if they could fix the boy. Zabier had lost all faith in healers after he'd been defrauded of a small fortune, while his mother was dying.

'Father's-voice?' She saw his expression. 'I knew it. He'll have me killed and get himself another wife. He killed his first two wives.'

Zabier didn't deny this. 'Have faith, my queen. You'll give him a healthy son.' It would amuse him to cuckold the king and see his own son on the throne. If he could convince Jaraile that her life depended on producing a healthy boy, he might stand a chance. She was as morally upright as Marantza had been. Mind you, he'd been a callow youth back then, and terrified of her father. King Matxin seemed to be able to look into his heart and know exactly what he was thinking or feeling.

The day Matxin died, he wanted to ring the church bells in celebration, but instead he'd ordered the bell ringers to sound a dirge. Marantza had been stoic, relieved by the time her father's suffering ended. Back then, he'd been so shy, he hadn't done more than confess his love and try for a kiss. For which she'd magnanimously forgiven him, then turned around and run off with Baron Nitzane. Curse him.

'Would it help if I prayed?' Jaraile asked.

'I'll pray with you.' He knelt, and she knelt with him. He pulled her closer, pressing her cheek against his chest. 'Say what is in your heart, my child.'

Her prayer poured out of her, revealing all her fears and the king's growing weakness. For all his boasting, Charald could not maintain an erection and, if he did, he couldn't get to his release. Zabier learnt all this from her delicately-phrased prayers.

Silently, he thanked King Matxin. Eight years of watching how that king manipulated and used people had trained him for this.

When Matxin came to power, he'd been afraid the king would order Hiruna's execution and hand Valendia over to the priests for sacrifice. Zabier had not dared to protest, as the king wanted ever grander offerings to impress the high church officials and keep his nobles in line, not even when those offerings included half-blood infants. He'd had to make himself cold inside to save Hiruna and Valendia. The Zabier who did those things was a different Zabier from the one who rubbed his mother's feet in winter and bought his sister musical instruments.

So different was he, that when Sorne had asked about half-blood sacrifices, Zabier had been genuinely horrified.

After living in fear for so many years, Zabier never wanted to be powerless again. He'd thought, when he took advantage of the holy-swords' insurrection and talked the king into sending Sorne away, he would replace Sorne in the king's trust. But Charald had proved a capricious master, and nothing anyone did satisfied him. These last three years had convinced Zabier he could not go on living like this.

Jaraile's hot tears seeped through his robe and warmed his heart. And elsewhere. Time to plant the seed of doubt in her mind. 'Tell me, do you welcome the king into your bed?'

'I do my best.'

'So did the last queen. She bore him one boy, then six blue babies.'

Jaraile swallowed. 'You think–'

'I think you must give the king a healthy son, or...' He waited for her to make the connection. It would be so much better if she came to him. 'Pray with me again.'

Poor little thing. She prayed so earnestly. And that top lip...

The door flew open. A shaft of light illuminated Zabier
with the queen. From where Zabier knelt, the king
appeared huge in silhouette. Zabier was grateful he hadn't
given in to the urge to kiss the queen.

'There you are, Jaraile. Praying again? Fat lot of good
that does.'

The queen sprang to her feet and made her bow. 'My
king, I–'

Charald ignored her. 'Despite your grand offerings,
Zabier, you and this True-man Warrior's-voice can only
come up with vague visions. Sorne used to offer relics, yet
his visions came true.'

Sorne, always Sorne. First his own brother Izteben, then
his mother and Valendia, and now King Charald.

'The gods are capricious, my king,' Zabier said. Matxin
had never worried if the visions did not come true. He'd
used them to justify getting rid of his enemies. Feeling a
fraud and desperate for visions of his own, Zabier had
resorted to the pure form of pains-ease to produce visions,
but even these did not come true. Now he took the pure
pains-ease because he liked the way it made him feel –
powerful. Only Utzen knew his secret vice.

'Forget the gods, I have more pressing problems.'

Zabier noticed the queen tensing, but Charald sent her
away. As soon as the door closed, he began to pace. Zabier
recognised the signs. He could go like this for days, hardly
sleeping, wearing out servants and nobles alike.

'A delegation of Wyrds wanted an audience today. I kept
them waiting. They stayed all day. They had the audacity
to say they'd come back every day until I saw them.'

Zabier lifted his hands. 'If you found out what they
wanted–'

'I know what they want. I want you to find a way
to use the gods against the Wyrds. I've seen the gods
devour half-bloods and T'En artefacts. Would they
accept a living full-blood? I suspect they would. I want
you to work out a way to harness the gods so we can

use them as a weapon against the Wyrds. I want to wipe out Cesspit City.'

'Sire...' Zabier could hardly speak, his mouth was so dry. 'If we turned the gods loose, they could...' *devour us all*.

'That's why you need to get Oskane's chest back from Nitzane. There's seventeen years of notes in there. Oskane set out to find a way to defeat the Wyrds. Put your priests to work.'

'Right away, sire.' Zabier made his bow and left.

GRAELEN FINISHED HIS meal and left the tithe-master playing cards with the old sea captain. They were having a wonderful time trying to outdo each other with outrageous tales. If you believed everything they said, the brotherhood feuds were ten times fiercer, the gifts more powerful, the duels more deadly and the women more beautiful when they were young.

He found Harosel waiting for him in his chamber.

'There's a rumour the king's son is deformed,' Harosel said.

'The barons will refuse to follow him if that's the case.' Graelen shrugged this aside. It had been three years since the all-father had told him there were no missing Malaunje infants but... 'There haven't been any half-blood babies delivered to the warehouse. Do you know if–'

'There's been any handed in to the other warehouse? No, but I can ask Paragian's people, and while I'm at it, I'll speak with All-mother Imoshen's port Malaunje.'

'Do that. And while you're out and about tonight, see if you can discover if the rumour about the king's heir is true,' Graelen said, wondering if it benefited the T'Enatuath to offer to heal the boy.

DESPITE THE T'EN sister's advice, Sorne had resumed his costume for the rest of the journey back to port. He saw field after field of dying crops. In Port Mirror-on-Sea, the drought was felt in the price of fresh fruit and vegetables. Dust billowed in the street, and in the royal plaza the trees drooped in the heat. Evidence of hard times, the church's poor-door courtyard was packed with the destitute. Sorne thought only of seeing Hiruna and Valendia.

It was almost dusk when he managed to slip into the Father's church. From the public chambers, he made his way through to the private corridors. There he hid until the bells rang calling the priests to prayer, when he made his way to the chambers of the Father's-voice.

Where he found Zabier's assistant, Utzen, hard at work.

'Yes? Do you have an appointment?' The old priest didn't look up from his work. 'The Father's-voice is not here. He was called to the palace.'

That suited Sorne. 'It's me, Sorne. I've come to see–'

'You...' Utzen went white. 'They told us you were dead.'

'Not yet. But I have lost my key, so if you'll just...'

'I can't. Only the Father's-voice has a key.' And clearly, he wasn't going to let Sorne past.

'I have to know. Hiruna...'

The old priest shook his head.

'When?' Sorne could hardly speak.

'The second winter after you sailed.'

A roaring filed his ears.

'Come back tomorrow, around this time.'

Stunned, Sorne did not object when Utzen summoned penitents to escort him out.

ZABIER RETURNED TO the church, deep in thought. If Charald was going to mount a campaign against the Wyrds, Valendia wasn't safe. He'd have to move her. The only safe place he could think of was the crypts. The old priest who'd shown him around had claimed the crypts predated the churches, and had been natural caverns. He'd shown Zabier paintings in caverns far below the earth. The old priest was long dead, and Zabier doubted anyone else knew more than a passage or two, from where they'd laid their own dead to rest.

He didn't want to shut Valendia away from the sun, but if it meant saving her life...

Opening the door to his private chambers, he found his usually unflappable assistant pacing.

Utzen hurried over to shut the door. 'I sent him away. I hope I did the right thing.'

'Who? Sent who away?'

'The half-blood who used to visit your...' He glanced upwards significantly.

'Sorne?'

'Walked in here, large as life, and asked me to let him in. He'd lost his key. I told him I didn't have one, and to come back tomorrow evening. I hope I did the right–'

'You did. Quick thinking.' Zabier found he was shaking. He would have to take Valendia down to the crypts tonight, and hide her.

'I told him about Hiruna. He asked, and I didn't see any point in lying.'

'Doesn't matter. Find five priests you trust and bring them here.'

As Utzen left, Zabier unlocked the door. Sorne was not going to turn Valendia against him. He ran up the steps, heart hammering.

She was eating on the terrace, but she sprang to her feet when he arrived. 'Zabier. If I'd known you were coming, I could have made enough for two. I'll–' She broke off, seeing his expression. 'What's wrong?'

'It's not safe here anymore. You need to come with me.'

'Why? What's happened?'

'The king's going to make war on the Wyrds.' *And Sorne's come back, but he can't have you.* He caught her hand. 'Get your things.'

She ran into her private chamber. He followed, and watched as she gathered her instruments. She wrapped them in her clothes, moving with natural grace. The sway of her hips, the curve of her waist, the way her long hair swept over her shoulder and fell past her breasts. She was fifteen, taller than him and very much a woman. She was too lovely for her own good. No man was going to lay a hand on her, not if he had anything to say about it.

She looked up as a thought struck her. 'Sorne's vision was right.'

'What?'

'Remember the message you sent to Adept Graelen?'

The message Zabier had burned without reading. 'Yes.'

'Sorne sent it to him because he'd had a vision of bad things happening to half-bloods.'

If he'd known this earlier, he could have claimed the vision as his own.

'What's made the king turn on the Wyrds?' she asked.

'I don't know. They've sent a T'En delegation to see him, and it's upset him. Just bring what you can carry for now. I'll get the rest to you later.'

'I have everything I want.' She rolled up in the blanket and swung it over her shoulder. 'I'm ready.'

He led her out into the main room. 'Are you sure there isn't anything else?'

'I have my instruments. I don't think... Oh, there's that.' She pointed to a camphorwood chest. 'I promised I'd mind it for Sorne, but he's not coming back.'

What could be so precious that Sorne would leave it here, rather than take it with him? 'Have you ever opened it?'

'Of course not.'

'Good girl.' He took her hand and drew her down the stairs. In his private chamber, he found a cloak and hood for her, drawing it over her head to hide her glorious hair. 'Keep your eyes down and hands hidden. Don't speak.'

His assistant and five priests had gathered in his study. They looked up expectantly when he entered. He didn't care if the five priests thought she was his mistress; only his assistant knew the truth.

At the door he told her to wait, then went back to his assistant, keeping his voice low so Valendia would not hear. 'Strip the apartment. Get rid of everything but the camphorwood chest by the entrance. Put that in my bedchamber. I want the apartment to look as if it has been empty for at least a year.'

Utzen asked no questions.

Taking a lamp, Zabier led Valendia to the nearest crypt entrance.

'We're going down there? I thought you'd take me—'

'Where? To the Wyrds? Do you think I want you dead?' He turned and held her eyes. 'Do you trust me, Dia?'

'Of course.'

He led her into the crypts. The upper tunnels had been finished with neat stone columns and arches. There were niches for lamps and statues, and antechambers where the remains of high-ranking church officials lay in darkness. The air was dry, dusty and cold.

'Was that a skull?' Valendia whispered.

He raised the lamp. It was a skull, sitting in a wall niche. 'Listen.' He turned her chin so that she looked at him. 'I have to hide you amongst the dead to save your life. But don't worry. I'll leave you a lamp and adequate oil to keep it burning. If anyone else but me comes, hide. I'll be back tomorrow with food, and we'll find you a safer place. You'll be all right for now. You have your pipes and books. You can play as much music as you like down here.'

'But no one will hear it.'

He handed her the lamp, then lit a candle for himself.

'Thank you, Zabier.' She hugged him. Soft curves, racing heart; a woman's body.

Seeing her there, with her copper hair glinting in the lamplight, surrounded by darkness, he was reminded of the she-Wyrd. But Valendia was not going to end up like her. Not even if he had to lock her away from everyone.

Back in his chamber, he lit a lamp and opened the camphorwood chest. After removing some foreign rubbish, he found two compartments. One contained a bag of stones, which he recognised as malachite. The other contained Oskane's journals, and some scrolls.

Not just any scrolls. They were the missing Wyrd scrolls, which no one had been able to find for the last thirty years. Oskane must have taken them.

He went looking for Utzen. In the private apartment above, he found one of the priests mopping the polished wooden floors. Through the glass doors, he saw his assistant and another priest pulling the flowers and vegetables out by the roots and stuffing them into a couple of baskets. Zabier had to hand it to him, Utzen was thorough.

Zabier drew his assistant aside. 'Leave that for him to finish. The king has given me a special commission. I need fifty of our best scholars. They must be discreet. If the king learns that they've gossiped he'll cut out their tongues.' The priests would believe this; the king's rages had become legendary. 'We'll set aside a large chamber for the work. The priests bring nothing in and they take nothing out. I have some precious scrolls and journals that need to be analysed. The king wants the answer to a very important question. How to destroy the Wyrds.'

SORNE WAS TIRED and hungry. The food the sisterhood had given him had run out yesterday. If this had been a small country village in one of the southern kingdoms, he would have offered to read fortunes in the local tavern. But, after seeing what had happened to the sisterhood's half-blood servant, he didn't want to risk exposure.

He bought a pie from a street vendor, then made his way to the wine cellar. The door was locked, but he forced it open and crept downstairs. When he lit his candle stub, he found the cellar just as he remembered. He would sleep here tonight, and leave a message in the morning.

If Graelen was in the city, they would meet here.

But he didn't expect it would be as easy as all that. He planned to take Valendia to the Celestial City, for he had learned one thing in his travels.

Wyrds were vastly outnumbered by True-men. For every friend Sorne had found, there had been a hundred who despised him on sight.

Chapter Fifty-Four

ZABIER HURRIED TO answer to the queen's summons, sick dread filling him. But if he wanted to win her, he had to protect her from the king. He found Jaraile in the corridor wringing her hands.

'It's the Wyrds,' she whispered. 'They're in the greeting chamber. They came first thing this morning, and they've been waiting ever since. Charald refuses to see them.'

'What do they want?'

'I don't know. He won't tell me and he's acting strangely.'

'Don't worry. Everything is going to be all right. I'm already working on it.' Zabier caught her hands in his and squeezed them. 'I'll go in and see him.'

'Oh, thank you.' Tears glittered in her eyes. 'I don't know what I'd do without you.'

Zabier found the king slumped in front of the fire, elbows on his knees, head in his hands. It was unusual to see him sitting still, let alone looking dejected. As Zabier cautiously approached, he realised the king was muttering under his breath.

Charald looked up and saw him. 'There you are. The Wyrds, they haunt me. It was all your idea, Oskane. You and Nitzel advised me. It's your fault they're here.'

Startled to find himself addressed as Oskane, Zabier took a step back. Jaraile had said the king was acting strangely. Was he losing his mind? 'Sire?'

Charald sprang to his feet. 'Arrogant Wyrds...' And he was off again, pacing and ranting, but at least he now recognised Zabier.

Zabier said all the right things and eventually managed to calm the king. Then he set out to discover why the Wyrd delegation had unnerved Charald.

'WOULD YOU CARE for another curried egg?' Kithkarne asked. The plump tithe-master had insisted they come prepared with food, drink and books to read, while they waited for the king.

Graelen resented the need for this but he had to admit he'd rather not go hungry. It was mid-afternoon now, and he was getting restless.

Just then a priest in rich robes entered, closing the door after him. Graelen recognised him as the Father's-voice, and thought of Sorne, who had been sent to Maygharia on the king's business only to be killed in the uprising.

The priest made a shallow bow. 'I am–'

'The Father's-voice,' Graelen said.

'At your service.' The Mieren smiled briefly, his gaze settling on Graelen's brotherhood torc, avoiding his eyes.

Graelen glanced behind him to Kithkarne, who was sitting elegantly, fanning himself with High Golden Age grace, as if he had not been polishing off pickles and curried eggs a moment before.

'Tithe-master Kithkarne, of Kyredeon's brotherhood,' Graelen introduced his companion. 'And I'm his assistant, Gift-warrior Graelen.'

'King Charald has asked me to discover the nature of your business.'

'It concerns the king's debt,' Kithkarne said, sorting through his papers.

As the tithe-master explained the origin of the debt and what it now amounted to, Graelen observed the Father's-voice. He wore the white robes of a priest, and a rich brocade vestment. A small, flat-topped cap sat on his head, and his hair hung down his back in rippling waves. In the shaft of light from the window, it had a gingery tinge. He was young, but then these Mieren lived such short lives. If he was twenty-five, his life was already half over.

According to Sorne, they could trust him.

'So there it is, the final figure,' Kithkarne said.

The Father's-voice looked at the number and went pale.

'I've made two copies, one for the king and one for his advisors. I assure you, the workings are accurate.'

Very slowly, the Father's-voice rolled up the copies and tied them neatly. 'This is a very large sum.'

'That's what happens when payments are not made and interest accrues,' Kithkarne said, somewhat primly.

'We are aware the sum has become unwieldy, and we understand the king spent eight years outside of Chalcedonia,' Graelen said. 'During this time, he could not have made payments. We are open to negotiation.'

'The king will...' The Father's-voice cleared his throat. 'I will speak with him. It is almost autumn cusp. King Charald has many official duties. I should think the earliest you could expect to hear from him would be fifteen days after autumn cusp.'

Graelen drew breath, but the old tithe-master beat him to it.

'Very well. You'll see us on that day.'

As they rode home in Chariode's carriage, Graelen complained, 'Why make us wait fifteen days?'

'We've waited over forty years. We can wait fifteen days.'

The carriage stopped at an intersection, and Graelen could hear Mieren arguing.

'This is all most diverting. Dragomyr would love to know our business with the king. He sent that pretty Malaunje woman to keep me distracted while one of his men searched my chamber.' The tithe-master's eyes twinkled and he patted his leather folder. 'Never leaves my side.'

Harosel appeared at the window of the stationary carriage. 'A word?'

Graelen excused himself.

'You play your games.' Kithkarne waved him off. 'I'll play mine.'

Graelen was grinning as he climbed out of the carriage.

Harosel drew him into an empty lane and pressed a folded scrap of paper into his hand. It looked like it had been torn from a broadsheet. On the top was Sorne's signal. Graelen's stomach dropped. 'Where did you find this?'

'Where do you think? In the wine cellar.' Harosel met his eyes. Despite his dry manner, he was excited. 'Only the three of us knew about the message drop.'

'Unless he told someone.' Graelen looked down, almost unwilling to open it. More than three years gone, two years dead... 'Why did you even check the cellar?'

'I always check when I'm in the port.'

Graelen shook his head and opened the message. 'This is his handwriting.'

'And it bears yesterday's date.'

'You read it?'

'In case it was a forgery. He'll be waiting there tonight.'

Graelen looked up. 'Almost dusk.'

'Do you want me to come along?'

'No. I can't believe... Everyone thinks him dead.'

'It's the best way to avoid assassination.'

Graelen laughed. 'What did you learn last night?'

'Nothing. My contacts have moved on, or weren't in their old haunts. I'll go back tonight and see if I can strike up a friendship with more of the king's palace guards.'

Graelen hesitated. 'Be careful. Dragomyr tells me two of his people were followed and beaten on the street.'

Harosel stiffened. 'I've been slipping into Mieren taverns and whorehouses since before you were born.'

'Right. I'm off to the wine cellar. See you tomorrow. By then, we'll both have something interesting to report.'

* * *

SORNE HAD SPENT the day wandering the port. Now he was tired and hungry, but looking forward to seeing Valendia. The news that Hiruna was dead had come as a blow. It made Valendia all the more precious to him. He'd timed his arrival with the evening prayer bells, and now he made his way to Zabier's chambers.

The assistant was ready. Utzen glanced to the connecting door. 'He's waiting.'

Sorne went through, found the little door open and climbed the steep, narrow stair. His heart raced in anticipation.

Even before he stepped into the apartment, he knew something was wrong. There was nothing, not a stick of furniture.

Zabier turned to Sorne, who brushed past him and going from room to room. All empty.

'Where is she?' he demanded. 'What have you done with her?'

Zabier gave him a sympathetic look.

'No...' He took a step back, his shoulders hitting the door frame. 'She can't be–'

'More than a year ago now.' Zabier's voice caught.

'How?'

'It was just after her fourteenth birthday. She complained of stomach pains. I offered to send for a healer, but she didn't want me to get in trouble for sheltering her...'

A moan escaped Sorne.

'Here, sit down.' Zabier led him out onto the terrace. They sat on the broad edge of the raised garden bed.

Sorne remembered Hiruna tending the vegetables and flowers, and how Valendia had played her music for him. 'I hope you–'

'I did. I overrode her wishes and brought in a healer. She went down very rapidly. He said there was nothing anyone could have done. I know it's a shock. I'll give you time.'

And Zabier went downstairs to his chambers.

Sorne stared at the screened terrace. This had been the extent of her world... it wasn't fair. Valendia had hardly lived at all.

He was so angry...

Sorne turned and pounded his fists into the empty flower bed. His hands sank deep into the moist, soft soil.

WHEN SORNE CAME down, Zabier was ready with an explanation for the whereabouts of his chest. He was going to say it had all been disposed of. But Sorne appeared too stunned to think.

Why did he have to come back? Zabier had grown used to the idea that he was dead, and now...

'What will you do?' Zabier asked.

Sorne shook his head and wandered away.

As Zabier watched him go, Utzen joined him at the door.

'Now?' his assistant asked.

'Yes. Now.' Zabier hated being forced to do this, but he had to protect Valendia.

The little man hurried off to alert the thugs who'd been hired to kill Sorne, weigh his body with stones and drop it in the bay, where it would sink without a trace. No one would know he'd come back from the dead, however briefly.

SORNE WALKED WITHOUT seeing. He had tried to hold onto hope for Hiruna, but her death had not surprised him. Valendia's death, however...

He heard shouts behind him, ugly jeers that turned the word *Wyrd* into a curse. Stepping into the shadows of a doorway, he saw a dozen palace guards drag an unfortunate Wyrd from a whorehouse opposite. The guards were followed by about two dozen True-men and -women, all eager to witness the Wyrd's humiliation.

'What's going on?' smeone called from a first floor window above Sorne.

'The king's guard caught a Wyrd spy passing himself off as a True-man. He was asking questions about the prince!'

Sorne flinched, for he had passed himself off as a True-man many times. Aware that he was risking his life, he followed the crowd. They were all so intent on the fate of the captive, no one paid him any attention.

Once Sorne had commanded men; now, he watched impotently as a shop sign was chosen, and a rope and a chair were found. Helpless to save the captive, he curled his hands into fists and felt the damp, gritty soil of Valendia's empty garden grind into his palms.

Damp?

There hadn't been rain for ages. The only way the soil could be damp was if someone had watered it recently.

He lifted his hands to his face and smelled fresh, fecund earth. This was not the dried, dead soil of an abandoned garden.

Zabier had had a day's warning. Enough time to take Valendia away, empty the apartment and strip the garden beds.

Zabier must have hidden her.

Hope filled him.

He looked up across the heads of the crowd to the badly beaten Wyrd. Several guards restrained him, while someone made a noose.

Was that...? Sorne stepped into the light as he recognised Harosel. His hand went to the sword hilt he no longer wore.

Harosel saw Sorne across the heads of the jeering crowd, and gave the slightest shake of his head.

The instinct to go to Harosel's aid was so strong Sorne found he'd taken several steps before he knew it. Again, Harosel shook his head and jerked his chin as if to say, *get out of here.*

Sorne didn't want to leave him.

The king's guards threw the rope over the shop sign, looped the noose around his neck and hoisted him onto the chair. Before it was knocked out from under him, Harosel yelled Graelen's name in what appeared to be defiance.

But it was a message for Sorne.

Graelen was here in the city. Maybe even in the wine cellar right now, just a couple of blocks away.

Sorne edged away as the crowd cheered Harosel's death throes. Backing off fast, he rounded the corner, then ran. He'd reached the end of the block when two men came out of an alley ahead of him.

He slowed to a walk, and veered to the other side of the street. As he passed a dark lane, arms reached out, caught him and pulled him off his feet.

He dropped and twisted, breaking their hold. Three men confronted him, one coming at him with a knife. Sorne side-stepped, grabbed his arm and pulled him off balance, before sending him head first into the nearest wall. The knife went flying.

As Sorne turned, a fist slammed into his stomach, right over his unhealed wound. He staggered, almost blacking out with the pain. One of his attackers tackled him, driving him into the wall. His head hit the boards and he fell to his knees, curling into a ball. His hand closed on a stone.

He panted through the pain. One of his attackers came at him. Waiting until the last moment, he slammed the rock into the thug's face. Heard the crunch of breaking bone.

It was a struggle to come to his feet. Everything hurt, everything was too much effort.

The last attacker lunged. Sorne saw the flash of a blade and only just managed to avoid it. They grappled. Somehow, he forced the knife up into the attacker's ribs. The man fell.

Sorne swayed. His vision came and went. Blinking blood from his eye, he saw three unmoving bodies. He had to get out of here.

After gathering his belongings, he stumbled into the alley mouth and pulled his hood over his head.

He needed to reach the wine cellar, but didn't know if he could walk that far. He could hardly straighten up.

Looking vulnerable in this part of town would get him killed.

The next corner seemed so far away and, when he got there, he spotted a dozen True-men coming towards him. They were shouting and boasting about the Wyrd they'd just seen strung up.

He'd never make it to the wine cellar.

Wasn't there a Wyrd warehouse near here?

Turning back, he found the right street and saw the sisterhood symbol over the warehouse door. Lit by a lantern, the door beckoned like a beacon.

But it was halfway down the block.

Meanwhile, the cold fire in his stomach was all but consuming him. Sorne staggered like a drunk. His sight came and went.

True-men passed him on the other side of the street. He half expected them to come after him, but they put their heads down and left him to stumble on.

Blinking, he saw the warehouse door in front of him and thumped on the wood. 'Let me in.' Remembered to switch to T'En. 'Let me in.'

A slot slid across. He turned the good side of his face towards it.

As the door opened, he threw himself inside. He felt hands dragging him in, and heard the door swing shut behind him. He fell to his knees, toppling forward. The polished wood was cold on his cheek. He just wanted the pain to stop.

'What's going on?' a woman demanded. 'Who is he?'

He was rolled over. It felt like his belly had been torn apart. He heard a piteous moan and realised it was him.

Someone made clucking noises of sympathy. 'He's been badly beaten. Do you recognise him? Check his travelling kit.'

'That's our sisterhood symbol. He must be one of ours.'

Sorne wondered if he should tell them he wasn't from their sisterhood, but the voices faded.

* * *

GRAELEN WOKE AS a cart trundled by on the street outside. He was stiff from sleeping on the wine cellar floor. Sorne had not shown up. Had he been delayed, or changed his mind? Or was it something more serious?

After removing all sign of his presence, he added a line to the message, saying he would be back tonight, and then went up the steps. It was a little after dawn and mist came up from the bay, growing thicker as he cut across the warehouse district, aiming for the road down to the Wyrd warehouses.

He glimpsed something out of the corner of his eye, and a sick feeling settled in his stomach, making his gift rise. He turned to look up the rise towards the east, where a body hung from a shop sign, silhouetted against the rising sun.

When he got closer, he could make out the beaten, swollen features. He staggered. 'Harosel.'

He had to lean against a shop front to steady himself. He'd sent Harosel out to spy amongst True-men; he'd known it was dangerous. His gift surged, but it was too late to help.

'Thanks be, you're alive!' Kithkarne startled him.

He turned to find the tithe-master with several Malaunje. The half-bloods hung back, giving him time to get his gift under control.

'When you weren't in your bed, we feared the worst.'

'I had a meeting.' He could hardly speak.

'So you weren't with him when...?'

'Do you think I would have let this happen?'

'Do you think you could have stopped them? Ah, lad.' Kithkarne put a hand on Graelen's shoulder. 'You sent him out, but he knew the risks.'

It was true, but it did not help. Contempt for Harosel's killers coursed through him. 'Strung up like a common criminal.'

Kithkarne gestured to the body. 'Cut him down.'

'Gently.' Graelen caught Harosel's cold, damp legs to support him as they sawed through the rope. 'I'll carry him.'

'We should make arrangements to get everyone who isn't a warrior back to the city,' Kithkarne said.

But Graelen wasn't listening. Was Sorne hanging from a shop sign somewhere? Was that why he'd failed to return?

Chapter Fifty-Five

As ALL-MOTHER, IMOSHEN received many messages from the sisterhood's estates, but this one from their warehouse in Port Mirror-on-Sea was unusual.

'They say a Malaunje staggered through their door, beaten and gravely ill,' she told Egrayne. 'He could be one of ours, but none of them know him and he can't answer their questions. They say he has a silver torc of foreign origin, and a ball of glass that glows when they touch it. They also say he has a wound that won't respond to their herbalist and they don't think he'll recover without help from Healer Reoden. I think I should bring him to the city and ask Ree to heal him.'

'Every favour you ask of her on behalf of our sisterhood has to be repaid. She would not be a good all-mother if she didn't hold you to this. Let me see.' Egrayne held out her hand. Imoshen passed over the message.

They sat on the roof garden, enjoying the sun, while Imoshen's infant daughter slept. The idea of holding the life or death of this unknown Malaunje in her hands made Imoshen uncomfortable.

Why did she think she would be good at this?

Egrayne returned the message. 'If he's one of our people, he might have important information. You have to weigh up whether that information is worth incurring an obligation to the healer.'

'That's easy. I'll send for him. We have a duty to protect all Malaunje.'

* * *

ZABIER'S HEART RACED as he realised this was what he'd been looking for. Night after night, he'd waded through reports compiled from analysing the Wyrd scrolls and Oskane's journals. Tonight he had the solution to the Wyrd problem.

He'd read both the report and the original passage in Oskane's journal. It had been an eye-opener for Zabier. He'd had no idea the scholar was so ruthless. The passage contained a description of Oskane's experiments on a captive T'En female. These tests had proven his theories about the extent of gift power. From the scholar's meticulous notes, it was clear he had been prepared to go to the king with this information just before Sorne had his first vision.

According Oskane, the Wyrds' greatest defence was not their gifts, but True-men's fear of their gifts. Bluff!

The scholar had given malachite pendants to the penitents who took part in his experiment. He'd told them the green stone would protect them from the Wyrd's gifts, but he'd made it quite clear in his notes that the stone was useless. It was the *idea* of the talisman that was powerful.

Everyone believed T'En could enslave with the power of their minds if they trapped an unwary True-man with their gaze. Oskane had proven this wrong. They could not compel with words alone, and they could not bend metal. The power of the full-blood Wyrds was limited by touch. Silverheads needed skin on skin to work their gifts, so he recommended wearing long sleeves and gloves. He also advised avoiding contact with their blood.

If they did overcome a weak-willed True-man and turn him into their slave, this left their physical bodies vulnerable. And if they disappeared, stealing the life of the True-men who were in contact with them at that time, it meant they'd sacrificed themselves to kill those men. And their numbers were few.

For three hundred years they had used bluff and trickery to keep True-men at bay.

Oskane believed King Charald could take the Wyrd city, albeit with heavy loss of life.

Would the king baulk at this?

At least now Zabier knew why there was a bag of malachite in the chest. He retrieved one of the talismans and slid the report into a leather folder, then went out through his study. 'I'm off to see the king.'

'What about...' His assistant glanced down towards the crypts.

He'd taken Valendia food and water again yesterday, but she complained she was lonely. 'She'll have to wait.'

The palace guards were used to him coming and going, and they ushered him through into the king's chamber. When he saw two of the barons had come to the king to resolve a dispute, Zabier hesitated just inside the doorway.

Originally from Dace, Eskarnor and Hanix had attached themselves to the king's army during the Secluded Sea campaign. They'd returned with him three years ago and been rewarded with estates close to each other. From what Zabier could gather, one was accusing the other of stealing his land. A forester had been killed, there'd been reprisals and now several men-at-arms were also dead.

Charald dismissed the barons with the injunction to 'stick to the original estate boundaries and no more reprisals.'

The barons strode, out bristling like dogs. One of them looked Zabier up and down, with the contempt of a fighting man for a man of the church.

Zabier stiffened. Perhaps it was time for another demonstration, to remind them of his power.

Charald beckoned him. 'Greedy, ambitious bastards. I suspect they're testing me. They've heard about Cedon. They think I'm old and weak, and he'll never sit on the throne. I should confiscate their estates and have them executed for treason.'

If it had been King Matxin, he would have had Zabier make an offering and announce the gods had told him of the barons' treason. Who needed proof when the gods could point a finger?

'A pox on the barons. In times of war, a king needs powerful barons. The rest of the time they're nothing but trouble, always after his throne.' The king paced, working himself up. 'And now Nitzane's returning to Chalcedonia, but he's left his son in Navarone. If I'd known he was going to marry and produce a healthy heir... Twenty years from now his brat will try to usurp my Cedon–'

'And there's the Wyrd delegation.' Zabier fed the fire.

'Don't get me started on the Wyrds.'

'That's why I'm here. I have good news, my king.' Zabier opened the leather folder, removing the report and malachite pendant. 'Oskane put the Wyrd gifts to the test and found their weakness. They need touch, skin on skin, to work.'

He handed Charald the report.

The king read it, then swore softly. 'Who would have thought a pious priest could think like this? He was more brutal than a war baron.'

'He anticipated you'd lose a lot of men taking the Wyrd city,' Zabier warned.

'Martyrs for the cause.' Excitement lit Charald's pale eyes. 'But first we must test Oskane's theory. There's a Wyrd winery near Nitzane's largest estate. I'll send those two trouble-making southern barons. You'll lead them–'

'Me?' Zabier gulped. 'I know nothing about warfare. I can't lead an army.'

'You won't need to. The barons and their men will do the fighting. You have to be there because this is a holy war.'

Zabier nodded, but he didn't like it.

Charald grinned. 'If Oskane's precautions fail and the winery Wyrds kill the barons, they get rid of the barons for me.'

'But won't the attack anger the Wyrds?' Sorne protested.

'I'll deny all knowledge and pay compensation. Meanwhile, they'll blame Nitzane because I'll give Eskarnor and Hanix one of his banners.' Charald shrugged. 'On the other hand, if Oskane's precautions work and the baron's kill the winery Wyrds, I'll summon all the barons and attack Cesspit City.'

Zabier's head spun as Charald went to the door and sent for Eskarnor and Hanix.

He strode back to Zabier. 'You'll march as soon as possible.'

SORNE NEEDED TO wake up. There was something important he had to do, but the pain kept dragging him under. Cold fire burned in his belly. At times he thought he was with Hiruna in the stable and she was nursing him. Other times, he knew he was in a sisterhood warehouse. Although he couldn't remember why, he knew it was important that they didn't discover who he was, and he knew they hadn't, because he heard them speculating as to his identity.

Someone tried to make him drink a tisane but he turned his face away.

'It will bring you relief, I promise.'

It would make him stupid, and there was something important he had to do. If he could just remember what it was.

'He won't take it,' the first voice reported.

'He's conscious again, then?' Someone touched him with the impersonal hands of a healer, but it was a T'En and their gift brought him relief.

'He's coming around.'

'Do you know who you are?' the T'En asked. A face came into focus above him: square jaw, strong nose, intelligent mulberry eyes. 'Do you know where you are?'

Sorne groaned.

'We're losing him again.'

'Listen to me,' the T'En commanded. He felt a little warming rush of power and was able to look up at her. 'We're sending you to the city, to Healer Reoden.'

He nodded, and hope flamed through his body, followed quickly by shame. Either he died of this wound, or the addiction he'd been fighting since he found that first artefact would make him a slave of the T'En.

He should kill himself now, but he didn't have the strength.

They carried him out to a cart. It might have been the same day, it was hard to tell. He heard them talking of collecting others from the port warehouses, and for a moment he knew where he was. Then the jolt of being lifted into the cart triggered another spasm and he lost himself to the pain.

ZABIER HAD BEEN utterly miserable on the journey to attack the brotherhood's winery. He was not a man of war, and had never claimed to be. Since coming to port at thirteen, he'd spent years learning church and court politics. Back in port, Eskarnor and Hanix had come to Charald as rivals, but on the journey to the winery they had united against Zabier. He did not know how to speak to the barons and their men, and the barons made it clear they despised him.

But tonight was different. Tonight, they looked to him for guidance. He raised the two malachite pendants and blessed them, hanging them around the barons' necks, saying, 'These talismans will protect you from the Wyrd's powers. While you wear them, you are strong.'

To each of their captains, he gave a malachite chip. Everyone had been warned not to let the silver-haired abominations touch them, and to avoid T'En blood. Then he went up and down the lines, blessing the men-at-arms. So many men, ready to kill for glory and reward. How many would still be alive tomorrow?

Zabier was grateful the barons did not expect him to take part in the attack.

He returned to stand in front of the church tent, raising his voice so it would carry. 'This is a holy war, to rid our land of Wyrds. Every man who dies here is a martyr, assured of a place with the gods!'

And they cheered. Zabier rather enjoyed the sensation.

TOBAZIM ACCEPTED THE compliments with a sense of achievement. Today his bridge had been officially opened. It did not matter that it was only his brotherhood who'd attended, and most of them had been involved in the construction. He was content for now. The bridge would still be standing long after he had gone, serving the needs of travellers.

At Gift-tutor Nerasun's signal, the kitchen staff cleared the meal away.

Tobazim looked around the courtyard. Lanterns hung from the tree, and a couple of braziers burned to warm old bones.

Tonight was unusual, in that not only was there the T'En table in the courtyard, but a long table had been set up for the Malaunje, and everyone celebrated together. Using hay bales for seats, mothers nursed babies, while elders watched little children dance in front of the musicians. Under the tree, two youths played pipes, three plucked strings, a boy kept time on the drums and three girls sang old favourites.

The T'En table consisted of him, Learon, the new youth and four scholars, all over eighty. Tobazim leant close to his choice-brother. 'Poor Athlyn, after we leave, he'll only have the scholars for company.'

'And those three pretty song birds.' Learon gestured to the girls. 'He'll have them all to himself. I almost envy him.' He blew the lead singer a kiss, and Paravia made a moue of disappointment. Tobazim knew she'd been sharing Learon's bed and was annoyed with him for leaving.

'In fact...' Learon drained his wine and came to his feet, dragging Athlyn with him. 'Come on, lad. We'll make a man of you tonight.'

Athlyn went bright red. 'I really don't–'

'Yes, you do.' Learon guided him over to the musicians. 'You really do.'

Tobazim grinned.

'Come on, Tobazim.' Learon beckoned.

'Leave the poor boy alone, Lear.' But he joined them anyway.

Outside the villa a dog barked, then stopped abruptly.

They made their way through the dancing children to the musicians. Paravia finished the song and settled her hands on her hips.

As Learon tried to cajole her with sweet words, a great clatter came from the kitchen and someone cried out. Conversations faltered. Even though Tobazim's first thought was that someone had dropped a pot on their foot, he felt his gift stir.

Over at the T'En table Tobazim saw Gift-tutor Nerasun send someone to check on the kitchen staff. Tobazim glanced to Learon. He had an arm around Paravia now, and was whispering in her ear. A smile tugged at her lips, and Tobazim knew she'd given in. Her two friends were eyeing Athlyn and whispering together. They giggled. The T'En youth looked like he was considering running away.

The drummer started a new rhythm.

The servant came running back, shouting. As he passed, Tobazim saw something protruding from between his shoulders. The servant's legs faltered and he fell. A knife was buried in his back.

Gift-tutor Nerasun came to his feet. Clearly, he'd spotted something in the passage to the kitchen. Old Nerasun gestured urgently to Tobazim.

Before he could move, Mieren men-at-arms poured through every opening into the courtyard, blocking any chance of escape. Tobazim glanced to Learon, who reached for his long-knives, but they were all unarmed. Mothers called their children. The young Malaunje men sprang to their feet, demanding to know what was going on.

Old Nerasun raised his arms. 'Sit down, everyone. I will speak with them. We are not at war.'

As he finished, a Mieren came up behind him and ran him through. There was utter silence for a heartbeat, then...

Women screamed, children shrieked and the Mieren men-at-arms attacked. Many of their people didn't even make it out of their seats; they were hacked down at the table, some made it a few steps, before they were cut down.

Paravia gasped and went to run, but there was nowhere to go. The three singers clung together. Tobazim saw a little girl crawl under the table. The musicians threw down their instruments, picked up chairs and tried to defend themselves.

Learon grabbed the nearest brazier by the base and swung it as four Mieren charged them. Hot coals sprayed their attackers. Tobazim pushed the girls and the drummer boy behind him. Athlyn just stood there, stunned.

Tobazim grabbed him by the arm. 'Protect them.'

A Mieren attacked Tobazim. He picked up a drum and brought it down on the man's head. As the man staggered, Tobazim kicked him in the belly and tore the sword from his hands. He'd been trained to use the long-knives, and it felt strange.

Learon swung the brazier, clearing a swathe around them, but more attackers kept pouring into the courtyard. And all the while, their people fell. They were vintners, not warriors. The old, the sick, the very young. The children...

Sickened, Tobazim fought to stay alive.

Learon jerked his head towards a knot of Malaunje youths who had united not far from the kitchen corridor. 'Over there.'

As Learon charged towards the defenders, Tobazim glanced over his shoulder and saw the singers grappling with two men-at-arms, who were trying to drag them off. He cut both men down, before grabbing the girls and shoving them in Learon's direction. 'Stay with Lear.'

Tobazim saw Athlyn standing unarmed between the drummer boy and a Mieren wielding a bloodied sword. Tobazim ran the Mieren through, tore the sword from his hand and gave it to Athlyn. The drummer boy took the Mieren's knife.

'Come with me.' Tobazim hacked his way through the men-at-arms to join Learon and the defenders. There they fought, gradually backing up. They were holding their own, but for how long?

In the melee, he shouted to his choice-brother. 'We have to get out. This is a massacre.'

Learon glanced behind him. 'The passage to the kitchen looks clear. Get them out. I'll protect your back.'

Tobazim pushed the young musicians towards the door and grabbed Athlyn. 'Get them outside.'

The circle of defenders contracted as they poured down the passage, until only Learon, Tobazim and six youths held off the men-at-arms.

Tobazim glanced over his shoulder as he fought beside Learon. Movement in the passage had stopped; they needed him.

He ran, pushing past the others until he came out into the kitchen, where he saw blood on the tiles, a headless torso and someone's legs protruding from under the table.

One of the singers, Tia, was weeping over the body of the old cook. Paravia had stopped to grab carving knives and choppers, and was handing them around.

Tobazim hauled Tia to her feet. 'Out the back. Quick. Everyone out.'

He pushed Tia through the door, and the others followed. The kitchen opened onto a paved area and the walled garden. On one side was a culvert that ran down to the river. If they could just get to the river and into the boats, the current would take them.

He turned to look for Learon and the other defenders, but there was no sign of them.

Tobazim had to ensure the others got out alive. 'Go now. Follow the culvert down to the river, where you'll find boats. Hurry, and don't look back.'

He sent them down, hoping they'd do what he said.

Because he was going back for Learon.

As the last Malaunje ran for the culvert, he turned and headed back into the kitchen. Half a dozen youths came running towards them.

'Where's Lear, Charane?'

'He set fire to the hay bales.'

Learon charged into the kitchen, bringing the smell of smoke. He laughed to see Tobazim.

The crazy fool was enjoying himself.

Learon grabbed him and hugged him. Then they were running. Behind him, the flames took hold; he heard men-at-arms shouting.

Tobazim plunged down the culvert. Skidding on leaf litter, he landed on his backside. Learon hauled him to his feet and they kept going. He heard shouts, but didn't know if the Mieren were coming after them.

Down by the river, he found the youths but there were no more boats.

'We'll have to swim,' Learon said.

'No. Get on the jetty.' Tobazim used the borrowed Mieren sword to hack through the ropes that held the floating jetty.

They nearly fell in the river as the makeshift raft dipped and wobbled. Everyone dropped to their knees. Then the current took them. As it swept them around the bend Tobazim looked back to the winery, which was now well alight. If they were lucky, the Mieren wouldn't realise they'd gotten away.

But so many hadn't.

Behind him, he heard the youths muttering, trying to make sense of what had happened. Why they been attacked?

'We just built a bridge for everyone,' Charane whispered. 'Why attack us? Why now?'

Further downstream, well out of sight of the winery, they found the boats pulled up on the bank, surrounded by those who had fled the fighting. Tobazim slid into the icy river and dragged the raft to the bank.

Once they were all ashore, Tobazim counted seventeen survivors. They stood shivering in the cold night air. Several of them were injured, and none of them understood what had happened.

Paravia pushed through the others and threw her arms around Learon, sobbing and kissing him.

'What should we do?' Athlyn asked. 'Will they come after us?'

Learon set Paravia down and turned to them. 'We have to go to the city. Have to report this to the all-father. We need justice.'

'It's a long way by foot,' Tobazim said. 'We'll have to travel at night to avoid Mieren. First we should hide the boats, hide everyone. Tomorrow, Learon and I will return to the winery, see if there are any survivors and discover who is responsible for this outrage.'

'Mieren.'

'Filthy Mieren!'

'Yes, but which Mieren?'

'What possible reason could they have for attacking us?' Athlyn asked. 'We haven't done anything.'

The others muttered in agreement.

Tobazim spotted the stable master. 'Maric, see to the injured.'

As the Malaunje moved off, Athlyn rubbed his arms, teeth chattering. 'I killed at least one Mieren. He'll come after me, try to drag me with him into death's realm. I don't have the training to survive that kind of attack.'

Learon went very pale. 'I must have killed a dozen.'

Tobazim felt the impact of their fear as he recalled the men he'd killed. But... 'Violent death confuses the shades of the dead.'

'What if they do find us?'

'I'll anchor you.' Because he had to. Conviction filled him. He was not going to die, ambushed by the shades of the men he'd killed in self-defence.

Responding to his certainty, they relaxed.

And just like that, he became responsible for all their lives – T'En and Malaunje.

TOBAZIM STOOD IN the blackened ruins of the villa. He held Baron Nitzane's banner in his hands. It made no sense. The winery hadn't had any trouble with the baron. Why would he send his men to attack them? He rolled the banner up.

Nothing remained of the villa other than shattered stone walls and collapsed beams, some of which still smoked. The bodies of his people had burned, along with some of their attackers. Thankfully several of the outbuildings had survived intact.

'Maric, take the others and check the stables.'

'They'll have taken the horses,' Learon said.

'They might have left blankets or tools. Check the outbuildings for food.' Tobazim picked his way through the broken masonry and charred timbers. He prodded something with his boot, revealing glowing coals.

'What are you looking for?' Learon asked.

He had hoped to find the silver nib his choice-mother had given him, but it would be a puddle of melted metal now. It was only a symbol; you could not kill the idea.

Tobazim looked up. 'There's nothing here for us to bury.'

The others returned with blankets, an axe and some ropes.

'They stripped the store rooms,' Maric reported. 'Took all the food. There wasn't much left in the stables.'

'Then we'll have to forage as we go,' Learon said.

'Seventeen people, three of them injured.' Tobazim had been thinking. 'We'll take the river west, then strike north for the city.'

Chapter Fifty-Six

IMOSHEN MET THEM at the door to the solarium. They handed her the injured spy's travelling kit; as they carried him through, she caught a glimpse of pure white hair.

'Did he say anything on the journey?' she asked one of the Malaunje who'd arrived with him.

'He was rarely lucid.' The man lowered his voice. 'The journey exhausted him.'

'To be expected. I've sent for Healer Reoden.' Imoshen thanked them as they left.

While the sisterhood's herbalist bathed the injured Malaunje and checked his injuries, Imoshen opened his travelling kit, which bore their sisterhood's symbol. There was nothing of an identifying nature in his bag, just a change of clothes and the two items of interest mentioned in the message. The stone on the silver torc was most unusual, but it was the glass ball that fascinated her. If she held it in one hand, nothing. If she cupped it in both, it glowed, pulsing. What did it mean?

Behind her, the herbalist gave a soft gasp. 'This is bad.'

Imoshen put the travelling kit away and crossed to the wounded man. He lay on a bedroll, pale chest bare, face turned away from her. As she circled him she noticed, although his body was badly scarred, he was not elderly. Young face, white hair and burns. Could it be...?

The Warrior's-voice had been sent south two – no, three years ago. The last she'd heard, he was dead, killed in the Maygharian uprising.

'This stomach wound.' The herbalist pointed. 'I've never seen anything like it. The skin's dead, but there's no decay.'

Catching sight of the ugly wound, Imoshen drew back. Her sight shifted to take in the empyrean plane, and she saw the wound was slowly but surely leaching the life force from him. How had he survived this?

Her sight returned to normal. 'Send for the gift-wright.'

The woman looked confused for a moment, and then her features sharpened with fear. She sprang to her feet, darting out of the solarium.

Imoshen was left alone with the white-haired Malaunje. She studied him.

'Are you who I think you are?' she whispered, as she placed her hand on his forehead and probed with his gift. As if sensing her power, he stirred, but even in this state his shields were solid. 'What did the Mieren do to you? Why did they tell everyone you were dead?'

And what would the T'En do to him if they knew who he was? She'd gained the distinct impression the T'En did not approve of the Warrior's-voice.

'...never seen anything like it,' the herbalist said, leading Reoden in. 'We've sent for the gift-wright.'

The healer sank to her knees opposite Imoshen.

The herbalist left, and Imoshen watched as Reoden ran her hands over the injured man's body, pausing over old wounds, studying how the recent wounds had healed. It seemed Reoden didn't connect this injured Malaunje with the deceased Warrior's-voice.

'Can you–'

'Heal him? Yes. But he won't get better unless the gift-wright can heal his stomach wound.'

Imoshen had guessed as much. 'I've never seen Ceriane at work. This should be interesting.'

But when the gift-wright arrived and examined him, she was not hopeful.

'His wound is of empyrean origin so he must be someone's devotee,' Ceriane said. Imoshen didn't correct her assumption, or identify him. 'His T'En should have brought him to me when it first happened. Then, I could have healed him, by drawing on the T'En's gift. Now...'

'Can't you do anything for him?' Imoshen pressed.

Ceriane lifted her bony hands. She was a thin, angular woman, who radiated determination. 'I'm a gift-wright. He has no innate power for me to work with.'

'If Ceriane can't heal his empyrean wound, then there's no point me healing his physical wounds,' Reoden said, her voice heavy with regret. 'He'll only suffer. He must have been suffering horribly as it is.'

'I think we can heal him,' Imoshen said.

Reoden and Ceriane sent her sympathetic looks.

'Sometimes it is kinder—' Reoden began.

'No, I really do.' It frustrated Imoshen that even these clever women could only see what they'd been told. 'When we go to the empyrean plane, our bodies are constructs, yet if we take a bad wound on the empyrean plane, our physical body will mirror that wound. While we are on the higher plane, if we have the time and the power to spare, we can heal the wound. When we do that, our physical body heals.'

Ceriane frowned. 'You're saying...'

'We take his essence to the empyrean plane and heal him there.'

The gift-wright and healer hesitated.

'Would it work?' Imoshen asked.

'It might,' Reoden admitted. 'But it's too dangerous.'

'She's right,' Ceriane said. 'The use of power would attract predators.'

'I'll defend you while you gift-work.'

'His physical body is weak. He might not have the will to hold his essence together on the higher plane,' Reoden warned.

'He's survived this long. I think his will is strong.' Imoshen looked from Reoden to Ceriane. 'Do you want to try it?'

The gift-wright tilted her head. 'I admit the challenge interests me. But he could die.'

'He's not getting better as he is,' Imoshen snapped.

Ceriane's eyes widened.

'Imoshen can be rather forthright.' Reoden grinned. 'Very well. If we knew who his T'En was, we could ask their permission. As it is, we'll have to wait until he wakes.'

'I'll ask him.' Imoshen returned to the bedroll and knelt. She placed a hand on his chest and let her power seep into him. His one good eye opened. 'We can try to heal you on the higher plane, but it's risky. If we fail, you'll die. If we do nothing, you'll linger like this as long as your will lasts.'

He swallowed. 'Water...'

She held his head and let him sip some water.

He lay back, and looked up at Imoshen. 'Will I become addicted to your gifts?'

Imoshen looked to Ceriane.

'He's already imprinted with his T'En's gift. It will protect him from ours.'

That's if he *was* someone's devotee, which he wasn't.

He closed his eye. 'Do it.'

Reoden knelt on the other side of the bedroll and Ceriane knelt at the head. They rubbed their hands together to help focus their gift in their palms, and placed their hands on the bare skin of his chest and his forehead.

'His defences are too strong,' Ceriane said.

'You'll have to lower your shields...' Imoshen said, and then realised she didn't know his name. She wasn't going to call him the Warrior's-voice in front of the others. 'What's your name?'

'Sorne.'

'I'm Imoshen. For us to get a grip on your essence, you'll have to lower your defences.'

'I don't know how.'

'Of course you do,' Ceriane snapped. 'We're trying to help you.'

'Think of someone you trust,' Imoshen said. 'This will lower your shields enough for us to get a grip on your essence.' But with the strength of his will, he should not be imprinted by their gifts. 'Imagine that person is here with us, now.'

'Does she have to still be alive?'

Imoshen winced for him. 'She only has to be alive to you. She would want us to help you.'

He nodded and closed his eyes. As he did this, Imoshen heard a woman singing.

And just like that, they were through.

Imoshen took on the task of making the empyrean plane conform to her will. They stood on a cliff top, on the island where she'd grown up. To her left, far below, waves crashed on the rocks. To her right, the land fell away steeply, to dunes and then more sea. A silvery winter sun warmed the earth, giving crisp colour to the grass and sea.

Imoshen circled the others, watching for predators.

Ceriane and Reoden knelt in the same positions as they had on the earthly plane. She could feel their intensity as they focused on healing him. As if attracted to their power, a shaft of sunlight pierced the clouds and illuminated the cliff top.

Imoshen could defeat a single beast, even a pack of scraelings, but she could not defeat the plane itself, and it was always hungry for T'En power. Now she felt it take an interest in them as a breeze swept in from the sea and the waves thundered below, clawing ever higher.

She scanned their surroundings, then returned her attention to the healer and the gift-wright.

On this plane, she could see Reoden's essence: her kindness, and the wound where her sacrare daughter had been torn from her. Here, Ceriane was beautiful in her determination and compassion.

Here, Sorne suffered from the blight of acts committed and regretted. He'd done something in his past that he carried like an open wound. This was why the empyrean plane had been able to get its claws into him.

Reoden and Ceriane battled, but Imoshen's raedan gift told her that until he could forgive himself, he would not fully heal.

She knelt opposite Reoden and reached out to Sorne.

Now she walked with him through a city ravaged by war. Packs of men ran wild in the streets like beasts. The innocent lay dead all around them. The city, the country... all lay in ruins.

They left the streets and entered a square. King Charald stood on the plinth of a toppled statue, while the men who were beasts worshiped him.

Sorne felt responsible for unleashing the king and his army.

Imoshen took Sorne's hand and pointed to Charald, exercising her raedan gift. The king's features dissolved to reveal he was as much a beast as the men he commanded.

Sorne could not be responsible for Charald's nature; the king would always seek the path of war.

Imoshen felt it the moment Sorne accepted this. Relief swept through him. She felt the power of the gift-wright and the healer as they repaired and restored.

Then something stung her forehead.

She opened her eyes. They were still on the cliff, but stormy clouds hung low overhead and the sea had risen. Waves crashed, showering them with spray that stung exposed skin.

Time to go back.

In another heartbeat, they knelt in the sisterhood's solarium once more.

Ceriane toppled sideways. Imoshen just caught her, but she couldn't save Reoden, who slumped beside her patient, head near his feet.

Imoshen laid the gift-wright down gently, and came back to kneel next to Sorne. He seemed to be sleeping. His face... the burn scars had healed, but the eye socket contained no eye, only smooth skin. As for the wound on his belly, it was now a single silver line.

She pulled up the cover and stood.

For a moment, the room swung around her. When her head cleared, she went out to the corridor, calling for warmed wine and food to restore them after gift-working.

And she sent for Frayvia, because she knew her devotee would want to meet the Warrior's-voice. Imoshen left Sorne in Frayvia's care, with instructions to call her the moment he recovered.

ZABIER HAD TO admit there was something to be said for victory. It made a man feel... As his gaze was drawn to Queen Jaraile he was grateful for his voluminous priestly robes. Tonight, he sat at the king's private table, sharing a meal with the barons. They spoke of the ease of the attack.

'...no one left alive,' Baron Eskarnor said.

'What, not even the children?' Jaraile went white.

'Little Wyrds grow into big Wyrds,' the king told her; he rolled his eyes as he turned back to the barons. 'How many of the full-blood T'En did you kill?'

The two barons exchanged looks. Zabier waited to hear the number. It had been growing during the ride back, and the fire had made it difficult to ascertain how many had been killed. Most convenient.

'At least twenty,' Eskarnor said. 'It was a small estate.'

'But they were fierce. Terrible fierce,' Hanix assured him. 'Pickings were poor.'

'Hardly any prizes for the men,' Eskarnor agreed. 'I thought these Wyrds were rich as kings.'

'You're thinking of Cesspit City.' Charald lifted his glass, eyes blazing. The king was heading for one of his manic states, and would sweep everyone along with him. 'To ridding Chalcedonia of Wyrds.'

'To victory.'

As they began to discuss the best time to attack, and the logistics of getting men and supplies near to the city without alerting the Wyrds, Jaraile came to her feet. 'If you will excuse me, sire.'

Zabier was too busy to watch her go.

'It won't take much to turn the people against ·the Wyrds,' Charald said. 'They've always hated them. Why, only recently, my palace guards caught a Wyrd spy in a whorehouse, sniffing around True-men. They strung him up as an example to his kind and not a peep did I hear from the port Wyrds. But we'll need more than one spy to justify an attack on their city.'

'A massacre?' Eskarnor suggested.

'But the Wyrds haven't...' Zabier fell silent as the king and his two barons turned to him, with the eyes of cold-blooded killers. He wanted to sink under the table, but if he didn't protest, he would look weak. 'I'm a man of the church. I–'

'The drought has meant another poor harvest,' Hanix complained. 'Our people need something to distract them. A war with spoils will–'

'The drought.' Zabier sat forward in his eagerness. 'We can blame the drought on the Wyrds.'

'What do they have to do with the fact that we haven't had decent rain in almost five years?' Charald asked.

'They don't worship the Seven.' Zabier looked from face to face, and saw them make the connection. 'The gods are angry. They're punishing–'

'Well done.' Charald clapped him on the back. 'We'll make a strategist of you yet. Send the Seven's priests out to spread the word. They can use their sermons to rouse the populace. Which reminds me, we'll need a vision from the Warrior's-voice to make the holy war official.'

This was the only thorn in Zabier's side. The king was firmly devoted to the Warrior god. Zabier was torn. On the one hand, this meant he didn't have to risk his life making the offering but, on the other hand, it meant his counterpart from the Warrior's church had the king's ear. 'Yes, sire.'

'For an undertaking of this scale, we need a suitable offering.' The king looked thoughtful.

'Even after our victory, the Chalcedonian barons may be wary of attacking the Wyrds,' Eskarnor said. 'They piss themselves whenever Wyrds are mentioned. Especially the full-bloods.'

'That's it!' The king slammed his fist on the table. 'We'll sacrifice a silverhead, one of those two T'En who came sniffing around here demanding an audience with me.' He gestured to Zabier. 'You'll capture them and keep one in reserve.'

'You want the Warrior's-voice to sacrifice a silverhead?' Zabier asked, greatly relieved he wasn't doing it.

'Of course. Why not?'

Zabier came to his feet. 'I'll make the arrangements now.'

He left while the king talked logistics with the barons.

How was he going to incapacitate the two T'En delegates? The old fat one would be easy, but the big one with the hard face...

He'd need pure pains-ease.

SORNE WOKE FROM a nightmare vision. He woke babbling of half-bloods and True-men and danger. Every time he closed his eyes, he caught glimpses of the frightened Malaunje and T'En children being loaded onto the cart.

'Bad dream?' a sweet-faced Malaunje woman asked.

He looked around. And it all came back to him. 'Where's the T'En woman?'

'There were three of them. Imoshen, Re–'

'Imoshen.'

She spoke to someone outside, then came back to him. 'She'll be here soon. You have time to bathe. I'll help you.'

She helped him up, and he winced in anticipation of the pain in his stomach, but it wasn't there. Looking down, he saw smooth, healthy flesh and a single silver scar.

It was such a relief, he felt like laughing.

The bathing chamber was as fine as any in King Charald's palace. He remembered Imoshen guiding him to the revelation that the king would have chosen the path to war without his influence. He had not been responsible for the massacre that had followed.

Hot tears fell from his remaining eye.

The Malaunje woman said nothing as she ran the bath, and helped him in. He was so weak, his arms shook. To think he had once been proud of his strength. Proud and arrogant...

'I'm sorry, I don't know your name.'

'Frayvia.'

'I'm–'

'Sorne. I know.'

And she sang under her breath as she ran soft but firm hands over his body. He felt his muscles relax. The dull ache in his collarbone was gone. Everywhere her hands moved, he discovered smooth skin where there had been scars.

'Are...' He almost didn't want to ask. 'Are there scars on my back?'

'Not a one.' She ran her hands down his back from shoulder blades to ribs, and the touch of her hands seemed to strip all those years of scourgings from him, taking away the anger buried deep inside to reveal the boy.

More tears fell, but they were happy tears, and they were washed away by the warm water she poured over his head and shoulders. When she reached for the soap again, he took it from her. 'I can manage.'

'I'll fetch some clothes,' she told him.

Rising from the bath, he looked into the mirror to see what had become of his face. He discovered the hair over his left temple was still missing, as was that eye, but where the burn scars had been was now just smooth skin.

The person in the mirror was familiar. He'd seen him somewhere before...

'Imoshen's here,' Frayvia said, as she returned and helped him dress. 'Do you want me to comb your hair?'

Two voices reached him. 'Who's–'

'Healer Reoden. She and Imoshen lead the two largest sisterhoods. The other one who worked on you was the gift-wright, All-mother Ceriane.'

He was deep inside the sisterhoods, surrounded by the full-bloods he had been raised to fear and destroy.

If they knew who he truly was, they would despise him.

'Come.' Frayvia led him out into the solarium.

When he approached Imoshen and the healer he could sense their gifts like the drumming of rain on a roof, but without the pain in his core, he did not feel a desperate need for their power. He was drawn to them, like the fire on a winter's night.

'You're doing well, considering it's only been a day,' Imoshen told him. 'How do you feel?

Raw – emotionally and physically. He didn't know what to say.

'You surprised us all,' Reoden said. She looked him over with interest. 'Any pain?'

'None, not even...' His hand fell to his stomach. 'I don't remember much, but I do know I'm in your debt. All-mothers Reoden, Ceriane and Imoshen – you saved my life.' He gave the obeisance of gratitude, hoping he'd remembered it correctly. As far as they knew, he was one of their sisterhood half-bloods.

'I'm sorry I couldn't rebuild your eye,' the healer said. 'There has to be something to work with, and–'

'Doesn't matter.'

'Sorne woke with a vision,' Frayvia said.

He turned to her, shocked.

She gestured. 'Go on. You asked me to get Imoshen so you could tell her.'

Did they all know who he was? And they had still healed him? 'I've had another vision–'

'Malaunje don't get visions,' Reoden said. 'The only half-blood who ever claimed to have visions was the Warrior's-voice, and he...' She took a step back and looked to him, and then to Imoshen. 'You knew?'

Imoshen nodded. 'I guessed. And I suspect he does get visions. After all, he suffered an empyrean wound, and Malaunje don't usually–'

'He's supposed to be dead. He's the Mieren king's spy.' Reoden said. 'What's he doing here?'

'Trying to tell us about a vision.'

'And you believe him? He could be lying.'

'I don't think he gave himself a gift wound, then turned up nearly dead–'

'What better way to win our trust?'

Sorne sighed as he realised he had no option but to tell them everything. 'I'm King Charald's unwanted half-blood son, raised in secret. I've been having visions since I was seventeen.' And he confessed how he'd been luring beasts from the higher plane with T'En artefacts. 'The power that's shed knocks me out and triggers my visions. These happen as I regain consciousness.'

Reoden looked dubious.

'I've been researching inheritable traits,' Imoshen said. 'I believe if Sorne had been born T'En, he would have been a seer, but he was born Malaunje. The visions would have been latent all his life, if he hadn't been playing around with T'En artefacts and lured the beasts from the higher plane. The surge of power triggers his visions.'

Reoden shook her head, but in wonder rather than denial.

'This vision was more detailed than the last one,' Sorne said. 'I saw half-blood and T'En children being herded onto a cart, while True-men jeered at them.'

'That's not likely,' Reoden said. 'T'En children are kept segregated.'

'Not by True-men,' Imoshen countered.

'Mieren,' Reoden corrected absently.

'Do your visions always come true, Sorne?' Imoshen asked.

He nodded. 'I think so. Some haven't come to pass yet.'

Imoshen turned to the healer. 'I think we have to take this seriously.'

'And do what? It could happen thirty years from now. Who do we tell? He might have convinced the Mieren he has visions, but the T'En aren't going to believe it. Can you imagine how Vittoryxe would react?' Reoden shrugged. 'Besides, if we revealed his identity, they'd say it was a trick.'

'I've an idea.' Imoshen caught the healer's arm. 'Ask your scryer to confirm his vision.'

Reoden glanced to Sorne, and led Imoshen away, where she conferred with her. Sorne saw Imoshen's face fall in sorrow.

He remembered Zabier telling him of Valendia's death, and in the very next breath he recalled that Zabier had lied to him. 'I have to go.'

'Go...' Frayvia repeated. 'Why?'

'My sister's being held prisoner by the Father's-voice. I have to save her.'

Chapter Fifty-Seven

GRAELEN SMILED TO himself as Kithkarne bustled ahead of him. The king had finally agreed to see them. The palace guard showed them to the usual greeting chamber.

'See.' Kithkarne gestured to the food. 'The king has come to his senses. He knows he must negotiate with us, and he's trying to put us in a good mood.' The plump tithe-master poured some wine and tasted it. 'My. That's surprisingly good. Have some.' He took a mouthful of tart, swallowed and licked his fingers. 'Now that is good. I must ask for the recipe.'

Graelen was less enthused by the hospitality. Harosel's death still left a bitter taste in his mouth. 'I'll be glad to leave this place.'

Kithkarne's sharp eyes fixed on him. 'You are not to blame for the actions of a mob.'

'I know that.'

'Sit down, lad. Celebrate.' Kithkarne poured him a glass of wine. 'By tonight, we'll have good news to take back to the all-father.'

He took a seat and tried the wine; not bad, and the pastries were surprisingly good.

Kithkarne put his leather folder on the table, then went to undo it, but his fingers fumbled with the ties. He blinked and frowned.

'No more wine for you,' Graelen tried to say, but his mouth was numb. Poison? His thought moved slowly, like cold honey, and when he tried to call on his gift, he felt disconnected from it.

As Graelen lurched to his feet, his chair scraped across the floor and the room reeled around him. He reached for the table to steady himself and went to warn Kithkarne, but the tithe-mater had his head on the table. Snoring.

Now? For some reason this seemed terribly funny.

They had to escape...

The floor came up and hit him in the face.

'KEEP YOUR GLOVES on,' Zabier told the priests. From Oskane's experiments, he knew the T'En had to be conscious to use their gifts, and these two were definitely unconscious, but it didn't hurt to be careful. He gestured to the plump, elderly True-man who had replaced Sorne as Warrior's-voice. 'My advice is to keep the silverhead drugged until the day of the sacrifice.'

The Warrior's-voice did not look happy, and Zabier didn't blame him. They all knew what had happened the last time True-men underestimated the dangers of the ceremony, and these were T'En, their people's ancestral enemy.

'Which one do you want?' Zabier asked.

They both stepped back as their priests trussed up the two full-bloods.

The Warrior's-voice grimaced. 'I'll have the fat one.'

'Very well. I'll take care of the other one.' Zabier was going to hide him somewhere deep and dark. See how much fight he had left in him after he'd been given nothing but water for days on end.

'What will you tell the other Wyrds if they come looking for them?' the Warrior's-voice asked.

'That they set off for Cesspit City. I can't help it if they were attacked on the way.'

The priests covered the unconscious T'En with blankets. Getting them across the plaza was easy enough, with a blanket thrown over the bodies in a cart. Halfway across, Zabier and the other priest parted ways.

Zabier entered the Father's church through a side gate. His priests rolled the Wyrd onto a blanket; it took six of them to carry him down the steps into the crypts.

Zabier had chosen an entrance that was a good distance from where he'd left Valendia, but they made so much noise struggling with the unconscious silverhead that he wasn't surprised when he saw a shadow following them.

'Go to the next corner and wait at the top of the stairs,' he told his priests, before hurrying back the way they'd come. Sure enough, Valendia was there, pale and ethereal in the candlelight.

She went to hug him, but he held up his hand. 'I'm on church business.'

'What's going on?' she whispered. 'Was that a body?'

'Yes. A fat old priest. We're going to put him away down below. Nothing for you to worry about.'

She nodded. 'Will you come visit me tonight? I get so lonely.'

'I know.' He felt awful. 'I'll try. But the king has me working on a new project.'

'I'm proud of you.'

He smiled and hugged her. 'Don't follow us. I'd have a terrible time explaining you to the others. There's already whispers of a ghost in the crypt.'

She laughed, but it wasn't her old laugh.

He left her, wishing he could do more for her. But what could he do, with the king planning a campaign against the Wyrds?

TOBAZIM AND HIS party approached the causeway in silence. They'd crossed Chalcedonia at night, avoiding all contact with the Mieren. Now they saw the enemy had access to the T'Enatuath stronghold. True, the Mieren wore the usual identifying red half-capes and they had to line up for inspection as they entered. But, once the gate guards were sure they were unarmed, they were allowed in. It did not look like their peoples were at war.

'What's going on?' Learon whispered.

Tobazim greeted the warriors on gate duty. The symbol on their arm-torcs told him they were from Hueryx's brotherhood.

'Why aren't the gates closed?' Learon muttered. 'Why are they still letting Mieren come and go?'

'Things will be different after we see our all-father,' Tobazim said. He had listened to enough tales of the city to make his way to Kyredeon's palace. They walked through the entrance, into courtyard and deep into the palace.

Busy Malaunje came and went on errands, while T'En strolled by talking and laughing. From their talk, they were looking forward to the winter's cusp feast. It all had an air of unreality.

Tobazim spotted a thin, older T'En man, who was inspecting a small child's foot.

'It's just a sprain. Keep her off it for a few days and she'll be fine,' the saw-bones said.

The mother thanked him and carried the little girl away.

Tobazim approached and made obeisance. 'I am Adept Tobazim of Vanillin Oak Winery. This is Adept Learon and Initiate Athlyn. We need to see All-father Kyredeon. I have three injured Malaunje.'

'Ceyne, inner circle, Kyredeon brotherhood,' the saw-bones introduced himself. 'You can't see Kyredeon looking like that.'

'We look like this because we escaped the massacre at Vanillin Oak Winery,' Learon said.

Ceyne glanced over his shoulder. 'Keep your voice down. Who was it, All-father Chariode? Hueryx?'

'It was Mieren, and I can prove it,' Tobazim said, indicating the banner he carried. 'They wiped out the winery. We barely escaped.'

One of Paravia's friends began sobbing softly.

'Hush, now.' Ceyne took her arm and led them to his chambers. As they all filed in, he looked them over. 'Your wounded seem well enough.'

'We need to see the all-father,' Learon said. 'This is war.'

Ceyne drew Tobazim, Athlyn and Learon aside. He gestured to the others. 'You Malaunje stay here. I'll be back soon to treat the wounded.'

'We're hungry,' the drummer boy said. 'Awful hungry.'

Ceyne smiled. 'I'll have food sent up. But don't talk to anyone.'

Outside, he stopped a passing Malaunje. 'Food for fourteen in my chambers.'

'Why mustn't they talk to anyone?' Tobazim asked, as they followed the saw-bones through the palace.

Ceyne hesitated. 'An attack makes Kyredeon look weak.'

'But we have to warn our people,' Tobazim said.

'When did the attack take place?'

'Seven – no, eight days ago.'

'Then why hasn't the Mieren king surrounded the city?' Tobazim looked to Learon for help.

'What if it was an ambitious baron, acting alone? Do you want to jeopardise three hundred years of peace?' Ceyne saw he had them wondering. 'Don't worry. Kyredeon's waiting on good news. When that comes through, he'll take this to an all-council. Come with me. You need to give your oaths of loyalty.'

GRAELEN WOKE TO a terrible thirst, a pounding head and darkness. The air smelt dusty, dry and old. The cold came up through the ground. He shifted and felt manacles around his wrists and feet.

Drugged. The brotherhood's best assassin, drugged. How stupid was he?

He'd failed in his duty to protect... 'Kith? Are you there? Kithkarne?'

No answer. Graelen opened his gift and probed the surroundings. He sensed no other life nearby. He searched farther; still nothing.

Clearly, the king had decided it was cheaper just to lock them in his dungeon than pay his debt. Didn't he realise there would be other brothers? Kyredeon had used diplomatic methods this time. Next time he would send an assassin, to make his meaning plain.

But it wouldn't be Graelen, because he was chained to a wall in the dark. Even with his gift-enhanced sight, he saw only oppressive darkness.

He crawled forward, feeling his way. The chains clanked with every movement. He felt cold, dry stone. There was an empty bucket for his needs, and another filled with water. He drank greedily, then stopped. What if this was all the water he had? He should ration it.

He found a blanket, but no food.

The extent of his chains told him he was against a wall.

He could segue to the empyrean plane, but that would achieve nothing.

If only he had a shield-brother, he might have been able to reach him via their link. But he had no one, and since Paryx's death, not one person would miss him.

But he was determined not to give in.

Rolling himself in the blanket, he prepared to sleep. As he drifted off, he thought he heard beautiful, haunting music.

SORNE SLEPT WITHOUT pain. It was a luxury he had not known for three years. And, when he felt soft curves pressed up against him, silky hair flowing over his skin and warm lips on his, he thought he was dreaming. But no dream had ever been this good.

Surfacing from a kiss that made his head reel and his heart race, he tried to think. 'Frayvia?'

'Who else?' She reached for him with determined hands.

He captured them. 'Why are you here?'

'Tomorrow, you go.'

'To save my sister.'

'So there is only tonight. You can't tell me you don't want me.'

'It will be dangerous. I can't take you–'

'I don't want to go with you. I want...' And she whispered in detail what she wanted from him, until he stopped arguing.

Later he lay there, heart gradually slowing after his exertions. If this was what women and men did together, why did True-men act like it was a crude, vile thing?

She trailed a hand across his hip, down his thigh and back up again. He'd no idea his skin could be so sensitive.

'I think it's disgraceful, the way you've been treated.'

He found her indignation on his behalf endearing, and rolled over. He kissed the spot where her jaw met her throat, under her ear, and felt her shiver in response. Such power...

'Doesn't it make you angry that the king refuses to acknowledge you?' she persisted. Earlier that evening, after the others had gone, she'd asked him why everyone thought he was dead, and he'd told her about Maygharia and Norholtz, and how Charald had betrayed him. 'You've done so much for him. You were his trusted advisor on the Secluded Sea campaign.'

'I used to feel angry, but I'd forgotten what life was like here in Chalcedonia. Associating with a half-blood tainted him. He had to distance himself from me. Besides, I wouldn't want the throne. All I've ever seen Charald do is fight to hold it. Every ambitious baron wants what he has. Even Nitzane.'

'Nitzane?'

'His son is Charald's heir, if the prince dies. No, I used to want power, but now I want something much more precious...' He lifted himself on one elbow to admire her beautiful curves, pale and perfect in the moonlight. 'Fray, I –'

She placed a finger on his lips.

He caught her hand and kissed her palm. 'Fray, I must save my sister. But after that, we could...'

She was shaking her head. He sat up, putting his back to her. What was he thinking? What did he have to offer a beautiful woman like her?

'Sorne...' She came to her knees and hugged him, her warm cheek resting on his shoulder. 'I can't leave Imoshen, I'm her devotee. I'm addicted to her gift.'

Shock and then anger ran through him. He turned in the circle of her arms. 'How could she do that to you?'

'When I was dragged through to the higher plane, she saved my life. It imprinted her gift on me. I am bound to it, but what we share is so much more.' She cupped his face in her hands, kissing him. 'So, you see, we only have tonight.'

And she pulled him down onto the bed.

He did not get much sleep that night, but he didn't feel the lack as he saddled his horse the next day.

'Here,' Imoshen said, putting a small metal disk in his hand.

He felt the gift infusion. 'Why give me this?' Was she trying to bind him as she'd bound Frayvia?

'Anyone from my sisterhood will recognise it. Go to our warehouse in the docks. They'll feed you and give you whatever you need.'

'Why are you helping me?'

'I was a prisoner once,' she said, simply. 'How will you know where to look for Valendia?'

'He loves her. It has to be somewhere close by and secure.' He tightened the straps of his travelling kit.

'Are you sure you want me to keep the orb?' Imoshen asked.

'See if your scholars can work out what it is.' Besides, if he took it with him and he failed, which was possible, it would fall into Mieren hands. 'You saved my life and asked for nothing in return.'

'You told us your vision.'

He shrugged. 'Which could come true in thirty years.'

'There is something you could do for me. If it looks like your vision could come true, let me know. You can leave a message with my sisterhood's warehouse in port. They'll send it to me.'

'You want me to spy for you?' Sorne almost laughed. He'd gone from being Oskane's weapon against the Wyrds, to protecting them.

Chapter Fifty-Eight

ZABIER DID NOT like the place the Warrior's-voice had chosen to hold the ceremony. Izteben had died here.

Since the Warrior's-voice was in charge, Zabier chose to stay well back. He could remember the moment he had almost been taken. The further he was from the priest, the better. His brother had saved his life. Everyone seemed to forget Izteben and Prince Cedon had died the night of that botched ritual. All they remembered was that it was the night King Matxin had come to power. Zabier fingered Oskane's ring.

From up here, he could see all the barons Charald had invited. After the offering and the vision, which would show him triumphant, Charald was going to reveal his war plans.

Watching the Warrior's-voice as he set up the offering, Zabier had to wonder: if Charald didn't believe True-men had visions, why go through with this?

Four priests escorted the T'En, who could hardly walk. Zabier cursed. He'd told that fool priest not to drug the Wyrd for the ceremony.

Plump and balding, with his fancy robe all rumpled and his face half asleep, the tithe-master wasn't going to impress the barons. He wanted to kick the Warrior's-voice. Men of learning only held the power they did because men of violence feared them. If these barons weren't impressed by the ritual, it undermined Zabier's power, too.

At least, they should be impressed that they had captured a T'En.

Charald strode out, decked in his war gear. Why a man would bother to wear plate if he wasn't going into battle was beyond Zabier, although the king did cut a striking figure in his finery. Strutting about down there, in glistening armour, you couldn't tell Charald was nearly sixty. He had the energy of a man of twenty as he gesticulated, finishing his speech with a flourish of his sword.

The barons cheered.

Well, they would, if they knew what was good for them.

Finally, it was time for the ceremony. Seeing the tithe-master slumped there, squinting at the lanterns, chains dangling from the two poles they'd tied him to, the barons muttered. As the Warrior's-voice went to make the first cut, one wit called, 'Watch out, he might faint and smother you!'

The Warrior's-voice glanced over his shoulder, before muttering to his priests, who approached the offering and each grabbed an arm. The Wyrd twisted and bucked. The Warrior's-voice fumbled the cut, spraying himself and the others with Wyrd blood. Zabier cursed. He'd warned them about this. Two more priests ran to help while the barons laughed and jeered.

Zabier could hear the Warrior's-voice yelling at his priests to hold the offering still. A pool of blood spread at the feet of the tithe-master, and the priests' breath began to mist with each exhalation. The ritual was working.

'They've got to get out of there,' he muttered, coming to his feet. 'Get out of there!'

But his voice was lost in the jeers of the crowd.

The offering went very still, lifted his head and called out something in his barbaric language. His voice sounded triumphant. Then he vanished, taking all five of the priests with him. Their clothes settled on the ground in the silence that followed.

Zabier realised the silverhead had just dragged himself and five True-men through to the higher plane, body and soul.

No one moved.

Then the god came through, ripping the posts from the ground as if they were sticks.

'Run!' Zabier screamed. 'Run for your lives.'

Because he knew it wasn't a god; it was a beast. He'd felt its claws when it grabbed him all those years ago.

He turned and ran. A single glance behind him revealed chaos, with the barons scattering and the king trying to stop them.

Please, let it get Charald. Him and his Warrior god. Let it get him.

Zabier did not stay to watch. He ran down between rows of overgrown vines to the clearing where they'd erected the tents.

The night lit up as if lightning had struck behind him and the ground shifted under him. He lost his sight and his footing, as a wall of air slammed into him. It sent him flying into the brambles. Someone collapsed on top of him.

He could have thrown them off – they were unconscious – but he preferred to stay where he was. If Charald survived, he would want to know why the Father's-voice hadn't intervened to save them from the Warrior god. How could he, when he'd been swept away with the crowd, trampled and left unconscious?

It was what he let his rescuers assume, when they found him and carried him down to the tents. Lanterns had been lit. The dead had been laid out; and servants and saw-bones tended to the injured.

'Terrible thing,' a priest muttered. 'Just terrible.'

'But then the gods should be terrible,' another said.

'Here he is, King Charald,' a servant announced, as Zabier was carried into the king's tent.

Charald had survived? That man had more lives than a cat.

At least seven of the barons were present, along with their captains. Zabier pretended to be disoriented. He needed time to learn how everyone was interpreting the events.

A man leaned over Zabier and held up his hand. 'How many fingers do you see?'

Zabier frowned.

The saw-bones shook his head and called for clean water and bandages. Meanwhile, Charald paced. They'd taken off most of his armour, and now he wore just the leather and padding.

'Did you see it?' he demanded of Zabier, as the saw-bones bathed his forehead. 'Did you see the bolt of power? The Warrior was pleased with our offering.'

'It was terrible,' someone whispered.

'The gods are meant to fill men with terror,' Zabier said.

A man strode in, demanding to see the king. He brushed aside the servants who tried to stop him. 'My brother the baron's gone. He just vanished.'

'Taken by the Warrior!' The king's eyes gleamed with holy fervour. 'Praise be.'

The new baron took a step back and said nothing, proving he was a sensible man.

'How many were taken by the Warrior?' Zabier asked.

'Ten, maybe fifteen. We're still trying to work out who is missing.' The saw-bones tied the bandage and moved off.

Charald took his place. 'You were unconscious. Did you have a vision? Did you see me?'

Zabier nodded; anything else would be foolish.

'And?' Charald prompted. He glanced around, to make sure everyone was listening.

'I saw you triumphant, marching across the causeway into the Wyrd city.' What else could he say? Besides, Sorne's vision had been of Wyrds being loaded into carts by True-men; the city must fall.

'Triumphant!' Charald raised his fist and words poured from him. 'I'll stage a tourney at your estate, Aingeru.' He pointed to an unsuspecting baron. 'It's a day's ride from the Wyrd city. On the morning of winter's cusp, we'll march towards the city and strike that very night while they're celebrating. Our holy war will be begun and ended in the space of a single night!'

And the barons cheered.

Zabier was glad he wouldn't be in the front ranks when they invaded the city. He'd just seen one plump old T'En kill five True-men.

But the tithe-master was dead, and there were hundreds of True-men, eager to avenge the priests' deaths.

Martyrs, to Charald's ambition.

GRAELEN DID NOT know how long he'd been here. It felt like days. At first he'd performed exercises to use up his gift, so that it wouldn't trouble him. Then, when there'd been no food and the water ran low, his gift had raged, along with his hunger. But that had passed and he'd come to the conclusion they'd chained him down here to die.

A distant noise reached him. It was high and repetitive. He tilted his head, listening. It wasn't the music again. No, this was a pitiful squeal, repeated over and over. He could feel his gift stirring.

Was that a glow?

His gift rose – and he'd thought it exhausted by deprivation. If someone was coming he'd...

What if he was mistaken?

Hope was a terrible thing, when he'd resigned himself to dying down here.

The glow gradually grew until it resolved itself into a tiny circle of golden light. As it came closer, he realised he was looking at a Mieren in a dirty brown robe, holding a lantern high in one hand while pushing a small trolley in front of him. The squealing sound came from one of the wheels.

All this time, he'd known of only the wall at his back and the stone under his feet. He'd thought he was in a locked room. Instead it was a tunnel, under the palace.

'Have you bought me food as well as light? How long have I been here?' He realised he was babbling. He was just so glad to see someone, even an old Mieren. All he had to do was get close enough to touch bare skin and he would have him and be out of here.

Hope burned in him, focusing his gift.

The man blinked and stopped the trolley. A line had been chalked on the stone. The man unloaded a basket of food from the trolley, then used his walking stick to push the basket across the line.

When Graelen reached for the basket, he discovered the chalk line was the extent of his range. He could just reach the food, and he drew it to him eagerly. Cheese, bread and pickles. His mouth watered.

A rapping noise made him look up. Now two buckets stood on his side of the line. He left the basket to retrieve them; a water bucket and an empty bucket. He took them back to his nest.

The man rapped the cane again and gestured for the two used buckets and Graelen pushed them to the chalk line.

'Is it day up there?' He thought he smelled sunshine on the man's robe.

The man put the lantern on the trolley and prepared to leave him.

'Why are they doing this? What do they want?'

The man pointed to his ears and shook his head. He couldn't hear.

Graelen slumped. For some reason it seemed particularly cruel, to send a man who could not talk to him.

There he went, taking the circle of light. Graelen watched until the tiny glow disappeared. Then he watched some more as the after-image lingered in his mind's eye. His gift seethed in frustration.

Graelen ate sparingly. The idea that the food might be poisoned or drugged crossed his mind but he had to eat, and they already had him.

Clearly, they were keeping him alive for a reason. As for poor Kithkarne... he hoped the tithe-master was still alive, but he feared the worst as the rumours of sacrifices returned to haunt him.

If they didn't plan to use him in some vile ceremony, why keep him alive?

Rage fired up his gift. Just let them try to feed him to the empyrean beasts. He'd shift himself to the higher plane, sacrificing his life so he could take as many of them with him as possible.

But he'd still be dead. And no one would know what the Mieren were getting up to.

He had to escape.

One of these times, the mute would slip, and he'd get close enough for Graelen to grab him. Especially if the manacle chain had been loosened from the stone. He worked on the bolts until his fingers bled.

Finally, he curled up on his blanket with his food basket hugged close to him. If the rats came after it, he'd scare them off.

He dreamed he was a boy again, impatient to leave the sisterhood. His older self wanted to tell the eager lad to savour this time. He would never know peace like this again.

He woke to a brief glimpse of a beautiful face, eyes watching him in the glow of a candle, long copper hair gleaming.

The candle went out.

'Wait. Don't leave me.' His gift leapt, eager and ready.

No answer.

Was that the softest of breathing?

'I won't hurt you. Please don't go,' he coaxed.

The image of that face stayed with him in the darkness. She was a Malaunje. He could not mistake that vivid copper hair. Was she a captive like him, stolen from the port Wyrds? Why would they take a beautiful young woman, and then lock her in the crypts? Was this where they kept the Malaunje before they sacrificed them? 'Did they drug you, or just grab you off the street?'

No answer. No sound.

Perhaps he was hallucinating. Was his power corrupting, like poor Paryx's? Fear rose in him, and his gift prickled across his skin.

'What is that?' she asked in Chalcedonian, her voice low and lilting.

He wanted to weep with relief. But she must have been away from their people a long time, if she'd forgotten the T'En tongue and the feel of gift power.

'How long have you been here?'

No answer.

He focused his power so that he could see in both planes. She had strong affinity for the gift. He could use this to lure her close and imprint his gift on her, and then she'd be eager to help him escape.

But he had taken a solemn vow to protect Malaunje from just this kind of manipulation. On the other hand, it was his duty to free her, even if she didn't know she was a prisoner.

'How long have you been here?'

'I've been locked up since I was four.' She relit the candle and he blinked. 'I've lost track of how long I've been down here.'

King Charald must have had another half-blood child like Sorne. Had he kept her by him until she was four years old, then locked her up? 'It's barbaric.'

'It's for my own protection.'

'It's still not right, keeping you down here. You should be living with your own kind, where they can appreciate your music. It is your music I've heard?'

'Yes...' She smiled shyly. 'I make it up. The music tells stories.'

'With your talent, you'd be sought after in the brotherhood.' Some high-ranking male would try to lure her to his bed. Graelen found he didn't like the idea. 'Free me and I'll take you to my brotherhood. I'll protect you.'

She seemed nervous.

Of course. After spending years alone, she was probably terrified of people. How old was she? Her body told him she was a woman, but she sounded young. In her late teens, he guessed.

'They said full-bloods were dangerous,' she whispered.

'I'm sworn to protect Malaunje. I would die to protect you.' And he meant it. The thought of what they'd done to her infuriated him. His gift surged and he wanted to use it.

'There it is again, like beautiful music on the edge of hearing.'

He had to rescue her. And this was his chance to tell her the truth.

But he hesitated. The Mieren who imprisoned her had been indoctrinating her for years. She might take fright and run. He mustn't lose her. He had to make her see the danger. 'They chained me to the wall.'

'I know...'

'They're going to sacrifice me to their gods–'

'No!'

'Malaunje have been going missing–'

'No!'

'Then why did they drug me and chain me down here?'

Finally, she said, 'He's keeping me safe. He wouldn't lie to me.'

But there was a thread of doubt in her voice.

'He's already lied to you,' Graelen guessed.

'He said you were a dead body. I didn't come back, until the mute brought down the food. A dead body doesn't need food.'

'Clever and beautiful.'

She looked up surprised. Had no one ever told her she was beautiful?

'What's your name?'

'Dia.'

'I'm Grae. I can get us out of here, Dia. If you unchain me, I can overcome the will of the True-men. I'll take you to the city and–'

'The Celestial City?'

'You've heard of it?'

'We can't go there. The king's going to attack the Wyrds.'

'What?' He surged to his feet, sprang forward and tried to grab her arm, tried to give her a taste of his gift, but she was too fast. In the scuffle, the candle went out.

He heard her backing away and strained against the chains as he switched to the empyrean sight. 'Come back, Dia. I'm sorry. I didn't mean to frighten you.'

'You tried to do something to me. I felt it.'

'I tried to share power with you.' Fool! He'd almost won her. But the thought of the Mieren king attacking his city... 'Dia, they're my people. I have to warn them.'

She backed up further.

'Dia?' Desperate, he pulled at the chains. 'Dia, I'm sorry. I shouldn't have tried to use my gift on you. But I have to warn them. Dia, come back.'

She turned and ran, until she was swallowed by darkness.

In a rage, he grabbed the chains, planted his legs against the wall and strained until his head pounded. Cursed. And tried again. Tried, until he was battered and bleeding.

And, all the while, his useless gift raged.

Chapter Fifty-Nine

SORNE WAS DRESSED as a beggar again. He'd ridden into the port on the borrowed horse and returned it to the sisterhood's warehouse. When he'd shown them the token, they'd offered him food, wine, fine clothes and a feather bed. He'd asked for their oldest cast-offs and a simple meal.

Now he shuffled down the streets, head bowed. It was strange – without his scars, he felt vulnerable. People used to glimpse those scars and look away. The bandage covered his eyes, and his hands were wrapped, so that it looked like he had only stubs of fingers.

If the Mieren found him, they'd string him up like poor Harosel.

The last place he'd known Valendia to be was the Father's church. If he had to slip inside, find Zabier and threaten him, he would. How had it come to this?

Everything started to go wrong when they came to port all those years ago. Oskane and Franto had taken Zabier away from them. Sorne recalled him bounding into their chambers, full of news about the crypts. He'd been fascinated by the tunnels under the church. Of course, Zabier would not send Valendia away, not when he wanted to keep her safe.

But Sorne had no idea how to get into the crypts. He passed the courtyard where the church fed the poor. It was filling up with the lame, the blind and the sick. Among them were skinny children with cunning faces and quick fingers. Food went into the hand and into the mouth, or it was lost. He'd fit in perfectly here.

Keeping his head down, he shuffled through the gathering. He had been planning to ask questions, but he heard the kitchen staff talking through an open window

'...killed the Warrior's-voice and four of his priests.'

'Four? I heard it was five.'

'Doesn't matter. Serve him right for trying to outdo the Father's-voice, I say.' Thump, rattle. 'Everyone knows silverheads are dangerous.'

The pots clattered and people shouted as Sorne took a spot under the window. At first he thought the Warrior's-voice had made a mistake while conducting a ceremony, but the mention of silverheads made no sense.

Then Graelen's suspicions returned to him.

Surely not. Zabier would never...

'It's not like we haven't got enough work.' The voice resumed. 'Now we have to pack for travelling. Why does the king want the Father's-voice at his tourney–'

'A tourney? That's not what I heard.'

Lowered voices, lost in clattering. He wasn't interested in what Charald was up to. At least the king wasn't making war for the moment. That was Charald's problem. Without a war to keep the barons occupied, he needed a tourney.

Sorne had no illusions about those men. He'd seen them at their worst, while they were conquering the kingdoms of the Secluded Sea under King Charald's banner. He was glad he was no longer the Warrior's-voice, making offerings and calling up visions to justify the king's ambition.

His duty was to Valendia now. He thought of her sunny smile, shut away in the crypts, and wondered if he'd ever known Zabier.

Sorne glanced to the old woman at his side. Her hands were curled into claws and he couldn't see her eyes for wrinkles. Trusting to her poor sight, he leaned closer. 'With winter coming on, it's a pity they don't open the crypts and let us sleep in there.'

'Sleep wi' the dead?' She gave a sharp laugh. 'That'll happen all too soon for the likes o' me.'

Through the window behind him, a commanding voice ran off a list of things required for the journey. Sorne caught Baron Aingeru's name. Why did that ring a bell?

'Mind you, they did open 'em up one winter when it snowed so bad th' trees split open. Come to think o' it, the entrance was near here.' The old woman lifted her head and looked around. 'No... it was th' old poor-door.'

'Old poor-door?'

'Afore the king built his new palace.'

Thirty years ago. Sorne hid a smile.

Just then, penitents came out with buckets of scraps and there was a rush for the food. In keeping with his disguise, Sorne grabbed a bit of soggy bread and retreated to gnaw on it, crouched under the window, where he heard the kitchen staff talking.

'...will have his holy war, one way or another. And now there's no Warrior's-voice, it'll be the Father's-voice the king turns to for his visions.'

Looked like the rivalry between the two largest churches was still going strong.

The old woman screeched and clipped a child over the ear. The urchin was too quick for her and made off with her dinner. She went to go back for more, but the penitents upended the buckets to show they were empty.

Sorne edged over to the old woman and offered her his bread. 'Show me the crypt entrance.'

She eyed the food, licking her gums.

He tore off a third of the bread and gave it to her. 'The rest when you show me the entrance.'

She grabbed it and sucked on it. Sorne took her arm and they hobbled out of the poor-door courtyard. She took him to the old wall of the original church grounds.

'Was just over there. Reckon no one comes back this way much. Reckon you could get in, but my old bones won't be makin' th' climb.' She held out her hand and he gave her the rest of the bread.

She smacked her lips and headed off.

Meanwhile, Sorne studied the wall. He'd have no trouble climbing it, but he'd need a lamp and maybe chalk or string to find his way around the crypt.

Holy war. The chatter of the kitchen staff returned to him. *The king would have his holy war.*

It all fell into place. Baron Aingeru's estate was less than a day's march from the Celestial City. That's why the king was staging the tourney there. Sorne knew how King Charald thought. He'd always wanted to crush the Wyrd city. With a vision from the Father's-voice to justify his ambition, Charald could call it a holy war and use the feast of winter's cusp as a diversion to attack an unsuspecting populace...

Sorne had to send word to Imoshen.

If he told the warehouse Malaunje now, one of them could get out the port gate before it closed. If he went down into the crypts, he could be all night looking for Valendia and still not find her. The messenger would be delayed by a day or more.

He'd have to come back for Valendia.

GRAELEN THOUGHT THE bolt was working loose. He'd wound scraps of blanket around his hands; the blood had made them slippery. So intent was he on breaking loose and so gradual was the approach of the light, that he almost didn't notice her until she spoke.

'You'll be forever doing it that way. I'll have to try to get the key.'

He dropped the chain and turned so quickly he almost tripped. 'Dia?'

'I couldn't leave you here in the dark. I couldn't let mothers and children die.' She placed the candle in a wall niche and frowned. 'I don't know why I couldn't see this before.'

'Oh, Dia.' He took her in his arms. His gift surged and he wanted to protect her. 'What they did to you was terrible. Shut away all these years. It's a wonder you turned out like you have.' And he kissed her.

He didn't mean to. She was looking up at him, with her heart in her face. She had no defences, played no games. She had such trust in him that he wanted to be the person she thought he was.

She'd never been kissed, he could tell. She drew back, surprised.

Then she pulled him down to her. Soft lips explored his. Her breath caught and she made a sound in her throat that made him want to throw caution aside. It was a challenge to hold back and let her set the pace.

She stepped away and smiled shyly up at him. For her, he could be the man he should have been.

ZABIER BROUGHT EIGHT burly priests with him into the crypts, to collect the big silverhead. He was not going to make the same mistake the Warrior's-voice had made with the tithe-master. If he'd had time, he would have drugged the Wyrd's food, but the king was organising things with his usual breakneck speed.

War, he had learnt, was all about the logistics: moving men and equipment, moving men's emotions to motivate them. To justify Charald's holy war, they needed a holy site to make the offering. But the nearest site was a day's ride to the north of Aingeru's estate, so they had to get there to stage the ceremony, then back in time for the attack before the evening of winter's cusp. His captive would have to travel in a heavy, barred wagon, draped with canvas to hide him from curious eyes. Even pulled with four oxen, the wagon was slow.

Time was running out, and Charald was not a man who accepted failure.

Which brought him back to the Wyrd. The king wanted a showy offering. Zabier wanted to survive. So he went down into the crypts with priests, armed with spears; great long things, with vicious heads. The Wyrd was already chained. A couple of wounds would slow him down. It didn't matter if he was injured when Zabier sacrificed him.

And just to be sure, Zabier had laced some wine with pure pains-ease. He figured the Wyrd would rather drink it, sleep and live another day, than have his throat cut. It wasn't as if he knew or even suspected what they had in mind for him.

Zabier was taking no chances. He didn't want the Wyrd aware of their approach until the last moment, so he warned his men to tread softly.

What he did not expect was to find his sister staring up at the silverhead, about to kiss him.

Rage poured through Zabier. He wanted to tear the Wyrd's throat out.

Utzen caught his arm.

Trembling with frustration, Zabier signalled the men to get into position, then strode in and caught Valendia by her glorious hair, dragging her back.

She cried out and clutched at her head, falling to one knee. Zabier slapped her hard, splitting her lip open.

'How could you? How could you go to him?' He gestured to the Wyrd. They had him up against the wall, a dozen spear points pressed to his throat, chest and groin. His eyes were wild and he gasped for breath. 'How could you let him touch you?

Valendia sprang to her feet. 'Don't hurt him.'

'Hurt him?' Zabier wanted to shake her. 'How could you do this to me? I've risked everything to keep you safe.'

His secret was out now. He would have to make these burly priests his supporters, buy their silence with prestige.

With this in mind, he confronted the Wyrd and gestured to the priests. 'These are my holy-warriors, an elite force who serve the Father's-voice. They will not hesitate to gut you on my signal.' He beckoned his assistant. 'Give me the sleeping draught.' A flask slid into his hand. He held it out to the Wyrd. 'Drink this. Drink it now, and drink it all, or...' He saw the way the silverhead was trying not to look at Valendia as Utzen helped her to her feet. 'Or I hand her over to my holy-warriors.' He was feeling so angry with her, he just might.

The Wyrd nodded and Zabier tossed him the flask.

As he drank, Zabier whispered to Utzen. 'I want you to take her away. Take her to Restoration Retreat.'

'It's a long way.'

'Take people you trust. Take whatever you need. She can have her music, but nothing else.' He turned. 'Did you hear that, Dia? You're going–'

Valendia was reaching to the Wyrd.

He cursed. 'Stop her.'

The holy-warriors went to grab her, but not before the silverhead gathered her in his arms.

'Don't just stand there!' Frustration made Zabier's voice harsh. The holy-warriors plunged in and pried them apart. It was sickening how they reached for each other.

Utzen had two of the burly priests drag her away.

With the holy-warriors pinning the silverhead, Zabier stepped in and swung at him, putting all his frustration into the punch. It slammed into the Wyrd's head and he dropped.

Hand throbbing, Zabier stepped back. 'Get him into the wagon.'

A little later, he met his assistant in a private courtyard, filled with busy priests and penitents.

'They saw me load her into my cart. But I kept her under a hooded cloak and no one knows who she is,' Utzen assured him.

Zabier pulled the flap back. Valendia was surrounded by provisions, and her arms were chained to the backboard. She glared at him through tangled hair. Her top lip had split and blood ran down her chin. Serve her right for betraying him, after all he'd done to keep her safe.

He let the flap drop. 'I'll go first.'

As he passed the other wagon, he pulled the canvas aside, to find his men chaining the unconscious Wyrd to the floor ring. He'd keep the silverhead drugged until the night of the ceremony.

A second cart followed, piled high with supplies for the supposed tourney. His holy-warriors had commandeered the seats and any perches on the cart. He mounted up. 'Open the gates.'

The gathered priests and penitents gave a tentative cheer, then a louder one. It warmed him. He hadn't expected it.

The gates trundled open to reveal a crowd gathered in the street outside.

He stood in the stirrup and shouted. 'Make way in the king's name.'

'Make way for the High Priest Zabier, the Father's-voice,' one of his holy-warriors yelled.

'Is it true the king leads a holy war?' someone shouted from the crowd. 'Is it true you take a Wyrd to be sacrificed?'

Zabier glanced to the wagon. Considering the logistics, it was inevitable the news would get out.

'Filthy Wyrd!' Something hit the barred wagon. Someone yelled abuse, several more took up the call. He could see people hurrying up the street, some swinging cudgels, some calling to others. At this rate, they'd never get out.

Men jeered, women screeched insults.

'Good people, good people.' Zabier tried to get their attention. 'I go on the king's business. Don't attack us when there are Wyrds right here in port–'

He got no further. The mob turned and took off towards the docks. He heard shouting and running feet, smashing windows.

About two blocks from the port's eastern gate, someone on horseback rode past them. He wore a hood and kept his head down.

'Wyrd!' someone yelled.

Several people dragged the half-blood from his horse and beat him; others swung a rope over shop sign. Zabier concentrated on getting his two charges out the gate alive.

SATISFIED THAT HE had fulfilled his promise to Imoshen, Sorne returned with a lamp and supplies. He had kept to back streets, so it had taken him a while to return to the old section of the church. Scaling the wall was easy. He had thought he might have trouble finding the crypt entrance, but the symbol for the dead was etched into a time-worn portico. He went down the steps and forced the doors.

Once inside, he lit his lamp and began a systematic search. Under the new section of the church, there were tunnels that were clearly used for storage and regularly visited. He avoided them.

There were wall niches piled with bodies, chambers with ornate coffins and walls of skulls. He kept a note of the turns and paces. He found tunnels thick with dust and others with a narrow path of footprints.

He found no sign of Valendia.

Half the night had gone when he discovered an empty tunnel, four levels down, that reeked of the gift. There were two bolts embedded in the wall, both a little loose, and a burned-out candle stub in a wall niche. But it was the residue of gift power that made his heart race.

The power was male and reminded him of Graelen. But the gift-warrior was the only T'En man he had ever been near; perhaps all male T'En power felt like this.

All he knew for certain was that a T'En man had performed some powerful gift-working here.

What had he been doing beneath the Father's church, and where had they taken him?

But his concern was for Valendia now. He searched the passages linking to the crypts of the other churches. He found the caverns where ancient people had painted images of themselves and their animals, and remembered Zabier talking about it.

The thought of Valendia, alone and frightened in this maze of tunnels, kept him searching until the oil in his lamp ran low. Frustrated, he returned to the surface.

Low clouds hung over the city as he emerged, and the sky was an odd colour. He smelled burning. Out on the streets, he heard the occasional shout, a scream and splintering wood.

Rather than leave the safety of the church, he scaled the nearest building and made his way to a rooftop where he could look down on the port city.

Sorne had witnessed cities under siege before, but he had never seen anything quite like this. Angry crowds surged through the streets. At least four pillars of smoke added to the pall over the port. He saw a mob smashing shop windows and surging inside to steal goods. They were sharing out the loot when another mob came along, and battle ensued over bolts of cloth and barrels of oil.

A madness had seized the city.

It was easily two days since he had last eaten, and hunger gnawed at him. He broke into the apartment where Hiruna and Valendia had lived. There he used the bathing chamber, before curling up to sleep on the floor of the main room. He could not help thinking of them living here, year after year, waiting for him to come, and now Hiruna was dead and Valendia was missing...

What a fool he had been to spend so much time chasing power and prestige. What had it gotten him, but the envy and resentment of other ambitious men?

In the middle of the night, he woke in a cold sweat.

What if the sisterhood messenger hadn't gotten out of the city? What if Imoshen hadn't called an all-council to warn the leaders of the brotherhoods and sisterhoods?

Climbing out onto the rooftop, Sorne saw that the clouds had cleared and the large, lazy moon had not yet set. To the east, a faint glow told him it was not long until dawn. At this time of day, only bakers and carters would be about. He decided to go to the west gate and wait for it to open.

Dropping down to the street, he found the mobs were not on the loose, but neither were the bakers and carters. Businesses were either shuttered, or their shutters had been ripped off and they'd been looted.

When he rounded a corner and found the sisterhood messenger hanging from a shop sign, he knew he wouldn't get out the port gate alive. He backed away in horror, and made his way down to the docks.

He felt like a coward for avoiding the Wyrd warehouses, but he knew what he would find. He thought of Graelen and wondered if he had made it out of the city. And he thought of Lysania, the Malaunje woman Graelen had used to lure him into the wine cellar. He hoped she had escaped with her little girl.

He searched the wharfs until he found a little dinghy with the oars still in it, and he did not hesitate to steal it and make his way across the bay.

Chapter Sixty

DRIVEN BY THE need to warn Imoshen, Sorne left the boat and stole a horse. He alternated between walking and riding to pace the horse. It was three days' fast ride west from the port to the Wyrd city, but he had to avoid the main road. Both the moons were nearly full; it would soon be winter's cusp.

The farm folk went about their business, preparing for the winter. Herds had to be culled, the best saved for breeding next year. Fields lay fallow or had been harvested, leaving them bristled like a man with a two-day beard. No one looked too closely at Sorne as he passed, and he got the impression they did not want to know why a lone rider was pushing his horse through their land.

Sorne came to a fork in the road. If he went north, he would come to a place called the Old Stones. If he went south, he would run across Baron Aingeru's estate and the king's tourney. If he went west, he could warn the city.

But he hesitated, because he knew the king would want a vision.

Riding had given Sorne time to think. The words overheard through the kitchen window of the Father's church preyed on his mind. He remembered Graelen trying to confirm rumours of Malaunje sacrifice, and he knew a T'En had been held captive in the father's crypts. He suspected that the silverhead was being taken to the Old Stones to be sacrificed.

If he went west, he would be able to warn the city. But that meant a T'En man would die, and he would be responsible for that death. It was he who had planted the idea that unclean places were holy sites.

The clouds hung low and dark. A storm was coming.

As he sat astride his horse in a copse of pine trees, debating his course of action, Sorne saw a closed wagon, drawn by four oxen, come trundling down the road. Three men in priestly robes sat on the seat, and another five or six rode behind. One of them reminded him of Zabier from a distance.

As the wagon turned north, the wind blew the canvas against the side of the wagon, and he saw the impression of bars. The captive T'En man would be in that wagon, and this was the Father's-voice going to meet the king to conduct the ceremony.

There was time to prevent the sacrifice and still warn the city. His decision made, Sorne followed the cart at a safe distance.

Lightning flickered within the lowering clouds and he hoped the storm would hold off until evening. Meanwhile, the wagon made its ponderous way through undulating hills occasionally broken by limestone crags. Sheep grazed, lifting their heads to watch them pass by.

At last he crested a rise and saw the Old Stones.

He led the horse back and left it tied to a tree, then climbed up to the crest of the hill and lay in the grass.

The standing stones had been erected on the highest hill as far as the eye could see. He'd expected them to be made of the local white stone he'd seen used in houses and fences, but they were tall and dark against the blue-black clouds.

To the left of the stones was a flat field, and it was here the king had set up camp. Sorne counted twelve banners, aside from the king's. Each baron would bring a man or two. With so many True-men, Sorne would need luck, the storm, and stealth to free the T'En and escape. More than luck, if they had the captive chained, rather than bound by ropes.

The setting sun's rays broke through the clouds, making the dark stones shine like black glass.

Sorne's stomach dropped as he relived the pinnacle offering that had gone so horribly wrong all those years ago. The memory of the night his holy-swords turned on him was burned so deeply, he flinched in pain.

But he was not turning back now.

The wagon had just arrived on the knoll beside the Old Stones. Between him and the camp was nothing but grass, cropped short by sheep.

No cover. He didn't like it.

The sun went behind the clouds, and the intensity of the colours faded. Now, it was a grey evening, under heavy storm clouds.

He would have to wait for night. As he waited, lightning flickered and the clouds seemed to come lower still. Rain would help hide him. But no rain fell.

Finally, he could delay no longer. He headed down the slope. The wind chose that moment to pick up, tearing at the cloud cover, revealing the rising moons. Lightning flashed, turning night into day, every detail clear. Thunder rumbled, growing louder as the storm drew closer. This would please Charald. The Warrior was said to throw lightning bolts.

Sorne hid from the camp, approaching from behind the bulk of the wagon. The wind rose in sudden gusts. It lashed the grass, driving the clouds faster across the sky.

No one sounded the alarm. He reached the wagon, and lifted the canvas to peer inside. In the darkness, he sensed male gift. It felt familiar.

A flash of lightning revealed the empty cage.

Heart pounding with disappointment, he crept to the far end of the wagon. Another flash illuminated the rise beyond the tents and the Old Stones on the hill top. A crowd of True-men made their way up the slope, forming a circle around their captive.

He'd left it too late.

Lightning struck the Old Stones, sending up a shower of sparks. The True-men shouted and cheered.

Cursing, Sorne skirted the camp, trying to get around to the far side of the hill. Between the wind, the racing clouds and the intermittent lightning, the night was full of movement.

As he reached the crest of the hill, a patch of moonlight illuminated the area. This close, the stones were enormous, each standing twice as tall as him; in the centre, he saw a crude stone table. Chains had been wound around it.

They were going to chain the warrior to the altar then spill his blood.

Trusting to the confusion created by the storm, Sorne crept to the corner of a standing stone and pressed his back to the black rock, watching the far side of the circle. He was just in time to see the first True-men enter the area.

Lightning flashed and thunder rolled over their heads. The men ducked. Sorne felt the stones reverberate with the low, angry roll of thunder.

More True-men followed the first few, moving towards the stone table. Short of dashing forward after a lightning strike, when the True-men were blinded, he did not see how he could reach the captive. And if he reached him, he did not see how they could both get away.

He should leave now and warn the city.

Lightning forked across the sky, revealing Graelen's pale silver hair.

He'd been right. It had been Graelen's gift he sensed in the crypt.

The T'En was bleeding from the nose, and one eye was nearly closed.

Sorne was not leaving Graelen to die.

Thunder hammered the Old Stones; they seemed to attract the lightning strikes. True-men ducked and cowered. Before they'd straightened up, lighting hit the stones again, sending sparks showering over them.

Some of the men dropped to the ground. Sorne could see nothing but the after-image of the lightning strike for several heartbeats.

The Warrior was in fine form tonight.

In that instant, Sorne made the connection with the man he'd seen in Imoshen's mirror after they had healed him. He had become the white-haired, one-eyed man of his first vision, the man Oskane had identified as the Warrior.

And just like that, he knew how to save Graelen.

He tore off his beggar's robes, and dropped the knife. Now he stood naked, his back pressed to the slick black stone. He waited, heart thundering, for the next lightning strike.

So far, the Warrior god had taken the ceremonial offerings in a flash of light. This time the god was going to give something back.

Almost as if the storm had been waiting for him to make this decision, a bolt of light streaked down and hit the stone to his right. Brilliant sparks flew into the air. The smell of scorched stone filled the night.

Blinded, he felt his way around the stone and took his place in front of it.

Thunder shook the skies, making the very earth tremble.

As Sorne's sight gradually returned, the after-image of the lightning repeated every time he blinked. He knew the True-men would suffer the same effect. They would see him pale and naked against the black stone, between each blink. The barons shouted and pointed to where he stood.

Only King Charald did not stumble back in shock. In the confusion, Graelen could have escaped, but he seemed stunned.

Sorne ran and jumped onto the stone altar, lifting his arms.

Graelen's eyes widened.

'Is it really you, Sorne?' The king had to shout to be heard above the elements.

'Sorne is dead. I was Sorne in my old life. The Warrior has returned me to this world.' And he dropped into a crouch, so that the True-men could see the smooth skin where his missing eye had been. 'See! He has healed me, but I bear His mark.'

Many came closer. But others, including Zabier, hung back. The man who'd been raised as his brother stared in horrified fascination.

Lightning flashed, laying his face bare. The True-men pulled back with awestruck cries.

'Your skin, the burns are all healed...' Charald was almost speechless.

'I've been reborn!'

'See,' King Charald roared. 'The Warrior supports my holy war. He's given me back my half-blood visionary!'

The barons and their men raised a tentative cheer, which was torn away by the wind.

Lightning struck the stones again, showering them with sparks. Too soon for Sorne's plan.

Momentarily blinded, he had to wait for his sight to return, then he pointed to Graelen. 'Bring the sacrifice here.'

They drove the male at spear point. He stumbled, and Sorne realised his arms were bound behind his back. Sorne reached down and caught the adept by the shoulders, felt the intensity of his gift. This was his one chance to speak privately.

Graelen beat him to it. 'They're going to attack the city.'

'I know. Warn them. When the next lightning strike hits the stones, drop off the table. Behind the tall stone at my back is a knife. My horse is over the hill.'

Sorne caught Graelen by the hair and pulled him to his feet. The way Graelen's gift beat on his skin, Sorne feared it would trigger a breach between the planes.

Lightning flickered through the clouds above them, as Sorne kept one hand on Graelen's hair and pointed to a man-at-arms. 'Give me your knife.'

The man obliged and Sorne held the knife high, praying lightning did not strike it. 'We seek your guidance, Warrior.'

'Praise the Warrior!' King Charald roared.

Sorne took his time lowering the knife. The moment he spilled Graelen's blood, the empyrean beasts would sense it and break the wall, coming for them both. He looked around, knife at the ready, waiting for the next lightning strike to hit the stones.

'We are your weapons, Warrior,' Sorne yelled, playing for time. Where was that lightning? He kept the knife poised. 'We need a sign.' *We need a lightning strike.*

The barons' men crowded close.

Lightning struck the hillside just beyond the camp.

'A sign!' King Charald cried. 'Make the sacrifice.'

Sorne looked up, praying for lightning to strike the stones, praying that the overflow of Graelen's gift wouldn't kill them both.

'Kill him!'

'Sacrifice him!'

'Cut him. Spill his tainted blood,' King Charald bellowed. Lightning forked in the clouds, but it was too far away to be useful.

'You tried,' Graelen said. 'I won't endanger you.'

'No.' If Graelen went to the empyrean plane, he'd die. Sorne felt the adept gather his gift.

Lightning flashed in the sky above but did not hit the stones.

'Let go.' Graelen met Sorne's eyes. 'Then pretend to cut me.'

He did. He had no choice.

Graelen disappeared. Even though Sorne had let go, he felt the wavering of reality as he was nearly dragged through to the empyrean plane.

The king cheered, the barons shouted and roared. No one seemed to notice that Graelen's clothes and the binding ropes had fallen to the stone.

Lightning hit the stones, showering them with sparks.

Sorne could have wept.

Instead, he dropped to the stone table and sprawled as if unconscious.

The True-men cheered. Charald ordered them to bring him down to the camp. They rolled him onto a cloak and carried him between them.

He'd failed twice over. He'd failed to save Graelen, and gotten himself trapped in the process. And he'd failed to warn Imoshen. He'd have to escape after he gave the king the vision he wanted and they'd fallen asleep tonight.

He would steal a horse, ride for the city.

ZABIER WAITED UNTIL Sorne had finished revealing his fake vision – the king's heir, whole and undamaged, sitting on the throne of Chalcedonia – and the king had left them alone so he could share a toast with his barons before breaking camp.

One of Zabier's holy-warriors had found Sorne the breeches, vest and thigh-length shirt of a priest. He sat on a chest and sipped a restorative wine that Zabier had asked another of his holy-warriors to bring. Now Zabier dismissed the two priests. 'Wait outside. We'll pack up the tent in a moment.'

Sorne looked up. 'You're not camping here tonight?'

Anger welled up in Zabier. He stalked over.

Sorne went to rise, but Zabier shoved him down. He did not doubt that the half-blood could best him in a fight, but right now Sorne was playing innocent.

'I know what you did.'

Sorne looked confused.

'I saw you two conferring. You didn't sacrifice that Wyrd. He went willingly to his death.'

Shadows haunted Sorne's face.

Zabier had to concede, he really was very good at appearing noble and troubled. But... 'I've read Oskane's journals. You and that Wyrd are up to something.'

'The gods took him.'

'There are no gods.'

Sorne looked up, surprised.

'You thought I believed? I've felt their claws on me. I know we summon beasts, and I know you just played the king for a fool.'

'Then why didn't you speak up?'

'And break the king's illusion?' Zabier shook his head. 'The only thing I can't figure out is why the Wyrd would go to his death without taking half a dozen True-men with him.'

Sorne looked away.

'You think you're so clever, but you've outsmarted yourself this time. Yes, you've got the king swallowing your visions again, but this time you're going to be working for me!'

'Why would I do that?'

'Because Valendia is not dead. I have her.'

Sorne went very still. 'You wouldn't hurt her.'

'Oh, no? I found her consorting with that Wyrd. She's a slut. All she can think about is fucking and sucking.'

Sorne flinched. 'How can you talk like that about our sister? She's an innocent.'

'Not anymore. And she's not your sister. Never was.'

Sorne blinked and swayed. He glanced down to the wine. 'What have you done, brother?'

'I'm not your brother. You're a half-blood. A tool, to be trotted out to perform sacrifices for me, and parrot my visions for the king.' Zabier leant closer as Sorne collapsed. 'You're so smart. Yet you never thought to look for trickery from me? Shame on you!'

And he called the holy-warriors in. They wrapped Sorne in a blanket and took him out to the wagon. Zabier felt a glow of satisfaction. Things were finally going his way.

* * *

GRAELEN WOKE IN the dim grey of dawn with his arms wrapped around Dia. He was naked, but warm. For a heartbeat he lay there, luxuriating in her soft curves. His gift stirred and he let the power slide over her skin; felt her stir in response, then stiffen as she woke.

'You came to me in the night,' she whispered. 'But you weren't even conscious. How did you do that?'

He was about to say he didn't know, when he remembered one of the stories he'd loved as a child.

'It had to be transposition. It's supposed to be a myth, but...' He shrugged. 'If I hadn't imprinted you with my gift before we parted, I would have been lost on the empyrean plane. But I thought of you, and the link we share brought me here. You saved me.'

He sat up, and saw that her hands were chained to the backboard of a cart. He'd soon fix that. They were surrounded by chests, sacks and barrels. Canvas covered the cart's frame. She shivered and he pulled up the blanket.

Life was good. He lived and he'd found her again. It was more than he deserved. Then he remembered the planned attack on the city, and urgency made his gift surge. 'What day is it?'

'I don't know, but it's six days since we left the port.'

That meant today was winter's cusp feast. 'Where are we?'

'In a covered cart, being transported to Restoration Retreat.'

'I meant, where in Chalcedonia?'

'I don't know. We went south, then east. We've been climbing since yesterday.'

If they were in the mountains bordering Navarone, then he had only a general idea of the area. He could take a horse and strike out for the city, but it might take him three days to find the route.

'What's wrong?'

Relief hit him as he realised he didn't have to warn the city. Sorne believed he was dead. Sorne would do what he could not. 'Nothing. Everything's all right now.'

A horse whinnied. Someone grumbled about the cold and another person told them to build up the fire.

Graelen looked to Dia. 'How many?'

'The old priest, Utzen, and two even older penitents. No one else would come with him.'

He nodded. 'I'm going to get the key to free you.'

'Don't get hurt.'

Her concern warmed him, but he wasn't the one who would be hurt. His all-father had asked him to kill his own kind to further his private ambition. Dia asked nothing of him, but he felt no compunction killing to protect her.

When he climbed out of the cart, he found one man working over the fire. Another was off with the horses, and he heard a third in the bushes relieving himself.

A little later, he sat by the fire with Dia as they watched the beans cook. The camp perched on a natural lookout high in the mountains. Chalcedonia spread out below them, pristine in the fresh light of dawn. Mist lay in the hollows. Perhaps he was selfish, but he was glad warning Kyredeon was no longer his duty.

Dia warmed her hands. 'Did you warn the city?'

'Someone else is doing it.'

'Good. Did you kill the three True-men?'

He didn't want her to be frightened of him, but he had to tell the truth. 'Yes.'

'Good. We cannot afford to let them go back to port.'

Her frank assessment made him smile.

'Why do you smile?'

'Because I'm happy.' And he hadn't been happy for a very long time.

Chapter Sixty-One

'GUARD DUTY TONIGHT?' Learon grumbled, adjusting his long-knives. 'When we should be celebrating?'

'Come on.' Tobazim glanced behind them as they crossed the brotherhood's courtyard. He couldn't see much through the archway into the next courtyard, but he could hear laughter, music and children singing. Soon the children would be in bed and the real fun would begin.

But not for him and Learon, nor for any of the Malaunje men who had escaped with them.

'He's punishing us,' Learon muttered as they took up position on the street, outside the front entrance to their brotherhood palace.

Tobazim elbowed him. 'Let Kyredeon's hand-of-force hear you say that and you'll spend a year on guard duty.'

It was meant to be a jest, but it had the ring of truth. Life in the brotherhood's palace was not what Tobazim had expected. He was used to the camaraderie of the winery. Here, there was a constraint he didn't understand. When he approached, people stopped talking. He didn't know if it was because the adepts and initiates had been told to avoid them, or because of something deeper.

'Everyone's celebrating but us,' Learon muttered, as they reached the palace's street entrance.

As if to prove his point, a dozen laughing warriors poured out of Chariode's palace next door. Despite the chill that held the promise of winter, they went bare-chested to show off their duelling scars, breeches slung low on their hips, heavy belts embossed with semi-precious stones.

None of them carried their long-knives. It was forbidden on feast nights. Too many potential duels.

Arm-torcs bearing the symbol of Chariode's brotherhood encircled their biceps, and their long pale hair had been threaded with jewels, which glinted in the street lamps.

It was all about display, tonight; not threat.

But display could be a form of threat. *See how rich and powerful my brotherhood is. We have no need to fear you.* Bluff and counter-bluff – the dance of brotherhood rivalry.

The warriors were singing at the tops of their voices as they waited for friends to join them before setting off.

Tobazim grinned. 'Looks like they've already started on the wine.'

'I bet they're making for the park and its secluded nooks. I heard some of the more daring T'En women slip away tonight,' Learon whispered. He nodded towards the sisterhood palaces, their domes and towers silvered by the double full moons. 'There's a chance of illicit trysting. But not for us.' He made a disgusted sound in his throat.

As Chariode's adepts waited for their friends, several of them turned to give Tobazim and Learon filthy looks.

Tobazim felt his gift leap to his defence and had to force it down. He sensed Learon doing the same. The others arrived, and all of them moved off through the archway onto the causeway boulevard.

'What was that about?' Learon whispered.

'I wish I knew.' They hadn't been allowed out of the brotherhood palace since they'd arrived. Kyredeon didn't trust them.

Chariode's palace was the closest to the causeway gate; the other brotherhood palaces stretched along the street past Kyredeon's, following the curve of the island. Now revellers poured down the street and wandered past them in groups, singing and joking, as they headed for the free quarter. Tobazim had read of the plays and dance halls, the way poets would challenge passers-by to a duel of rhyming couplets. He wished he'd lived in the Early Golden Age, when the city's buildings were first raised and his gift would have been appreciated.

'Look.' Learon gestured up the street. 'None of the other all-fathers have bothered to put anyone on guard duty tonight.'

He was right. All the brotherhoods' palaces stood wide open. Tobazim shrugged. 'The causeway gate's shut and the Mieren have all gone home for the night.'

'So, what's the point of ceremonial guards?'

'Prestige.' Which begged the question. Why did their all-father feel the need to reinforce his prestige? What had to happen before he could safely reveal the attack on Vanillin Oak Winery?

'Lear...' a sweet, husky voice sang.

Tobazim glanced over his shoulder.

Paravia glided through the gate to join them. On the floors above, balconies overlooked the street. Tobazim could hear laughter and the occasional squeal of delight. It sounded like some of the brothers were getting into the revelry early.

'Paravia...' Learon's voice held genuine regret. 'You shouldn't be here.'

'I brought you some wine.'

'We're on duty.'

'He's right, Paravia,' Tobazim said. 'This isn't the winery. If the hand-of-force caught us drinking...' He shuddered to think.

'Why are you even on guard duty tonight?' She was indignant for them. 'It's a feast night. None of the other brotherhoods are going to come banner-stealing–'

'Actually, it's a very good night for banner-stealing.' Learon caught Tobazim's eye. 'Kyredeon seems to dislike All-fathers Chariode and Hueryx. If we stole their banners, we could win stature and sweeten him up.'

'Oh...' Paravia stamped her foot in mock annoyance, then sidled up close to Learon. 'You don't want to go banner-stealing when you could be meeting me.'

Tobazim looked away so he wouldn't have to watch Paravia's busy hands. But T'En warriors from other brotherhoods saw what she was up to as they went by and whistled appreciatively.

Tobazim was about to remind Learon of his duty, when his choice-brother caught Paravia's hands and turned them away, saying, 'I finish at midnight. Go have some fun 'til then.'

She kissed him and darted away.

'Not too much fun without me,' he warned.

She laughed.

Learon adjusted himself. 'Midnight can't come too soon.'

IMOSHEN WAS GLAD the official duties of her evening were over. She returned to her chambers with the intention of singing baby Umaleni to sleep, but found Iraayel, Saffazi and Bedutz playing with her. Seeing their heads bent over the baby, she realised their hair was darkening to silver-grey. They were no longer children, but neither were they adults. They would keep growing until they were twenty-five, and it would take years for them to learn to master their powers.

It was good to see Bedutz. She hadn't seen much of him recently. He was focused on joining the brotherhood, and there was a lot of anger in him, as if Vittoryxe's rage had taken root. But, seeing Umaleni in his arms, she was reminded of the boy she had met all those years ago when they first arrived in the city.

Her gift flexed and she read him. Holding the baby soothed him. She came over, placed a hand on his shoulder and opened her senses. His gift, usually laced with aggression, was now leavened with compassion.

And in that instant, she understood what Imoshen the Covenant-maker had not. By removing the T'En children, infants and nursing mothers from contact with the men, she had removed the soothing effect they had on the aggressive male gifts. Once the men were surrounded by nothing but more men, their gifts responded to each other, always spiralling towards violence. The covenant had made them more dangerous.

'Time for me to put Uma to bed,' Imoshen said.

They each gave the sleepy infant a kiss and Imoshen went through to the nursery, where she found Frayvia sitting on the window sill. Clearly, she missed Sorne.

Imoshen lay down next to Umaleni to feed her, and Frayvia came over to join her.

'He could come live in the city,' Imoshen said softly. 'I'm all-mother; I'd accept him into our sisterhood.'

Frayvia rolled her eyes. 'I don't think he's a tame Malaunje.'

Imoshen smiled.

A little later, she wandered out to find Iraayel and Saffazi sitting on the floor in front of the fireplace, playing cards.

'I won, I have a sisterhood!' Saffazi crowed.

'That was luck, pure luck! You always take ridiculous risks.' Iraayel threw his cards down with a laugh.

Egrayne's choice-daughter rolled her eyes. 'What fun is life, if you can't take risks? Another game?'

Iraayel leaned forward to collect the cards and noticed Imoshen. 'Oh, did you want to go to bed?'

If she said yes, they'd leave and that would be the end of their game. Iraayel had turned sixteen yesterday. The thought of him having to join Chariode's brotherhood in a year's time horrified Imoshen.

Although he'd spent the last three years studying martial arts with great focus, seeing him there playing cards with Saffazi made her realise how very young he still was. Yet all too soon she would have to declare him dead to her. The covenant was wrong, and she intended to change things, but she would not be in time to save her choice-son from the challenges of brotherhood life.

Her only consolation was that Ardonyx would be on Chariode's inner circle, and he would keep an eye on her choice-son.

If Ardonyx returned from his voyage of exploration. He *had to* return. He didn't even know they had a daughter.

'Can we stay? Please say we can,' Saffazi cajoled.

'You can play, too,' Iraayel offered.

Imoshen laughed. 'Stay as long as you like.'

She went through to the nursery, where she found that Frayvia had returned to the window sill. Imoshen sat next to her.

Iraayel's laughter reached them.

'You're soft,' Frayvia said.

'I won't have him for much longer.'

TOBAZIM HAD BEEN listening to other people drinking and laughing all evening, and it was getting on his nerves. Music from at least three different sources reached him. Groups of merry-makers had wandered the streets of the brotherhood quarter earlier, but they were mostly up in the free quarter now, or inside the brotherhood palaces.

Something clattered loudly, metal on stone. It seemed to come from Chariode's palace.

'Can't be long until midnight now,' Learon said, reaching down to adjust himself.

The volume of noise from Chariode's palace doubled, and the music stopped mid-tune. Deep male voices rose in anger. Something smashed, the tinkle of broken glass clear and high above the hubbub.

'A fight,' Learon muttered. 'Too much wine. Some old slight remembered. Someone out for pay-back.'

A scream, short and visceral, made Tobazim's gift surge. He forced it down.

'Their hand-of-force will step in and separate them,' Learon said, 'then call for their voice-of-reason to sort it out.'

But the furore rose in volume.

Tobazim and Learon exchanged looks.

Next came the unmistakable clash of metal on metal, followed by agonised screaming.

Learon swore. 'Chariode's people are under attack!'

Tobazim ducked into the palace gate-tunnel. 'Help me with the gates.'

Learon thrust his big shoulder behind the heavy gates. After initial resistance, they creaked and eased shut. Tobazim threw the bolts.

They ran through to the first courtyard.

Here, within the palace walls, the sound of fighting was muted, and could easily be mistaken for rowdy roistering. Until a shriek rose and was cut off abruptly.

'It's the winery all over again,' Tobazim muttered.

They sped through into the palace, past those still caught up in the revelry and those long past carousing.

Hand-of-force Oriemn stood in the corridor outside Kyredeon's door, talking to the saw-bones, Ceyne. When Oriemn spotted them, anger flashed across his face.

Before he could berate them, Tobazim reported, 'Chariode's palace is under attack.'

'That's none of our business.'

'A Mieren attack is none of our business?' Learon demanded.

'What makes you think it's Mieren?' Ceyne asked.

'It'll be a rival brotherhood,' Oriemn said. 'Or a leadership challenge. You're new to the city, you don't know our ways.'

Tobazim glanced to Learon. Had they overreacted?

Running boots made them all turn.

'Mieren attack!' a warrior reported as he hurried towards them. 'They've breached the lake-wall and broken into Chariode's palace.'

Learon cursed. 'I told–'

'Quiet,' Oriemn snapped. He turned his attention to the messenger. 'How do you know this?'

'I come from the rooftop garden. Women and children are pouring onto Chariode's roof, calling for help.'

'We must–' Learon turned to go.

Oriemn caught him by the arm. 'You do nothing until I give the order.'

'But–'

The hand-of-force shoved Learon up against the wall, forearm across his throat. 'Nothing.' Oriemn's gift flared to reinforce his words. 'Do you understand?'

Learon did not look happy, but he nodded.

'We've shut the palace's street gate,' Tobazim reported, trying to divert him. 'But we only have our long-knives. They'll be armed with swords. We need–'

'You need to shut up.' Oriemn turned the full force of his gift on Tobazim.

'Do as he says,' the saw-bones advised.

'Come with me.' Oriemn gestured to the warrior from the rooftop. He strode into Kyredeon's chamber, shutting the door behind him. They waited.

And they waited.

Learon swore and went to stride off.

Ceyne caught his arm. 'If you disobey a direct order, he'll execute you.'

'I know, but women and children are dying.'

'Believe me, I share your frustration.'

Tobazim was having trouble controlling his gift. 'What's the delay?'

Ceyne glanced in both directions and gestured for them to come closer. 'My guess is, Kyredeon's waiting for Chariode's warriors to bear the brunt of the attack, before coming to the brotherhood's rescue. He wants Chariode weakened and indebted to him.'

Tobazim felt sick. 'How can you follow him?'

'He's the all-father.' Ceyne grimaced. 'He holds our lives in his hands.'

Athlyn arrived at a run. 'There are armed Mieren in the street.'

Learon turned to Tobazim.

'What are you going to do?' Ceyne asked.

'The women and children need us,' Tobazim said. 'Come on.'

He led them up the steps at a run, heart pounding. When they reached the roof, the cries of the women and children drew them to the edge. Kyredeon's palace roof was lower than Chariode's. Only a short gap separated the two buildings, but it was too far for the children to jump, and the mothers couldn't leave them.

Tobazim looked around for something to bridge the gap. He spotted a long garden trellis. His gift told him it was sturdily made and would support the weight of adults. He raised his voice. 'Over here. Give me a hand with this.'

The others saw what he intended. Between them, they uprooted the trellis and carried it across, stood it on its end and let it fall. It clattered into place.

The mothers sent the nimbler, older children across first, but there were still the babies and toddlers to come.

Tobazim noticed a canvas awning, and threw it across the gap as well. The mothers sat their little ones on the canvas and they slid down into the arms of the waiting rescuers.

While this was going on, Learon jogged to the far end of the roof, which overlooked the street. After a moment, he returned.

'It's bad. Mieren fill the brotherhood quarter. They're pouring up the causeway boulevard towards the free quarter.'

'All those revellers...' Unarmed, drinking and eating. Tobazim ran to the far end of the roof to see for himself. Judging by the volume of invaders... 'The causeway gate must be open.'

'We should close it,' Learon said. 'We need to gather a party and fight our way there. Once it's closed, the Mieren will be trapped. We can overcome them and hunt them down.'

Tobazim caught his arm. 'First we have to make sure the palace will hold. Then we close the causeway gate and take back the island.'

This time there was nowhere to run to.

IMOSHEN WOKE AS a particularly raucous cry drifted up from the courtyard below. Her gift tried to rise and she forced it down.

'The celebrations are noisy tonight,' Frayvia whispered. Sitting up, she pushed the hair from her face. They'd fallen asleep on the window seat.

Something tipped over and smashed. They heard running feet and shouting.

Annoyed, Imoshen came to her feet. 'Stay with Uma.'

She left the nursery to find that Iraayel and Saffazi had fallen asleep in front of the fire, holding hands with their heads together.

Surprised, she was about to say something, when a scream echoed up from the courtyard.

Iraayel snapped awake. She felt his male gift surface as he rolled to his feet.

Saffazi frowned, lifting on one elbow. 'What's going on?'

'I don't know.' Imoshen felt a sick lurch of fear. Had the brotherhoods attacked?

Shouts, running feet, a shriek cut off too soon.

Iraayel hauled Saffazi up, and the two sixteen-year-olds looked to Imoshen, eyes wide with fear, gifts on alert.

'Come with me.' She slipped through the greeting chamber and out into the corridor. It was empty, but she could hear shouting, shrieks, smashing glass and running feet.

She would be able to see what was going on from the top of the grand staircase. When she reached the balcony overlooking the main entrance, she saw half a dozen Mieren below, looting and smashing. If they were here, in the highest palace of the sisterhood quarter, that meant they were all over the island city.

'We have to get the T'En children to safety,' Imoshen said, drawing the other two out of sight.

As she headed back the way they'd come, Bedutz led several T'En lads round the far corner.

Imoshen signalled for silence and beckoned them. When they reached her, she was enveloped in roused male gift. Saffazi shifted, uncomfortable with the sensation.

'There are Mieren on the ground floor,' Imoshen whispered.

'I don't believe it,' Bedutz muttered. 'Why are there Mieren in the palace? We're not at war.'

'We need weapons,' Iraayel whispered. 'Where's the hand-of-force? She should be organising our defences.'

Imoshen suspected everyone was scrambling to find weapons and hold the rooms they were in.

'Wyrds!' A man yelled from the top of the stairs. 'Filthy Wyrds.'

With a roar, a mob of Mieren charged them, weapons raised.

'Go save the children.' Iraayel pushed Imoshen away. 'Everyone else, with me.'

Imoshen hesitated. Iraayel ran toward the men. He grabbed a tall brass statuette from a sideboard as he ran, and swung it like a club, sending two Mieren flying. Saffazi darted forward to snatch a fallen sword and Bedutz snatched a second blade, and the younger lads followed their lead.

Imoshen didn't want to leave them, but she had to.

She ran along the corridor and around the corner, discovered old Tiasarone with a huddle of young T'En children.

Scooping up a little boy, Imoshen led them to her chamber. As she opened the door and ushered them through, she saw Iraayel and the others battling to drive half a dozen Mieren back to the top of the stairs.

'Take the children through to the nursery. Here's the key. Lock every door after you,' she told Tiasarone.

As soon as the inner door closed, Imoshen ran to a chest and threw the lid open. She hauled everything out, removed the false bottom and retrieved the sword that once belonged to Imoshen the Covenant-maker.

Sword in hands, she ran out into the corridor, finding Iraayel and the others trying to hold the stairs. Imoshen charged, swinging the sword. She took down two Mieren before embedding the sword in a column.

Iraayel pushed her aside and grabbed the hilt. 'Block the stairs with the sideboards. We need a barricade.'

She nodded and grabbed several of the smaller boys to help her. Iraayel tore the sword from the column. She heard the sharp clash of metal on metal.

The sideboards were very heavy and Imoshen and the lads struggled to drag them. Bedutz and Saffazi left Iraayel to hold the stairs while they built the barricade.

Once they'd barred the stairs, they had to finish off the last few Mieren still on the balcony. Imoshen saw a youth of fourteen bring a statuette down on one attacker's head. Two of the lads dragged the Mieren away and threw him down the stairs. He took several others with him.

The lads cheered. But for every enemy that fell, two more fought to breach the barricade. Imoshen ran to the railing. A glance below showed Mieren pouring through the entrance. They divided, some coming straight up the grand staircase, others charging off into the ground floor rooms.

Iraayel swung the sword, with Bedutz and Saffazi on either side of him. Hacking, chopping, cutting the invaders down. It was butchery.

The clatter of metal on metal, the deep shouts of their attackers – the roar of battle drummed on Imoshen's ears. She saw a boy of thirteen go down under a Mieren. The man lifted his arm to drive his sword through the boy's chest. Imoshen leapt for the Mieren, touched the back of his neck and pulled his life force out of him, sending the man's essence to the higher plane.

He dropped. Bedutz shoved the Mieren aside and hauled the boy to his feet.

The distinctive ululating warcry of the sisterhood warriors reached her from the ground floor. Their defenders had rallied.

The attackers at the top of the stairs thinned, until the last few Mieren turned and ran. The T'En lads drew back, and bent double, gasping to catch their breath. Saffazi grinned, covered in blood, a wild light in her eyes.

This time, when Imoshen looked over the balcony, she could see the bloodied marble floor. Their attackers fled, chased by a dozen warriors, both Malaunje and T'En.

'After them,' Iraayel cried.

'Don't go downstairs,' Imoshen told him. 'Go up to the top floor. Go through our palace room by room, flush out any attackers who have already reached the higher levels. We don't want any nasty surprises.'

He nodded and led the others along the corridor. As he rounded the bend, Imoshen's hand-of-force appeared from the other direction, with several bloodied warriors.

'You're all right.' Arodyti hugged her, then pulled back. 'We can't find the T'En children.'

'They're safe in my chambers. I sent Iraayel with Saffazi and the lads to the top floor to flush out attackers.' Her mind raced. 'We'll need to bring the wounded to the solarium.'

They heard a sharp cry, which suddenly stopped.

'It's still dangerous,' Arodyti told her. 'Stay here.'

'I'm the all-mother. I can't hide.'

'Of course she can't,' Egrayne said, joining them. 'But you're not going to take any risks either.'

'As soon as our palace is secure, help the others,' Imoshen told Arodyti. She was worried about Reoden. 'When that's done, make sure the sisterhood quarter is safe, then–'

'Then report back,' Egrayne said.

'We need to make sure the island is secure,' Imoshen added.

'The brotherhoods are already doing that.' Egrayne slid an arm around Imoshen and drew her away. 'You need to come with me.'

'I should check on the children.'

'Soon. There's something you need to see.'

She led Imoshen up to the tallest tower.

'Good idea,' Imoshen told her. 'We can assess the damage from here.'

Then she saved her breath for climbing the steps. From the top of the tower, she spotted several fires down in the brotherhood quarter and the free quarter, but... 'The brotherhoods have managed to close the causeway gate.'

'Look.' Egrayne pointed to the lake shore.

Dotted along the slope to one side of the town were hundreds – no, thousands – of flickering camp fires.

Imoshen's heart sank. She had come here seeking sanctuary, looking for a safe place to raise her child. Now she had another child, but this was no longer a safe haven. 'The city's besieged.'

VITTORYXE FOUND IMOSHEN and Egrayne coming down from the tower.

'The city's under siege,' Imoshen said. 'We're trapped.'

'We're going to need someone to deal with King Charald,' Egrayne said, looking at Imoshen. 'We need a causare to unite us.'

Vittoryxe could not believe it. Everything fell into that woman's lap. 'Imoshen...'

'Exactly. She's a raedan.'

'No.' Imoshen looked genuinely frightened by the idea. What was wrong with her? Didn't she realise what an honour this was?

'You're the most powerful of the all-mothers,' Egrayne said.

'What about one of the all-fathers?' Imoshen suggested.

'Oh, I'm sure they'll all want the role, but would any of them be suitable?' Egrayne looked past Imoshen to

Vittoryxe. 'Do we want an aggressive man intent on making the Mieren pay for what they've done, or someone who can read King Charald and manipulate him?'

'We want Imoshen for causare,' Vittoryxe said, and the words were sour on her tongue. Somehow, Imoshen had stolen everything she had ever wanted.

Acknowledgements

A book does not just arrive, it takes a long time in the gestation and many people play a part. I would like to thank my writing group, ROR, who read the first draft of a book set in this world over ten years ago. Thanks to Marianne de Pierres, Margo Lanagan, Maxine McArthur, Tansy Rayner Roberts, Trent Jamieson, Richard Harland and Dirk Flinthart.

I would like to thank my agent, John Jarrold, and my publisher, Solaris, who have been so supportive. Solaris chose the cover artist, Clint Langley, for both King Rolen's Kin and The Outcast Chronicles. Everyone comments on Clint's great covers.

My special thanks goes to my editor, Jonathan Oliver, for his input in pulling the series together and to David Moore, for saying it was worth it.

ISBN: 978-1-78108-012-2 • US $7.99 / CAN $9.99

ROWENA CORY DANIELLS

EXILE

BOOK TWO OF THE OUTCAST CHRONICLES

For over three hundred years the mystics have lived alongside the true-men, until King Charald lays siege to the mystic's island city.

Imoshen, most powerful of the female mystics, is elected to negotiate with the true-man king. The male mystics still resent her, but she has an ally in Sorne, the half-blood, who was raised by true-men. Even though he is vulnerable to her gifts, he gives Imoshen his loyalty. In return, she gives him the most dangerous of tasks, to spy for her.

She negotiates exile for her people. They must pack all their valuables, reach port and set sail by the first day of winter. But to do this, they have to cross a kingdom filled with true-men who are no longer bluffed by their gifts. Meanwhile, there are mystics living in the countryside, unaware that their people have been exiled.

King Charald announces any mystics who remain behind after they are exiled will be hunted down and executed.

 WWW.SOLARISBOOKS.COM